Dor Slinkard is an unstoppable storyteller. Be it through writing or voice, her stories will enthral. Inspired by life, especially as a jillaroo in outback Australia and later as a racehorse trainer, her imagination thrives. In her lasting marriage to Wade, a jackaroo and now horse trainer, they have produced two children and they, in turn, five grandchildren.

For the Love of Patrick is the first of three independent family sagas.

Dedication

Without the support of my husband Wade, who is
my in-house proof-reader, and a great many friends and editors,
my stories would not be.

To Margaret Mooney, my lifelong friend and English guru, to Denise
Doraisamy, a tireless teacher and editor, and to Brian Clarke, my chief
editor, who have all sprinkled their magic and turned my unruly writing
into understandable English. To my dear friends who are too numerous to
mention, but who know they are appreciated in helping to make the stories
the very best they can be. To Michael Cybulski, my agent from New
Authors Collective, for his amazing support with all publishing matters.
Thank you all.

I would also like to dedicate this book to the memory of one of Australia's
greatest horse trainers – Guy Walter, who was an avid reader and would
question me every time we met, 'How's your novel going, Dor?' I'd tell
him, and he'd reply, "I can't wait to read it!"
Guy passed away with a sudden heart attack May 21 – 2014, age 59.

And, of course, to the characters, whom I believe are real. Though unseen,
their voices pass through time and space to writers
who then tell their story.

Dor Slinkard

FOR THE LOVE OF PATRICK

AUSTIN MACAULEY PUBLISHERS™

LONDON • CAMBRIDGE • NEW YORK • SHARJAH

A CIP catalogue record for this title is available from the British Library.

ISBN 9781787101173 (Paperback)
ISBN 9781787101180 (E-Book)

www.austinmacauley.com

First Published (2017)
Austin Macauley Publishers Ltd.™
25 Canada Square
Canary Wharf
London
E14 5LQ

Part 1

Chapter 1

Blessings

South Australia, 4 July 1892

The full moon cast its fading shadow over the convent, as young Sally hugged her baby for what she feared may be the last time. Every atom of courage was needed to wrap him snug and leave him on the doorstep. Thinking the nuns would soon be up, she lifted the door knocker and let it fall. After a final gaze at her baby, Sally hurried to hide behind the nearest tree. Holding the trunk, she sensed its strength and the life coming from within. It had withstood the test of time and now she'd have to do likewise. She prayed she'd see a smile once they'd found him. Only then would her guilt lift a little.

The door opened to reveal a small girl, six-year-old Betty, still in her nightdress. She looked from left to right, but saw no one, before she glanced down to notice the sleeping baby. Flicking her sleep-mussed hair behind her shoulders, Betty smiled, bent down, and with awkward care picked him up. "Never mind, little one. We'll look after you." Betty held the baby to her heart, then turned and shut the door.

Sally's fist pressed tight against her mouth to muffle the sounds of grief. She then ran from the scene. This memory would go deep—very deep.

Betty beamed with delight at her new-found treasure: a live doll, and at this very moment, all hers. As she walked head-down to the kitchen, her eyes met a pair of black shoes. The hem of a nun's habit almost covered them. Betty's heart raced as she looked up into the face of Mother Matilda. She swallowed quickly and launched into her plea.

"Can we keep him, Mother, please? I want to, I mean, could we call him Patrick? That's if he's a boy."

With a stern look from Mother Matilda, Betty handed the baby into her outstretched arms. Without a word, Mother Matilda continued into the kitchen, placing the child gently onto the scrubbed wooden table. She unravelled the blanket and clothing to determine the baby's sex then turned to Betty.

"Well done, Betty, indeed it's a boy. But this is a home for girls, y' know that."

"Yes, Mother, and all the more reason to keep him. He'll have so many mothers here. We can all look after him." Betty had an answer for everything. The tension broke and Matilda smiled at Betty, seeing her enormous capacity for love and compassion. This touched Matilda, who remembered the day Betty was brought to them, a homeless waif, heartbroken after losing her mother.

Trying to hold back tears, Betty gave her reasons. "We're all young, Mother, so we can look after him forever. We'll grow old together before we die." Tears welled and trickled down her cheeks. Oh, how Matilda wished she could make everything right for all the girls. She hugged her favourite orphan.

"I'm too soft, that's what I'd be, Betty. But y' know I'll have to be puttin' it past The Mother Superior when she comes a-visitin' next week. Now let me warm some milk for our little baby Patrick."

Matilda's words soothed Betty's anguish and in a much happier tone she asked, "Do you like his name, Mother?"

"Yes, I was just wishin' it were Saint Patrick's Day, so we would all be warmer. Now go stoke up the fire, Betty. We don't want the baby ta be dyin' of the cold, now do we?" At the age of thirty-six, still holding onto her Irish beauty, Matilda sat in the convent kitchen with the baby boy in her arms, feeling he was indeed Heaven-sent. Every now and then, her heart ached for a baby of her own, the one she knew she could never have. Smiling into his blue eyes, Matilda crooned an Irish lullaby.

Rocking back and forth, she fed him milk through a large teat used for the poddy lambs given to the convent by her Da. Each spring, Matilda was happy for the girls to take care of the lambs, before they went home to be turned into Sunday roast. A secret Matilda would never disclose.

"Thank heaven," she would say, when her Irish father, whom she called 'Da', assisted in many ways at the convent. He did so, seeing he lived nearby.

Betty hurried off to do Matilda's bidding. Before too long, young girls dressed in nightgowns arrived in the kitchen, and with sleepy faces they peered at the baby. Betty proudly proclaimed. "I found him on the door step. He's been 'bandoned, so he's all ours. His name's Patrick."

The girls were in thrall of the baby boy who Mother Matilda was now cradling, as if it were second nature. In an effort to control the excitement building, she raised her voice over their buzz of conversation.

"Now, girls, despite baby Patrick's unexpected arrival, it's not Saint Patrick's Day. In fact, it's American Independence Day." Matilda warmed to her subject.

The history teacher in her couldn't refrain. She decided to give the girls a short history lesson—always the opportunist, Mother Matilda.

"Do y' know, girls, why the Americans celebrate this day?" She asked as if nothing unusual was happening. She felt she didn't need to explain to the girls why she was nursing a baby boy in her arms. It had happened, she accepted it and so should they.

"Well, do y'?"

"No," they chorused, their eager faces watching Matilda burp the baby over her shoulder.

"Well, then. Americans celebrated their Independence Day after defeating the English, who were not at all pleased, when the colony wanted t' run things for themselves. And t' commemorate their independence from Britain, they had a huge celebration with lots o' fireworks." She then stood and paced the room, all the while rocking the infant.

"In Australia, we have another fireworks celebration. Who can name it?"

"I know!" shouted Lizzy. "It's Guy Fawkes Night!"

"Well done, Lizzy. I'm pleased you've been listenin' t' m' History lessons!" Matilda looked down at the sleeping baby. "Interestin', wasn't it?"

"Could we set off some firecrackers tonight and celebrate our very own baby? Please, Mother?" Lizzy pleaded, with her usual manipulative grin.

"No, Lizzy. Now don't be getting too excited about our very own baby. As I said t' Betty, I'll be puttin' it past The Mother Superior. She'll be visitin' next week t' check on us. So be off with y' now and get dressed. The porridge'll soon be ready. And there'll be no money spent on fireworks!" Matilda called after the giggling group.

She sat down, gazing tenderly at the infant. "I do hope the Good Lord knows what He's doing, Patrick, m' boy." Her thoughts were disturbed by Sister Catherine.

"Heavens above, Mother, what do you have there?"

Matilda looked up, her blue eyes sparkling. "He's God's gift, Sister."

"I think you should get a second opinion on that, Mother!" Sister Catherine exclaimed wryly.

Matilda gave a hearty laugh. "Yes, I am. I'm goin' t' ask Mother Superior what we should be doin' with him when she comes t' visit next week. But in the meantime, we have t' be carin' for him, Sister."

Sister Catherine peered over Matilda's shoulder. "Oh, he is a dear little thing. It is a boy, you said, Mother?"

"Yes, it was the first thing I checked, Sister."

"Well, as you say, Mother, it'll be left up to the Reverend Mother, but I think it's a real shame we can't make our own decisions." Sister Catherine sighed. "I suppose we'll have to inform the police? I'll do it if you wish, Mother."

"No, don't bother. I'll do it, Catherine. All in good time," Matilda replied cheerily. She had no intention of informing the police.

For the rest of the day, happy chaos filled the convent school. Prayers were extended to their new charge and for the "birth mother", who God only knew why had given up her baby. Matilda was forever grateful that the wealthy doctor, whom she'd liked and respected very much, had bequeathed to her—not to the church—his magnificent blue-stone mansion. His wishes were that his home be used as an orphanage and a school for homeless girls. Plus, he'd stipulated in his will that Sister Matilda, as she was then, was to be in charge for as long as she lived. It would only belong to the Catholic Church on Matilda's passing. This was legally binding and although the bishop was not impressed, there was little he could do about it. Mother Matilda lit a candle every day for her generous doctor, hoping the good doctor was more than pleased she was fulfilling his wishes. How could she not, he'd touched her deeply when he'd said, "I admire you, Matilda, for your indomitable spirit and your strong sense of duty to others. I believe you to be a saint already."

His wishes for the substantial wealth he'd left behind were to directly benefit troubled and homeless girls, and not to line the pockets of the Church hierarchy. "All matters concerning my Will are water-tight, Sister. My lawyers have made sure of it." This, he relayed to Matilda, only days before he passed away.

The week before Mother Superior's visit, the home had been scrubbed from top to bottom in her honour. Sisters and girls, handy with a needle, had worked with loving detail, sewing Patrick's nightgowns. Using his great skill, Mother Matilda's Da had fashioned Patrick's rocking cradle, using the timber he'd felled from a gum tree that had sat too close to his cottage.

A different feeling had overcome the girls and nuns alike. Sister Catherine declared to Mother Matilda, "Why, it's as if the Saviour Himself has been born, Mother. This child has brought out every ounce of love and compassion held within my heart. And the rest of us, I'm sure."

This was the mood of the orphanage that met Mother Superior as she walked through the enormous front door. Smiling faces, clean, neat young girls, respectful nuns and the entire place glowing. The aroma of lavender oil suffused it all. Never before had Mother Superior been greeted with such a warm reception, so she began to harbour a little suspicion.

"And how are we, Sisters, girls?" Before they had time to answer, Matilda guided her by the arm.

"Well, if ya'd just come this way, Mother Superior," Matilda said, while ushering her into her office, warmed by a hungry fire.

Mother Superior, short and plump, with rounded cheeks and spectacles sitting precariously on the end of her nose, breathed in the calming fragrance of lavender before she sat heavily in Matilda's armchair.

"Tell me, Matilda, do I detect something different about this place?"

"Well, it's just the girls are so happy to be havin' y' visit. They've worked so hard t' have everythin' spick and span, just t' show y' how capable they are. They're all growin' up now, y' know, and they can help care for anythin' that comes their way."

Mother Superior, from the moment she'd been met with unusual ceremony, suspected a cover-up, or perhaps a favour to be wrangled. "You're rambling, Matilda. Now tell me what's happened."

Matilda was hesitant. She'd rehearsed this moment in detail for the past week, but when confronted by Mother Superior's stern look, decided to get straight to the point. "Well, it's like this, Reverend Mother ..."

"Please call me Adele, Matilda, we're out of earshot."

"Alright, Adele," Matilda took a deep breath. "A week ago, I sent young Betty t' open the door t' an early-mornin' knock; sometimes we get produce given t' us by the local farmers and they leave it at the front door. Anyway, Betty couldn't see anyone until she looked down to find," Matilda paused, "a beautiful baby boy."

Adele's eyebrows shot up.

Matilda then hurried on. "We knew you'd be comin' in a week and he needed t' be cared for until then. So, I know it's your decision, Adele, and I shouldn't be sayin' this, but it would break all our hearts if he had t' go t' a boys' orphanage, especially with the rumours of cruelty bein' so rife. Now, I'll be leavin' the decision t' you, of course, knowin' you'll be sayin' a prayer t' the Almighty for His guidance, and won't be makin' any hasty decisions ..."

Adele smiled at her friend's unease and chose to ignore the implied warning. Instead, she asked warmly, "May I see the baby, Matilda?"

"T' be sure, Adele. I'll ask Sister Catherine to bring him to y'."

Matilda released the breath she'd been holding, and rose hastily then vanished through the doorway. Adele sat back in the chair, taken aback by the news. It was not entirely unusual for a baby to be left; after all, this was an orphanage. A girl would be no problem, but a boy? Adele had to admit that it would be her heart versus her head in this situation. She was in a quandary as to know what to do. Sister Catherine was quick to bring Patrick into the room and hand him to Adele. She cradled him in her arms and smiled down at the squirming baby.

"Oh, he's beautiful, Matilda! And he looks a picture of health. Have you given him a name?"

"Yes. Betty named him Patrick."

"I think it suits him. He's wriggling a lot. Does he need to be fed?"

"He's always hungry, Reverend Mother. But he's a good baby, he causes no trouble, only dat all the girls love him and want t' nurse him all the time. So I'm afraid the only problem will be tryin' not t' spoil him. Well, that's if we get t' keep him, until he's maybe adopted out, or goes into one of dose very strict, heartless, cruel boys' orphanages. Oh, I've heard such terrible stories about them, Reverend Mother."

Adele smiled at Matilda's blatant attempts to make her feel guilty. "Now, now, Matilda, there's no need to get carried away. Tell me, who's in charge of feeding him? Doesn't he interrupt the school lessons?"

"No, Mother, there's always one of us that can feed him. We keep him in the classroom while the girls are workin' on their studies. One of us Sisters feeds him when it's time. My Da made him a fine cradle that swings; Patrick loves it. It puts him straight back to sleep. Havin' him here has made the girls more attentive in class and much more responsible. They're learning through their hearts, t' care for and look after somebody else and not t' be selfish. And it's comin' so natural." Matilda made the sign of the cross and prayed that Adele would let them keep Patrick.

"I really don't know the right thing to do at this point, Matilda. Could somebody take him from me? I need to think about it over a cup of tea."

"Of course, ya'd be needin' a cup a tea, Mother." Matilda threw her hands to her face. "Oh, it's been remiss o' me, and after you've had such a long journey and all, God bless y'. And y'll have to be tellin' me how things are in the big city."

Sister Catherine, who had been waiting in the wing, took Patrick from Adele. Snuggling him close to her chest she walked to the kitchen then placed him in his wooden cradle. Not a single sound had come from the baby. It was as if he knew not to make any trouble, or the consequences may be grim.

The two women enjoyed their chat over a pot of tea in the warm kitchen, turning their heads every now and then to smile and coo at Patrick. His blonde curls and perfect features held their hearts. Matilda was pleased Mother Superior would stay until Monday, as she thought this would give Adele time to be as charmed by Patrick as they were. She was appreciative of Adele for dwelling on the problem and her compassion so far. Matilda smiled over her cup of tea, before attempting to manipulate Adele further, with information she thought would please her.

"My Ma will be bringin' the apple pies and clotted cream tomorrow after Mass. And Da's killed a lamb for us t' roast."

Matilda was forever grateful they had Da to help out with the food rations. The doctor's money, she knew, would not last forever.

"Oh, Matilda, you girls are spoilt! You're making my mouth water. But now I'd like to go and see how the young girls are getting on with their school work." The fact the girls were well behaved and had improved with their English and Maths gave Adele confidence that they were indeed handling the baby situation well. Moving among them, inspecting their writing and numbering skills, Adele was overcome with a sense of unity about the place. Her thoughts drifted to the baby. *Maybe it would work out—just until he was old enough to be sent to a boys' orphanage. Or, as Mother Matilda had suggested, they might just find good people to adopt him. It's also possible his mother may return to reclaim him. Sometimes people hit with hard times, have their lives turn around for the better, then they're once again able to care for the children they'd abandoned.* Adele consoled herself with these ideas. After a hearty lunch of Irish stew and plenty of damper to soak up the gravy, Adele and Matilda ambled through the well-kept gardens of the convent. A crisp, winter breeze bit into their faces and their hands became icy cold when picking oranges. Adele admired Matilda, but there seemed a touch of envy in her voice.

"You're very lucky, Matilda, to live in such a pleasant environment, and it's nice to see the girls appreciating everything you and the Sisters do for them."

Matilda smiled at her short, plump confidante. "I know, Adele, and I t'ank the Lord each day f' m' blessings, but y' know it's not always this peaceful. Sometimes we get the odd girl who stirs up the others, just like a rebellious angel in Heaven. Or we'll have a Sister who comes here determined the rod should not be spared. I have m' own way of doin' things and it seems to work itself out in the long run."

Adele had to agree with her. "That's why you should think of going on to bigger and better things, Matilda. You could help more children with your loving ways. Show those stern priests and bishops how it should be done. It amazes me how we praise the God of love and mercy, but then some of us within the Catholic Church take steps to punish and burden with guilt the ones who are weak and misguided."

Leaving the convent at any point of time, especially now with baby Patrick in her care, was totally unacceptable to Matilda.

"I must admit, Mother, I'm selfish, I'm totally satisfied with m' life here. I don't wish to be doin' anythin' else, even if the conditions of our benefactor allowed it. And I truly feel that baby Patrick has been sent to us for a special reason. I pray t' God t' forgive me m' selfish ways, but each time I do, He sends something else which pleases me."

15

Matilda paused, orange in hand, "Like just before the wee baby came, I said goodbye t' young Lucy Jones. Remember, the girl who was disowned by her parents after she'd been raped at thirteen and became pregnant? After her baby died at birth, she wouldn't talk to anyone f' two years. It was as if she'd been struck dumb by the fear and trauma. Well, she finally left here a confident young lady of eighteen. We found her a wonderful job as governess for a good family in Melbourne." Matilda threw the orange into the air and caught it, grinning at Adele. "Now, if that didn't give me great joy, nothin' ever will."

"You work hard, Matilda, and you deserve all the pleasures God can bestow upon you."

"I'm only doin' God's work, Mother. That's what gives me the pleasure."

Mother Superior held no further discussion with Matilda on whether baby Patrick should go or stay. Adele was thinking of the difficult time she was having with the Bishop of Adelaide. He was of the old "fire and brimstone" age, which angered her. Rumours of harsh punishments and meagre rations in some of the boys' orphanages around Adelaide ripped at her heart. She felt not enough was being done by the powers that be to correct this. *I'm not about to tell an actual lie, but at the same time, do I need to tell the Bishop about baby Patrick?*

Monday came, and Mother Superior readied to go. A spare piece of apple pie was wrapped in cloth by Matilda and handed to her.

"Thank you, Mother Matilda, I can't believe there was a crumb left of that delicious pie, enough for me to take on my journey home." She crossed herself before smiling.

Adele waved goodbye to the line-up of young girls and Sisters. She then looked deep into Matilda's eyes and, with her finger to her lips, she nodded. Their secret would be safe. Matilda watched the horses as they champed on their bits, and then reared slightly before leaning into their harness to begin the long haul to Adelaide.

Chapter 2

A Second Chance

After receiving rides from various strangers and walking many miles in between, Sally came upon a boarding house in Adelaide City. She'd intended to ask for food and lodging in return for work, but she arrived in an exhausted stupor. She was trying to summon up enough energy to walk down the path and knock on the door. But it seemed Sally's energy had left her and the sky began to spin before she collapsed.

As fate would have it, Jonathon Darcy was strolling along the pavement. This young man, new in town, was taking in the sights and getting his bearings. The last thing he'd expected was to see a young woman lying on the path outside a boarding house. His immediate reaction was to run to her aid although, Jonathon feared, the girl might be dead. Leaning over her slight frame, he placed his fingers on her neck. A pulse told him she was still alive. In a few strides, he was down the path where he banged several times on the door, calling, "Please! Can somebody help me?"

The door opened to reveal a plump, red-headed woman, wearing a white mob cap and wiping her hands on her apron.

"Yes, sir, what's the problem?"

"There's a young lady who appears to be very ill lying outside your establishment. May I bring her in until I fetch a doctor?"

The woman folded her arms, assuming the "young lady" would be nothing more than one of the street urchins who sometimes came looking for a handout.

"No, I'm afraid you can't. She belongs in the poor house!"

Jonathon then remembered how he'd experienced a similar situation himself, before a kind gentleman had taken him in off the streets of London. "Madam, please, have a heart. This poor girl is unable to walk. She's near death."

"I'm sorry, sir, but this is a respectable boarding house and not for the likes of her!" she exclaimed, while pointing her finger at the unconscious girl.

Jonathon would not relent. "I have money. Please accept a payment just to take her inside until I fetch a doctor." He held out a handful of coins. The woman's eyes glinted. Money, especially two shillings, was hard to come by. She pocketed the coins. After Jonathon gathered the girl in his arms, the woman ushered him into the sitting room where he lay her on the couch.

"Now, madam, where is the nearest doctor?"

"It's Mrs Murphy to you, sir." She'd taken note of his high-brow pronunciation of the English language. "The only doctor worth getting is Dr Forster. His rooms are about four blocks away."

After Mrs Murphy gave him directions, Jonathon strode out towards the doctor's surgery. He was almost breathless when he arrived, but once settled, he introduced himself to the doctor and explained the situation. The doctor collected his medical bag and set off to the boarding house with Jonathon. It hadn't taken Dr Forster long to assess the young woman's condition. He put his diagnosis to Jonathon.

"In my opinion, Mr Darcy, this poor girl is simply lacking proper nourishment and is suffering from sheer exhaustion." He looked squarely at Jonathon. "If you want to help her, Mr Darcy, then I suggest you leave her here and pay Mrs Murphy to feed and care for her. Otherwise, you could hire a cart and take her to the poor house where she may or may not recover."

Jonathon prided himself on his better judgment and inherent compassion. This was one of those moments. *Surely this young woman deserves more than the poor house can offer. Obviously, something terrible has happened for her to be in such a state. But this situation is not what I need in my first few weeks of arriving in the Colonies. I've come here to start my own law firm, not to rescue damsels in distress. But how can I not? Especially when someone reached out to me when I was young and destitute.'* Jonathon continued to look long and hard at the slender young woman on the couch. *How could she be in this predicament? Why did someone so beautiful seem to be all alone in life? What has happened to make her travel to the point of exhaustion?* These questions swirled in his mind until he asked, "How much do you charge for board and lodgings, Mrs Murphy?"

"Usually, it's three shillings a week. But she's so poorly, I'll have to nurse her too." Mrs Murphy made a few quick calculations. "So, I'd say five shillin's."

"Alright, I'll pay the five shillings, but you must care for her very well. I'll visit every day to make sure you do."

Mrs Murphy became indignant, retaliating, "You needn't bother t' check on her every day, Mr Darcy. I'm a woman of m' word and well respected in the community!" She then rose from her seat to accept the bottle of tonic which Dr Forster handed her, along with strict instructions.

"The girl is to be fed only nourishing soup and milk, Colleen, plus the tonic for the first week. She has to be left where she is until she's regained the strength to walk up the stairs."

"But this is the guests' sitting room, Doctor."

Colleen Murphy's protest was without conviction. Sometimes her business of caring for boarders, the daily chores and the enormous amount of food she needed to prepare and cook each day wore her out. Compassion was not always easy to elicit, but under these conditions, despite her formidable appearance, her heart seemed moved at the sight of this helpless waif. In Colleen's estimation, she needed the care of a mother.

Dr Forster sighed. "I'll send a screen to put around the couch so no one can see her, Colleen. I think in a day or two she'll be feeling better. Now, go and get some hot water and wash her down. Put a clean nightgown on her and make some of that chicken soup you're famous for. But first, offer her plenty of sugar water to drink when she wakes."

Before Mrs Murphy had time to move, Jonathon placed a hand on her arm. "No, please wait, Mrs Murphy. I'll carry her upstairs to whichever room you wish. I think she should be in a proper bed."

Dr Forster agreed and so Jonathon gathered Sally up in his arms once again. "Please show the way, Mrs Murphy."

Colleen Murphy's demeanour had softened by the time Jonathon put the young woman on the bed. Looking kindly at him, Colleen assured Jonathon, "I'll take good care of her, Mr Darcy. The poor little waif, she's so pretty. I'll try to find out what happened to her when she wakes."

The doctor took his leave, followed by Jonathon, who was now satisfied the girl would be well cared for.

Over the next few days Jonathon went about the business of settling in and inspecting offices to find just the right premises for his law firm. He felt excited about Adelaide. It was definitely a new, bustling city, surrounded by expansive cattle and sheep stations. Business everywhere was still booming, despite the great drought.

On the day Jonathon had arrived in Adelaide, he had sat on a park bench reading the *Adelaide Gazette*, when a local farmer sat down beside him and commented on the headlines, 'Drought Takes its Toll'.

"I see ya readin' the *Gazette*, mister. Well, I'll tell ya, the graziers are made of tough pioneer stock, so a drought won't finish them. You can bet on that!'

Jonathon smiled and continued to read another story in the paper:

From the gold mines in Ballarat, not far west of Melbourne, and all the way through the Australian countryside to the diamond mines of Western Australia, the opportunity to make a fortune is proving to be a great attraction to many foreigners. However, before the drought, the Chinese, Irish and Italian immigrants had been coming to Australia in droves. Not to mention the English. Now that South Australia is gripped by a severe drought, only a small percentage of the first influxes are making the long journey to South Australia.

The story continued. *However, Adelaide has been most fortunate, as nearby Broken Hill is now mining successfully for silver and lead, therefore, business in Adelaide City has only been slightly compromised.*

Yes, Jonathon could see how the country had definitely been on the brink of a population explosion and that's why he could see that his future was here. Another reason, of course, was his mother. Before she'd died, she said that the Australian colony would be the place she'd like to go and live. "We could make a new life for ourselves there, Jonathon. I hear it's warm, and the land is so rich and the seas so blue, you would think you were in Paradise."

Jonathon accepted the fact that his coming here was because of his mother's dream and the money left to him by his benefactor, Mr Angus Darcy QC. So now in South Australia, Jonathon intended to pursue the dream of the only two people he'd loved: his mother and Angus Darcy. Of course, there was his father and although he could only remember him vaguely, as he'd died when Jonathon was seven, he knew him to be a kind and loving man.

On arriving in Adelaide, Jonathon had been advised to stay at the Graziers Club, which was quite extravagant for its time. He was a little surprised to see the furnishings were of such regal splendour. The interior walls were covered in crimson and gold brocade wallpaper, and the furniture was probably crafted from imported rosewood. Jonathon took pleasure in feeling the silk curtains which hung luxuriously to the floor. The light green carpet, he'd been informed, was made from the finest New Zealand wool. He took no time at all to settle himself amongst the splendour. He also enjoyed the company of some of the wealthiest cattle barons who frequented the club on their visits to Adelaide. He felt sure his future was set.

Chapter 3

Sally's Relief

It was not until the following morning that Sally woke to the aroma of homemade biscuits. Sunlight streamed through the window. She was lying clean and warm between crisp sheets and a feather quilt, and watched dreamily as a pair of wily wagtails built their nest in the jacaranda tree directly outside her window. "Thank you, God," she said out loud, while having no idea how she came to be where she was. She tried to remember the final moments before passing out, but the memory of having to give up her baby stabbed her.

Trying to turn her mind from grief, she looked about the room. A washbowl sat on the bedside table, along with a face washer, a towel, and half a glass of milk. Her carpet bag had been placed on top of a chest of drawers. Her dress, washed and pressed, hung over the back of a chair. Aware of footsteps and voices rising up the stairs, Sally sat up as they became louder. Two women appeared, smiling at her from the doorway.

"Oh! Thank the Lord, you're awake," Mrs Murphy said cheerily as she walked towards the bed, all smiles, and red curls peeking from her mop cap. Alongside her was an unimaginably beautiful woman, her raven hair tied loosely in a bun, her eyes deep pools of violet.

"Hello. My name is Bernadette Jones," the woman said, then turned towards Mrs Murphy. "And this is Colleen Murphy, the owner of this boarding house."

Sally smiled coyly. "I'm very pleased to meet you both. My name is Sally. If you don't mind, how did I get here?"

As Colleen laughed at her bewilderment, Sally managed a wan smile before Bernadette spoke.

"Well, let me begin by telling you, Sally, that a Mr Darcy happened to be walking by and noticed you had collapsed outside Mrs Murphy's boarding house. He carried you inside and then fetched Dr Forster, for whom I work. Such a kind young man Mr Darcy must be. He's offered to pay for your care until you're well. That's assuming you may not have the funds to do so yourself?"

"I have no funds, I'm sorry, but I cannot allow him to do that. I shall work for my board." Struggling with the bed clothes, Sally had almost managed to climb out of bed before Colleen grasped her by the shoulders.

"Oh, no you don't, young lady! You'll be getting back into bed until you're good and strong. Look at the likes of you, as weak as a kitten!" Mrs Murphy tucked Sally smartly back into bed.

Bernadette added, "Yes, Mrs Murphy's right. You must rest and not worry about a thing, Sally."

Earlier in the kitchen, the two women had been discussing Sally's predicament. They could only imagine what may have happened to her before she reached them.

Gentle in her approach, Bernadette inquired, "Would you like to talk about how you came to be here, Sally?"

Sally began to cry. "Please, you've been so kind to me but—I can't—I can't talk about it…" Her tears trickled down her cheeks.

Bernadette sat on Sally's bed. "I'm sure you'll tell us your story whenever you're ready."

Mrs Murphy bustled towards the door, exclaiming, "I'll be up with some porridge soon and after that, I'll be running you a hot bath."

She left, while Bernadette sat holding Sally's hand. "You're a very lucky young lady, Sally. The Lord has guided you to the right place. He knows we'll care of you."

Chapter 4

All Things in Place

Five days had passed since Jonathon left Sally in the care of Mrs Murphy and he'd not found the time to visit her again. He was kept busy, looking for offices to lease and to settle in. On this, the fifth day, Jonathon decided to have a light lunch in the Graziers Club before walking the dusty streets of Adelaide to view yet another premise. He suspected it would probably be as unsuitable as the ones before it. His thoughts then lightened. *I may find time this afternoon to visit the young lady at the boarding house.*

Jum Watt lifted his head as Jonathon walked into the dining room. Liking the look of the young man, Jum stood to shake his hand and introduce himself. "Hello there, I'm Jum Watt. And you, sir, are …?'

Jonathon looked Jum in the eye. He could tell straight away by his handshake that he was of strong character, perhaps an ally. "My name is Jonathon Darcy."

"Care to join me, Jonathon?" Jum asked, pulling out a chair.

"Thank you, sir, don't mind if I do. I'm new in town and after a quick bite, I'm off to find suitable premises from which to run my law practice."

Jum raised an eyebrow. "Law, you say? Well, you just might've found your first customer. I'm looking for a good lawyer to tie up some mining land in the west and I'm not getting on too good with the wife, so a divorce could be on the cards." He reached for the whisky bottle and poured a measure into two glasses.

"Oh, that's a shame," Jonathon was taken aback by the man's straightforward talk.

"No, it's not, Jonathon. She can't have children, and she's become bitter and frigid."

"Well, I'm still sorry, Mr Watt; it's a sad tale."

Jum laughed boisterously, throwing his ruggedly handsome head back. "I like the look of you, Jonathon," he said, raising his glass, "but are you tough enough for this country?"

"Yes, I'm sure I am, sir. But that doesn't mean I must be heartless," Jonathon took a mere sip of his whisky.

Jum leaned back, half-shutting his eyes, a wry smile curled one side of his mouth. He focused on this refined young man before he made his decision. "I always go on first impressions. I like you, Jonathon Darcy, so I'll give you a go." Clinking his glass against Jonathon's, Jum downed the contents. The talk over lunch was all about their pasts and where their families had hailed from. Both men had interesting and similar starts to their fortunes. They both had generous benefactors and both had lost their parents at an early age.

Jonathon looked at his gold fob watch, declaring in genuine surprise, "Goodness, look at the time! I must meet a gentleman downtown. He's to show me another office to let. It's on the north side of the city, adjoining the park. I'm sorry but I'll have to hurry."

He stood and shook Jum's hand, with the same degree of strength that he'd received earlier. "I thank you for your company, Mr Watt, and perhaps your future business." Jum then poured a final glass of whisky and watched in amusement as Jonathon walked away, a little unsteady.

Hurrying along, Jonathon went over the address in his head, as he'd left the paper he'd written it on in his room. He waited outside the office building for some time until he began to think, *Maybe I have the wrong address.* At that moment, Jum came striding along, laughing at Jonathon's surprise.

"It's all right, Mr Darcy, or Jon, if I may call you by your Christian name?" He didn't wait for an answer. "I'm the owner of the building. I had to get the key from my offsider. I thought I might as well show you myself, seeing we're going to be doing business together."

"I must say, Mr Watt, you took me by surprise and yes, you may call me Jon, but I'd prefer Jonathon."

Jum smiled at Jonathon's correctness and proceeded to show him the way up the stairs and into the office. Jonathon gazed around the room, *Mmm, it's very generous. Large windows overlooking the parklands and a more than ample fireplace. My desk will go there. Yes, it will be a very impressive office, once furnished.* Before walking into the main office they'd passed through a small waiting room. Jonathon turned back to view it.

Jum remarked, while pointing, "This room's smaller, Jon, but there's still plenty of space for your secretary and your clients to wait in comfort."

"It's perfect, Mr Watt. How much per month?" Jonathon asked, quite enthused.

Jum took Jonathon's hand in his and looked him straight in the eye. "Call me Jum. I don't like being called Mr Watt, as I'm not that sort of bloke, Jonathon. I'm informal, one might say." He gave the hint of a laugh. "Now, why don't we work it out as we go? You keep a tally of hours you work for me and see how many customers come your way. If you're successful, Jonathon, then I'll charge you plenty, if not, you can have it cheap."

Jonathon's eyebrows shot up. "I think we should draw up an agreement, however, Mr Watt. I mean Jum."

"My handshake is as good as any agreement you'll get around here, Jonathon!" he said, shaking Jonathon's hand. His grip tightened and his large palm, covered in calluses, felt rough against Jonathon's much softer skin. Jum's enthusiasm escalated.

"I'll have all the right furniture brought in straightaway, Jonathon. I also know a young woman who's looking for secretarial work. And I may just have your first client." Jum's heavy footsteps echoed upon the floorboards as he paced the room. "He's a bloke I know who's been wrongly accused of stealing. I knew his old man. He was a real honest bloke, so I can't imagine the son being any different." He stopped and turned to face Jonathon. "So, I'll tell him to come see you tomorrow morning, say, ten? Let's seal it with a drink and dinner tonight at the club. What do you say?"

"Yes. Yes, of course, Mr, ah… Jum," Jonathon replied, mentally preparing himself for a long night ahead, if lunch was anything to go by. "I have some business to do with the manager of the Bank of Adelaide this afternoon, Mr Watt, and it may take up my entire afternoon. I don't think I'll be able to help with the furnishing."

Jum shook his head to confirm. "Don't worry about a thing, Jonathon. It'll be all ready and waiting for you in the morning, along with your new secretary, Mildred Morrison, and your first client, Tom Coutts. And call me Jum, remember."

Walking away, Jonathon shook his head in disbelief. This was like a dream. When would he wake up? He couldn't believe his luck. He sensed his mother in heaven was sending the right people his way. How else could he explain it, first, Angus Darcy in England, and now Jum Watt in Australia?

An evening of guaranteed business deals and introductions to many of Jum's friends and acquaintances was followed by dinner and wine, after which the men retired to the smoking room for port and cigars. Jonathon had enjoyed two ports before peeking at his watch. As he did so, one of the Club's valets entered and addressed Jonathon with meticulous pronunciation.

"Mr Darcy, I have taken the liberty of drawing your bath, as you requested."

His forced accent amused Jonathon, and it took all of his composure not to laugh. He was sure this young man was just a glorified jackaroo. The valet's appearance at that point had been well planned by Jonathon, as he didn't want the evening to turn into an all-night binge. Turning to Jum, Jonathon explained, "I'm a little weary, Jum. It's been a busy few days, so if you'll excuse me?"

"Ah, we'll have to toughen you up, Jon, but I'll let you off tonight!" Jum swilled his port and asked the waiter for another, along with a whisky chaser. As Jonathon left, he passed yet another man dressed in the same attire as Jum's: Harris Tweed jacket, in shades of brown and beige, light blue shirt, cream-coloured brushed cotton trousers, and polished brown leather riding boots. *The uniform of the graziers*, Jonathon thought. He nodded at the man in acknowledgment, then heard Jum's raucous greeting.

"Bertie, good to see you, mate, come 'n have a drink with me!"

The bath had been drawn for Jonathon in one of the many bathrooms at the Club. Jonathon lay back in the hot soothing water. *Here I am, I've survived the arduous boat trip from England. Encountered the strangeness of the Australian landscape, endured the endless road from Port Melbourne to Adelaide, then found a poor young woman outside a boarding house, and finally I met the amazing Jum Watt. What a journey! I truly feel Jum is a man of his word. I'm sure he'll have all details secured for my first day at the office. Yes, this will be a remarkable feat in itself.*

Relaxed and content, Jonathon slid into bed, when suddenly a pang of guilt hit. He hadn't kept his promise to visit the girl. It had been five days since he said he would. *I'll go tomorrow after lunch.* His last thought calmed his conscience.

His sleep was deep and dreamless before the morning light came streaming through an opening in the drapes. He blinked and turned to look at the time on his fob watch—it read 9.30 am—Jonathon's heart raced. He needed to be dressed and in his office within thirty minutes for his first official appointment. If he made it, it would be a miracle.

After running most of the way, he slowed up only when he'd reached his door. He then walked calmly through, pretending he'd just savoured his breakfast, read the paper and strolled to work. Jonathon kept up the pretence, thinking his client may be there waiting. He couldn't afford the impression of being disorganised.

"Good morning, Miss," Jonathon stepped closer to the desk and whispered, "I'm so sorry. What was your name again?"

She whispered back, trying to hide her amusement, "It's Miss Morrison, sir."

Jonathon then straightened his jacket, smiled and asked, "Well, who do we have here, Miss Morrison?"

"This is Mr Tom Coutts, Mr Darcy. He's a little early." She stood and waited for Jonathon to enter before ushering Mr Coutts into the office.

Jonathon indicated a seat to his client. He then settled himself and said, "Please take a seat, Mr Coutts. What seems to be the problem?" It transpired that Tom had been accused of stealing from his boss, someone he'd been working with for the last five years.

"Why would I bite the hand that feeds me, Mr Darcy?" he asked, as he sat perched on the edge of the leather chair opposite Jonathon's desk.

"Indeed, why would you?" Jonathon replied. Jonathon then called in Miss Morrison who, in excellent shorthand, took a detailed statement from Mr Coutts. The meeting lasted an hour, after which Jonathon was convinced of Tom Coutts's innocence. He shook Tom's hand and told him, "Try not to worry, Mr Coutts. I'm sure we can win this case."

Jonathon now had the opportunity to inspect the furniture Jum had supplied. He smiled at the fact that he'd tried hard not to be impressed when first entering the room. Jum's effort had obviously been to create the feel of opulence. Jonathon ran his fingers over the polished desk, and opened and shut stationery drawers with childish delight. He walked around the room, admiring the paintings on the walls and the richly embroidered Turkish rug. *Jum Watt certainly is an incredible man— this office makes me look very successful. I have never met anyone like him, and perhaps I never will again. Yes, he's like a tornado, that's what he is. If you don't go along with him, I'm sure he'd spit you out—broken.*

After missing breakfast, Jonathon was ravenous. "Please take your lunch break now, Miss Morrison. I'll be back in two hours, thank you." This would give him time to eat and then visit the girl.

He chose to eat in a neat little tea house before walking to visit Sally, enjoying the midday sun warming his shoulders. When he'd run to help the young lady, he hadn't had the time to notice the small, manicured garden in front of the white-washed boarding house. He paused now to take it in. A wooden swing seat, made for two, sat under a jacaranda tree, and a row of yellow rose bushes lined the path to the front door. He knocked, expecting to be greeted by Mrs Murphy. After a few moments, the door opened to reveal a very different lady. Jonathon almost stepped backwards, so startled was he by her beauty. She was tall and slim and her magnetic violet eyes seemed to look straight into his soul. The woman smiled, showing a slight gap between her otherwise perfect white teeth.

"Yes, sir, may I help you?" she asked politely.

Jonathon was momentarily lost for words. "Ah um, yes… yes, I was here about a week ago. I helped a young lady… could you please…"

Bernadette interrupted, once she realised who he must be. "Of course, do come in, sir. You must be Mr Darcy, the gentleman who helped our Sally?"

"I'm sorry. I assume you mean the young lady who was taken ill. I must confess I haven't been to see her since I called the doctor. I was not aware of her name."

"Please forgive me. Let me introduce myself. I'm Bernadette Jones. I assist Dr Forster."

Bernadette smiled, offering her hand to Jonathon, who knew from her firm handshake that this woman was not only beautiful, but formidable. *How strange, to shake a woman's hand. The colony certainly has developed strange customs,* Jonathon thought.

"Pleased to meet you, Miss Jones. How is Miss, er, Sally, is she recovering well?" Jonathon asked once he'd followed Bernadette into the sitting room.

"Sally is quite well, Mr Darcy. It's been near a week now, although she still seems a little fragile. Sally's resting in her room, however, I'm sure she'll want to meet you. I must thank you, on her behalf, for what you're doing. Please take a seat. I'll shall go and inform her you're here."

"Thank you, Miss Jones. That would be very kind." Bernadette smiled in acknowledgement and left, while Jonathon sat daydreaming out of the window for what seemed a long time.

"Hello, Mr Darcy."

Jonathon turned to find Sally standing there. When she held out her hand to him, instead of shaking it, he bent and brushed his lips over her knuckles. He immediately felt foolish. "I'm so pleased to meet you. Sally—isn't it? I say, you're looking much better than when I last saw you. Would you prefer I call you Miss—?"

Sally interrupted him. "No please, Sally is fine." With her heart pounding from the unexpected intimacy, Sally managed to say, "I have to thank you, Mr Darcy, for your help and kindness. I don't know when I'll be able to repay you. But I promise I will, just as soon as I have a job." Her blue eyes fixed on his with determination. "That was the reason I came to Adelaide, to find work. I never realised how far it was from the small country town where I lived. I'm afraid my strength ran out. Thank you so very much for helping me, well, saving my life, actually."

Jonathon was touched by her sincerity. His heart had raced when he held her hand and now the idea, that this sweet girl may be another blessing sent to him by his mother, excited him. "It was my pleasure, Sally. I was there at the right time, it seems. Are you up to sitting outside?"

Sally nodded. He opened the door for her and together they sat on the veranda chairs. Jonathon watched the swing seat under the jacaranda tree, as it swung back and forth in the breeze. "I love swing seats. They remind me of our garden in London. If I had to sort out a problem with my studies, or even a personal problem, I found the swinging calmed me and helped me think more clearly."

"I admit I've never sat in one, Mr Darcy, but I can see what you mean. It's like being rocked as a baby." Sally's words suddenly caught in her throat. Tears welled. Jonathon noticed. "Sally, please. Is anything wrong? Do you feel unwell?"

"No, I'm alright, thank you, Mr Darcy." Wiping her tears, she lied, "I'm just so grateful for your kindness; it's touched me more than you can know. Please forgive me."

Sally made a visible effort to compose herself before asking, "Perhaps you'd tell me a little about yourself, Mr Darcy. You're obviously from England?" Her smile was forced. More than willing to dispel the tension, Jonathon told Sally everything he could think of, from when his father had died, to his gentle aristocratic mother being disowned by her family for marrying beneath her station. He went on to explain how his mother had suffered and died from an unknown cause and how he, as a young boy, was left alone.

"But I never stole or begged," he said, pride straightening his back. "I would ask to work in exchange for food or money. I spent my days in the better part of London in an effort to find work with people who could afford to pay, or at least give me a decent meal. That was where I encountered Mr Darcy. He had been returning from his wife's funeral and found me knocking on his front door. I was about to see if any work was available."

Jonathon lapsed into silence for a few moments. He was trying to think of how he could best explain to Sally the relationship between Mr Darcy and himself. "I suppose some people want to be alone after such heartbreak, and some people need company. To maybe take their mind off their sadness. It was the latter with Mr Darcy, so he asked me to come in, much to the disapproval of Millie, his house maid." Jonathon gave a cheeky grin. "But, I soon won her over. We became quite close."

"You mean," asked Sally surprised, "he took you in to live with him without a second thought?"

"Yes, he was the kindest, most intelligent man I think I've ever met. He legally adopted me. Angus Darcy was a high-powered lawyer in London. I was ten years old when he took me in. He must have seen something in me which led him to believe I could be a scholar. Mr Darcy probably recognised how my mother's 'breeding' had paid off." Jonathon had the grace to look embarrassed by this revelation.

"You see, my mother insisted I be bought up as a young gentleman. Mr Darcy simply continued the training. I was very lucky to be taken in by him, both into his home and heart." Again, Jonathon paused. "However, I think I did him a favour by giving him something to do after his wife died—a kind of project, if you like." Jonathon blushed and turned his head, before looking directly at Sally. "But please do tell me something of yourself, Sally."

Sally gave a feeble cough and almost whimpered. "I must beg your pardon, Mr Darcy, but I'm still very weak and need to rest."

Jonathon stood and bowed. "Oh, I am sorry. I've been rambling on about myself. Of course, you must be tired." He escorted her back into the sitting room where Bernadette Jones sat reading. Sally stopped at the foot of the stairs, offering her hand to Jonathon. He held it briefly in his but gave her a lingering look.

"It was very nice to meet you, Mr Darcy. Thank you for coming. I hope you will visit again soon." Sally blushed and hurried up the stairs. This was the first time in her life she'd received any sort of attention from a young gentleman. A delightful shiver ran through her body.

"Yes, I'll return tomorrow after lunch, Sally, if I may?"

Bernadette jumped in. "Yes, please do, Mr Darcy."

Jonathon enjoyed walking around Adelaide. Each day he would notice something different, even strange, be it a bird, a wildflower or a tree. The openness of this country was almost unfathomable. He then hurried back to his office, taking the path through Adelaide Parkland. Ducks and swans floated carefree around the large lake in the centre of the park. Children holding their mothers' hands skipped along, occasionally stopping to pick up a stick or a stone to throw in the lake. They stood on the edge, watching the missile splash into the water, causing ringlets to appear, increase in size, then disappear. It filled Jonathon's heart with expanding warmth, a longing maybe, that one day he and his own children would be doing the same. Yes, he was ready to work hard and think of a family. He only wished his mother were here, walking beside him. His thoughts turned to Sally; her beautiful face, her skin so pale and soft. He wanted to hold her in his arms when she cried. He asked himself: *Why can't I show my true feelings? Why am I so reserved, always studying and judging every situation, never spontaneous in showing what I truly feel? Does it come from the warning, or perhaps, I should say, strong advice from my adopted father?* "Choose your love wisely, Jonathon. It's best for one to be married before consummating. It's much safer in terms of contracting syphilis and, of course, it is the morally correct thing to do. Please follow my advice, do not under any circumstances fornicate with young women."

Miss Morrison was arranging a vase of flowers on her desk when Jonathon returned to his office. "Oh, hello, Mr Darcy, did you have a nice lunch?"

"Yes, I did, thank you, Miss Morrison. Has anyone called?"

"Mr Watt came looking for you, and a Chinese man, Dr Liu, I think he said his name was. He came peddling some sort of concoction. He said it cleansed the blood and gave good health. I told him to go away."

"Well, Miss Morrison, if Dr Liu calls in again, please be polite and tell him, yes, I am perhaps interested in purchasing some of his tonic." Jonathon thought it could perhaps be just what Sally needed. "Did Mr Watt say when he would return?"

Miss Morrison glanced at the clock on the mantelpiece. "Yes, he should be back any moment."

Jonathon sat back in his leather chair. He was about to go over Tom Coutts' statement when Jum came bursting through the door. Without a word said, he sat in the client's chair, then lowered his head, he seemed to be mulling over something. He then looked up at Jonathon who eyed him tentatively.

"Jonathon, I must tell you, I have to tell someone, my heart's about to jump through my bloody rib cage! I've just seen the most beautiful woman in the world! I was on my way to make travel arrangements to go west when she passed me in the street. I tell you, she's amazing. I had to follow her, without her knowing, of course. She went into Dr Forster's office. I waited and waited for her to come out and when she didn't, I went inside. She was sitting at the front desk and she asked me if I'd come to see the doctor. I said, 'No, I've come to see you'." Jum laughed at his own temerity.

"Now, most women would've scorned me for being so forward, Jon, but she just laughed and said, 'I'm sorry, but there's nothing I can do for you, sir'. I said, 'Yes, there is. You can have dinner with me this evening', and she said, 'Come back at five o'clock'. Christ! I don't even know her name!" Jum stood and ran his hand through his hair and paced the room. "She left me tongue tied after that."

Jonathon lent backwards, amused at Jum's overwhelming excitement. "Do you realise, Jum, that you've told me all of that without drawing breath? Are you usually this way when you see a good-looking woman?"

"Good bloody looking? I'm telling you, Jon, she's a goddess!"

Jonathon laughed, and then thought for a moment. "I think I know the woman. She must be new in town if you haven't seen her before. She may be a Miss Bernadette Jones, the woman who's helping to look after Sally. She works for the doctor."

Jum's brow crinkled. "Really, but who's Sally?"

"Oh, I am sorry, Jum. It seems I've been too preoccupied with my own affairs to mention her. When I first arrived in town I was walking down the street and noticed a young lady had collapsed outside Mrs Murphy's boarding house. I paid Mrs Murphy two shillings to have her taken inside while I fetched the doctor." Jonathon went on to tell Jum the whole story.

"Well, I'll be buggered! How long are you going to keep paying her way?"

Jonathon shrugged. "As long as it takes for her to get well, I suppose. Sally's promised to pay me back when she finds work."

"I'll make bloody sure she does! I'll give her a job on my property, Bulkawa. Now you'd better make sure she doesn't skip town on you!" Jum gave him a wolfish grin. Still beaming, he left the office.

Jonathon listened to Jum's farewell to Miss Morrison, before thinking about his "skip town" statement. *I like Sally, even if only on face value, as I don't know anything about her. However, I feel she won't let me down. Even if she did, it's against my nature to abandon anyone in trouble, especially a young lady. The money doesn't matter to me, but funnily enough, I think Sally does.*

Chapter 5

Time to Take Store

Twelve months had passed since that day and Jonathon had kept a journal.

New tracts of land are being opened up and there are so many opportunities for this fast-growing population. This past year, my business has grown beyond my imagination. But I'm not sure if some of my clientele are perhaps conveying their true circumstances. It seems to be, what Jum refers to as, "telling the truth, the whole truth and something resembling the truth". I'm a truthful and compassionate man, but I should get tougher and more cunning if I want to remain successful in this society. Jum always relates to me how very proud he is to have me as his friend and I have become one of his closest confidantes. There's very little I don't know about Jum now. I've consolidated his mining deals, and handled his divorce, which could have been nasty if it weren't for my tactful handling of the proceedings. I sound a little smug, I guess. But I'm sure I literally charmed Jum's ex-wife into believing she would be far better off without him. It did help that Jum was extremely generous in paying her enough money to keep her in fine fashion for the rest of her life in Sydney. In truth, that was the main reason the divorce was as amicable.

Despite my business success and my victories in court, I have to admit, I'm a little jealous of Jum's happiness with his new love, Bernadette Jones. I harbour an attraction towards Sally and I torture myself by not speaking about this when I have the chance.

I'm so shy around women. While I'm grateful to Jum for employing Sally on Bulkawa, his sheep and cattle property, this means I rarely see her unless I make a visit there. I think Jum, being an intuitive man, has not failed to notice my attraction for Sally. I'm sure he knows, but I have to work up the courage to approach Sally honestly. Yes, that's what I'll do.

Sally, after saving nearly every penny she'd earned, was ready to repay her debt to Jonathon. She decided to share this fact with Jum. Nervous with the thought, she brushed down her dress and pushed her curls into place before knocking on his office door.

"Come in, come in," said Jum, not looking up from his paperwork.

Sally opened the door and stood to attention in front of Jum's desk. "Please excuse me, Mr Watt, but I have been saving my money and I would now like to pay Mr Darcy the money I owe him. Will he be coming here soon?"

Jum, somewhat amused, lent back in his cowhide chair and said with a grin, "No, he's not coming here soon, Sally. But I'll tell you what, because I'm grateful for your hard work over the past twelve months and saving to pay back my friend, I'll take you to Adelaide with me next week. You can pay him back there. I'll even buy you a new dress and you can have dinner with us as a reward for your hard work and honesty. How would you like that, young lady?"

Sally was taken by surprise. "You are too kind, I, I—don't think—sir. Well, what I mean to say is, yes, yes, of course, I would like that. Thank you, Mr Watt."

She left hastily, fearing Jum would hear her heart pounding. *Oh, my goodness, I'll have to walk in the garden for a moment to steady myself. How will I ever be able to contain my excitement when I see Jonathon and dine with him in Adelaide? This is the only time in the past twelve months when my feelings for another have overridden those I feel for my son. I pray, dear Lord, that the nuns have kept him. Has he been adopted out? If so, are his new parents loving and kind to him? Maybe if I tell Mr Watt about him, he would understand and allow me to bring him here. Now another problem is tugging at my heart, dear Lord. This deep affection, perhaps love, I have for Jonathon Darcy. Try as I might, I cannot help but think of him near every minute of the day. I need your guidance, dear Lord.*

Sally walked quickly through the garden to Jum's chapel. After crossing herself, she knelt at the altar. *Dear God, please help me to make the right choices. I want desperately to see my son and be assured he's alright. I know my love for Jonathon may never be returned and I'm prepared for that. But if Jonathon should see it in his heart to love me back, I promise to make him a good wife. Dear God, please forgive me my sins and please give me the guidance I need. And most of all, I trust in You, dear Lord, to take care of my beloved son. Amen.*

Sally stood, feeling some of her burden had lightened and hurried back to the kitchen. She didn't want to be reprimanded by Frieda, the cook.

"Where has y' been, girl? I need y' to stoke up the fire. JW has called for scones with his afternoon tea." Frieda was up to her elbows in flour, making scones for Jum, the man she'd helped raise since he was a young boy. While she kneaded and probed the dough, she shared her love to prattle.

"Y' know, Sally, well, I don't think y' do know, because I haven't told y' before, our Jum was the only child of the head stockman for the original owners,

Mr and Mrs Watt. Then Jum lost his ma from pneumonia; she was only young too. It was a sad day." Frieda gave a sigh. "Then not long after that with his father bein' killed in an accident on the property, well, Jum had no one to take care a' him."

Sally listened intently as she placed his afternoon tea cup and plate on the tray.

"Jum was legally 'dopted, y' know, by Mr and Mrs Watt, they treated him as their own. They had a daughter afore they 'dopted Jum, but she died wit' the croup. She weren't even two yet. It were such a sad time, poor Mrs Watt, she were heartbroken. She never got her strength back ta go on with another birth, ya know. So, she gave all a' love and affection t' young Jum. They give him the best of everythin', includin' a private school education. Yep, everythin' that was good, he got. Jum was a strong and determined lad. No 'fancy talk' as he called it, rubbed off on him, but he was canny. He become friends with young men who's got powerful connections. Yes, well-healed, well-spoken young men, dey was. They'd come here on school holidays and all of 'em have stayed close to Jum." Frieda paused to have a chuckle. "He's so open and generous, be our Jum, but ya wouldn't want t' cross 'im. Y' mark m' words, Sally, those that has 'ave lived t' regret it. He'd be a strong character, Sally." Frieda rolled her eyes for effect. "Such a talent to makin' money too, I never met the likes of 'im before. Jum be one of the most respected men in Adelaide, y' know, if not da' whole country! Now I don't know why I'd be tellin' y' all this? I suppose it's because I've come ta really like y', girl, and I know JW does too."

Sally noticed the look of pride on Frieda's wrinkled face, as she loaded the scones in the oven. "Thank you, Frieda, I like you too, very much and I agree. Jum, I mean Mr Watt, is an exceptional man, he's just offered me a wonderful gift." Sally then told Frieda what had just happened. Frieda wasn't surprised.

The buggy trip into Adelaide gave Sally time to reflect. *I feel my only chance of winning Jonathon's love is to be respectable and one who pays her debts. But I'm determined to ask Mr Watt if I may have two days off while in Adelaide. I'll use the time to travel back to Brinton and see if my baby is still at the convent. I can hardly imagine how much he's grown. Does he look like me? Is he walking yet? Dear Lord, please allow me to see for myself.*

It was mid-afternoon by the time Jum delivered Sally to Mrs Murphy's boarding house. "Hello Mrs Murphy…" Before Sally could say another word, Colleen had embraced her so warmly that it was more like a rugby tackle.

"Oh Sally, but you look so beautiful! I can't tell y' how happy I am to be spendin' time with y' at last. I look forward to your letters, but seein' ya in the flesh, well, that's a different thing altogether, we have so much ta' catch up on."

"I know, Mrs Murphy, you're right. So much has happened, but what you don't know is all the wonderful in-betweens!" Catching the aroma of something delicious wafting down the hallway, Sally asked, "Mmm… what is that I smell cooking, Mrs Murphy?"

"It's a new curry recipe given ta me by Bernadette. She's got some real exotic recipes, she does."

They indeed had a lot to catch up on. While they waited for the kettle to boil, Sally gave Colleen the news about her plans to take a trip back to Brinton, plus her dinner engagement and the new dress Jum had promised to buy her.

"That's wonderful, Sally. Now I don't want to appear rude by changin' the subject, but did y' hear our dear Bernadette be gone into politics?"

"No, the boss doesn't discuss anything personal with me. And I don't see Bernadette as often as I'd like to anymore."

"Well, she be busy, Sally. It seems she's taken her stand on somethin' she called 'women's rights'. She thinks women should be allowed ta vote. I suppose that's fair. We work just as hard as the men, and we're just as smart. Do y' agree, Sally?"

"Yes, of course I agree. I've read a lot about it in the newspapers. Mr Watt has them delivered. How far has she gone with it, I wonder? Is Mr Watt on her side?" Sally tilted her head upwards toward the ceiling, deep in thought.

"Of course he is, Sally! He'd chop his right arm off if she told 'im to. I've never seen a man so smitten with a woman in all m' life. I don't, for the life of me, know why they don't just get married!" Colleen sighed in exasperation.

Sally declined to offer an opinion on the topic and so changed the subject. "I do hope Bernadette will be having dinner with us tomorrow night. I'd love to hear her views on politics. So many interesting things are happening at the moment, it seems."

Sally became lost in thought again until Mrs Murphy declared, "Of course she'll be there! Jum won't set foot anywhere in Adelaide without her. And please don't be tellin' me, Sally, that y' want to be joinin' the Suffragette Movement too?"

Sally laughed. "No, not really, I mean how could I possibly join, living where I do? But I would like to learn a lot more and understand how the government works, particularly where this country is heading."

"Well," said Colleen, standing to clear the table, "I know the country isn't heading here to do the washing up!"

Jum had booked into the Graziers Club and was about to have a stiff whisky when he thought the better of it. *If I get the taste I'll find it hard to stop. God knows I need all my faculties when I make love with the woman I desire more than anything else in the whole bloody world.* He decided to bathe instead. Not wasting time, he washed then dried himself, generously splashing cologne over his face after shaving. He brushed his teeth with bicarbonate of soda and smiled into the fogged-up mirror. As he started to dress in his tailored grey suit, a thought crossed his mind, *I'd be a damned sight more comfortable in my moleskins and blue shirt. But out of respect for Bernadette, I'll struggle with this bloody stiff white shirt— bastard of a thing!*

Downstairs and striding through the foyer of the club, he refused several offers to join his friends for a drink at the bar. "No thanks, not tonight, Bill!" He whistled as he left the club and strode towards Bernadette's residence. A cold mist cast an eerie glow around the lighted gas lamps, for those who ventured out in the evening. Appearing out of the mist, an old woman stood on the corner selling flowers. She graced a knowing smile.

"Violets for your sweetheart, mister?"

Startled at first, Jum recovered and accepted the small bouquet that she'd thrust into his hand. "Yes, of course, thank you." *How does she know what's on a man's mind?* "Here you are, madam, one shilling, plus two shillings for reading my mind."

"God bless y', sir!" she called, disappearing into the gloom once again.

Stopping at the foot of the stairs to straighten his tie, Jum took a deep breath. "Ah yes, the stairway to heaven," he murmured.

In the open doorway, a soft light cast Bernadette in silhouette. Jum stood almost transfixed, admiring her perfect body through sheer chiffon. The violets he threw on the dining table, just after he'd slammed the door with his foot.

Their bodies entwined never to part, until every ounce of love had been given from their longing. Lying naked in the afterglow, their bodies warmed by the open fire, Jum felt relaxed and confident enough to ask Bernadette the question he'd asked her many times before. "Please marry me, Bernadette. I need you every night, not once in a bloody blue moon!"

She laughed out loud. "You would soon tire of me, my love."

"Not in a million bloody years," he said, rolling over on top of her and pinning her arms down. "I'm not letting you up until you agree to marry me. I'm tired of asking you." He rained soft kisses on her mouth, her neck and her breasts until it aroused the passion in her once again.

Chapter 6

Not Even in Sally's Dreams

The scent of drifting blossom pollen made Sally sneeze. She was to meet Jum at ten-thirty for their shopping spree. Dusting down her plain grey dress and straightening her sensible hat, she waited patiently outside the Graziers Club. Jum, with his enormous stride, came up from behind and caught her unawares.

"Oh, Mr Watt, you gave me such a fright!"

"Never mind, Sally, here I am! And now we're going to buy you the prettiest dress we can find." He studied her hat with disapproval, then said bluntly, "And a new hat!"

Once in the department store, Sally stood amazed; she'd never before set foot in such a large building. It was full of everything one would ever need, from dinner plates, saucepans, furniture, pharmacy items and clothes. Sally's head began to spin as she moved from one miraculous sight to the next. Jum simply smiled. Holding her by the arm, he guided her through the store to the Ladies Fashion department, sat himself down on a brocade sofa, and said, "I'll just wait here and read the paper, Sally. You find what you like and try it on." Store-bought dresses were something of a novelty. This was like a wonderland for Sally. To be able to see a dress already sewn and ready to wear! After scooping up as many dresses as she could manage and with the young shop assistant chasing after her with others, Sally soon chose her favourites. She held up two gowns before Jum.

"I'm sorry, Mr Watt, but I cannot decide between these two." Sally flounced the dark blue one, more suited to evening wear, then held it up against her slim frame. She did the same with the soft yellow day-dress, then cocked her head to one side and asked, "What do you think, Mr Watt?"

"Well, I think if you can't decide, Sally, then we'll have to buy them both!" Jum grinned at the shocked expression on her face.

"This is something I have never dreamt of, Mr Watt. You are too generous."

Jum simply waved his hand. "Go put the yellow one on, Sally. I want you to look your best for Jonathon when we meet him."

His remark gave Sally reason to think, or hope. Perhaps Jum knew something she didn't. She soon appeared before him looking radiant, her cheeks flushed pink and her blue eyes sparkling. She twirled around, lifting the skirt a little to show off the flow of the pale-yellow dress. Jum suddenly noticed her old, lace-up boots.

"Bloody hell, Sally, you can't be wearing those old boots! Let's go buy some new ones, shall we?"

After buying two pairs—one, a delicate black for evening and the other, of all things, a pair of white leather boots for the day time. Sally was overwhelmed and nearly fell over when walking along the street, her head down admiring her new white boots.

Next stop the milliner. This shop was just around the corner from Jonathon's office. Sally's hands trembled while placing the hat she'd chosen, one with the red plume to set off her yellow dress. She smiled meekly, and with a quiver in her voice, she said, "I cannot thank you enough, Mr Watt. I don't know what I've done to deserve such kindness."

"Just being you, Sally, is thanks enough. I happen to think you're a very special young lady." He opened the door for her, but not before throwing the bag of old clothes in the garbage bin. Sally gasped and he laughed.

"Hello, Miss Morrison, I see you're still keeping the place looking lovely with your wildflowers."

"That's actually lavender, sir, but thank you very much. I'll just let Mr Darcy know you're here."

"No time for formalities." Jum burst through the door into Jonathon's office. "Hello, Jon," he boomed, leaning his large frame across the desk to shake Jonathon's hand.

"Jum—I wasn't expecting you until tonight?"

"Well, I'm here now, Jon, and I've got someone with me, who wants to pay you back some money they owe you." He called out, "Come in, Sally!"

Jonathon sat pinned to the seat. The shock of Sally's transformation stunned him momentarily before he sprang to his feet, offering her a chair. "Oh, my Sally, but don't you look lovely and so well. Please, won't you take a seat?" With his eyes unable to leave the spectacle before him, he sat awkwardly.

"Mr Darcy," she said formally, straightening her posture. "I have come here today to pay back the money I owe you and to thank you once again for your kindness."

Jonathon had not only paid for her keep but had supplied her with a modest wardrobe of clothes. Sally handed him a small roll of pound notes tied in string. Feeling slightly embarrassed, he pushed the money back across the desk.

"I really didn't expect to be repaid, Sally. It was a simple act on my part, and I'm sure you would have done the same under the circumstances. Please, keep the money. I'm sure you need it far more than me."

"No, sir," Sally said with conviction, as she pushed the money back towards him. "I would be unable to live with myself. You see I now feel free to continue with my life and save for my future and the future of…"

The men waited in silence for her to finish. Sally lowered her eyes and clasped her hands in her lap. Jum, curious, asked, "Do you have two futures to care for, Sally? What were you about to say?" Jum wanted to know whereas Jonathon thought nothing of it, being far too distracted by the way Sally looked.

"I only mean, Mr Watt," lifting her eyes to meet Jum's, "that I may, in the future, go into some sort of business for myself."

"Well, why not young lady? You're a hard worker and smart too. But you know, you've never told us where you came from, not even your surname."

"I'm afraid, Mr Watt, as I've told you before, I have no family left. I'm now alone in the world. I came from a very small country town about fifty miles south-east of Adelaide. My surname is Smith, a very common name, I'm afraid." Her next words came out in a rush. "However, I do have a friend at an orphanage back home, and I was wondering if I may ask for two days to visit her?" Sally sat in silent prayer, almost regretting what she'd just said, until Jum answered.

"I don't see why not, Miss Sally Smith," said tongue-in-cheek. "We have quite a bit of business to do, don't we, Jon? Should take a few days, eh?"

Jonathon closed his mouth and swallowed. He then made an effort to shift his attention from Sally to Jum. "Yes, yes, of course, Jum, a few days at least."

"Have you got time for some lunch, Jon?" Jum asked.

"No, I'm afraid not. I have clients all afternoon, but I'm looking forward to dinner this evening. Will you be joining us, Sally?" Jonathon used his question as an excuse to look at her again.

"Mr Watt has kindly asked me, so yes, I will be joining you. Thank you, Mr Darcy."

Jum immediately stood, holding his hand out for Sally to accompany him. "It looks like just you and me for lunch then, Sally. We'll have a bite to eat, and then I'll take you to the coach house to book your return journey. Just to make sure you come back. We'd miss you if you didn't, wouldn't we, Jon?"

Jum smiled at his loaded question, noticing the admiration his friend was showing for Sally. Before Jonathon was able to reply, Sally came back indignantly at Jum's accusation.

"Of course I will return, Mr Watt! I would never ever let either of you gentlemen down. Not after the enormous generosity I have received from you both. Why, I could never…"

"We know, Sally, we know," Jum said, easing her discomfort. "See y' tonight, Jon." Jum escorted Sally from the office, taking her arm in his.

Jonathon sat down again, staring at the wad of pound notes in front of him. *I'll give it back. Yes, on the day Sally opens her own business.*

Jum and Sally shared lunch in the new Chinese restaurant where the cuisine according to Sally was "absolutely tantalising". Her over-reactions to almost everything kept Jum amused. He enjoyed them as much as he did the food.

Later they wandered around Adelaide city, admiring the architecture of the many churches and the ones being built. After nearly an hour's stroll, Jum handed Sally the money for her coach ticket, then pointed her to where she could buy it. Sally was more than relieved when Jum trusted her to go alone. She was concerned about him knowing her destination.

Returning to the boarding house, Sally held mixed feelings about the upcoming dinner. *It will be the most extraordinary evening of my life. I've never dined in a restaurant before, except for my lunch today and that I would forever describe as exotic. Today has been wonderful; I find it hard to believe how relaxed I have been in Jum's company. It was fun being able to show my feelings openly. But this evening I'll be so nervous. I'll have to watch my manners and make sure I don't give away my secrets.*

After lingering in a long luxurious bath, Sally dressed in her dark blue evening gown. Admiring her image, she spoke to her reflection in the mirror. "I love the low neckline," she giggled. "It's very daring, I think." It had a row of dainty rose buds sewn close together where she ran her hand over the curves of her breasts. Then she let a cheeky smile form on her face.

"I simply adore this gown and I think it to be perfect for this evening." A blush spread across her face. "I look most glamorous. I do hope Jonathon will notice." She giggled as she went down the stairs. Mrs Murphy stood below to greet her.

"Oh, but you look so lovely, my dear!" She handed Sally a small, monogrammed handkerchief. "I make these handkerchiefs in my spare time. It's not much, but I'd like you to have it. A lady never goes out without a fine linen handkerchief," she added.

Sally gave her a hug. "Thank you, Mrs Murphy, I'm so nervous. I hope I don't make a fool of myself."

"Of course ya won't, Sally! You look and behave better than many a society lady I've known, so don't y' worry. Just be yourself, m' dear. That's the best advice I can give ya."

Colleen patted Sally's arm and peered out of the window. "Oh, now here's the carriage. I shan't be waitin' up for y', Sally, I know you're in good hands."

After travelling for a short while, the carriage stopped in front of Bernadette Jones's residence adjacent to the botanic gardens on the north bank, the most fashionable part of town. Sally breathed in Bernadette's heady perfume, moments before Dan the driver handed her into the carriage.

"Hello, Sally, it's so good to see you. How beautiful you look. I just love your dress!"

"Thank you, Bernadette. Mr Watt has been so kind. He bought me this dress, plus another day dress, as well as a new hat and two pairs of shoes! He's also paid for a coach ticket so I can return tomorrow to my home town to see if…" Sally stopped. She could have kicked herself.

"See what, dear?" asked Bernadette.

Sally thought quickly. "Oh, Alice, a friend of mine who's in an orphanage there."

"How old is she? We may be able to find her a job, if she's old enough, that is."

"Oh no, she's not old enough to work and she's been quite unwell."

"That's a shame. Anyway, I hope you have a pleasant journey, Sally. I'll pray that your friend Alice regains her health. You leave tomorrow; is that right?"

"Yes, that's right." Anxious to change the subject, Sally continued, "I haven't seen you for such a long time, Bernadette. I thought perhaps you may have joined Mr Watt today. We had such fun choosing my dresses."

"Yes, I know all about it, Sally. I would have loved to have been there. However, I'm quite involved with the Women's Movement. I also spent three hours today assisting Dr Forster." Bernadette gave a deep sigh.

"It's been far too long since I've visited Bulkawa. I miss it. But I have so many commitments here in Adelaide. I seem to run out of time to go anywhere. So, tell me Sally, how are things going on the property?"

"Oh, things are fine, as usual, but…" Sally hung her head and added, "Well, I miss your company, Bernadette."

"Oh, Sally, you're so sweet." She reached for Sally's hand.

"Thank you, Bernadette. You seem to be more beautiful each time I see you. I don't mean to be presumptuous, but would you and Mr Watt be thinking of marriage?" Bernadette's laughter filled the carriage. "He hasn't put you up to this, has he, Sally?"

"No, not at all. I just think, and so does Mrs Murphy, you simply make such a handsome couple."

Still smiling at the thought, Bernadette announced, "We've arrived at the Graziers Club."

Both men stood waiting outside, looking handsome in their finest attire and smelling of expensive cologne. Sally's heart skipped a beat when Jonathon entered and kissed her on the hand.

The candlelit ambiance of the restaurant oozed romance. It was everything Sally hoped it would be, even more so, as it sat opposite the seashore. Sally breathed in the tang of the salty air while listening to the waves folding onto the sand. *I feel magical, as if I don't belong to myself this evening. And now the talk and laughter of the people I most admire have taken me to another level of consciousness, almost as if someone is playing music that only I can hear.*

Gratefully, there was no mention of where Sally had come from, or where she would go to tomorrow. She took a vested interest when the conversation turned to politics and the Women's Movement. She asked intelligent questions and showed enthusiasm about becoming involved. Sally believed strongly in the contribution women made to society. Bernadette Jones, it seemed, was becoming a strong force within the women's suffrage movement and gave praise to a woman she admired greatly.

"You mark my words. Catherine Helen Spence will end up with a seat in Parliament one day soon, or my name's not Bernadette Jones!"

Sally had been reading about Miss Spence in the newspapers. "I very much agree with Bernadette. We women are simply beginning the inevitable —"

"Bloody hell, Sally, you sound like a politician already!" Jum said. He was amazed at the substance of this young lady. He knew there was something about Sally, but this evening she'd held her own, especially when discussing the future of women.

'How far did your schooling go, Sally?" Jum asked.

"Of course, I've learned to read and write, Mr Watt, along with arithmetic. However, I kept learning by reading as many books as I could. The man my mother worked for had an expansive library. I've always loved to read and learn."

"Was the man a scholar of some sort, Sally, or just a clever business man? What was his name? Maybe I know him."

Sally spoke hesitantly for the first time that evening. "He... he was not a very nice man. I really would prefer not to talk about him, if you don't mind, Mr Watt. Except to say, yes, he was a scholar of sorts, clever and cunning." Sally's demeanour stiffened as she spoke. "Please forgive me, but I'll say no more on that subject."

Jum raised an eyebrow. He was not usually told to mind his own business. On the other hand, this trait of strength was what Jonathon was looking for in a woman. He sat back and smiled at Sally for some time. It began to unnerve her.

"What I just said, Mr Darcy, did you find it amusing?" she said, surprised at her own confident manner, under the watchful eye of Jum.

"No, on the contrary, Sally, I thought you showed wisdom far beyond your years."

"I'm twenty-one, Mr Darcy, old enough to vote!" she replied in an even manner.

This elicited raucous laughter from Jum. It took him a while to pull himself together enough to apologise. "I am sorry, Sally. It wasn't what you said but the way you said it. Well done, my girl!" Jum shook his head. "I think we've got more than we bargained for here, Jon!"

"Yes, Jum." Jonathon then turned to Sally, "However, I must apologise on behalf of my friend and myself if we have caused you any offence, Sally."

"Apology accepted, Mr Darcy." Her girlish presence returned and she giggled, and everyone then relaxed. Their seafood dinner was delectable. Sally savoured every mouthful, truly appreciative of this culinary experience. After dessert of fresh raspberries folded through vanilla ice, their conversation became informal. Jum then coaxed a group of acquaintances to join them.

Stories and jokes Jum had recently heard were reiterated. Sally laughed at the humorous quips, but privately observed Jum's charismatic effect on others. She also studied Jonathon's reaction to Jum's extroverted approach to life. *Does Jonathon wish he were more like Jum? It's hard to judge, as Jonathon's a man of few words. He's so well-mannered and thoughtful, qualities I admire. I dream about having a future with Jonathon, but I know it's silly because I know we are worlds apart. However, I realise I'm more suited to a quieter type of man, rather than the overwhelming personality of a man like Jum.* She also took note of Bernadette's physical attraction to Jum, which certainly was intense. *Will they end up married, or will the flame of desire flicker and die?* She was lost in thought when Jonathon approached her.

"Would you care to take a stroll along the beach, Sally?"

Shocked a little, but determined to remain poised, Sally accepted. "Oh, that would be lovely. Thank you, Mr Darcy."

"Please call me Jonathon, or Jon if you wish."

They left the jovial group, he taking her arm, and they crossed the road.

"It may be a little hard to walk on the sand, Sally. Would you prefer to walk along the road?"

"Would you think badly of me, Jonathon, if I took my shoes off and walked on the sand? I've never been to the seaside before."

His eyes seemed to dance. "Of course, please enjoy yourself, Sally."

With Sally's inhibitions set free, she delighted in playing games with the waves, lifting her dress and running back and forth. Jonathon became aroused when catching a glimpse of her delicate ankles. Pausing every now and then to pick up a seashell, Sally forgot about how revealing her neckline could be until she rose and saw the look in Jonathon's eyes. He lent forward, held her face in his hands and kissed her lips, gently at first, then with increasing passion, until he stepped back.

"I'm so sorry, Sally, perhaps we should return to the restaurant."

Sally's euphoria was replaced with embarrassment. Her enjoyment of the evening dissolved as she watched Jonathon turn and walk away—two steps in front of her.

Chapter 7

The Journey Home

Spring could be a volatile season in Adelaide. Sometimes, the winds blew with such force that the days could be colder than winter. But shielded out of the wind, the sun beamed a warm promise that summer was on its way. It was sunrise, and a bitter wind from the Great Southern Ocean ripped through Sally's clothes, even though she was rugged up in a woollen dress, warm coat and scarf. She'd also borrowed a blanket from Mrs Murphy. "It's t' tuck over y' knees on the coach ride, Sally," she'd said. The clock struck seven when Sally arrived to take her seat.

Sitting in the corner of the coach, she gathered the blanket up around her and then pretended to be asleep. A difficult task, as everyone seemed to want to know everyone else's business during the long journey. After four hours of intolerable babble and bone-shaking bumps, she was relieved to hear the driver call, "Brinton, next stop!"

The buckles on the harness clanged together as the horses shuffled slowly to a halt. Their snorting, mixed with fine dust, sprayed over Sally as she stepped from the carriage. She collected her bag, brushed herself down and looked around. *Yes, everything looks the same, except for the general store. It's been whitewashed and the veranda poles look so nice painted red and white. Oh, and pots full of red geraniums—lovely. Must be new owners, as the previous owners would never have gone to so much trouble.*

The tiny school house sat next to the general store. Sally remembered it well, as she watched the children run outside to play. She then tried to imagine the day when she'd openly wait for her son after school. But if that day ever came, it would be a few years away. Sally shook herself back to reality. Now she was actually here in Brinton she felt nervous as she began walking toward the orphanage. She took a mind's journey back to her own childhood. The only time she ever came to town was when she was a child and she'd accompany her mother to buy stores. *I'd be in the cart and gaze towards the distant Adelaide Hills and my imagination would fly.*

The feeling of leaving Birch behind, if only for a short while, gave her hope. It was her imagination that saved her, apart from her mother's love and wisdom.

She wondered if Bob, her favourite workman, was still with Birch. Bob was the only one Birch trusted to take her mother into town. Birch never worried about their returning as he held something over everyone's head, including Bob's. Sally was never allowed to enter the store. They were Birch's orders. Her mother Harriet would say every time, "I'll be quick, Sally", and then she'd return with a candy bar. Harriet would notice how forlorn Sally was while she'd watched the children play in the schoolground. Her school lessons were given by Mr Birch, or "that man", as Sally used to call him. It always amazed Sally why her mother would stay working for him.

"Why can't we leave here, mother?" she'd ask.

"One day, when you're old enough I will tell you, Sally. Just be a good girl and do what Mr Birch tells you. Learn all you can, it will help you in your life to come."

Sally was seventeen when her mother passed away. It was after a short but serious illness. Only days before, Harriet had finally told Sally the truth. She could remember every word her mother said, as if it were yesterday.

I'm an ex-convict, Sally. I was arrested for a minor theft in England, in fact it was stealing an orange for my dying mother, something for her to enjoy before she passed. I was sent to the colonies at age sixteen. I endured the ravages of the voyage only because there was a light of hope that came when I fell in love with Charles. He was the Captain of the Guard on ship. At first, I'm sure he took pity on me, but then he came to feel genuine love for me and I for him. Charles promised to marry me as soon as I was released into his care. However, in Sydney and shortly before this was to happen, he was fatally injured whilst leading other guards in the capture of an escaped convict. I was young, Sally, there was nothing I could do except serve out the remainder of my term in prison. But when Cecil Birch came to the prison looking for workers, he seemed a refined, well-mannered man. He promised us we would be paid handsomely. I thought it would give me a new beginning and a life for you, Sally, my unborn child. Birch took me from Sydney to his property in South Australia. From that moment on, he threatened—if I ever tried to leave after my detention period expired, he would accuse me of theft. I would be returned to prison and you, my darling daughter, left at his mercy. His threat made it impossible for me to escape, as Birch had never kept his agreement to pay me for my duties. I had neither money nor anywhere else to go.

Sally remembered with hatred how, after her mother's death, Cecil Birch kept her prisoner. Without her mother there to defend her from his depraved appetite, it wasn't long before Birch forced himself upon her. She begged and pleaded with him but to no avail. When she realised she was pregnant she was repulsed then horrified, but Birch left her alone after that. She contemplated killing herself and her unborn child. But as her pregnancy progressed, she felt the need to protect the innocent life inside. It was her blameless child who gave her the strength to survive and plan her escape.

As Sally's eyes filled with tears at her bitter memories, she proclaimed aloud, "I've returned for one thing only, and that is to discover what has happened to my beloved son. No one will recognise me, especially now I look like a young lady."

Opening her carpet bag, she placed the folded blanket inside and continued on her way to the orphanage. For no apparent reason, a rainbow appeared and spread its soft colours above the orphanage. Sally took it as a sign from God that she may at least see her son. Edging closer she stood admiring the grand two-storey house. It looked like a monument to design and wealth. Standing outside the imposing iron gates in the shadow of the ghost gums, Sally pondered what she should do. *Maybe I should knock on the door and pretend I'm looking for someone. Yes, I should do it now. But I'm so nervous, can I trust my emotions? If I were to see him up close, I just know I'd break down and cry. But I must try.*

A moment before she took her first step towards the front door, she heard a high-pitched call. "Patrick! Patrick! You come here, young lad!"

Her breathing stopped when she caught a clear view of a toddler, giggling and trying to run away from the nun chasing him. His blonde curls bounced as he jogged along. With her habit flapping about her legs, the nun gained ground. She scooped him up and threw him into the air. His laughter was so loud that Sally felt the vibrations through her heart.

"I'm tellin' y', young man, you'll get a paddy-whackin' if y' don't stay put and eat y' lunch. Y' want to grow to be big and strong, doncha?"

Smiling down upon the boy, the nun led him by the hand until they disappeared behind the house. Sally was in turmoil, torn between gratitude that he was being cared for and jealousy, because someone else had given him his name, Patrick. Longing to hold him and speak his name, she strained to see him once more, but to no avail. Her heart began racing with indecision. *What should I do? Should I run inside and demand they hand him over to his real mother? Or be content that he seems loved and cared for?*

Sally dragged herself away, still thinking about what to do. After a short time, she looked up and noticed the door of a small chapel lay open. Within, the Virgin Mary held her baby Jesus. The scene depicted in stained glass sent forth a light so bright it bathed Sally in shafts of colour. She fell to her knees, releasing the emotion she'd harboured for so long, crying as if the piercing rays were being driven through her heart.

"I have so much pain and anguish, dear Lord, please help me."

When her tears finally subsided, she sat in quiet reflection. It was some time before she could raise another prayer to the God she knew, in her soul, existed.

"Dear Lord, please help me, give me a sign. Should Patrick stay here with the nuns, or should I reclaim him and take him back with the chance that Mr Watt and Jonathon will understand?" Crossing herself, she then sat silently, waiting. Waiting for a sign, any sign, but none came. Disappointed, Sally left the church. She decided reluctantly to stay at the inn for the night until the coach returned in the morning.

Walking back past the orphanage, Sally stopped every now and then, again wondering what to do. Should she knock on the door? This was her last chance to be close to her son, for the time being, but would she break down and confess the truth? Because she'd paid Jonathon almost all she had, there was very little money left. She could hardly take Patrick with her now.

I'll have to return to Bulkawa. I'll work hard and save, I'll be independent, just in case Mr Watt won't keep me on with a child. I could at least save enough for us to go somewhere else, somewhere where nobody would know me. But maybe I could take a risk that Jum would understand and accept my child? Perhaps I could tell him my husband had died and I had no money to raise Patrick, therefore I had no choice other than to leave him at the orphanage. Then there's Jonathon— kind, intelligent Jonathon. Would he ever forgive me for not telling him the truth in the first place? Everything is so complicated; it seems there is really only one choice for me.

Sally stood taller, and looking skywards, said to God, "I'll make a new beginning, that's what I'll do. I've seen my son, he's healthy and happy, that's all I need to know until I've saved the money to collect him. I'll take him to Sydney where we'll start a new life!"

Relieved she'd made her final decision, Sally continued her walk to town, trying to clear her mind and enjoy the walk. She admired the wildflowers in full bloom, especially her favourite, Sturt's Desert Pea. She'd pick one carefully, so as not to spoil its perfection. Along with a wild daisy, it reminded her of Patrick. *I'll place the flowers in a special book to remember this day—a diary, yes, of course, I'll write a diary and preserve the flowers for myself and Patrick. One day, I'll give it to him, when he's old enough.*

As she walked, Sally reached for the blanket and wrapped it around her shoulders. The lengthening shadows had brought a chill to her back. She walked for another fifteen minutes before arriving at the inn. Pulling her bonnet down to hide her face, she whispered to the bartender. "Do you have a room to let for the night, sir?

He returned a whisper. "Have y' the money, miss?"

"Yes, sir. Well, I think so, how much?"

"It's a shilling for the night, includin' damper and tea in the mornin'."

Sally dug deep into her purse, counting out the change on the counter but she was a halfpenny short. "If I don't have the damper and tea, sir, will you accept this?"

He said nothing, but took the money and then walked around the bar to show Sally to her room.

Three customers stopped talking to watch and listen to this unusual request. Not many travellers stopped at this town, let alone a young lady looking for a room for the night. It so happened that the one of the customers was Bob, Birch's station manager. As Sally's voice had sounded familiar, he left his stool to take a closer look. She felt his presence and pulled the blanket up around her ears, before she hurried off behind the publican.

Bob called, "Don't I know you, miss?"

Sally's heart pounded. *I know that voice.* Panicking, she pushed past the publican to enter her room. Turning quickly, Sally shut the door in the publican's face.

He shrugged it off, saying, "She's a shy one."

"Do y' want some hot water to be brought to y' room, miss?"

"No, thank you. I'm very tired. Please leave me be!" Sally bolted the door and pushed a chair under the knob for extra protection.

Bob returned to his stool, alongside his mates, with his forehead furrowed in thought.

"Who'd y' think that was, Bob?"

"Oh, just someone from the past, Joe, I think. Don't worry about it. It doesn't matter."

Bob continued to drink his beer, although he knew who the girl was. *I have to decide what to do now, now that the old bastard Birch is dying. I know Sally won't come with me willingly, but why has she come back?*

Deep in troubled thought, Bob remembered how Birch had sent him out many times, across the surrounding districts, to try to find Sally and her baby. He'd even asked the nuns at the local orphanage if they had an abandoned baby boy. Their answer was, of course, "NO!" Each time Bob came back empty-handed, then Birch made things even harder for Bob and his family. Like everyone connected with Birch, Bob was intimidated and blackmailed. As Birch took on only ex-convicts from Sydney, it was not difficult for him to threaten to turn them in to the authorities on trumped-up charges. Bob knew that the ones who had attempted to stand up to Birch or walk away, including children, had mysteriously gone missing. Bob's common-law wife, Dawn, was an Aboriginal woman and so Birch threatened to hand them into the do-gooders who would take his wife back to her settlement and his son to the mission, to be adopted into a white family.

Sally paced the room, expecting at any moment a knock on the door from Bob. It must have been two hours before she relaxed, thinking he'd drunk enough beer to forget about her. The muffled talk coming from the bar had diminished, now Sally had to decide whether to leave and find somewhere else to hide, until the coach came in the morning, or hope Bob had left for home. Emotionally and physically drained, she lay on the bed and pulled Mrs Murphy's blanket up before sleep led her into unconsciousness. Sally was unaware that Bob was keeping a silent vigil. Sometime during the night, she woke to feel a wet cloth being pushed hard against her face, then blackness.

Becoming conscious only when the first rays of sunlight fell on her eyes, Sally felt her body bouncing about in the back of a hay cart. She was covered with a blanket and lying beside her was her small carpet bag. Brushing the hay from her face, she struggled to sit up in an effort to find out where she was, and who was driving the cart. In her weakened state, this was impossible.

When the cart eventually came to a stop, Sally clung to the railing for support and peered out. Her heart plummeted at the sight of Birch's homestead. Spurred by energy generated from pure fear, she threw herself from the cart and began to run, only to be caught by Bob. Sobbing and struggling, Sally pleaded, "No, Bob! No! Let me go! Please, let me go!" Then not a word was said, as he dragged her back to the prison that she'd prayed always to be free from.

The stench of decaying flesh hit Sally like a blow to the head. She gasped at the sight of Birch's wasted frame lying on his bed; his face grey, contorted with pain. Dawn stood over him, applying a dressing to the gaping hole in his thigh, with what looked like boiled leaves and roots.

"Hello, Sally. I think Birch got real bad blood. I do my best with bush medicine but he too sick, I reckon." Dawn never took her eyes off the wound, which was full of infection and turning black at the edges. It made Sally sick to her stomach.

Upon hearing Sally's name, Birch opened his eyes staring, as if to assure himself it really was her. "Oh, Sally, it is you." His voice strained, as if every word took an enormous effort to utter. "Why did you run away? Where is my son?"

Sally's sick feeling turned to unleashed rage. "How could you even dare to ask such a question?" Her eyes blazed with hatred. "You're a monster!"

She lunged forward, spitting on him. Bob pulled her away, holding her tighter, frightened Sally would kill Birch if she had the chance. Still struggling with her,

Bob tried to explain the situation. "Sally, I have to tell you something, something that'll change both our lives!" Sally took no notice, instead she lunged forward once again. Bob grabbed and shook her violently.

"Sally! Please listen! Mr Birch wants to leave his property to your son. I had to find you and bring you here, so he'd leave me money in his will too. It'll give us all a new start in life. Doncha see, all ya have to do is bring the boy here and say Birch is his father and he'll sign the will. It'll be legal once he signs. Please do it, Sally, I've seen the will and met the solicitor bloke."

Sally stopped struggling. Looking directly at Birch, she said coldly, "The baby's dead!"

Birch's eyes widened in disbelief, "That can't be true," he hissed. "How did he die? Did you murder him? Yes, you killed him because he's mine, didn't you?" Birch tried to move but the pain sliced into him like a knife.

Sally gave a bitter laugh and spoke contemptuously. "No, I'm not like you, you evil bastard. The baby took ill and died on the way to Adelaide. I buried him beside the road." She smiled grimly when seeing the pain in Birch's eyes. "I hope you rot in hell!"

Suddenly, Sally was surprised at what she'd said and felt guilty. *Dear Lord, forgive me, I've never sworn before, or intentionally told a lie, especially one this shocking.* She then recalled the words her mother would say to her as a child, whenever Birch had been especially harsh. *Whatever Birch is, Sally, we must be the opposite. Whatever he thinks, we must think differently. Always stay true to the Lord and to yourself.*

Sally's rage had left, and the strength of her mother's love flowed through her so completely that she felt invincible. Lifting her head to look directly at Birch, Sally took a deep breath. Calmly, and with restrained composure, she spoke.

"Do one good deed in your life, Cecil Birch, or as sure as I'm standing here, you'll burn in hell. I want you to give everything to Bob, yes, give him the lot. I don't want anything to do with you or your money. The child has gone and now let me go. God only knows how much pain and suffering you've caused and what crimes you've committed. Probably even murder. Pray for God's mercy and forgiveness, Cecil Birch, then do this one good deed before you leave us."

Sally turned and left the room, walking through the house to the veranda where she sat on a wicker chair with her head in her hands. Several minutes later, she became aware of Dawn standing beside her. "Birch be dead, Sally. Heart took him. Bad blood and pain of lost baby."

"He didn't have a heart, Dawn. He was evil through and through."

"Everybody has heart spirit, missy. Sometimes go to bad land but find way home, just before fly away forever."

"I hope you're right, Dawn," Sally said wearily.

Bob came to join them. "What are we gonna do now, Sally?" He was at a loss without a final signature on the will to seal his future. Sally's look was full of compassion for her friend.

"I know he had no family in Australia and he had no friends here, Bob. So, there's no one that needs to be informed except the solicitor. Did he know Birch was ill? Do you remember his name?"

"I think he was a Mr Peterson, but it was a year ago now when he was here. And Birch never left the property after that. I think he was waiting for you and the baby to come back, Sally. That's why he wouldn't go to the doctor, I reckon, after that bull gored him in the leg."

Like a shot from a gun, Sally was struck with the answer. "You take over the property, Bob. Bury Birch where no one will find him. Sell his sheep and cattle." Sally spoke with authority. "No one will suspect anything because you were the only one he'd ever trust to take his stock to the sale yards and then bring the cash home with the receipt of sale."

She managed a wan smile. "Make a new life for you and your family, Bob. You deserve it—we all do. None of the other workers here will shed a tear; just make sure they get a share of the profits. Take what you can and leave. Tell the others to do the same. The solicitor would only outsmart you and it would end up costing you lots of money to settle it in the courts. So keep it simple, just take what you can and go. Birch was a recluse. He had no one who visited or even cared for him, so do as I say Bob and everything will be alright."

"What about you, Sally? What will you do?"

"I want to forget this place and that Birch ever existed. I want absolutely nothing except to visit my mother's grave. I know she's with me in spirit. I felt her presence here today. And then I'll return to Adelaide where I have dear friends waiting for me."

"I'll do what you say, Sally. You always were the smart one." Bob had the good grace to look ashamed. "I'm glad you escaped, Sally. Tell me though, did the baby really die?"

Sally chose not to answer; instead, she stepped off the veranda and began the long walk through the paddocks to the hill where her mother lay buried. The steep climb left her breathless, but invigorated by the fresh air. White cockatoos screeched before landing on the branches of the old grey gum which grew above her mother's grave. The birds looked down on Sally, who, as a young girl, had taken refuge with her mother under the same tree. It was there they would read the Bible, talk about the wonders of the world and discuss what book from Birch's library Sally had been reading. Sally would often ask her mother about her family and her upbringing in England, but Harriet refused to ever speak of her past, instead she'd always apologise, saying, "I'm sorry, Sally, it's too painful for me to discuss these things, perhaps another time. We must live for the future, Sally. The past is over and done with. One day, I know you'll leave this place and make your own way in life. I'll make sure of it. Please keep in your heart the important lessons from the Bible and then think of the wonderful world you are yet to discover. There are far better people and far better places than this, my dear child. Please believe me, Sally. If you keep faith and love in your heart, you won't go wrong."

Sally's tears flowed as she recalled her mother's words which had now cleansed her soul and washed away the horror of the last few hours. Feeling renewed and ready to start her new life, one that would make her mother proud, Sally picked a small bunch of wildflowers and placed them reverently on Harriet's grave. She kept one to put in her diary, the one she would begin on her return to Adelaide.

"Oh! Adelaide!" Sally exclaimed, before running down the hill and then back to the homestead. She almost knocked Bob over when he appeared from behind the stables. "Whoa, Sally, I was just coming up to get you. Dawn said I should take you back to Adelaide. I'll even hitch the old bastard's show horses to the buggy. I know I shouldn't speak ill of the dead, Sally, but in his case, it's good riddance. It should only take a few hours to get you home. I'll camp for the night just out of Adelaide. There's a place I know where I can shelter and tether the horses." Bob added earnestly, "I won't ever tell anyone I know you, Sally. Dawn says the past should all be left in the past. You need to find happiness for you and your son."

Sally smiled knowingly at Dawn, who stood with her arm around their son, Earl. "Thank you, Bob. I'll just say goodbye to Dawn and your boy. He's grown so much; he looks just like you."

Chapter 8

More Secrets

"Dear Holy Mary, Mother of God—it can't be!"

The unmistakable carriage belonging to the Bishop of Adelaide had just arrived at the orphanage, unannounced. He was now gathering his black gown up around his knees, taking huge strides towards the front door. Matilda ran to be ahead of the situation and flung orders to Betty as she did.

"Hurry up, Betty! Go and make sure Patrick stays outta sight. But just in case, put the pink dress on him, and try and keep him quiet!" Matilda gave Betty a shove to get her on her way. "Quick! Quick! Up the back stairs! Patrick's with Sister Catherine. Tell her what's happened."

Betty ran for her life, while Matilda cut across the garden, showing a remarkable turn of speed in an effort to put a halt to the Bishop. Matilda made it just in time, skidding to a halt right in front of the Bishop, blocking his path to the front door. She tried desperately to catch her breath and welcome him.

"Well, hello—Y' Grace! Ah—and what—what brings you out—here? What a—a pleasure it is to be havin' y' visit." Matilda grabbed his hand, kissed his Holy ring then continued, still breathing heavily. "Although, saints preserve us, Y' Grace, it would have been nice to know you were comin'. We coulda made such a fuss. But we've been busy with our house chores today, so I'm afraid the place is still a bit of a mess."

Matilda was backed up to the door, holding on tight to the handle. The Bishop seemed in a great hurry to enter the orphanage. "Please don't worry about that, Mother. I won't be staying long, just as long as it takes the driver to put a shoe back on one of the horses that he threw a couple of miles back. I told him, just get me here so I can have a nice cup of tea. And I'd be grateful if you could show me to the lavatory first, Mother, quickly, if you don't mind!" Beads of sweat had begun to break out on his ruddy face.

"Why certainly, Y' Grace, would you like a turn around the garden first?" Matilda took him by the arm.

"No, I wouldn't! Thank you, Mother," indignant at her stalling, "I'd prefer to see the lavatory, if you don't mind!" He gently but firmly pushed her aside to open the door.

"Now where is it, please Mother? Refresh my memory." He mopped his brow.

"It's down the hallway on the right, next to the laundry and the kitchen," Matilda told him, then almost yelling, she added. "It's a proper inside water-closet, not an outside one, Your Grace. Although we do have one of them, too, it comes in real handy if there's a rush, sometimes there is, y' know, with twenty females in the house." She smothered a laugh while watching him waddle away like a duck on its way to the pond. Matilda went to the kitchen and busied herself, putting the kettle on the stove and bringing out her finest china, along with an apple pie, made by her Ma. Little Betty stuck her head around the door and winked at Mother Matilda, who winked back, before immediately throwing her arms towards Betty, in a "go away" signal.

The Bishop entered, his smile of relief changing to one of delight at what he saw on the kitchen table. "Well, well! What do you mean, Mother, 'no time to make a fuss'? This looks wonderful! Apple pie is my favourite—and clotted cream! I must say, this is a real treat." He licked his lips in anticipation.

"Only the best will do for you, Y' Grace. My Ma makes the apple pies. She's quite famous for them—well, around here, anyway. Would y' prefer to be sittin' in the parlour? It's much more fittin' for those such as y'self."

"This is fine, Mother," he said as he brushed her concerns aside. Then he settled his generous backside into one of the chairs, so as to indulge. Matilda felt sure this was, as the Bishop said, just a quick visit and so she began to relax a little. However, she closed the kitchen door, a sign the girls understood that she was not to be disturbed. Not wanting the conversation to become political, although Matilda would have dearly liked to have asked him how the poor young boys living at the Adelaide orphanages were doing. Had the rumours of cruelty been squashed? But upsetting him was the last thing she wanted to do, so she began firing questions at him.

"How are the new buildin's in Adelaide progressin', Y' Grace? And do y' think the Catholics outnumber the Protestants in the city, Y' Grace? Isn't the seaside a lovely place t' visit? I enjoyed the ocean very much when I was at the convent in Adelaide, studying history. Yes, I miss the ocean." She said with a sigh. "And have y' heard anythin' about the new steam-driven cars in Melbourne? I hear they'll soon be everywhere, all around Australia, or so they say. Do ya think they would be takin' over the horse and buggy, all in due time of course?" She paused for only a moment, then noticing his mouth was full of pie, she continued. "D' y' think women'll be allowed to vote in the near future, Y' Grace?"

Matilda had bombarded him with questions, never waiting for his answer. The Bishop seemed more than happy with the lack of opportunity to get a word in edgewise, as it allowed him to devour two large slices of apple pie and three cups of tea. Picking up the last crumb of pastry with his fingertip, he looked at Matilda.

"I must thank you for your hospitality, Mother. I have to be leaving now." He heaved himself out of the chair and proceeded with haste towards the front door, praying silently that the horse had been shod and he could be on his way. The Bishop stood in the doorway, about to bid Matilda farewell, when Patrick came galloping through the hall with Betty in fast pursuit. Patrick was frantically ripping the pink dress off. It now flapped over his eyes and he ran straight into the Bishop.

"Oh, my goodness! And who might we have here?" The Bishop looked down at Patrick, who was making every effort to rid himself of the offensive garment. "That's such a pretty dress, you're not being ungrateful, are you? If you are, then Mother Matilda will have to reprimand you severely," he warned Patrick. "What's your name, child?" He took hold of Patrick's arm with far too tight a grip for Matilda's liking.

"Me Patwick!" he yelled at the Bishop.

Mother Matilda gently took Patrick from the Bishop's grasp. "Please don't mind *her*, Your Grace. *She's* a real little tomboy."

Looking up with bull-frog cheeks, all puffed up with disdain at being dressed like a girl, Patrick yelled again, "Me PATWICK!"

Mother Matilda, smiling through gritted teeth, tried to calm the recalcitrant child. "Now *PATRICIA*, be a good little girl. You go with Betty, now," she glared at Patrick. Such was the strength of her gaze, he temporarily fell silent. Scooping Patrick up, pushing his face into her shoulder, Betty made sure he was unable to say another word.

The bewildered Bishop asked, "I didn't think you took them in that young, Mother?"

"Well, Your Grace, that'd be true but sometimes, well, the good Lord sends us a real challenge—and it wouldn't be right of me t' be lettin' Him down now, would it, Y' Grace?"

Matilda offered her sweetest smile, handing him another piece of pie.

"No, quite right, quite right, thank you, Mother." His eyes lit up with the proffered pie. "This certainly is the best apple pie I have ever tasted. You should come to Adelaide and visit sometime, Mother," he added, sincerely hoping she would never take up his offer. "Goodbye, Mother, and God bless."

Matilda waved as the carriage disappeared from view. She made the sign of the cross, saying fifty Hail Marys before she decided it was time for a meeting.

Matilda rang the dinner bell, to be used out of meal times only for extraordinary meetings or in an emergency.

The sound of running feet could be heard from every direction in the house. As usual the grand dining room was the venue. All nuns sat to attention at the long rosewood table which had ample room for sixteen diners, and so the older girls joined the nuns. The younger ones sat crossed-legged in front of Mother Matilda, who stood, as usual, in front of the fireplace. It was the worst possible place she could stand, had it been a cold winter's day. She would inevitably do this on cold days, blocking the heat from everyone else in the room, save her own posterior. It was the only time she appeared selfish to the girls, but they knew how she hated the cold. "It's the only t'ing that God has given us here on Earth that I'm not truly grateful for," Matilda would say.

This day gratefully brimmed over with the warmth of late spring and therefore no logs blazed within the hearth. Wearing her most serious expression, Mother Matilda proceeded to lay down the law. "Now Sisters, girls, I've called a sudden meeting to tell y' what a close call we've just had with the Bishop. If he'd a got the slightest wind of what was happenin' here with our Patrick, he'd a been surely scooped up and taken t', well, should we say, a home where the love is sparse and the punishment plenty. We don't ever want that t' happen t' our darlin' Patrick, now do we?" Matilda paused for effect and then continued, "We'll have t' be workin' out a better plan for these unexpected cases. Y'll have to jump to it, like a fire drill. Now, mind you, it may not happen again, and usually we have plenty of warning. But just in case it does, here's what we do!"

Matilda went on to explain her simple but brilliant plan to make sure no one would ever suspect they were hiding a little boy, although sometimes he proved to be a real handful for all of them. "And anoder t'ing, we can't be lettin' Patrick get outta hand. He has us all worked out at present, and he's gettin' away with far too much. Some good old-fashioned discipline will be applied from this moment on," Matilda said as she looked sternly at the assembly. "Or as God is my witness, we'll pay for it later!"

She inspected the horrified faces of each girl, some even putting their palms to their cheeks in dismay. It seemed Matilda needed to press her point home even further.

"I'm tellin' y' if we don't all pull together, he won't know what's struck him when he gets out inta the real world. We've created a Heaven on Earth for him here. And while that's all well and good, he'll be soon growin' into a man and he'll be expectin' a terrible lot from the poor unsuspectin' woman who marries him!" Matilda paused, making sure they were all paying attention. "From now on, we're goin' to be usin' a naughty corner. If he misbehaves and doesn't do as we say, then he must stay there for five minutes. If that doesn't work, he's to be sent to me for a smack on the bottom. I'm the only one who should hand out any physical discipline." Matilda gave the ghost of a smile. "If we all go smackin' him he'd end up black and blue. So, does everyone understand what I just said?" They all nodded. "Are there any questions?"

No, but smacking him—not one of them would ever even think about smacking him! Mother Matilda was totally wrong there. Just before the meeting, Betty had finally managed to wrestle Patrick down for his morning nap. However, he'd since woken up and managed to climb out of his cot. After running and tumbling down the stairs, he opened the door of the dining room, toddled in, teddy bear under his arm, long blonde curls, pink cheeks and a dimpled smile that would melt ice.

"Milky?" Patrick had asked angelically. Every girl and woman jumped up as one—except Matilda.

"Oh Patrick, did you wake up, our darling little man? Come on, we'll get milky for you." Sister Catherine beamed at the precious child after she'd gathered him in her arms. The group followed, leaving Matilda standing all alone in front of the fireplace.

"Well, to be sure, Dear Lord, it seems I've made a very strong impression," she said, her eyes rose to the heavens. After going into the kitchen and telling the besotted lot she was off to see her Da, she strode out the front door admonishing herself.

"I'm too soft, that's what I am, but I'm goin' to get tougher! Yes, I am. I'll have a talk to Da—he'll help me, and dear Lord, You'll have t' help me too," she said, looking again up into the heavens and pointing her finger in that direction.

Da's property was nearly an hour's walk, or fifteen minutes by buggy. Matilda walked. She needed to clear her mind in an effort to reassure herself that this situation with Patrick was truly what the Lord intended. It wasn't going to be easy. The child was obviously spoilt and she seemed too weak to control matters. *No, not weak, just kind*, Matilda tried to convince herself of this, while going over the many trying situations she'd had with Patrick, until finally she reached the cottage.

"Ma's little piece of Heaven," Matilda exclaimed. The well-kept garden appeared like an oasis among the golden rye grass. They'd been blessed with rain in the area, unlike most of Australia, which had been hit with one of the worst droughts on record. Da's cattle and sheep looked fatter than she'd ever seen them. Matilda was about to knock on the door when Da opened it first.

"Oh, May," he said, taken by surprise, his blue eyes sad and his expression clouded.

"I was just about t' go get the doctor. Your mother's feeling poorly." Regardless of the circumstance, both Da and Ma never relented from calling Matilda by her birth name.

"You go quickly, Da. I'll stay with her, and don't be worryin'," Matilda said, hurrying into the cottage. Her mother, Florence, was lying in bed, looking as white as the sheets.

"Oh Ma, what's the matter?" she whispered as she stroked her mother's greying hair.

"I don't know, May, but I feel the Lord is with me so I'll be fine." Florence managed a weak smile as she patted Matilda's hand.

"Well, you just rest, Ma. D' you want me to read to y'?"

"That would be lovely, May." Florence sighed and folded her hands on the counterpane. Matilda inspected the bookcase.

"Oh, I see ya've kept all m' old history books. I'll read to y'all about London Town and the famous buildings. Knowin' that'd be y' home town, Ma. How would y' like that?"

Matilda could never resist the chance to delve into a bit of history.

"Now I know I'm not going to die, May. If you thought I were, you'd read from the Bible and yes, London was my home town until I met your dear father." Florence laughed, coughing at the same time.

"Well, of course y' not goin' t' die, Ma! What nonsense! You've never been real strong, but you've always got over these little turns." Matilda pulled a chair to her ma's bedside. She read aloud about the Tower of London and the Traitors Gate, where they would sail the prisoners down the Thames and through the opening in the brick wall on the river bank. She read when it was built, who built it and how long it took to build. Excitedly, she told her Ma of all the famous people who had been hung by their necks from the gallows, until Florence stopped her.

"Please, May, is there not a romantic novel among the books? To tell the truth, I've never had the same passion for history as you."

Matilda closed the book. "I'm sorry, Ma. Would y' be up to hearin' the problems I'm havin' with wee Patrick?"

"Yes, of course, May, but first, would you mind making me a cup of tea. It always helps if I have a problem."

Matilda went to the kitchen, setting the kettle to boil, and while she waited, found some fruit cake. She made the tea just how her mother liked it—strong with just a dash of milk—and took it all in on a tray.

"Here we are, Ma." Matilda stood over her sleeping mother.

"Oh, well, I'll not waste it." She left to sit in Da's armchair and enjoy the tea. After a while, Matilda drifted off to sleep, only to be woken by the sound of the door banging shut. "Oh, Da, I musta dropped off. Ma's asleep, where's the doctor?" Matilda sat up and rubbed her eyes. The drama this morning with the bishop and the long walk seemed to have worn her out.

"The doctor will be comin' soon, May. He has t' deliver a baby. I'd best be checkin' on y' Ma. If she's sleepin' soundly, then I'll drive y' back to the convent."

They entered Florence's bedroom together. She'd just woken up.

"You're lookin' a wee bit better, Ma. D' y' think if I made y' another cuppa, Da might be able to leave y' for a while? The doctor will be here shortly. Da says he'd just finished delivering a baby." Matilda felt torn between her duty to her mother and her responsibilities at the convent. "If I wait much longer, it'll be getting' dark and I'll miss the evening prayers," Matilda started to explain, but her mother cut her short.

"Of course, May, I'll be fine."

"I won't be long, my love," Da said, giving Florence a kiss on her forehead. "If the doctor comes while I'm gone, try and remember what he says, maybe write it down, so I'll know what to do." Florence smiled and waved them on their way.

Matilda sat in the buggy alongside Da and told him all about the problems they were having with Patrick. "I'm havin' trouble being firm enough with the Sisters and the girls, Da. It seems Patrick has every one of them wrapped around his little finger."

Da chuckled, then offered. "May, I tought y' had a serious problem, it's not surprisin'. Ah, that Patrick's a charmer, but you'll have t' be tough t' be kind. In the long run, it's all about fair and consistent discipline. Then he'll grow up ta respect y', but only if y' take control now." Da shook the reins to hurry the horse along. "Of course, I would love ta help y' more, but with your Ma the way she is, with her health and all. Well, it takes me all me time ta do the chores and look after her. If I had a little one too, I couldn't cope, neither could ya ma."

Matilda leaned her head on his shoulder. "Oh, I know, Da, and I'm certainly not expectin' y' to take him home! I'll work it out. I've always laid down the law to the young girls who come our way and I've always shown them love, by rewardin' 'em when they do well and punishin' 'em when they misbehave. But havin' a baby, especially a boy, it's just—well, it's different. I don't know what it is about Patrick, he seems to have a magnetism we just can't resist." Hearing how besotted she sounded herself, Matilda had to smile before Da wiped the smile from her.

"You could always adopt him out, May," Da ventured.

"Oh please, Da!" Matilda sat up straight. "I've been prayin' every minute to the Lord for His guidance. And I'm either not listenin' to Him, or He's not tellin' me. I know I keep sayin' it, but I'm sure Patrick was sent to us for a Divine reason."

Da nodded his head, not wanting to give May his honest opinion, which was that she'd simply fallen in love with the little fella, as they all had, and she didn't want to give him up. Lowering beneath the horizon, the sun gave forth its final light, silhouetting the convent and the gum trees. Matilda was struck by its reverence. "Look at that beautiful sunset, Da, it's one of God's paintings." They sat in silence for a moment admiring the scene before Matilda kissed him on the cheek.

"Thanks for the ride home, Da, and please let me know if Ma gets any worse. We'll all be sayin' a prayer for her. Now you take care too, Da."

Chapter 9

Reunited

Colleen Murphy became more anxious as time slipped by. She'd expected Sally home by twelve-thirty and it was nearly four o'clock. *Maybe she's takin' a stroll through the city streets before comin' home.* Colleen tried to keep herself busy but her mind was preoccupied with the worry that Sally may not return. *What if she's met with foul play? It can be dangerous for a young woman travelling alone.* Every so often she'd walk outside to look down the road. As the clock struck four pm, the front door swung open. Colleen hurried out of the kitchen, head down and wiping her hands on her apron.

"Sally! Where on earth have you been? I've…" She was startled to see Jum Watt standing inside, looking, as usual, like he owned the place.

"Hello, Colleen, is Sally not here?" he inquired, one eyebrow cocked.

"No, I'm afraid not, Jum. I'm quite worried about her. She should've been back b' twelve-thirty."

Jum placed his hand on Colleen's shoulder. "Try not to worry, Colleen. The coach may have stuck trouble with one of the horses. I'll go and check, I'll be back shortly." He, too, felt a little concerned. However, he was also trying to contain his excitement over the news he'd come to deliver. He thought the better of it now, as Colleen was showing signs of genuine distress. Jum made another effort to assure her before he left.

"I'm sure she'll be right, Colleen, so please don't fret."

At the coach house, the clerk answered Jum, "All coaches have run to schedule, Mr Watt."

"Thanks, Percy," Jum said, his brow creased as he walked away. *It's unthinkable she wouldn't return from—shit, I don't even know where she was going.* "Jesus, I hope she's alright," he said aloud. "Shoulda found out a lot more about her. Bloody hell, what if something's happened to her?" Jum's imagination ran riot. *Oh hell, what if she's been bashed and robbed and her body thrown away somewhere in the remote bush. How will I break the news to Jonathon?* Jum moaned at the prospect.

"Mr Watt! Mr Watt!" Sally called as she ran towards him.

"Oh, b' Jesus, Sally, you've had me worried! Where have you been, girl?" Jum flung his arms around her, holding her tight. Sally, totally ignorant of the fact she had made a Lazarus-like entrance back into Jum's arms, was a trifle overcome by the enthusiasm of his embrace. She extricated herself with some difficulty.

"I'm all right, Mr Watt, really I am," she assured him breathlessly. "Really. I am!" She took a step back and straightened her hat which had been pushed askew. "I'm so sorry, Mr Watt. I missed the coach. But I was able to arrange a ride with a friend."

Jum, relieved and happy to see Sally, was at the same time pleased that no dark shadow would now fall over his own good news. News he was anxious to share. Unable to wait a moment longer, he began to explain.

"Well now, Miss Sally Smith. Allow me to give you some good news. But I must explain. I did go to Mrs Murphy's, to tell you both, but she was far too worried about you. So, I told her I'd go and find out what had happened to your coach, and here we are." He paused for effect.

"I've just won myself the best thoroughbred racehorse in the whole of Australia! So, we're all off to the races tomorrow!" Jum's eyes fairly burned with fervour.

"My goodness, how did you manage that?" Sally was agog with surprise. Walking briskly together, he began to tell her the whole story.

"It was late last night when I got back to the Graziers Club and this Pommy bloke was there. A real big shot, telling everyone he'd just imported the best thoroughbred in the land, all the way from England." Jum looked down at Sally and was pleased she seemed to be listening.

"He'd brought the horse here to Adelaide, where it's been in training to win the big race tomorrow. The race is a prelude to the Melbourne Cup. And then, of course, he'd planned to win the Cup itself. I started talking to him and found out he was a professional gambler. One thing led to another and before I knew it, we were right into a very serious poker game. I'll say one thing for him. He's a better gentleman than he's a poker player!" Jum laughed, shaking his head.

"He said if he had to pay the money he owed me, it would break him financially. So I said, 'Just give me the horse and we'll call it even.' And because it's a stallion, and I'm a good bloke, I told him he didn't have to pay for a service. Yes, any of his mares could have one free service—every year!" Jum laughed again in his usual raucous manner. "So, Miss Sally Smith, I now own the favourite in tomorrow's feature race at Victoria Park. Freelance is his name. He'll then be prepared for the Melbourne Cup in November. I've got the best trainer and the best jockey, so we can't go wrong." Jum seemed as excited as a kid on Christmas morning.

"How wonderful for you, Mr Watt. I'd love to see him race." Sally still found it hard to believe how open and generous this giant of a man was. *I'm going to try and be more like him. Everything just seems to go his way—it must be his positive manner. Yes, put everything that's just happened behind you, Sally. Be positive and think positive.*

As they continued walking to the boarding house, their conversation returned to Sally's trip and the friend she'd been to visit. She had to invent the details and make a passable attempt at being excited about her time away. This was difficult, considering what she'd been through, but Sally relied on her instincts for survival. She'd learned to keep secrets close to her heart. Jum seemed to accept her story and went on to explain his arrangements for the races. By this time, they'd made it back to the boarding house.

Colleen sat waiting anxiously, peering out of the front window. The moment they arrived she flung the door open. "Oh, Sally, I've been so worried about y'!" Tears glistened in her eyes as she hugged Sally against her generous bosom. She then ushered her inside, and turning back to Jum, she asked, "Would y' like to come in for a drink, Jum, or dinner perhaps?"

"No thanks, Colleen, I've other plans and now I'm late. Sally will pass on my good news." Jum tipped his hat and walked away, then turning, he called, "Oh yes, and you're expected to come along, Colleen. The more the merrier!"

Jum then walked through the gate and headed in the direction of Bernadette Jones's residence. Colleen began fussing around the kitchen, announcing happily, "I've made some nice mutton stew, Sally. Now go and freshen up. There's only you and me for dinner. Oh, and a young man who's only arrived today. He'll be boarding with us for a few months. He seems a respectable young man. We'll all have a good chat over dinner."

Sally pulled her curtains closed and removed her plain brown frock, letting it fall to the floor. She emptied the water from the earthenware jug into the basin, then stripped off her undergarments. Soaping up her cloth, she gently washed her body, feeling the warmth caress her skin and set off her imagination. *Jonathon's hands are sliding over my breasts, my hips. My skin is tingling with the pleasure.* Suddenly, Birch's face appeared, she shuddered with revulsion and dropped the washcloth back into the basin.

Entering the kitchen, Sally noticed the back of a young man who sat talking to Colleen. Blonde curls hung over his shirt collar, looking exactly the same as Patrick's hair did. Sally's heart skipped a beat. He laughed at something Colleen said and Sally stood transfixed.

"Sally, Sally? Are y' alright?" Colleen asked, the wooden spoon suspended in mid-air.

'Oh, yes, I'm sorry, Mrs Murphy. I was just thinking of somebody, I mean, something. I'm sorry. It's just, well, I'm very tired."

"Come, sit down here, m' dear. Have a chat with young Paul here and I'll be gettin' y' dinner, then it's off to bed with y'! I can't imagine how exhausted y' must be after all y' travellin'." Colleen placed crusty bread and a pot of butter on the table as she spoke.

"Now, Paul, this is Miss Sally Smith, the lovely young lady I was just tellin' y' about."

Paul stood. "It's a pleasure to meet you, Miss Smith," inclining his head after the greeting.

"Thank you. I'm sorry, I didn't hear your surname?" Sally asked.

"I suppose it is a common enough name," Paul grinned. "My name's Smith, too. Paul Smith."

Sally began to speculate. *This is like a dream, showing me what my son will look like when he grows to be a man. The darker blonde curls, the intense blue eyes, the full lips, the fulfillment of my son's childish features.*

Colleen interrupted Sally's thoughts by placing a large plate of stew in front of her.

"Now come on. Eat up, you two."

They ate in silence until Colleen asked, "Now, Paul, how long did it take y' t' come t' South Australia by train from Sydney?"

"Nearly four days, Mrs Murphy, due to the railway lines having different gauges. It's silly really, they should all be the same. It would save a lot of time and trouble. I can tell you I was more than pleased when I reached Adelaide."

"I suppose y' would be, Paul. Now tell us about Sydney. Is it far more populated than Adelaide? How does Adelaide compare? Is the harbour as magnificent as I've heard?"

Before he could answer just one of these questions, Colleen continued, "How did y' become a stock and station agent, Paul?" The toing and froing took the pressure off Sally. Now that her hunger had been satisfied, she desperately needed to sleep.

"Please excuse me. I hope you don't think I'm rude, but I'm so tired, I'm about to drop. I must retire." Sally stood, smiled and left the room. As she began to climb the stairs, she remembered she hadn't told Mrs Murphy about Jum's racehorse and the races tomorrow. Retracing her steps, she was about to enter the kitchen when she heard Colleen say, "It's a strange coincidence, Paul, you two havin' the same name and, y' know, y' even look alike." Tempted as Sally was to wait for Paul's reply, her guilt at eavesdropping prevented her, so she coughed and then entered the kitchen.

"I'm sorry to interrupt, but I forgot to tell you the news, Mrs Murphy. Mr Watt won himself a racehorse in a poker game. He wants us to join him tomorrow at the Victoria Park races to watch his stallion race. I think he said the horse's name was Freelance. Well anyway, Dan will collect us in Mr Watt's carriage at lunchtime. I'll tell you the rest in the morning, Mrs Murphy. Goodnight once again."

Colleen sat stunned for a moment. "Well, I'll be blown away! You never know what that man's goin' t' come up with from one moment t' the next. I hope y' get to meet him, Paul. He's like a giant whirlwind but a lovable one." She laughed, shaking her head when suddenly her hands flew up to her cheeks in mock dismay.

"Oh crikey, I haven't got a thing t' wear! I'd better get crackin' and tart somethin' up!" She leapt to her feet and began clearing the table. Seeing no one else was there to help her, Paul offered.

"No, no, young man, this is woman's work! I'll be through it in no time, and then I'll have t' be goin' through m' clothes to see if I've somethin' decent t' wear, otherwise, I'll have t' make a dash to the department store and buy a dress off the rack." She stopped mid-wipe and marvelled, "Isn't it a wonderful thing, Paul? Just fancy being able t' do that these days! What will they be comin' up with next?" Colleen laughed while bidding Paul goodnight.

Sally wearily brushed her teeth, something she'd never forget. *My mother would always pull me out of bed if I hadn't cleaned my teeth.* She smiled at the memory of her mother's gentle reprimand. Sally paused, toothbrush in hand. *What an exciting day it will be tomorrow. No doubt Jonathon will be there, I hope I see that glimmer of admiration in his eyes. Oh, that tender feeling of his warm lips on mine. Dear God, it was so lovely.* Charmed with the memory, she entered her bed and drifted into a deep, contented sleep.

Colleen was up early the following morning. The fact she'd stayed up half the night to reinvent a lovely but old dress she'd tucked away, did nothing to dampen her enthusiasm for the day ahead. "Sally dear, your breakfast's ready, your favourite, bacon and eggs, Sally…"

Not a sound came from the room. Colleen opened the door and crept over to the bed.

"I'm awake, Mrs M."

Colleen stood back startled. "'Mrs M'? My goodness, Sally, I haven't been called that since m' husband died. He used to call me that, he did! And do y' know what else is peculiar? He used to love goin' to the races, he did. Now, come on, young lady, we have t' be spendin' a bit of time dollin' ourselves up. Not to say you'd need much, bein' as pretty as a picture. Breakfast will be gettin' cold, so hurry up, m' dear!"

Paul and two other boarders sat at the breakfast table. "Good morning, gentlemen," Sally said before sitting beside Paul.

"Good morning, Miss Smith," was the chorus, before Paul continued the conversation he was having.

"Yes, Jim, our property's at Rouse Hill, near the Hawkesbury River." Paul boasted. "We grow the most amazing crops. It's the best soil in New South Wales."

Normally, Sally would have asked questions but this morning her mind was preoccupied with the day ahead, particularly on how she would style her hair, after her long luxurious bath, of course. She finished her breakfast and was about to go up to her room when Colleen stopped her.

"Now, tell me again, Sally. What time are we to be picked up in Jum's carriage?"

"Twelve o'clock, Mrs M. Do you mind me calling you that?"

"No, not at all. I think we know each other well enough now, Sally, to be informal. You can call me Colleen if you like. I can't tell y' how excited I am! And I'm feelin' lucky. How about you?"

"Yes, very lucky, Colleen." Sally put her arms around the plump, redheaded woman and gave her a squeeze. "We're going to have a fine day, Colleen. I can feel it in my bones, as my mother would say."

Sinking her body into the hot water to which she had first added a few drops of lavender oil, Sally began daydreaming. *I'll be the sweetest smelling lady at the races. My new yellow dress has already impressed Jonathon. I'll be happy and vibrant, yes, I'll behave with confidence and speak intelligently. My hair will be arranged, as artfully as I can make it, under my fashionable hat. Surely Jonathon will find me completely irresistible!'* A girlish giggle escaped. *Yes, this day will begin our never-ending love for each other.* She then scolded herself. *Oh Sally, you're fantasising, you really don't believe what you're saying, or why you would even dream about a man who you know you could never have. You know Jonathon's kiss was a moment of weakness on his part, probably too much wine.*

Ten minutes before they were due to be picked up, Sally waited in the parlour with nervous anticipation. Thankfully, before too long, Colleen appeared at the head of the stairs, wearing a pale green organza gown that hung bell-like from her generous hips. Pointedly, she did her best to swan down the stairs. Sally watched in silence, overcome by the attractive appearance of her friend. Her red hair piled becomingly under a large brimmed hat of darker green. The colour certainly suited Colleen's complexion. It seemed to tame the ruddiness of her skin. A fine dusting of face powder, and the touch of rouge she'd applied to her lips, took ten years off her age.

"How d' I look, Sally?" she asked when descending the last step before striking an exaggerated pose.

"Oh, Mrs M, you look so elegant! I love your dress, the colour, and the hat! Where did you buy the hat?"

"Do y' really like it, Sally? I made it m'self from material I'd put away in the cupboard. I made the roses too!" Colleen gently touched the roses she'd sewn intermittently around the crown of the hat.

"You're very clever, Colleen. You look beautiful." Sally then escorted her down the path to wait outside for the carriage.

"Thank y', Sally, we may as well show ourselves off in our finery outside."

Within a minute, two men passed by. They actually paused to take an appreciative look while tipping their hats. Two ladies also stopped in their tracks and commented, "How lovely you both look."

"Thank y', we're off to the races at Victoria Park, y' know. Just waitin' for our carriage," Colleen airily informed their admirers.

Jum's carriage, drawn by four beautiful red bays, arrived. The driver, Dan, a normally hard-working jackaroo on Jum's property, jumped down from the driver's seat.

"Ladies, if I may?" He tipped his hat, opened the door and handed them in to the carriage. "You both look beautiful," he added as he closed the door, careful to make sure their skirts were well out of the way.

Sally then duly complimented Dan on his appearance, and she'd caught a waft of Jum's cologne. "You smell delightful, Dan. I thought perhaps Mr Watt and Bernadette would be accompanying us in the carriage?"

"I took them earlier, Sally. Jum, I mean, Mr Watt, wanted to make sure everything was alright with Freelance, his horse, and with the marquee. He's hired a real beauty for his guests. That includes us and he's ordered plenty of grog and tucker. Mr Darcy was going to come along with us in the carriage but he's just bought himself two new horses and a buggy." A paddock with ample shade trees had been assigned for the horse-drawn transports and their drivers. However, Jum, thoughtful as always, had organised a young lad to tend his horses so that Dan could join them.

As Dan helped the two women out of the carriage, Sally commented, "I was just saying to Colleen, Dan, how handsome you look, and your new suit would have been such a waste if you'd had to stay here with the horses."

"Thank you, Sally, but I'm not really used to gettin' togged up like this." He ran his finger around the inside of his starched collar and tugged at his waistcoat.

"Now before I forget," Dan handed Sally a pound note. "Here you are. Jum gave us this to have a bet with."

"Oh, my goodness, I can't take this! This is a month's pay!" Sally handed it back.

"No, no, please take it, Sally. I'll get in to big trouble if you don't."

"Well, I'll share it with Mrs Murphy then."

"No, you don't understand. He's given me the same for Mrs Murphy, too." Dan produced another pound note and Colleen grabbed it.

"Well, I'll be blowed if I'm going to turn down an offer like this," Colleen said, tucking the money into her purse.

Sally smiled. "Our dear Mr Watt certainly is a very generous man. I would even say he's a great man!"

"Yeah, he's a great man alright, Sally, and a great boss. Now, let's have some fun, ladies," Dan said, hurrying them along. The marquee had been erected on the lawn near the winning post, leaving only just enough room for the public to have full view of the races. Sally's mouth fell open when she entered. White linen clothes covered each table, and silver candelabras sat dead centre. Bowls of seasonal fruit, dishes of nuts, dried apricots and dates, along with platters of cheese and cold meats, plus fresh crusty rolls adorned a long trellis table. Drink waiters, dressed in white shirts, black trousers and bow ties, attended to the group of friends and well-wishers. Huge barrels of ice cradled bottles of French champagne. The main buffet table held silver platters full of prawns and plump oysters, with smaller bowls brimming with black caviar.

Sally stood astonished. *I don't think there's anything that can compare with Jum Watt's generosity.*

Jum spotted the group and forced his way through the admiring throng, declaring, "You look more beautiful than ever, Sally." His attention then turned to Colleen. He added, with a wink. "You too, Colleen, I think you might find yourself a fella today!"

Colleen flushed, tapping Jum's arm in a playful reprimand. Jum then stood back, hands on hips and gave Dan the once over—head to toe. "Well, Dan, if you don't look as flash as a rat with a gold tooth! Now don't be fillin' yourself up with too much rum. Just take it easy, Dan." Jum spread his arms expansively. "Now I want you, my friends, to have a great day and mingle with the other guests so don't be shy. They're a wonderful group of people, from all walks of life and they're a real friendly bunch. The food is the best money can buy, so tuck in! Now may I get you two beauties a glass of champagne?"

Colleen laughed. "Oh, be off with y', Jum, we can take care of ourselves." With a glint in her eye, she added, "Well, I'll be off too. I have t' see the bookies and back a winner, and thanks for the money, Jum!"

Jum excused himself, and Dan headed straight for the bar. Sally stood alone, admiring the ladies dressed in the height of fashion. She took note of how they held themselves elegantly, drifting from one conversation to the next. She felt her elbow being taken hold of, and turned.

"Oh, Mr Darcy, how are you?" Sally surprised even herself with how calm and collected she sounded, especially as her heart felt like it was going to jump from her chest. Jonathon smiled—almost seductively. *Oh no,* Sally thought, *here we go again!* She felt weak in the knees.

He noticed her falter a little and escorted her to a table. "Please sit down, Sally, you must be exhausted after your trip. Jum tells me you missed the coach home. You had him and Mrs Murphy terribly worried until you returned. Thank heavens."

"Yes, that's right, Mr Darcy. I missed the coach and yes, I had to ask a friend to drive me back to Adelaide. But I'm here now and that's all that matters. Well, I mean to say…"

"Yes, that's all that really matters, Sally. Now, let me find you something to drink. Have you ever drunk champagne before?" Jonathon asked.

"No, I haven't, Mr Darcy."

"Please call me Jonathon. Remember?" He raised an eyebrow.

"Well, Jonathon. Do you really think I should?" she asked coyly.

"I don't think one will hurt you, Sally. After all, this is a day of celebration. And what better way to begin than with a glass of 'champers', as they call it."

She didn't have to wait long before he returned with a selection of the delectable seafood. "This is only starters, Sally. I'll be back with the champagne." Sally took the opportunity to have a silent talk to herself. *Now, Sally, you must be calm and confident. After all, Jonathon's intelligent and he wouldn't be interested in a scatterbrain.* Sally then took a deep breath and composed herself.

"Here we are, Sally." Jonathon placed a bottle of French champagne on the table along with two crystal champagne coupes. After filling them both, he seated himself opposite, raising his glass to hers. "Let's drink a toast, shall we. Here's to a successful day all round!" The crowd soon began to gather in front of the marquee to watch the first race. Sally drank her champagne far too quickly and when she stood up, she felt a little lightheaded. "Shall we watch the race, Sally?" Jonathon asked, offering his arm. Sally nodded, grateful for his support as he escorted her to the rail.

Ten fine thoroughbreds lined up behind the starting tape. The starter held his hand high for what seemed like ages, warning the jockeys. "Keep your charges still! Steady now, steady your horse, Jimmy!" A hush fell, just before the rope pinged back and the horses surged forward. They were met with a mighty cheer from the crowd as they galloped past.

Colleen then appeared beside Sally, after having to shove her way through the multitude. "I've backed The Pirate! Number four!" she shouted.

Sally shouted back, "I'll help you cheer, Colleen. I haven't had a bet!"

Once the horses were in the home straight, it appeared to be a battle between number four and number six. The crowd went wild, as the two fought it out over the last fifty yards, with the rest of the field two lengths or more behind. One final bob of the head and number four was the winner by a nose.

Colleen, overcome with the thrill of backing the winner, yelled, "I put me one-pound note on him to win! I'm gunna collect a bloody fortune!" As she looked as if she were about to faint, Jonathon stepped forward and held her up.

"Mrs Murphy, are you alright? You shouldn't become so excited. It may cause a heart attack!"

Laughing wildly, Colleen quipped, "My dear late husband, Fred, died of a heart attack, Mr Darcy, and I don't think it was 'excitement' that killed him! Anyways, I've good reason. I've just won meself a bloody fortune!"

"Well, Mrs Murphy, won't you join us for a glass of champagne to celebrate."

"Only a quick one for me, Mr Darcy, I'm on a roll. I have t' go back and study the horses so I can pick the next winner."

Still bubbling with her good fortune, Colleen joined them inside the marquee, helping herself to a dozen oysters and downing a glass of champagne. She then dabbed her lips with a linen napkin. "Well, thanks for that, now I'd better get back t' business!"

She was off in a flash, while Sally and Jonathon watched, laughing as she charged through the crowded tent.

"If she loses the lot, Jonathon, it won't matter because Mr Watt gave us each a pound to bet with."

"Yes, I've never met anyone like him, Sally. He lives like there's no tomorrow. I wish I could enjoy life a little more, without being so conservative."

Sally spoke tenderly. "I also admire him." She held back the words she would have liked to have said. *But he's no better than you are, my darling. In fact, if it weren't for you, I wouldn't be sitting here right now, enjoying the very best life has to offer.*

Instead, she said, "I will always be in his debt, as well as yours, Jonathon." When saying this, she dared place her hand over his. Jonathon looked down and smiled, then threw her a look that could have told his next words.

"Please, Sally, I don't want you to be grateful to me forever, it's not the way a relationship should begin," his voice was quiet with emotion. His eyes showed the intensity of his feelings.

"Sally, in all the time I've known you, I've tried to like other women. I've taken them out to dinner and done my best to enjoy their company." He paused and held her hand. "I'm afraid, well, I shouldn't say afraid, Sally. I should say I'm very pleased that no other woman has come close to you. The feelings I have of deep affection and, indeed, love for you, Sally, are genuine." He kissed her hand and looked again into her eyes. "Please, tell me you feel the same, Sally?"

She sat dumbfounded. This was beyond her wildest dreams! Almost stuttering her words with the shock of his admission, she replied, "Jonathon, of course—of course, I love you! I don't know what to say. I can only say that I've hoped and prayed some day you would love me too, the same as I have always loved you." At that very moment, Jum and Bernadette appeared, her arm through his. Jum looked from Jonathon to Sally with a wry smile.

"So, what's happening here, Jon? You look like all your Christmases have come at once, mate?"

Jum then noticed Jonathon's hand entwined in Sally's and went straight in for the kill. He slapped Jonathon on the back. "Well, I reckon y've finally backed the winner, Jon!"

As usual, Jonathon shrank a little under Jum's enthusiasm. He returned, in a strained voice, "I was just telling Sally, Jum, I have feelings for her. Is that alright with you?"

"Alright? Of course it's bloody alright! I was wondering when you two were going to get around to it! And by the way, I've just asked Bernadette to marry me for the tenth time and she's accepted—finally! So let's have a drink to love and marriage." Jum raised the toast, then sensing Jonathon and Sally needed to be alone, Jum and Bernadette left.

Sally and Jonathon remained at the table, discussing their future together. Sally's head had begun to spin. *I wonder, is it from the champagne or the talk of love? I don't know, and I don't care. It's like a beautiful dream.* Sally's dream became a reality when Jonathon proposed marriage. I needn't tell you her answer. A hum of excitement filled the air, minutes before the main race of the day was about to be run.

Jonathon suggested, "Come on, Sally, let's get a good vantage point to see Freelance win!" He took her by the hand. "Excuse me, sir. Excuse me, madam," he nudged his way through the crowd, towing Sally behind, until they were directly in front of the winning post. Jum stood in the mounting enclosure, talking with Harry, the trainer, and Jimmy, the jockey. After Harry had given his instructions to Jimmy, he turned to Jum and asked if he agreed with them. "Well, I was just about to tell Jimmy to go to the front and stay there!" Jum then slapped Jimmy on the back. "Good luck, Jimmy, there'll be a wad of notes waiting for you when you come back the winner."

Jum then ushered Bernadette to the members' grandstand, where they had a front row view of the race. His trembling hands lifted the binoculars.

Bernadette noticed, "Are you nervous, my love?"

"I have to be honest, Bernadette. I've never been so bloody nervous in all my life!"

"Well, I suppose you've set yourself up for the highest of highs, Jum. But on the other hand, if Freelance fails, you're in for a big, embarrassing thud." She sat closer to him, rubbing his arm. "Always remember, my love. If you fall, I'll be right there to pick you up. Good luck, darling."

Jum's nerves rose when the pedantic starter held the field a moment too long. Jum said loud enough for the people around him, "Oh, for Christ sake, let them go! How good do you want the bloody line?"

Jum didn't have to wait a second longer. The tape flung back and the horses bounced forward in a good even start. Freelance settled in his customary position, near the tail of the field, only two horses behind him. The tearaway leader increased his margin with every stride, until he was ten lengths in front. With one mile left to race, Jum wasn't concerned, as Freelance looked to be galloping well within himself. But when only half a mile was left to go and the other horses hadn't changed position, Jum was beside himself.

"Get going! Bloody hell, what's that eff'n' jockey doing? Get going, Freelance! Jimmy, get him going! Go, Freelance, go!"

With the leader tiring over the last quarter of a mile, Freelance took off in an attempt to round the field, only to be bumped by an erratic horse that ran him off the track. Not to be outmanoeuvred, Jimmy found a clear run down the outside fence and smartly gathered in his rivals. The leader still remained, but Freelance was gaining on him with every stride. Jum and Bernadette, in defiance of members' etiquette, stood to cheer him on.

"Go, you beauty. Go!"

With every stride, Freelance narrowed the margin until his head was clear of Volunteer, who ran a gallant second. Jum threw his hat in the air before grabbing Bernadette by the waist and lifting her high off the ground. They were ecstatic. "You bloody beauty!" Jum called. "Nothing compares to this!"

Bernadette asked, laughing, "Nothing, my love?"

Jum's speech was hilarious. "How damned lucky am I? I won Freelance in a poker game and now he's going to win the Melbourne Cup!" Jum finished by doffing his hat and bowing to the crowd.

"Everyone's welcome to my marquee for celebration drinks!" This announcement was met with resounding cheers.

It became impossible for Jonathon and Sally to get close to Jum, with what seemed like the entire race crowd taking it in turns to pat him on the back and congratulate him. They simply gave up. "We'll have more luck catching up with Jum later, Sally. Anyway, I want to show you my new buggy."

Sally floated in a state of happy delirium as they walked arm in arm, to where Jonathon's two-horse buggy was being tended by a young boy.

"Gee, thanks, mister," the boy said when Jonathon handed him two shillings.

Sally reached into her purse and did the same. She noticed the boy had grown out of his clothes and had no shoes. He couldn't believe his luck.

"Thanks Mrs, my mum'll be real happy. This'll feed us for a couple of weeks! Thanks Mr and Mrs Darcy."

Jonathon turned to Sally. "That sounds good, doesn't it, Sally?"

"Yes, it certainly does, Mr Darcy."

"Well then, my dearest Sally, shall we go home?"

Chapter 10

The Wedding

Three days later and Jum was reluctant to leave Adelaide. However, the drought was taking its toll. "I have to make decisions, Bernadette, about which stock to feed and keep for future breeding, and which stock needs to be grazed on the public stock routes, or 'the long paddock', as they call it. I'm sorry, my love, I hate to leave you, even for a minute."

In the past three days, the four friends had decided that in three weeks' time, they'd share a double wedding at Bulkawa. This would be ten days before Jum and Bernadette would travel to Melbourne and attend the Melbourne Cup.

"I can't tell you how happy I am that you'll accompany me to Melbourne—at last, Bernadette, as my wife and not my mistress." He levelled his gaze.

"And I think it's a great idea to have Sally stay with you before the wedding. You'll be able teach her about—you know, what it takes to be a 'good' wife." Jum winked. "You know what I mean, my love."

"Of course, Jum. I have the credentials, don't I?"

Jum then walked over to Sally, his gaze symbolic, almost father-to-daughter.

"Looks like I've lost you as an employee, Sally, but gained you as a good friend. You know Jonathon's not only my closest associate but I also look upon him as my younger brother. Anyway, the wedding will be just the start of our celebration heading towards the Melbourne Cup. Bernadette and I have decided to go early to Melbourne, the day after the wedding. Then after the Cup we've booked passage to Bernadette's homeland, Hawaii."

Sally couldn't help herself. "Hawaii?" she repeated in surprise.

Bernadette laughed. "That's right, Sally, I've never told you. My mother was a Hawaiian princess and my father, an English missionary. Apparently, it was love at first sight." She smiled, placing her arm around Sally. "I'll tell you all about it in our time together."

The two women stood with their arms linked, waving Jum goodbye. Bernadette then led Sally up the steps and into her townhouse.

"This is your room, Sally."

"Oh my, it's lovely, Bernadette, and your home is beautiful. Are you sure you don't mind me staying?"

"Not at all, Sally." Bernadette sat on the bed. "Come sit next to me. I think it's a wonderful idea! I'm so happy for you and Jonathon, and Jum thought as I did that you may like someone to help choose your bridal gown. And with any other question you may have about marriage, seeing you lost your mother." She paused when Sally let out a sad reflective sigh.

"It must have been hard for you, Sally, left all alone to fend for yourself. Please consider me as not only your friend but your confidant. If you wish to talk to me about anything, anything at all," she studied Sally's faraway look. "I know it can be difficult sometimes, but it helps when you're able to share your concerns."

Sally hung her head. "The past is in the past, Bernadette. My mother used to say that. 'It's no good dwelling on the past, Sally, we have to look forward to the future.' She always said that, so if you don't mind, Bernadette, I would like to think that this day will be the beginning of my new life. I hope you understand I don't want to appear ungrateful, not after all you've done for me."

Sally then brightened. "But I would love to hear about your family and your childhood. It must have been so different living in Hawaii! That's if you don't mind, of course?"

"Of course I don't mind, Sally. Come on, unpack your things and I'll make us a cup of tea and we can talk." Bernadette paused in the doorway, her head turned to Sally.

"I know we have plenty of time before the wedding but if you need to talk about anything," Bernadette gave a sideways glance. "You know what I mean, Sally, what happens between a man and a woman, the lovemaking." She noticed Sally's cheeks turning pink and so she levelled her look. "I assume you'd know some things, Sally. I'm sure your mother would have talked to you but you may have more questions. I'm here to help and listen. Please don't be shy, I'm a woman of the world. I've had many lovers." Amused at Sally's shocked expression, Bernadette said, "I'll get the tea".

While Sally unpacked, her insecurities began to surface. *How am I ever going to explain my loss of virginity to Jonathon? How am I...?*

"Tea's ready, Sally."

Sitting opposite Sally at the dining table, Bernadette began. "So, Sally, my dear, have you anything you want to talk about, concerning what I mentioned before? I don't mean to press you, not at all, it's just that I may be able to put your fears to rest. Then we can get on with our wedding plans, it's going to be such fun, don't you think?"

"Yes, I think it will be wonderful."

Sally sat sipping her tea, reflecting, before she spoke. "I miss my mother terribly, Bernadette. She died when I was seventeen but she taught me everything I know and what to expect in the outside world and how to behave in society. Every spare moment we had, we read together, therefore my knowledge so far has been gained mainly through books."

Sally raised her eyes over the rim of her teacup. "Mother did tell me the facts of life, Bernadette, if that's what you mean. She gave me a book to read, *The Circle of Life*, so I know everything I need to know, I suppose."

Sally flushed, seemingly unable to meet Bernadette's gaze, she lowered her eyes and drew the cup of tea up to her mouth and sipped. Bernadette noticed her discomfort but chose to continue.

"I know you may think me presumptuous, Sally, but did your mother only cover the clinical side of producing a baby? I know the book you've read only covers that. I'm sorry, Sally, maybe I'm not going about this the right way."

Bernadette placed her cup in its saucer and came around the table to sit next to Sally and hold her hand. "Sally, what I mean to say is that making love to your husband should be the most wonderful experience. A real woman enjoys making love every bit as much as a man does. If you satisfy your husband in bed, then there should be no need for him to take a mistress. And if he satisfies you," here Bernadette gave Sally a dazzling smile, "then you're a woman blessed. There's nothing more pleasurable. Did your mother tell you that?"

Bernadette paused, reached across the table for her tea. Drinking it slowly, she gave Sally time to think. No response came, so she continued.

"I know you truly love Jonathon, Sally, and he loves you and I know in my heart your union was meant to be. But remember, the first time you make love, because you're a virgin, it may be a little painful. I promise you though, it will become less so and far more pleasurable. Just relax and let yourself be taken by his love and everything will happen from there on. It's such an important part of marriage, for both of you. Enjoy it, Sally, that's what I'm really trying to say. So many women have gone through their lives hating sex, after being told by their mothers they should just lie still and put up with their unpleasant, wifely duties, when, in fact, it's the opposite."

Sally took in what Bernadette had said. Leaning her elbow on the table, her cheek against her hand and with a dreamy faraway look, she gave Bernadette the suspicion that she was already, in her mind, making love to Jonathon. To bring her back to reality Bernadette asked, "Now, is there anything else you want to ask or talk about?"

Sally sat upright. "Oh! No, thank you, Bernadette, I love Jonathon with all my heart. I'm sure I'll be able to do as you say." Sally became shy. "But there is one thing, I... I'm... I'm not a..." Sally stopped abruptly.

"What is it, Sally?" Bernadette asked.

"It doesn't matter. It's not important."

"Well, in that case," said Bernadette, getting to her feet, "let's go shopping!"

Harris Scarfe Department Store was "the place" to go for bridal couture. They had an abundance of different fabrics to choose from, and the in-house seamstresses would create their chosen style. It took no time at all before both women had their measurements taken in readiness. They browsed and discussed the wedding gown sketches while considering different veils, necklines, sleeves and the fullness of skirts. They were overwhelmed with the elaborate beading and lacework available. Finally, their decisions had been made.

Happy with their choices, they agreed to lunch at Bernadette's favourite café. It overlooked the botanic gardens. If it were a nice day, Mr Dipietro, one of the first Italian free settlers to open a restaurant in Adelaide, would carry a table outside for his "Bella Bernadetta". And he did just that, on this the most beautiful of days.

He made Sally giggle, with his act of a broken heart, now that his beautiful Bernadetta was getting married to another man. Kneeling before Bernadette, he pleaded.

"How coulda ya breaka my heart, Bernadetta!" He cried, wiping away imaginary tears, until his chubby wife appeared, hitting him over the head with a dish cloth.

"Comma inside and do some work, you no-good lazy mana—inside!" Turning to Bernadette, she apologised, "I ama sorry, Miss Bernadette, he's a foolish a man. I bringa you some of your favourite spaghetti and some vino for two." She turned, smiling at Sally. "Oh, such a pretty girl—she your sister?"

"No, Maria, this is Miss Sally Smith. Sally is soon to marry Mr Darcy, the lawyer."

"Oh, mama mia, you have plenty bambino, you so pretty!" She said, pinching Sally's cheek between her thumb and forefinger. Sally had never heard an Italian accent before and was most intrigued. The whole scenario was like watching a stage show. After Maria had left, Sally confessed to Bernadette, "I don't know what I've done to deserve such happiness. I can't thank you enough."

"We're the lucky ones, Sally, it's not very often you find a dying flower, care for it and it blooms beyond all imagination. I don't know anything about your past, Sally, but I know you will have a wonderful future with Jonathon." Bernadette hoped then that Sally may be a little more forthcoming.

Sally's eyes filled with tears. Bernadette gently wiped them dry, asking, "Tears of joy, I hope?"

"I've led such a sheltered life, Bernadette. Well, in one way I have. I rarely left the property where we lived and my mother worked. And now it seems all of my dreams are coming true, in a world I thought maybe only existed in books and my mother's imagination." Sally stopped abruptly, leaving Bernadette wanting to know more.

"I wish you'd tell me more about yourself, Sally. I feel you have secrets you don't want to share. Secrets which may trouble you forever, especially if you're unable to confide in a friend. I want to help you, Sally."

Sally longed to unburden herself. She was about to begin when Mr Dipietro appeared, singing and dancing around with a plate of spaghetti balanced on each hand.

"Signorinas, your spaghetti witha my special sauce, justa for you, I'ma comin' right back with some molto bene vino!"

Sally's train of thought was broken with the entertainment. All she could do was laugh, enjoy the wonderful food and meet other acquaintances of Bernadette's who'd stopped to talk. After lunch, they ambled through the gardens, taking time to admire their surrounds, when suddenly, Sally stopped. Walking toward them was Paul Smith, the young man who was staying at Mrs Murphy's boarding house. He was arm in arm with Jonathon's secretary, Mildred Morrison. Sally introduced Paul to Bernadette.

"And of course, Bernadette, you know Mildred Morrison, Jonathon's secretary?"

Mildred nodded, smiling at Bernadette while Sally looked quizzically at Paul.

"I didn't realise you and Miss Morrison knew each other, Paul?" Sally asked.

"Yes, we met when sitting on the same park bench." He turned to smile at Mildred. "We were enjoying the scenery; it was the first day I arrived in Adelaide. We met again at the races, and we've enjoyed each other's company every day since." He smiled lovingly at Mildred, who seemed to be glowing with enthusiasm.

Bernadette noticed Sally staring at Paul, as if in a trance. To break her friend's reluctance to move, she offered, "It was very nice to meet you, Paul, and you, Miss Morrison. Maybe you would care to join us for afternoon tea one day soon? I live on the north side of the gardens, number thirty-four Park Street. Perhaps even tomorrow afternoon, say four o'clock?"

"That would be very nice, Miss Jones," Paul replied, turning to Mildred. "What do you say, Mildred?"

"Yes, that would be very nice indeed, although I'll have to check with Mr Darcy first. I usually don't finish work until five."

Bernadette smiled sweetly. "I'm sure Sally can arrange that for you, Miss Morrison." Giving Sally a nudge, Bernadette asked, "Won't you, Sally?"

Snapping out of it, Sally responded, "Yes, yes, of course. I'll speak with Jonathon."

"So, until tomorrow, Paul?" Bernadette said as she almost dragged Sally away, but at the same time she was totally intrigued. This young man, Paul Smith, looked as if he could be Sally's twin brother, and having the same surname, she began wondering. *The way Sally looked at him, it was like she was mesmerised by her own reflection.*

"So, tell me, Sally, who is the mystery man? He looks so much like you, and he has the same surname. He must be related?"

"I don't know, Bernadette," Sally answered honestly. "I've only met him twice at Mrs Murphy's. Paul comes from Sydney, or just out of Sydney. Some place called Rouse Hill, near the Hawkesbury River."

"You should know that part of the country, Sally, since you've read so many books. That's where the convicts took arms against the military, in 1804, only it was called Vinegar Hill then."

"Oh yes, of course, I've read about it."

"Have you asked Paul about his family? Maybe he's related to you?"

Sally didn't answer, instead she turned her head, looking into the distance. Bernadette was getting nowhere with Sally in her dream-like state, and so she relented with a sigh.

"Oh well, we'll find out more tomorrow."

A bright morning sun and the sound of tinkering woke Sally. She yawned and stretched, thinking it was Bernadette in the kitchen. She rose slowly, put her dressing gown on and made her way to the kitchen, where she found Bernadette, dressed and making breakfast.

"I hope you like scrambled eggs, Sally?"

"Yes, I do, thank you, Bernadette. Do you want me to do something? I'm very good at cleaning, washing clothes, even mending. I'd like to help you while I'm here."

"No, it's alright, thank you, Sally. I have a lady who comes once a week to clean, so I just keep the place tidy. I'm off to work today. I help Dr Forster when he needs me. I enjoy it. You know, I think I would have liked to have been a doctor, or at least a nurse."

Bernadette brought the skillet to the table and served up the eggs. "So, Sally, you'll have to keep yourself amused until I return at three o'clock. Perhaps you could make the scones and sandwiches for our afternoon tea with Paul and Mildred?"

"Oh yes, I will. I make very good scones. Frieda, Mr Watt's cook, taught me. But I best go and see Jonathon about letting Mildred leave early from work. I've also told Mrs Murphy I'd drop by for morning tea, so I'll be quite busy until you come home."

"That all sounds good. Enjoy your breakfast. I'll see you this afternoon." Bernadette dropped a kiss on the top of Sally's head and swept from the room.

Sally began worrying. *I don't know why I should be looking forward to seeing Paul again, especially with Bernadette being so inquisitive. It may lead to trouble.*

Later, Sally found Colleen in her kitchen.

"Hello, Mrs M!"

"Oh, my dear Sally, how's it goin' with Miss Jones and all the weddin' plans?"

Sally went on to fill Colleen in on all the details, and then asked, "Mrs M— Colleen, I've spoken with Bernadette and we wish to ask you, would you do us the honour of being our Matron of Honour?"

Colleen gasped, and lent back in her chair with hand on heart.

"Of course, I accept. 'Tis the greatest honour that's ever been bestowed on me, m' dear. Thank you so much, I can hardly wait!" She dried the tear of joy and then broke the news she'd been anxious to tell.

"And now I have t' tell y', Sally, I've made plans to go home to England for a holiday." Colleen nodded in silent agreement with Sally's look of surprise.

"Yes, that's right, m' dear. I haven't seen m' two sisters or m' elder brother since I came to the colonies as a young bride. Fred, m' late husband, wanted to come here and try his luck in the gold fields and it wasn't long before we did indeed strike it lucky. Fred gave me his word of honour that when we gathered enough gold, we'd settle down in Adelaide and open a respectable boardin' house. But now, after twenty years of not havin' seen m' family, and finally havin' enough money, well, I long t' go home." She saw Sally's brow crease in concern.

"Oh, only for a holiday," she chuckled. "Yes, only for a short time, I won't be leavin' y' altogetha." Colleen took a deep sigh before placing the cups and saucers on the table. Her shrewd eyes searched Sally's with intent.

"Now, Sally, m' decision must be to either sell the boardin' house, which I really don't want ta be doin, or t' find someone who'll run the place for me. For, say, nine months?" She could almost hear Sally's thoughts clicking over.

"So, what do y' think, Sally, are you up for it?" She paused with the teapot mid-air, waiting for her answer.

"I for one would certainly take up the offer, Colleen. I don't want to lose you. I mean it sincerely when I say that I've come to look upon you as my second mother. The other reason is I want to be a real partner in my marriage with Jonathon and not just a dutiful wife who sits at home waiting for her husband to return from work. Of course, I'll have to discuss this with Jonathon. But I would love to do it. We could move in after the wedding. When are you planning to leave, Mrs M?"

"Well, I won't be goin' anywhere until I've seen y' married, m' girl. Just to hear you say you think of me as y' second mother, brings tears t' me eyes. Thank y', Sally. You are an angel!" Colleen laughed.

Over their cup of tea, both women shared laughter, remembering Colleen's winning day at the races. "It's paid for m' passage home, y' know that, Sally. I still can't believe how lucky I was!" Colleen paused and shook her head. "But y' knows I'm smart enough to know it only happens once, or maybe twice, in a lifetime. So, I'll now be puttin' it to good use, the same as I did when m' hubby and I built the boardin' house. Oh, how I wish my Freddy was travellin' home with me," Colleen said, putting her teacup down.

Seeing her sadness, and without hesitating, Sally walked around the table and gave her a hug. "He's never left you. You know that, Colleen. You must feel his presence sometimes, the way I do with my mother." Sally then gave Colleen a kiss on her cheek, "I must be off now. I'll have to talk to Jonathon about your proposal. Oh, and also about letting Mildred leave a little early this afternoon, so she can come to afternoon tea with Paul."

"Yes, I know all about the buddin' romance between the pair. So, there you go, Sally, I'm one up on y'!"

Sally walked along with happy thoughts of her and Jonathon living at the boarding house. *It would save us a lot of money. I only hope Jonathon will agree.* Holding her head high, Sally almost bumped into Paul, who came walking from the opposite direction.

"Oh Paul!" Sally exclaimed, laughing while apologising for nearly knocking him over.

"I was just on my way to ask Jonathon about Mildred being relieved from her duties a little earlier today."

"I'm afraid you won't find her there, Sally. She's not well," Paul said as he removed his hat.

"Oh, that's a shame, poor Mildred. Will you then be coming alone, Paul?"

"No, I'm sorry, Sally, we'll both have to miss it, if that's alright?"

Sally suddenly registered a wonderful thought. *This change of plan was heaven sent.*

"Certainly, Paul, we'll have afternoon tea another day." Sally paused a little, "Do you have a minute to talk, Paul, I'd like to ask you a question?"

"I do, but not for long. When I discovered Mildred was ill, I made an appointment with a client wanting to buy some cattle before they go to auction."

Paul indicated a bench seat bordering the path. Sally sat next to him, wondering for a moment how to broach the subject.

"Paul," she said hesitantly, "I've been thinking whether we may be related in some way. You must admit we do look alike, and with the same surname, I was wondering if there may be a family tie. May I ask you where your father came from before settling in Australia?"

"Yes, of course, Sally, and it does seem too much of a coincidence, the resemblance and the surname, even though it's a common one. I'll be happy to tell you all I know and see where it leads us." Paul smiled then took a deep breath.

"My father's name is Ted, well, Edward, is his real name. He came from England to New South Wales as a free settler. His father, my grandfather, died when dad was only young and then, when my grandmother became ill, Dad went to work in the coal mines. He had to try and keep his mother alive. His wages were used up by doctor's bills, the rent, and food. His money didn't go far, as he also had a younger sister to care for."

Sally thought she may have found the link. "So, your father had a sister. What happened to her? Did she stay in England or come here with him? What was her name?" Sally leant forward with anticipation.

"My dad never knew what happened to his sister, Harriet." Sally's heart skipped a beat at hearing her mother's name. Paul noticed her surprise but chose to continue.

"He'd camp out near the coal mines, which were miles away from London. But on Sundays he'd come home with his pay. One day, when he was about eighteen, I think, he came home to find his mother dead and Harriet gone. He never understood how his sister could leave their dying mother." Paul hung his head, his expression pained.

"My father was heartbroken but he searched for Harriet. He never found her. Then one of the neighbours told dad she'd been dragged off by the police in London Town. Dad went to the London prison, and then to the docks from where they transported the prisoners to Australia. The men who ran the English prisons in those days were a heartless, arrogant lot. Well, anyway, the chief record keeper told dad bluntly, 'Nobody ever gives their right name. I can't find her here,' and then he slammed the book shut."

Sally sat spellbound as Paul continued.

"I suppose they thought it was a good way to begin a new colony, by sending not only hardened criminals, but also those poor blighters who stole while merely trying to survive in hard times. So, with no family left, dad decided his only chance was to work hard and save his money. By the time he was twenty-one, he'd saved enough money for his passage to Australia. He soon found a job with a grazier but first he checked the prison in Sydney. They had so many women named Smith, plus most had left, to who knew where? So he gave up.

Then not long after he'd settled in his job, he met and married my mother. She was the daughter of the man who owned a property next to where my father worked, at Rouse Hill. My grandfather, Mum's dad, was a wonderful man. He took my father on as his partner, once he'd married Mum, of course. Granddad never had a son of his own, so he loved my father like his own son. Then when I was six, my mother died giving birth to my sister. The poor little baby died two days later. I don't think Dad ever got over it. He's never remarried. He puts all of his grief into working the property. My grandfather was also heartbroken—he sickened and died several months later." Paul paused, ran a hand distractedly through his hair, looked up and pushed on.

"I was taught the hard way, Sally, hard work and respect for the land. But Dad understood when I said I wanted to be a stock and station agent, mainly because I'd like to travel around and see Australia. So now I get to travel all around this great country and meet lots of different people, I love it." He swivelled around to face Sally, "That's about it for my story, so what about yours?"

Sally knew now exactly what had happened to Paul's aunty Harriet. Delighted in finally knowing that they were related, Sally would apprise him of the facts, some of which he and his father obviously had not known.

"Thank you for being honest with me, Paul. I must tell you now; my mother Harriet is your aunt." Sally noticed Paul's expression was more of interest than surprise.

"My mother would never divulge to me where she came from, or what had happened to her before she came to work for her degenerate master. I have to say degenerate, because he was. But finally, on her death bed, she told me her secrets. She said she had to feed and care for her sick mother while her brother Edward (Ted) was working in the coal mines.

"Having no money at the time, she took the chance of stealing a few oranges for her mother to enjoy before she passed away. Unfortunately, she was caught. She was rushed through the courts and was shipped to the colony of New South Wales, all within a few days of being apprehended. Which I think, as you say, was an extremely harsh punishment for such a minor offence. With no one to care for her, our grandmother would not have survived very much longer. It was my mother's deepest regret, to think that her mother must have died alone."

They sat silent for a moment considering this sad fact, then Sally asked, "Could you keep a close secret, Paul? You may tell your father, but only him. Please don't tell another living soul, and ask your father to do the same. Can I trust you, Paul?" Sally's look was so earnest, pained even, that Paul agreed without hesitating.

"Yes, Sally, you have my word. I would never intentionally hurt anyone. So yes, you can trust me," he smiled and took her hand. "We're family, after all."

"I will start at the beginning. My father was the Captain of the Guards on board the convict ship and then at the Sydney jail. At first, he felt sorry for my mother. She was a beautiful young woman in such a dreadful situation. Then every night he would take her out of her cell and give her decent food to eat. His affection grew into real love. My mother, of course, fell in love with him, and before long, well…" here Sally blushed, "well, here I am. I'm the product of their love."

Sally went on to tell him how her father was shot and killed while trying to capture an escaped convict. "It was a tragedy, because my father, Charles Keegan, vowed to marry my mother as soon as she was released. They truly loved each other, Paul. Had he lived, our lives would have been so different." Paul seemed touched if not sympathetic.

The Cecil Birch story was the hardest to tell, but it felt good to at last be able to talk to someone, someone she knew was family and who would not betray her. During and after her heart-breaking tale, Paul's eyes welled with tears. He held her close and said, "Cousin, I promise never to divulge your secrets to anyone, especially about Patrick. I give you my word of honour, Sally. I will never say a word of what you have told me to another living soul, except for my father when I see him. I won't even tell him in a letter, as it might venture into the wrong hands."

Sally needed to ask one more question. "When my mother told me on her death bed she'd been a convict, she also told me she had a brother back in England. She'd written to him, many, many times but never received a reply. I think this broke her heart more than anything." Paul jumped in.

"I can assure you, Sally, my father never received any letters from her. Probably because he never went back to their rented house, he moved to another village, closer to the mines, and boarded with a miserly old woman. He told me he had to bury his money or she'd steal it from him. And the main reason he saved his money was to come to Australia and find his sister, who he suspected had been shipped here. Then they could start a new life together. I don't know, Sally, maybe the old lady didn't give him the letters, or they just never found him. And with everyone calling him Ted, not his real name Edward, maybe no one made the connection?"

Satisfied they had discovered the truth, as hard as it was to bear, they embraced for some time, offering each other support before Sally drew back.

"I must go and see Jonathon now, Paul. I have good news. Mrs Murphy has asked me to run the boarding house while she returns to England to see her family."

Paul hugged and then kissed her on the cheek. "That's wonderful news, Sally! Goodbye, cousin. I promise you, your secret is safe with me, and congratulations on your engagement!"

"Thank you, Paul. You have no idea how I have longed to unburden myself. I know I can trust you, you're family. And, of course, you along with Mildred will be invited to our wedding." Glowing with happiness, she hurried along, feeling as if she'd grown three feet taller with the removal of her guilt. Soon she spotted Jonathon walking towards her.

"Jonathon," Sally said surprised, "I was just coming to see you. I have so much to tell you. You know Paul Smith? Well, we look so much alike, and his surname is Smith. Of course, you already know that. Anyway, we talked and talked and traced our family tree and, yes, we are definitely related. Isn't it wonderful? I now have a cousin." Sally said with enthusiasm, hoping this particular line of conversation would not go any further.

"Yes, that is wonderful, Sally. Was that the only thing you were coming to see me about, your new-found cousin?" They linked arms before turning and heading back towards his office.

"No, Jonathon, that's a very long story. I'll tell you tomorrow," she said, wishing to avoid telling the story, tomorrow, or any other day. "Actually, I have something else to ask you."

"And pray tell, what might that be, Miss Smith?"

By the time they'd reached his office the whole business of the boarding house had been discussed. Jonathon thought it a wonderful idea. He had no objection to women working in business and remarked on how efficient Miss Morrison had proved herself to be. Sally paused at the foot of the steps, asking Jonathon if he'd known of the relationship between Mildred and Paul.

"Yes, as a matter of fact I do. There's been some talk of Mildred going to New South Wales with Paul after our wedding. So, I'll have to find myself a new secretary."

"Goodness, that was quick, Jonathon! They must be truly in love. He didn't give that away in our conversation, although we didn't broach the subject." Sally looked a little bewildered.

"I know Mildred's not at work today. Paul told me she was ill. Would you like me to help you, Jonathon? I have nothing else to do now that they won't be coming for afternoon tea."

"Why not? It should be fun having you at the front desk, we can kiss—in between clients."

She slapped his arm, laughing as they climbed the stairs.

The wedding date had been set for the third week in October and all plans had gone smoothly to the day. Recently, the property had benefitted from an inch of rain. It was enough to settle the dust and wash the garden. The small chapel had been newly painted, and the shearers' quarters were scrubbed to the boards. New beds were brought in with fresh clean linen, ready for overnight guests. Of course, a separate space had been curtained off and set aside for the women. Every inch of the homestead had been spring cleaned. Wang and Chong, trying their best to have the gardens perfect for the wedding day, ran around to the point where they kept bumping into each other. Jum had hired the best caterers in Adelaide and warned them, "Only the very best food and wine will do."

The scene was set for the most extravagant wedding the neighbours could remember, despite the fact the rest of the country was still affected by the depression. If anyone dared comment about Jum's profligate lifestyle, he would answer, "Well, my friend, there are winners and there are losers, and that's all there is to it. But be assured, I'll always lend a helping hand."

Mrs Murphy, as their Matron of Honour, was dutifully helping both women into their bridal gowns. "I still can't believe you've asked me, a fat old lady, to help the two most beautiful women in Adelaide. I just can't believe it!" she exclaimed.

"You can't believe it?" replied Sally. "What about me? I was found dying on your front door path by my future husband. I'd hardly met a stranger before, let alone a handsome lawyer, and look at me now!" Sally beamed a smile at Colleen but inside felt a little shaken, thinking momentarily of her past, especially her son, Patrick. Holding onto so many secrets gave her reason to feel weak at times.

With the weather perfect and the gardens manicured to perfection, everything it seemed had been organised to the minute. Guests chatted happily among themselves while anxious bridegrooms waited at the altar with an outward show of patience. It was standing room only in the tiny chapel after the first fifty guests took their seats. Bernadette had entreated the Bishop of Adelaide to conduct the ceremony. He had been in two minds, knowing Jum was an atheist. However, the Bishop could not refuse Jum's generous donation. Bernadette was under the impression the Bishop had agreed to preside over the ceremony for one reason only, and that was, she, Sally and Jonathon were all devout Catholics. The Bishop, however, had taken a more practical approach, thanks to Jum.

The bridal music began when the two women, both breathtakingly beautiful, entered the chapel, arm in arm with Dan. With no fathers to give them away, Jum had decided Dan was 'good looking enough' to at least escort the brides down the aisle. A hush fell over the assembly as the brides made their way to the altar. Both women held bouquets of perfumed roses cut that morning from the garden.

Bernadette had defied custom by wearing a white gown, cut to accentuate her slender waist. Sally's frock was a simpler design, but elegant nonetheless.

"Your youthful beauty would outshine any dress, m' dear," Colleen said, when Sally had confided her fears that her dress was too plain.

As the grooms turned in unison, not one drop of regret ran through their veins when they took their brides-to-be from Dan. Jum had promised Bernadette he would be on his best behaviour during the ceremony. But after thirty minutes of what was, to him, an unintelligible Catholic ritual, he whispered to Bernadette, "How long does this bloody thing go on for?"

"Shush!" was all she said.

Finally, the nuptials were complete, and Jum proclaimed, "Halle-bloody-luiah! Let the party begin!"

The celebrations progressed throughout the afternoon and into the evening. Torches were set ablaze, accompanied by stars forming the Southern Cross. A full moon cast its golden light so bright that shadows appeared. Under this magical sky, Paul danced with Mildred. As they waltzed around the dance floor, he asked, "Mildred, would you do me the honour of becoming my wife?" And he spun her around twice before she could answer.

"Oh yes, Paul! Yes!"

"If we sneak off early," he whispered, "I can show you how much I love you, Mildred."

After accepting to marry Paul, and under the influence of both love and a little too much champagne, she giggled her agreement.

Dan had decided to stay sober. He had his eye on Mary, the daughter and only child of the grazier on the neighbouring property. *While it's not my sole motivation, the idea of marrying Mary and taking over her father's property when he becomes too old, of course, is a compelling thought.* Dan walked in his bow-legged way towards his prey.

"Mary," he said, his opening line sincere, "you look beautiful this evening. May I have the pleasure of this dance?"

Too overcome to speak, Mary held onto his extended hand and accompanied Dan to the dance floor. After several turns around, he suggested they take a stroll. Mary more than willingly accepted the offer. Dan soon found a secluded spot to plant a passionate kiss upon her lips. Thus began their romance and Dan's well-planned future.

It seemed love was in the air that evening, as Colleen had also found herself enjoying the company of Bob, Jum's blacksmith, a widower for four years. Flattered by his attentiveness and his compliments, Colleen was transported back to her youth. Bob made more advances by kissing her on the cheek. Sometime later in the evening, he told her how much he enjoyed her company and how beautiful he thought she was. He also asked her whether they could see each other more often.

Colleen regretfully informed him, "I will be leavin' for England next week, Bob, and I'll be stayin' for six months."

Silenced momentarily by this unexpected news, Bob then suggested, "I tell y' what, Colleen. I still have family back in England. Do you think there's room for me on the boat?"

"But Bob, what about your job here with Jum?"

"Oh, he won't mind. I'm training a young lad and he's working out real good. He should be able to handle everything while I'm gone."

Colleen's brow furrowed in thought, if only for a moment. "This is all a bit quick, Bob. But yes, I think it would be nice t' have company on board the ship."

Bob placed her hand in his. "Would you care to dance, Colleen?"

"I haven't kicked m' heels up for such a long time, Bob, but let's give it a go, shall we?"

The revelry continued into the small hours of the morning, in fact, the sun was rising when Jum, still inebriated, reeled towards Jonathon with rum in hand. He then placed his spare hand on Jonathon's shoulder. It steadied him from falling.

"Now, young man," he was trying to focus his vision, "I, Jum Watt, well, I wancha t' know I'll alluss be y' friend." His heartfelt speech was interrupted by a fit of hiccups. "But (hiccup) I need to know (hiccup), yes, I need t' know why y' still (hiccup) here with me an' not with y' bewdiful (hiccup) bride?" Jum shook his finger.

"Y' should be makin' love (hiccup) t' Sally RIGHT NOW!"

Jonathon, stone cold sober and embarrassed by Jum's outburst, whispered, in an attempt to put an end to his friend's advice. "I will, Jum, but I need to have peace and quiet, you know, to be in our own home, with privacy."

Jum staggered only a step away, and trying not to laugh, he stage-whispered back, "Well, y' not like me, Jonno, nothin' puts me off!" (Hiccup).

"I want this to be special, Jum. You see, I've never made love to a woman before."

As soon as the words had left his lips, Jonathon knew he'd made a mistake. Jum burst out laughing and fell to the ground. When his hilarity showed no sign of abating, Jonathon looked down upon his drunken friend with a degree of disdain and said stiffly, "It's not that funny, Jum!"

"Like bloody hell it's not! Christ, Jon, I had me first when I was twelve! How old are ya? Thirty?"

Jonathon turned on his heel and left Jum still laughing and trying, unsuccessfully, to lift himself off the ground.

Chapter 11

Back to Work

A recovery party was held the next day at Bulkawa for those guests who had been invited to stay and for those who had simply been unable to make it home. The cook, doling out bacon and eggs with slabs of toast was, as Jum so aptly put it, "busier than a one-legged man at a bum-kicking competition".

The morning gave the newlyweds the opportunity to mingle and catch up on local news and gossip. Jum's next door neighbour, Jack, Mary's father, had heard about Jum's enormous win on Freelance at the races.

"How did you go about getting all that money out of the bookie, Jum?"

"I only got half of it, Jack. He didn't have enough to pay the rest, so I told him to write it in his book for Freelance to win Melbourne Cup. He gave me three to one, not a bad price, I reckon. Freelance is a certainty to win. Harry, the trainer, said he's never come across a horse as good as him. He reckons there's not a horse in Australia that'll be able to beat him over the two miles!" Jum boasted loudly enough for all to hear.

"Well, good luck, Jum, and by the way, your young jackaroo, Dan, seems to be a good chap. I know he wouldn't be working for you if he wasn't. But I need to ask because Mary seems very keen on him. She wants to go out on a picnic with him next weekend and she asked if he could come for dinner tomorrow night."

Jum was quick to speak up for his favourite jackaroo. "Dan's a fine young man. Hard worker, respectful, likes the rum a bit but what young bloke doesn't? No, mate, he's an honest fella. I wouldn't knock him back as a son-in-law!" Jum laughed, but Jack only smiled and thanked him for the reference.

As they waved their last guest goodbye, the four friends let out a huge collective sigh. Once in the sitting room, they sank back onto feather cushions. No one seemed to have the energy to speak, until Bernadette yawned out her words, "I hope we're not leaving too early tomorrow, Jum. I'm exhausted."

"No, my dear, I've booked an evening passage on the Intercolonial. Thank God the train won't have to stop to change gauges. Yes, it's about bloody time they realised their mistakes. It will be very leisurely and you'll have a few days to shop before the Cup. We'll also be dining with a few influential friends of mine in Melbourne." He turned to Jonathon, "You haven't changed your mind, Jon? I'd really like you and Sally to be there, mate."

"No, I'm sorry, Jum, too much business on, and Sally has to learn the run of things at the boarding house before Colleen leaves for England. But we'll have a proper honeymoon one day." He smiled in Sally's direction.

Jum listened, although his attention had shifted. "That reminds me, Jon, I seem to remember hearing something about Bob, my blacksmith, having taken a shine to Colleen. And now he wants to go to England with her. I had a damn good laugh about it but I suppose I owe it to him. He's worked on Bulkawa for near twenty years without a bloody holiday."

The girls were especially pleased to hear about the budding romance. Bernadette then added more gossip. "I think we inspired love last night, my dear, with Dan planning Mary's courtship. Then a friend of mine caught Mildred and Paul in the men's quarters, in what could be considered a rather compromising position." They all laughed, then Frieda interrupted.

"Would anyone like dinner or just a snack with a cup a tea?"

Sally stood, indicating the chair she'd vacated. "I tell you what, Frieda. You sit down here and I'll make us some sandwiches and a pot of tea. You've worked so hard ordering those caterers around and then helping with breakfast this morning. You must be exhausted!"

"I always did like that young lady," Frieda quipped.

Sally's extreme tiredness had not completely drowned her longing for Jonathon. Last night was understandable, too many people to talk to, too much food and wine. But tonight, Sally expected Jonathon to be in a romantic mood. She would throw caution to the wind and think of something, anything, which would explain her loss of virginity—after he'd made love to her. However, Jonathon seemed tense and a little withdrawn.

"Is something wrong, Jonathon?"

"I… I feel embarrassed, Sally, I must confess, I've never been with a woman before. I'm afraid I may disappoint you, or even worse, hurt you. I feel a bit of a fool actually."

Brushing the hair from his forehead, Sally consoled him, "Oh Jon, you dear wonderful man, you could never disappoint me. We can learn together about the pleasures, which are now ours to enjoy."

Sally gently touched his face before she kissed him. Their kisses grew passionate and arousing. Jonathon reluctantly stopped and turned Sally around and undid the buttons of her dress, sliding it over her pale shoulders. He kissed the nape of her neck. It sent shivers down her spine.

"I'll be back shortly, Jon. Please get into bed and turn the lamp down low."

She closed the adjoining bathroom door. Leaning against it, she gazed at her vision in the mirror, hardly recognising the young woman who stood before her. Sally pulled the pins from her hair, allowing her curls to cascade down her back. She removed her clothes and then a little nervous, she joined Jonathon.

The silkiness of her skin heightened Jonathon's desire. He drove his action quickly until euphoria overcame his new-found sexual pleasure. Sally was slightly amused at his eagerness because it gave her no time to experience total satisfaction. But her heart now filled with even more love for this gentle man who was her husband.

"My darling, Sally, I love you so much."

She heard the raw emotion in his voice and took joy in his sincerity. At the same time, Sally was relieved at his obvious naivety about a woman's body. Jonathon hadn't realised she was not a virgin.

It was eleven am before Bernadette and Jum waved goodbye to Sally and Jonathon.

"See y', mate, wish us good luck in the Cup. I'll telegram you when we win, Jon!"

Bernadette hugged Sally tight. "Goodbye, Sally, take care. I'll miss you."

Jonathon then asked Sally, knowing very well it was too late, "Am I being selfish, Sally? Would you like to have gone to Melbourne?"

"No," she looked at him levelly. "I'm truly happy here with you, Jonathon. I want to make a home, for us—our family." Jonathon squeezed her waist. Standing together in silence, they waved Jum and Bernadette goodbye, watching as they disappeared from view.

"You know, Sally, we may not see them for nearly six months by the time they travel to Hawaii and back. I'll miss them terribly."

"Me too, and with Colleen leaving for England, we'll just have to enjoy each other's company, Jon, or we'll be in trouble!" Sally poked him gently in the ribs with her elbow.

He turned to kiss her, before patting her bottom. "Well then, Mrs Darcy, let's hitch up the buggy and get back to work."

Deciding half-way home to pull up and have a rest, Jonathon tied the horses under a tree where there was relief from the heat, with a soft breeze cooled by the deep shade of the leaves. He then attached hessian nose bags half-full with oats to the horses' nuzzles and sat with his back against the tree while gathering in the picture of Sally rubbing the horse's sweaty patches and then offering them water.

Jonathon said, "I'm not being lazy, Sally. I'm simply mesmerised by your caring for the horses, before yourself."

Setting the water down, Sally walked towards him and confessed. "I love you, Jonathon, with all my heart. We're alike, you and I. Giving and thinking of other beings before ourselves, it comes from within. I feel our strong hearts together will make a difference in this cruel world."

Sally knew, slowly but surely, she would execute her plan to bring Patrick home, and this was the beginning. Jonathon said nothing; he didn't have to, his love shone through in his eyes. Kissing him with passion, Sally felt him respond. He wanted to have her right there and then, to make love in broad daylight. However, his usual manner of correctness overrode his desire. And so he pushed Sally gently away.

"I'm so hungry, Sally... for... for lunch," he finished lamely, trying light-heartedly to disguise what he felt was an inappropriate lustful urge at that time of day.

"Shall we have the sandwiches and fruit cake you packed?"

Sally knew better than to force herself upon Jonathon. *He's so coy but it doesn't mean he does not love me. He's reserved, slightly prudish and I love him for it.* She went about opening the muslin-wrapped parcel containing their food. Later, after unloading their bags at the boarding house, Sally took in the welcoming aroma of Colleen's chicken soup.

"Oh, you are a darling, Mrs M. This is just what we need. Thank you."

"That's alright, m' dear Sally. We're all a bit weary and this is a simple supper."

"Let's tuck in, as Jum would say," Jonathon said with a smile.

Sally then asked, "Where's Paul this evening, Mrs M?"

"He's havin' dinner with Miss Morrison's parents, and I think he's gonna ask her father's permission for Mildred's hand in marriage." Colleen gave a knowing wink. With hand on chin and brows furrowed, Sally asked, "Now what relation will their children be to me?"

Jonathon replied without a moment to think, "They would be, if they were to have children, Sally, your second cousins, once removed."

"Well, I'm very pleased. Because I know, Jonathon," she said in the demeaning manner intended, "I will have many more relatives, I can just tell by the way they look at each other." Sally gave him the 'I know better than you about such things' look.

Sally bathed, not lingering as she usually would in the tub, as more pleasurable things awaited. Jonathon chose to wash himself from the china basin in their bedroom. Naked, he slipped into bed feeling a little more confident after their previous night of lovemaking. Sally paused, as he laid open the bed clothes. Kissing her gently, Jonathon's hands began to explore her body. Over the fullness of her breasts, the curve of her hips, then between her thighs. Sally moaned, arching her body to meet his gentle touch. She became lost in the pleasure of their union, her hips involuntarily rising to meet his, her hands cupping his buttocks. Feeling every cell of her body come alive, it was unbearably beautiful, and she cried out. The dam had burst, wave after wave of immense pleasure washed over them, leaving both weak and breathless. Jonathon abandoned himself to the sensation, never wanting to let her go, while Sally cried tears of joy.

"Oh, Sally, I never dreamt anything could be so wonderful."

"Nor I, my darling."

The days ahead were extremely busy. Jonathon's law firm was now among the most respected in Adelaide; so much so, he took on a young university student in his last year of studying law who needed part-time work.

"This will be perfect, Sally. Phillip can do most of my investigation work. If I think him suitable, after he's graduated, of course, I might just offer him a junior partnership. And now Mildred's officially engaged to Paul, she'll soon be moving to New South Wales. So, I'll have to find a new secretary. Actually, I'm interviewing a young lady today."

"I'm run off my feet as well, Jonathon. Colleen seems too busy packing and saying goodbye to friends to help out much. But she hasn't forgotten about Freelance winning the Cup. She told me that she gave Jum her money, with her orders, 'Put it on his nose, Jum!' I think I'll follow her tip. She seems to know how to back a winner!" Sally laughed, through tired eyes.

The day had arrived for Colleen to leave. Regrettably for Sally, Colleen was all packed, ready and waiting for Bob to arrive with Dan, who was driving them to the sea port.

"Now have you got everything you need, Colleen? You must be so excited and I'm so pleased you have Bob to take care of you on the journey." Colleen nodded in agreement, smiling at Sally's assumption of Bob's capabilities. Colleen then began to pace anxiously as they had to be at the dock by nine-thirty. It was a quarter past eight when the carriage finally arrived in a cloud of dust. Colleen almost ran with her ports and threw them up to Dan who stacked them in the luggage carrier.

"Hang on, hang on, that's my job! I'll look after you now, Colleen!" Bob said, scurrying to finish the packing.

"I'm sorry I can't be at the dock to wave you goodbye, Colleen," Sally said with a catch in her voice. "I'll miss you very much."

They managed a final embrace before Colleen entered the carriage and Sally called, "Goodbye from Jonathon, Bob, he asked me to give you his best wishes for your journey," as she waved them off.

Colleen, for once in her life, was too preoccupied with her voyage ahead to cry. Suddenly Sally felt apprehensive. *How will I ever be able to manage running a boarding house?* But then her thoughts focused on Jonathon. *I'll find my strength through Jonathon. My whole world now revolves around him. Patrick will always be in my heart, but that's different. One day soon I'll tell Jonathon about Patrick, but not today. I have two new boarders coming. Beds have to be made and I have the evening meal to prepare.*

She set back to work.

Chapter 12

Melbourne

Four days of travelling, plus interludes, and Bernadette and Jum finally arrived in Melbourne. Before booking into one of Melbourne's most exclusive hotels, The Victoria, they made a brief visit to Flemington Racecourse where Freelance was stabled. Jum met up with Harry, the trainer, and his new strapper. After shaking hands and looking into the beady eyes of the boy, he asked, with a sideward glance, "Where's the other lad, Harry?"

"Oh, he shot through, Boss. Dunno where he's got to."

Jum's gaze remained on the lad. "And where do you hail from, boy? What's y' name?"

By this time, the boy hung his head, wilting under Jum's scrutiny.

"Just out bush, spent a lot of me time breakin' in stock horses. Me name's Jock." He twisted his cap in his bony hands.

"Fair enough. You look after my horse, Jock, or there'll be trouble. Y' hear me?"

"Yeah," the boy answered, still unable to meet Jum's gaze.

Jum opened the stable door and stepped in to give the huge horse a pat. "You're a champ, you know that? And you're gunna win the Cup next Tuesday." Freelance whinnied, nodding his head. They all laughed, except Jock, who was still looking at the ground, kicking dirt with his boot.

"Jesus, he knows he's gunna win, Harry!"

Bernadette, also a horse lover, joined in to pat Freelance.

"You'll spoil him, missus, and he won't wanna run. He's a bit of a sook, you know," Harry's eyes glistened with mischief.

Jum was quick. "Not in a race he's not, Harry!" He then continued with pride, "I'm gunna stand him at stud at Bulkawa after he wins the Cup, Harry."

"He's got plenty a wins in him before you need to retire him, Boss."

"I know that, Harry, but to tell you the truth, I've never been as nervous as the day he won in Adelaide. This game will end up giving me a bloody heart attack."

98

"If y' don't mind me saying so, Boss, maybe if y' didn't gamble so big, you might just enjoy it for what it is—a great day out with friends to watch your horse race."

"You have a point, Harry, but that's not who I am. I'm a gambler. That's how I've succeeded in everything I've done. I follow my instincts and take a punt."

Jum sat silently as they travelled through the city streets, Bernadette knew there was something on his mind, "Penny for your thoughts, Jum?"

"It's nothing, just a funny feeling I have about that kid. Well, he's probably not a kid, more like twenty, but he's a skinny little bugger. I didn't like his beady eyes. Looks like a cunning little bastard, so I might just tell Harry to get rid of him."

Jum flicked the whip at the horses. He needed a whisky. "Get up, boys!"

"You know best, Jum. As you say, you've always followed your instincts and most of the time you're right." Bernadette smiled at her own observations.

The Lord Mayor's dinner, held to celebrate the coming Melbourne Cup, was graced by one hundred hand-picked aristocrats. Bernadette stunned everyone with her charm, wit and alluring beauty. She and Jum soon became the highlight of the gathering. However flattering the evening was to their egos, there came a time for them to retire, although perhaps a little too early, as far as their host was concerned. They excused themselves, explaining they were very tired after their long journey from Adelaide. All eyes turned for one last look at the handsome couple.

"Leave 'em wanting more," Jum whispered to Bernadette, as they turned for one last smile. Despite there being a small degree of truth in the excuse they'd given, the desire between the two lovers had been brewing all evening. They were hardly through their bedroom door when Jum held Bernadette close, kissing her fervently while undoing the buttons down the back of her gown. Smiling seductively, Bernadette stepped away, sliding the red taffeta dress from her shoulders. It rustled to the carpet, her nakedness now revealed. Jum stood captivated.

Preferring the tease to the rush, Bernadette ran her nails over Jum's naked chest. His tongue then followed the line of her torso to where he knew it would drive her wild. Her fingers curled around the back of his neck and her involuntary moans begged him not to stop.

Jum had planned for the following day to be a day of shopping in the most elegant boutiques Melbourne had to offer. Potted flowers sat outside every café and shop along the city streets. Flags of every description seemed to wave a welcome.

Bernadette, delighted at the scene, asked Jum, "Does the Melbourne City Council go to this much trouble only for the Cup Carnival, or is it 'the done thing' all year round?"

"Well, my love, Melbourne is a little more upper crust than any other city in Australia. I'm sure they keep up appearances all year round."

Walking arm in arm, admiring the city's architecture and discussing their stay, Jum gave Bernadette the rundown of events once again. "Tonight, will be a great occasion, Bernadette. The band usually plays until midnight and then there'll be plenty of champagne toasts made to the horses and jockeys running in the Cup. That'll suit me," he said with a wink. "And the garden party at Government House tomorrow should be enjoyable for you, my dear, seeing how you love gardens. Then I'm sure you'll be enchanted by an evening at the opera. Yes, the Melbourne Opera Company is the best there is. Well, I've heard it is, I've never been," he finished softly.

"Don't worry, my love, we'll have one day of rest and relaxation before dining with Harry and his wife, Bessie. Together we'll celebrate our imminent win on the eve of the big race."

Entering the palatial department store, Bernadette felt a shiver of excitement. "Oh Jum, you know nothing delights me more than dressing in beautiful gowns. Not that I'm vain. I would be just as comfortable in a sarong, strolling along the beach in Hawaii. I simply admire beauty in everything, be it art, or a beautiful garden, but especially in the design and creation of these magnificent gowns. They take my breath away."

Her chosen evening gowns were placed in a fitting room. Each and every one looked amazing on Bernadette as, one at a time, she paraded them before Jum.

"This is when your royalty shines, my dear. You were born to be a queen."

Bernadette laughed. "I've told you before, Jum, if it weren't for my European father maybe I would have been Queen of Hawaii—one day." She paused for a moment. "That's silly because I wouldn't be born; I'd be somebody else." Bernadette had a delightful laugh.

"You should be a queen anyway, Bernadette, you're not only beautiful on the outside but you have a beautiful spirit."

"You're always right, my love, so I won't argue." She sighed, acting out the insincerity of what she'd just said. Inadvertently, Bernadette had just reminded Jum to see Harry and tell him to get rid of that kid and find someone else.

"I don't want to rush you, Bernadette, but I'd like to go and talk with Harry. You'll probably need to rest up a bit for this evening anyway, so I'll take you back to the hotel and then I'll go. Is that alright with you, my love?"

"Yes, of course, Jum. I'm so excited though, I don't know whether I'll be able to rest."

With shopping bags in tow, Jum escorted Bernadette into their room, kissed her goodbye and suggested, "Have a sherry, my love. It'll help you relax."

100

"I will, Jum. Take care. I'll see you later, my darling."

Jum arrived at the stables and called out, "Harry? You there, Harry?"

Jock was sitting in front of Freelance's stable, whittling on a piece of wood. He looked up through narrow eyes, holding the knife in a threatening pose. It took Jum back for a moment. Regaining his composure, he asked bluntly, "Where's Harry, Jock?"

The boy didn't move. "He's down the pub." He dropped his head and added in undertone, "Where I should be."

"What did you say, Jock?" Jum asked, leaning forward.

"Nothin'," the boy mumbled and went about his whittling.

Casting a final, suspicious glance at the boy, Jum turned on his heel and left.

The bar was crowded, full of rowdy racing experts, all claiming to know the winner of the Cup. Smoke and the stench of sour ale filled the air. Jum blinked in an attempt to quell the sting in his eyes, before pushing his way through to where Harry was sitting on his own, apparently lost in thought.

"Hello, Harry."

"Oh, g'day, Boss. What brings you to this hole?"

"I'll come straight to the point, Harry. I don't trust that kid, Jock. There's just something about him I don't like. I want you to get rid of him."

"Oh, he's alright, Boss, just a bit rough around the edges." Harry's smile seemed a trifle insincere. "Don't get upset about him, Boss."

Harry was unaware that discounting Jum's misgivings was a big mistake. Tight-lipped with anger, Jum reached forward and grabbed a handful of Harry's shirt, drawing him off the barstool, until he was close enough to whisper menacingly.

"Listen to me, Harry. I'm gunna say this one more time. Keep him away from my horse. If you don't, I'll give the horse to another trainer and I'll find my own strapper."

Harry held up his hands in surrender. "Sure, Boss, I'll tell him to go. But it won't be easy to find a good kid to guard him day and night until the Cup."

"Just do it, Harry, or I'll be taking Freelance from you." Jum released Harry, turned and strode out of the bar, knocking shoulders with men who were ready for a fight. Jum totally ignored their remarks. "Wotchit, mate!" and "Y' lookin' for a fight?" Jum was angry—too angry for his own good. He decided to drive his horses to the better part of town. *The Melbourne Club, that's a good place for a man to have a drink and calm down.*

When entering the club, Jum noticed a group of men he knew and thought he'd share a drink, and then hesitated. *On second thoughts, I need some time alone. I just can't shake off that uneasy feeling, I've never felt like this before and I reckon that kid has something to do with it.*

After downing two double whiskies, Jum felt a little more relaxed and so chose to approach his acquaintances. Before he realised, he was about ready to order his sixth scotch when his friend, Barnaby Stuart, one of the most popular members of the club, asked him, "Aren't you going to the Cup Eve Ball this evening, Jum?"

Jum wrinkled his brow. "Oh Christ, I'd betta get going, thanks Barney. The missus'll tar 'n' feather me!"

Barnaby smiled knowingly and placed his hand on Jum's shoulder. "Your lovely wife, Bernadette, did not appear the type of lady to do such a thing, Jum. If you don't mind me saying so, she's the most beautiful woman I think I've had the pleasure of meeting."

Jum knew Barney to be a gentleman and so took the remark in the spirit in which it was made and slapped him on the back. "No, I don't mind y' saying so, old chap. I'm very proud of her—and my horse, Freelance! Let's not forget Freelance!" Jum waved goodbye, a little unsteady as he left.

Barnaby Stuart, or Barney as everyone called him, had been at the Lord Mayor's dinner the night before, where he had met and had been quite impressed with Bernadette, especially when they'd spoken animatedly of politics and business. Barney had also used their time alone to appreciate Bernadette's beauty, as he had already been admiring her from a distance. Barney was a widower. He thought, *If Jum ever did the wrong thing by Bernadette, I wouldn't mind being the one to pick up the pieces.* He watched Jum leave before he too left to be ready in time for the Cup Eve Ball. The thought of meeting the beautiful Mrs Watt again made him quicken his pace.

Trying to hide his inebriated state from Bernadette, Jum walked directly past her into their bathroom, stripped off his shirt and submerged his head in a basin full of cold water.

"I've ordered a bucket of black coffee," Bernadette said calmly, when Jum appeared semi-naked before her. His smile reflected his lascivious thoughts, his voice low and husky.

"I know what'll do me more good than coffee, Bernadette," he said stripping off.

She returned the smile, moving with feline grace towards her naked lover. Her long fingers caressed his back, her lips settled on his neck. Jum lead her by the shoulders and almost threw her onto the bed, tearing at her skirts.

"My God, Bernadette, you don't know what you do to me!"

Bernadette raised her hips so he could remove her petticoats. "Oh yes I do, my darling," she laughed and drew him upon her. "Indeed, I do!"

All heads turned as the final guests to arrive were announced at the top of the stairway leading to the ballroom.

"May I present the owners of FREELANCE, Mr and Mrs Jum Watt!"

"My queen," Jum said softly, extending his arm upon which Bernadette placed her gloved hand. They descended the stairs, smiling, taking in the admiration, which was evident on the sea of faces below. Bernadette's gown, a simple dress made of fine satin with champagne chiffon overlay, was perfect. Delicate diamantes and pearl beads surrounded the upper part of the bodice, which encased and accentuated her curves. A similarly beaded sash encircled her waist and the shimmering fabric hung from her hips, training off at the back. A matching tiara, also set with diamonds and pearls, created a regal splendour. Not one of the two hundred women attending this function could come close to her radiance.

The evening was proving to be a great success. Jum met all the influential men in the room, using his raw charm and intelligence, while Bernadette basked in the unconcealed admiration from both men and women. Overnight, they had become Melbourne Cup royalty and they bathed in the glow of their future successful life together. Holding Bernadette close as they danced the last minutes of the night away, Jum whispered, "I love you so much, Bernadette, my heart would break if anything was to happen to you. Stay close to me, my love. I want to keep you safe for the rest of our lives."

Bernadette welcomed this confession but at the same time she thought it a little odd and out of character from Jum's usual brash declarations. "I'd never leave you, Jum. Why do you say this? Do you have something to tell me?"

"No, I'm just raving. Take no notice. I'm tired, I'm—oh, never mind. It's just—I love you so much." Jum paused to kiss her passionately, unworried by what anyone else might think. After returning to their hotel room, they made love with such fervour, it was as if it were their very last time. Not once during the night did they leave each other's arms as they slept.

"I'm off to Mass, Jum."

It was eight in the morning and Jum was still in need of sleep. After he'd pulled the pillow over his head, Bernadette could just hear him muffle the words, "Bloody Church!"

"I heard that, Jum. You'd better make friends with God. Remember the Cup!"

Since she was young, Bernadette had committed to following the Catholic faith even though her father had been a Baptist minister. He, being an open-minded and intelligent man, had said, "As long as one believes in the same God, it doesn't matter which door one goes through to find the Lord." He'd been a devoted husband to Bernadette's mother, who also had leanings toward Catholicism, particularly the stories told about the Catholic saints. Bernadette's parents had died some years ago while trying to save their Hawaiian people from a measles epidemic. Her brother survived, but unfortunately it left him unable to have children. Therefore, there were no heirs to continue their particular royal lineage.

This fact concerned Bernadette who had, at that time, left her homeland at the age of fourteen to be educated in England. Her heart, she said, would remain in Hawaii but her love of travelling and seeing the world tempted her adventurous spirit. Now her heart seemed torn between Australia and Hawaii.

The Church of Saint Francis stood as one of the most amazing churches Bernadette had ever entered. Stained-glass biblical scenes adorned each window. They reflected dancing rainbows as the sun shone through the vivid colours. Bernadette lit tall thin candles for the people she loved. Her spirits lifted when the choir of young boys began to sing, their innocent voices seemingly coming straight from heaven.

On this morning, the Bishop included special prayers for the jockeys and the thoroughbreds who, on the coming Tuesday, would take part in one of the most celebrated events in Victoria, the Melbourne Cup. It appeared, to Bernadette, the race took precedence over everything in this state and was fast becoming the highlight of every horse-loving Australian. On Cup Day, bets were taken in every large city in Australia through to every small country town. The telegraph lines went mad once the winner was announced.

It wasn't often Bernadette sang her homeland songs, especially in Hawaiian, but today, as she walked back to the hotel after her spiritual healing, she sang a Hawaiian song of thanksgiving, as a reminder of where she and Jum would spend the next three months, in her beloved Hawaii, after Freelance won the Cup.

"You look magnificent, my darling," Jum said, as Bernadette twirled around in her fashionable floral print skirt. She placed a large brimmed picture-book hat on her head, trimmed with the same floral fabric as her skirt. They chose to leave the carriage on St Kilda Road and walk to Government House through the Royal Botanic Gardens, as it was such a lovely day. Melbourne was unlike Sydney, which was "a tangle of goat tracks", Jum would say when visiting there. When in Melbourne he would justify his opinion.

"Melbourne's been mapped out and planned; they've made it easy to find your way around. Why couldn't they have done the same in Sydney? Bloody fools, that's why!"

The manicured lawns surrounding Government House sat framed by flowers and scented shrubs. The perfume of gardenias and jasmine filled the warm, still air. A feeling of quiet grace was accentuated by the perfect weather. Waiters in black and white uniforms cruised among the guests, offering champagne and chicken sandwiches. It seemed the same aristocratic crowd was invited to each of the special events held in honour of the Melbourne Cup. Bernadette and Jum recognised many faces from their previous engagements and were introduced and passed around to each, like a box of chocolates. After two hours of repeating the same conversation with the same people over the past four days, Jum had had enough. He took Bernadette by the arm, excusing himself and his wife from their company and steering her towards the hotel.

When out of earshot of the other guests, Bernadette voiced her disapproval. "I trust you have a good excuse, Jum. I was enjoying my conversation with your friend, Barnaby Stuart. He believes strongly that all women should be voting and even standing for their place in Parliament."

"Well, I'm sorry, my dear, but I have something more important on the agenda. So please forgive me." They returned to their hotel room in silence, but once inside, Jum locked the door. Bernadette stood motionless, confused by his manner.

"What is it, Jum? What's wrong?"

"Nothing's wrong," he said in a somewhat humble and apologetic tone. He stepped forward and placed his hands around her upper arms. She could feel his fingers tighten through the thin chiffon of her blouse.

"I just want you to know, Bernadette, it wasn't because of me I didn't have children with my ex-wife. So this is important, I really want to make a baby, our baby. Do you agree?"

She threw her head back, laughing. "Oh Jum, is that all? I thought something terrible had happened. Come here, you funny man." Cupping his face with her hands, she kissed him passionately then led him by the hand to their bed.

Bernadette chose to wear a black velvet gown to the opera. A small spray of exquisite black feathers held together in a ruby-encrusted clip decorated her hair. By now, every lady of any social standing was anticipating what she would wear. Tonight, they were not disappointed. After being enchanted, Bernadette was moved to tears by the opera, *La Traviata*, a sad tale. Bernadette had all the attention from "the Melbourne social set" at the after-show super, and it was beginning to tire her. She pleaded a headache, while chatting with the ladies.

"Are you alright, Bernadette"? Jum asked as they were being driven back to the hotel.

Squeezing his hand, she whispered, "Yes, I'm fine, Jum. I just think we should get back to the business of making babies!" He couldn't help but laugh.

Jum fumbled with the key to the point where Bernadette took it from him. "Haste makes waste, my love, so let's not waste a moment." She placed the key in the lock, turned it only once and it opened. Like children, they ran to the bed and threw themselves upon the satin coverlet, stripped each other with eager hands and made love, quickly at first, then slowly, until they were both exhausted.

"That should do it!" Jum said as he smacked her on the bottom.

Bernadette rolled over sighing, contented. "Good night, Jum. Only one more day and the Cup's yours."

"You mean 'ours'. What's mine is yours, Bernadette."

The morning sun steamed through the window, given passage by the curtain the butler had forgot to close. Jum yawned, stretching out to his wife.

"Let's have an easy day and an early dinner with Harry. What do you say, darling?"

Bernadette raised her arms above her naked body and placed them under her head then turned to face Jum, enticing him to put his mouth to her nipples. This soon stimulated her senses.

Noon arrived before they had pried themselves from each other. The two ravenous lovers then ordered a hearty brunch to be delivered to their room. With her hunger satisfied, Bernadette suggested, "Let's go and see Freelance now, Jum."

"I thought we'd wait until after dinner. You know, tuck him into bed and wish him good luck for tomorrow. Anyway, I spotted something in a shop window. I want to show it to you, and if you like it, Bernadette, it's yours."

"Oh Jum, you don't need to buy me another thing. I have plenty of everything and all I really need is you." However, Jum had his way.

Melbourne had not only presented them with a warm welcome from the highest echelons of society, but also fine weather. Another glorious late spring day greeted them as they left the hotel and strolled to the most exclusive jewellery shop in Bourke Street, the main shopping street in Melbourne. Stopping in front of the shop window, Jum pointed to a solid gold, lady's wristlet watch.

"This, my love, is now the fashion for telling the time for ladies. Do you like it?"

"Like it? I love it! But no, please, Jum, it would cost a fortune!"

Jum took no notice and walked inside the store, where he looked the shopkeeper in the eye and almost demanded, "Wrap up the gold wristlet watch in the window, if you please, sir."

The salesman hesitated, thinking Jum may pull out a revolver, as he'd never had anyone, especially in the current economic circumstances, buy something without asking the price first.

"Well, go on! Wrap it up for the lady," Jum ordered, his patience wearing a little thin.

"Certainly, sir, that will be one hundred pounds," he said cautiously.

Bernadette's mouth dropped open as Jum handed over the cash.

"Silly to wrap it up, I suppose. Why don't you put it on, my love?" Jum beckoned the jeweller over and said, "Show my wife how to fasten it, there's a good man."

"May I, madam?" He was delighted to have been asked to place the watch on Bernadette's wrist. "You will find, madam, well, if God is willing and that you hopefully live that long, this watch will last many, many generations. It was made by the finest craftsmen in Switzerland." He smiled and thanked them for their business. Reluctant to let an opportunity go by, he added, "Is there anything else I can help you with? Sir, madam?"

"No, thank you," said Jum. "I'll give you a tip though. Back my horse Freelance in the Cup tomorrow."

"Certainly, sir, thank you. I always close the shop at noon so I'm able to go and watch the great race. Good luck, sir, I hope he wins." By now he was following them out of the shop and waving them goodbye. "Well, I never," he said to himself, his face flushed with the success of a hefty sale.

"Shall we walk through the Flagstaff Gardens, Jum?" Bernadette asked a little wistfully, as she was feeling quite different today, without knowing why. She was unaware that the first hormonal changes of pregnancy were taking effect.

"Jum, do you think we will be this happy forever?" Bernadette asked while gazing at her gold wristlet watch.

"Of course, my love. With you, everything is possible." Jum stopped, turned to his wife and kissed her.

On their return to the Victoria Hotel, Jum booked a table for four in the Grand Dining Room, where they would meet Harry and Bessie at six-thirty. Back in their luxurious room, Jum suggested, "Let's have a naked nap before dinner, my darling." Naturally, she took up his offer.

While dressing for their evening ahead, Jum told Bernadette of his plans for later in the evening. This included going to see Freelance after dinner and then having a pre-celebration drink with his trainer, Harry. "I hope you don't mind, my love."

Bernadette gave an almost inaudible sigh. "Of course, I don't mind at all, but please take it easy. I don't like to be a bore, but there'll be plenty of time for celebrating after Freelance wins the Cup tomorrow." Bernadette kissed him on the cheek and straightened his tie, adding, "I would have liked to have given Freelance a pat myself. Why can't we all go after dinner, then you could drop me back and then you can have a drink with Harry?"

"No, my love, it's too much mucking around. It'll wear the bloody horses out driving around all night, so I'll drop Bessie home first. They live right near the stables."

Bernadette refrained from pointing out the faults in his reasoning, but knowing Jum so well, she accepted his mind was made up. Fussing a little with her hair, she announced brightly, "I'm ready, we may as well be at the table waiting instead of the other way around. After all, they are our guests."

"Certainly, let's go."

Moments after being seated, Jum spotted Harry. "Hello, Harry. Nice to see you and you too, Bessie." He stood to shake Harry's hand and then pulled out a seat for Bessie. "Bessie, you haven't met my wife, Bernadette."

Bernadette held her hand out across the table, "I'm delighted to meet you, Bessie."

Bessie nodded, smiling, fiddling with her clothes, seeming a little self-conscious.

Jum nailed Harry with the look of a tiger, about to pounce on his prey. "You got rid of that boy, didn't you, Harry?"

Bernadette gave him a nudge, thinking it was hardly an appropriate opening to a formal dinner. Jum felt the nudge and turned to Bernadette. "Well, I wouldn't enjoy my meal if I knew he was still there."

Harry smiled. "Of course, Boss, I got rid of him. I got a nice style of boy now."

"That's good, Harry, now we can enjoy our evening. Ladies, they serve a wonderful lobster mornay here, so I suggest we all tuck in."

Sometimes Bernadette felt embarrassed by her husband's earthiness, but at the same time she had to laugh at the boy inside this enigmatic man, the man she adored. She was also used to her beauty sometimes making plain women feel either jealous or uncomfortable. Never wishing for this to happen, she tried to put Bessie at ease, by asking her questions about herself.

"You know, Bessie, secretly, I'd love to have red hair, and your dress is beautiful, the colour flatters you."

Bessie flushed a deep pink. "You can't be serious, Bernadette, I hate red hair."

Bernadette's reply was quick. "I shouldn't really call it red, Bessie, it's more a lovely chestnut colour. You're very lucky."

Bessie was grateful for Bernadette's kindness, and they relaxed a little.

Jum had been right about the lobster. "It's out of this world!" Bessie commented.

"I suppose it is. I've never tasted anything so delicious," added Bernadette with a giggle.

Their conversation had not yet focused on the Cup but it was on Jum's mind. The Victoria Hotel was alcohol free and was actually called the Victorian Coffee Palace Hotel, proud to cater for more-refined clientele. Eventually, Jum came up with an excuse.

"I hate to interrupt you ladies, but it's going to be a long and exciting day tomorrow. I think we should try and catch an early night."

Bernadette gave Jum a side glance. She knew he needed a drink and she wished she were going with him but, of course, it would be most improper for a wife to drink in a bar with her husband. After shaking hands with Harry and embracing Bessie, Bernadette promised, "I shall join you at the races tomorrow, Bessie. We'll have such fun, don't you think?" She then took Jum by the lapels and gave him a little shake before kissing him goodnight. "Be careful, my darling. Give Freelance a pat and a big hug from me."

"I will. Don't worry, sweetheart, I'll be back before you know it."

Driving the buggy past the stables, Harry asked, "Why don't we stop and check the horse now, Boss?"

"No, Harry, if Bessie comes too, she'll get her lovely dress dirty and I don't want to leave her all alone in the buggy."

"Yeah, makes sense," Harry responded.

A block away, they bid goodnight to Bessie. Jum then turned the horses around and gave them a flick with the whip. "Bloody hell," he said as they passed one pub shut after the other.

"We'll have to go to the Melbourne Club, Harry. They stay open all bloody night if the members need a drink!"

They arrived just in time, as the young bartender was about to close. When Jum stuffed a few folded notes into his hand, he not only opened the bar, but also welcomed Harry, who was not a member. Jum's confidence in winning the Cup, plus their strategies for the way Freelance should be ridden, became more and more definite with each whisky. An hour of solid drinking and Jum could barely hold his glass. He decided it was time to take Harry home. Swaying, with his arm around Harry's shoulder, Jum was almost bent in half with the difference in their height.

With slurred speech, he proclaimed yet again, "My horse, Freelance, is gunna win the Melbourne Cup! Or my name's not Jum Watt!"

He continued to drivel on about everything and anything that came to mind, including his wife. "If anyone ever touches her, I'll kill 'em, Harry. I'll kill 'em, I will. I luvva, y' know that, Harry!"

"Yeah, Boss, I know. Do you want me to drive the horses home?"

"No bloody way! I'm in control here, Harry!" Jum flicked the reins in the direction of horse's rumps and then slumped in his seat.

Just as well the horses seem to have a vague idea of where they're heading, Harry mumbled under his breath. Laughing, they sang dirty ditties all the way until they pulled up in front of the stables.

"Hey, Harry, there's a light on in the stables. Ya didn't leave the bloody lamp on, didya?"

"No, I didn't, Boss. Maybe it was the new lad."

Together, the two drunken men half-fell, half-climbed out of the buggy. Harry stopped outside for a pee while Jum strode on unsteadily. He entered the stables and blinked, trying to focus on the two men who stood before him. Jum then realised that one was the bookie who he'd won the money from in Adelaide. The other was Jock, the sacked strapper. Jock was holding onto Freelance's head collar, trying to administer something into his mouth. The new stable boy, Ernie, lay very still on the floor beside Freelance's stable. He appeared to be dead.

"What! What the fuck do y' think y'…?" were the last words Jum Watt uttered, as the bullet from a Smith and Wesson revolver went straight through his heart. Harry stumbled into the stables as another shot was fired towards him. The culprits ran from the scene and Harry fell to the ground, grazed by the bullet. He then reached out to Jum.

"I'm so sorry, mate. Those bastards, I'll get 'em!"

He tried to stand but fell again, sobbing. It was some time before he regained his composure. By this time, Ernie had come around. He sat up, blurry eyed but able to make out his boss, Harry, who sat beside another man lying in a pool of blood. He hesitated when Harry called to him.

"Come help me up, Ernie! Tell me what happened!"

"I don't know, Boss," the boy rubbed a hand over his face. "All I can remember is bein' grabbed from behind and then I blacked out."

"So ya didn't see who did this, Ernie?"

"No, Boss, I didn't see nothin'. Is he—is he dead?" Ernie asked nervously, his face pale.

Harry swallowed and took a deep breath.

"Yeah, mate. He's dead."

Chapter 13

A Time to Mourn

Jum Watt was a special man, honest, loyal and steadfast. Jum was the finest friend a person could ever have and he was a devoted and loving husband to Bernadette. I'm sure I speak on everybody's behalf when I say that his amazing generosity was beyond comprehension. Jum was a man of his word and highly respected by all who knew him. He will be sadly missed.

That was part of Jonathon's eulogy.

For nearly twelve months after Jum's death, Jonathon had been like a pup shaking a rag doll, not resting in his efforts to help track down and bring the murderers to justice. Although he had not prosecuted the case himself, as he was too close to Jum not to lead with his emotions, he and his new junior law partner, Phillip Morgan, had tried everything to help the police apprehend the criminals.

Now, on the morning of 12 December 1894, the case was officially closed. The men responsible for the senseless killing were behind bars, waiting to be hung by the neck in one month's time. Bernadette had kept her passage aboard the ship bound for Hawaii. Despite the devastating events in her life, she took her place alongside her brother and his wife, helping to govern the people of their nation. They, in turn, gave solace and compassion to Bernadette in her time of grieving. Her grief had been assuaged by the birth of a beautiful baby girl she named Adelaide.

Sally and Jonathon had produced a baby boy. Sally found some peace in being a mother once again. Their baby, now three months old, was named Angus, after Jonathon's benefactor, Angus Darcy. This baby had bonded Sally and Jonathon together more than she could have imagined. She had to almost throw Jonathon out of their home to go to work, as to break the trance he had on his son. At this stage, the child looked so much like Jonathon. The worst times for Jonathon were when he had to leave them and travel to Bulkawa for a day or two, where he still kept the accounts. He'd promised Bernadette he would do it.

Over the past twelve months, Sally had welcomed the heartfelt letters from her uncle, Ted Smith, in Sydney. She'd never disclosed to Jonathon the whole truth about her past and her family, but he seemed happy for her to have found a lost relative.

"My uncle Ted said one day soon he would come visit us, Jonathon. I can't wait to meet him."

"That's wonderful, my dear," was all Jonathon ever said, in an almost patronising way. Sally thought it a little strange how Jonathon seemed to play down the excitement she felt at the prospect of finally meeting her uncle. But she shrugged it off, as she had to do with Jonathon from time to time.

Uncle Ted's promise of "one day soon" had not yet eventuated. Secretly, Sally was a little relieved, despite being confident that her uncle Ted would keep her secret hidden. However, with one slip of the tongue, she would have to tell the complete truth to Jonathon, and she was still not ready. Sally sat reading the most recent letter from her uncle.

"Oh, Jonathon, Uncle Ted has written. Paul and Mildred have a grand baby boy. They've called him Jum. I suppose it wouldn't matter if we named our second son Jum, would it, Jonathon?"

"No, of course not, Sally, and we'll do just that." He then kissed her on the head, adding, "I have to leave for Bulkawa now. I'm so pleased to know Dan's doing a great job, although he's been lucky with the seasons lately. They've been perfect, just the right amount of rainfall at just the right time. It now appears Jum's decisions about what stock to keep for breeding have proved to be wise. His legacy will live on for many generations. At least that's something, I suppose."

Both Jonathon and Sally assumed Bernadette would leave things as they were at Bulkawa, for the time being anyway. She'd told Sally in her letters that the memories would be too painful if she were to return too soon, although she welcomed the news of the murderers having been caught and punished.

Dan and Mary had become engaged, and the wedding was to be in two months' time, on Mary's twentieth birthday. Dan had accepted Bernadette's generous offer of Mary and Dan, when married, living in the main homestead. He wrote:

Dear Mrs Watt,

Mary and I would be honoured and enjoy very much living in the homestead. We will certainly care for it, as if it were our own.

Bernadette wrote back, saying she was delighted, and prayed they would fill the corridors with laughing children.

Mrs Murphy was now Mrs Thomas. She and Bob had married while in England, where both families had united in a jovial wedding. After the happy occasion, they'd returned to Australia like two love birds. Bob had set about repainting the boarding house and helped with everything and anything his "doll face" (as he called Colleen) wanted.

Sally and Jonathon had settled into a quaint new three-bedroom cottage, just on the outskirts of the city. Sally loved her new home and having been able to pay cash for it never failed to astonish her. She could hardly believe they actually owned it!

Sally took great pleasure in gardening, particularly growing her own vegetables and tending her rose garden. Jonathon had also built a chicken coop large enough for six layers. He'd wanted a much grander home, but Sally insisted, "This home is good enough, Jonathon. Plus, I want to save money for our children's future and not waste it on an extravagant lifestyle."

While Jonathon's business boomed, the people who paid him were few, rather than many. Jonathon was unable to refuse those who needed his help. However, Jum had left his friend a tidy sum of money in his will, and he'd bequeathed Jonathon's office to him. They were now comfortably off, without being wealthy.

Sally counted her blessings every day, but still could not help but daydream about Patrick and what might have been. In fact, she had done something that was a little more than daydream. Exactly six months earlier, when she had been almost seven months pregnant with Angus, Sally had returned to the orphanage and, summoning courage and audacity, had told a white lie to Mother Matilda. Knocking nervously on the door, Sally had come straight to the point before any pleasantries could be exchanged.

"Hello, Mother, my name is Mrs Sally Darcy. I've come seeking a young girl, the daughter of a friend of mine. I thought perhaps she may have found her way to your orphanage." Her cheeks flushed pink with the guilt of telling of a lie.

Mother Matilda welcomed her inside, after having taken an immediate liking to the pretty young lady. They chatted for some time about the missing girl and what she looked like, and why Sally thought she may have found her way there. Matilda then showed Sally around the grand house, after Sally had asked. "I'm extremely interested in the architecture of this two-storey home, Mother. May I see where the girls take their school lessons, and do you have a play room of some sort, maybe for the younger children?" Her thoughts were conniving. *Perhaps Patrick's in the play room?*

Sally had been right; Patrick was still there, playing in the room set aside for extra school activities. Her heart raced when Mother Matilda stopped in the doorway.

"God forgive me," Matilda said, making the sign of the cross, mistaking Sally's gasp of delight as one of surprise. Matilda quickly confessed. "This is Patrick, our little secret. We didn't have the heart t' send him t' a boys' orphanage, after him bein' left with us as a wee baby."

"Hello, Patrick," Sally said, as her arms automatically spread. When Patrick ran into them, Sally's eyes filled with tears. She blinked, trying to disguise her overwhelming emotions, and laughed at the little boy—her son. He'd happily kissed her on the cheek and then pulled his head back to look and say, "You got water on your face, lady!"

"Well, they're tears of joy, Patrick. I was just thinking I hope the baby I'm about to have is as lovely as you are." Sally kissed him back, hugging him tight until Mother Matilda, slightly bemused by her actions, asked, "Would you like a cup of tea, Mrs Darcy?"

"Can Patrick come too, Mother?"

"Yes, of course. Come along, young man. He loves his cuppa tea and a biscuit, don't y', Patrick?"

"Yes, Mother," he replied sweetly.

In the kitchen, Patrick chose to sit on Sally's lap, cuddling into her warmth. Mother Matilda gently scolded. "Now hop down, Patrick. Mrs Darcy's goin t' have a wee baby and she can't be pickin' y' up all the time."

Sally clung to him. "No, please. It's alright, Mother. I love children."

After a time, enjoying her conversation with Matilda and, of course, the immense pleasure of holding her son once again, Sally knew it was time to leave. She pried herself away from Patrick.

"I'm sorry, Mother," she looked down at Patrick with a smile, "and Patrick, but I must leave now. I've made arrangements for the driver to pick me up and take me back to Adelaide. He's probably waiting outside."

Standing in the doorway, Sally asked Matilda, "Could you please tell me, Mother, if the young girl I have been seeking happens to find her way to your orphanage? I'd also like you to accept a donation from my husband and myself." Sally smiled sweetly and handed her the money. "And would it be alright for me to visit again? I sometimes come by this way to visit a friend."

Overcome with the generous donation, Matilda welcomed her suggestion. "Yes, of course, Mrs Darcy, we're most grateful for your donation. Please come and visit us anytime. I truly feel as if we may be kindred spirits. Strange, I know, but sometimes we meet people who God has sent to us for a reason. I think this might be such an occasion." Matilda gave her a searching look. She then held Sally's hands.

"Goodbye and God bless y', Sally Darcy. Oh yes…" she'd just thought to remind Sally. "Please don't tell another living soul about Patrick. I beg y', or we may just lose him to a boys' orphanage."

"No, of course not, Mother. You are to be congratulated. Patrick is a fine young boy." Sally bent down and held Patrick close. She kissed and breathed him in before taking one long look into his big blue eyes, thinking, *He is of my image; it will be amazing if Mother Matilda doesn't eventually put two and two together*.

"Goodbye, Mrs Darcy. You come back soon!" Patrick said solemnly as he waved her goodbye. She laughed, wiping away tears of joy. Smiling all the way home, with her heart in a state of euphoria, Sally decided to ask Jonathon if they might adopt Patrick. While she was still not ready to tell him the whole truth about how Patrick came to be, she thought if he agreed to adopt Patrick, then he would surely come to love him as she did.

Back home, Sally threw her bonnet onto the hall stand where it landed on the hook. Jonathon watched somewhat amused, especially when she removed her leather gloves and threw them with the same accuracy onto the shelf below her hat. He noticed the change in Sally. *It's late in the evening. She should be exhausted. But her eyes are sparkling, like she's just witnessed a miracle.*

She hugged and kissed him, then announced happily, not thinking for a moment he would object, "My dearest Jonathon, I have just met today the most amazing little boy at the orphanage! I have fallen totally in love with him! I thought, if you were in agreement, we might adopt him. He would be a wonderful friend for our baby when he, or she, is born and he could keep me company while you're away. Oh, Jon, I know you'll love him as I do! He's so affectionate and intelligent and, well, he's just plain lovable!" Sally exclaimed in a rush.

She had no doubt in her mind that Jonathon would agree enthusiastically to her request. However, he sat back in stunned disbelief, thinking Sally's behaviour may have been something to do with her having her first child. The nurturing instinct had obviously overwhelmed her.

But witnessing Jonathon's silence, Sally felt she could still persuade him if he gave her a chance. "Please, Jonathon, if you would only visit the orphanage with me, I'm sure you…"

Jonathon interrupted. "My darling Sally, I think you are overtired and I must confess this has taken me quite by surprise. I'll warm you up some milk and then we'll go to bed as it's very late." Jonathon stood closer and placed his arm around her shoulder. "We can talk about this in the morning, Sally. Things will be a lot clearer then."

He held her close, ushering her into the bedroom. All the while Sally protested, until he said once again. "We'll discuss it in the morning, Sally." Mollified by his pledge, she allowed Jonathon to undress her and slip the nightgown over her head. He then tucked her into bed, where she waited for her milk.

"Here we are." He'd noticed she'd drifted off and so sat, studying his sleeping wife, thinking. *Whatever would make her think I'd agree to adopt a little boy? It's bizarre. Why would she want to adopt a strange child when she's pregnant with our own child?*

Jonathon usually woke at sunrise, and this morning was no different. However, the fact his first client had changed his appointment gave Jonathon time to spoil Sally with tea and toast in bed. She woke to Jonathon's breakfast call and opened her eyes to see a food-laden tray.

"Oh, thank you, Jon! I think I would have slept all day!"

Once the tray had been balanced, Jonathon sat perched on the end of the bed. Sally filled her mouth with toast and marmalade. Once she'd swallowed, she laughed, "I can't believe how hungry I am all the time, Jon!"

"Well, you are eating for two, Sally." He took a deep breath and held her hand in his.

"Sally, about what you said last night, I don't want you to be upset, but I do want you to understand my feelings, and my point of view. I will begin by saying I think if our baby was already born, and for some reason we were unable to have more children, I would consider adopting the little boy."

Sally opened her mouth to interrupt. "Please, Sally, let me explain, I have to be truthful. I think it would be most unfair on our first child to have to look up to another child who is not a blood relation to him or her. Who is, in fact, a total stranger?"

Sally felt the dagger twist in her heart. "But Jonathon, you don't understand…"

With Jonathon's accusing look, ice ran through her veins. *I've seen that same look in court, when Jonathon cross-examines criminals. He's judged my situation without compassion. He hasn't taken into account my feelings at all.* She began to cry softly. *No amount of tears will work, not this morning, not when he's in one of his thinking modes, when his emotions are completely squashed by his logic.*

Jonathon took the tray away and held her in his arms. "Please, Sally, I don't want to hurt you, but we must be rational. We have to look at the future, not just this moment. You're most vulnerable in your condition. I think it must be like nature building up the love inside you, so you have all that is needed to care for our own child. What about the young girl you go to the orphanage and visit, Sally? Can we help her? Maybe she can come live with us. She may be able to help you with the baby and do a little housework?"

Sally stopped sniffling. Sometimes she amazed herself with the speed of her answers. "She's going to be a nun!" she had blurted out.

Sally's memories of that first emotional visit to the orphanage, and Jonathon's refusal to adopt Patrick, would interrupt her daily chores, and now her thoughts were interrupted by Jonathon's return from Bulkawa. Sally kissed him before placing the kettle on the stove. She then sat and listened while he explained how things were on the property.

"I'm so pleased with Dan. As I've said before, he's doing a great job with everything, Sally, especially with the breeding of Freelance. The stallion has a full book of mares and he looks magnificent." Jonathon dipped his head a little. "Although the place still holds an aura, as if Jum still lives there." Tears began to well. "I'm sorry, Sally, I've become emotional." He paused, blinking away his stress.

Sally put her hand on his. "I understand, Jonathon. Go on if you can."

"I'm fine until I get out there, Sally. You may think me fanciful, but it's as if Jum's walking beside me. I planted a Queen Adelaide rose at the head of Jum's grave. When I stood to say a prayer, a warm breeze suddenly blew the petals and they fluttered all around me. I knew he was there, Sally. I felt him. Why did he have to go?"

He turned to her for comfort and immediately Sally held him, rocking him back and forth. "I can only tell you, Jon, my faith in the Lord gives me strength. I trust all things happen for a reason and while it's hard for us to understand, I'm sure He has a plan. Remember, Jon, we never die, we just go home."

At that moment, baby Angus's cry beckoned them to his crib. "Hush, little baby, don't you cry," Sally sang, picking him up to offer him her breast. Sitting opposite, Jonathon became entranced by the sight of his wife suckling their child. The life in his brown eyes returned as he watched the tiny miracle he'd helped create. *Yes, they are my responsibility now. It's all I've ever wanted since coming from England. One day, Angus and I will go walking in Central Park. I'll smile as he throws stones into the lake, waiting for the ripples. We'll play cricket together and ride horses through the bush.* His demeanour saddened. *But I still miss you, Jum, I know I should be happy, I have a son now and he's the reason I need to move on with my life. I know it hasn't been an easy time for anyone who was close to you. You were such a force in our lives. But perhaps now I should look to the future. The past should be laid to rest.* Jonathon smiled at his future sitting before him.

Chapter 14

Growing Up

Patrick's fifth birthday was celebrated on the fourth of July, not his official birthday. Mother Matilda had guessed he was about two months old when he was left on the doorstep and not knowing his correct birth date, they decided each year it would be celebrated on this day. There was going to be a magnificent show of fireworks, courtesy of a recent addition to the town. A Chinese man, named Dr Liu, had been travelling around town, purporting himself to be "Vely good Chinese medicine doctor." Apart from claiming to be an expert in healing all ailments, Liu made excellent firecrackers.

Dr Liu had arrived at the orphanage unannounced. His timing was impeccable on this particular day, as little Betty was struggling to breathe, due to a severe asthma attack. Mother Matilda had done all she could to relieve Betty's suffering and was in a state of panic when she opened the door to Dr Liu. After listening for only a moment about his healing skills, Matilda practically pulled him into the room where Betty sat gasping for air. She prayed every second that the Good Lord had sent this unusual Dr to them.

After a speedy diagnosis, Liu went about boiling up different herbs. He then placed Betty's head over the steaming brew, draping a towel over her head to trap the fumes. Liu then injected acupuncture needles into certain pressure points. Very soon, Betty began to breathe normally. Mother Matilda cried, praising the Lord and Liu.

"It's nothing short of a miracle! Thank you, God! Thank you, Dr Liu!"

The following Sunday at Mass, Mother Matilda asked the parishioners to give thanks to God for sending Dr Liu to them in their time of urgent need. Her public accolade had decided Liu's future in Brinton. Liu then remained in town for a few weeks after curing some of the local people. However, as business lessened, he packed his bags and headed off to another district but not before making a final call on Mother Matilda.

"I give you special medicine for Betty and strict instruction, what to do in no-breath attack," Dr Lui advised.

Matilda thanked him and bade him farewell, thinking she would never see the good doctor again. However, three months later, he showed up at the orphanage. "Hello, Mudda Mat, I set up shop next to town store now. I see your mudda, she not well, you give her this medicine, she no takes from me. Maybe she takes from you, Mudda Mat. She then pays me for next lot, yes?"

"Yes! Yes, of course, Dr Liu!" Mother Matilda was delighted see him. "Would you like to come in and have a cup of tea?"

"Yes prease, Mudda, my China tea I show you how. Yes, thank you." He bowed and entered the orphanage, following Matilda down the familiar corridor to the kitchen. Liu proceeded to make his Chinese tea, accompanied by running commentary. "First, put tea in pot—this much, yes?" He glanced up to make sure Matilda was paying attention. "Pour boiling water over tea into tea pot, wash away dust. Tip dusty water out. Pour more boiled water again, yes? Now wait two minute. Liu has special tea for evelything. You no sleep, sick belly, pain in head. You name it, I got it." He flashed a toothy grin. Matilda laughed, totally intrigued and entertained by this funny little man with a long plait hanging down his back. His brown eyes gleamed with life as he spoke of his immense desire to help people, not only with medicine, but with logic—simple, uncomplicated logic. Matilda then sat captivated, listening about where he had come from and why he had chosen Australia as his home.

"What's China like, Dr Liu, and which part of China does your family come from?" Liu described in detail. "My China country vely picturesque, huge winding rivers and, most interlesting, my family heritage almost lost in many battle with Mongolian raiders. Great numbers of family members also die, perish when build Great Wall of China. They buried in Wall forever. I came from long line of warriors. It necessary to learn the skills of healing, Liu first began journey with teachings of vely old man, living in my village and also from glandmother. I watch and rearn. They work together, help heal many Chinese soldiers, including high Officer. I come more and more intelest in medicine, and vely less in fighting. This reason, I leave homeland and come to Aderaide. No fight here."

Matilda placed her hand on his and looked him in the eye. "I'm pleased you did, Liu, but why did you choose Brinton as the town to settle in?"

"Ah yes, ever frowing creek make it easy for me to glow herb and medicine prants. Land also cheap," he told Matilda over a third cup of tea. "And maybe I rucky. Find gold in creek." He giggled. "I travel round country sometime, sell medicine. This country free, no tyranny here, here, evelyone equal, I write to family, they must come. This best country in world, I think. I like you, Mudda Mat. You good woman, you have good heart. Your mother has not so good heart, vely sick heart. I try make strong. Maybe I fix with good Chinese medicine, yes?"

Matilda smiled. "Yes, Dr Liu, we pray you fix."

Liu's return visit had been six months before the celebration of Patrick's fifth birthday. Dr Liu had made not only fireworks, but a huge pâpier maché dragon and a small figurine of a Chinese girl for Patrick. Both unusual gifts were painted in red and gold, China's national colours.

"Maybe one day, Patrick, you travel to my rand. You see people look like this beautiful girl and BIG fire dragon." Liu pushed the dragon aggressively towards Patrick. The girls screamed, but Patrick stood his ground and giggled.

Matilda's ma had made Patrick's birthday cake in the shape of a soldier, including his hat. Icing sugar she'd coloured red and black was used for his uniform. This was the highlight of Patrick's day, until later. But meanwhile, everyone, including the nuns, took part in a sack race. They became hysterical when unable to control the yards of fabric plus the hessian sacks at the same time. They soon fell over in fits of laugher. Lizzy was about to win the race but decided to let the birthday boy win.

"No, Lizzy, that's not fair! You slowed up, you mustn't let me win! I wanna win by myself!" Patrick was still gruff with her when she smiled and said, "Look behind you, Patrick."

It was Da, who'd previously made an excuse to be late. He walked slowly up to Patrick, leading a white pony of perfect confirmation. He was a rare gift. Patrick's mouth dropped. He stood motionless as Da handed him the pony.

"Happy birthday, Patrick."

Patrick whispered, "Is he really mine, Da?"

Mother Matilda stepped in. "Yes, Patrick, he's really yours and you have t' thank Ma, she swapped her best milkin' cow f' him."

Patrick dropped the pony's lead and ran straight to Ma, wrapping his arms around her. He thanked and kissed her many times before letting go.

Kneeling before Patrick, Da looked him in the eye. "Now, young man, this is a very big responsibility y' have now. Y' have to be carin' for y' pony, feed and water him every day and give him plenty of exercise. He'll be happy out in the paddock behind the orphanage, but water is the most important thing, so make sure he has plenty every day."

"I'll look after him, Da, I promise. I'm gunna call him Sergeant. Can I ride him now?"

"Yes, but I'll lead y' round today, Patrick. And then twice a week I'll come and give y' lessons so you'll be able to ride him on y' own soon." Da continued proudly. "I used to be a jockey and ride in races when I was a young lad back home in Ireland. Have I told y' that, Patrick?"

"No, Da, but tell me all about it now please."

Mother Matilda hadn't been too sure about the pony idea, but today she had second thoughts. *Da's promised it'll keep him out of trouble and teach him responsibility. I truly hope this'll be the case because, although he's happy most of the time playin' with his wooden soldiers, the ones Da's carved for him, he often gets himself into scrapes. I hate t' look up when he's climbed a tree and then yells t' me, "Look at me, Mother, I'm on the lookout for the enemy, I'm a soldier." Or he's up on the roof, workin' up the courage to fly.* Matilda remembered with a shudder. *Oh dear Mother of God, what about the time when Betty caught him by the pants, just as he was about to investigate the well in the back garden. Head first and legs about to follow, "Let me go, Betty, you can pull me up later!" he said. "Yes, when you're dead and drowned!" our dear Betty had t' grunt out the words, with the physical effort it took her t' save him. Yes, I'm beginning t' t'ink a pony just might be the distraction Patrick needs, Dear Lord.*

Half an hour later and Da was tiring from leading the pony around. He'd pointed at the setting sun. "See Patrick, that's how y' always know which is east and which is west, it might be helpin' ya one day if you're ever lost," he said, while nonchalantly slipping him off the pony.

"I'll never get lost, Da. My pony Sergeant will always be with me and he'll know his way home!" Da laughed, but at the same time, wondered if he'd unwittingly put an idea into this young adventurer's head. After letting the pony go and watching it trot around the five-acre paddock, Da helped Patrick bucket the water up from the well.

"Come on, Sergeant, here's some water!" Patrick splashed the water and Sergeant came cantering up before plunging his muzzle into the bucket. "There, you see, Da? He knows his name, and look, he's very thirsty!"

Suddenly a whistling sound broke into their chatter before an explosion.

"Look, Da," Patrick pointed to where Dr Liu was setting up his fireworks. One had gone off accidently, followed by another.

"Gee whiz!" Patrick said as he was enthralled, but stayed where he was, watching to see if his pony needed more water. Da noticed his responsible action, and how the pony hadn't flinched with the firework explosion.

"You're a good pair, you two, you're both very brave," Da said ruffling Patrick's hair, then guided him by the shoulder to where Dr Liu was apologising.

"Big mistake, solly, I get right this time!"

With each explosion came gasps of, "It's magical", "Amazing", and "Spectacular" from the captivated audience.

"One of God's masterpieces, with a little help from Dr Liu," Mother Matilda said, while in awe. "Not even the heavenly stars can outshine Liu's display this evening."

Dr Liu wasn't finished yet, he had another show in store. He'd asked them all to sit in the grand dining room. With the enormous oak table pushed to one side, the nuns and Ma and Da sat on chairs at the rear of the room, while the rest sat crossed-legged on the floor in front of them. With the fire stoked and burning bright, the smell of fresh eucalyptus permeated the room and was inhaled through their sniffling, winter noses. Mother Matilda, as usual, sat closest to the fire.

Dr Liu had set up a large block of wood, resting between two carpentry horses. He now entered the room, dressed in the traditional Chinese Kung-Fu apparel, including a black satin belt tied tightly round his waist. He bowed to the group then began his display of this ancient art. His muscular legs lifted well off the ground as he flung them aggressively towards the transfixed audience. "Hi-*ya*! Hi-*ya*!" he called with each agile movement. He flung his body into contortions and then leapt almost as high as the ceiling.

This went on for several minutes until the grand finale. Patrick had sat entranced, watching every precise movement. Finally, Liu stood motionless with his eyes focused on the block of wood. Suddenly, he took three quick steps forward and, in a chopping motion, brought the side of his hand down on the wood. "HI-*YA*!" he screamed. Amazingly, he had chopped the wood in half. Then he took his final bow. Applause exploded in the room before Patrick stood up to imitate Liu. When finished, he bowed, emulating Liu.

Liu came to his side, grinning, "If Mudda Mat let me, I teach you Kung-Fu, Patrick."

"Oh no," Matilda said, wagging her finger for emphasis, "there'll be none o' dat for Patrick!"

Da had also been amazed with Liu's display, and felt he should put a bid in. "Now, May, he's a boy! It's good f' boys to learn self-defence. Let him learn."

Liu shook his head from side to side. "No want trouble. I cause no trouble! Just say good for boy to learn. Liu agree with Da."

Matilda was quick to finish the discussion. "We'll be talkin' about this tamorra. We've had enough excitement f' one day! Now come on, everybody, off t' bed!" The nuns and the children filed out of the room, still buzzing with the events of the day. Matilda noticed Ma looking a little pale. "You best be stayin' here tonight, Ma. It's been a big day."

"I'll be fine, May, I'll have a cup of Dr Liu's tea, then we'll be on our way." She patted May's hand, smiling the way she always did when trying to hide the tiredness and pain in her heart. "I'll put the kettle on. You get the girls and Patrick settled. I'm alright, but thank you, my dear."

The convent lay blanketed in heavy mist, the dawn air damp and chilly. Matilda, after her morning prayers, called out from the kitchen to Betty and Lizzy, who were, as usual, stoking all the fires in the main rooms. "I'll put the porridge on now, girls!"

They giggled after mouthing what she'd just said, knowing full well she said the same thing every morning, at the same time.

"I'll go get the sleepy heads out of bed, Mother!" yelled Lizzy.

"Thank y', Lizzy."

Lizzy gasped in shock and tore down the stairs. "Mother! Mother! Patrick's gone!"

"Oh, Holy Mother of God," Matilda dropped the bowl that she was about to set on the table and ran from the house, calling, "Patrick! Patrick, where are ya?"

A faint voice came through the fog, "I'm here, Mother, with Sergeant."

"Oh, Patrick, to be sure, y'll be catchin' y' death of cold! Come here right now!" Anger had replaced her relief.

"It's alright, Mother, I was just feeding Sergeant the oats Da's left for him. He loves them—come look." The pony had his head at the bottom of the bucket, licking up the very last grain.

"I hope you didn't give him the whole bucket of oats, Patrick?"

"No, of course not, Mother. Da said only a small tin full in the morning and a biscuit of hay at night and I filled his water again, because he'd drunk it all. We'll have to get a bigger bucket, Mother."

"Yes, yes, all right, we will, Patrick, but f' now, you need ta be gettin' inside, young man, and be puttin' some warm clothes on." Matilda smiled fondly at the little boy who she was beginning to admire, not only love but truly admire.

Patrick had been reasonably attentive in class before his birthday. However, given the opportunity, he'd preferred to play with his wooden soldiers under the desk until he was discovered. This meant detention and so he'd often miss out on play time. Happily, from his fifth birthday onwards, he concentrated on his school work. The reason? He would be able to spend extra time with his pony. Also, Mother Matilda had offered something.

"If y' concentrate on bein' a good student, Patrick, I'll be lettin' y' have lessons in Kung-Fu with Dr Liu." She'd preferred to see this as an incentive rather than a bribe and so Patrick became diligent with his studies. And it wasn't too long before he'd picked up some of the basic skills of Kung-Fu. Soon after this achievement, he'd bewitch the girls by riding Sergeant bareback and jumping him over a fallen tree in the paddock. Something he would never do, if he knew Mother Matilda was watching.

Visits from Mother Superior became more frequent, as she too, had fallen in love with Patrick. Never coming empty-handed, she'd bring a toy soldier for his collection. Still sporting his long blond curls and eyes of an intense blue, he'd throw himself into her arms, kissing her and thanking her effusively.

Mother Matilda made sure she never ever missed their greeting. Smiling and nodding, she'd say, "Ah yes, I told y', Adele, see he's charmed y', too."

"Do we have any defence against this boy, Matilda?"

"Not really, but not everyone would be as beguiled by him as we are, Adele. And yes, we've survived so far from the Bishop findin' out about him bein' here. I pray to God I'm right and this is where he should be—I know it's not with the likes of the fire-and-brimstone lot."

"No, that would be a terrible thing to do to the boy," Mother Superior agreed, and then asked, "You've only had the one close call, Matilda?"

"Yes, thank heavens, we've been warned each time whenever there was goin' t' be a visit from the Bishop. Da always comes to collect Patrick and takes him home for the day, so it works out well." Matilda thought for a moment then added, "Patrick's old enough now t' know the consequences. If the priests were t' find out he was here, well, I don't know what we'd do. All I can say is, it's just as well we have y'self and the good Lord on our side, Adele."

Chapter 15

Adelaide

The month before Patrick's birthday, Sally held her three-year-old Angus close to his birthday cake. "Angus, blow out the candles, darling." He blew gently but unfortunately, mostly spit came from his full lips. Nevertheless, they all clapped and Sally passed the cake around. Jonathon was proud of the colourful donkey piñata he'd made for Angus. It now hung from a tree and he watched as the children screamed with joy, bashing the poor donkey mercilessly in order to relieve it of its hidden treasures. This brutality made Angus wail.

"Oh, don't cry, my darling, it's alright." Sally picked him up and walked inside.

Jonathon sat silent, taking it all in, thinking, *Angus should have been made to stay here and see it's all in fun, but no, as usual, Sally has had her way.*

Later, Sally returned to the party alone. "I'm so sorry for leaving. It's all been a little too much for Angus. He needs to sleep now." The guests were happy to party for a little while longer. However, Sally's frequent admonitions to the children and adults alike made them feel a little uncomfortable and so they left. But Colleen stayed back to help Sally clean up. Bob and Jonathon both offered to help, but Colleen flicked the tea towel.

"Go and enjoy a quiet beer together and let us girls have a chat on our own." She turned to Sally once the men were out of earshot.

"I know it's probably none of m' business, Sally, but don't you think you're molly coddlin' Angus just a wee bit too much?"

To avoid Colleen's gaze, Sally kept washing the dishes. "You sound like Jonathon, Colleen. He says the same thing. But Angus is—well, he's just a baby."

"I have to be tellin' y', Sally. He's not goin' to be just a wee baby forever," Colleen returned drily. "Just make sure y' let him grow to be a boy, then a man and that means lettin' him get used t' things. You can't always be there to protect him. He has to learn most things the hard way, Sally. Even today, Jonathon had made that piñata especially for him and I'm sure Jon would have held him and showed him there was nothing to be afraid of, if ya'd given him a chance."

"I know, Colleen," said Sally, as she passed another plate. "I know I'll have to let go. I can feel it is causing trouble between Jonathon and me. I know I simply take charge of everything to do with Angus. Yesterday, Jonathon wanted to take him into Adelaide City to play in the park, just the two of them. But I made up a feeble excuse so they couldn't go. I just can't bear to let Angus out of my sight."

Placing her plump hand on Sally's shoulder, Colleen turned her around. "Y' know, Sally, if you were to be havin' another baby, you'd be needin' more help from Jonathon t' take care of Angus. That might not be such a bad thing."

"And making the baby might just help our problems too!" Sally smiled, blushing at her quip.

Chapter 16

Hawaii

Bernadette sat on the ocean shore, sifting sand through her fingers, watching her three-year-old daughter toddle towards the water and then run away from the last reach of the waves. Bernadette felt, as she always did, that Jum was sitting beside her, laughing in his raucous way at his daughter's antics. She asked herself: *When will this ever end, dear Lord? Will there be a day when there's only Addy and me? When will the palpable presence I feel since Jum's death ever fade, along with the memory of his touch, his love?*

Bernadette's days of mourning had turned from weeks into years. Her thoughts were suddenly broken by a man's voice behind her.

"Hello, Bernadette."

Turning she looked up, her hand covering her eyes from the sun.

"Barnaby Stuart," she said softly, unsure for a moment if it might be an apparition. She blinked, before realising it really was him. Stunned, she sat back on her heels.

"Barney! It is you! What on earth are you doing here?"

He seemed a little nervous, shifting his weight from one foot to the other. Taking off his straw hat, he began smoothing the brim with his long elegant fingers. Then pointing to a spot on the sand next to her, he asked. "May I?"

"Of course, please sit." Bernadette rearranged her sarong and sat cross-legged on the sand as Barney lowered himself awkwardly beside her, trying not to stare at her bare legs. Bernadette's near naked body looked more alluring than he'd ever imagined.

Barney took a deep breath and let it out, before speaking. "I've—ah—I've recently set up a business here, Bernadette. I've begun exporting tropical fruit seeds to Australia. Queensland seems to have the ideal climate to grow pineapples, bananas, mangoes etcetera and we're soon to reap the rewards."

He glanced sideways at Bernadette and admitted shyly. "I've been to Hawaii several times but I've never worked up the courage to come and see you, Bernadette." He began to sweat with nervous anticipation. "I thought after more than three years you may—well, I don't know what to say. I feel, and have always felt …"

Bernadette's attention was diverted from Barney by a high-pitched wail coming from the beach. For a second, her eyes had left Addy, and in that moment a large wave had knocked her over. Bernadette rose smoothly and ran to collect her. Returning with a sobbing child perched on her hip, she said, "I'm sorry, Barney. What were you about to say?" she asked distractedly, as she used the hem of her sarong to wipe away Addy's tears.

"Oh, nothing really," Barney said as he got to his feet. "She's so beautiful," he added, stretching out his hand to touch Addy's cheek.

"What is her name?"

"Adelaide, but I call her Addy." Barney nodded with a grin.

"Are you happy here, Bernadette? Will you ever return to Australia?"

"One day I will, Barney, when Addy's ready for school. My memories are still too painful for me to return at the moment." Suddenly, if only to break her constant thoughts of Jum and Barney's intensity, she said brightly, "I'm so sorry, Barney. I should have offered sooner, but would you like to come to my home and have some refreshment? It's such a hot day. Lily, our housemaid, makes wonderful lemonade."

The temperature dropped about ten degrees after they'd walked out of the hot sand and through the tropical rainforest to Bernadette's home. It was built in a style that in Australia had become known as a "Queenslander", white weatherboards, a generous veranda all around, sitting high off the ground on stilts, and a widened staircase that added an air of grandeur. Pink frangipanis and lush ferns surrounded the house, with the rainforest a perfect back drop.

Bernadette spoke Hawaiian to Lily, who then smiled at Barney as she took Addy from Bernadette's arms.

"Lily will return with the lemonade once Addy's in her crib. So, tell me, Barney," she asked as she led him to a cane chair on the verandah, "How's Melbourne?"

Barney sat and wiped his brow with his handkerchief, embarrassed to make a minor confession. "I've moved to Adelaide."

"Oh really, Barney, I would have thought, with Queensland being the location of your business, if you were to move anywhere it would be there?" Bernadette raised an eyebrow.

"It's far too hot and humid for me there, Bernadette. It's alright to visit, but I'm afraid this continuous heat does me no good. I find it hard to breathe." He wiped the perspiration from his brow again, flapping his handkerchief as if it were a fan.

Bernadette noticed, clapped her hands and a boy came running. She introduced him to Barney. "This is Ahio, Lily's son. His name means 'whirlwind'."

Smiling sweetly, Bernadette simply nodded and Ahio pulled the cord attached to a large woven fan. He spoke a few words of Hawaiian, which Bernadette translated. "He says this is his job, because his name means 'wind'."

Barney flashed a smile before speaking. "I find your people wonderful, Bernadette, so happy and keen to please. Their attitude to life is refreshing. If I could only bear the heat, I'd love to live here."

Sitting back in her oversized cane chair, Bernadette took note of Barney's suit and bow tie, not to mention the woollen socks and his heavy shoes. By force of comfort and nature, Bernadette would shed her unsuitable English clothes the moment she hit Hawaiian shores. Now adorned in a colourful pink sarong, her velvet skin a much deeper tan and with a pink frangipani blending into her long black hair, she looked every inch the Hawaiian Princess.

Barney sat admiring her beauty, while feeling a little self-conscious. Although he thought himself to be good looking, in a refined, cultured sort of way, he was certainly not the rugged, handsome man Jum had been.

Bernadette broke the silence. "Barney, come with me." He followed her involuntarily, transfixed by the subtle swaying of her hips. Before he realised, they were standing in her bedroom.

"Take your clothes off, Barney, and put this on."

His heart began racing and his body stood rigid when Bernadette handed him the sarong. Finding his coyness amusing, she giggled. "Come on, Barney, it won't bite you! I just want you to feel comfortable and a damn lot cooler. I'll be on the verandah when you're ready."

She turned and left, shaking her head, thinking unbidden thoughts. *If Barney were Jum, well, we wouldn't be leaving the bedroom, and Jum would've dressed in a sarong from the moment he arrived, dropping it in an instant to swim naked alongside me. I must stop thinking these things,* she admonished herself. *It only brings me loneliness and a longing for something that has gone and will never be replaced.*

Barney joined her on the verandah, showing his "farmer's tan", white legs and chest, arms brown from the elbows down. He smiled self-consciously. Bernadette smiled sweetly and poured the lemonade. "There now, don't you feel more comfortable, Barney?"

"I feel a little silly, well, undressed to say the least, but yes, I do feel much cooler. Thank you, Bernadette." He took a long drink and remarked how refreshing the lemonade was.

"You know, Barney, if you dressed like a native, you would enjoy this land a lot more. Have you seen our wonderful waterfalls and inland lakes?"

"No, I'm afraid not. I usually do my business and leave. I've never taken the time to look around much," he confessed.

Bernadette sipped her drink contemplatively. "Where are you staying?"

"The Royal Hotel."

"Why don't you come and stay with us? And then I'll show you some of the wonders of this beautiful country. Have lunch with us, and then go get your things, that's if you have a couple of days to spare?" Barney began to feel more relaxed and happily accepted her invitation.

The lunch of baked fish and tropical pawpaw salad they savoured slowly, as they did with the fermented coconut and pineapple juice. Their conversation finally turned to Bernadette's passion—the women's political movement in Adelaide.

"I was so pleased to have read the good news about Catherine Spence. It seems the suffragettes have finally made headway. Just fancy, she got thousands of votes, and became the first woman in the world to run for parliament. I'm so pleased for Catherine. I must write her a letter of congratulations!"

"You must, Bernadette. And it's only the beginning, you know. One day we may have a woman as prime minister!" he said before taking another sip of the wine she'd poured.

Bernadette's demeanour softened as she leant back in her chair, remembering how much she'd enjoyed both the company and her former conversations with Barnaby Stuart. *I know he respects my opinion and he's not just paying lip service to my ideas, because we've argued quite heatedly over different aspects of politics. But it seems we share the same vision of what the future should be for Australia and women in general.*

The wine had relaxed Barney enough for him to acquire a little Dutch courage so he walked to the Royal Hotel still dressed in his sarong. He smiled as he nodded to the Hawaiians along the way, who seemed amused at this very white man wearing their national dress. Barney was quick to pack his bags. Not in his usual manner—pedantically folding tailor-made suits and shirts. He shoved everything into his case and skipped down the stairs, almost tempted to slide down the banister into the foyer. An adolescent feeling of recklessness had overtaken him as he gladly signed himself out of the hotel. Bag in hand, he walked briskly towards Bernadette's house.

Bernadette's laughter swam in the air as he walked up the pathway. "Aloha, Barney, come. I'll show you the guest room. Unpack and then we'll take you to our private lagoon."

"This is heavenly," Barney remarked, after pushing his way along the jungle path. A smooth rock ledge gave easy access to a cascading waterfall, white lilies seemed to be dancing with the flow. Bernadette and Lily, uninhibited, shed their sarongs. Holding Addy in her arms, Bernadette then glided into the water and turned waving for Barney to join them. Unsure about dropping his own sarong, he hesitated.

"Relax, Barney, we won't look and, remember, when in Rome, do as the Romans do. Come on, Barney, the water's so refreshing." Bernadette beckoned him again. Defiantly, he threw the sarong to the ground. Never had he felt such freedom.

Addy's charming giggles blended seamlessly with the gurgling of the waterfall and the cries of the tropical birds in the jungle. They took it in turns to launch Addy gently in the air and then to catch her as she splashed and screamed with joy.

Barney soon felt completely at home, a feeling which, on reflection, had surprised him, considering he was so far removed from his usual sphere. After some time at play, he confessed he was a little cold.

"There you are, Barney, I told you. If you dressed and acted like a native, you would soon feel cool and comfortable."

He had to admit Bernadette was right, *but would I behave in this way for any other woman? NO! It seems Bernadette's able to talk me into anything. I must admit I'm a little daunted by the thought. I've been well and truly hypnotised and now, I'm sure I would go through the fires of hell if she needed me too.*

Bernadette smiled sweetly. "Come, Barney, let's enjoy our Hawaiian sun. It'll warm and brown you. And then you'll not only dress and act like a native, but you'll look like one." Her giggle was music to his ears. They spread themselves like lizards on the sand, the brightness of the sun forcing their eyes to close. Listening to the waves lift and crash on the nearby beach, Bernadette spoke softly.

"Barney, can you hear the waves telling you their story? They're like us, they're born of the sea to travel through different currents until their end. Then they return to the ocean to be reborn and start all over again."

Barney listened for a while, his voice low. "You're right, Bernadette. I truly believe we all have many journeys to experience before the end."

Addy played happily, building castles around them, without a care.

Chapter 17

A Helping Hand

Sally sat alone in Central Park. Occasionally she glanced up to admire the flowers and birds that the park their home. She enjoyed the peace and tranquillity while writing in her diary, an enjoyable duty she performed each day while waiting for Angus. He was now four years old and attending a newly founded kindergarten. She was grateful for the rest given she was six months pregnant with Jonathon's second child—her third.

She kept the diary diligently, ordered by dates and events, along with her feelings. She'd also pressed wildflowers and recorded their common names. Below that she wrote the name of the person whom the flower reminded her of. It gave Sally some comfort, thinking perhaps that: *One day I hope Patrick will read my diary. I can only pray he will understand that I've always included him as part of my family. I now long for the end of each month when I visit him at the orphanage. I'm so proud of him. He's growing to be such a fine scholar and he's mostly well behaved, except for the few misadventures Mother Matilda has told me about. I'm simply astonished at his horsemanship. I can hardly believe it when he stands on his pony's back, cantering him in a circle. Thank heavens for Betty who seems to be always there to pick him up if he falls.*

Sally looked forward to her visits that gave her not only the opportunity of being close to Patrick, but Mother Matilda's friendship, which had become an important part of her life. Sally would never leave without donating some money, knowing it usually went to buy the girls and Patrick new shoes or the like. She laughed when she'd heard the children had nicknamed her "Mrs Sally", and "new shoes Darcy". All this and more was written in her diary, *the whole truth and nothing but the truth*, as she'd promised herself. Sally hid her diary beneath a loose floorboard under her bed. While she admired Jonathon for many things, she was sure his understanding of her true story would not sit well with him. Knowing that he would look upon her differently, she'd written:

Everything in Jonathon's life has to be tagged and filed. Yes, all things must fit into place before his judgment is to be made. It's just the way it is with Jonathon.

He judges everything. Maybe he will become a judge one day? But he needs never know about my diary. It is intended only for Patrick to read. I've not written it to invite Patrick's forgiveness. That may be impossible. But I do pray for his understanding, once he's grown into the fine man I'm sure he'll be. Sally penned those last thoughts and closed her diary. It was time to collect Angus.

Her fierce protection of Angus had been weakened as Jonathon had become more involved. Slowly, Jonathon had established a stronger bond, beginning as a friend, not a father figure. And in return, Angus grew to love his father more each day. Jonathon was proud of the fact that at four years of age, Angus was able to give him a run for his money in a serious game of chess, something Sally considered might be a world record.

Walking briskly away from the park, Sally overtook an elderly man who was dirty, poorly dressed and coughing painfully. He stumbled and nearly fell against her. She stopped and offered assistance, her hand supporting his elbow. "Where are you going, sir? Perhaps I could help you get there?"

He coughed uncontrollably, trying to get the words out. "I'm—tryin' to make it to the poor house. I'm—I'm sick, need to rest a bit."

His face was grey and unshaven, his eyes full of pain. Sally's heart went out to him. "Just rest over here, sir, on the park bench. I'll take you home with me and then I'll call the doctor. You won't have to go to the poor house, nobody should."

Sally remembered Jonathon's kindness and what would have become of her if he hadn't helped. "I have to go and collect my son now, but I promise, I'll arrange a coach to take us home, so please don't move until I return. What is your name?"

"Rupert, Mrs."

Part of Sally thought her actions rash, perhaps reckless. Jonathon wasn't at home so she was on her own with Angus. Was this wise? But the idea of just taking him to the poor house was intolerable. Sally picked Angus up and hurried to the nearest coach depot where she spoke to a waiting driver.

"I need you to drive us to the park first, I have to collect an elderly gentleman who is waiting there. He's very ill. You can then drive us home please. I live three miles from here."

The driver helped her inside, then slapped the horses with the reins. "Hup, boys, trot on!"

Rupert had waited. He had no choice, other than to accept her kindness, or lie down and die where he was. He was too tired to care. Angus's expression was quizzical as he watched his mother hurry over to the old man and then look up to the driver.

"Please, driver, can you help me with poor Rupert? I need to get him into the carriage and then you can take us home please."

He jumped down to help, but couldn't refrain from offering his opinion. "If y' don't mind me sayin' so, missus, he'd be better off in the poor house."

Rupert coughed before he caught his breath. "He's—he's right, missus, please just take me to the poor house. That would be a kind enough gesture. I'm—I'm grateful for your concern." As he pleaded all the while, they helped him into the carriage. Angus's concerns were also squashed when Sally agreed to let him sit alongside the driver. "Be very careful, Angus, hold on tight now." *He's probably safer in the fresh air anyway,* she thought.

Sally tried again to persuade Rupert to come home with her, telling him the story of how Jonathon had helped her when she needed it most.

"I need more than help, missus. I need a miracle," he smiled briefly. "Please, I'm ready to go. I've lived me life and most of it was good. I just fell on hard times, that's all. Now it's time to go and be with me dear wife, Myrtle, and ask the Lord for His mercy."

Tears always came easily to Sally, and this was no exception. Rupert noticed, smiled and then patted her hand. "Don't you worry, missus. You've been very kind to an old man."

"I'll say a prayer for you then, Rupert. 'Dear Lord, give this poor soul peace, forgive him of his sins. And please let him be reunited with his beloved Myrtle in Heaven. Amen'."

Sally reconciled her decision and called to the driver. *At least he'll have a bed to lie in when he passes away. I'll not just drop him outside, like a stray dog though, I'll go inside and see that he's taken care of.*

"Please, driver, can you wait?"

"Me name's Henry, Mrs, and yes, I'll wait."

"Well, Henry, could you chat with Angus until I return?"

Sally was greeted at the door by an older woman. "Well, well. What have we here?" she asked, taking Rupert's arm to help him inside. After apprising the woman of the situation, Sally then drew a pound note from her purse.

"Please, madam, take this, I'm sure I can trust you to give Rupert food and care for him in his last hours?" She pressed the note into the woman's hand. "I'll return tomorrow to see how he is."

"Of course, my dear, you've been very kind and be assured we will make him comfortable in his final hours." She touched Sally's cheek gently before calling for assistance. "Go home now, and may God bless you, my dear."

Deep in thought, Sally walked toward the coach and looked up when Angus announced, "Look, Mama, Henry said I can drive us home!" Angus held the reins and sported a grin from ear to ear.

"Well, look at you, Angus! You're all grown up. Listen to Henry now." *He's beginning to resemble Patrick, not physically, as he has the dark hair and brown eyes of Jonathon, but they possess the same adventurous spirit.*

Angus's baby features were disappearing and the fine, chiselled face of his father was beginning to emerge. Yes, Angus was the image of Jonathon, whereas Patrick was beginning to look more and more like Sally each time she saw him. She'd even noticed Mother Matilda studying their features and worried that Matilda may be about to ask some serious questions.

The day had culminated in a new adventure for Angus as he'd never been allowed to drive coach horses before and he just couldn't wait to tell his father. "You know, Mama, Father said I could go with him to Bulkawa one day soon. Will you come too?"

"Yes, of course I will, my darling. It's not really that far away and the government is building a railway track so we can all go by train soon. Would you like that, Angus?"

"Oh yes, I'd love that, Mama."

"Well, you can go to bed right now and dream about it."

There was never a problem putting Angus to bed, as long as he was read a story first. Jonathon was usually the one to do this and when he did, he would ask Angus to look closely at the words after he'd finished each sentence and then he'd ask him to repeat them. This exercise was paying off, as Angus could read simple stories. And on this particular night, he tried to read Sally his entire book. She was most impressed.

"I must congratulate you on your fine achievement, Angus." He then gave her the meaning of "congratulations" and "achievement". Sally shook her head. "You're going to be a lot smarter than me when you grow up, Angus."

"No, Mama, you're very smart." Sally couldn't win, so she cuddled him. "I love you so much, Angus, and I look forward to giving you a baby sister—or a brother to play with."

"If you don't mind, Mama, could you make the baby a boy? I'd really like a brother. I truly feel I'll have a brother soon, because I've said my prayers to God. Then the next time you can make me a sister."

"I'll try, my darling."

A hot, oppressive night kept Sally in a restless state of sleep, although she thought it was probably due to Jonathon's absence rather than the heat. Jonathon took his responsibilities at Bulkawa seriously. He would never let Jum down, dead or alive. After Jonathon's previous visit to Bulkawa, he'd confided in Sally. "I know this may sound strange and I know I've mentioned similar things before, but yesterday I truly felt Jum's presence. I could even smell his familiar cologne and the aroma of his cigars. I sat back in Jum's chair and laughed at all the fun times we'd shared together, as if he was going over them with me. In that moment, I actually saw Jum, just as it was the last time he said goodbye. I must have dwelt on this picture in my mind and drifted off into a reverie. I heard Jum's voice loud and clear say, "Bring Bernadette and Addy home before you leave, Jon."

Sally tossed and turned in her sleep, troubled by the words "before you leave, Jon". *Where was he going? Jonathon has no plans to leave Adelaide. He loves it here and he feels duty bound to keep things going at Bulkawa until Bernadette comes home.*

Unable to sleep, Sally made her way to the kitchen, intending to warm some milk, hoping the fuel stove hadn't gone out completely. Standing by the embers she began to perspire profusely, when from out of nowhere, the coolest of breezes drifted through the kitchen. Throwing her head back, she opened the neck of her nightgown to capture it, thinking it must be a cool change. She then opened the door, only to meet the still-suffocating heat. The breeze suddenly stopped. Puzzled, she returned to the table, sat drinking her milk and thought of Jum, feeling him close. It didn't frighten her at all; strangely, it calmed her. Relaxed, she went back to bed and fell asleep.

"Mama, Mama!" Angus shook his mother until she woke.

"Oh, my darling, it's morning! Have I slept in?" Sally stretched and yawned out her first words. "Let's have some breakfast, Angus, then I have a surprise for you. What say we go see Mrs T and ask her to spoil you? Then Mama can go visit the poor, sick man we helped yesterday?"

"I don't want you to go there, Mama! He's sick and you might get sick too!"

Sally laughed, patting the bed for him. "I won't get sick, my darling, I promise." She rubbed her swollen belly. "God will look after me and your brother."

"In that case, Mama, I suppose you can go." Angus brightened visibly, "Do you think Mrs T might make me some jam biscuits?"

Sally ruffled his hair. "When doesn't she make you jam biscuits, Angus?"

They cuddled while Sally sang his favourite nursery rhymes. Angus then sang her a song Bob had recently taught him. He began confidently.

"Paddy McIntyre, an Irish man of note,
Fell into a fortune and bought himself a goat.
This goat of McIntyre's, he had an appetite,
One morning for breakfast he ate some dynamite,
A packet of matches and a quart of kerosene,
He went down the backyard and drank some glycerine.
He came by the fireside and didn't give a hang,

He swallowed a great big spark
And exploded with a bang!
Now if you ever go to heaven
You can bet a one-pound note,
That the angel with the whiskers on
Is Paddy McIntyre's goat!"

Sally laughed, and ached with it.

"It's a funny song, isn't it, Mama. I wouldn't buy a silly goat like that! You know, Mama, I have an appetite, but I don't want dynamite for breakfast. I want two eggs from Henrietta, my favourite hen."

"Yes, sir," she gave a mock salute. "Right away, your Lordship!"

"But Mama, I want to get the eggs myself!" Saying this, Angus jumped from the bed and ran outside to the chook pen where he found three brown eggs. He carefully carried his cargo into the kitchen. "Soft-boiled please, Mama."

Sally sat watching as Angus dipped his bread soldiers into the egg and then, with surgeon-like precision, he gently scraped the white from the inside shell until it was cleaned of every trace.

"You know, Angus, you have the hands and the brains to be a surgeon. Do you think you would like to be a surgeon when you grow up?"

"I will have to think about it," he said as he pushed the plate towards Sally. "There Mama, I'm all finished."

"Well then, let's clean up and walk to Mrs T's, shall we?"

The cool morning air offered only short relief from the hot windy day to come. Pleased she'd made it to Colleen's boarding house before noon, Sally sat fanning herself, sipping on cold lemon tea while explaining to her friends about the unfortunate man she intended to visit.

"Whatever is y' thinkin', Sally m' dear?" Colleen asked in disbelief. "He's probably riddled with the pox or some other dreadful disease!"

Sally became indignant. "I really feel I have to go, Colleen. After all, I'm a great believer that God sends us duties to fulfil. I feel so sorry for this poor man, Rupert. It seems he's had neither luck, nor kindness, from another soul since his dear wife passed away."

Colleen was most concerned and said as much. "Y' doesn't know what conditions he may have, Sally. Y' have y' own family to worry about. And as you say, he's just waitin' for God to take him, so he can be reunited with his wife. Please don't feel duty bound t' go, Sally, you've done all y' can for him."

Colleen wrung her hands in genuine distress, then a reluctant Bob agreed to drive Sally to the poor house. They sat silently, neither wanting to confront the other with what they were thinking until they were almost there, when Sally spoke her mind.

"I assure you, Bob, this will be my last visit. I just need to say goodbye, as I promised."

Taking one hand from the reins, Bob then placed it on Sally's shoulder. "You're a lovely young lady, Sally, I know how much the missus loves ya, and she'd hate to see you get sick, that's all. She loves y' like a daughter, y' know."

"I love her too, Bob, but I'll be fine, so please don't worry."

Bob smiled knowingly and put his hand back on the reins, before pulling his horse up in the shade of a peppercorn tree. Sally took a deep breath and another look at the building, which she'd only just read about in a newspaper article.

The Adelaide poor house was originally constructed by community-minded volunteers. Scraps of any materials offered went to putting the four walls and a roof over the heads of less fortunate souls. However, the government has recently stepped in (just before the election), supplying new timber, along with professional tradesmen to extend and rebuild most parts of the building.

Accepting Bob's help as she stepped down from the carriage, Sally stood for a moment, lamenting the poor souls within. *Perhaps a new name would also be appropriate, rather than "poor house", as it might offer a little more solace to its inhabitants. Why can't they call it a "refuge"? It would sound more comforting. Maybe I should write a letter to the government about changing the name?*

Her thoughts were interrupted by the manager walking briskly toward her. "I'm sorry, missus, you can't come inside. We've been shut down. We're in quarantine. I was just about to put the sign out front."

Taken back, Sally asked, "What for, sir, what's happened? I was here yesterday. I brought an elderly gentleman here. I've returned to see how he is getting on."

"I'm so sorry, missus. I know who the man was and I'm afraid he died early this morning. The doctor said he had tuberculosis. It's highly contagious. I suggest you go and see your doctor, missus." He looked pointedly at her swollen belly, "Especially in your condition."

Sally felt faint as she turned to Bob. "What have I done, Bob?"

Bob helped her back into the carriage and headed straight to Dr Forster. For the entire journey, Sally held her hands protectively over her unborn child. Dr Forster seemed more than happy to see Sally. He'd delivered young Angus into the world and was looking forward to the next arrival.

"Sally, how nice to see you. I was going to drop by for a cup of tea on my way home this evening, just to see how you were feeling. Only twelve weeks to go now. Do you think it might be a girl or a…" The stricken look on Sally's face made him pause.

"What's wrong?" he asked, coming from behind his desk. "Tell me, Sally. What is it?"

He took her hand and then she told him the whole story, before admitting her worry.

"I may have put myself and my family at risk of contracting tuberculosis, Doctor."

"Try not to worry too much, Sally, we'll just have to wait and see. Tuberculosis does have an incubating period, sometimes up to a month, or it may be slightly longer, before you show the symptoms. It usually begins with coughing, feeling extremely tired and night sweats. I suggest you leave Angus with Colleen and Bob for a while, just to be on the safe side." He crossed the room and took a bottle from the medicine cabinet. "Take this tonic each morning, Sally, and do nothing but rest. And try not to worry. You're young and healthy so I suspect you'll be fine. I'll send for Jonathon to come home."

"How long will I be quarantined for, Doctor?" a tremor evident in her voice.

"At least four weeks. All we can do is wait now. And as I say, Sally, you're young and healthy, so the risk should be less. But please do as I say."

"And Jonathon?" Sally asked, her eyes welling with tears. "Must he stay away too?"

"He must wear a mask and stay away from you as much as possible. The closer the contact, the greater the chance of spreading the disease. Actually, he shouldn't really go near you at all for a month, Sally. But knowing Jonathon, I think that would be impossible."

Dr Forster escorted her outside and gave Bob the prognosis.

"We'll take good care of Angus for as long as need be, Doctor. Colleen and I will do anything we can for Sally and Jonathon, so there'll be no problem at all with having Angus staying a while."

"Thank you, Bob. Now Sally, I'll drop in every night to see how you are feeling. Try to think good thoughts."

Bob pulled his horses up outside Sally's home. "I won't come in, Sally, if that's alright?"

"No need to, Bob, I won't be long. I'll just go and pack some clothes for Angus."

Sally returned with a bag of clothes and Angus's teddy bear.

"Tell him I love him, Bob, and this is just for a short while. Tell him I have to rest as the baby seems to want to come early. He'll understand. Please don't tell him what's really happening."

Sally returned to her silent home, feeling emotionally drained and exhausted, but somehow mustered the energy to fill the bath tub with lukewarm water. She smiled as she added a few drops of lavender oil. It brought back the memory of her first night, making love with Jonathon. Lying back, welcoming the coolness of the water, she prayed.

"Dear God, I pray my time spent alone and resting will give me the strength to accept whatever You have in store for me. I must also beg You that it will be a lifetime spent with my children and my husband. I'll try not to worry, God, I'll leave it up to You."

Without drying herself completely, she donned a loose cotton robe, made a cup of tea and placed it with two pieces of bread and jam on the bedside table. She plumped up her feather pillows and made herself comfortable. The novel she intended to read sat perched on her distended belly, but it soon fell unread to one side.

This was how Jonathon found her in the morning. Kissing Sally on the forehead had made her stir. She opened her eyes and smiled. "Oh, Jon, I must have dropped off for a while."

"Darling, its ten o'clock in the morning. What time did you go to bed?"

Somewhat bewildered, she answered, "I think it must have been yesterday afternoon, about four o'clock."

"I came as quickly as I could, Sally. Dr Forster has told me everything. I know in my heart you will be fine, darling. I love you." He bent to kiss her again, but she pushed him away.

"No, Jon, you must wear a mask. Please do as the doctor said."

He put his hands up in surrender. "Yes, yes, Sally, if you say so. I'll get you a cup of tea."

"Thank you, darling. I'll get dressed."

Sally walked into the kitchen and laughed at the sight of Jonathon with a handkerchief tied around his face, looking like a bank robber. He aimed a fork as if it were a gun. "Stick 'em up!" he growled.

Obediently, Sally put her hands above her head. "I have no money, sir, please spare me! I'm only a poor young lady. All I can give you is my love."

He held her in his arms and Sally cried into his chest. Jonathon kissed her lips through the handkerchief. This made Sally laugh, before she whispered, "Everything will be fine, Jon, I know it will. I'm so sorry for putting us in this position."

He stroked her back. "Yes, we'll all be fine, Sally."

Angus sat opposite Bob at the kitchen table where they shared a pot of tea and jam-filled biscuits. The chessboard lay between them, open and ready for their first game together. Philosophical about his mother, Angus assured Bob. "I'm not going to worry too much about Mama, Bob. I'm sure Dr Forster is just being careful and I'm positive this new baby will be as strong as I am," he said, with the conviction of a grown man.

Bob smiled, shook his head wondering. *How did an old head come to be on such young shoulders?*

"I'm sure y' right, Angus, and I wouldn't be surprised if you become Prime Minister one day. Now come on, young man, how about that game of chess? You'll have to teach me though, I'm not as smart as you are."

"Oh, don't say that, Bob. You're a very clever man, I heard father say so," Angus said sincerely, which made Bob smile. "Why, you can do so many things I can't, Bob. But I don't think I want to be Prime Minister yet, not at my age. Mother said I'd make a good surgeon. Maybe I'll do that first."

Bob laughed even louder. "You're a real character, Angus. I'll give y' that!"

Meanwhile, Sally had to push Jonathon out of the door. "I think it is best you go to work, Jon, and perhaps stay with Angus at the boarding house. I'll be alright. Dr Forster has promised he'll visit me on his way from the surgery every night. And if anything happens, I can call our neighbours, Penny and Wally, to go and fetch you."

Jonathon stood, reluctant to leave. "I'll not have a bar of that, Sally. Besides, don't you remember they're leaving soon? They're going bush, remember? Wally bought the Dougherty farm forty miles out. I'll be home for dinner, Sally. To tell you the truth, I think the doctor's being a little overcautious."

He finally left, tipping his hat before he blew her a kiss. The unrelenting heat seemed to penetrate every part of Sally's body. Normally, the heat wouldn't bother her, however, being over six months pregnant, it was taking its toll, both physically and mentally. She'd kept her spirits high for Jonathon, until she'd closed the door. "I need to rest for a while. I feel awful."

Jonathon presumed *his* tiredness was due to the huge workload of keeping Bulkawa running, as well as his own thriving business. In his office, Jonathon accepted a letter delivered by his secretary, Alison. He studied it for a moment. *Bernadette usually corresponds with Sally. I wonder why Bernadette is writing to me.*

Dear Jonathon,

I need you to look at investing my money in Barnaby Stuart's tropical fruit business. It has begun to really thrive so I'm sure it would make a fruitful investment. Ha ha!

Addy and I are enjoying Barney's company very much. He's a wonderful man. I'm sure you will come to like him as we do. Yes, I must say, Addy and I are extremely fond of him. We will be returning to Adelaide soon, but only staying for a short while. I cannot express how much I miss you and Sally, and I'm longing for the children to meet each other. I trust and pray you and Sally are well, Jonathon, and looking forward to your second child.

Bernadette's letter distracted Jonathon from his concern for Sally. He couldn't help but smile, knowing how much Sally would love to see Bernadette, especially after so long apart. And of course, her daughter, Addy, who would be near five years, close in age to Angus. It was exciting news to take home to Sally.

The hot day lingered into an oppressive night, sapping Jonathon's energy. He'd tried in vain to catch up with clients and court cases. But eventually gave in to tiredness and hitched his horses for home, but first he made a stop at the boarding house.

Colleen opened the door. "Oh, I'm sorry, Jonathon, I've just put Angus to bed. But I'm sure he'd love to be woken by his dad and have a cuddle." Colleen seemed more than happy to see Jonathon, although her heart feared the worst was still to come.

"Father!" Angus said excitedly. "I knew you would come, that's why I'm not asleep. I've been waiting." He jumped out of bed to embrace his father.

"God bless you, Angus. I hope you understand why you're here with Mrs T. Mama just has to rest for a while."

"A good thing, I think. Mama should rest, especially in this heat."

Was it pride in his son's ability to fathom and reason these things that brought such emotion to Jonathon, or was it pure unconditional love? Jonathon asked himself this question before he sat and listened to Angus read *him* a story. Once finished, he assured his son. "Your reading has improved, Angus, so well done, my boy." Jonathon sighed and held Angus to his chest. "Everything will be fine, Angus. I love you more and more every day, if that's possible."

"I'm sure it will be, Father. And I know you will be very pleased to hear that I'm teaching Bob to play chess. It won't be long and he'll be able to compete with me very well. Tell Mama I love her and I miss her very much and she should do as the doctor says."

He then hugged Jonathon before whispering. "Don't worry, Father. Mama will be fine."

Jonathon stroked his son's dark hair, dwelling on the thought of how much they looked alike and how much they *were* alike, in many ways, especially when it came to logical thinking. They were both kind and intelligent, but somehow lacked a certain passion, something his great friend Jum Watt had had—for everything.

Sally hadn't long woken when Jonathon walked through the door. He put his mask on and went to her on the couch where she'd been all day, her face flushed and her eyes feverishly bright. Placing his hand on her forehead, he said. "Sally, you're a ball of fire. You're burning up, my love."

"I feel very weak, Jon. I suppose it's just the dreadful heat and falling asleep for so long."

"I'll draw you a cool bath, Sally, it'll bring your temperature down while I make us some supper." He helped her into the bath tub and sat on the edge, wetting her forehead with the tepid water, when a loud knock startled him, and he almost ran to the front door.

"Dr Forster, come in, I'm so pleased to see you. I was just thinking perhaps I should call on you."

"Well, I've saved you the trip, Jon. I always call in, just in case." A brief smile brushed Jonathon's face before his brow creased. He whispered, "I'm concerned about Sally, Doctor. I haven't long returned home to find her asleep and she seems to be burning up. I've just helped her into a cool bath."

"It may not be what we think it is, Jon, so don't be too concerned. I'll take a look."

Sally voiced her irritation at having to leave her bath so soon. "Shoosh, Sally," Jonathon tried to calm her down while drying her and putting on her favourite nightgown. "I'll help you into bed, Sally. Dr Forster wants to check your blood pressure and your temperature."

Sally's temperature was up to 100 degrees, even after a cool bath. The smiling doctor took Jonathon by the arm into the kitchen. "I don't want to panic you, Jon. It may be just a harmless fever. The baby's heartbeat is fine, so that's a worry off our mind." He placed his hand on Jonathon's shoulder. "Use cold compresses to keep her temperature down. And make sure she drinks plenty of water. I'll drop by on my way to the surgery in the morning, but please come and fetch me if she gets any worse through the night. But try not to worry."

He gave Jonathon a comforting pat on the arm and a smile before he left. *Don't worry, he says. How can I not worry?* Taking a deep breath and, with his most reassuring smile, Jonathon approached Sally with the tonic and a promise.

"If you are a good girl and swallow your medicine, Sally, I shall give you a sweet."

Sally managed a wan smile. Took her medicine and drank her water. "Jonathon, may I please have a cup of tea now? And perhaps some bread and jam?"

"Of course, my love," he hastened to the kitchen, exhausted, but more than happy to meet her requests.

The morning came too quickly, it seemed for Jonathon. Wearily he reached across to feel Sally's forehead. "Are you awake, Sally? How do you feel? Oh good, your temperature's gone."

"Yes, I'm feeling much better, thank you, Jon."

"I really don't want to leave you today, Sally, but my work is piling up. Do you think you'll be alright?"

"Yes, of course, I feel fine. Please don't fuss, you need to go to work."

"I'm not fussing," he hesitated, knowing there was something he'd forgotten to tell her.

"Oh, yes, I've just remembered, Sally. I received a letter from Bernadette yesterday. Her intentions, along with Barnaby and Addy of course, are to visit us. They should be leaving Hawaii today."

Sally jumped out of bed. "Oh, that's so exciting! When will they arrive? I can't wait to see Bernadette. There's so much to do!" She rushed to the window, exclaiming in horror. "Oh, my garden, just look at my poor garden, Jon, I must use the bath water to save the plants. They're all dying. What will Bernadette think of me, letting my garden die?"

Jonathon took her firmly by the shoulders. "Hey Sally, please stop. You're supposed to be resting. I'll hire a gardener to see to your plants. Please calm down, or I'll have to stay home and make sure you do."

He led her back to the bed, even though she protested every step of the way.

"Really, Jon, I feel much better now. Oh, I'm so happy, I just want everything to be perfect for Bernadette and Addy. I wonder if she's fallen in love again with— who did you say his name was?"

"Barnaby Stuart, surely you remember Barney? He's been mentioned in each of Bernadette's letters. Apparently, he was a friend of Jum's."

Jonathon tucked Sally back into bed and gave her a glass of water. "Here, drink this, Sally. You must remember when Bernadette spoke of the Barnaby Stuart she'd met in Melbourne? Anyway, I'm pleased she's found a gentleman to keep her company. Now Sally," Jonathon spoke sternly, "promise me you'll rest. We don't want this fever to return, do we?"

Sally thought for a moment, her fingers drumming on the counterpane. "Oh, of course, I remember him now. Bernadette said he's a very nice man, Barnaby Stuart. Yes, she calls him Barney, that's right. Addy adores him, too. You know Jon, it must be my pregnancy. They say women become absent-minded when pregnant." She offered a smile so becoming that Jonathon forgot about the mask and kissed her on the lips.

"I'm going to draw myself a bath, Sally, and if you feel up to it, I'll then cook you bacon and eggs for breakfast."

"Yes, of course, my darling, I feel fine—and I'm starving. I don't think I've eaten much lately."

Lying back against her fluffed-up pillows, Sally tried to remember when Bernadette had first mentioned Barney. *Was it when they first met in Melbourne? Or was it when he went to Hawaii? Oh, well, I don't suppose it really matters as long as Bernadette's happy.*

The time of Sally's quarantine seemed to pass quickly. The first two weeks she'd spent doing as the doctor ordered, especially after the fever had affected her more than she was willing to admit. The next two weeks she'd busied herself, preparing for Bernadette's visit. The new gardener, Sally loved.

"I'm so happy, Mr Mark. Just look at what you've achieved with my new flower beds. It's amazing. And you've done such an excellent job of salvaging my old garden and the vegetable patch. Thank you so much."

Dr Forster paid regular visits, firstly on his way to work and again on his return home. He was more than pleased to see her back to her normal self. "You look wonderful, Sally."

"Thank you, Doctor. I'm so happy, I feel like a new woman, although I miss my boys." Dr Forster assumed she meant Jonathon and Angus.

"I console myself each day by writing them letters and I'm counting the days when I'm able to go to Adelaide and buy…" Sally paused, realising if she mentioned a diary, she may make a slip and tell him about her first and secret diary.

"What do you need in Adelaide, Sally, perhaps I could buy it for you?"

'Oh, nothing really, Doctor, I was just thinking how wonderful it will be to feel free once again." Sally bid him farewell, before going directly to where she'd hidden her diary. Her heart sank when it opened unassisted, on the page where she'd written about her heartache of having to leave Patrick at the orphanage. Closing her eyes, trying to smother the memory, she held it against her heart for a moment and then returned it to its hiding place, promising, *I will begin a new diary, fit for everyone to read, once my third child is born.*

Chapter 18

All Things Must Change

Bernadette accepted Barney's hand as they embarked on the magnificent sailing ship. Addy, every bit as beautiful as her mother, was intrigued by the sailors scurrying to obey the captain's orders. She welcomed the first rays of morning sun on her face, her tiny hand waving farewell to family and friends. Addy was perched on Barney's shoulders, squinting into the sun. "They all look like big ants now, Barney. I can hardly see Anakala and Anake."

He laughed. "Your uncle and aunt will be the same size as they were when we return to shore, Addy. It's just we are moving further away. All things will remain the same until we come home. I promise."

His calm, caring explanations always soothed Bernadette's soul. She was now totally in love with him. The moment she realised this, it felt like the final bolt had been fitted to a sailing ship, allowing it to float. Her life was now complete again and her thoughts drifted back in time.

I will never again experience what I had with Jum, but over these past three years, you, my darling Barney, have slowly filled my aching need. I was meant to love and be loved in return. Sometimes I feel Jum may have sent you to me. I harbour no guilt when making love to you. Instead, I have felt a grateful joy, which slowly but surely has diminished my pain. Thank you, my darling.

Barney's sun-streaked hair danced in the wind. He turned, smiling at Bernadette, whom he knew kept her personal thoughts to herself. "You've been thinking about me or us. Was it all good, Bee?" He placed a gentle kiss on Bernadette's cheek.

"Yes, my love, it was all good."

Over two miles from shore, the mainsail took full advantage of the southerly trade winds. The masts stood tall and strong while the sails strained against the sheets. For Addy, it was hard to believe that this ship would carry them all the way to Australia, the Great Southern Land.

Meanwhile in Adelaide, Jonathon had bought Sally's second diary before she had time to make the trip to the city. Slightly disappointed she hadn't chosen it, she reprimanded herself for telling him she wanted one. However, excitement soon overcame her frustration when she opened the wrapping, to find it was almost identical to the first book. The cover was made from black leather, with the word "Diary" written in gilt.

"Thank you so much, Jonathon, I shall begin writing the day after our baby is born. It's a mere four weeks away now, darling. I can't wait, and to think it will be near the time of Bernadette's return. I'm feeling on top of the world this morning."

The truth was that Sally was still feeling occasional high temperatures and overwhelming tiredness, which she hadn't let on to Jonathon. "I'll begin my spring cleaning today to be ready for Bernadette. That's how well I feel, so I'll scrub the kitchen from top to bottom. Then I'll wash down the fuel stove as best I can and I'll not forget to throw every drop of water on my plants."

"Please don't do that, Sally. I'll ask Colleen if we may use one of her maids for a day or two. Just rest, my dear. Read a book. You love reading, it'll help you relax."

Sally let out an exasperated sigh before she bid Jonathon farewell, assuring him, "I will sit and read all day, Jonathon, don't worry." She said this, with no intention of doing so.

Finally, after four hours of hard labour, Sally made a cup of tea and sat in her favourite chair. This was a colourful tapestry armchair she'd had crafted for Jonathon. However, she took pleasure in its comfort most days. "Yes, it's much cooler in here. I'm pleased I closed the curtains early this morning."

It was autumn and the debilitating heat should have left South Australia by now. However, this was a different heat. It suddenly welled up within Sally, along with extreme dizziness. Placing the cup down on the small round table was no easy feat, with her hands beginning to tremble. "Sugar, that's what I need. I need sugar," she said to herself.

Struggling to lift her heavily pregnant body out of the chair, Sally made it a little unsteadily into the kitchen. With her hands still shaking, she managed to butter the bread and heap her homemade jam on top. Leaning on the kitchen table for support, she ate quickly, hoping it would revive her strength. Instead, her legs suddenly gave way and she collapsed, unconscious.

Some hours later, Jonathon returned to find Sally semiconscious. Dr Forster now stood beside Sally's bed with stethoscope in hand, waiting patiently for Jonathon to finish his gentle reprimand.

"I told you, Sally. I would organise help for you. Why did you do so much? You must take care, my love." He brushed a loose curl from her forehead and stood admiring his pretty young wife before Dr Forster asked, "Please step aside, Jon. I need to listen for the baby's heartbeat again." After listening, he smiled at Sally and then looked at Jonathon. "I need to talk to you, Jon. Outside please."

"No!" Sally protested. "You can tell me too, Doctor! What's wrong? What's wrong with my baby?"

Hesitant to answer, as he feared the worst, Dr Forster confessed. "Sally, I'm unable to hear the baby's heartbeat. It was faint ten minutes ago, but I'm afraid I can't hear it any longer. We're going to have to get you to hospital straightaway."

As Dr Forster took hold of Sally's hand, she suddenly grimaced in pain and then grunted her words. "That can't be true, Doctor, I'm having contractions. The baby's coming, I can feel it. It's alive, it wants to be born!" Her face screwed up in agony. She yelled, "Help me, God! Help me, please!"

"There's no time to get her to the hospital now, Jon. You'll have to help. Boil some water and bring clean sheets, quickly."

He turned his attention to Sally. "Now, try not to push until I say so. Breathe deeply and relax. That's right." He repeated his orders, while Sally tried with all her might to do as he asked, but the pain was unbearable. It seemed this baby was not going to help her. The work needed to bring him into the world would be all hers.

When he feared she was going to pass out again, Dr Forster offered her smelling salts.

"Come on, Sally, don't give up! Just one more push and he's out! Come on, be brave, just one more push!"

Sally somehow found the strength to push the head and then the shoulders of her stillborn baby girl out into the world. Dr Forster tried for fifteen minutes to revive the baby, before reluctantly giving up.

Sally had since passed out and by this time her pulse was very weak. Placing her wrist down on the bed, he ordered, "Quickly, Jonathon, hitch your horses! Sally's bleeding internally. We have to get her to the hospital quickly!"

Trying not to panic, as it would only waste precious time, Jonathon methodically but hastily hitched the team; the back seat of the buggy he made comfortable with feathered quilts and pillows. They gently placed Sally upon them, with Dr Forster sitting beside. He lay the baby girl in her arms, noting the spreading crimson onto the quilt. As soon as they reached the hospital, he called out.

"Quickly nurse, get the operating theatre ready! Time is of the essence. If we can stop the haemorrhaging, we may be able to save her. Hurry." After two hours, Dr Forster appeared before Jonathon who sat slumped, head in his hands while praying for a miracle. Looking up, he saw Dr Forster's broad smile and leapt with joy. Holding him tight, Jonathon sobbed.

"Thank you, thank you, Doctor."

"She's not out of the woods yet, Jon. Although I do feel confident I've stopped the bleeding. She's still very weak. I'm afraid Sally has lost a considerable amount of blood."

"But she's alive!" Jonathon felt such passion, such relief, such gratitude. He also began to feel a little guilty that it took a near catastrophe to bring his passion to the fore. "Can I go and see her?"

"Yes, Jon, but if she wakes, don't stay too long. She needs to sleep."

Jonathon lent over to kiss Sally, just as her eyes blinked open. She struggled to speak.

"Jon, the diary –"

"Sally, my dearest, I bought you a diary. Don't you remember, darling? Please don't worry, just sleep."

Trying in vain to lift her head, but devoid of strength, Sally mumbled incoherently. "Mother Mat... Patrick... bed... floor... diary..."

"Shoosh, Sally, I'm here and I'll be here when you wake up. Please don't worry, Sally. Please sleep, and don't worry." To silence her, he kissed her lips then waited.

"Diary—the diary," Sally spoke with effort before she collapsed into deep sleep.

Dr Forster entered the room. "Would you like a bed brought in, Jon, so you can sleep next to Sally?" He added, "Matron suggested it. She knows Sally very well. I'm not sure if you're aware, Jonathon, but Sally would come into the hospital most days and read to the patients. Sally told Matron she had some time to spare while Angus was at school. Matron has just reiterated what a lovely young lady Sally is and so you must be a very nice man."

He placed his hand on Jonathon's shoulder, and smiled. "It's not often we get a compliment out of her Royal Highness, as we call Matron," he said softly, trying to lighten the moment.

Forcing a return smile, Jonathon answered, "If it's not too much trouble, Doctor, I'd like that. May I ask another favour of you? Would you be able to inform Mrs T about Sally?"

"Certainly, Jon."

Within minutes, the bed was brought in and Jonathon pushed it as close as possible to Sally.

The baby girl, some weeks premature, was wrapped in a white crocheted shawl by the Matron. It was unusual for her to become sentimental, but on this sad occasion she took time to ponder. *What a wonderful life you'll be missing out on, blessed with parents who would have loved and cared for you dearly.* Before placing her in the hospital morgue, Matron said a silent prayer. *Dear Lord, please accept this innocent soul. May she join Your angels in Heaven, Amen.*

The following morning brought a brief cool change, accompanied by a sprinkle of rain and then a heavy humidity that promised heavier falls. Colleen cussed. "Oh, I hate this blessed weather, I perspire so. But the Dear Lord knows I have no time t' worry about such things at the moment."

Bob walked into the kitchen and, thinking perhaps they had another boarder, he looked around. "Who was y' talkin' to, doll face?

"I was just talkin' to m'self, Bob, tellin' m'self I have to be hurryin' to have Angus dressed in his finest clothes to visit his poor sick mother in hospital. And I have t' be havin' m'self looking at least respectable, as well as havin' everythin' spic and span before we'd be leavin'."

Taking a deep breath, trying to calm herself, she then called out. "Angus, come on me, darlin'. We're off t' see y' mama now!"

Colleen straightened her frock, the one she'd worn to the races that day, now five-and-a-half years ago. Bob left to wait for them in the buggy, thinking how over the past four years Angus had endeared himself to them both. Their relationship was definitely as a family should be.

"This is really kind of you to take me to see my sick mummy, whom, I believe, you love like a daughter." He paused to search both faces. "I have to tell you I love you both very much and I've decided I would like you to become my grandparents. You don't have to adopt me legally, we can just have an agreement. Would that be alright with you?" Angus asked in all seriousness.

If Colleen had been slightly flustered before this moment, she completely lost her composure. Laughing, crying and shaking like a bowl of jelly, Colleen felt her eyes disappear into tear-filled creases.

Looking in dismay at her reaction, Angus continued. "Are you alright, Mrs T? Do you want to be my grandmother?"

Bob, always calm and with a wry sense of humour quipped, "I think I'm up to it, for sure. What about you, doll face? Give the boy an answer."

Grabbing hold of Angus, Colleen kissed him on the head. "I would very much like t' be y' ornery grandma, Angus!"

Angus sighed, "No, not ornery. It sounds like a donkey. Honorary is the word."

"Yes, Angus, my answer is most definitely yes!" Colleen said, trying to be serious.

Not expecting Sally to look so pale and drawn, Colleen stood in shock, but tried quickly to disguise her concern. Smiling, she bent over to place a kiss on Sally's cheek.

Sally's eyes, ringed with shadow, half-opened and settled on Angus. "Patrick," she said hoarsely.

"No, Mama, my name's Angus," he replied matter-of-factly.

Smiling, feebly holding out her hand, Sally repeated his name. "Angus."

"Your hand is so cold, Mama, I'll warm it up."

His small hands gently rubbed against hers, eventually bringing back the warmth.

Colleen, still in shock and not really knowing what to say, began telling stories. "You know, Sally, Angus has been teachin' Bob how t' play chess. And he even makes jam-filled biscuits better than I do m'self."

Sally seemed to be taking it all in. However, it was hard for Colleen to know, as she lay so still, her eyes closed. Colleen turned when the door opened.

"Father, father," Angus cried. He jumped into Jonathon's outstretched arms, hugging him tight. "Father, I miss you and Mama very much, but Mrs T and Bob have agreed to be my grandparents. Isn't that a good idea?"

Jonathon laughed, "I think it's a very good idea, Angus."

Colleen gently placed her hand on Jonathon's arm, her head lowered in an attempt to hide her sadness. "We'll be leaving you alone for a while, Jonathon."

Jonathon nodded and sat down with Angus on his knee. He spoke softly. "Angus, I think this may be as good a time as any to tell you what happened." He hung his head, hesitating for a moment, then looked up into Angus's innocent eyes. "Your baby sister has died, and gone to Heaven. And now Mama is very sick."

Angus considered his own emotions for some time before he came to fully understand the gravity of his father's words. He then wept uncontrollably. Jonathon carried him from the room, out to the gardens surrounding the hospital. They walked, hand in hand, until Angus's tears subsided.

"It's not fair, Father. I was going to have a baby brother. I wanted a brother more than anything." Angus stopped in his tracks to look questionably at his father. "Do you think God has made a mistake and that's why He took the baby girl back to heaven?"

The fact Angus had already consoled himself with his own explanation put a smile on Jonathon's face. "I don't know, Angus, we'll find out, I suppose, when we eventually go to heaven."

"Do you think Mama will get better soon? When she does, can she try again to have a baby brother?" Angus studied his father's face for a moment. "Mama looks very, very sick. Don't you think, Father?"

Choking back tears, Jonathon answered, "Yes, she does, Angus, and now we can only pray she gets better. Then I'm sure she'll make you a brother. Do you want to go back and sit with Mama now?"

"Yes, I need to sing her my funny goat song. Mama loves it; it makes her laugh. I'm sure it will make her feel better."

Sally hadn't moved, her eyes remained closed, however, she became conscious of their presence. She coughed feebly before trying to tell Jonathon what she knew she must.

"Jon, there's a diary—under the bed—Angus has a brother."

Jonathon felt his heart heave. *Surely, she's delirious? She's talking nonsense.* "What do you mean, Sally? Angus has a brother? Are you dreaming, my love?"

She forced the words out. "No. His name's Patrick. Take Angus there—to the orphanage."

Angus heard Sally loud and clear. "Mama said I had a brother. Father, I heard her. Where is my brother, Mama?"

Every ounce of Sally's strength had been consumed with her effort to speak. She lay unconscious.

Holding Angus close, Jonathon sat in silence, looking at Sally and wondering why on earth she would say such a thing. Unable to fathom the answer, he reluctantly decided it was time to go home. "Come along, Angus, we'll come back and see Mama later."

He kissed Sally on the lips before he left.

Colleen and Bob were on their way back into Sally's room as Jonathon and Angus were leaving. Jonathon shook Bob's hand.

"I think we should all leave Sally to sleep for a while, Bob. I'll take Angus home with me and bring him back in a few hours. Thank you so much for your help. I don't know what I'd do without you." Jonathon hugged Colleen tightly before leaving.

Father and son walked towards the exit. And Colleen watched, desperately wanting to chase after Jonathon and ask about Sally's chances of survival. Bob knew instinctively what was on her mind and so held her back. "This isn't the time, love. Let him go. All we can do is pray. How about we stop by the church on the way home?"

Colleen nodded.

The entire way home, Jonathon remained silent, while Angus kept busy practising his goat song. "I need to sing it really well for Mama when we go back to the hospital, Father."

Their home seemed dank and empty as Jonathon went about slowly, gathering up the sheets used during the birth. He tried desperately not to cry at the thought of having to bury the tiny body. *I'll have to give her a name and a proper funeral, probably long before Sally's well enough to attend, although knowing Sally, she'll insist on being there.*

Jonathon sat motionless on the bed, staring into space. Memories of his mother surfaced and how he'd nursed her until she died. "That isn't going to happen again," he said aloud. "I can't lose Sally, not my first true love. Surely, God, You wouldn't be so cruel?" With great effort, he forced himself to shed the thought and continue his domestic duties.

The bread and jam Sally had half-eaten remained on the kitchen table. Dried to a crisp, Jonathon threw it in the chook's scrap bucket.

"Angus!" he called.

"Yes, Father." The little voice came from behind him.

"Oh, there you are, Angus. Could you please take the scraps to the chickens and make sure they have lots of water, and collect the eggs, please?" After Angus left the room, Jonathon began talking to himself. "You have to keep going, Jon, for Angus. He needs you to be strong. Don't give in. Sally's still alive. She won't die. You won't let her die."

Angus excitedly ran back through the kitchen door. "Look, Father, six eggs!"

He held them up for Jonathon to see. "We can have eggs for dinner. Can you make them just like Mama? She makes them soft in the middle and cuts up bread into soldiers."

"We don't have any fresh bread, Angus." Jonathon said, angry at himself. *I don't even know how to make bread! How could I be a grown man and not know how to make a simple damper?*

Angus sensed his father's anger, mixed with sadness. With the compassion one would expect from an adult, not a child of five, he said, "It's alright, Father, we can have scrambled eggs. You don't need bread with that." He managed a cheeky grin.

Jonathon laughed, shaking his head. "What would I do without you, Angus?"

Scuffing his son's hair, he thought again how much alike they were.

"Now, Father," Angus said formally, "can you do something for me?"

"And what would that be, my boy?"

"Well, I was just thinking about what Mama said, you know, about me having a brother. She said the diary was under the bed. Can we have a look to see if it's true?"

Tired of hearing the word "diary", Jonathon sighed, "I know where her diary is, Angus, I bought it in Adelaide only the other day. It's sitting on the dresser in the living room."

"I know that diary, Father, but it has nothing written in it, I just had a look. There must be another one."

Jonathon had to think for a moment. *Do I really need to know if Sally has secrets, especially now, when everything seems to be drowning me?*

"Father," Angus tugged on his trousers, jolting Jonathon's attention back to his initial question.

"Alright, we'll look, Angus, but please don't be disappointed if the diary doesn't exist. Your mother's very ill and sometimes when people are so ill, they say silly things."

"I'll be just a little sad, Father, because I really want a brother more than anything."

Jonathon glared at Angus. "I don't think you mean that, Angus. I think you'd want your Mama to be well again before you have a brother to play with."

"Yes, of course I would, Father," he said indignantly, then in a small voice, he added, "but I really would like a brother, Father."

Reluctantly, Jonathon went to his bedroom. Angus followed closely, saying, "Mama said it was under her bed, under the floor, Father."

On his knees, Jonathon lifted the loose board he found directly under Sally's side of the bed. And there was the diary. With his pulse racing, Jonathon settled on the edge of the bed, studying the front cover. Gilded scroll ran around the edge of the well-worn black leather book. What surprised Jonathon, as he hesitantly opened the first page, was the neatly pressed wildflowers, along with the names of the many people they knew, plus a few he didn't know. Then at the bottom of each page, Sally had explained why each particular flower reminded her of that particular person. *Jonathon,* she wrote, *is the Queen Adelaide Rose, so pure and correct; Jum, the Sturt's Desert Pea, roaming wild and free. Angus is the waterlily, which I admire so much when sitting beside the lake in Adelaide Park. Patrick reminds me of the wild daisies, happy and young.* The name "Patrick" sent a shiver down his spine.

Jonathon turned to Angus. "It's going to take some time for me to read this book, Angus. I'll explain what Mama has written when I'm finished. This book is really only meant for me to read at the moment. It's for adults. Do you understand?"

"Yes, Father, I'll just sit and read my own books. I understand. I only want to know about my brother."

Jonathon sighed, thinking, *it's no use saying anything else until I've read the diary.*

Dumbfounded and shocked, Jonathon continued to read of Sally's heartbreak, with intermittent words of joy. After the final word, he sat motionless before closing the diary. He held the pages tightly together, as if each word could be crushed out of existence.

Angus noticed his father had finished and he was now staring out of the window. Cautiously he asked, "Do I have a brother, Father?"

Jonathon was unable to speak, so many different emotions flooded through his heart and mind. Finally, he answered his son in the simplest way possible. "Yes, you do, Angus. Patrick is your half-brother."

"What does that mean, a half-brother?"

"It means Patrick had a different father. Your mother gave birth to him before she met me."

"But I don't understand, Father. Why didn't Mama stay with the first daddy?"

Jonathon remained still, his expression blank. He answered bluntly. "He died."

"When can we go and get Patrick, Father? Will he come and live with us?"

Jonathon let out a huge sigh. "I don't know yet, son. We have to get Mama better first, and then we'll see. I'm going to take you to Mrs T's for a while. I need to talk to Mama alone."

"You mean Grandma and Grandpa," Angus corrected him.

Jonathon managed a slight smile, but couldn't help but go over in his mind the words Sally had written about him. *I can't believe she'd think I wouldn't understand her situation. It makes me so angry—angry because Sally has never confided in me about Patrick. Didn't she respect me enough to know I would be compassionate and I would most definitely understand her dilemma? What affects me even more than that is what she has written in the diary, about me being a judgmental heartless fool? She hasn't used exactly those words, but I know it's how she felt.*

Jonathon's normally well-mannered horses sensed his anger, shying away from his rough hands. As he slapped on the leather harness, they pawed the ground and champed their bits fretfully. Jonathon pulled Angus aboard roughly and flicked the reins urgently. Usually the trip to Adelaide took fifteen minutes. Today the horses responded to Jonathon's outward show of anger. They pulled up, blowing, in front of the boarding house in nine minutes flat.

Upon hearing the carriage, Bob took a quick look out of the window and ran through the door to greet Jonathon, fearing he was bringing sad news. Bob wanted to bear the brunt of it, before telling Colleen. Jonathon appeared angry, not at all what Bob had expected.

"I need to see Sally alone, Bob. Could you look after Angus please?"

Angus jumped happily into Bob's arms, "I have a half-brother, Bob, I mean Grandpa."

Bob flew an enquiring look at Jonathon.

"I'll tell you about it later, Bob. I have to go—thanks."

The nurses were all wearing muslin masks. They walked to and fro quickly, the sudden change in the atmosphere disturbed Jonathon. He stood for a moment taking in the seriousness.

"Mr Darcy, Mr Darcy!" Matron was right in front of Jonathon before he acknowledged her.

"What's going on, Matron?" He was confused but at the same time, sensed the worst. Matron immediately handed him a mask. "I'm afraid we have an outbreak of tuberculosis, and I'm so sorry to tell you, Mr Darcy, but your wife is one of the patients afflicted."

She placed her hand on his shoulder as a kind gesture, but it only offered Jonathon the certainty Sally was leaving them. "Please come this way, Mr Darcy. Dr Forster wants to have a word with you."

He followed in slow motion, not wanting to hear the words confirming his worst fears—"Sally's dying". He knew in his heart she would soon be lost to him forever. *Dear God, please allow me at least a minute to say goodbye, to tell Sally I love her and ask for her forgiveness.*

Jonathon walked away from the Matron, before running to Sally's room.

"Mr Darcy! Mr –" Matron paused, having second thoughts. "Dear God, give him one precious moment."

Sally lay within the golden glow of the sunset, her curls cascading over the pillow and her skin, a perfect alabaster. Jonathon stood in awe of her peaceful beauty and felt his anger disappear. Without opening her eyes, Sally felt him there. "Jon, I, I …"

"I'm here, my love." He placed a gentle kiss on her cheek.

"Please forgive me, Jon," were the only words she could manage.

Jonathon whispered. "I've read the diary, Sally. Please forgive me, I never wished to appear judgmental. I would never have judged you for what happened. It was out of your control. I love you with all my heart, I love everything about you. I would have understood about Patrick. It breaks my heart to think what you went through, then having to give up your son. I promise you, Sally, I'll bring Patrick home. Home where he belongs." Jonathon took hold of her hand and squeezed it. "I'll go tomorrow, Sally, please stay with us, don't leave us. We'll be a family, and we'll have another baby girl. The boys will love her. We'll live on a farm. Children love farms and as you wrote, Patrick is such a good rider, he'll be able to teach Angus. They can both ride their ponies together and—and—" His voice broke, he'd lost control. Weeping, he nestled his head on her breast.

With one last ounce of energy, Sally lay her hand on his head before it slipped away. Jonathon looked up to see her lips curved in a smile. He lay his head down upon her breast again, feeling his heart break.

Dr Forster quietly entered the room, placing his hand on Jonathon's shoulder. "I respect your grief, Jon, I'm so terribly sorry, but I need you to know. Sally had many serious health problems, which inevitably lead to her passing."

Jonathon kept his head against Sally's breast while listening in silence to the doctor's explanation.

"Sally's heart was not strong. I fear she had a congenital weakness, but we will never know for sure. And, of course, losing so much blood in the birth didn't help matters. We've also detected the early stages of tuberculosis. I must tell you how very sorry we all are, Jonathon. Everyone who knew Sally loved her dearly. I'll help you in any way I can."

Dr Forster gripped Jonathon's shoulder briefly, and then left him to feel the final rays of light vanish from his life.

Chapter 19

My Brother, Patrick

Jonathon left the next morning for the orphanage. Once there, he introduced himself to Mother Matilda before giving her the sad news. He then handed her the diary.

"This is Sally's diary, Mother. It will give you time before the funeral to understand why Sally visited the orphanage so often." He looked pleadingly and asked, "I trust then you may be able to explain to Patrick some of what Sally has written?"

Matilda simply nodded before seeking solitude in her office, where she read all of what she'd expected. In the meantime, Betty introduced Jonathon to Patrick. They talked freely of Patrick's interests and adventures, which sometimes made Jonathon laugh.

"When I grow up I'm going to be a soldier. I want to ride my horse into battle. Do you like riding horses, Mr Darcy, or do you always drive your buggy?" Jonathon took an immediate liking to this young boy who was the image of Sally. After nearly an hour of what Jonathon thought to be an enlightened conversation with the young boy he would soon call "son", Mother Matilda joined them, with the diary in hand.

"My dear Mr Darcy, I now know the reason the good Lord sent Patrick to us. He has a plan for everythin', and although we may find it hard t' fathom sometimes, we must be strong and follow his wishes." She paused to ruffle Patrick's blond curls.

"I'm pleased to say, Mr Darcy, while others t'ought me selfish for keepin' our beloved Patrick, I knew in m' heart it was the right t'ing t' do." Stepping forward, Matilda embraced Jonathon before asking, "Would you like to take tea in the kitchen, Mr Darcy, or may I call you Jonathon?"

"Of course you may, Mother."

"Well then, Jonathon, I will now speak with Patrick alone, while Betty prepares you a cup of tea."

He felt sure Mother Matilda would lead with her heart when divulging the reason to Patrick for Sally's visits. He also knew the guilt he was still feeling would have shown in his delivery. Mother Matilda truly felt the Lord was with her, as she had little trouble explaining things to Patrick.

"Patrick, m' dear boy, y' t' be knowin' that Mrs Sally Darcy was y' real mother, y' birth mother. And now her husband, Mr Jonathon Darcy, is going to have y' go and be livin' with him and y' half-brother, Angus." She paused to see Patrick's eyes welling with tears. She wiped them dry.

"What about my real father, Mother, where is he?" Patrick brightened a little with the thought.

"Your birth father died suddenly and that's all I can tell yer now." She held him to her chest. "Don't be frettin', Patrick. We'll always be here if y'd be needin' us. The few days we have left together before the funeral will give y' the time t' adjust t' the idea of livin' with your new father and y' brother Angus. I can assure y', Patrick, Mr Darcy is indeed a very fine man and I'm sure he'll be lovin' and treatin' y' as his very own son. Y' may be a little young t' be understandin' the reasons why y' mother never took y' home with her. Y'll just have ta trust m', Patrick, when I tell y' you're not old enough t' read her diary. However, when y' are, you'll find all the answers y'd be needin' and y'll be very content with Mrs Darcy's reasons. Do y' have any questions, Patrick?"

"No, Mother, I always liked Mrs Darcy, that's why I was crying. It's nice to think she was my mother. And I'd rather call Mr Darcy, Da, if I may?"

Matilda stood and embraced him. "Let's go then, shall we. We'll say hello ta y' new Da, or y' Dad, whatever he wishes."

"Mother. Patrick," Jonathon nodded and then blurted out before any formality could continue. "The most amazing thing has just happened. Betty, only minutes ago, experienced a vision. She spoke with Sally."

Matilda said not a word. Instead, she smiled knowingly and took him by the arm. "Would you care to join me in our chapel, Jonathon? Together we will thank the Lord for His guidance and pray for Sally and baby Millie's departed souls and for our dear boys in their future together."

Chapter 20

Time to Start Anew

The mourners filed past the open casket, crossed their chests and offered a silent prayer. Patrick held Mother Matilda's hand as they stood to view his mother and half-sister, Millie.

Jonathon had named Millie in honour of old Mr Darcy's housemaid, the woman who had become Jonathon's surrogate mother. Angus followed his father and after saying a prayer, he placed a bouquet of wildflowers on Sally's chest, then moved forward to hold Patrick's hand. Patrick smiled down at Angus. The funeral ceremony ended with an announcement.

"The wake is to take place at Mrs Thomas's boarding house."

Jonathon was expecting many friends and acquaintances to attend so Colleen had offered her home to accommodate the throng. He greeted and expressed his gratitude to all who had come to pay their respects. Soon tiring from the effort, Jonathon found a quiet spot to sit alone and began to yearn over the married couples chatting quietly. *That's how it should have been for Sally and me. Instead, she's gone and I'm left alone with two boys who I'll have to find the strength and courage to raise on my own.*

With Mother Matilda keeping a close eye on Jonathon, she was able feel his emptiness. She dearly wanted to console him, but felt he should be left alone, at least for a while. Moments after the last friends and acquaintances had left, Matilda took note of the boys sitting together on the floor talking. *They seem happy. I'll go and have a wee talk ta Jonathon.*

As she walked past, she heard Patrick say, "I have Kung Fu lessons once a week with Dr Liu." Patrick then hung his head. "Oh, I forgot, I won't be at the orphanage anymore. I'm coming to live with you, Angus." He then brightened a little. "Do you think Dad will let me bring my pony with me? I could teach you how to ride him, Angus. His name's Sergeant and I ride him bareback—over jumps!"

Angus's eyes lit up. "Really?"

Matilda took the liberty of sitting beside Jonathon without asking. "I can see how tired y' are, Jonathon. It'd be hard for y' to find the time t' grieve, if y' have ta be takin' care of two small boys. So, what do y' think if I was ta take the boys home with me f', say, a month? I t'ink it maybe the best; well, for the time being anyways. It'll give y' some time to mourn and have a rest. Y' need to be lookin' after y'self now, Jonathon." Matilda waited for his answer.

"Yes, I'd really appreciate that, Mother. I must be honest, I feel far too tired and emotionally drained to care for two small boys at the moment. Thank you for offering and I'm sure the boys won't mind."

"No, I'm sure they won't mind at all. And m' da's fit and healthy, so he'd love ta be helpin' look after the boys. Y' take as long as y' need t' feel well and strong again, Jonathon." Matilda placed her hand gently over his.

"Yes, I will, thank you, Mother, and now I must apologise to everyone. I need to go home and sleep."

Bob, also concerned about Jonathon, offered to take him home and collect clothes for Angus. "You need to rest, Jon. Angus can stay here with Mother Matilda and Patrick. Leave your horses here. I'll look after them and then I'll come by tomorrow with your buggy. Maybe you'll be rested enough to drive me back home then."

Relieved with Bob's offer, Jonathon accepted. He went solemnly to the boys and placed a hand on each of their shoulders. "Angus, you now have the brother you've always wanted, and Patrick, you now have a family who will love and care for you, the same as Mother Matilda. We'll soon be together but I need to mourn your mother and regain my strength. I need time alone to do this. Do you understand, boys?"

They replied in unison, "Yes, Father. Yes, Dad."

Jonathon's heart suddenly swelled with Patrick's token of trust. *Dad. Yes, it sounds good and right.*

"Mother Matilda will take you boys home to the orphanage for a short while," he said then paused to take note of the expression on Angus's face. He seemed a little unsure.

"I think you'd like that, Angus. Patrick can teach you how to ride his pony."

"Yes, I will and I can teach him Kung Fu too!" Patrick said.

Angus's strength remained until Jonathon waved him goodbye. His heart broke and tears flowed like rain. Patrick's blue eyes also filled. Holding them close on either side, Mother Matilda watched as Jonathon and Bob disappeared down the dusty road.

"Come on, boys, I t'ink we're goin' t' be havin' a nice time, stayin' with our kind Mrs T t'night, and then we'll be catchin' a fine coach that'll take us to the orphanage tamorrow."

Trying once more to cheer them up, she offered, "And we'll play a game. We'll count how many kangaroos we see on the way home, and for every one you see, I'll give y' a toffee. What do y' say about that, boys?"

Patrick forced a smile, while Angus tried to control his sobbing. Patrick placed his arm around Angus and asked, "If you feel like it, Angus, maybe you could teach me how to play chess?"

"Yes, but not now, Patrick," Angus said, wiping his nose and eyes with the monogrammed handkerchief Colleen had made him.

Mother Matilda would be held to her word. Angus spotted five kangaroos as they travelled the country road. Patrick whispered, "Don't eat all your toffees, Angus. We can get the girls to do our chores if we give them sweets." He then went on to tell Angus all about the orphanage and the daily routine. Angus appeared most interested in everything Patrick had to say. Angus then asked intelligent questions about the countryside.

"You know I've never ventured further than Adelaide City. It's most interesting."

Angus sat back and took it all in. The soft glow and dancing shadows of this unique landscape began to comfort him. White cockatoos in their hundreds swooped and screeched their way from one tree to the next, flying so close together at times they appeared like clouds in the sky. Grazing sheep dotted the paddocks where the breeze rustled the rye grass. Occasionally a drover appeared, ambling by on his horse behind his cattle, their bellowing hanging in the air, mixing with the clip-clop of the horse's hooves and the hum of the coach wheels. This new experience, if only for a short while, took away the pain of Angus's loss.

After almost five hours, and many stops to drop off the other passengers, the coach finally pulled up in front of the orphanage. "Oh, my goodness!" Angus exclaimed, his brown eyes wide open with admiration. "Is this mansion built with Willunga blue-stone?"

Mother Matilda was finding Angus to be extremely unusual. He seemed to have the intellect of a man, and a well-educated one at that.

"You're amazin', Angus," Matilda observed. "How do y' know all these t'ings for one so young?"

He crinkled his brow unwittingly, a habit when asked a question. "Well, Mother, if I see something I don't know about, I just ask an adult, and if they are unable to answer me, then I ask my father to look it up in a book. Sometimes we go to the Adelaide Library. I love to learn about everything," he said with conviction and arms spread wide.

"Y' ta be congratulated, Angus. I t'ink Patrick will be able to learn many t'ings from y'."

"And I from him, Mother Matilda," Angus said with a huge grin focused on his older brother.

Betty stood first in the line, alongside Lizzy and then the rest of the nuns and girls who had been given an abridged account of the diary. They too were deeply saddened by the loss. Both Lizzy and Betty had recently decided, when they turned sixteen, they would join the convent together, as Novices. After such a sad loss for the boys and with the thought of becoming nuns, they were unsure if they should greet the boys with the joy they felt in their hearts. They held back a little, until Patrick asked cheekily, "Where are my cuddles and kisses, girls?"

With this they laughed, kissed and embraced him, before greeting Angus the same way. He soon became overwhelmed, as every girl, plus the sisters, one by one held him close. Mother Matilda finally broke it up, calling out as if she were giving instructions to a football team.

"Alright, everyone, that'll do. Angus Darcy will be stayin' with us for a wee while. His da needs time to mourn his dear wife, our beloved Sally Darcy, who has passed into God's care. And may the good Lord rest her soul. I can't be tellin' y' how much poor Mr Darcy's feelin' his terrible loss, so we all have t' be kind and thoughtful t' Angus and Patrick and look after them at this sad time."

"We will, Mother," came the assurance from all the girls who were still offering the boys their deepest sympathy with just one more hug.

Turning her attention to Patrick, Matilda spoke quietly, "Patrick, Angus can sleep in your room. I'm sure you won't mind."

"NO, Mother, he's my brother!" he answered stoutly and with that, he took Angus by the hand. "Come on, Angus, I'll show you our room."

Two single wooden beds sat on opposite sides. Angus looked back and forth. "Just for tonight, Patrick, can I move my bed closer to yours?"

Patrick was about to call him a sook, but thought better of it. "Yes, of course you can, Angus."

Heaving and puffing, they pushed the beds together until they became one.

"There, that's better, Angus. Now let's go get something to eat."

At the head of the stairs, Patrick held Angus back and peered around, "Okay, coast's clear!" Patrick slid down the banister, something he would forever be in trouble for—if he were caught!

Angus watched with open-mouthed admiration. "I'll do it next time, Patrick."

The girls had eaten lunch, but Betty had made extra egg sandwiches and put them aside for Mother Matilda. Unaware Patrick would be returning with Angus, it was more than a pleasant surprise for Betty. Her heart would simply break if she were never to see Patrick again. From the moment she'd found him on the doorstep, Betty felt he belonged to her. Indeed, some days she worried deeply about whom she loved more—God or Patrick.

Patrick sniffed out the leftover sandwiches and scoffed them down with a glass of milk. Angus ate his like a gentleman. Patrick then grabbed a piece of apple pie, before taking Angus by the arm, mumbling with his mouth half-full, "Come on, it'll be dark soon and we won't get to ride Sergeant."

Betty had returned to the kitchen, just in time to hold the door open to expedite their escape. Patrick jumped up with precision, planting a milky kiss on her cheek. Angus giggled. He then watched in awe as Patrick whistled and the pony came galloping straight toward them. Patrick offered the pony a piece of pie.

"See, Angus, he loves apple pie. Come on, meet Sergeant."

Angus climbed through the fence, excited by the prospect of having a ride. He stroked Sergeant's neck and face. "Can I ride him now, Patrick?"

"Of course you can! Have you ever ridden a pony before?"

"No," Angus confessed, "but father has led me around on his carriage horses. I always wanted a pony. Mama says when I'm older I can have one." Angus blinked trying to hide a tear.

"How old are you, Angus?"

"I'm nearly five. My birthday's on the second of June."

"Really! I'm seven on the fourth of July and we always let off firecrackers on my birthday. You'll meet Dr Liu. He makes the best fireworks ever. He lives in town, but he comes here to teach me Kung Fu."

"I can't wait to meet him, so when will he come?"

"Now let me see, today's Saturday, so he'll be here on Monday. Tomorrow we'll see Da. He comes to Mass in the morning and stays for lunch. He brings two legs of lamb nearly every Sunday morning, so we can have a roast. I hate peas. Don't mind 'em raw. We've got a veggie garden. I'll show you later." He turned to Angus, smiling, "You can have a ride now."

The heady odour of horse's urine, mixed with the earthy smell of straw, made Angus sneeze.

"Bless you!" said Patrick. "This is where I saddle Sergeant, see, there's my saddle and bridle." He pointed to a rack on the wall where they hung. "The most important thing is to do the girth up tight. Sometimes, horses breathe in lots of air when you girth them up. Then when you start riding them, they blow it out and the saddle slips—with you on it!"

The two brothers had a laugh, and then Patrick gave the girth one last mighty heave.

"I'll ride him a little bit first, Angus. Just to brush off the cobwebs and then I'll put a long lead on Sergeant and give you a lesson. I'll have you ridin' like a champ in no time, brother."

Matilda dreaded bookwork and her procrastination would cause it to pile up until she could no longer avoid it. After packing a few personal items away, she'd taken her tea and sandwich in her office. That was over an hour ago, and she was now looking for any excuse to be relieved from the drudgery of numbers and notes. Being responsible for documentation of all things concerning the convent was the only thing she didn't enjoy. *I'd rather chop wood, or scrub floors, or look after Patrick.*

"Oh, the boys!" she suddenly yelled. She hadn't checked on them, or put anyone else in charge. After finding no sign of them inside, Matilda opened the kitchen door to be almost blinded by the late afternoon sun. She squinted, looking to see if what she thought was true was, in fact, true. Yes, it was Angus bent over, holding onto the pony's neck for dear life. Patrick stood calmly, lunging Sergeant around in a circle, giving orders.

"That's good, Angus. Now sit up straight and try to keep your bum in the saddle!"

Matilda's heart skipped a beat; she thought at any moment Angus was going to fall—and he did. Matilda's black habit streamed behind her as she ran to where Angus sat on the grass, "Jesus, Mary and Joseph. Are y' alright, Angus?" Matilda pulled him to his feet while brushing him down. Patrick doubled up with suppressed laughter. Matilda threw him a stern look.

"It's not funny, Patrick!" she scolded before she turned her attention back to Angus. "Are y' alright, m' boy?"

"Yes, thank you, Mother. Patrick says I have to fall off ten times before I can call myself a rider." Angus forced a smile, when in actual fact he wanted to cry, more from shock than physical injury. Matilda escorted him inside while telling Patrick firmly, "That's enough ridin' for t'day, Patrick. Put your pony away, then come inside and have a bath. It'll soon be dinner time."

Matilda gave Angus a hug and a kiss on his head. "I'm sorry, Angus, I shoulda kept an eye on y'. I t'ought I could trust Patrick," she added, looking over her shoulder.

"No! Please, Mother," Angus protested, "it's all my fault. I wanted to ride Sergeant and Patrick made it look so easy. He even stood on the saddle while Sergeant cantered around the paddock!"

"Oh, he did, did he? Well, there'll be no more showin' off from him! Now, come on, Angus, I'll run y' bath."

The orphanage at dinner time was a completely new experience for Angus. Chatter was allowed, as long as it didn't become too boisterous. He'd never sat at such a large table with so many people, except perhaps at Mrs T's boarding house, where sometimes there were six extra guests. After Mother Matilda had said Grace, they ate heartily. Angus was distracted from his sadness when humorous stories, especially the ones about Patrick, made him smile. Patrick didn't seem to mind. He laughed along, although sometimes he'd roll his eyes with their exaggerations.

The fire had been lit in the grand dining room as the late autumn weather had turned cold. After dinner, Mother Matilda sat close, as usual. It was what she called "their precious time". The girls would take it in turns to read part of or all of a short story. Screams of terror, tears and sometimes uncontrolled laughter filled the room as the story unfolded, each girl trying to outdo each other with dramatics to act out the plot. Angus had tried in vain to keep his eyes open, but finally fell asleep with his head on Patrick's lap. Mother Matilda leaned toward Sister Catherine and whispered, "This is what I was hoping for, Sister. He's asleep. I didn't want him to be lyin' awake t'inkin' of his Ma."

Sister Catherine, used to carrying Patrick to bed, volunteered, "I'll carry him to bed, Mother."

Patrick then offered. "Angus may wake up, Sister, and I should be there for him."

Catherine ruffled his hair. "What a kind brother you are, Patrick."

As the dawn sun streamed in, Angus awoke to the sound of girls talking and rushing about. They were in a hurry to be dressed in their best clothes, their hair brushed and tied back in ribbons, porridge eaten and dishes done, all in time to be ready and on their way to the chapel for early morning Mass. Inquisitively, Angus looked out of the bedroom door.

Patrick yawned then called to him, "Don't worry, Angus, they take all morning to get ready for Sunday Mass. You'd think the King of England was coming." He rolled over.

"But shouldn't we get dressed now, Patrick?"

"All in good time, brother." A little bewildered, Angus sat on his bed, feeling as if there was something he should be doing. "Shall I go and feed Sergeant some oats, Patrick?"

Suddenly, a pillow nearly knocked Angus off his bed. He grabbed it, got to his feet, then glowered at Patrick.

"You want a fight, brother? I have pillow fights with Father. You can't beat me," Angus threatened through gritted teeth. Lunging forward, he whacked Patrick over the head with all his strength. Together they managed to spread the contents of two feather pillows throughout the room. They called a truce when Mother Matilda appeared in the doorway, with a look Patrick knew well.

"Boys, y'll be cleanin' up this mess and be puttin' every single feather back inta the pillow cases—after Mass! Now, go and eat y' breakfast and be dressed and ready t' walk t' chapel in ten minutes!" Matilda's hands left her hips as she turned to walk through the door. Patrick knew not to show any sign of cheek when Matilda was in this mood. He turned to Angus. "We got off lightly, thanks to you, Angus. I'd have been in big trouble if you hadn't been here." He put his arm around his brother. "Now, do you like porridge, Angus?" Angus nodded and they headed down the stairs together, leaving a trail of feathers in their wake.

"You look like chooks!" shrieked Suzie, who sat eating her breakfast in the kitchen.

"Don't sit near me!" warned Judith.

"Eat your porridge, boys!" Betty snapped, in an uncharacteristic display of ill-temper, then immediately apologised.

"I'm sorry, please forgive me. I'm not feeling well today."

The fact was, she felt jealous of Angus. Patrick seemed no longer hers; she'd lost him to his brother. Betty prayed silently to God for His forgiveness and busied herself at the sink. Duly chastened, the boys exchanged looks and proceeded to eat their porridge in silence.

The small orphanage chapel was full of parishioners. Sally had always told Angus, "Prayers are to be said to heal one's soul." However, while looking at the Virgin Mary, Angus thought his heart would break. The vision reminded him so much of his Mama holding his baby sister. Matilda tried in vain to comfort him, until Da thought it best to carry him outside. Holding and patting Angus gently, Da murmured, "Angus, did y' know m' dear wife has not long left me? She's gone t' heaven, just like y' mama and baby sister, but y' know, Angus, I truly believe in m' heart that I'll see m' beloved wife one day, when the dear Lord decides it's time for me t' go home, too. Y' know, if you talk to y' mama, she'll hear y', all the way up in heaven."

Da's blue eyes blinked as he looked up, pointing to the sky. Angus was not satisfied with this explanation and asked petulantly, "But I don't understand. Why did God want Mama to go?"

Da sighed, before he told the truth, "I don't know, Angus, but there must be a reason and one day the good Lord'll tell y'. Y' must have faith and believe y' mama and Millie are in a much better place." Giving him a hug, Da then lowered his voice, "Now Angus, what y' have t' do for them is t' be strong and make 'em proud a y'."

Angus sniffed back tears, half-smiling at Da.

"Do y' want t' go back inside, Angus, or would y' like t' walk for a wee bit? We can look for the wildflowers y' mama loved so much."

"Let's walk, Da." Angus looked up at the tall old man, whose gentleness so reminded him of his own father. They began walking, but turned back in unison upon hearing running feet. Patrick had caught them, breathless and, without a word, he took hold of Angus's hand. The three walked on in silence.

Chapter 21

Bernadette Returns

Nearly five weeks had passed since the boys had left with Mother Matilda. Jonathon's health had not improved; he'd been working long hours, mainly to stave off his loneliness. His cough had persisted and an overwhelming tiredness prevailed. But he'd told no one of this, not even Dr Forster. Nothing was going to stop him from bringing his boys home. He needed them to take away his empty feeling. They would be his solace, his reason to keep living and, of course, he'd told himself they would both need him, especially Angus, who'd been so very close to his mother. He knew Patrick had been deeply saddened, perhaps more than Jonathon could possibly know. He felt that he owed it to Patrick and Sally, to take him in and treat him as his own son. The thought of the brothers with him as a family touched him deeply.

The day promised to provide perfect weather for his journey and the autumn leaves would remind him there was a season for everything.

Miss Marjorie Gibbs had been recently hired by Jonathon to care for the boys and do light housekeeping duties. She had fine credentials, having worked as nanny of three boys for a well-respected English family. However, they'd only just returned to their home in London where she was not needed. Marjorie seemed a contented soul, a little on the chubby side, with curling red hair, but her charming smile reminded Jonathon, just a little, of a youthful Mrs T. She went about her unpacking this morning while singing happily under her breath. Marjorie respected the fact that Mr Darcy was still grieving for his wife and she thought it may be a little insensitive to sing aloud. Her room was quite spacious and, despite knowing Mrs Darcy had almost died there, she thought the home had a lovely feel to it.

Jonathon, busy hitching his team to the buggy, looked up as Miss Gibbs made her way to him from the house. "Yes, Miss Gibbs?" he enquired politely.

"I just wanted to tell you, Mr Darcy, I'll have everything shipshape when you return tomorrow."

Jonathon stopped in his tracks. *Ship- ship-... Oh yes, Bernadette should've arrived in Adelaide by now. I hope all is well. I'll make enquiries on my return.*

"Thank you, Miss Gibbs, I'll see you tomorrow with the boys." He tipped his hat, coughing loudly at the same time.

Marjorie frowned, saying under her breath, *He should see a doctor about that cough*. She smiled, waving him farewell, and said aloud, "Poor Mr Darcy, he seems a very kind man, and quite a handsome one at that," as she went to tend the washing.

The roads in South Australia were usually dry and dusty in autumn because rainfall came mostly in spring and winter. This year was no different and, after the long scorching summer had finally given way to autumn, the country was left desperate for rain. An hour into his journey, Jonathon coughed furiously into his handkerchief, blaming the dust, when he discovered blood. Pulling his horses up straight away, he reached for the canvas water bag and drank thirstily. "Just the dust," he said, convincing himself, as he pushed his horses on.

Sad memories still plagued him and try as he may, he just could not erase the image of Sally lying in her coffin with baby Millie in her arms. It was this memory that tortured him. If he believed God could have taken him, then and there, he would have gladly joined his wife. Tears ran unheeded down his cheeks before, once again, he realised the purpose of his journey.

"My God, what will I look like when I arrive at the orphanage?"

Determined, he focused his thoughts back on the boys and the good times they would share in their future together. He would have them educated at the finest school in Adelaide. They would not want for anything. Whatever sport they pursued, Jonathon would be there to cheer them on. *Yes, I will be there for them always, we will be comrades. I don't want to be an authoritarian. More like their guide and mentor.* "Just like my father would have been to me, I'm sure," he said aloud, and held that idea as he clicked his horses into a canter.

Marjorie Gibbs had been very busy all day, cleaning and scrubbing the house, while grumbling a little. *Mr Darcy should have had this place cleaned before I arrived. After all, I'm a nanny, not a housemaid. I'll speak with him when he returns, or...* She paused, at the washing line, *maybe not at the moment. He has so much sadness to bear.*

Marjorie began singing sweetly again as she hung the washing on the line before she stopped suddenly, her ear turned to the front of the house. *Did I imagine a knock on the front door? There it is again.* She walked around to the front of the house where she saw the slender back of a tall woman who was holding the hand of a little girl, her long black hair reaching her waist. They stood waiting, looking at the front door.

"May I help you?" Marjorie called.

"Oh, my goodness, you startled me!" Bernadette said, turning and putting her gloved hand up to her heart.

"I'm sorry, I didn't mean to." Miss Gibbs held her hand out to Bernadette. "I'm Miss Marjorie Gibbs. I'm Mr Darcy's new nanny. How do you do, Mrs…?"

Bernadette shook Marjorie's hand. "I'm pleased to meet you, Miss Gibbs. I'm Bernadette Watt. I'm a close friend of Mr and Mrs Darcy. This is my daughter, Addy. We've only just arrived from Hawaii. This is our first port of call, so to speak; we've come straight from the docks. It seems we've been at sea forever and I just couldn't wait to see my dear friend, Sally. I mean Mrs Darcy."

"I'm very sorry, Mrs Watt, you obviously don't know." Marjorie looked deeply concerned.

"Don't know what, Miss Gibb?" Bernadette asked anxiously.

"Mrs Darcy passed away over a month ago and Mr Darcy isn't here. He's gone to pick up his two boys from the orphanage, where they've been staying for a while."

Bernadette almost fainted; she had to lean against the wall of the cottage for support. Miss Gibbs immediately went to help her. "Are you alright, Mrs Watt? Please let me help you inside. I'll make you a cup of tea."

Addy seemed confused. She'd never seen her mother behave like this. Bernadette was always so composed and in control of every situation. Miss Gibbs noticed Addy's concerned look and so spoke kindly.

"Now, Addy, we'll help Mummy inside and I'll bring you some lemonade and a piece of chocolate cake. I made it just this morning." Looking up at Bernadette, she asked, "Would you like a cup of tea, or perhaps something stronger, Mrs Watt?"

"I think I need a brandy if you have any. Thank you, Miss Gibbs."

Bernadette sat in Sally's favourite armchair, staring blankly, feeling so very numb. *Choosing to come here first before going to see Colleen has been a big mistake. Colleen would have sat me down and prepared me for the shock. It's too late now.*

Remembering Sally's smiling face and her charming personality brought back the memory of their shared wedding. Then the day at the Adelaide races when Freelance had won. It all came flooding back. Yes, Jonathon had proposed to Sally that day. How excited Sally had been to talk it over with her. Bernadette had become like Sally's elder sister.

And now the mention of two boys at the orphanage. What was this? What was Miss Gibbs going to tell her? Bernadette sat, so shocked that she was unable to move or even cry at the moment. *Why hadn't Jonathon written me? Well, of course, with the storm and loosing valuable time, his letter may have gone missing.*

Addy held her mother's hand. It was all she could do, as Bernadette seemed to be in another world, a world of sadness.

Miss Gibbs went about preparing the drinks in the kitchen, while admitting to herself: *How stunningly beautiful Bernadette and her daughter are. They look so exotic. How intriguing, Hawaii, of all places.* Marjorie carried the drinks into the sitting room.

"Thank you, Miss Gibbs." Addy said politely, as she took the glass of lemonade carefully from the tray.

"That's okay, Addy," replied Marjorie, smiling at Bernadette and handing her the brandy in a fine crystal glass.

Bernadette drank it quickly and asked bluntly, "When will Jonathon return?"

"He should be home tomorrow afternoon, Mrs Watt."

"Do you know how Mrs Darcy died?" Bernadette's questions were fired rather than asked. Suddenly, she realised how she was speaking to the young woman.

"Please forgive my rudeness, Miss Gibb. It's just the shock of it all."

Marjorie replied, "No, please forgive me, Mrs Watt. I should have sat you down before telling you. I should have broken the news gently and not while you were standing at the front door. I am so sorry." Marjorie then went on to tell Bernadette all of what she knew, which was quite a bit more than what was written in the newspapers at the time.

Many more questions from Bernadette and answers from Marjorie continued for some time, before Bernadette reminisced about Sally. Their years spent in friendship and of how she'd helped Sally after Jonathon found her near to death. Bernadette appreciated the young woman's quiet attention to her stories and her seemingly genuine compassion. Sitting on the floor beside her mother, Addy took it all in.

Marjorie continued, "Hundreds of people went to Mrs Darcy's funeral. It was so sad, with the baby and all."

Bernadette shook her head, still thinking it to be an almost unbelievable tragedy. They sat in silence for a while. Then, unable to keep her opinion to herself any longer, Miss Gibbs had to tell them.

"If you don't mind me saying so, I think you are the most beautiful woman, Mrs Watt, and you, Addy, are the prettiest little girl I have ever seen." She blushed. "Could you please tell me what it's like? Hawaii, I mean?"

Bernadette smiled, "Thank you for the compliments, Miss Gibbs."

Then, with a faraway look in her eyes, she said, "Hawaii is peaceful, beautiful, it's my home. I love Hawaii and my people." But with harsh reality quickly taking over, Bernadette felt she had to leave. "I'm so sorry, Miss Gibbs, I'm unable to talk any more, but I've enjoyed your company. I must return to the city now as I have a friend waiting for me."

Bernadette stood and looked into Marjorie's kind, hazel eyes. Taking her hand, she confided, "It all makes sense now, about Sally I mean, having an older son in an orphanage. Many times I thought she held a deep sadness in her heart, not just her mother dying. It was something much deeper. It seems now her story was so heart wrenching that she couldn't divulge it to anyone. It's such a shame. I would have helped Sally. I loved her very much." Bernadette's eyes welled with tears.

"Thank you again, Miss Gibbs. Goodbye. I've no doubt we'll meet again under happier circumstances." Kissing each other on the cheek and feeling the dampness of each other's tears, they bade farewell. Bernadette had hired a coachman who by now had waited patiently outside for nearly two hours. Pleased to see them walking towards him, he jumped down and helped them on board. Soon, they were with Barney at their hotel, and Addy spoke openly again.

"I know you're sad, Mummy. You must have loved Sally very much."

"Yes, I did love Sally a great deal, Addy. I wrote to her every month and told her everything about our lives in Hawaii. She also wrote to me every month. Do you remember me showing you the letters from Sally that came all the way from Australia?"

"Yes, I do. They had red and black stamps on them. You told me they should have kangaroos on them, to show everyone they were from Australia, not England."

Bernadette smiled. "Yes, I remember, and one day I'm sure they will. Well, anyway, Addy, Sally was my beautiful young friend and she has now gone to Heaven."

"I'm sad too, Mummy, and I'd like to meet Angus and Patrick and tell them I feel so very sorry for them both, and Mr Darcy too." Addy slipped her small hand into her mother's.

"You will, my love. They'll be coming home tomorrow. We'll meet them then." Bernadette sobbed as Barney rocked her back and forth, Addy began to cry too, feeling her mother's heart break. After some time and through sheer exhaustion, Bernadette's grief had lost its intensity.

Barney asked, "Can you help me take Mummy's dress off, Addy? Then we'll tuck her into bed."

"Yes, Barney," Addy said with a whimper. She then bustled about, doing things for her mother, while confiding in Barney, "I've changed my mind about being a sailor, Barney." With a determined look, she declared, "I'm going to be a doctor when I grow up, so I can save all the sick people. I don't like seeing Mummy cry. If this is what happens, when the people you love, die, well, I just don't want anyone to die!"

Addy then kissed Bernadette on the cheek. "Sweet dreams, Mummy."

Enjoying the luxury of eating dinner in their hotel room, and then having their first good night's sleep after being on the ship for so long, Addy woke first to the sound of heavy rain beating on the tin roof. She slithered out of her mother's bed, tiptoed across the floor, and whispered to Barney, "Are you awake, Barney? Mummy's still asleep and I'm hungry."

"No, I'm not asleep, Addy," Bernadette broke in.

Addy ran and climbed back into bed with her. "Are you feeling better, Mummy?"

"Yes, my lovely, beautiful, gorgeous child."

As Addy snuggled in, Bernadette began tickling her until, between peals of laughter, Addy begged her mother to stop.

"That's what I like to see, everyone happy." Barney beamed, stretching and trying to get over his uncomfortable night on the couch.

"Poor Barney, I'm sorry to have been such a burden. You should have left and slept in your own room." Bernadette rose and hugged him. "Now I need you to do me another favour, Barney. I'd like you to come to the boarding house with me this morning and meet Colleen." She kissed him on the cheek.

"I really need your support, Barney, as this, too, will be a sad day. But I promise I'm over the worst of it. I was suffering from the shock of it all yesterday. I'll be sad for some time, I know, but I feel I'll be able to cope better if you come with me. You will come with me, won't you?"

In a voice only Bernadette could hear, he said. "To the end of the earth, if need be, my love."

After kissing her hand, he smiled broadly at Addy. "And you, Miss Adelaide, if it stops raining this afternoon, I shall take you out sightseeing." In a very posh voice, he continued, "What do you say, Miss Adelaide, would you care to visit the Adelaide parklands and feed the black swans?"

Giggling, Addy returned in the same manner. "Of course, Mr Barnaby, I would be delighted to join you for a stroll in the park."

Walking in the rain never bothered Bernadette, in fact, it was one of her favourite things to do in Hawaii. However, on this day they borrowed a large black umbrella from the concierge before they left the hotel. Addy thought it wonderful, as she'd never walked under such a thing. In Hawaii, nobody cared about the rain and certainly never used an umbrella. They clung together, walking the short distance from the hotel to the boarding house, although Addy wanted to keep walking under the "black cloud", as she called it.

Bernadette knocked tentatively and Colleen opened the door, her eyes wide open in disbelief. She blinked rapidly a few times before throwing her arms out. Barney collapsed the umbrella and shook the water off before Colleen, without a word spoken, ushered the three inside. She then managed to speak through her sadness and tears.

"There are so many things to talk about, so many things."

Embracing Colleen, Bernadette murmured, "I know Colleen. There, there. Time will heal." After Bernadette introduced Addy and Barney to Colleen, Barney peered through the window and noticed the sun was out and shining bright.

"It seems the weather has finally cleared, Addy. Would you care to take me up on my promise?"

They left and Bernadette then led Colleen to the couch. "Now, you sit here, Colleen, I'll put the kettle on." Bernadette found Bob sitting at the kitchen table talking to a man, aged perhaps in his late fifties, with greying, blond hair. They immediately stood and Bob introduced him. "This is Ted Smith, Bernadette. Sally's uncle."

Bernadette was slightly taken back. However, she managed a smile and shook his hand. Ted inclined his head, before explaining things to Bernadette. "I'd come to Adelaide to surprise Sally. It seems I'm too late. I'm finding it hard to believe that after all the letters I wrote, promising Sally I'd visit and when I finally got a chance, well, she's gone." He hung his head and blinked away a tear, then looked up. "Paul always told me what a lovely, young woman Sally was. He also told me about the sad life she'd led, until she'd met with all of you wonderful people." Ted's eyes welled with tears again.

Bernadette wanted to hug him, but considering they were practically strangers, she chose instead to speak on a more positive note. "I believe you have a grandson, Ted, named after my late husband?"

"Oh, yes!" This triggered the response Bernadette wanted from him. He laughed through his tears. "He's a real little tiger, that Jum. He keeps us all busy. Mildred said they named our little Jum well, because your husband was a whirlwind, too. I'm so sorry you lost him because he sounds like a great bloke. By the way, Mildred's pregnant again. That's the reason they didn't come with me."

The kettle began to boil and Bob, who'd kept silent until now, gently placed the best china cups on their saucers, and turned to Bernadette. "You go and talk to the missus, Bernadette. I'll bring the tea and cake in to you."

"I will, thank you, Bob." She then turned her attention back to Ted. "I would really love to talk with you further, Ted? Are you staying here or somewhere else in town?"

"I'll be staying here tonight then at the Graziers Club tomorrow night. I'll be on my way home to Sydney the next day."

"Well, maybe we can talk later. I'll try and calm Colleen down."

Ted smiled, nodding, "I'd like that."

175

Many happy memories of shared times soothed the sorrowful women as they sipped on their tea. The men had stayed in the kitchen and left the ladies to their mourning. However, after some time, the women's laughter brought Bob into the sitting room. With great relief, he exclaimed, "I haven't heard you laugh like that since before the funeral, my dear. It sounds so good. Could us blokes have a listen to what you're laughing about? Come in, Ted, the ladies have some funny stories they want to tell," Bob called out.

Ted's spirits also lifted when he heard about the many happy moments they'd shared as a close group. When the laughter slowly faded, they sat smiling, remembering the beautiful spirit Sally was and, of course, the larger-than-life character of Jum Watt.

Bernadette thought it appropriate to drink a toast. "I know the Irish celebrate the life of their loved ones, rather than mourn their death. I truly believe this is the way it should be. We were all lucky enough to be able to help Sally and be a part of Jum's love and generosity. Sally's life, up until she met with us, must have been miserable, except for being with her darling mother."

Bernadette turned to Ted. "Your sister, Ted, and what heartbreak you must have felt. Sometimes this can be a cruel world, but Sally, and you, rose above your misery and created lives full of love and faith." Bernadette raised her eyes to the freshly painted ceiling and remarked, "I trust Sally's faith has been fulfilled and she is now in Heaven smiling down upon us." Turning to Bob, she asked, "Bob, if you would be so kind as to share your best whisky, we'll have a drink to the memory of two great people—Sally and Jum."

Bob sprang out of his chair and unlocked the cabinet which held his finest whisky. Together they raised their glasses and drank a toast. "Cheers! Here's to the human tornado Jum—and to our beautiful Sally!"

Meanwhile, Addy and Barney were walking through the parklands where raindrops glistened on grass. "Why is the grass so brown here, Barney?"

Barney's thoughts had drifted back to Hawaii and how he missed it. Maybe it was because he felt he'd entered into Jum's territory here. It gave him a sense of uneasiness. He took a moment to answer. "Well, my dear Addy, Australia is a very dry continent."

Once again he was mindful of Hawaii and how green it was.

"What does that mean, 'con-ti-nent', Barney?"

"Australia is a big island with some islands a bit away from it, one of which is Tasmania. Australia is called a continent because of its massive size. Australia is also very dry, so most of the time the grass is brown because it needs rain. Tomorrow, you'll see the grass will turn green because it's rained today."

As Barney went on to explain many things about Australia, Addy listened while they sat watching the black swans glide around the lake. After being satisfied with his teachings, she asked, "Barney, can I go and feed the swans now?"

"Of course, Addy, just don't go too close to the edge of the lake."

This gave Barney time to think of what he was heading into. He was reluctant about going to Bulkawa, or "Jum's territory" he called it and he was trying hard to find a reason to change his mind. *I should be strong and just say no, even though on many occasions, I've told Bernadette, I would follow her to the ends of the earth. But going to Bulkawa is certainly pushing the limits. I'd feel an intruder. When I'm in Hawaii with her, it's so different. I think it's because it's a place Jum had never been to.*

Addy tugged on his hand. "Barney, I'm hungry. Can we go now?"

He smiled, "Yes, of course, silly me, it's lunchtime. Let's have a treat, shall we, Addy? We'll have lunch in a café before we return to Mummy."

Later, the sound of laughter rocked the boarding house just as Barney knocked at the front door. He raised an eyebrow towards Addy then when Bob opened the door, Barney said, "Well, this sounds much better. Celebrating life, are we?"

Bob laughed, "Yes, that's right, Barney. I'm sorry we didn't meet before. I'm Bob, Colleen's hubby." He shook Barney's hand. "We were just about to drink our fifth toast to our dear departed loved ones."

Removing his panama hat, Barney asked, "Do you mind if I join you, Bob?"

"I'd expect you to, Barney, come in." Bob poured a generous slurp of Chivas Regal into a fine crystal glass and handed it to Barney. "Cheers!"

Colleen, after sculling her sixth whisky, attempted to lift her hefty frame off the settee where she'd been sitting for some hours. It took Barney and Ted's combined effort to pull her up onto her unsteady feet. "I'll jus' be gettin' us all somethin' t' eat, t' soak up summa tha' alcohol," Colleen announced in an almost drunken stupor.

Bernadette swayed into the kitchen after her. "I think we should just make sandwiches, Colleen, we may be too drunk to cook, and we may burn the house down!" Bernadette thought her own suggestion hilarious and leaned on the kitchen table to stop from falling over, laughing. After an inebriated effort, the women produced an abundance of sandwiches: lamb with chutney, and cheese with pickle. They sat them on a large China-blue platter in the middle of the kitchen table, and Colleen called out, "Come 'n help y'selves, everyone!"

With their hunger sated, Bernadette asked, "Will you come with me tomorrow, Colleen, to meet Jonathon and the boys?"

Addy jumped in, "Don't forget me, Mummy. I want to meet the boys."

"Of course, you'll come with us, Addy. I think Barney has business to attend to tomorrow, so it will be just us girls." Bernadette held Colleen's hand, "I think it was best we didn't go today, Colleen. Let the boys settle in, although I think Jonathon's going to need our support, as well as the boys. I'm looking forward to seeing them, especially Patrick. How sad and difficult it must have been for Sally, to keep him a secret. Not to mention what Patrick must be going through. We must help in every way we can."

"Of course, we all will," offered Colleen. The men nodded their agreement.

Chapter 22

Jonathon

When Jonathon had finally pulled the horses up at the orphanage, the air seemed harder to breathe, dust lined his throat and sweat beaded his brow. He slid listlessly from his buggy and dragged his feet along the path to the front door. Lifting the door knocker, he leant against the cool stone wall, remembering how he'd felt when he was last there; tired, and an emotional wreck after Sally's death. But he felt differently today. Jonathon now accepted the fact that he was very ill and he feared, like Sally had, that he was about to put his family in jeopardy. Only now in this moment could he understand the guilt she must have felt, not only through endangering the health of her family, but perhaps denying them a parent.

Jonathon needed desperately to see Angus and yes, of course, Patrick. This was his overriding motivation, the passionate desire to see his boys. "If anything happens to me, I know Mother Matilda will help the boys," he said in an effort to assuage his guilt. "It can't be tuberculosis, please don't let it be. It's just that I'm so tired."

The door finally opened. "Yes? May I help you, sir?" Betty asked brightly, not recognising Jonathon at first. She then gasped at his state, and she guided him inside immediately. "Are you alright, Mr Darcy? You don't look well at all."

Jonathon coughed weakly. "Yes, I'll be fine, thank you, Betty. I'm just a little weary from the trip. May I have some water, please? And my horses must be tended." Jonathon heaved and coughed as Betty helped him into the dining room, sitting him down on a comfortable chair. She then ran to find Mother Matilda.

Jonathon threw his head back, trying to quell the nagging cough, mindful once again of what he might be doing by coming here; he knew very well there could be grave consequences. "May God forgive me," he said aloud, as Mother Matilda walked into the room. She went to him and felt his forehead, also taking note of his harsh cough.

"Betty, please fetch some water for Mr Darcy and then ask Patrick t' tend t' Mr Darcy's horses. He's then to ride with haste to Dr Liu and ask him t' please come straight away!" Her tone was urgent.

Betty hurried from the room, returned with the water and ran off again to find Patrick. Patrick and Angus were in the games room, vowing one day they would both be soldiers. To prove their bravery, they'd made a small cut on their fingers and pressed them bloodied together, promising their undying loyalty. Betty stood at the door horrified.

"What in the name of God...?" She started, and then realised it was not the time to reprimand them. Regaining her composure, she spoke calmly, "Patrick, Mother Matilda wants you to ride to town and fetch Dr Liu quickly. But first you must tend to Mr Darcy's horses."

Angus jumped up and Betty held him back. "I'm sorry, Angus, you must stay here until you tidy up your play things. But wash your hands first." Then she added in a more sympathetic tone, "Yes, Angus, your father is here but he's not well, so you must stay calm and wear this mask before you go downstairs to say hello."

The blackest of dread hit Angus's heart. He knew what was about to happen. Without speaking, he quickly picked up the toys. As Betty watched him, she wondered, *how many times do we have to go through the agony of losing the ones we love? It's not fair, it's just not fair!* Angry at God perhaps, though she did not mention His name.

Angus reached for Betty's hand after she'd tied a cloth mask around his face. Jonathon had not moved. His legs stretched out in front of him and his head lay back, trying to ease the constant coughing. Tears of remorse ran down his face, feeling bereft at the thought he may be leaving Angus and Patrick without a father. He wouldn't see them grow. *This is not how it was supposed to be; so much death in so short a time. I'm going to fight this, I am.*

"Father, I'm here. It's Angus."

Struggling to sit, Jonathon greeted Angus with a weak smile and a joke. "It's a bit early for the mask, Angus, or are you about to rob me?"

Running straight into his father's arms, Angus held on to Jonathon so tightly it brought on another coughing spasm. Unsure of what to do in this moment, Betty took hold of Angus, but the memory of being forcibly removed from her dying mother overwhelmed her.

Matilda's entrance, with wash basin and water in hand, put a stop to Betty's indecision. The look on Matilda's face, when she saw Angus cuddling his father, said it all. She went to Angus and gently but firmly moved him away. Trying then to control her fear and anguish, Matilda said confidently, "Now, Angus, your father will be fine. Dr Liu is on his way here now. I have t' be washin' your Dad's face and hands. He's been on a long dusty journey. You best go with Betty and help her make us a cuppa tea. There's a good boy."

Matilda, angry at herself for not warning Betty to keep Angus well away, even with his mask on, scolded herself. *This has t' be done properly, Matilda. T'ink, woman, t'ink!' I'll tend to Jonathon first and then I'll tell Sister Catherine we'll have to be in quarantine until the crisis has passed.*

Although Patrick didn't like the reason he was galloping his pony, he did love the feeling of freedom. The warm breeze became a wild wind, whipping through his blonde curls as he stretched along Sergeant's neck, urging him on. Patrick imagined he was in the army, charging the enemy. His heart filled with pride for his trusty pony, carrying him through bullets and bayonets, dodging every one. Sadly, the fantasy ended when he skidded his pony to a halt in front of Dr Liu's shack by the creek. Sergeant's sides heaved and his coat was lathered with sweat. As Patrick leapt off Sergeant, he called, "Dr Liu! Dr Liu! Come quick. Dad's very sick and Mother Mat wants you to come. And bring all your medicine. Please hurry!"

Straightening up from tending to his garden, Dr Liu responded, "Which dad? Who dad? You mean Mother Mat-dad… who dad?"

"Angus's dad, Dr Liu, my new dad, Jonathon. Quick, come on, he's really sick!"

"Yes, yes, I come vely quickly." Liu cast his eyes over Sergeant. "You take care of pony. Small drink. No go home so fast." Liu hurried into his house but turned in the doorway. "Patwick, you put horse in cart for me, be much quicker."

Patrick harnessed the horse with the precision and confidence of an adult. He then ran to the creek and filled a bucket of water for Sergeant. "Just a little drink, Sarg, or you'll get a bellyache. We won't have to gallop home so fast. I'll let you decide how fast you want to go." Patrick stroked the pony's neck as he drank. "We'll wait a bit, Sarg. I'll let you get your wind back."

"Yes, you good master, Patwick, very good horseman. See you there." Liu urged his heavy cart horse from a trot into a lumbering canter.

Matilda, after having taken Jonathon's shirt and boots off, lay him down on the floor, placing a pillow under his head. She'd been washing him with cool water to bring his raging temperature down while praying to the Lord for help. During this time Jonathon had become delirious.

"Sally… wait… Sally," he was mumbling, when Dr Liu came into the room.

"I get medicine ready quick, in kitchen. You keep praying, Mudda Mat."

Angus sat at the kitchen table with Betty and Lizzy, with both young women trying their best to comfort him. Betty offered the truth. "It's something all of us must go through, Angus. But some children, like the three of us, have had to bear the most terrible heartbreak of all. It's the worst pain ever to lose a parent." Betty gave him a hug.

"We'll be here for you always, Angus. Lizzy and I will do everything we can. We'll pray every minute of the day for your father to be well."

The door suddenly swung open. "Liu here now. I make your dad better for you, Angus. Yes!" Liu said with conviction.

Angus grinned. "I know you'll help, Dr Liu. May I watch and learn what you're doing with your herbal medicine?"

"Yes, of course, and one day you may help people, just like me. You girls go help Mudda Mat, bring proper bed in room. Close door, write sign 'KEEP OUT'. Room only for Jon, Mudda Mat and me. You put mask on. Only stay one minute, yes?"

"Yes, Doctor."

"You stay help me, Angus. You not be with Dad until medicine work, okay?" Liu regarded him, eyebrows raised.

"I understand," Angus said, stoic in his reply, "Let's begin, Doctor."

Meanwhile, Betty and Lizzy had dragged a wooden bed down the stairs on a carpet mat and slid it into the dining room. Clean sheets and blankets were folded on top. "Do you want me to make the bed, Mother?" Betty asked. "I would really like to stay and help you nurse Mr Darcy."

"If anyone else is going to be stricken, it will be me, Betty. Not you nor anyone else."

Upon seeing the tears in Betty's eyes, she added gently, "I appreciate y' offer, Betty, but I need you and Lizzy t' keep things runnin' with the girls and all. And I'm thinkin' Dr Liu should take the boys t' Da's. He'll look after them for a wee while, until the crisis is over."

Betty returned to the kitchen and kept Angus from following Dr Liu into the sick room.

"No, Angus. You come with me and together we'll write the sign to put on the door, just like Dr Liu said."

Sitting at Mother Matilda's desk, they had full view of the road and the path leading to the front door. When the sign was nearly complete, Angus heard and then saw Patrick trotting Sergeant past. He ran to greet him, while Betty remained gazing out of the window, tears welling once again at the idea of losing Patrick. Maybe forever, if Jonathon survived. The thought that he might not survive gave Betty a momentary glimmer of hope, before she felt ashamed. *It's wicked to think such a terrible thing! How could I be happy knowing Patrick would stay, only because of his father's death?* Placing her hands together, she prayed. "Dear Lord, please forgive me this sinful thought. I wish Mr Darcy to live more than anything. It's just... I love Patrick nearly as much as I do You, Dear Lord. Please forgive me."

Patrick turned when he heard Angus running towards him. "Hey, Angus. Come help me wash Sarg down. He did a great job, you know. He's such a good horse." With Patrick on one side and Angus on the other, they washed Sergeant nice and clean. "You can let him go in the paddock now, Angus, and I'll get his oats. I'll give him a little extra because he's worked so hard."

Angus smiled, proud that Patrick trusted him with Sergeant.

Liu gave Jonathon his oral medicine and then placed acupuncture needles in particular areas of his body. "This helps him be calm and strong to fight illness. Before too long, Jon high temperature drop. I wait—you see."

Mother Matilda's sigh was one of relief. "I'm most grateful t' y', Dr Liu. Once again y've helped us in a time of great need."

All details for the quarantine of the orphanage and Jonathon's care were discussed over dinner. It was also decided that Da would pick up the boys in the morning. Liu would tell him this evening. Matilda had written a letter to Colleen about Jonathon's condition, hoping that it would arrive as quickly as possible. It included the words: *Please don't worry about the boys. They are being taken care of, but please pray for Jonathon.*

Chapter 23

Bulkawa

Bernadette and Colleen sat in the kitchen of the boarding house, devastated by the news. Neither knew what to say or do. Bernadette reached out for Colleen's hand across the kitchen table. "You know, Colleen, we're powerless. There really isn't anything we can do for the time being, apart from informing Marjorie. I'll tell her, and if she feels she needs to find another job, well, of course, then she must. However, I would like her to stay and care for the house and garden. At least until more news comes to us of Jonathon's condition. She seems a lovely young woman, I'm sure she'll oblige. Let's have a cup of tea."

While filling the kettle at the sink, Bernadette glanced over her shoulder at the older woman and smiled, albeit a little tremulously. "You keep your chin up, Colleen. I really like the sound of this Dr Liu and what's even more comforting, Mother Matilda has such great faith in him."

She placed the cups and saucers on the table, making an effort to conceal the tremble of her hand. "Let's be positive, Colleen. As we know, Jonathon's fighting only one condition, tuberculosis. Whereas our dear Sally had heart problems, compounded by losing so much blood in giving birth." She turned the teapot several times then poured. "I have a feeling Jonathon will fight hard and win this battle," Bernadette said with more confidence than she felt.

"Yes, Bernadette, I'm sure you're right—but those poor boys!" Colleen sighed heavily and they drank in silence, lost in thought.

"You know, Colleen, I'm not sure if Barney is looking forward to staying at Bulkawa. He's fallen in love with Hawaii. He'd return tomorrow if he could."

After saying that, Bernadette became wistful, thinking about their carefree life in Hawaii, but she soon shook herself back into the present. "Of course, Addy's very excited about going to the property. She loves Australia and wants to see everything, including all the different wildlife. There's plenty of that on Bulkawa," Bernadette said with a smile then gazed out the window, contemplating.

"Maybe I'm being a little unfair, insisting Barney comes to Bulkawa, but we're heading in the right direction. We can board a carriage from there to Sydney and then board the train to Queensland. We need to inspect our plantations."

Colleen looked surprised, "Your plantations?" She'd forgotten about them.

"Yes, remember, Colleen? I'm an equal partner with Barney in his tropical fruit business. Jonathon drew up the contract just before we'd left Hawaii. We signed it yesterday and, I must say, Jonathon's new partner is a fine young man and seems to be running things extremely well." She thought for a moment. "I should go and tell Phillip the news. Actually, I'd better go now. I have so much to organise before tomorrow."

Bernadette walked around the table to put her hand on Colleen's shoulder. "Together we'll help the boys and Jonathon, Colleen. I'll be away only six weeks, including our quick trip to Queensland. You could telegram me at Bulkawa and let me know before the end of the week if you need me. I'll just need to know before we leave for Queensland, although I'm sure Barney's quite capable of going on his own this time. If that's the case I could come back to Adelaide."

Colleen patted Bernadette's hand. "Well, as y' say, Bernadette, we can only pray and keep in touch with Mother Matilda." She looked up into Bernadette's eyes.

"My dear Bernadette, you're like a daughter t' me, the same as our dear Sally was. And of course, Angus has already adopted Bob and me as his grandparents." She managed a giggle. "I suppose that'll include Patrick too. And now Addy as well. Oh my, but Bob and me are goin' t' be busy!"

Thankful she was on her own, Bernadette was able to go quickly about finishing her business before they had to leave in the morning.

Barney had offered to take Addy to the park again. Every Friday an elderly man came to give pony rides to the children, costing only tuppence. "I'm going to have to go to the bank for more funds, Addy, if you don't hop off the pony. I've run out of money."

It was not very often Addy disobeyed. However, ponies had become her passion ever since Barney bought her a velvet horse that she named Sailor. They were inseparable, and now Addy wanted to ride the real thing—all day. Barney didn't mind really. He sat and thought of how tired he was of the Graziers Club and all the big notes. But never the less, Barney tried to pry Addy's hands from the reins.

"Now, be fair, Addy, the sun's going down, the pony's tired and so is Mr Plumb. Give the pony a pat and thank him for the ride."

"Do you think I'll have my own pony when we go to Bulkawa, Barney?"

"We'll see tomorrow. Maybe Mummy has a surprise for you."

Addy's brown eyes widened. "Oh, Barney what colour is it? Is it a boy or a girl? What does it look like? Oh, I can't wait!" She jumped into his arms.

He laughed. "Don't tell your mother I told you. You must keep it a secret. Act surprised, or I'll be in big trouble. I'm not going to tell you any more about it, so don't bother asking, young lady," Barney said, wagging his finger with mock severity.

The following morning Addy was first up, dressed and waiting. "Hurry up, Mummy! I can't wait, I'm so excited we're going to the farm. Come on!" She tugged at the blankets covering Bernadette, who would have preferred another hour of sleep.

"Alright, Addy, but first you must eat some breakfast." The breakfast tray, laden with fruit, eggs, bacon, bread, jam and coffee, had been delivered to their room some minutes earlier, giving Bernadette a few moments longer to linger in bed.

"Anyway," she added sleepily, "we can't leave without Barney."

"No, of course not, Mummy, he's really my daddy now, isn't he?"

"Yes, he is and one day soon, Barney will legally adopt you as his daughter, because we have decided to be married. Would you like that, Addy?"

"Oh! Yes!" Addy jumped on the bed and threw her arms around her mother's neck, her dark velvety hair obscuring her mother's face. She then sat back and asked, "Will you have another baby, Mummy?"

At this, Bernadette sat up, a little shocked. "Mummy's getting a little too old to have another baby, Addy. Would you be upset if I didn't?"

Addy considered for a moment. "No, but it would be good to have someone to play with like I play with my friends in Hawaii, especially Billy." She hung her head sombrely.

"Are you missing Hawaii, Addy?" Bernadette asked gently.

"Yes, I am, but I miss Billy more."

Holding her close, Bernadette rocked her back and forth, thinking how she also missed her homeland and the laughter of the two children running and playing along the sand. A knock on the door broke their reverie.

"Come in!" Bernadette was never one to wait upon formalities, or care if she were dressed, looking her best for visitors.

Barney opened the door. "Good morning, my beautiful girls! Are we ready for our journey?" He tried to maintain a light-hearted mood when, in fact, he knew he was going to resent every minute of being at Bulkawa. He felt something was telling him—even warning him—not to go, but he kept assuring himself it was nonsense. There was really nothing to be concerned about.

Dan and Mary had been happily living in the spacious homestead at Bulkawa where, of course, Bernadette had not been since her marriage to Jum. Therefore, her coming home was indeed a very special occasion. The home had been spring cleaned, the gardens manicured to perfection, and Frieda, the cook, was overwhelmed with excitement. She'd been trying out new recipes, sewing new aprons and had polished the silver until it gleamed. Privately, she thought it strange for Bernadette to be bringing Barnaby Stuart to stay, but she shrugged it off. Life had to go on.

When he was alive, Jum's presence at Bulkawa was overwhelming. Now after his death, his lesser presence had not disappeared, it seemed. Each person there had become accustomed to Jum's "ghost" in his or her own way. Dan and Mary's three-year-old son, Billy, was frequently seen talking and laughing into space. For some time, they suspected he had an imaginary friend, which was most understandable, as he was an only child. Curious, Dan asked him, "Who is it you talk to, Billy, and what does he look like?"

"He's a big man, Daddy. He's nice and laughs a lot, and his name's Jim."

"Jesus, I'm not imagining it then," Dan muttered to himself. He'd swear he had heard Jum's voice many times when out mustering—"Go left, mate. They're over there, Dan." And Jum's "ghost" was always right. Dan would find the lone steer in a gully, or a stray sheep lying behind a clump of saltbush. Then there was a memorable time when Billy had climbed out of his cot and had gone tracking across the garden toward the dam. Dan had, for no apparent reason, a feeling there'd been a warning; yes, an urgency to return to the homestead. He galloped his horse back, still wondering why he was doing so, until he saw Billy about to step into the dam. Where did that warning come from? *I know it was Jum.*

Around the dinner table that same evening, he'd asked off-handedly, "Has anyone else, apart from me and Billy, seen or heard Jum lately?"

Frieda gasped and dropped her fork, her face ashen. "I thought it was only me and m' imagination."

Mary joined in. "I've been in Jum's office many times and I've seen his chair move." She looked from Dan to Frieda. "One day I'm sure I actually saw him. He smiled at me and then sort of faded away. But I never felt scared," she added.

"Me neither," said Frieda.

"Well," Dan said light-heartedly, "you'd better set another place at the dinner table from now on, Frieda. It seems we've ignored our dear friend." Dan made an expansive gesture towards an empty chair. "Come on, Jum, have a seat, mate!" The moment the words left his mouth, the vacant chair moved out. Dan was the only one who didn't jump with fright. Mary half-stood, preparing to run. The four jackaroos, spruced up as usual for the evening meal, stood with uncertain

187

expressions on their faces, Moments later, Dan's laughter exploded, "That was me! I moved the chair with my foot!"

They all stared blankly at Dan, not remotely amused by his prank. Still chuckling, Dan gave an order, "Sit down, y' silly buggers. Jum won't hurt you! Let's welcome him. It seems he doesn't want to leave us just yet. Maybe he's just waiting around to see Bernadette?" Dan raised his wine glass. "Let's drink a toast. Here's to Jum and Bernadette!"

Dan's hand suddenly trembled and the red wine spilled. He forced a smile, knowing he had absolutely no control over the glass. He knew Jum was telling him to "pull his head in", just as he had on so many occasions. "Well," Dan said, "it seems I've had enough to drink already. I'm sorry, Frieda, I've ruined your tablecloth."

"Oh, don't be silly, Dan! I'll have it out in the mornin' after a soak in the tub with bicarb."

Mary was anxious to change the subject, as it seemed now she would have to accept Jum's presence, even if it wasn't in a physical form. She then turned her attention to Marcus, the latest jackaroo Dan had employed. "I'm so glad your sister Rose is coming to help with the bookwork, Marcus. It's been a very sad time with Sally passing away and, of course, losing Jonathon's company for a while. He's had so much to deal with lately, the poor man."

Before Marcus could reply, Mary turned to Dan. "That reminds me, Dan. There's a letter addressed to you on the desk; it's from Mrs Thompson. Don't you think you should open it before you go to bed? It's been sitting there for some days now."

"Yes, of course, Mary, I've been so busy sprucing up the place, I haven't had time to open the mail."

With the conversation no longer about Jum, the diners continued with small talk about the stock and the weather. After they'd said goodnight to each other, Dan went to the office to read the letter. With no sign of Jum anywhere, he sat safely in Jum's leather chair and tore open the envelope. "Bloody hell," Dan swore after he'd read the bad news. He rose from the chair and called down the hall to Mary. She came quick, still holding a tea towel.

"What's wrong, Dan?"

"Come in. Sit down, Mary. I've got some really bad news. Jonathon's held up sick at the orphanage. It seems he has tuberculosis." Dan buried his face in his hands and Mary rose from her chair to put her arm around him.

"I'm so sorry, Dan. It's been one terrible thing after the other. We'll pray every day for Jonathon's recovery." She squeezed his shoulder. "I'll go get us a brandy, dear, to help calm the nerves."

Dan broke down and wept. "Too much bloody sadness for those poor little fellas. How will they ever cope, especially Angus?"

Mary returned with two generous measures of brandy. Normally she'd disapprove of his drinking hard liquor. Dan, it seemed, behaved much better on beer or wine. But just one glass of brandy before going to bed, Mary thought, would help them both sleep. He held the glass up to her after gulping it down. "Please, Mary, just one more? Then we'll go to bed."

She smiled and conceded.

While travelling to Bulkawa in their hired coach, Bernadette felt it an ideal opportunity to give Barney a detailed description of the property and the amazing homestead. "You'll love the home, Barney. It's surrounded by wide verandas. It's so wonderful to sit there, just admiring the scenery. The home has eight large bedrooms, four bathrooms, a grand dining room and a ballroom, where Mr and Mrs Watt held the most extravagant evenings with music and dancing. Two large offices are decked out exactly the same, with beautifully crafted timber furniture and leather chairs. Shelves filled with leather-bound books line all four walls. And an enormous, cowhide rug is a feature on the floor," Bernadette said with some pride.

"The elder Mrs Watt chose to keep the décor in her office the same, as it gave her a feeling of power, or at least that's what old Mr Watt used to say, apparently." Bernadette paused a moment to see if they were as interested as she was. They smiled and she continued. "The different wallpapers for the homestead were chosen by Mrs Watt, through a European mail order catalogue. Each bedroom evokes a different country, which makes the home extremely interesting and all the guests seem to look forward to being transported to another country on each visit."

Bernadette saddened when she said, "Sally and Jonathon spent their nuptials in the 'French Royale' room." She blinked away a tear. "Mrs Watt also created a Hawaiian theme in the sunniest, north-facing bedroom. She had an artist paint palm trees and tropical plants on the walls. Bamboo furniture and shutters on the windows complete the illusion of being in Hawaii." Stating both facts brought on melancholy, so the tour ventured outside to the paddocks.

"The property covers forty thousand acres and the paddocks closest to the homestead have water bores. There's also an underground spring which Jum turned into a swimming hole. It's not too far away from the homestead—walking distance, in fact. We had our picnics there. Jum always said, 'It's not only for the Bulkawa residents, but also our neighbours. This underground spring is very rare, especially in this part of the land, so I make sure we can all enjoy it.' There's a diving board and a lovely garden surrounding it. It's like a secret oasis in the desert."

Bernadette then remembered, "Oh yes, our neighbours on both sides built a fire pit, in appreciation of Jum's generosity and hospitality. Of course, this meant we had many a good time with our friends. We each took it in turns to donate a beast for cooking and we really enjoyed those homemade beer competitions. One could only imagine the fun!"

She looked at the strain on Barney's face, but chose not to comment. "I think we should rise above our recent sadness and invite the neighbours to join us at the waterhole for a barbeque in memory of Jum." She put on a Mona Lisa smile before looking out the window.

This all sounded wonderful to Barney. However, he wanted no part of it. Already he felt the need to turn back to Adelaide. Addy listened to every word her mother had said. Barney sat in silence and although he'd tried to look interested, he was actually kicking himself for his weakness in agreeing to come here.

"Here we are!" Bernadette announced, as they entered the avenue of silver birch trees, all standing over sixty feet tall. Golden leaves fluttered like confetti on and all around the coach. Recent autumn rain had also been kind. Swathes of late summer grass still covered the sometimes-parched earth.

Addy giggled, her face tickled by the leaves, after she'd poked her head through the window when seeing a kangaroo hop by. "Look, Mummy, I've seen ten kangaroos now. And she's got a baby popping out of her tummy, so I've seen eleven."

This delightful child would forever save Barney from taking life too seriously. "Haven't you forgotten the grandmother, Addy, and there must be a father, so that's thirteen. Oh yes, there must be an uncle and an aunty so that makes fifteen."

Addy giggled. "You're funny, Barney."

Entering the gardens surrounding the homestead, Bernadette noticed a new railed paddock with a wooden shelter. Dan had written to her, saying he needed to build a shelter. It was to house two ponies. Dan had timed their breeding to perfection, as he wanted the ponies old enough and well trained by the time his son, Billy, and Addy were ready to begin riding.

"They're calm enough for any small child to ride," Dan had told Mary earlier, when she'd watched her son being led around the garden by his proud father.

Addy spotted the ponies grazing. "Mummy, look! Barney, are they my ponies?"

Bernadette looked at him accusingly. "You didn't tell her, did you, Barney?"

"Well, not exactly. I just said you may have a surprise for her."

"You're partners in crime, you know that?" She turned to Addy. "It was supposed to be a surprise, Addy, but yes, one is yours. The other pony is Billy's."

"My Billy?"

"No, darling, Dan's little boy's name is Billy, too."

190

"Oh," she said, momentarily disappointed, then looked up at her mother with a cheeky smile. "I'll just have to be happy with my pony then!"

A few minutes earlier, Bluey, the Aboriginal stockman had told Dan, "They be comin' now, boss." He could feel the vibrations of the coach with his bare feet, all within a mile radius, it seemed.

The troop had lined up.

Bernadette was the first to step from the carriage. Brushing down her long skirt, she then looked up to see Frieda with her hands over her mouth, and obviously trying to hold back tears. Bernadette understood. She embraced her and then shared Frieda's bottled up grief.

Barney stood with Addy in his arms, before placing her down, so as to be formally introduced to the line-up. Finally, there was Dan, who shook Barney's hand, then Bernadette's.

"You'll meet the new jackaroos tonight at dinner, Mrs Watt. We've also got three Aboriginal families working here now. They're living down by the creek and, of course, you know Pete, the blacksmith, and the gardeners, Wang and Chong. They'll come over soon and give you their welcome gifts. We've had a reasonable season, so things have been made a little easier. Plenty of time to celebrate your visit," Dan said with a friendly smile. He then looked down, "And who do we have here? It can't be baby Adelaide!"

Addy's smile was confident. "Everyone calls me Addy. I like it a lot better than Adelaide and I'm grown up now. I'm five. Can you please show me my pony, Dan? I would really, really like to ride him now."

Dan looked to Bernadette for approval.

"No, not now, Dan," she looked down to Addy. "After we unpack and settle in, Addy, then you can go meet your girl pony. Billy has the boy pony. You can ride tomorrow when we're all rested from the trip."

Addy, obedient as usual but a little reluctantly, said, "Yes, Mummy."

However, she would have loved to have kicked up a fuss—stamp her feet and pout as she had seen other children do. But her nature and breeding determined that she was to do as she was told. Bernadette was of royal lineage in Hawaii, not just her mother. Addy thought it made it mandatory for her to obey.

Bernadette chose to stay in the Hawaiian room, as she thought it best not to test her emotions by staying in the room she and Jum had shared. Barney, after inspecting every room with interest, chose the one decorated in a Spanish theme. This room intrigued him to the point of taking the red cape from the wall and donning the matador's hat to partake in an imaginary bullfight. He was caught by Addy who giggled then joined him, pretending she was the bull.

"That is what this place needs—more fun and laughter!" Dan exclaimed as he was drawn in by the sounds of merriment. He leant on the doorway and clapped his hands at the performance.

Barney, worn out and breathless, grinned. "How about a beer, Dan? I could sure do with one."

"Bloody oath, I declare the bar open!"

Feeling relaxed after the beer and with his fears of the unknown quashed momentarily, Barney was happy to take Addy to meet her pony.

"She looks like my Sailor, Barney. Can I call her Sailor even though she's a girl?"

Barney tilted his head, overdramatising his thinking, at which Addy became impatient.

"Well, I'm going to anyway, because she looks like him. She has a soft brown coat and black mane and tail."

"You can call her any name you like, Addy. Remember, you said you wanted to be a sailor when you grew up?"

"No, I don't any more, I want to be a doctor. Remember, I told you, Barney. I want to make everyone better." She stood on the fence, feeding the ponies apples. "Sailor's beautiful. I can't wait to ride her tomorrow, Barney."

"I'll ride along with you, Addy. There must be a nice quiet horse I can manage. I'll lead your pony off my horse because you're not quite ready to ride on your own just yet."

"I know, Barney, but you can teach me to ride every day while we're here. You will, won't you, Barney?"

"We'll see. I may have to go to Queensland a little earlier. You can stay here with Mummy. And Dan, I'm sure, will give you riding lessons." He lifted her from the fence.

"That's enough now, Addy. Let's go and get ready for dinner. Apparently, we have to dress up a bit, so you can wear the pretty dress we bought from the department store."

Enjoying some girly fun, Bernadette and Addy began dressing in their best for this special evening. "Thank you," Addy said, looking beyond her reflection in the mirror.

"Why did you say 'thank you'?" Bernadette asked.

"I thought it was Barney standing behind me, Mummy. I thought he said, 'You're beautiful.' I said, 'Thank you' but I looked again and he was gone."

"Well, whoever it was, they're right. You are beautiful, Addy." Bernadette smiled reassuringly, but at the same time, her experience earlier led her to ask herself a serious question about Jum's spiritual presence at Bulkawa. While she'd been relaxing in the bath an hour earlier, thinking of her times spent with Jum in this home, Bernadette suddenly felt his presence. It felt as if Jum were there.

"I'm imagining this," she'd said aloud, shrugging it off, and had closed her eyes, preparing for the feeling to be gone once she opened them. But with her eyes closed, she suddenly felt the sensation of his lips kissing hers. It immediately rekindled the passion for her lover that she thought she would never feel again. His kiss lingered until her loins lifted involuntarily, her longing for him making her ache with pleasure.

"Oh, Jum," she'd whispered huskily. She gasped when feeling the hot waves of pleasure surge again and again, as she writhed and moaned in ecstasy, daring not to open her eyes, for fear he may leave her. She felt insatiable, wanting and needing the thrill of their mutual desire, every nerve in her body had tuned to his touch. She'd felt his strong hands slide over the fullness of her breasts, his mouth tantalising her nipples and had heard his whispered words of love. She couldn't help but cry out with the pleasure it had brought.

Addy, in that moment, had knocked on the door. "Are you alright, Mummy?"

Bernadette sat up, startled and somewhat embarrassed at having made love with a ghost. "I'm going mad," she said before pulling herself up from the tub. "Yes, Addy, yes, I'm fine. I just stubbed my toe." She found it impossible to wipe the smile from her face.

Bernadette now sat on her bed, staring blankly out of the window, not even noticing the magnificent glow of the sunset.

"Are you alright, Mummy? What are you thinking?"

The question brought her back into the moment. "Oh nothing, my dear, darling child. Let's go down to dinner. Mary's parents will be joining us this evening. It will be nice to see them again. Maybe we can ask them to help us organise a barbeque down by the swimming hole. We'll invite all the neighbours. What do you say, Addy? Would that be fun?"

"Can my pony come too?"

Mary's parents, Jack and Christine, were wonderful company and seemed extremely happy with their son-in-law. Of course, they adored their grandson, Billy, and hinted he needed a sister or a brother to play with. It didn't really matter as long as it was as healthy and robust as Billy.

Barnaby was enjoying the various conversations, ranging from his, or their, tropical fruit business, to politics and how a newly formed Liberal Party was becoming stronger in its force to take over the United Australia Party. Both parties sat to the Right in politics. All agreed that the Liberals should be the one to govern this now free society. Normally, politics was a taboo subject at dinner parties, however, after it seemed they had all agreed on the same principles, that particular conversation was short-lived.

Bernadette then held a captive audience after Mary had asked her to explain what life was like in Hawaii. She went on to paint an alluring picture, almost swaying as she described the soft salty breezes central to her warm carefree existence in her homeland.

Barnaby sat head in hand, forgetting his manners and leaning his elbow on the table, transfixed by Bernadette. Her voice was music to his ears, transporting him back to his adopted homeland.

"Oh, my goodness, it sounds so wonderful, Bernadette! I think we should all sail to Hawaii tomorrow and stay all winter. When are you returning, Bernadette?" Christine was ready to pack her bags.

"I would love you to come and visit us, Christine. We'll be returning in eight weeks' time, although it may be longer if I'm needed to help Jonathon."

A silence descended with the sobering thought of Jonathon's fight with tuberculosis. Then Bernadette continued with some good news. "However, I believe the shipping companies will soon have steamships ready for the journey. After our last experience on the sailing ship, I'm sure it would be much safer. But, in saying that, we did all survive one of the most ferocious storms I have ever experienced."

She noticed the nervous expressions on everyone's faces at the mention of this and so added quickly, "But usually it's smooth sailing all the way—and lots of fun." Bernadette went on to amuse them all with stories of the entertainment supplied by the passengers, including her own performance of the hula dance.

Christine was intrigued. "Bernadette, we would love you to show us how you do the hula. Would you please do us the honour?"

"No, I'm sorry, Christine, not tonight, maybe at the barbeque." She smiled coyly, feeling embarrassed she'd even dared tell the story. "That reminds me, I was going to ask for your help, Christine, in rounding up the neighbours to join us for an afternoon around the swimming hole. I think Jum would have loved that. We'll celebrate his life and tell funny stories. We've never really taken the time to do that." She looked at Barney. "I'm sure you will have some stories to tell about Jum, being an old friend of his, Barney?"

Smiling, albeit through gritted teeth, Barney nodded, but was in fact thinking, *What the bloody hell are you trying to do to me, Bernadette? It's not as if we're in a platonic relationship—I'm fucking you. Dammit! You were Jum's wife. Don't you understand?*

Bernadette noticed his cold stare and knew she'd pushed Barney too far and so turned to Christine. "Do you think the barbeque is a good idea, Christine?"

"Of course it is," she replied then looking at her husband, added, "Isn't it, Jack dear?"

"Yes, yes, of course, a great idea! We'll get on to it in the morning. When do you want the barbeque to be, Bernadette? The weather might hot up a little in the next few days. Good weather always makes for a good time, they say, especially at the swimming hole."

Bernadette agreed. "The sooner the better, Jack. We haven't a lot of time to spare, as we're off to Queensland to inspect our plantations in two weeks' time, so how about the Sunday before we leave?"

"No worries at all. I'll pass the word around." Jack raised his glass and everyone followed.

According to tradition, the men took their cigars and pipes, along with a decanter of port, into the smoking room. This evening, the oncoming chill of autumn was kept at bay by the Indian summer night, so the gentlemen chose to sit on the west-side veranda. Heavy bamboo chairs, well furnished with feather cushions, gave them comfort. Jack was the first to take a seat, while all the time covertly studying Barney's faraway look.

"It must be a little hard for you to be here, Barney, with so many memories for Bernadette to cope with. I don't think I'd have the courage to come here, as you have. Mind you, we're enjoying your company and little Addy, of course. She seems to think the world of you." Jack lit his pipe, while settling his body into the ample feather cushions. He'd noticed over dinner that Barney looked more than a little uncomfortable whenever Jum's name was mentioned.

"Yes, I must admit it is difficult, Jack. I'm even thinking I should leave the day after tomorrow." Barney sipped his port, reflecting. "I don't think Bernadette understands how I feel. We were a perfect couple in Hawaii, but this is Jum's place, and I feel like an intruder. Ever since landing in Adelaide I've fought with myself about coming here. I've tried to explain to Bernadette how I feel, but she says I'm just being silly. 'How can a dead man threaten our relationship?' she says."

He stood stargazing, wishing he was looking at them under a Hawaiian sky. "I've promised to take Addy riding tomorrow and I can't let her down." He swilled down the last of his port. "I'll leave on Thursday, Jack."

"I don't blame you, Barney. I think young Dan can tell you a story or two about how our Jum has decided to hang around. He really hasn't left, you know."

"Christ, Jack, we don't want to scare the bejesus out of him!" Dan butted in, then stood to join Barney, leaning on the other side of the veranda post. "Don't worry, Barney. Ghosts can't hurt you, mate." Dan put his arm around the post to tap Barney on the back.

How sick Barney was of the whole thing, sick of his ambivalence. *I've made cut-and-dried decisions all my life and I don't need to be patronised now.*

He voiced his decision again. "I've made up my mind. I'll go alone to Queensland. I think Addy would appreciate it more, being left here to ride her pony, rather than taking the long trip. Bernadette doesn't really need to go with me. I'll meet them both at the dock in eight weeks. I don't mean to be rude, gentlemen, but I'm a little weary so I'll say good night."

The two men watched in silence as Barney disappeared through the doorway. Jack waited until his footsteps had subsided, before speaking in a loud whisper. "I still think he's bloody brave coming here in the first place, Dan. I really like Bernadette, but she seems to have such a strong hold over men. I've never seen such magnetism before in any woman. Not saying she does it on purpose, but by Christ, she's a goddess, a femme fatale, and she must know it. I wish Barney luck in telling her his decision."

"Yes, I agree, Jack, and on that note, I'll bid you goodnight." Dan paused a moment. "You may as well stay here, Jack. It's getting late and you know how Christine loves to sleep in the French Royale room." Dan gave him a conspiratorial wink and a fake punch on the arm as he walked passed.

The ladies had begun to yawn and so chose to retire to their respective bedrooms. Christine made her way to the veranda. "Come inside, Jack. We're going to stay the night. It's too late to be hitching up the horses and driving home." The following silence was broken by a girlish giggle.

"And you know how I love my favourite room, *mon chéri!*"

Jack rose slowly from his chair, rolling his eyes. He was not feeling up to any romance this evening, or putting on a French accent, as Christine insisted he do when staying in the *chambre d'amour*. However, he tapped the tobacco from his pipe and replied dutifully, "Yes dear, I know how you love that room. I'll be there directly and I'll then tell you what Napoleon once said to Josephine." He sighed with a knowing smile.

"That bloody rooster!"

As usual, Dan woke an hour before he needed to, because of "the bloody rooster", which avoided being captured every day. It was a rogue, a devil in feathers. "I'm damned sure Jum has something to do with that fuckin' Houdini chook! I'll catch the bloody thing and wring its neck!"

Mary protested. "Oh please, Dan, stop swearing at the poor thing. Can't you just roll over and have a kip?"

"Listen, Mary, if I do, he'll know, and then he'll start crowing again. And when I get up, he'll stop. I'm telling y', Mary, it's Jum who sets him up to it."

Mary smiled, rolled over and lifted the bedclothes up over her head. Dan followed her actions and within ten seconds, the rooster crowed even louder, or was it because it was now sitting on their window ledge?

"That's it! I'm gunna get the gun and shoot the bastard!" Dan hurled the bedclothes back and sprang out of bed. He stormed toward the gun cupboard which was in the office. While fiddling in the drawer for the keys, he heard a man's voice say, *No, don't shoot it, Dan*. He looked around—nobody there.

"Oh, for Chrissake, Jum, you're dead! I hafta run this place on my own now! Don't y' have somewhere else to go—Heaven or somethin'?"

Bernadette opened the office door. "Dan, did I just hear you talking to Jum?"

Dan threw the keys on the desk in anger. "You weren't supposed to hear that, Mrs Watt. I thought I was the only one up."

"Well, tell me. Were you talking to Jum?" She needed to know she wasn't going crazy and that somebody else saw and spoke to him.

"I suppose I was. Everybody does. He's still here, you know, and that bloody rooster! Well, I reckon Jum sets him up as my alarm clock and I don't need to get outta bed that early. I was gettin' a gun to shoot him, but I'm sure it was Jum who just said 'No, don't shoot it, Dan'. What do you reckon, Mrs Watt?" He averted his gaze, scratched his head and waited for her reply.

She smiled wryly. "Well, Dan, if you think Jum's still here and still trying to tell you what to do, then let's show him who the boss is now. Get the gun, Dan, and let's go rooster hunting!"

If it wasn't Dan and Bernadette's laughter chasing the bloody rooster around the garden, it was the missed shots that woke the entire household. Finally, the job was done, and the two assassins finished with a firm handshake.

Breakfast at Bulkawa was deemed a social occasion, especially when guests stayed overnight. They tucked into a full country breakfast of lamb chops, bacon, fried tomatoes and eggs, while sitting on the east veranda, at the later than normal time of ten o'clock.

Barney sat across the table from Addy, smiling, as she was about to devour another serve of pancakes and treacle. "Let's not eat too much, Addy. It's not good for us when we're riding. And don't forget, Frieda's packed us a picnic hamper— a feast fit for a king—and all his men!"

Dan nodded in silent agreement at the abundance of Frieda's packed lunches. "That reminds me," said Dan, "I have to check on the horses."

He excused himself and left to make sure Bluey had the horses tacked up and ready. Addy also excused herself to run after him. Dan turned, waving for her to catch up. "Come on, Addy, keen as mustard, aren't ya? I can't wait for Billy to be old enough to ride out with me."

"Bluey, you got horses ready for Mrs Boss?"

"Yeah, they all saddled 'n' ready."

Sailor greeted Addy with a whinny. After only one meeting, it seemed that the pony knew her. Excited by the "welcome", Addy ran straight at him. Dan's large hand reached out, grabbing the back of her shirt. "Addy, slow down, y' gotta stay calm around horses. They sense everything, you know. If you're frightened, they know it and if you run at them, they run away."

Addy stood listening to Dan's advice, wanting to learn all she could. Dan led Sailor out, placed the reins over his head, and then gave Addy a leg-up. He led the pony across the yard while Bluey followed, leading the black gelding and the dappled grey mare towards the homestead.

Frieda was ready and waiting with the picnic hamper. "I don't know how far y' goin', Addy, but I reckon y'll last a week on this lot if y' get lost."

Anxious to be on her way, Addy asked her, "Where are they, Frieda?"

A moment lapsed before Barney and Bernadette appeared. Bernadette effortlessly mounted the sixteen-hand-high grey mare, after refusing to be legged up by Barney.

Dan held some concern about them losing their way, so he offered his compass to Barney. "Are you sure you don't want me to ride with you, Barney?"

"No thanks, Dan, I have some matters to discuss with the girls alone."

Bernadette threw him a look of surprise, before turning her mare's head, adding, "We'll be all right, Dan. I still remember my way around."

Dan handed Barney the rope attached to Addy's pony. This would be her first riding adventure, and definitely not her last. Addy already had a strong bond with the property, though she didn't know it yet, but one day it would be all hers.

Bernadette trotted off in front, her mare's neat hooves kicking up the dust. She was the first to reach the garden gate and so leaned over, lifting up the slip rail to bring it around, allowing Barney and Addy through.

Looking back, Bernadette said, "Look, Barney, doesn't the garden look wonderful? Those saplings were planted just before the wedding. I can't believe how much they've grown!" She turned to him, smiling. He gave no answer. Bernadette took no notice and continued with a guided tour as they ambled along.

"Old Mr Watts was a lover of trees, and when most graziers cleared their land of the trees and scrub, even some of the ancient gums, he'd allowed nature to have its way. I think he must have been a very wise man, you know, Barney. He'd seen other properties blown away in the wind and he understood; preserving the trees and scrub would stop erosion. His plan seems to have worked. Especially in drought time, as most of the scrub around here is edible for the stock and it also protects the top soil from being blown away in the hot northerlies. Plus, it provides shade, and shelter in winter. However, come the annual muster, it sometimes makes it difficult to find stock, if they're hiding in the scrub."

Needing then to feel the wind in her hair and the power beneath her, Bernadette said, "I'm just going for a gallop." Barney nodded his approval. Leading Addy on her pony had meant that Barney and Addy were having to go slow.

Bernadette hand-galloped circles around them. Barney looked on, admiring her slender figure leaning forward over the front of the saddle, urging her mare to go faster, her long black hair streaming out behind.

"I'll be able to ride like that soon, won't I, Barney?" Addy looked longingly into Barney's eyes.

"All in good time, Addy. We shouldn't 'over-face' ourselves, and the same applies to our horses."

"What does that mean, Barney?"

"It means that we should never quickly take on anything that's too big for us, including fences."

"Well, I still think I should like to ride like Mummy soon. I'm going to be a great rider, Barney!"

He could only smile at this overconfident child.

They'd ridden some miles before Barney noticed an enormous rock jutting from the earth. "Is that where we're headed, Bernadette? It certainly is an outstanding landmark."

"Yes, it is. It's always seemed to me as if the earth is wearing it like a piece of jewellery. From the top, you can see almost to Adelaide. Jum and I would often come here and sit for hours. 'Jum's top-of-the-world rock', he'd call it." Deepening her voice, she then reiterated Jum's words. 'Don't say this is God's own country, Bernadette. This is my country, my land, as far as we can see.' I suppose he didn't want to offend my spiritualism, so he said," again lowering her voice, "'and with you sitting alongside me, Bernadette, it's my Garden of Eden. I'll give you that much.'" She let a little laugh escape before she dismounted.

Barney now felt like he'd be committing some kind of sacrilege by climbing their domain. He dismounted from his well-mannered black gelding, finding his legs to be a little stiff after their long ride. They tethered their horses below the rock in a narrow strip of shade. The sun was at its highest, directly above them.

Bernadette shaded her eyes with her hands and looked up. "Let's have some water before we begin. It's such a long, hard climb. Then, if you're not too hungry, we can wait and eat our lunch at the waterhole on the way home."

"Sounds good to me," Barney said, giving Addy a wink.

"Good. Then I suggest we climb with bare feet, as the leather soles of our boots will slip against the rock. I'll go first, and then you follow me, Addy. Barney, you go last, just in case we fall," Bernadette cautioned.

Barney quipped, "Certainly, madam, I'll catch you both if you fall. But Addy, you may have to pull *me* up. My bones are a little achy after the ride." He groaned and bent to pull his boots off. Addy laughed, clipped the lead rope on, and Barney tipped his hat.

"This is just wonderful," Barney said with a sigh. He stood at the top, admiring the expansive view. Bernadette placed her arm around his waist.

"Barney," she said cautiously, "you told Dan you needed to talk to us?"

Barney said nothing, but moved closer to the edge, thinking, *Maybe, just maybe, I'd be able to last out my stay here. After all, it's a magnificent property and I haven't seen or heard Jum's ghost since I arrived.* Wiping the sweat from his brow, he turned to look Bernadette in the eye.

"Well, as you know, Bernadette, I've had mixed feelings about coming here. I felt uncomfortable—and I must admit—almost fearful about being on Jum's land. But standing here and looking out for miles, it's as if we were on top of the world. Well, I can't say if I've changed my mind entirely about leaving tomorrow for Queensland, but I'm thinking about it." He spoke his next few words quickly so as to quell her look of surprise.

"I was going to tell you yesterday, Bernadette. But now I'm having second thoughts. I think I'd find it hard to leave you and Addy here." He shrugged and looked away, then added, "Maybe it's the fear. You'd never want to leave this place?" He turned again to face Bernadette.

There was a silence.

"I love you with all my heart and soul, Bernadette, and I look upon Addy as my own daughter, but I couldn't possibly live here forever, and I suspect you and Addy could. I suppose if I go tomorrow, it'll give us time to think things over, even if you decide to live half the year on Bulkawa and half in Hawaii." He returned Bernadette's level gaze.

"I'll wait in Hawaii for you, Bernadette. I'll understand and accept your decision."

Addy, until now, had remained silent, knowing not to interrupt adults while they were speaking seriously. However, she'd heard the conversation, or really, what Barney had said. "Barney, please don't go. I want you to stay with us!" Flinging her arms around him, she begged. "Please, please don't go, Barney."

He held her tight before sitting her down. "Addy, sometimes adults have to make difficult decisions. I'm sure you wouldn't want me to stay and be unhappy in a place where I never felt I truly belonged. It's up to your mother to make the final choice, about how and where you live your lives." He looked deep into her eyes. "My dearest Addy, I love you so much, and when you love somebody so much, you want to give them everything, even if what *they* want is not what *you* want. Do you understand?"

"Um, I guess so," Addy said, hesitant in her reply. "But I don't understand why you don't like it here—I love it!"

"It's too complicated to explain, Addy. You just have to accept I have reasons you won't understand until you're older."

Bernadette had listened to his gentle wisdom, realising once again why she loved him. Barney took nothing—he only gave. However, she knew she and Addy had to make peace with this land, which would hopefully stay in their family for many generations to come.

"So, Barney, you've made your decision. You'll leave tomorrow for Queensland?" Bernadette didn't wait for his answer. "I'll be disappointed not seeing the plantations, but I know you understand why I can't leave here, not until Addy has had her fill, and I also need to ease out of my past with Jum while we're here." Bernadette gave Addy a squeeze.

"It seems now, Addy, you'll have your wish of riding every day for some time. We can also sort out your schooling in Adelaide. When you're ten years old, you'll go to boarding school. As much as I don't want to see you go, it'll be good for you to have really close girlfriends and have the chance to concentrate on your studies."

Addy shuddered inwardly at the thought of leaving her mother and Barney. However, Bernadette knew that she wouldn't have to consider this for another five years.

The sun had cast its shadow east of the rock. They decided they'd best be on their way. A clear sky allowed the full force of the sun to sear the earth and all that inhabited it, and so they readily agreed on a quick ride to the waterhole.

"I can trot now, Barney, so let's go faster. I'm hungry and I'm hot. Can we swim in the waterhole after lunch?"

"I think that's a very good idea, Addy," Barney said. He watched amused at Addy bouncing around in the saddle. "Addy, listen to me. When I say 'down', that's when your bottom must sit in the saddle. When I say 'up', stand in your stirrup irons. Ready? Here we go. Up, down, up, down, up, down!"

Before too long, Addy had the rhythm and Barney kept up instructions until she'd mastered the rising trot, and then he taught her how to sit to the canter. "You're a fast learner, young lady!"

"This place definitely has a tropical feel to it," Barney said, as they stood on the bank of the bottomless waterhole. Maybe that was the reason it was the darkest of blues. Palms towered above and a thatched roof hut gave shelter to table and chairs. "Look, Addy, there's a diving board so I'll teach you to dive later."

"Barney, don't be silly. I can dive already!"

"Oh, that's right, you can do everything, Addy. So, can you eat sandwiches?" Barney felt a little more relaxed, perhaps because this place reminded him of Hawaii. He turned to Bernadette.

"I feel a lot happier now you've listened to me, Bernadette, and we know where each of us stands. But mind you, I think I could get used to the life here."

They devoured their sandwiches, especially Barney, who'd eaten three before he lay back in the sun, cooled a little by the gently swaying fronds.

"This is like Hawaii, Barney," Addy remarked while looking up at the palm trees.

"We could all live here, you know, Barney, because every time we miss Hawaii, we could come here and think we were home."

"You just said it for me, Addy—home. That's where I want to spend my life. Hawaii." Raising a speculative eyebrow, he craned his neck to look at Bernadette. "But maybe I could get used to this place for *half of* the year."

"Barney, you surprise me! One minute you want to leave and next you're saying you wouldn't mind sharing your time here." She leant over and kissed him tenderly. "You have always amazed me, my darling."

Giggling at the sight of them kissing, Addy pleaded. "Mummy, can I go for a swim now, then you can kiss some more?"

Barney leapt to his feet. Bernadette's kisses always aroused him, so he needed to cool down. "I'll test the water first, Addy, there might be a big shark in there and he'll eat you all up!"

She giggled as he ran to the diving board. Springing high off the edge, Barney sliced through the water, leaving barely a ripple.

"Show off!" Bernadette called before lying back down.

As Barney began to rise from the depths, a debilitating cramp suddenly crunched his stomach. The pain was excruciating. Straining desperately to reach the surface, he felt his lungs begin to burn with gulps of unwanted water. Struggling furiously, he tried with all his might to force his way to the top.

"Mummy, Mummy! Barney hasn't come up!"

Addy had been waiting on the bank to applaud when he rose. She took a deep breath, and without hesitating, dived in. Precious time elapsed before she broke the surface. Gasping, she duck dived again.

"No, Addy, no! Come out, I'll find him!" Bernadette was yelling at Addy who'd disappeared. *Don't panic, don't panic!* she told herself. *Take a deep breath and remain calm.* She filled her lungs and dived into the abyss.

In his fight to get to the top, Barney's strength had been just about exhausted. He had almost reached the point of reconciling with his fate—this was the end—when he caught a glimpse of Addy sinking lifelessly past him. With all the mortal strength he could muster, he grabbed for her body. The relentless pain which had been holding him down suddenly evaporated, and he was somehow almost catapulted to the surface with Addy limp in his arms. He'd never felt such urgency in his life. He gasped and coughed water from his lungs as he dragged her from the pool, laying her on her back, his hands looking enormous on her small body as he turned her on her side.

Bernadette struggled from the water, overcome with joy at seeing them both on dry land. Barney was patting Addy firmly on the back, forcing the water out of her lungs; she began to cough and splutter as Bernadette reached them. She threw her arms around Barney and sobbed. He took no notice; he was still giving all his attention to Addy. Finally, Addy opened her eyes and said weakly, "I couldn't find Barney, Mummy. I ran out of breath."

"It's alright, my darling. Barney's here, and he saved you from drowning."

Addy smiled faintly before closing her eyes, drifting off to sleep in Barney's arms.

They sat in silence, the whole episode so unreal that they were unable to discuss what had happened. On the slow ride back to the homestead, they could only think that it was a greater power that had been responsible for saving them.

Barney kept his plan in place and left alone for Queensland the next day, although they decided to shorten their stay to six weeks. This would give Barney enough time to visit relatives in Melbourne and give Addy time, under Dan's tuition, to become the competent rider she'd wished to be. However, Bernadette stipulated one point. "Only one thing will change our plan, Barney. If I'm needed in any way to help Jonathon and the boys, I will stay."

Chapter 24

A Future — With the Help Of Friends

After many months of expert nursing and Dr Liu's refined medicine, Jonathon seemed well over the worst of his illness. In fact, today he felt supremely alive. Dr Liu's herbs had worked wonders, not to mention the acupuncture and pressure-point massages. The prayers from within the orphanage, needless to say, helped heal Jonathon both physically and spiritually. He sat up in bed feeling, if not entirely his old self, certainly much, much better. Mother Matilda and Dr Liu looked on very pleased, nodding their heads in agreement.

"Yes, he's with us again, Mudda Mat. He cured."

"I'm telling y', the Lord Himself has sent y' to us, Dr Liu."

"Yes, this is the first time in months I've felt well enough for a walk in the garden. I think a bit of fresh air would do me the world of good," Jonathon said. The winter's chill caused Jonathon to shudder so Matilda draped a woollen blanket around his shoulders.

"Here now, y' can't be catching y' death of cold, not after all the hard work put into savin' y' in the first place!" she joked, while wrapping him snugly. Matilda then turned to Dr Liu. "Do y' think it's too early to be sending out news that our patient has beaten this wretched virus?"

Nodding his head up and down repeatedly, Dr Liu laughed at seeing Jonathon stride out toward the front door unaided. "Yes, of course, Mudda. Oh, boy, look him go! He all better, I think. Yes, vely much I think—he all better now. I keep treat him, so he's gone home in no time. Yes, vely good, vely good. I go tell Da, bling boys now, come see."

Jonathon, desperately needing to see the boys, replied, "Oh please, Liu, if you think it's safe, please go as soon as possible." He turned to Matilda. "I'm really hungry, Mother. Is there any chance of a piece of that apple pie Betty makes so well?"

Matilda hurried inside and returned with a huge piece, smothered with clotted cream.

"Now sit down here, Jon, in the sun. You know m' Da made this garden seat. I don't know what we'd do without him. Oh, and he's been so good with the boys. I can't wait to see their faces. What a great blessing this has been. We'll have a party! Yes, an early birthday party for the boys and a celebration of your recovery. Then soon as y' feel fit enough…"

She paused here, thinking how she would miss the boys terribly.

"You and the boys will be leaving us now."

She hung her head trying to quell her emotion. Jonathon placed his hand on her shoulder.

"You don't think it's the last you'll see of us, do you, Mother? I could never repay you for what you and Dr Liu have done for me, for us. I'm sure I would have died without your care." He looked up at Liu.

"And you, Doctor, for your amazing knowledge in healing my condition. We're all a family now. We'll visit often and I want you to come and stay with us whenever you can. That means you too, Dr Liu."

He stretched his hand out to Liu who was standing in front of him, bowing.

"No wully, no wully. I vely pleased and happy for you, Jon and boys, to have father back live with them, see them grow into good men, I think." Liu continued bowing. "I go now, tell Da."

Da was in the backyard of his house, stacking the wood supply, with Patrick and Angus helping. Liu could hear the echo of an axe falling on dry wood and hurried in his shuffling way around the corner to see them.

He announced, "Good news, vely good news! Father Jon all better, no danger no more, all better!"

Immediately dropping the wood they were about to stack, the boys ran with open arms to greet him, grateful he was the reason their father was alive. After the initial shock, Da dropped his axe and came to join them, clapping Liu on the back.

"Mudda Mat has big, big party, yes! We celebrate boys' birthdays and good long livings before you boys go home with father Jon. I make best fireworks ever! Mudda Mat says you, Da, to bring boys to see father. It all safe now, all good now. I go make fireworks. Happy, I happy, vely happy!" He began walking backwards, bowing as was his usual custom, then turned kicking his heels up, before leaping into his buggy.

"Giddy up, good horsey, giddy up!"

When the boys had come to live with him, Da had named their group the Three Musketeers. They stood glued to the spot until Doc Liu had disappeared from sight, stunned by the welcome news.

"Well, boys," Da said, breaking the spell, "I t'ink we should all scrub up now before goin' t' visit your father." As the boys ran inside, Da shook his head laughing. He'd never seen them as eager to wash and spruce up. He was still smiling, but when pouring water into the wash basin, he began to feel a little sorry for himself. The thought of not having his two "young men" around to break the loneliness made his heart ache. He reminisced.

I taught 'em both how t' ride—well, Angus mostly. Patrick's just a natural when he's around horses; his intuition seems t' be one step ahead of both man and beast. Yes, he's a born natural, alright. I thought it was a shame though that Dr Liu wasn't able t' give 'em Kung Fu lessons whilst he was treatin' Jonathon. But Patrick took it up t' teach Angus all he knew about the art. This had had its moments.

Da shook his head and chuckled, thinking about the few black eyes he had to soothe with a piece of prime steak. He smiled again at another memory. *I was real proud how dey worked right alongside me when shearing the sheep and then helpin' move the cattle on their ponies.* Da remembered the day he bought Angus his first pony. *Ah, that was a grand day, takin' them to the cattle sales where I bought the pony.*

Da had apologised to Angus because the pony wasn't as good looking as Sergeant. He was an old swayback. "I can't afford anyt'ing better at this stage, Angus, but he'll do y' well enough 'til you can ride a wee bit better."

Angus was beside himself with excitement. "Oh Da, he's a beauty!" he'd said. 'I'll look after him, Da. Thank you so much. I think I'll call him Buster, because I hope I don't have any more busters!' Patrick near doubled up with laughter, and Angus had a good laugh too but it was mainly at Patrick.

I'll miss playin' chess with 'em every night. Angus taught me and Patrick well. But each time he'd be leavin' us scratchin' our heads about how the hell we didn't see that move comin'.

Da hoped he had taught the boys their school lessons properly. He gave thanks to Ma for caring for all the books, pencils, and slates. They had been still in fine condition, left over from Matilda's schooling. He was duly impressed that even though Angus was younger by two-and-a-bit years, he'd been able to help Patrick with his reading and arithmetic. Da tried hard to keep his admiration to himself, as he'd never wanted to make Patrick feel inferior.

It mighta been so with the schoolin', but Patrick levelled the field with his physical ability. So, I can say it was a great mix, as each boy seemed to admire the

*other for their talent, instead of competing against each other. I saw how they
helped each other overcome any weaknesses. It made m' heart sing, it did.*

As Da lathered his hands, he put his reflections to the side for a moment. He
had a rare ability to accept all things which came his way, both good and ill. He
thought again on how sometimes he'd see the cunning and mischief in Patrick, or
notice how Angus was learning to think for himself, rather than simply following
Patrick as usual into a hellish scrape. He thought Angus to be wise far beyond his
years, but then everything was quite different with Angus. *Where would his
intelligence lead him?* Da wondered. *Maybe Prime Minister one day?*

"Come on, Da, we're ready." The boys stood behind him, hair slicked back,
clean shirts and Sunday trousers on. Da grimaced as he splashed the cold water on
his face, mainly to rouse himself from his melancholy. "What about the horse and
buggy, boys? Have y' got old Jimmy hitched up and the ponies tied secure t' the
back of the buggy?"

"Yes, Da, we did it in five minutes flat. Let's go!" Patrick said as he handed
Da his clean shirt. They watched impatiently as he put it on and buttoned it slowly.
Anxious to get going, but also needing to ask him something, Patrick nudged
Angus, then vice versa. Da noticed.

"What is it, boys, do y' need to be tellin' me somethin' or askin' me
somethin'?"

Patrick threw Angus a look, as if to say, "you ask him", so he did.

"Da, we were thinking. Just to show our father how we've learnt so much by
living with you, and you teaching us everything, you might let us take it in turns to
drive the buggy—to the orphanage?" They looked hopefully at the old man.

Da decided to play along with the game. He frowned. "D' y' really t'ink I'd be
puttin' me life in y' young hands, especially when Jimmy's not so amiable?"

"But Da, we've got to know him. He likes us, and you let us drive him around
the paddocks!" Patrick never liked to take "no" for an answer.

"Ah, yes, but that's a different matter. Out on the road Jimmy could be takin'
fright and bolt. That'd be the end of us." He lowered his head for effect.

Patrick was quick with his comeback. "But Da, you'd be sitting right beside us
to help pull him up!"

"Oh, so y' won't be throwin' me in the back like a sack of spuds then?"

"No, of course not, you'll be second in command—sitting right in the middle
of us," Angus assured him.

This struck the final chord and Da broke into laughter, ruffling their well-
groomed hair. "Oh, be off with y' now, and bring poor old Jimmy around the front
of the house. I'll be there directly."

Mother Matilda spread her arms, and the boys snuggled into her warm embrace, while Jonathon stood back to view the scene. He was well aware of the fact that he could have been looking down on it from Heaven.

"Anyone for a cup of tea?" Jonathon asked. He was near bowled over with a tackle from Angus, while Patrick held back, a little uncertain, until Jonathon drew him firmly to his chest.

The kitchen hummed with the chatter of a crowd as the kettle boiled. In no time, they devoured the best biscuits because Matilda was not paying her usual attention to such things. Laughter and plans for the boys' early birthday party became a proverbial screaming match, before a gruff Mother Matilda dismissed the girls.

"Go to the Chapel, girls. Give thanks to the Lord for His mercy! And don't come back until y've all said one hundred Hail Marys and done some weedin' in the garden in front of the Chapel!"

They scurried off. "There now, that'll get rid of the noise for a while," she said, smiling at Jonathon, and then poured herself another cup of tea.

Da stood and asked the boys to go outside with him. Out there, Da opened up. "I'll help y' take care of y' ponies, m' boys, and y' know I'm gunna be missin' y' somethin' terrible. I really think 'tis about time I had a good look at what's been happenin' around Adelaide Town. So, it won't be too long and I'll be comin' t' stay with y' for a wee while. And in the school holidays, I'm sure y' dad won't mind y' comin' here for a week or two. What do y' reckon?"

"Oh, yes! That will be perfect, Da," they said, almost in unison.

Jonathon felt he was now on a mission to guide his two young boys into manhood and help them towards purposeful lives. Boarding school would begin the following year. He would organise it on his return, giving him a good seven months to get to know Patrick, and for the three of them to bond as a family. Yes, he would begin the new century with enthusiasm. He'd told Mother Matilda of his plans while they sat sipping on tea in the kitchen.

The night before the family left for Adelaide, the fireworks celebration lit up the sky above the orphanage. Everyone strained their necks to take full view of the sky set ablaze with Dr Liu's magic.

Betty and her three apprentice cooks had demonstrated their culinary skills, producing everybody's favourite apple pie and sausage rolls. Da had also set up a spit, to roast a lamb, serving the succulent meat on hot damper along with Betty's prize-winning chutney. It was a joyous occasion which held both happy and sad reflections. Jonathon took note of the many tears shed, as everyone reflected on how different the place would soon be, without the boys.

Betty packed the leftovers in a calico cloth and gave them to the boys for their long journey home. Having the two ponies tied to the back of the buggy would slow them down a little, so Jonathon made a promise.

"If either horse or man becomes too tired, we'll camp out overnight to break the journey." Of course, the boys had previously decided to become extremely tired half-way home, as the promise of a camp-out sounded too good to refuse.

In the yard early next morning, their boots cracked the thin blanket of a crisp white frost as they readied for their departure. The long goodbyes began and as more tears flowed, they were on their way.

Mother Matilda stood alone, watching the final cloud of dust settle and listening to the sound of trotting hooves fade into silence. She then glanced upwards. "Y' take good care of 'em now, Lord."

After three hours of their journey, it was time to rest and enjoy their sandwiches. Once settled, Patrick asked many questions. He wanted to know all about his mother, although he understood their entangled lives could never be explained in a few hours. He was anxious to know more about Sally. At the end of some lighter stories he told about her, Jonathon gave Patrick the assurance he seemed to need.

"Your mother loved you dearly, Patrick. She never abandoned you. It seems I may have unintentionally influenced her with many of her decisions. But I promise you now, Patrick, I will make up for my mistakes. I will love and raise you as your mother would have done." Patrick embraced Jonathon, mostly to hide his tears. The three then decided to set up camp.

"It seems my strength has not fully returned, boys," Jonathon admitted. Later, they gathered wood for a fire and stoked it up, then huddled close together on top of the ground sheet and under a generous supply of blankets Da had packed.

Sadness soon overcame Jonathon, only this time it was for the loss of his best friend, Jum, and the fact he'd also missed seeing Bernadette and Addy before they'd set sail for Hawaii. He tried to put his sadness aside by focusing on the sparks shooting into the starlit sky.

In his heart, he knew Sally's starlight would shine upon him and her boys forever.

Part 2

Introduction
Adelaide 1908

Ten years had passed since Sally died and the boys reunited as a family. Jonathon's health had steadily improved and his law practice had become the most successful in South Australia. He had, therefore, earned enough funds to purchase the grand home he'd always wanted. We now find the boys celebrating their birthdays in the grounds of the mansion.

Chapter 1

The Birthday

The day had been sundrenched and warm, unusual for a winter's day in South Australia. A balmy breeze strayed from the north, bringing with it a delightful evening. An enormous marquee covered the tennis court, which became the enclosure for the one hundred partygoers. Jonathon had hired the most popular quartet to entertain his guests, and he'd made sure an endless flow of fine cuisine would keep the buffet table full all night.

As usual, Patrick and Angus shared their birthday celebration each year on the fourth of July. However, what made it unusual was that this date was neither of the boys' birthdays. It had been the date when baby Patrick had been left in the care of Mother Matilda. One could say it was for the love of Patrick that this day was deemed memorable. Angus didn't seem to mind the fact that his birthday fell some weeks prior, as he'd prayed to have a brother and was more than willing to share everything with him.

The revelry began at seven pm with Emily Tompkins arriving on time. Emily was Patrick's playmate at the moment, having the same adventurous spirit and the same intense interest in the opposite sex as Patrick. She whispered in his ear, "I've snuck in two bottles of rum to spice up the punch, Patrick."

"This way, Emily. I'll show you," he said with his most charming smile.

Standing directly in front of the punchbowl, Emily distracted all-comers with her flirting ways. She titillated the men with her décolletage and paid flattering comments to the women. This gave Patrick time to pour the rum into the bowl and dispose of the bottle under the table. Before walking away, they each downed three glasses, commenting innocently, "We're very thirsty." The alcohol immediately added a pink glow into Emily's cheeks and a twinkle in her eye. Excited by this transformation, Patrick led her by the hand to the crowded dance floor where he held her close, before slowly dancing her out of sight through a side opening in the marquee.

He was intent on finishing what they'd sometimes begun. After all, Emily was now sixteen, the age of consent, a fact that gave Patrick licence to perform his slow art of seduction. This he'd already performed many times. Firstly, under the guidance of an experienced prostitute named Molly, and later with numerous other willing females. Patrick had enjoyed his first and totally fulfilled sexual experience one afternoon two years before. It had begun when he'd first met with Molly on his way to his father's office. Patrick had taken a short cut, which took him past "Bordello Lane", as most people called it. Molly was not one of the garishly painted wenches he'd sometimes seen. She had a certain quality, a true and natural attractiveness that stopped Patrick in his tracks. Smiling seductively, Molly glided up to him and whispered in his ear, "If you pay me two shillings, I can show you how to make a woman beg for more, my lovely."

The timbre of Patrick's voice and his physique made him seem older. "I have one shilling, madam." Molly would never have agreed to such a low price if it weren't for her thinking, *I'd do it for you for nothing*. Undressing him with her eyes, she said, "One shilling will be plenty for you, my lovely."

It was the beginning of Patrick's sexual liaisons and education. Once a week, he'd meet with Molly who taught him everything there was to know about how to please a woman. She'd also happily acted out every fantasy Patrick could throw at her. In the end, she did the slow dance of lust for nothing, such was the charm of her student. And tonight, Patrick thought, Emily was going to experience some of what he'd learned.

Young nuns, Betty and Lizzy, had arrived a little late to the party, due to their final mass at eight pm. Trying not to be impressed by the grandeur of the house as they entered the marble foyer, they each held Jonathon close and blessed him. His eyes filled with tears, as memories came flooding back of the Little Angels, as he'd called them. It was many years since they'd both cared for him while he convalesced at the orphanage.

"It's so good to see you both," he said, looking at them closely. "I know I shouldn't say this, but it's a shame your beauty is wasted on the church. Please forgive me, but you are such lovely looking young women."

Both women blushed at his compliment, although Jonathon had really only meant Betty. But how could he leave plain Lizzy out? She certainly wasn't ugly, just very plain, whereas Betty had blossomed into a real beauty. Something shone from within her which captivated him. Her perfect features sculptured on alabaster skin set off her alluring green eyes, and a trace of chestnut hair showed where her wimple had slipped. Tall and slender, Betty effortlessly carried her height with regal composure as they walked together down the expansive garden steps towards the party. The happy crowd was bathed in an orange glow emitted by the fires and permanent gas lights. Laughter, chatter and music filled the air. Betty paused momentarily, marvelling in the freedom of the young and the beautiful. A fleeting pang of jealousy tried to spoil her pure thoughts as a part of her yearned to be loved as a woman.

"Now let me find Patrick and Angus for you," Jonathon said, after looking around. "No, I can't see them."

Just as he'd said that, Angus spotted them. Pushing through the crowd he called, "Betty, Lizzy!" Holding his arms out for the usual big hug, he asked, "How long has it been—two years since I've seen you both? So, how's the nunhood?"

They both laughed and Betty replied, "Very good, very good indeed, thank you, Angus. But it's always nice to come out into the real world and see the people we love so much." Giving him a kiss on the cheek, Betty then smiled at the young woman standing beside him. Angus noticed.

"Oh, please excuse me, I've forgotten my manners. Sister Lizzy, Sister Betty, I'd like to introduce my friend, Jennifer Rose. Jennifer's father is a doctor. I'm leaning towards being a doctor, you know." His head lifted with pride while Jennifer smiled coyly. Betty and Lizzy offered their hands to her at the same time.

"Pleased to meet you, Jennifer," the two nuns said together.

Jennifer giggled and shook their hands. "Pleased to meet you too, Sisters."

Betty asked caringly, "And you, Jennifer, what would you like to do with your life?"

Looking straight into Betty's eyes, she proudly proclaimed, "I'm going to be a barrister and then a judge."

Trying not to be shocked by the confidence in her proclamation, Betty answered, "Well, they're both very worthy professions and just think, you and Angus will have fine examples to follow in each other's fathers."

Betty's thoughts then drifted. *How enjoyable this evening will be, meeting many different people and feeling a certain freedom. I'm so pleased we were given leave to stay overnight.* On their way to the party, Betty had admitted to Lizzy, "This will be the most exciting time in my life so far, Lizzy." Betty had never ventured further than the convent school in Adelaide, where she'd become a novitiate, or Mother Matilda's orphanage, where she now lived while waiting for a permanent posting. Both young women were, of course, hoping to stay and teach with Mother Matilda at the orphanage. Lizzy had passed with honours in mathematics, and Betty with honours in literature. Such skills, they knew, would make them a welcome addition to any Catholic school in South Australia.

"May I fetch some refreshments for you, Sisters?" Jonathon asked.

"Oh, please don't bother, Mr Darcy, we're quite capable of looking after ourselves and we would love to mingle on our way to the buffet table, wouldn't we, Lizzy?"

"Yes, yes of course, Betty. The food looks scrumptious."

After filling their plates, they moved on to the punchbowl but it was almost empty. A noticeably inebriated young man stood beside it, smiling. He helped them pour the last of the punch into their glasses. Swaying slightly, he then said, "I surely hope they bring some more of this wonderful punch, Sisters. It does have a hell of a good punch to it!" He laughed raising his glass. "Enjoy, ladies!"

Smiling back at him, their mouths too full to speak, they raised their glasses and followed the food down with a mouthful of punch. After the burning rum had made passage down their throat, they looked at each other with shocked expressions. With a shudder and a slight cough, Betty wondered what was wrong with the punch.

"Should we tell Jonathon?" asked Lizzy.

"Let's wait and see what the next mix holds, Lizzy. It may have been the last drop that tasted strange." She raised an eyebrow, "Or it could have been spiked."

"Betty, I really don't know how you became so worldly! 'Spiked'? Is that what they call it when somebody adds alcohol?"

Betty nodded a yes and then with her plate and drink in hand, she found them both a seat within the enclosure. Once satisfied by the delicious cuisine and calmed by the alcohol, they looked for old acquaintances to talk to. It wasn't too long before they heard Doctor Liu's voice.

"Come on evelyone, come ov' hea. Firewoks bout to start. Come on, huwy, huwy!"

The Sisters chose not to interrupt Lui's concentration. They stood close by to where he was working. However, Doctor Liu, cunningly attuned to his surrounds, turned slowly to face the nuns. With a broad smile and his usual bow, he said, "I so happy to see you, Betty, Rizzy. We talk for wong time after firewoks."

They returned a smile to his low bow. All guests soon gathered to watch this spectacular pyrotechnic display. Betty gazed in wonder. "Liu's extraordinary. I think his talent has reached new heights, Lizzy." With that said, Betty was transported back to when she'd witnessed fireworks for the first time. It was Patrick's fifth birthday. How she missed him terribly.

Suddenly her attention was caught by the movement of two figures running up from the woods. While unable to identify their faces, she did notice Patrick's blond hair. The night sky had been lit up with another skyrocket. He ran ahead of a young woman, pulling her along by the hand. His hair remained long and unruly, but he had grown and filled out into manhood since Betty had seen him.

She turned away from the scene, trying to banish her thoughts. *I wish he was holding my hand. I know he's been exploring, probably lusting after that young woman.* "Stop it," she said softly to herself.

Lizzy turned towards Betty. "What did you say, Betty?"

215

"Oh nothing," she murmured, "I just wish this display would never STOP."

After fifteen minutes of splendid fireworks, the night faded back into darkness. Liaisons seemed to be taking place everywhere. Parents and servants began searching for their charges who were nowhere to be found. Colleen and Bob bustled around, gathering up all the young lovebirds they'd caught holding hands in the dark or kissing behind trees. Some were falling into each other's arms as they danced, unaware of anyone wanting to make a speech.

Jonathon took note of what Bob and Colleen were doing to help establish some control over the young people. "Thank you, Bob, Colleen, but I really need the boys to be here now for the speeches and the cutting of the birthday cake. It's getting late. Have you seen them?" Jonathon asked, as he looked around.

"Oh, never mind, here they are." He stood proudly as the two young men walked through the crowd with arms wrapped around each other's shoulders, as was their custom. Tinkling his glass with a spoon to claim attention, Jonathon then spoke. "Everyone, please excuse me. May I have your attention please? I would like to say a few words." He paused and smiled as wolf whistles and a few calls of "Good on ya, mate," were directed at the brothers before they stood next to him. Silence then prevailed. Most people had known the true story of the family, but it was rarely mentioned. When it was, it was never met with criticism. People's adoration of Jonathon and the boys had grown over the years.

Jonathon began his speech as he always did. "I'd like to make a toast to the memory of my darling wife, Sally. How I wish she could be with us this evening." The crowd murmured sombrely, "Here, here." Jonathon continued, "Let us now drink to the memory of my dear friend, Jum Watt."

He went on to regale the crowd with loving and funny stories of his two sons. Jonathon finished by saying, "Patrick, after graduating, will be heading for England, where he will attend The Royal Military Academy Sandhurst. His future in the Army as an officer, I'm sure, will be an honourable one. And Angus has aspirations of being a doctor. I feel whatever profession my sons take on, they will serve with honour and compassion. I would now like to make a toast to Angus and Patrick!"

After blowing out the candles on his cake, Patrick looked up and caught sight of Sister Betty. He almost knocked the cake over in his urgency to reach her. Picking Betty up by the waist he twirled her in the air, as if she were a child. Betty shocked everyone by delighting in the greeting, throwing her head back and laughing shamelessly, until one of the many upright Catholic parents ordered Patrick to stop. "Put that nun down this instance!"

Jonathon came to the rescue, taking the offended gentleman by the arm, explaining calmly, "The two have been brought up as brother and sister, Michael.

216

To Patrick, Betty will always be family. And it's been years since they've seen each other. They were simply overjoyed to be reunited." The man nodded grudgingly, seeming to accept Jonathon's reasoning.

The clock had struck two am before the last guest left and the weary friends entered the main living room. Patrick, holding Betty's hand, and Angus with his arm through Lizzy's, sank heavily into the luxurious sofa. Jonathon chose to sit in his tapestry armchair, the only possession he'd brought with him from the cottage. The chair was special, as Sally had designed it and then had it made just for him. Placing his arm lovingly around Betty's shoulders, Patrick leaned over to kiss her cheek. He then looked into her eyes and said, "I miss you, Betty. I wish you weren't a nun. You could come and live with us." Betty blushed and her eyelashes fluttered.

"Patrick! Please don't speak to Betty in such a way. She belongs to Christ now. Have some respect," Jonathon said, a little shocked.

"I do, Dad, I just can't help speaking my mind through my heart," Patrick's eyes were wide with sincerity.

"Yes, that's right, Father," Angus joined in. "You know how he is, and Betty's like his real sister, even more than a sister!" Immediately realising what he may have insinuated, Angus tried to make amends. "You know what I mean, Father. Betty, well, she almost saved his life and yes, she looked after Patrick like a real sister would have."

Betty was secretly enjoying the conversation. She'd never experienced attention from the opposite sex, not since Patrick had left her. She longed sometimes to return to their days spent at the orphanage, when he would lay soft kisses upon her neck and place his small hand on her breast. She'd been quite possessive of Patrick back then and would scold the other girls if they went near him. He belonged to her. With the memories of those special intimate times spent alone with Patrick and being so close to him now, Betty began to feel the weakness of the flesh struggling with her vows of chastity. She rose to excuse herself.

"I'm rather tired, gentlemen, so I must say goodnight." She beckoned Lizzy to follow her. "Come, Sister."

Somewhat relieved by her decision, Jonathon immediately offered to guide them to their room, saying, "Marjorie would have shown you the way, Sisters, but she's gone to bed. Yes, Marjorie was absolutely exhausted. You know, Sisters, I don't know what I would have done without her and, of course, Colleen, Bob and Doctor Liu. They've been my strength, my rock through all of my trials and tribulations."

Jonathon continued to praise his close friends as he escorted the nuns up the grand staircase into their opulent chamber, the blue room, as he called it. The brothers stood silently watching their father as he led Betty and Lizzy up the stairs.

Before disappearing from view, Betty turned, smiling down at Patrick. Angus was unable to read her smile, but Patrick could. There was no mistake—it was the smile of a warm, loving woman—not a nun.

Chapter 2

Manhood

The following morning, near midday in fact, Patrick became a little downhearted after finding Betty and Lizzy had departed early. However, his disappointment lasted only until Emily Tomkins paid him a visit, flirting in her promiscuous way.

"It's a lovely day for a drive in my new buggy, Patrick. Mummy purchased it especially for me just this morning. Would you care to join me?" Her tone of voice suggested that riding in her new cart was not the only thing on her mind. Angus stood beside Patrick, admiring the beautiful palomino cob with the princess carriage to match. It was like something out of a storybook.

"Oh, it's so beautiful, Emily," Angus said with excitement. "May I come too?"

Emily frowned at Patrick, who then put his hand on Angus's shoulder.

"Not today, brother. Next time. Tell father I'll be gone for an hour or two, will you. There's a sport."

Still not catching on to the silent language between the two, or the condescending manner in which his brother had spoken to him, Angus sauntered away to find his father. Jonathon sat in his office, knee deep into urgent business. He had an important court case coming up and needed to be well on top of it before the coming Tuesday. Normally, he would never work on the Sabbath, but this was an emergency. A knock on his office door startled him.

"Come in. Come in if it's important!"

Looking up to see the sorrowful expression on Angus's face, Jonathon asked, "What's wrong, son?"

"Oh nothing, Father, it's just, well, Patrick asked me to tell you he's gone for a ride with Emily Tomkins in her new buggy. I could have gone with them, but they wouldn't take me."

Jonathon couldn't help but be amused.

"Never mind, son, it's all part of growing up. One day you won't want Patrick to accompany you when you'd rather be alone with your girlfriend."

"Girlfriend! I hope he doesn't get that serious with her. She's a spoilt twit!"

"Angus! I've never heard you use that expression. Please don't denigrate young ladies."

"She's no lady, Father, and I'll say no more on that subject!"

Jonathon's pen dropped as did his mouth. In his son's manner, he'd just seen and heard Sally.

"Are you alright, Father?"

"Yes, yes, Angus. It's just that your mother used that same phrase once. And in the same manner when referring to someone she didn't trust or like very much." Jonathon paused for a moment and then admitted to Angus, "I still miss her very much, son."

He sat for a moment staring into space, remembering Sally's sweet smile. He then looked at Angus, his own image. "Come here, Angus, you're not too old to give your father a hug."

They embraced for some time before Jonathon tapped him on the back. "Let Patrick make up his own mind who he likes and who he doesn't like, alright?"

"Yes, Father."

"Now let me get on with my work please."

Angus was quite happy then to forget about his initial hurt and turn his attention to a school project he needed to finish.

Patrick was also quite happy to find a secluded spot off the beaten track and seduce Emily Tompkins in broad daylight, covered only by the dancing shadows of the gum leaves.

As Emily lay on her soft silk dress, her nipples sat erect with excitement, and perhaps the slight chill of the winter's day. After undressing quickly, Patrick stood above her, his muscles twitching in expectation, and smiling with the confidence of a man twice his age and with just as many willing conquests under his belt. He would now accept her offerings with pleasure. Patrick needed women to want him. It wasn't in him to force himself upon the opposite sex.

"I adore women, every bloody inch of them," he had once confided to his school mate, Thomas, when discussing their sexual pursuits. "The taste, the smell of women—it consumes me like a drug. And why not, Tom? I'm young, I'm not married, and I'm free to have as many women as I want and need." And now, Patrick and Emily lay entwined after Patrick's perfected art of making love had sent her to heaven, and until the cool air had forced them to dress. As Patrick was buttoning up his fly, Emily, already dressed, asked with a slightly demanding tone, "Do you love me, Patrick?"

Patrick had never lied. Well, not a bad lie, only tiny ones to save his hide from Mother Matilda. He'd thought a little too long about his answer it seemed.

"Well! Tell me, Patrick. Do you?"

"Yes, I suppose I do, Emily. In a way. I love making love to you."

Emily pouted. "That's not the same. I mean do you love me as a person, as a woman? Are you going to marry me?"

"Emily, I love everyone. I'm just a loving kind a bloke. But as far as marriage, I'm too young for that."

With his honesty proclaimed, Emily stormed over to the cart, lifted her skirt, and jumped in. After grabbing the reins, she flicked the pony so hard with the whip that he reared before taking off down the road.

"Emily! Emily, what about me!" Patrick called. "Bloody hell," he barked, throwing his hat on the ground and cursing vulgarities before setting off on the walk home—five long miles. Angus was the first to see Patrick when he'd returned, well after dark. They'd crossed paths on the staircase, Angus on his way to dinner and Patrick on his way to the bathroom.

"Hello Patrick. What happened? You don't look too happy?" Angus grinned with justification. It was obvious that Patrick had had a bad experience with Emily Tompkins that afternoon.

"Just a bit tired, Angus. Tell Dad I won't be down for dinner."

Angus gloated, knowing sooner or later he'd get the full story out of him. After all, his father was an extremely good lawyer, an expert at getting people to spill the beans, so to speak. Angus thought he too had the talent for cross-examination. Jonathon was already seated at the long rosewood dining table when Angus entered the room. At the same time, Miss Marjorie Gibbs placed the dinner plate laden with roast lamb and vegetables in front of Jonathon.

"Thank you, Marjorie," Jonathon said with a smile and then turned to Angus.

"Where's Patrick? Has he not returned from his buggy ride?"

"Yes, Father. He's having a bath and said to tell you he doesn't want any dinner."

"Oh, is he not well then?"

"No, I think he's just tired from all the excitement of the weekend."

"That's a shame. This is his favourite meal, prepared beautifully by Marjorie."

Jonathon eyes showed noticeable warmth toward Marjorie as she placed a plate in front of Angus. She then sat opposite Jonathon with her own dinner. "Thank you, Jonathon. I do my best," Marjorie said, returning the same admiring glance.

The boys' ritual every Monday morning was for Jonathon to drop them off at boarding school before he drove two miles further to his office. Usually the brothers were very chatty, boasting of great feats they'd accomplished on horseback. However, this past weekend was all about celebrating their birthdays so the talk was of who said what to whom, and who danced with whom, and who couldn't dance at all. And who kissed whom behind the mulberry tree. Angus began asking Patrick about his buggy ride with Emily and what he thought of her, intellectually.

"Well, Angus, she's not the brightest young lady I've ever met, but she certainly makes up for it with entertainment value."

"Really, what do you mean by entertainment? Surely, she's not clever enough to be witty. Does she dance for you, or sing to you perhaps?"

"Yes, all of that, Angus. And what about your friend, Miss Rose? Does she sing and dance, or does she just talk about boring school projects?"

Jonathon was pleased he'd finally arrived at their school as the conversation was beginning to sound condescending. He hoped they would sort it out before next weekend. He'd never witnessed this behaviour between them before. "Here we are, boys, back to work. It's time to forget about your young lady friends."

In the school ground, their friends greeted the brothers enthusiastically. The age of consent, it seemed, had met Patrick's friends with ample testosterone. The younger boys could only imagine what these older young men related to in their quest for the opposite sex. They sat listening in awe to their intimate conversations. But this trivia began to bore Angus. Life to him held far more important things than the exploration of a woman's body. The clanging of the school bell broke through their laughter.

Patrick's concentration on his school work was forever in doubt, although with a little more diligence towards his studies, he may have been in the top ten per cent of students. He knew this, but chose to put in just enough effort to get by. His dream of becoming a soldier was still on track. Actually, it was growing stronger every year. Whereas with Angus permanently looking forward to his return to school, his passion for learning had never wavered. He'd also become a national identity, reaching champion status in the game of chess. There were no players his equal once he'd defeated the reigning chess champion of Adelaide. This was a thirty-five-year-old university professor within their school. After Angus had considered many offers to travel interstate to take on challengers, he chose to leave it there; his studies were far too important. Angus had also become more and more interested in Doctor Liu's Chinese medicine. He'd spend as much time as possible with him, learning all he could about his wondrous cures of so many ailments. Even some of his teachers would ask Angus for his opinion on what to take for a continuous back pain, migraine headaches, arthritis etc. He revelled in his knowledge, plus the fact he'd rarely had to confide in Doctor Liu for a back-up opinion. The road to medicine seemed well-paved for Angus.

The days spent at boarding school could never end quickly enough for Patrick—for Angus, never slowly enough. However, both young men were enthused by the prospect of returning every weekend to their horse pursuits. And so, the ritual of school and study continued, with rewards to be had at the end. Both young men were especially looking forward to this coming weekend for the annual fox hunt at Lord Milne's estate. After the chase, they would attend their first formal ball to be held in the ballroom of Lord Milne's palatial home.

Chapter 3

The Hunt

The stoutly built Lord Milne was also the Master of the hunt. This meant he wore the master's boots of highly polished black leather with a mid-brown band around the top. Sporting an imperial moustache and finely tuned English accent, he was adorned in the finest red woollen jacket and white breeches. He welcomed his guests enthusiastically.

"Jonathon, old chap, so good to see you out of the office. I see you're not riding today?"

"No, your Lordship, too much work to do after dropping the boys off. I thought the fresh air and the splendid drive may clear my mind for the never-ending workload ahead."

Lord Milne's expression shifted from a broad smile to a look of concern. "You do know, Jonathon, life's not all about work. We do have to play sometimes. It keeps us sane and happy, old chap. Why don't you stay, relax a little and then attend the ball this evening? It would do you good to dance with a young lady." He laughed at his own proposition, twirled his moustache and continued in a sombre manner. "You cannot live the rest of your life with a memory, Jonathon, not even a memory as beautiful as your dear Sally. It's time to get back into living and enjoy yourself before it's too late. There's no crime in that, my friend." With this advice, Lord Milne left Jonathon to ponder.

However convincing Lord Milne was, Jonathon was not going to stay. He instinctively knew this was not the time or the place to take up his Lordship's offer. In his usual manner, Jonathon had been for some time weighing up the thought of, or more precisely, his feelings for Marjorie. Ambling home alone in his buggy was an ideal opportunity to think things over. His awakening by Lord Milne may have come just in time. Was it gratitude for Marjorie's care and always being there for him and the boys since Sally had died? She'd never taken up with anyone else. Actually, Marjorie rarely left the house. Why?

Marjorie had been a rather plump girl when she began her duties with Jonathon, but in the last ten years, she'd blossomed into a slim, lovely looking woman. She often spoke to Jonathon of her desire to travel and, under his suggestion, she'd become a constant pen pal with Bernadette. This correspondence had fuelled her dreams of adventurous journeys all around the world.

Reining his horses to a walk, Jonathon asked himself, *Why hasn't Marjorie ever asked me for leave so as she could travel? Heaven knows she would have saved enough money and she has such passion to do so. Could it be she has feelings for me? Is this why she's stayed?* He'd noticed her loving smiles many times, especially when the boys were at school.

"Am I stupid? Have I dug myself into a rut, so much so that I'm unable to see or feel what's going on around me?" he said aloud, in order to answer himself.

"Yes, I am stupid, and yes, I've dug a huge hole for myself. I miss the love and tenderness of a woman. I'd be very content to have Marjorie as my wife. She's almost my wife now. No one else would ever care for me as she does. She's selfless and gives her all. Oh, dear God, help me find the words to ask her to marry me. But first I'll begin by apologising to her, for not seeing what I now believe to be true. She loves me and, of course, the boys. I know it's a different love from the love I had for Sally. But, nonetheless, it is a sincere love I feel for her."

Elated at his decision, Jonathon hurried his horses up to reach home as soon as possible. Smiling all the way, he felt Sally had given her blessing. He knew now the weight of his never-ending workload and his caring for the boys would be truly shared. He was sure the love and passion he would receive from this lovely woman would soothe him into that magical place. "Yes," he said, after thinking of the fulfilment one enjoys, when all avenues of love are satisfied.

Once home, Jonathon handed his horses to the junior stable boy and ran briskly toward the kitchen door. *What made me choose the kitchen door? Of course, it's where Marjorie usually is.* He swung the door open, reminding himself of Jum Watt, the way he'd stride out. Never just opening the door, he'd swing it back as if to say, "Here I am, world, aren't you pleased to see me?" Inside the kitchen, Marjorie sat sobbing, her head buried in Colleen's shoulder. Jonathon stopped abruptly. Shocked, his heart immediately went out to her.

"What's wrong, Marjorie? What's the matter, dear?" Walking closer, he gently placed his hand on her shoulder. With his touch she sobbed harder, holding onto Colleen, who in turn gave Jonathon a look of despair while patting Marjorie on the back.

"There, there, Margi. It'll be alright, I'll be tellin' Jonathon if y' like?"

Through her sobbing, Marjorie managed to compose herself. "No, I'll tell him, thank you, Colleen." Rising from her chair, she asked Jonathon to follow her into the smallest sitting room, the room where they'd sit by the fire and read together while the boys were at boarding school.

Marjorie took two deep breaths to calm herself. "I've gone over what I'm about to tell you, Jonathon, for many years now." She then hung her head for a moment, as if to gather her final strength, and looked up through saddened eyes, "I have to leave you, Jonathon. I want to travel, and if God is good, I will find a husband. A man who will love me as a woman needs to be loved. I'm thirty years old now and some may say I've already missed the boat."

She looked into his brown eyes, searching for a glimmer of hope and then continued, "Now I will be truly honest with you, Jonathon. I have loved you. Not since the first day I saw you, as I was too young and you were still in mourning for your beautiful wife. But my love has grown stronger over the years, as I've realised what a truly remarkable man you are, so kind and gentle, never hurting a soul." Her speech quickened, "Except the ones who deserve to be hurt and locked up in prison."

Jonathon could have stopped her right there, putting her out of her misery. But if the truth be known, he was enjoying her sincerity. It furthered the awakening he felt on his journey home. Only this time his thoughts were coming from Marjorie's pretty lips.

"I know I would never be able to find a man like you, Jonathon, not even if I travelled to the end of the earth. You must understand, Jonathon, I've spent my last years here praying and hoping you would feel even the slightest love and attraction for me. I finally realise now I've wasted my time, which is the reason I was crying with Colleen. This day is the beginning of the end for us."

Marjorie hurried the last sentence, as she felt tears welling once again and so hung her head waiting for him to respond with, *I understand Marjorie and I wish you well with your travels.*

Jonathon had remained silent throughout her confession, but at that moment he walked towards her. Looking up, Marjorie met his outstretched arms, only to fall into them and cry even more. Holding her tight, he took in her softness and scent, realising he'd missed the feel, the smell and the touch of a woman so much.

"Marjorie, my dearest, please hear me as I tell you. I love you and I apologise with all my heart for shelving my feelings before this."

Her crying stopped but she chose to stay in his arms.

Jonathon knew he should be more ashamed of hurting her but he was too elated to feel much guilt. "My dear Margi, I was thinking all the way home as to how I would ask you to marry me. So now I will ask you. Will you marry me, Marjorie?"

Marjorie laughed and cried so loud that Colleen came bursting into the room. Marjorie broke away from Jonathon to hold Colleen. "Oh Colleen, Jonathon has just asked me to marry him!"

"Well, my girl, have you answered him?"

"No. Oh yes, YES, I will!" And she rushed once more to his arms.

In a soft voice, Jonathon said, "You know now that God is good. Your prayers have been answered. You've found the man who truly loves you, and we'll take our honeymoon overseas. So, you'll finally travel abroad as you have wished. I'm well overdue for a holiday, as I know you are too. We'll discuss where you would like to go over dinner this evening." He then asked Colleen if she and Bob would join them on this very happy occasion.

Meanwhile, back at the hunt, Patrick was finding it difficult to follow Lord Milne.

"He's too bloody slow, Angus. He can't ride to save himself! Even the bloody hounds are out of sight. Stuff this, I'm taking the lead." With that, Patrick bounded ahead of Lord Milne with Angus in fast pursuit.

"Hey there, I say, get back in the ranks, you lads," Lord Milne called, red faced and out of breath. He watched as the two-raced past. Of course, he was a little upset, but he knew he was past being master of the hunt. Never one to make a scene or put anyone off side, Lord Milne accepted the move and victory to another rider.

"What's going on, your Lordship? Damn rude of those young blokes to take over, against all etiquette. I'll fetch them back. They've been forging ahead all morning."

"No, no don't bother, Freddy. I gave them the go-ahead. Not feeling up to the chase today. I think I'll retire. Let them lead the way. And if you don't mind me saying so, they are the most competent riders here. I'll see you back at the homestead for lunch." Lord Milne was so breathless he had trouble getting his sentences out. Tipping his hat at his fellow hunters, he gave the sign he'd retired.

Patrick couldn't help himself. Whenever there was a challenge, no matter how big or wide the fallen tree, he'd urge his horse to take the highest and widest part. Directly behind him, Angus found courage in his brother's shadow. The rest of the riders admired their leader's bravery and elite horsemanship but chose the narrow easy way. The hunt continued for over two and a half hours, with only a few minor casualties along the way. To appease his guests' concern about any injuries, Lord Milne had hired an attractive young nurse from the Adelaide Hospital, Helen Groves. It was her day off duty, so she was more than pleased to drive the medical buggy and be on hand.

Jennifer Rose, Angus's girlfriend, had accompanied Helen in the buggy. Her reason for riding in the buggy rather than being in the hunt was that the fast pace and tackling the uneven jumps truly scared her. The two young ladies had spent the morning chatting and catching up on the local gossip. Helen, after becoming acquainted with Jennifer, who'd mentioned she was a close friend of Angus Darcy, felt confident to confide in Jennifer her feelings when she first met Patrick Darcy that morning.

"This morning, Jennifer, at the introductions…" Helen hesitated for a moment. She still held concerns about divulging what she'd felt. "Perhaps I shouldn't tell you this, Jennifer, but I simply must tell somebody. I just couldn't believe how my heart really raced the moment I was introduced to Patrick Darcy, especially after he lingered with a kiss on my hand. His amazing blue eyes gazed into mine and he asked if I was staying for the ball this evening. My reply was far too swift for my own liking." She let a giggle escape before continuing, "I said, 'Yes, yes I am, Patrick and I would like very much to dance with you.' I blushed, thinking, how shocking. A girl doesn't ask a boy to dance! Why did I say such a thing?"

Helen laughed out loud, before looking at Jennifer's horrified expression. She knew then not to go any further. What Helen didn't know was that Patrick had had similar thoughts. *Yes, another easy conquest. I'll be safe tonight from Emily Tompkins. The likes of her and her common hotel-owning mother would never be allowed to set foot on the grounds of the snobbish Lord Milne. My evening, therefore, will be free so I can execute my plan of making love to yet another beautiful young woman.* He then spared a kind thought for Emily. As he totally disagreed with snobbery, it was a waste of time, especially a good time.

Lord Milne held onto his chest as the pain had increased. He'd only just made it back to the homestead before collapsing from his horse. Thankfully, his gardener saw it and ran to him while calling for help. Mable, the Lord's cook, panicked when seeing her boss in such distress. She called out, "Quickly, somebody get the nurse!" Mable had been with the family for many years and became even more distressed when fearing the worst. She tried to make Lord Milne comfortable on the ground where he lay. Because he was large and overweight, she thought he would be hard to move, and any attempt to do so may cause him more pain. As Lord Milne gasped for breath and moaned in pain, Mable began to pray.

Their youngest jackaroo, Adam, had ridden off at a flat gallop to find Nurse Helen. It took him only ten minutes to find her because she was returning with a young man on board. The young man, thankfully, was Angus. When his horse had shied, Angus smacked his leg on a tree trunk. Although in pain, he was enjoying the trip home with the girls and remained amused at his brother's quip.

"Ah, ya just did that on purpose to get in the cart with the girls, especially Jenny."

Patrick gave him a wink before he threw him up effortlessly into the wagon. Nurse Helen pulled the horses up when she saw the jackaroo riding straight for them.

"Come! Come quickly, the boss is havin' a heart attack!"

Angus miraculously overcame the pain in his ankle and jumped up to grab the reins from Helen. He'd just about caught up with the galloping jackaroo when he skidded the horses to a halt. Angus jumped off and after examining Lord Milne, he said, "Yes, he's having a heart attack."

Turning to Mable, Angus said, "I think I'll be able to help him but it'd be better if Doctor Liu was here. Oh, never mind, he's overseas anyway, don't worry. I'll do my best."

Then Jennifer cut in, "My father's a qualified doctor, Angus. He should be the one to attend Lord Milne. This situation needs a professional doctor, not any stupid Chinese medicine you can give him!"

Mable chided herself for not sending for the doctor. "Oh, why didn't I think of Doctor Rose? Adam, I'm sorry, please hurry and find Doctor Rose." Mable called out to the young jackaroo. "Ride for your life, Adam."

The last thing Angus wanted to be was disrespectful, but he knew Doctor Rose was not half the doctor that Liu was, especially in his knowledge of medicines and cures. Angus composed himself and concentrated on the exact pressure points where he could relax the patient and relieve pain. Luckily, he had brought with him his medicine bag, which was full of important antidotes and cures. Doctor Liu had given him this bag as a reward for learning the procedures he'd taught him. "You smarter than me, Angus, you take three years to learn. I take ten, you good man, you use medicine wise.' Liu had said as he handed him the leather Gladstone bag. The bag came with instructions on the dose and medicine to give for each complaint.

Angus pleaded with Jennifer. "Will you forget about who's right and who's wrong for a moment, Jennifer? Please go to my room quickly and bring me back my medicine bag. I promise you, it will help Lord Milne."

She replied fervently, "I've just told you, Angus, I don't believe in that Chinese hog wash, nor does my father!" She stood, defiant.

Mable threw an angry look at her, thinking, *if you were mine, I'd give you a hard slap for that remark*, before she said, "I'll get your bag, Angus. You just do your best for the boss. I'll do anything to help."

Mable ran as fast as she could while Angus worked hard at what he'd been taught. When she returned with the bag, Nurse Helen was kneeling beside Angus, taking particular interest in what he was doing.

Calmly, Angus asked Helen, "I need you to press on this point for sixty seconds and then return to this spot. Alternate there, until I return. I must mix the medicine correctly to help his blood flow." After this acupuncture procedure, Mable noticed her boss becoming calmer and thanked God for Angus. He took no more than a minute to mix the medicine before he asked, "Please help me sit him up, Mable. You help too, Helen." Angus then administered the medicine orally.

"Swallow, there's a good chap, Lord Milne, now swallow again. The quicker you get this into you, the quicker you'll recover."

After the medicine had been taken, Angus took over from Helen, who sat in awe of this confident young man.

"You're truly amazing, Angus. Who did you learn this form of medicine from?" Angus went on to tell Helen the story of their wonderful Doctor Liu from the beginning.

Jennifer, whether it was jealousy, or seeing her father riding towards them, stomped away.

Doctor Rose, a small man about forty years old and with possibly limited knowledge in cures for heart attacks, barged his way through the onlookers, demanding, "I'll take over now thank you, Angus."

His manner was aggressive so Angus took a deep breath, not wanting to lose his temper.

"With all due respect, sir, Lord Milne is beginning to come around. I have just administered herbal medicine. It will soon make his blood flow faster and hopefully clear the blockage. If he follows my advice and keeps on taking the medicine, it will considerably lower his risk of heart attacks and…"

"Oh rubbish! I'm a real doctor. Now step aside, young man, I need to have a look at him."

As Doctor Rose went to grab Angus by the shoulder, a hand came from the crowd and grabbed Doctor Rose by the arm.

"That's my brother you're about to push away, sir, and as far as I can see, he's already saved Lord Milne's life. There's no need for you to move any closer, other than where you stand."

Patrick's tone of voice and tight hold on the doctor's arm gave him an unmistakable message. The doctor turned and walked away.

Finally, Lord Milne managed a grin toward Angus. Patrick then took charge and asked everyone to give them room.

"Thank you, everyone, it seems now that Lord Milne is feeling much better." Patrick placed his arm around Mable's shoulder.

"Mable, could you please see to the lunch for the guests. We'll wait here a while before moving his Lordship inside. A warm blanket for his Lordship would be most welcome too. Thank you."

Patrick then looked with pride at Angus and shook his hand. "Well done, brother. Liu will be proud of you."

Angus's expression was more of relief than pride as he smiled and then looked down at Lord Milne.

"You seem to be feeling a little better now, your Lordship," Angus said.

"Yes, thank you, Angus, I now realise what people say about you is true. You're a very intelligent young man, well beyond your years. I'm sure you'll make a very fine doctor."

Lord Milne turned to Patrick. "Your father has told me you are headed for Sandhurst to become an officer. Take my advice, son, and study hard. The army needs brave young men like you. But I'll give you some advice. Using your brain will keep you alive, Patrick. There's no good being a brave dead hero. Yes, my lad, strategy is the greatest weapon."

As Patrick listened to this advice, he changed his opinion of this man, whom he thought at first to be a doddering old fool.

"Thank you very much for your advice, sir. But please save your strength."

"Yes, quite right. I am very tired, Patrick."

Angus then stepped in. "You will soon feel strong enough to enter the house, sir, but then you must go to bed and take this medicine every four hours."

"Yes, Doctor," he said with a cheeky smile. Struggling, he then lifted his hand up to pat Angus on the back.

"Please, Angus," he said, then looked toward Patrick, "and you too, Patrick, would you kindly take charge of this evening's proceedings, as you have done this afternoon. Please make sure my guests have a wonderful time." The boys nodded and helped Lord Milne back to the house and up to bed. Later, Patrick sat watching his younger brother dress in his formal evening attire, and thinking about the tiff between Angus and Jennifer that day.

"Angus, you must be heartbroken after Jennifer's disappointing behaviour."

"No, not at all, brother. I hold no physical attraction towards Jennifer. However, I thought her to be a more sensitive, intelligent human being than what she displayed to us today."

"You make me laugh, Angus. You're such a bloody cold frog."

With the devil in him and a twinkle in his eye, Patrick then said, "I should lead you astray tonight, brother. I think it's time for you to experience the sensuous warmth of a young woman's naked body, thrusting your manhood deeper and deeper until you both cry with orgasmic ecstasy. There's nothing better, I'm telling you."

Angus held his head high. "I'm not ready for that sort of thing, thank you, Patrick. I'll tell you when I am and you can lead me astray then."

He offered Patrick his hand, but instead Patrick grabbed his wrist, giving him a severe Chinese burn.

Angus cried out. "You bastard, Pat!"

He began to fist up, while Patrick laughed hysterically. "I just wanted to get you feeling something, brother."

Placing his hands around his head and crying like a baby, Patrick whimpered, "Please don't hurt me, Angus. Please don't hurt me. I feel things much more than you do."

Angus lowered his fists. "I'll let you off this time, brother." Angus messed his hair and said, "Come on, let's join the party."

With their arms wrapped around each other's shoulder, the two walked into the ballroom, looking so handsome that they turned heads. Young women giggled and whispered, gazing sideways at the most admired young men in the room. Although Angus was two years younger than Patrick and two inches shorter, he was still tall at five feet ten. The two soon parted company, as Angus knew his brother needed to play the room.

On the prowl with his lethal charm, Patrick spoke with his eyes to every young female who looked his way. He decided, *I'll waste no time dancing with pretty little things too young to seduce. Nurse Helen will do. She'd be around twenty, I think, and very attractive.*

He'd already made up his mind to faze Emily out, sensing the danger there. Emily was too immature and demanding. He'd seen the warning signs. He then swore silently to himself. *No woman is ever going to tie me down, not until I'm well and truly ready, which may be never.* His search for Helen was interrupted by a group of men standing talking together. They beckoned Patrick over and complimented him on his riding ability. They commented on how proud he must be of his younger brother knowing so much about medicine, especially as he was so young.

"It's truly amazing," one gentleman said.

"Ah yes, gentlemen. But you know my brother is a genius at whatever he pursues. From the age of ten, he's challenged and won every chess game with the best players in the land. My father is so proud of Angus." Patrick paused and smiled. "I'm near to hopeless at the game, although if I were moving pretty young ladies around a chess board, I may just conquer him!"

The group laughter had almost stopped when he caught an off-putting comment. "You mean Angus's father." Patrick turned and stared at Cedric Mott, the father of a boy he detested at school.

Patrick replied through gritted teeth, "Jonathon Darcy is my father. My sperm donor is dead. I've been legally adopted by Jonathon Darcy. Therefore, he is my father. He's our father."

Cecil Mott smiled smugly and walked away. The men had remained silent as they'd witnessed the confrontation, but all patted Patrick on the back as he turned back to them. Patrick smiled, bowed his head and excused himself.

Luckily, before Patrick could, Angus found Nurse Helen and took her to a secluded veranda. *One up on you, brother*, he thought. Not that Angus had anything else on his mind, other than explaining to Helen how he truly believed in Chinese herbal medicine, even though it was frowned upon.

"And you know, Helen, most of our medicines come from plants and fungi, even leeches are used to rid the body of bad blood and rotten flesh. So, I cannot imagine why our medical professionals don't own up and admit that we need this knowledge. Especially so, where in foreign lands their people have existed for thousands and thousands of years and the techniques Doctor Liu has shown me for relieving pain are unobtrusive and work incredibly well. You saw it yourself today." Angus hadn't come up for breath with his information when he noticed Patrick walking towards them. Patrick stood before them, giving Helen a look Angus knew so well. It was never hard to guess what Patrick was thinking; his animated good looks gave him away every time.

"Oh, don't stop on my behalf, Angus, I'm sure Helen was riveted by your conversation."

Angus knew when he was defeated.

"It's okay, Patrick, we've been talking for some time now. Would you like me to get you a glass of punch, Helen?"

Helen smiled sweetly, "Thank you, Angus, that would be lovely."

Holding his hand out, Patrick gave Helen his look of desire and demanded, "Let's dance."

The music changed from a quick fox trot to a soft romantic waltz. Patrick lowered his head, his lips resting on her swan-like neck.

"You look magnificent in red, Helen, it suits your soft white skin. Skin I would love to explore."

Kissing her softly on the neck he then aroused her with his tongue before giving a gentle bite. It made her flinch but she wanted more. This sensual experience, along with the sensation of his well-muscled body holding her close into his loins, began her fire within. Patrick felt her melt in his arms. He gazed around the room. It was packed, so slipping away would not be difficult. As they ran across the moonlit lawn, Helen shivered.

"It's cold out here, Patrick."

He turned and smiled, "I'll soon warm you up, Helen."

A small wooden garden shed lay just outside the garden's boundary. It was well hidden by trees and shrubs. Earlier, Patrick had placed two blankets and a bottle of Clare Valley shiraz inside the shed. The red wine had been a real find, as it was a vintage blended by the monks of the local Clare Valley monastery, masters at winemaking. The wine was usually kept safe in Lord Milne's underground cellar, but not tonight. Patrick had prepared for his indulgence.

Opening the door for Helen to enter, he then followed, closing it gently before he slid the bolt. She watched his every move, until her eyes closed when his lips began kissing hers. He was so gentle she barely felt him undressing her. As moonlight streamed through the cracks in the aged wood, he stood back to admire her nakedness. This is what he'd loved ever since he'd found a peephole in the orphanage bathroom. It enabled him to watch the unclothed young girls washing themselves. Patrick believed girls were to be adored, loved and worshipped. Helen was not shy, at least not tonight. She'd made love before, with her first boyfriend, but that was an awkward unromantic event, more like an animal relieving himself. This young man, Patrick, gave forth such a sensual aura, she could do nothing but relinquish control and enjoy him.

Knowing what she was about to do was wrong, as she'd only just met him, Helen still wanted to make love to him like nothing else mattered. This evening she was prepared to be properly and thoroughly seduced by this devil in angel-disguise. Her body tingled with sensuous expectation. Patrick gently cupped her breasts in his hands, kissing each nipple. This sensation alone was almost too much for Helen to bear. She moaned and he stopped to lay her down on the blanket. Helen had full view of him undressing, which he did with the art of a professional stripper. She couldn't help but smile when he dropped his pants and exposed his erection. Parting her legs, she placed her slender arms above her head to give Patrick licence to perfectly seduce her.

She was duly sent into rapture, but was mature enough not to say, "I love you, Patrick," which is what she truly wanted to say. Instead she kissed his chest to prevent her words from escaping. Heaven then slowly slipped away as he eased himself off her.

"I'd love some of that wine you have, Patrick."

His lips brushed her forehead before he rose.

Helen smiled. "You thought of everything, Patrick. When did you prepare this?"

"This afternoon, when no one was looking."

"You were pretty sure of yourself then."

Patrick raised his eyebrow and grinned.

"With all due respect, my lovely Helen, you gave yourself away when you said, 'I'd love to dance with you, Patrick'. I knew then you'd like to do more than dance. So, I planned our escape and I'm bloody glad I did, aren't you?" After pouring two glasses of wine, he turned his charm on Helen. *The smile of a conqueror,* she thought. Giggling, Helen agreed with his assumption, she then lay back, admiring his naked masculinity.

"You are truly magnificent, Patrick. How old are you?"

"You don't need to know that, Helen. I'm old enough and that's all that matters. And I suspect you are too. Cheers!" They drank quickly, and began once again their slow indulgent pleasure of the flesh. Helen, however, knew that Patrick had to be less than eighteen because of the tweed jacket he'd worn in the hunt; it was to be worn only by the junior riders. She didn't care, she loved him. Every tiny hair on his body, every magnificent inch of him, and his dreamy come-to-bed eyes, and his blond curls, which she'd love to have herself, but most of all his sincere admiration and love for women. At the same time, she knew in her soul he was never meant for one woman alone. Helen was convinced God had sent him to the lucky ones. Only they would understand and appreciate him. She decided then she'd be more than happy to be part of his harem.

Chapter 4
Dilemma

Two months later and the warmth of the spring sun filtered into Patrick's classroom. Fresh air flowed through wide open windows. This was his favourite time of year. He sat daydreaming, as usual, only half-listening to the boring maths teacher.

"Thank God," Patrick said aloud, when the bell finally rang. It was his last class for the day. Tomorrow would be Friday, and on Saturday he would be home riding the cross-country course, playing soldiers, battling with his brother and other friends who had joined them.

"Girls and warfare. That's all you care about, Patrick!"

Angus had said this to him, not so long ago, when Patrick pinned him down after jumping from a tree, pretending to be a sniper. On that particular day, Patrick had ridden off in front of Angus, disappearing into the densest part of the bush. Angus called out and searched for some time before becoming anxious. The next thing Angus knew, Patrick had silently propelled himself from high up in a tree, and landed on the back of Angus's horse. He then pulled Angus to the ground and pinned him there.

"You're dead, brother!" Patrick said, before kissing Angus on the cheek.

That was when Angus had given his appraisal on Patrick's interests. However, he was interested in Patrick's methods in training his horse to stay quiet and still in one place. His talent with horses never ceased to amaze Angus.

"I suppose you have the same special, almost hypnotising gift with women too."

Patrick threw his head back laughing. "You suppose, brother! Of course I do and I'll teach you when you're ready. Remember, I'm just waiting for you to give me the go-ahead."

"How did you do that with your horse, Pat, to keep him quiet where is he?"

"I'll show you and then I'll teach you. I thought if I could train a dog to stay, I should be able to train a horse." And so began the lessons.

It was now Friday afternoon and they were finally released from school. Two familiar people waited at the school gate in separate buggies: Bob, Colleen's husband, in his buggy and Emily Thompson in hers. Patrick looked from one to the other, whereas Angus jumped aboard with Bob, giving him a hug and a robust handshake. Emily sat with a sour expression on her face and said, "You'd better come with me, Patrick. I have something very important to tell you!"

Patrick's heart fell. Instinctively he knew Emily's demanding tone was not just about him putting off her advances. *I'm studying, I can't make it today. Sorry, Emily,* this had been his excuse. It had also been three months, almost to the day, when Patrick had let his juices flow with Emily's. Just as well, he thought, that Dad and Marjorie are on their honeymoon. Marjorie had opted out of the big wedding, telling Jonathon she'd rather they just travel abroad for three or four months, as soon as possible. Jonathon was more than pleased to accommodate her wishes.

Patrick had been sneaking out at night lately, keeping up his romance with Nurse Helen, who had her own educated ways of killing semen. So the freedom from that concern made for their heightened sexual pleasure.

Now Patrick sat silent in Emily's buggy, thinking, *If only I'd known Helen's method, the two times I actually fucked Emily, none of what I suspect is about to happen would have.*

"You're very quiet, Patrick. Something bothering you?" Emily asked condescendingly, as she drove her Cobb out of town.

Patrick thought, *Of course she's smug, knowing she has something over me. Did she think I would do the right thing and marry her, just because she's carrying my baby?*

He tried to chirp up a little to hide his concern. "No, no, there's nothing bothering me, Emily."

Like bloody hell there's not. He then tried to muster a cheery note once again. "So, tell me, Emily, how are you and what have you been up to? You look well."

Patrick gave her a brief smile, certainly not his usual come-to-bed smile. She was offended and angry. He'd insulted her. Patrick didn't seem to want her and yet she did nothing but dream of him day and night. Especially at night, when she could actually orgasm just thinking about their lovemaking.

Emily flicked the whip hard on the Palomino's rump, making it gallop so fast even Patrick became worried. "Hey, hey Emily, what are you trying to do, kill us both!"

He grabbed the reins and pulled the horse back to a jog, before pulling it over to the side of the road. Then Emily began to cry.

"For God's sake, Emily, what's wrong with you?" Patrick's yelling was not what Emily needed. She needed him to hold her, make love to her. His aggression made her wail even louder. She sounded like a wounded cow until Patrick had the good sense to hold her tight. After his warm caress, she calmed down a little until she yelled through a flood of tears.

"I'M PREGNANT!"

Patrick's worst fears were realised. "Well, what do you want me to do about it?" She didn't answer Patrick's question, instead she kept crying.

Immediately he regretted saying the words, especially in the harsh tone he'd used. "We're too young to be married, Emily, and I know you don't want to be tied down with a baby."

She screamed uncontrollably and began punching his chest.

Oh Christ, think, Patrick! he told himself.

Holding her arms to prevent her from hitting him again, Patrick spoke much more sensitively. "Emily, please listen to me. I've been telling you the truth about not being able to see you. I've been studying hard to make a future, one I've considered you to be part of. If you go ahead with this pregnancy, it will ruin everything. I'm only seventeen, hardly old enough to support a wife and child. I'd have to leave college and work all day and night in the mines!"

He knew he wouldn't, but it sounded convincing. Emily began to control her crying and listened. "You wouldn't want that to happen, now would you, my dear Emily?"

Patrick knew he was beginning to win her over, so he continued to talk while holding her close. She seemed to stay calm if he held her. "Let's do something about this problem and then we can make plans for our future— when the time is right."

She began weighing it all up. So far, she liked what she was hearing, especially about *their future!*

"When I've completed my studies and graduated, I'll become an officer in the army. I'll then be able to keep you in the fashion you so deserve, my dearest." Kissing her softly on the head, Patrick then smiled, proud of his own charm.

Emily answered while still sniffling. "Well, what do you think we should do, Patrick?"

"All we have to do, Emily, is for you to take a small amount of medicine. Once, or twice at the most and all our worries will be over."

"Is it that simple, Patrick? Are you sure? And where will you get this medicine, from your Chinese doctor, no doubt?"

Her cynicism annoyed him, but he couldn't afford to lose his temper. Calmly he answered, "I do not divulge my secrets, Emily, just trust me. It won't take long and it will only cause you a little discomfort. We can ask your mother if you may spend the weekend at our home. Colleen and Bob are there to supervise us. We'll host a young people's gathering to play tennis for the weekend beginning tomorrow, Saturday. This will give us cover to be alone tonight and for you to take the medicine."

Looking her directly in the eye, Patrick then tried to find a shred of intellect in a mind he thought to be truly devoid of it. "If you agree, Emily, then I'll turn around and we'll go and ask your mother."

Patrick then panicked a little with what he hadn't considered. "She doesn't know you're pregnant, does she, Emily?"

"No, of course not, I've kept it to myself. I'm too ashamed to tell anyone." Emily kept whimpering so as to take advantage of Patrick's body being close to hers. *Well, at least she's listening to reason.*

A feeling of great relief overcame Patrick; he felt confident. *With help from Angus, we'll fix the problem quickly, tonight to be exact. Bob and Colleen are pushovers, especially if Angus wants something special to happen at home. Therefore, it shouldn't be a problem to ask a few friends to stay over for a weekend of tennis. This will take the attention away from Emily. I'm certain Angus knows the right formula to mix for abortions. After all, Doctor Liu has taught Angus absolutely everything.*

Mrs Ruby Tomkins, Emily's mother, was a young and very attractive woman. She was more than pleased for her daughter to be asked to stay at the illustrious home of the well-respected Jonathon Darcy. Not too many people of notoriety paid Ruby and Emily any attention, except for the few well-respected gentlemen who very discreetly kept Ruby's company on the occasional dark night. Ruby Tomkins had actually blushed when Patrick laid his charm on her, that afternoon, kissing her sensuously on her hand and paying her a compliment.

"If you don't mind me saying so, Mrs Tomkins, I would not be mistaken if I called you Emily's sister and just as beautiful, of course."

Ruby giggled like a schoolgirl when, in fact, she was a hard-nosed business woman, with a well-acted coy demeanour. However, she thought, *this young man could charm the pants off any girl—or woman. Not too many males could produce such a feeling in me. I'd love to seduce him right now.* As Ruby's bust heaved and her pulse raced with her naughty vision, she licked her lips. Without taking his dreamy eyes from her seductive looks, Patrick mirrored the lust that seemed to be welling up between them. *Just as well he's about to leave*, Ruby thought when her daughter walked happily from her bedroom carrying her overnight tote bag. Noticing the look on her mother's face, Emily immediately took hold of Patrick's arm, bidding her a blunt farewell, and dragged him from the room.

On the way to Patrick's home, they called upon some of his friends. All accepted his invitation, saying they would be there first thing in the morning to play tennis and stay for the weekend. All was going well, so far.

However, the plan soon met with a hitch. When Patrick confided his problem to Angus when they were alone, Angus exploded. "NO, definitely not! As a doctor, I will be sworn to save lives, not take them."

Patrick was outraged. "But that's it, brother, you're not a doctor yet! You haven't taken the oath. I know you can get rid of this problem. Please, Angus, put yourself in my position."

Angus fumed at his brother's request. Storming to the window he stood defiantly, looking out across the darkening sky, and his reply was firm. "That's it, brother, I would never put myself in your position! And an innocent baby should not be got... rid of, as you put it."

"Maybe not, Angus. Maybe you're right about the baby. But please try and put yourself in my shoes. I know it's hard for you to understand at the moment, for as you've said, you're not ready, but when you are my brother..."

Angus stopped him right there, almost yelling, "I'll be married, PATRICK, and the baby will be planned!"

Patrick's patience with his brother's holier-than-thou attitude was beginning to aggravate him so much so he wanted to plant one right on Angus's chin. Instead he kept his cool. He put his argument across another way.

"Ok Angus, just think of it this way. Do you want Emily as your sister-in-law? You know how much she annoys you, so do you want me to be tied down with someone I don't love for the rest of my life. For Christ's sake, Angus, I'm only seventeen. If you love me, you'll mix the bloody stuff and give it to her. I know you know how to do it. Liu's taught you almost everything he knows." Patrick sat riveted on the bed, watching the expression on Angus's face slowly become thoughtful. So, he waited patiently for the reply. Finally and solemnly, Angus looked Patrick in the eye.

"You know I don't want to do this, Patrick. It's against everything I believe in. But, as you've just put it, yes, I do love you, every bit as much as I love my parents. I always wanted a brother, maybe it was a plan from God himself to send you. I don't know. But I do know we're here on earth to learn lessons, and I don't want you to keep learning the hard way. But I do want you to learn. You mustn't go around getting young women pregnant, just for your own pleasure. If you promise me you'll change your ways with young women, then I will do this for you."

Patrick tried hard not to laugh. Angus had left himself wide open with his righteous attitude. *Change my ways? That could mean a different position, perhaps the girl should be on top. Yes, I'll try it next time with Nurse Helen.* Without saying a word, Patrick turned and took hold of the Bible which sat on the bedside table.

"I, Patrick Darcy, do swear on the Holy Bible, that I will change my ways with young women."

When Angus agreed, utter relief flooded Patrick but he kept his expression veiled. Then he took off quickly to find Emily. She was in the kitchen chatting with Colleen. He waited until the ladies had finished their small talk before he asked.

"May I please speak with Emily alone, Colleen?" Smiling at Colleen's look of surprise, he continued, "It's about what we should buy for a mutual friend's birthday next week."

Emily was, as usual, two steps behind his intellect, so she placed her head to one side. "What are you talking about, Patrick? We don't have a friend with a birthday next week?"

Colleen thought nothing of it and so continued preparing the dinner while singing her favourite song, *I'll walk you home again, Kathleen.*

Escorting Emily by the arm, Patrick said, "I'll remind you, Emily, if you come with me."

With trembling hands, Angus handed her the drink. "I'm sorry, Emily, but you'll have to agree to take this. Do you know what it will do?"

Hanging her head for a moment she then rose to look Angus in the eye. "Yes, I do. Patrick says it will cause an abortion, but with only minor discomfort. Is this true?"

"As far as I have been told, this is true, Emily. It should begin to work within a few hours. You may need another dose, if nothing has occurred before morning. You must go to the toilet as soon as you feel any cramping pain and please stay there until you have passed all of the blood."

Emily took the cup hesitantly from his hand, then quickly swallowed the bitter fluid. Sitting beside Emily, with his arm around her, Patrick said, "Remember, Emily, this is for the best—our future."

She nodded, wishing the taste would disappear from her mouth. Angus offered her a sweet toffee. "Thank you," she said kindly before sucking and slurping noisily on the toffee.

Patrick felt at ease and a little surprised that Emily was actually being sensible. He kissed her on the head and then rose. "Well then, let's all freshen up for dinner, shall we? Colleen will be ringing the dinner bell soon." Helping Emily up from his bed, Patrick escorted her to her room and assured her. "You'll be fine, Emily. I'll see you downstairs for dinner in ten minutes."

Closing the door behind him, he gave thanks to the Lord. Within seconds he was confused. Why would he thank the Lord, who would look upon him unfavourably? Patrick took it back and thanked Doctor Liu instead.

They had dinner in the kitchen because it was only Bob, Colleen, Patrick, Angus and, of course, Emily. It was far more informal and cosy than eating in the large regal dining room. Patrick did his best to cheer up the gathering by telling funny stories. However, a strained atmosphere hung between Angus and Emily. Colleen noticed and asked, "Are yer alright, Emily? You've only played with yer food, and hardly eaten a thing?"

"Yes, I'm fine, Mrs Thompson. I'm just tired and not really hungry, I suppose. I hope you will excuse me. I'm feeling very tired and need to go to bed."

"Of course, m' dear, you do look a little peaked. Go and get y' rest so you can enjoy the tennis tamorra. I'll be makin' some real treats for y' hungry young people. I know Angus will be pleased. I'm makin' his favourite Cornish pasties." Colleen threw him a glance, but Angus smiled only slightly while looking down at his half-eaten dinner. Not the usual thank-you Colleen would receive for such a promise.

"Oh dear," Colleen responded, "it seems we're all a wee bit under the weather this evenin'. Maybe we should be havin' an early night. I'll save the apple pie for tamorra."

Patrick had licked his plate and immediately quipped, "Oh, no ya won't, me lovely Colleen. I'll be havin' some a dat delicious pie now!" Colleen shook her head amused, as she piled his plate high with a large piece of pie and clotted cream.

During the night, Emily woke with the expected cramping pains. She found her way to the bathroom while clutching a large towel between her legs to prevent blood spilling onto the floor. Not long after, Angus thought he was disturbed in his sleep by his deceased mother, Sally. He looked around, but there was no one there. He was sure he'd heard her voice saying, "Angus, Angus, wake up dear, Emily needs you." Angus walked sleepy-eyed to the bathroom where he heard Emily moan. He whispered through the keyhole.

"Emily, can you hear me? Are you alright?"

"I don't know, Angus," she said half-sobbing, half-groaning. "I've been bleeding and in pain for over an hour now. I feel faint. Please help me."

Angus opened the door and approached her. He was shocked by the whiteness of her complexion. He had to think clearly. *Yes, I know how to stop bleeding. Massive doses of strawberry tea leaves, but do I have enough?*

"I'm just going to mix you something to stop the bleeding, but first I'll get you something sweet to give you energy. Just stay there. I won't be long." Angus went quickly to Patrick's room and shook him. "Wake up, wake up, Patrick. You'll have to go and sit with Emily. She's losing too much blood. I'll have to mix something which will stop it."

Patrick rose, thinking he was in a dream. Angus gave him another shake. "Patrick, go now and sit with Emily, hold onto her. Can you hear me? Go to the bathroom. I'll be back in a moment."

Angus's heart was pounding like a drum. He thought it was nerves, or was it pride in his knowledge and ability to administer medicine—he wasn't sure. Boiling

242

up the strawberry tea, Angus was hoping he was actually saving her life now. He worried he'd given her too much of the mixture in the first place. He was only fifteen and began to form doubts but then he focused on his ability and the knowledge of correct procedure. This drama gave Angus a view about his future. Straining the liquid and leaves through a piece of cloth into a large jug, he then carried both upstairs. He was pleased to see Patrick sitting close to Emily, gently stroking her back. Angus handed Emily the tea in the jug and asked her to drink it all. The three then sat for another long hour until Emily said, "I feel much better now the bleeding's stopped."

Angus said, "You best wash yourself and then apply the cloth of strawberry leaves to your private parts." He felt quite pleased with himself but he knew he could not quite trust Emily's temperament or mental stability, even though she'd behaved in a mature, even brave manner. He decided to make sure Emily and Patrick were sworn to secrecy.

"We are never, ever, to divulge this to another living soul. Do you both agree?"

Patrick chimed in straight off the bat. "Of course, Angus, we're all in this together."

Emily stalled and then said, "My pledge will be given, only after Patrick has given his word of honour that he will keep his promise to marry me, once he is an officer in the army, of course." Patrick's heart fell; it was as if his life had just ended. He sat silent until Emily prodded him.

"Well, Patrick, it's up to you now, or the secret will be out."

Bloody blackmail but this isn't the moment to challenge her. "Yes, yes of course, Emily. Now let's get you up so you can go about washing your private parts, as my brother so modestly put it." Patrick laughed a little, trying to lessen the blow, trusting she wouldn't see the disdain in his smile. After Emily's personal clean up, the brothers then put her back into bed and then quietly covered up all traces of evidence. Emily soon fell into a deep sleep, dreaming of the day she and Patrick would marry.

Patrick hugged Angus for some time before returning to his room. No verbal exchange was necessary. Angus was a little concerned at how his brother would ever get himself out of the marriage he'd promised to Emily. A cheeky smile brushed his face as he drifted off to sleep. *Whatever it takes, Patrick will win with his brilliance and cunning. It's one of the many traits I admire in my brother.*

Chapter 5
Homecoming

Only a glimmer of guilt shaded Patrick throughout the week that followed. Angus, however, would toss and turn at night and spend most days asking their priest for forgiveness, although he never divulged the whole truth. Angus felt only a little relief from the Hail Marys he'd been ordered to say. He really had no one to confide in fully until Doctor Liu returned from China. When Liu arrived a week later with his usual happy exuberance, Bob jumped up from his seat in the kitchen. "How are you, Liu, I'm so pleased you're back," he said shaking Liu's hand with gusto. "My rheumatism is killing me. Must be the cold weather and Angus has run out of the medicine."

Doctor Liu bowed. "No wully, no wully, Bob, I fix chop-chop. Where's boys and Colleen?"

"I'll call them for you, Liu, they're all upstairs. They'll be so pleased to see you're home safe."

While Bob was gone, Liu placed all the medicines he thought Angus may need on the kitchen table, and a large amount of one-hundred-year-old tea, neatly wrapped in fine silk. It was to be given to the Darcy family, as a gift from Liu's relatives.

Angus ran down the stairs, bursting into the kitchen and hugging Liu like his long-lost friend.

Friendly formalities and welcome homes were exchanged, then Liu asked Angus for his medicine bottles, saying he would replace all the medicine he had used. Angus knew straight away Liu would question why he'd used the drugs he had. Thank heavens for Colleen, as after she'd welcomed Liu home, she ordered them out of the kitchen.

"I have to be gettin' dinner ready now, so be off with y'. Go out t' the garden shed t' do all that medicine sortin', or I'll be getting' all that stuff in me cookin'. You'll be stayin' for dinner I hope, Doctor?"

Liu nodded. "Yes pwease, yes pwease, Colleen."

Being alone in the shed gave Angus the opportunity to talk with Liu about Emily's problem. "Doctor Liu, I don't know where to begin to tell you. I have perhaps destroyed your faith and trust in me and…"

Liu had been studying the medicines missing and butted in.

"You help young girl be rid of baby?"

"Yes, I'm so ashamed, but I had to help Patrick. He's my brother, I love him, and he's too young to be married, especially to a girl he doesn't love."

Angus's stomach turned with the thought that this may still happen.

"Don't wully, you vely smart boy, Angus! Patrick owes you big favour, one day he lepay, I sure young girl owe you too, bad choice, have baby no one want. In China, it happen all time. Evelyone has to eat. If no food, new baby say goodbye before it born. See you in next life, baby." Liu placed his arm around Angus, and continued. "You know, Angus, one day you save many rives, make up for this baby spirit. It just goes home to your God. Come back when leady."

This reminded Angus of his own laudable work with Lord Milne. Somewhat relieved and almost elated now, Angus confided in Liu, just how good it made him feel to be able to help and maybe even save Lord Milne's life.

Liu laughed. "There you see, no wully!" Liu looked again at the medicines.

"Young girl rost brud, I think plenty, you give her all the tea. This is good thing. I think you very good Chinese Doctor." They sorted the medicines, made an ample supply of rheumatism draft for Bob, and returned happily to the kitchen. Doctor Liu had brought back many gifts for everyone: a silk scarf for Colleen, a pair of silk slippers for Bob, and silk dressing gowns for the boys.

"I reave these plesents for Margi and Mr Jon when they leturn. I tell you, this country Austraya, vely best country in world, I think. I tell evelyone in China, come to Austraya, mostwy good people here, vely good life, plenty food. I think one day half Austraya people, half Chinese live here!" Liu laughed in his usual contagious way and continued with his prophecies.

"I think you boys have baby sister soon. Father and Margi make good love and have baby girl. I bet you. You rike a bet, yes?"

Loving a gamble, Colleen came in straight away. "I'll put a pound note on it, Liu. They'll have a boy, for sure and certain!"

Liu responded, "I give ten shilling to one. No boy, only girl."

When they all jumped in, agreeing with Colleen it would be another boy, Liu rubbed his hands together. "Easy money, yes, vely easy money."

Chapter 6
The Escape Plan

Nurse Helen had not only remained Patrick's lover but a good friend and confidant. He'd therefore confided in Helen the problem he'd had and was still having with Emily. Helen took it well, as it was not unexpected. However, one problem remained: how could he gently but firmly remove Emily from his life? This was proving difficult. A fine line hung between giving Emily enough attention so as not to anger her, and just enough attention so she didn't suspect his final rejection.

Patrick had managed to persuade Emily before she'd left him on their tennis weekend, not to tell her mother of their pending engagement, as he wanted to do it properly. "I will propose marriage at a family dinner party, Emily, after I graduate from college, when my future, our future, is sealed."

Emily was bursting at the seams in more ways than one, not only with the excitement of Patrick's promise. But it appeared she'd taken to comfort-eating lately, as she was unable to take sexual pleasure with Patrick after he'd told her he feared another pregnancy. "Emily, I'm very sorry." So, she ate incessantly to dull her lustful feelings. This gave way to a cruel but nonetheless workable idea that Patrick had thought up and now confided in Helen.

"Emily has become so enormous. I know it may be cruel, but I have an idea on how to be rid of her from my life. It concerns the seductive looks and sensual touches I receive from her mother on my rare visits."

Helen sat up, eager to hear his intrigue. She pulled the blanket up to cover her naked breasts. Patrick smiled cheekily, pulling the blanket back down.

"You know I like to look, Helen."

She pulled it straight back up. "I'm bloody cold, Patrick. Now tell me your plan."

"Well, what if Emily was to catch us, meaning her mother and me, in a compromising position. Would Emily blame herself for becoming fat, or would she blame her mother for seducing me?" He smiled his most devilish smile and continued. "Surely she wouldn't blame me, Helen. After all, I'm only seventeen and her mother should know better than to seduce a young man, especially her daughter's boyfriend!"

246

Helen lay back laughing; laughing so hard she began crying. Patrick leaned back on his elbows, ignoring her laughter, going over his plan. He then threw Helen a serious look and ordered her to stop laughing. "Helen, I need your help."

"Me? What can I do? Hold Emily down while she watches her mother seduce you?" She began laughing again.

"No, but you can send Emily a note. Tell her you want to meet her, say it's something about me she should know. Give her the time and place. It'll give me time to call on her mother knowing Emily's out with you. Also send a message to her mother asking whether, at the same time, a certain wealthy gentleman with a proposition could meet her. The interesting letter will make sure Ruby is home. Give me half an hour and we should be right into it when Emily and you come home to her mother's apartment."

"Patrick, please, why would I want to go home with Emily?"

"Because she'll be so devastated after you tell her I have a congenital heart problem and I may not live too much longer. You then, my dearest friend, will accompany Emily back to her home, as you will have previously told her you will help her tell her mother the terrible news. You see, Helen, our dear Emily will be so distraught she'll need your help. This news about my heart condition was, of course, a complete confidentiality. You just thought Emily should know, as you knew how much in love with me she is."

Helen's eyebrows lifted in amazement. "But I don't know Emily."

"You will. I'll invite her, along with Angus and you, to afternoon tea at my favourite tea house. You'll pretend you're good friends with Angus. I'll give her lots of attention so she'll swoon all over me."

"Patrick, you truly amaze me." Helen said while shaking her pretty head in wonder.

"I've just heeded some good advice from Lord Milne, that's all. Strategy will win the war. This is my war and I plan to win it!" Patrick rolled on top of Helen before swinging her over on top of him. "I'm pleased I changed my ways with young women. Thank you, brother."

Patrick's well-thought-out plan began two days later, starting with afternoon tea. Emily was notably impressed that Angus had finally found himself, if not a girlfriend, at least a very nice lady friend in Helen. Eating had become a real addiction for Emily. It fascinated Patrick as he watched her devour cream cake after cream cake. With his wicked sense of humour, he couldn't help but whisper in her ear. "Oh Emily, I can't wait for you to savour me like that cream cake."

She giggled, exposing the cream that had built up on her front teeth. Helen looked down so as not to laugh and then contained herself. She actually felt sorry for this poor girl, but she had no second thoughts about pulling the plug on Patrick's plan. She knew very well of the dire consequences if it didn't work. Angus had been told and while he didn't exactly like it, he thought it to be a brilliant strategy.

"Yes, now you're thinking, Patrick, a dirty plan but one that should put an end to this long arduous prologue. Her mother won't want to be dammed for seducing a young man, especially Jonathon Darcy's son, and Emily will blame herself for getting fat and unattractive. Brilliant, brother," Angus told Patrick the day before the plan was to unfold. Today in the teahouse, however, Angus felt Emily needed to be helped.

"Being overweight is not healthy, Emily. You should definitely curb your eating habits. It may lead to all sorts of health problems."

But the look on Emily's face told Angus in no uncertain terms to mind his own business. It seemed his brother loved her anyway, especially after his loving remark about licking and savouring her body like a cream cake.

Patrick then disappointed Emily. "Well, Emily, what Angus said is true. We don't want you to become ill now, do we?"

Her bubble had just been burst. She'd been hurt, injured and began to cry.

"There there, Emily," Patrick held her close, winking at Angus. "We just want you to look at your best and feel at your best for," he whispered, "you know our secret, Emily." She sat up from pressing her head into Patrick's shoulder.

"I'm sorry, I do know you're right, Angus. I'll begin my diet tomorrow."

Immediately after saying that, Emily reached for another cake. All eyes stared, especially when she defended herself. "This one's not as fattening as the cream cakes. It only has a little sugar coating on it. Here, try one, Helen, they're lovely."

"Thank you, Emily," Helen said graciously.

Two days later, a knock on the door sent shivers down the spine of Emily's mother, Ruby. The expectation of meeting with a handsome stranger was titillating. Two days prior, she'd received the mysterious note.

Dear Ruby,

You do not know me personally, for I am a shy but very wealthy widower. I have admired you from afar for some time. I wish to speak with you alone about my feelings. I also have a business proposition which I'm sure you will find too good to refuse. May I have a private meeting with you in your rooms, the day after tomorrow at precisely 4pm? I will knock four times. If you do not open the door within ten seconds, I will leave.

Yours sincerely,
Your most sincere admirer
D O M.

Wait a minute, Ruby thought, *it's 4 pm, but I've heard only two loud knocks.*

"Oh hell, I've got to get rid of this person." She opened the door and was shocked to see Patrick leaning on the door frame, smiling at her with dreamy blue eyes.

"Hello, Mrs Tompkins. Is Emily home?" Patrick's look told Ruby he wished she weren't.

"No, no, she's not, Patrick, and I'm expecting someone, so if you'll… umm, excuse me."

Ruby had hesitated, only half-wanting to close the door on this dream opportunity. But then, at the bottom of the stairs, a derelict old man with a bunch of flowers appeared. When he saw Patrick talking to Ruby, he turned and hobbled away.

"That's strange, Mrs Tompkins," said Patrick, "do you want me to fetch him? Was he the person you were waiting for?" (It had not been hard for Patrick to find an old man needing to make a quick quid in this day and age).

Amused at Ruby's disappointment, Patrick took her gently by the arm. "You don't really want me to leave, do you, Ruby? I'll wait here in the living room for Emily, if you like?"

Ruby quickly put her disappointment aside. Just looking at him was enough to arouse her lust. "Let's not wait too long, Patrick," she said while trying to coax him into her bedroom.

Patrick stopped, when noticing a fur rug in the middle of the lounge room floor. *This will be perfect, we'll be in full view of Emily when she comes home.*

Drawing Ruby into his arms Patrick kissed her passionately. She became a mad woman, tearing at his clothes, kissing him impatiently. *Oh Christ, slow down, this has to be timed right*, Patrick thought.

"Woo, let's take our time, Ruby. Allow me to explore your beautiful body."

He wasn't lying. Her ample breasts were still young and full, the curves of a real woman, not the slender hips of a boyish young girl, her flawless skin smooth to his touch. Ruby stood motionless as he delivered his artful slow seduction.

Although twice his age, Ruby had never experienced such perfect lovemaking she felt blessed beyond her senses. To have this young Herculean man admire and then make magnificent love to her voluptuous body made her feel as if she were the only woman in the world. Ruby melted to the floor and climaxed within seconds.

Patrick's timing was down pat. On their second time around, Ruby was on top of him. This had been the perfect position when Emily and Nurse Helen found them. Emily flung her hands across her eyes in horror. She trembled violently and let out a blood-curdling scream. Helen quickly closed the door to stop any rescuers from running up the stairs. Embracing Emily, she held her head into her chest to muffle her crying.

Helen then spoke calmly, "I'll take Emily home with me, Mrs Tompkins. She can stay with me for the night. We'll return in the morning for your explanation, if there is one." Helen guided Emily by the hand and closed the door. The two young women walked down the stairs, one distraught and one pleased the plan had succeeded.

"God bless, Helen," Patrick said before turning to his victim.

"Well, Ruby, what are we going to do now? This affair will be all over town before too long. There's no doubt about it. My father is due home next week. He won't be pleased with me. However, I know he'll be very upset with you. Very bad thing, you know, the older woman leading a young son astray. Tut-tut."

"This was a set-up, Patrick. I thought you loved my daughter?"

"If so, madam, why would you take the gift of my virginity away from Emily? Not a nice thing to do to your poor little daughter. I suggest you accept the offer of purchase for your hotel and move out of town, before the gossip mongers have their say."

Ruby barely heard his final words because she was laughing about his claim to being a virgin. Lying naked on the fur rug, Ruby asked Patrick, who'd begun dressing, "How did you know I had an offer for my hotel?"

"Remember, my father's a lawyer, Ruby. Anyway, it's common knowledge. Emily's been bragging about the large amount offered all over town."

Ruby almost yelled, "That stupid girl!"

"On that note, madam, I shall leave you to deliberate your decision."

Ruby sat back down on the rug, watching Patrick walk away as if nothing had happened. She then asked herself, "Where the hell did he come from? Outer space? No man I've ever known could make me feel that way. I'd do it all again if it meant he would stay for just one more time."

Jumping up she ran and opened the door. "Patrick, Patrick!"

Patrick looked both ways before he crossed the road, but his smile soon disappeared when he saw Peter Mott, the boy he most detested, along with his father, the man who'd made the remark about Jonathon at the hunt club ball. Peter walked towards him with their usual smiling-assassin grin.

"Patrick, you seem happy! It's shame your girlfriend has just passed by, sobbing as if someone had died. I do hope she's alright. Have you just come from Ruby's apartment? Of course, they do say Ruby Tomkins would make any man happy. Nurse Helen, who you know very well, is looking after Emily. I suggest you find out what the matter is, or perhaps you already know. Good day to you, sir." Mott tipped his hat and walked on.

Patrick's fists clenched but he chose to remain silent, instead he fried Mott with a hateful look. His initial decision was to go home and leave Emily with Helen. However, Patrick began walking aimlessly, going over the recent events in his mind. Before he'd realised it, he was walking in the direction of Helen's flat and so he continued there.

The walk did nothing but confuse his thoughts. He was hoping his plan would be a simple open and shut case. *But what if Emily forgives me and damns her mother. Oh fuck, what have I done?* His mind kept jumping from one scenario to the next, until finally, a little shaken, he knocked on Helen's door. Helen appeared, rolling her eyes, as if to ask—what are you going to do now, Patrick? He composed himself, kissed her on the cheek and walked towards the distraught Emily.

"Emily, stop crying, please listen to me."

With that, she threw herself onto the floor, kicking and screaming. "HOW COULD YOU! HOW COULD YOU, PATRICK!"

He turned to Helen, who shrugged her shoulders, saying, "I can't help anymore. This is your problem, Patrick." She was nonetheless intrigued as to what he would say, or do, with this uncontrollable young woman. He turned to Emily once more, this time with venom in his voice.

"It's obvious, Emily, that you don't love me enough to keep yourself slim and attractive for our future together. It is also obvious your mother loves and lusts after me, as it was she who seduced me!" Helen had to cover her mouth to prevent the laughter from escaping. He glared at her, before he continued. "Therefore, our future together, Emily, could never be. How can I possibly love both you and your mother? You will just have to forget about me, Emily. I think your mother should take the generous offer on her hotel. You should both leave town and forget I ever existed!"

Suddenly, Emily stopped crying and then with as much hatred as she could muster, she stood up and spat back. "NO, PATRICK, YOU AND I will leave town. Yes, you and me. Not my mother. OR ELSE, I will tell the world your brother aborted my baby—AGAINST MY WILL!"

Patrick's fist clenched and for the first time in his life he wanted to actually punch a female. It took every ounce of his self-control not to. Somehow, he was able to hold his composure. "Emily, dear girl, you can't prove a thing and who is going to listen to you against my well-respected brother. Tell me who?"

He then prayed she'd back down. Instead Emily came at him again, looking as if she were possessed by the devil, staring him in the eye. "I WILL MAKE THEM LISTEN!"

Not budging, Patrick stared just as hard back at her. "You will be classed as a mad woman, Emily, and be locked up. Remember, my father's a lawyer. He has a vast network of influential friends. I'm sorry, Emily, but the only way out of this is that you and your mother go on a holiday together, and reconcile your differences. Sell the hotel and make another life for yourself somewhere else."

Emily's tear-matted hair hung limply around her chubby shoulders, and tears began to well once more. Patrick's heart then softened and went out to her. He held her to his chest and Emily felt like putty in his arms as she spoke softly, "Oh Patrick, I love you so much. I couldn't live without you." Patrick looked hopelessly at Helen, who'd come to the rescue with a sleeping draft. "Here you are, Emily, drink this. It will calm you down. I'll be right here when you wake up. You'll feel much better after you rest a bit."

Emily took the draft and swilled it down. Patrick helped her into Helen's bed and covered her with a warm blanket. "There now, Emily, go to sleep. You'll feel better when you wake." He sat on the bed for some time, rubbing her back until she drifted off. He then stood to embrace Helen.

"Thank you, my dearest friend, I'll be forever grateful. And hopefully, when Emily wakes she'll know I'm right." He kissed Helen on the forehead and left.

Ruby lay back among perfumed bubbles in her oversized bathtub. Lamenting her experience with Patrick, she weighed up the love and the guilt she held for her daughter. *Is it my fault Emily's spoilt? I've tried to give her all the things I never had. God knows I've used cunning, good looks and sex appeal to give her a far better life than I had. I was lucky to survive the ravages of the long journey from England at fourteen. I had to do what I had to do, but it was all for her.*

Ruby sighed deeply after her self-justification. She knew she'd been one of the lucky ones with her beauty and ample bosom. When straight off the convict ship, she'd been indentured as a house maid to an oversexed and repulsive barrister. He slept in a different bedroom from his ugly wife, which gave him an open door to Ruby. And so it was inevitable that Ruby would fall pregnant. That's when her blackmail plan began.

"Money, lots of it, or I'll talk," Ruby threatened him.

For the two years Ruby lived with the barrister and his wife, he'd certainly received his fair share of sex from Ruby, as did she, his money. He'd explained to his wife when she'd asked why Ruby had become so fat. "She eats too much, dear. Just a little plump around the middle."

He laughed it off, until two weeks before Ruby was due to give birth, she was sent on her way with a decent wad of extra cash. With her cunning and lucky gambling streak over several years, Ruby had accumulated a huge bankroll, enough to buy the Grand Hotel in Adelaide. This was where she intended to put her past behind her and become a well-respected lady. However, because her acting ability to play this role was only amateurish, Ruby was transparent to the upper classes from the moment she arrived.

But using bribery, she was finally invited to some of the finest dinner parties and distinguished balls. However, with this new disaster, Ruby knew her world in Adelaide had ended. A problem she wasn't particularly worried about, as she was a master at reinventing herself. Her daughter's forgiveness troubled her more than having to leave town, so she prayed to the God she prayed to only when she needed help. After taking a calming bath and two sherries, Ruby later drifted into a deep sleep. She dreamt about accepting a large amount of money for the hotel, and then she and Emily drove out of town in a fine coach, smiling and holding hands. When she woke, she knew God had sent her His answer.

Meanwhile, Jonathon and Margi returned from an amazing four-month journey around Europe. On their final leg, they took time to visit Bernadette and Barney in Hawaii. For two glorious weeks, they laughed and relaxed in tropical splendour. The only thing which had saddened them was they were shown only photos of Addy as she was in England at boarding school. Now at home, they were greeted by Doctor Liu, Colleen, Bob and, of course, the boys. Pandemonium reigned as they handed out their gifts. Doctor Liu accepted graciously the most perfect medicine bag he'd ever seen, handmade in black English leather.

"Oh my goodness, I fit all medicine nice and neatry. You good man, Jon, and you good woman, Margi. I know you have beautiful baby girl, in five month time."

Margi almost fainted with shock. "How on earth do you know that, Liu?" Margi asked while holding onto her stomach. Her small bulge had been well disguised with the latest draped fashion, nothing clinging anymore in Europe, even the hats were beginning to change dramatically.

Liu's laugh was contagious. "Sorry, oh so sorry, I let cat out of bag. Liu just knows things sometimes. Don't know how, just does, evelyone happy, vely happy yes pwease."

Angus was the first to congratulate them, impulsively hugging Margi and then shaking his father's hand. "Well I'll be damned, Father, another Darcy." Turning to Liu, Angus said, "I won't mind paying you the money, Liu. Let's hope you're right and it's a girl. Hey, wouldn't that be wonderful?"

Patrick followed Angus with the congratulations. "It doesn't really matter. We'll love him or her whatever."

Margi welled up, expressing her love and appreciation for everyone. "I promise to be a good friend to you boys. Not so much a mother, just a good friend as always. Oh, what am I saying? Nothing will change, except I am now married to your wonderful father."

What Liu hadn't divulged was Sister Betty had had one of her premonitions and so told him about Marjorie's baby girl that was going to be born.

Chapter 7
Angus's Initiation

It was the day before the fourth of July, the day the brothers shared their birthday. This year Patrick would turn eighteen and was determined to achieve top marks to give him certain passage to Sandhurst. It appeared to be the only way to follow his dream of being an officer as the Australian Government had not yet set up a military academy. He was not fussed about a huge celebration for his birthday this year.

Sharing the same convictions as Patrick, Angus felt his studies now were more important than a huge party. And so, the brothers decided they would share a simple boys' night out on the town. Patrick explained it to Jonathon. "It will be just a quiet evening, Dad, dining out with a few friends in Adelaide."

"Yes, I agree, Father." Angus said, "I'd simply like to spend a night in Adelaide City with Patrick and a few close friends. I'll teach Patrick how to behave himself in public, as a young gentleman should. I hope this is alright with you, Father?"

Jonathon laughed at his younger son taking the mickey out on his older brother. "Of course, Angus, I'm sure Patrick would appreciate that."

"Well, that's all settled then. Thank you, Father, we'll be having dinner at the Glenelg seafood restaurant." After this, Patrick noticed a faraway look on Jonathon's face.

"Are you alright, Dad?" Patrick asked.

Jonathon sat silent, looking as if he could see something, something Patrick was unable to see. Then after some moments, he said, "Yes, I'm fine, Patrick. It's just that I haven't been to that restaurant since going there with your mother. That was the very first time Sally had ever dined in a restaurant. She was beautiful, intelligent, and funny. I fell totally and hopelessly in love with your mother that evening." Jonathon sighed after a long pause, lingering on the thought. Patrick wrapped his arms around Jonathon, holding him so tight Jonathon felt at one with him, as if Sally were there. He patted Patrick's hand.

"I love you, son. You make your mother proud. She loved you too, with all her heart. I just wish I could have listened to what Sally was trying to tell me all those years ago. Please forgive me, Patrick."

"Now come on, Dad, this is a joyous time, with a new baby on the way and another beautiful woman to love. I know my mother in heaven is more than pleased." Patrick's friendly punch to Jonathon's arm brought him out of his melancholy.

"Yes, you're right, Patrick, I promised Sally on her death bed I'd do my very best for both of you boys and I think making myself happy has a lot to do with that, don't you?"

"We couldn't agree more, Dad... Father."

Patrick had planned and rechecked all avenues for their memorable evening. This included a scrumptious seafood dinner before Patrick would introduce his younger brother to the pleasures of a woman's naked body. Knowing very well Angus would not be in it without a fight to keep his holy virginity, Patrick planned to spike his drink with an aphrodisiac he'd found in Angus's medicine bag. Then Molly, who Patrick still frequented, would initiate the plan.

Molly had promised Patrick she would do her very best to make Angus's first time a night to remember. After all, she'd been paid well and he was Patrick's brother. Surely, he'd have some of his brother's libido and sensual prowess. Molly just couldn't wait to make love to yet another of the Darcy boys. She loved introducing sex to clean young flesh.

Saturday morning arrived and Angus felt a buzz of excitement about dining in the city without his parents for the first time. He suddenly felt all grown up. "Wake up, Patrick. It's the fourth of July." He paused, brow furrowed. "Did we ever find out the actual date of your birthday?" he asked as he sat on the end of Patrick's bed.

"Piss off, Angus. I'm still sleeping!"

"It appears not, brother. Not unless you're talking in your sleep."

"Oh, cut the bloody Pommy accent, will ya," Patrick muffled from under the pillow.

"You too will have the Pommy plumb in your mouth when you reside at Sandhurst."

"No, I bloody won't!"

This time Angus's remark caused Patrick to retaliate physically, as he whacked Angus over the head with the pillow. "Ok, it's on, Pat!"

As usual, the two got stuck into it until the noise filtered through the home and Jonathon called, "Stop fighting, boys!"

Even if it were only in fun, they had over the years taken no prisoners with some very expensive china. Jonathon's voice had echoed from his bedroom where Margi and he cuddled, laughing at the boy's antics.

"Oh shit, Angus, what does this remind you of?" Patrick asked, as feathers fluttered wistfully around his room.

"Just as well Mother Matilda's not here, Pat, or we'd be in big trouble."

"We bloody well will be anyway if you don't clean it up, Angus."

"Me. Why me?"

"'Cause you're the youngest and you started it."

"No, I didn't. You hit me first."

With that Angus jumped on Patrick, wrestling him to the ground. Not being able to control his laughter, Patrick thought, *I hope he attacks Molly like this for his sex tumble tonight.*

"Stop laughing, Patrick. I can't win if you keep laughing. Stop it."

This only served to make him laugh louder. Margi finally came to investigate the ruckus.

"Will you boys ever grow up?" she said with a chuckle. "Happy birthday to you both once again, but please clean up the mess before you come down for breakfast, there's the good lads."

The aroma of perfectly cooked bacon and eggs brought them running. "So, have you cleaned up your mess, boys?" Jonathon asked before taking his first mouthful.

"Father, with all due respect, we're young men now. Patrick is eighteen and I'm sixteen, and now to answer your question. Yes, we have."

Jonathon shook his head, smiling. "So, young men, tonight will be your first night out alone in the city. Please behave in the manner you have been brought up. I'm not saying don't have fun with your friends, but be careful. There are scoundrels lurking in dark alleys at night."

Patrick almost spat his tea out, laughing, "Dad, I have to repeat what Angus just said, 'with all due respect', do you really think any scoundrel would stand a chance against Angus and me. Remember, we're karate champions."

"Oh yes," replied Jonathon. "I keep forgetting about that. Well, God help the scoundrels!"

Later, the brothers were spruced up for the evening and presented themselves to their father.

"How do we look, Father?" They stood shoulder to shoulder, dressed in new tailor-made suits made from the finest Peppinella wool. Margi was the first to congratulate them on being the most handsome young men she'd ever seen, before planting a kiss on Jonathon's cheek.

"Except your father, of course."

Jonathon had to agree, not about himself, as he'd always felt shy about his looks. He took no notice of flattery. However, if you gave him a compliment on his work and the successful outcome of his victory in court, then yes, he would appreciate it.

After Jonathon approved of their attire, he asked, "What time should we expect you home?"

"Would it be alright, Dad, if we stayed at Thomas's this evening? His home is in the heart of Adelaide," Patrick asked nonchalantly.

"Of course, Patrick, it sounds the sensible thing to do after a late evening."

The evening was chilly, as is usual in July. Margi, forever caring for her boys, placed a warm rug over their knees. Once out of sight they pulled the demeaning item from their laps, and threw it into the back of the buggy.

"Now, the night awaits us, Angus. Are you excited about your freedom? What do you fancy for dinner?" Angus almost drooled his words.

"Yes, I am excited and yes, I can hardly wait to have a huge freshly cooked lobster. What about you?"

"You live to eat, brother, whereas I eat to live. I eat anything, although I do love oysters."

"Ah yes, they're an aphrodisiac, which of course you don't need, Patrick, so go steady. Or I'm afraid you may just seduce our waitress on the restaurant floor."

Patrick laughed so loud it set his horses into a trot. "I'd better not waste a moment then, Angus. Maybe I'll have time to seduce two waitresses." He flicked the whip for effect, "Hup, boys."

Remembering the aphrodisiac he'd wrapped and placed inside his jacket, Patrick felt slightly guilty that Angus may not yet be ready for this experience. But, Patrick would soon be in England and unable to orchestrate Angus's sex education. So, this night had to be it. Patrick was also pleased he'd thought to tell his father they'd be staying at his best friend Thomas Norman's home in Adelaide City. And doubly pleased that Thomas would be accompanying him to England, where together they'd enrol at Sandhurst. Yes, Patrick had planned this evening with precision, especially with Thomas telling his father he'd be staying at Patrick's home. And because the two fathers barely met, the boys assumed their fathers would never know the truth. Patrick drove the horse and buggy to the nearest livery stable a block away from the restaurant. Thomas and the brothers' mates from school drove past in a hired coach. When spotting Angus and Patrick walking, Thomas called, "Hey, you didn't walk all the way did you, Pat?"

"No, we ran," Patrick returned dryly.

The interior of the beachside restaurant intrigued Patrick. He studied the mural of sea urchins and the secluded dimly lit booths to one side of the restaurant. He smiled as he visualised his mother sitting there with Jonathon.

"This way, gentleman," the waiter brought Patrick's attention back.

They were shown to a larger table, set for six in the middle of the restaurant. Patrick thought it to be conspicuous, in full view of well-respected businessmen and their families.

This is definitely not the place to let my guard down.

With his head buried in the menu, Patrick ordered a dozen oysters, and a whole lobster for main course. Looking up, he handed the menu back to the waitress, whom he recognised as one of his willing conquests.

"Thank you, ah, ah, Jane."

"No, Patrick, it is I who have to thank you." She leant over and whispered, "Don't forget to have a good look at your oysters before you devour them, Patrick." She smiled at the others and left.

"Jesus, Pat, don't hog all the girls, mate. Leave some for us!"

Thomas loved jibbing Patrick about his affairs with women, not that Thomas wasn't good looking, he just didn't have the libido or the charm of Patrick, it seemed.

"Don't worry, fellas, there'll be plenty left when I'm finished," he replied arrogantly.

Angus felt uncomfortable but smiled. *Why does everything have to revolve around women and sex with him?* However, he was not about to let Patrick spoil his first night out on the town. Choosing to change the subject, Angus spoke of politics, horses, and medicine. Because the present company was well educated and intelligent, they were able to converse freely on each subject. Even Patrick was grateful for the change in conversation, as he was being recognised by several young women and their parents. It began to unnerve him.

Enjoying his oysters to the point of savouring them as he would other pleasures, Patrick couldn't help but order another dozen. Angus noticed and raised an eyebrow. "Brother, please remember what I've told you about oysters."

"I might just try the effect a little later tonight, Angus. See if you're right."

"Oh no you won't. I'm not waiting in the cold for you to have your fun."

"You won't have to, Angus. I'll take good care of you." Patrick winked at Thomas.

Angus noticed. "What are you up to, Patrick?"

Patrick slapped him on the back, and laughed. "Don't worry, brother, I'm only kidding." He turned from Angus and began talking to Thomas about how he was looking forward to his officer training at Sandhurst. Thomas, however, had only just heard some bad news.

"I've just heard today, Pat, that bloody Peter Mott has enrolled at Sandhurst and he'll be on the same ship as us."

"Don't worry, Tom. I'll have him walk the plank. We'll get rid of that bastard somehow. I reckon his old man's worse than him though, he creeps around everywhere, trying to dig up shit on anyone he thinks is of a higher standing." Patrick shook his head in disgust. "I'll warn Peter he may as well join the enemy because he has no friends amongst us, same as his father. That bastard has gained his wealth by undermining people, taking short cuts in business, bribery. I'm sure that's why he's the most hated man in Adelaide. But at the same time, he's bloody powerful within the local council. And it's all due to bribery. That's what Dad says."

Thomas added, "And besides that, they're fucking ugly. Long thin greasy hair, small and lean bodies without an ounce of muscle, noses you could hang your bloody hat on and Peter's face is covered in acne. Repulsive is the word I'd use for the two. And, you know, Mrs Mott is a rare sight outside of her home. She's totally controlled by him."

"Poor woman," Angus said sympathetically. "I remember the day I tipped my hat to say good-day and she simply scurried off with her head down, as if she was scared to death of anyone recognising her."

Bertie, one of the boys at the table, lived not far from the Motts. "Yes, every now and then I walk past their home and I hear Mrs Mott screaming as if she were being whipped." Bertie then added, "We all know he belts his wife. Maybe we should set up an ambush and catch him in the act. I'd love to punch the shit out of him and his piss weak son."

Thomas agreed. "I hate weak men, especially those bastards who bash women. I'm in, so let's give him a hiding." Patrick took hold of Thomas's hand and shook it firmly, and Angus followed.

"Yes, I'm definitely in. I'd like to throw a few karate kicks at them!" Angus said.

Patrick gleamed with pride at his young brother's eager pledge and thought it may be the right time to slip him the aphrodisiac.

"Dad's organised this bottle of champagne to make a toast. But only one, so I reckon we should go to a sly grog place I know and have a nightcap after this one, lads," Patrick declared.

Angus looked shocked. "Patrick, I don't think we should."

Sometimes Angus, with his holier than though attitude, could be a proverbial pain in the arse. And so, from being proud of Angus one minute to being anxious to be rid of him into Molly's care, Patrick answered quickly and emphatically, "Well, I bloody well think we should, Angus!"

With that, the others agreed, and Thomas came in to support his best mate.

"Come on, Angus, you're a big boy now. Let's have a little fun," Thomas said then plonked his arm around Angus's shoulder. "Drink up, Angus, here's to our bright futures. Here's to life, love and happiness."

Angus shrank in his seat. He knew he was outnumbered and needed to do exactly what they suggested. Grow up a little. *Letting my hair down every so often can't be all that bad.* Unknowingly, he sculled the aphrodisiac-infused champagne to loud cheers of approval.

With the night turning even colder, they took relief in entering the coach Thomas had thoughtfully hired for the evening. Their coach driver, a young man named Eddy, was taking over from his father. He was intrigued to know where they'd like to go next. When Patrick told him, he answered, "Yep, I know the place. The old man goes there a lot, usually to fetch me."

They laughed, knowing they had the right driver for the night. "Come in and join us for a night cap. What's your name?"

"Eddy. Thanks, I will."

Patrick opened the door to a smoky haze. It shrouded a seedy bunch, some dour and some laughing raucously. Overly made-up young women, seemingly on the prowl for a quick quid, sat hanging off and groping men's knees while older women flaunted their wares by rolling their hips in that unmistakable way at any taker. Most men, it seemed, were under the influence and had succumbed to easy pickings.

The scene repulsed Angus. Patrick glanced at his young brother and knew he needed a little softening, so Patrick ordered a bottle of whisky.

"Come on, Angus, this'll warm you to the sights of how the other half live!"

"I don't know if I'm at all interested in how the other half live, brother."

"Well, Angus, when you become a doctor, you'll have to deal with all sorts. They're not that bad, just out for a good time after a hard day's work. Now drink up!"

Tinkling their glasses together, they sculled the burning fluid then shook their heads and blew loud gasps of "Haa!" After the initial shock, Angus became calm. Patrick noticed the change and whispered to Thomas, "Better not let him get too drunk, Tom. He needs to have some sense left."

With the bottle of whisky near finished, Patrick suggested, "Come on, let's go. I know another place that's classier than this dive."

Patrick talked with Eddy about where to go, and asked if he would like to join them, there'd be plenty of fun for all. He accepted eagerly. They bought another bottle of whisky to drink on the way but Patrick was careful to give Angus only a sip. Angus had certainly loosened up and he began to sing.

"At least he's a happy drunk," Patrick said, feeling pleased with the progress. Angus responded with a playful punch on the arm.

"I'm not drunk, brother, just happy!"

"Good, that's how it should be."

Inside "Molly's Establishment", as it was called, Angus tried hard to stand without swaying. "Oh, this is a much better place, Pat," Angus said, slurring slightly as he studied the interiors. "I love the red embossed wallpaper and all these beautiful young women. Don't they look nice!"

As he surveyed the room, Molly slinked over to him. "You're a handsome young man yourself, Angus. Here, let me take your jacket. It's warm in here. Allow me to introduce myself. My name's Molly." Molly, nearly as tall as Angus, carefully and artfully removed his jacket, breathing heavily on his neck as she did. It sent a shiver of pleasure down his spine.

"I know your brother very well, Angus. He tells me you're going to be a doctor, and you may be able to help with the pain I have in my lower back." She winked at Patrick who was being attended to by a nervous young Eva. Because Eva was only sixteen, Molly had arranged for Patrick to be her first client so as to ease Eva into the business.

"If you follow me, Angus, I'll show you exactly where the pain is." Molly took him by the hand, and Angus followed happily, telling her innocently, "I'm not so good without my medicine bag, Miss Molly. Perhaps I should have brought it with me?" Angus then laughed out loud. "How silly! How would I know you had a pain in the back? How would I know I was coming here?"

His rowdy laughter brought on a bout of hiccups. He asked, "Where am I by the way?" (Hiccup, hiccup).

"This is an exclusive tavern, Angus."

"Oh well, that's very (hiccup) nice. It's better than the tavern we've just left. Terr- (hiccup) -ible place, full of drunks and (hiccup) whores."

Molly was finding it hard to concentrate her finesse on this charming, half-inebriated young man. He was amusing her to the point of distraction although she managed to gather her composure. "Now let's be a little more serious, Angus. My back is so painful so would it be better if you looked at it without my clothes on?" Her coy smile fooled Angus and he began to feel embarrassed for her.

"Yes, yes of course, Molly. I'm going to be a (hiccup) doctor, you know, so the naked body is just an instrument to (hiccup) observe and treat." Angus's ego told him to act professionally.

"Well, you can treat yourself to my naked body anytime you like, Angus," Molly said sensuously. Angus found that remark intelligent and witty. Throwing his head back, he laughed so much his stomach began to hurt.

Oh my God, this is going to be hilarious. I love him already, Molly thought when she opened the door to her bedroom where everything was pink and fluffy. Angus's attention was drawn to it like a moth to a flame.

"This is an amaz- (hiccup) -ing room, Molly. I've never seen, well, I've never seen anything quite so pink and fluffy!" he chuckled.

Molly stood next to her bed and turned to ask sweetly, "Would you mind undoing my buttons?"

"Certainly, Molly, you will need only to (hiccup) drop the dress around your waist and lie face down (hiccup), on your..." he chuckled again, "very pink bed!" He began laughing hysterically.

Molly was beginning to think Patrick should have brought Angus when he was sober as she felt sure the job could not be done in his present state. She'd never experienced such a reaction, but how precious he was, how lovable. She just wanted to hold him tight to her breast. Perhaps she should just tell Patrick that he'd passed with honours, and let this young man hold on to his innocence, until he chose to make love to the girl of his dreams. But, Molly was a true pro and had been paid handsomely to do the job, one she was going to enjoy. She ignored Angus's orders to drop the dress to her waist. Defiantly, she let her dress fall to the floor then turned to face him, naked. Shocked, Angus hiccupped twice, "Oh my goodness, you have a lovely body, Molly." He then cleared his throat and deepened his voice, "From a doctor's point of view, that is, yes, clinically speaking."

But a strange feeling began to stir within Angus. His penis became erect, and a lustful longing he'd rarely experienced took over his senses. Before he gave in to the need to kiss Molly and make love to her, he said in regret at not letting this newly found passion take its course.

"I think you should turn around, Molly, so I can inspect your back."

Molly smiled, knowing she now had him. He was all hers. "Of course, Angus," she cooed, slithering face down onto her satin bed cover. "But my back feels better if I lie on my back and spread my legs," she whimpered.

As she rolled over, Angus's heart broke into a gallop when she revealed something Angus had never seen before.

"I'm sorry, Angus, it hurt too much lying on my stomach. I think perhaps I should stand and show you where it hurts."

He became transfixed, physically unable to move, as she loosened his tie, unbuttoned his shirt then his trousers. Molly's eyes spoke while her fingers fondled his erection. Angus could do nothing but accept the pleasure. His body craved more of her soft touch when Molly slithered her body down against his, until her moist lips slowly brought him to the point where his body shook with ecstasy. Angus, still in heaven, breathed deeply, taking in this incredible feeling.

Molly rose to whisper in his ear, "Come lay with me, Angus."

He had succumbed to his professional seducer. Lying alongside Molly in a blissful trance, he felt immense gratitude for his ethereal experience. Tears moistened his eyes. With his head nestling on her soft breast, he truly believed a feeling this good could not possibly be sinful. He also realised that Patrick had set him up, and thought, *I'll thank him in the morning.*

"Oh, thank you, Molly," Angus groaned before placing a lingering kiss on her neck.

She whispered, "We haven't finished yet, Angus. I have so much more to teach you."

"I'm sure you do. But how's your back, Molly? I'd really like to enter you now." And he chuckled.

The morning brought with it a crisp frost, and Eddy's comment, "Just as well I threw a rug over the poor bloody horses. It's freezing!" He took off their nosebags and flung the rugs off their backs. He then gave the orders. "I'll take Patrick and Angus to the livery stable first and then I'll drop you boys off home, alright?"

Suddenly a voice came from behind the group. "Good morning, gentleman." It was Cedric Mott. "I trust you all had a pleasant evening. I've heard the women in there are clean at least."

Patrick wasn't waiting for a second chance. Spinning on his heels, he came face to face with the ugly low-spying bastard and grabbed his lapels. With lethal power, he pinned Cedric up against the coach. In his anger, Patrick had finally captured his prey.

"You say a word to anyone about what you only think happened here last night and I'll cut your balls off and feed them to my dog. DO YOU UNDERSTAND?"

"Don't waste your time, Patrick, he's got no balls," Bertie quipped in his usual dry manner. "Anyway, he can wait. I know a few blokes who'll save you the energy, Pat".

It was the first time Cedric Mott's smug look had disappeared. A look of genuine fear showed on his face before Patrick released him. He straightened his attire and hurried off.

"Fuckin' hell, if we don't do something about that bastard," Patrick said, shaking his head.

"Don't worry, brother, let's use strategy. Remember, it always wins the war," and Angus put his arm around Patrick's shoulder. "What amazes me is how he sneaks around all hours of the day and night, trying to catch someone doing something wrong or unlawful. He must go home only to bash his poor wife."

Patrick stood back to have a good look at Angus.

"Do I detect something different about you this morning, Angus?" Smiling with pride, Patrick held Angus close to his chest and then at arm's length. "Yes, I think I'm looking at a true blue, red-blooded man right now. Am I right, Angus?"

"Yes, you finally got me, Patrick. Well done, both beautifully and strategically planned."

"Are you going to let us in on what happened last night?"

"If you don't know what goes on between a man and a woman, Patrick, then nobody does." The group, including their newfound friend Eddy, broke into raucous laughter.

Chapter 8
Leaving for England, 1910

Patrick and Thomas had accounted for all possessions and procedures before boarding the ship. Nurse Helen, Patrick's friend and lover, who'd known from day one he would be gone but thanked the lord she was still part of his life, gave a sad farewell. Probably the only mission not to be accomplished before departure was the gang bashing of Cedric Mott and his son, Peter. The thought of losing control and killing the pair stopped them from carrying out the plan.

As Patrick now stood on board alongside his mate, Thomas Norman, both men waved to a crowd of friends and loved ones. Patrick was conscious of Peter Mott standing not too far from them. There was no one there to wave Peter goodbye or wish him well, and Patrick felt a moment of pity for him.

Angus had to leave the wharf earlier, as the tears streaming down his face became an embarrassment, especially now he'd been initiated into manhood. Since his first evening with Molly, "the fine lady of the night", as Angus called her, he'd established a relationship with her. He'd taught her how to play chess, and they'd converse for hours about many things, including her profession.

"I've finally accepted your profession as necessary, Molly," Angus told her. However, he'd only once tried to persuade Molly that life had much more to offer.

"I love sex, Angus, and if you want to hear the truth, yes, I think we prostitutes have a very important part to play in the greater scheme of things. Just let's enjoy our time together before you meet the love of your life." He had left the dock to cry on Molly's bosom.

Jonathon stood proud alongside the glowing Margi, who had baby Millie in her arms. They returned waves of goodbye, while Colleen and Bob, along with Doctor Liu, Mother Matilda, Da and Sister Madeline (Betty), called their farewells.

"Good luck, boys. Bon voyage. We love you, Patrick. Take care, Thomas."

"Don't forget to go to mass every Sundee, Patrick, and say y' prayers every day. God speed!"

Matilda couldn't help herself, although she would have liked to also warn Patrick to quell his passion with the opposite sex. But, of course, it was not the correct protocol. So, she relented, justifying her decision by saying a silent prayer.

The huge steamship blew its deafening horn as anchors were hauled in. It seemed to take no time before the coast line had disappeared into the horizon. Patrick stood starboard, feeling an unleashed freedom and excitement about his future. After long hours of study, and with a great deal of help from Angus, he'd graduated with distinctions. Now his dream of becoming an officer in the King's army had begun. About twelve hours into their journey, Thomas began to feel the surge of the sea take a toll on his stomach.

"Bloody hell, Pat, I hope I don't have this feeling all the way to England," Thomas moaned.

Patrick searched in his personal 'medicine' bag that Angus had packed him.

"Ah ha, I've found it. Here it is, Tom. It says, 'sea sickness'. Come on, mate, take this. I'm sure it'll work if little brother has made it."

Looking further into the bag Patrick found the magic potion for abortions, also the serum used to kill sperm within two hours of intercourse, plus a concoction for lessening the libido. Patrick laughed at the instructions written on each bottle:

PERSONAL: PATRICK'S USE ONLY.

Patrick chose to enjoy his time on board as best he could, so he'd spread his charm around, meeting with other passengers and listening to their stories. Such was his nature. Thomas, whenever the sea sickness medicine was doing its job, remained by his side. On their first evening, they dined with a refined middle-aged couple, the Bakers, who were on their way to visit their daughter, Felicity. She was attending Badminton Girls' School in Bristol. Patrick sat opposite Mrs Baker and tilted his head after hearing this.

"That rings a bell. Badminton, yes, I know, my father has a friend whose daughter attends that same school. She'd be sixteen now, the same age as my brother. Her name's Adelaide Watt-Stuart. Adelaide was adopted by Barnaby Stuart after her mother was widowed before Adelaide was born. I've only seen a photo of her when she was about six years old; pretty little thing, long black hair. They call her Addy."

Patrick then seemed in a world of his own as he rambled on for some time about Addy's beautiful mother, Bernadette, being such a close friend with his dear belated mother. Telling the stories he'd been told by his father and mother, Patrick had also remembered on occasions at the orphanage, when Sally would natter on to Mother Matilda about her friend Bernadette, who lived in Hawaii. Hawaii always seemed such a foreign land to Patrick, a faraway place with untouchable people. Just when he was about to meet Bernadette and Addy, life turned them in a different direction. A twang of guilt flushed his face.

"I'm so sorry, Mrs Baker, I've been talking too much. Please tell me, where in South Australia do you live? Would your daughter Felicity know of Addy? I'm extremely interested as there may be further connections between us."

Mrs Baker had been amused and intrigued with the stories about Patrick's friends from Hawaii. Especially with his story of Bernadette's first husband, Jum Watt, whom she'd heard of as being a well-respected business man, and how sad it was when he was shot and killed over a racehorse. But at the same time, Mrs Baker was anxious to speak.

"Yes, Patrick, a thread does join us. Our daughter Felicity is in the same class as Adelaide Watt-Stuart, or as you say, Addy. They're best of friends. Unfortunately for us though, Addy has never taken up our offer to come and stay with us. She usually stays with her parents in Queensland on one of their many tropical fruit properties. Or she returns to Hawaii when on school vacation."

"I can imagine that, Mrs Baker. It seems Addy's an illusion." Patrick sat back, amazed at the coincidence and then continued. "You know, I took little notice of my father when he delighted in reading aloud the letters Bernadette sent to him, or should I say Mrs Watt-Stuart. And I'd always refuse the opportunity to go with him to her property named Bulkawa. It's about thirty miles west of Adelaide. The property was owned by Addy's birth father, Jum Watt, before he died. I know this because my father, Jonathon Darcy, was Jum Watt's lawyer and closest friend. My father still maintains the books and the final say on the monetary issues with Bulkawa."

Patrick took a deep breath accompanied by a sigh. He then combed his fingers through his blond curls. The Bakers were good listeners, so he went on. "My brother, Angus, always loved going to Bulkawa with Dad. Apart from the property, he loved the train trip, which is very convenient, as it runs through the property. So instead of waiting for the nearest station, the driver would slow up at the same point every time. Dad and Angus would jump off, and Dan the station manager would meet them there. Angus just couldn't wait to jump." A wry smile accompanied a tear that smudged Patrick's blue eyes.

"You seem to be missing your family already, Patrick?" Mrs Baker said. She must have been about forty-five, was attractive and had a voice Patrick could have listened to all night. He nodded.

"Yes, I suppose I am."

Ernest Baker coughed to clear his throat and then spoke with a rather large plumb in his mouth. "Well, I must say, young man, and I'm sure my dear wife would agree, your stories were riveting. Yes, quite riveting. You are right though about our connections. We do know your father, not socially you understand. He acted on our behalf when we purchased an abandoned property about forty-five miles north-east of Adelaide. Strange story this one." His brow crinkled, as if he was still trying to fathom the answer to his own story. "It seems the previous owner, a Mr Birch, died and was buried one hundred yards from the homestead. It appeared he had no family to be informed of his death. The lawyer, who'd taken care of all his affairs, apparently died, just before Birch died of tuberculosis, I believe. Nobody seemed to care about looking any further into Birch's business, or if he had remaining relatives, so the case was simply closed."

Patrick said, "That was how my mother died—from tuberculosis."

"Oh, I am sorry, Patrick, darned awful business. It's taken too many lives; dreadful, simply dreadful," Mr Baker said.

Mrs Edwina Baker returned to the conversation. "It's such a lovely property and we've done wonders with it. Still, my favourite thing is to climb the hill nearest to the homestead, where I can see for miles. I sit under the tree there, a ghost gum…" Her voice became wistful. "There's an unnamed grave on the hill that bares only an old wooden cross, but somehow I feel at one with the spirit there. I'm sure it's a woman. I speak with her, and what's so unusual is that the grave's always surrounded by wildflowers, even in winter." Edwina looked at the men's doubtful expressions and smiled, a little embarrassed. "I know it all sounds silly but the Australian countryside can be a lonely place for women, especially with Ernest travelling so much due to his evolvement with the South Australian Government. I wish he hadn't insisted on sending Felicity to England for her schooling."

Mrs Baker hung her head, not wanting to face her husband's sad expression after her complaint. Her pouring of emotion, especially to a stranger, tugged at Ernest's heart. He knew he'd overlooked her needs more often than he should have. He simply put his hand on hers and while looking at Patrick, he sheepishly confessed. "I wasn't going to tell my dear wife this, but we're not going to Badminton for a mere visit." Edwina's expression became full of hope. She looked up waiting for him to finish. "We're going to bring Felicity home!"

Normally, Edwina was in control, well trained in holding all emotions in, but Ernest's confession was a complete surprise, one which overcame all of her inhibitions. Patrick smiled at Thomas who'd been silent all through the conversation. Both young men applauded her kissing and hugging, and with tears of joy. At that, they rose and bid their new companions goodnight.

Patrick lay awake in his bunk, plagued with a feeling he had about the story the Bakers had told him, about the property they'd purchased, especially the tree on the hill and the grave. It was as if someone was trying to tell him something, to send him a message. He slept restlessly that night. Unfortunately, he was wakened far too early, when he heard Thomas moan with seasickness. When Patrick jumped up, he hit his head on the bunk and shouted, "Oh fuck!"

A groaning Thomas responded, "No thanks, mate, not in the mood."

"Ya silly bugger, I just hit my bloody head. Here take this medicine. Just as well Angus gave us plenty so it should see you through, Tom."

Thomas swallowed the pleasant-tasting liquid and within ten minutes he was feeling human again. Patrick sat on his bunk, his head resting in the palms of his hands, thinking of the nagging mystery. He'd never known the whole truth about his mother's past and never really wanted to, until now. The grave on the property that Mrs Baker had spoken about: was it something to do with Sally? He felt sure there was a link. The day before the boat sailed, Jonathon had told Patrick, "Your mother's diary will wait until you return from England. You should be mature enough then to understand the troubled story it holds." While this mystery haunted Patrick, he decided to write home to ask Jonathon about Mr Baker's property. What had Jonathon known of this place before he'd closed the deal with the deceased estate division? Did it have any bearing on his mother's life? He then tried to put the matter to rest.

Peter Mott had kept very much to himself. He had no choice, it seemed. However, every now and then, Patrick would feel sorry for this lame creature. *Perhaps now Peter's away from his father's influence, he may just lighten up a little and drop his forever spying and creeping around like a gutter rat.* As much as Patrick was repulsed by him, he confided in Thomas, "Let's have a talk with Peter and see what makes him tick."

"I never thought I'd ever hear you say that, Pat. He's the biggest fuckin' worm I've ever met!"

Patrick remembered the times at school when Peter followed him, spying, when Patrick had smoked cigarettes behind the outhouse, or how Peter eavesdropped when Patrick had told his friends about his sexual experiences with girls. Peter had reported Patrick's bad behaviour to the principal. Thank God, most of the time these troubles were kept quiet from Jonathon.

"Yes, I know, Tom, but he's been trained by his degenerate father so maybe we can get him to repent. I feel a bit sorry for the poor bastard. How would you like to go through life looking like him?"

Thomas rolled around, laughing so hard he couldn't stop.

Patrick lay waiting silently on his bunk. "Have you finished now, Tom?"

"Oh my God, I was laughing because I imagined you trying to line him up with a girl. And the girl all goo-goo-eyed over you. I tell ya, mate, no matter what you did, you couldn't make him pretty."

"I know that, Tom, but we could clean him up a bit, mentally too. Get him out of the dobbing mode, teach him the rules of being a good sport." Patrick was serious but Thomas was not so sure it could be done.

270

"A leopard never changes his spots, mate. Now let's have breakfast."

"I also know that, but we may have to bunk with him at Sandhurst. And one day maybe we'll have to fight alongside him. Better start training him now to be on our side rather than having him stab us in the back."

Peter Mott sat on his own, eating breakfast with his head almost buried in it.

"May we sit with you, Peter?" Patrick asked, standing over him, his breakfast tray laden with all that was offered.

Peter almost choked. "Yes, yes of course." With eyes lowered, he asked, "You've not come to poison me, have you, Patrick?"

"I suppose I should, but the truth is, we've come to make a truce, Peter. We're all going to the same place so there's no need to remain enemies. God knows, one day we may have to fight side by side. What say we put the past behind and join together as Aussies in a new land?"

Patrick placed his tray on the table and offered Peter his hand. Peter's handshake felt like a cold wet fish, and Patrick released it perhaps too soon. Thomas reluctantly shook Peter's proffered hand. *Not a good beginning. This is going to take a hell of a lot of patience and understanding. Still, I'm here to grow as a man, and having to deal with all sorts will be part of my education and journey in life*, Patrick thought. He then ate in silence, letting Thomas interrogate Peter as to why he chose the same military college as them, and why he even chose to be a soldier.

"If you don't mind me saying so, Peter, you don't seem the type to be a soldier. You're more the type to work in a bank or be an accountant?"

Peter coughed to clear his throat and give himself time to answer. "I know what you mean, Thomas. I may not be as physical as you gentlemen but I'm interested in other avenues of warfare."

Patrick finished his mouthful, just in time to blurt his reaction. "As a BLOODY SPY, you mean?"

Thomas laughed, whereas Patrick only smiled.

"Well, Patrick, I may be good at it," Peter answered proudly.

Patrick slapped him on the back. "I couldn't think of a better person for the job, but you'll have to pass the physical first. I think we'd better start training you on board or you might be sent home after the first gruelling week."

Thomas agreed. "Bloody brilliant idea, Pat, so let's get started. I'll be in charge!" He turned to Peter, while trying to hold his laughter. "Right, I want you to do one hundred pushups on deck. Now!" Thomas then gave him a nudge. "Let's go!"

Peter had no excuse to refuse Thomas's order, although he'd searched for one. He was outnumbered and outmanoeuvred. Naked to the waist, the three young men found a secluded spot on deck where they strutted side by side, proceeding with the one hundred pushups. Unfortunately, Peter nearly collapsed after twenty feeble attempts. Taking no notice of him, Thomas and Patrick continued, trying to outdo each other. The sun's bright rays soon coloured Peter's skin a deep shade of pink, making it look slightly better than the celluloid skeleton it was. Peter sat still for a moment, admiring Patrick's tanned torso, until Patrick ordered, "Get going, Peter. You'll do the hundred if it takes all bloody day."

Patrick then wondered: why in the hell he was trying to be a do-gooder when he'd rather throw Peter overboard, as he'd first planned. *My mother, that's who it is. Too much of my beautiful mother in me.* He felt her spirit flow constantly through him, especially when there was a lame duck to be saved.

"The pain is excruciating. I'm exhausted," Peter gasped as they were helping him back to his cabin and after nearly thirty minutes of intense exercise.

"We'll be back in two hours for a run around the deck, fifty times! Rest while you can, Peter," Patrick said before he slammed the door shut. Peter groaned.

"We may just kill him unintentionally, you know that, Tom."

"Let's do it anyway, Pat. I don't care what you say; that bastard won't change."

Thomas rarely opposed Patrick, however, on this point, he thought himself to be right. Peter Mott was definitely not worth the time or the effort.

The final leg of the journey was under way. They'd faced the blustery winds of the wild forties with ease and had rounded the Cape of Good Hope with little trouble. It seemed a blessed journey, but one which Patrick would prefer not to do very often. He knew his legs were meant to be wrapped around a horse or a woman, not swaying with the constant movement of the ship. Also, being held in such a confined space for so long began to take a toll on his disposition.

While on board, Peter Mott had not endeared himself at all to Patrick or Thomas. It seemed he was devoid of enthusiasm, a sense of humour, or any natural charm; especially with girls. Peter had simply taken no notice of the girls on board.

"Weird, he's bloody weird," Patrick declared.

He'd come to this conclusion after watching a girl—certainly not pretty, a rather plain one—actually smile and flutter her eyelashes at Peter. It was a shy attempt at sexiness. Peter's attitude towards her was obvious: he was not interested one bit. Thomas had it all worked out.

"He's in love with you, Pat."

"Oh, fuck off, Tom. She was no catch, that's all."

"WELL, EXCUSE ME. Is he a catch?"

Patrick sat thinking, before replying, "Well, at least we've tried to make him human. He certainly looks a lot better now, slightly muscled, a decent tan and the haircut you gave him gives his pinhead volume. All I can say is, we've tried, but he's beginning to give me the creeps!"

"I'm telling you, Pat, he loves you. He's a bloody queen."

"I don't care about his sexual preference. But if he ever touches me, I'll kill him."

Their final days and nights on board had become a tedious countdown. There were only so many things young, fit, virile men could do on board a ship. Patrick had forgotten how many times Mrs Baker had shown pictures of their lovely daughter, Felicity, together with Addy. And on this, their final night, it was no exception. Mrs Baker once again showed the pictures. Patrick had never imagined any young woman could be as beautiful as Miss Adelaide Watt-Stuart. However, when he looked at the photos, he displayed ample diplomacy and always concentrated on Felicity. "Felicity is a lovely looking young woman, Mrs Baker. You must be so proud of her," he would say for the hundredth time.

"Yes, I am, Patrick, and she has a magnificent voice. I'm going to have her trained for opera when we return to Australia. Although she's very intelligent and is sure to want an academic career first, and then a family, of course." Mrs Baker's look of admiration towards Patrick was unmistakable.

"It all sounds wonderful, Mrs Baker. I shall endeavour to be in the audience when Felicity makes her opera debut," Patrick said through clenched teeth.

"I'm sure Felicity would be delighted, Patrick. I'll keep you informed, I'll write letters and send photos of Felicity, along with news of her singing career."

Chapter 9
Love at First Glance

"No time for breakfast, Tom, we've slept in. Come on, get up. Let's get off this bloody ship!"

Thomas was still slightly groggy, but nonetheless in good humour, as his immediate reaction was of escaping seasickness.

"Yes, Pat, I'm with you. Let's get out of this den of intrigue and false claims!"

Patrick shook his head, not catching what Thomas was insinuating. Maybe it was about his slap and tickle with the daughter of a boxing champion on board? Who knew? Who cared? Patrick's urgency was more to the point of running for miles and feeling the freedom and sureness of solid earth beneath his feet. They packed their bags quickly and only minutes later, they'd arrived on deck, ready to run for their lives.

Mrs Baker was the first to say goodbye. "Please keep in touch. We're friends now and so we must hear all about how your training at the Academy is coming along." Mrs Baker glowed with enthusiasm while speaking with Patrick and would not let go of his arm.

Mr Baker stood back patiently then came forward when he had the chance.

"Goodbyes are always difficult, gentlemen. We sincerely wish you both well and, yes, please do write. We would love the occasional letter. It was so nice to meet you both, such honourable young gentlemen." He then shook their hands firmly.

Patrick bowed his head and bade them farewell. "It will be my pleasure, sir, and Mrs Baker. Thank you again for your company. Goodbye."

Colour Sergeant William Knight had been sent from Sandhurst to pick up the three cadets in a horse-drawn carriage. A very proper English gentleman was William Knight. He stood smiling, waiting at attention. After shaking hands and having a short, informal conversation with the Colour Sergeant, Peter, and then Thomas entered the carriage. But for some reason, Patrick turned his head before entering, as if something or somebody had told him to do so. With one foot on the step and the other on the ground, he froze. Addy stood not too far from him, talking with Felicity. It was as if Patrick's life, before this moment, had never existed. His heart rate rose dramatically. Addy's face, now alive and animated, drew him like a magnet. An intense power forced Patrick to ask William a simple question.

"What time do we have to be at Sandhurst, Colour Sergeant?"

"Why do you ask, Mr Darcy?"

"Just tell me, will you!"

Patrick's urgency, it seemed, made William nervous. "Well now, let me think. After arriving at Sandhurst, you'll have time to settle in and read any mail which has reached Sandhurst prior to your arrival. Then a formal afternoon tea will be served, so all new cadets will meet their officers on a cordial note before you get blasted for doing the wrong thing! Ha, ha. So, you should definitely arrive before then."

Patrick, losing his patience, asked again. "Just tell me what time I have to be there, Colour Sergeant."

"Oh, quite right, Mr Darcy. I'd say three pm, on the dot."

Patrick then flung himself away from the carriage.

"I'll see you later, Tom. Cover for me if I'm late."

Nothing Patrick ever did surprised Thomas. He watched in amusement as Patrick made his way towards Addy. He just caught a glimpse of Patrick kissing Addy's hand before their carriage moved away. "Well, well, she must be special!" Thomas said aloud, without realising he'd done so. Peter glanced at world outside.

As the coach rolled along, Thomas gazed out the window, admiring quaint picture-book cottages lining the narrow route. The greenest grass he could have imagined carpeted the fields. It was so different from the Australian bush. It'd been a shame they took no time to dwell in London, he thought. However, Colour Sergeant Knight was proud to have driven them past the city. It appeared the most amazing building Thomas had ever seen. Peter sat, not impressed by anything. The only words he'd muttered without any emotion were, "I trust Patrick will make it back to Sandhurst on time, or there's sure to be trouble waiting for him."

Thomas felt like throwing him out of the carriage, but knowing where the act would take him, he chose to go against his feelings of disgust and replied calmly. "You'll never have to worry about Patrick. He can look after himself. He'll be there on time." Thomas wasn't going to let this worm spoil the joy of his new experience.

After travelling at a slow pace for about two hours, William called out, "How would one of you chaps like to take the reins? I need to do a pee."

Thomas jumped up before Peter had time. "I will."

"Oh, that's a good chap."

As Thomas sat in the driver's seat waiting for William, thinking he seemed to be taking his time, he heard galloping hoofs and a familiar voice. "I knew I'd catch ya!" Patrick pulled up alongside the carriage on a sweating bay thoroughbred.

"Oh my god, that felt good!" Patrick's eyes gleamed with pleasure.

"Who felt good: the girl or the ride, Pat?"

Patrick laughed between gulps of air. "Mate, I'm in love! I couldn't stay long though. Mrs Baker—I think wants me to marry her daughter, Felicity. It's too complicated to explain, just like the horse I stole!"

Thomas shook his head, smiling at his mad mate. "Tie him to the carriage, Pat, and then tell me all about it."

William returned, amused at seeing that Patrick had already caught up with them. "I say, I've heard about you chaps from the colonies, darned good horsemen!"

He tilted his ruddy face and asked quizzically, "I say, where on earth did you find such a fine thoroughbred?" William began rubbing the sweat off the gelding's neck with a towel.

"Thanks, Colour Sergeant, he needs that and a drink too. Got any water on board?"

"Of course, Mr Darcy, we never travel without water for the horses. Darned hot today!"

Patrick took a swig, only to spit it out upon hearing William's words. "HOT, if you want hot, mate, come to South Australia and I'll show you bloody hot. One hundred and ten degrees in the shade and that's one of the cool days!"

"Is that a fact?" William asked in disbelief.

Patrick slapped him on the back. "Now would I lie to you, Colour Sergeant?"

William's face screwed into a frown and sweat trickled from his brow. He looked questionably at Thomas.

"He's pretty much telling the truth, Colour Sergeant."

"Oh my goodness, I cannot imagine living in such heat. How on earth do you survive?"

"A lot of skinny dipping," Patrick said before giving him a nudge and a wink.

"Let's go, Colour Sergeant, we've got some soldiering to do."

Once in the carriage and on their way, Patrick confided in Thomas. "I've just met my one true love, Tom. Her name's Adelaide Watt-Stuart. Addy was waiting with Mrs Baker's lovely, but not for me, daughter Felicity. Oh yes, and the horse I borrowed is from a nice old fella named Lord Fogarty, a graduate of Sandhurst. He's a great old bloke. I met him inside a London tavern. I introduced myself and bought him a drink. After another drink and some small talk, I felt the need to bare my heart." Patrick held his hand up to his heart and gave a mock sigh.

"So I told him all about us coming from Australia to enter Sandhurst. He became excited and said he'd done his officer training there. Anyway, we talked for a while and then I had to tell him about Addy. I said, 'Lord Fogarty, I have just met the woman I know in my heart I will love for the rest of my life. However, sir, I think my love-at-first sight may well deem me late for Sandhurst, unless I'm able to purchase a horse fast enough to get me there on time.' He's a real funny old bugger, Tom. He congratulated me and said. 'Well done, young man, a good soldier should always enjoy a woman's company before the battle begins!' He asked me to follow him. I still find it hard to believe, but he handed me one of his ex-racehorses and said, 'I'll send a groom to fetch him later. Good luck, Mr Darcy!' I bet he's laughing about the cheeky young Australian, who may have just pulled his leg, but I think he liked me anyway." Patrick's assumption had been correct.

Lord Fogarty had walked home, reminiscing. "Darcy, Darcy, I remember that name." He said it repeatedly until he finally recalled old Angus Darcy, being one of the finest gentleman lawyers in London. "I must ask young Darcy if he's related. Nice young man. Yes, I like him very much," he'd said aloud.

"Addy gave me her address, Tom. She's staying two more years at Badminton until she finishes her exams. I'm telling you, Tom, I've never felt like this before. I was tongue tied and my hands trembled when I held hers. I don't know what's happened to me, I just can't stop thinking about Addy." He gave a deep sigh, leant back and stretched his legs across the carriage, accidently rubbing the sleeping Peter Mott's leg. Immediately, Peter opened his eyes and smiled at Patrick.

"I told you, Pat," Thomas muttered, so only Patrick could hear him.

When seeing the sign, 'Sandhurst', Patrick's heart soared. The impressive white stone building stood stoically, with a backdrop of dark green forest highlighting its whiteness. Artfully crafted pillars stood in front of the massive entrance which lead to the officers' rooms and main office. The manicured grounds surrounding the quadrangle were, at that moment, devoid of soldiers. Colour Sergeant William Knight pulled the horses up outside the main entrance. Patrick, ever since he was a little boy, had only ever imagined this military academy and now he was actually standing in its grounds. He was feeling a little overcome, especially when Major General Hawk greeted them.

"Welcome to Sandhurst, men." He was middle aged and seemed a refined gentleman. There was no mistaking the Major General's pleasure in admiring these two fine specimens of manhood. However, his expression changed when he studied Peter Mott. Although the boys had spruced Peter up and made him look at least alive instead of a walking corpse, Peter still fell way below the standard of Patrick and Thomas.

As Colour Sergeant Knight drove the horses toward the livery barn, Hawk noticed the bay thoroughbred trotting along behind. "I say, do you men know anything about that horse?"

"Yes sir, I was loaned the horse while in London. A Lord Fogarty, sir, an officer who graduated from Sandhurst many years ago, he gave me the use of the horse while I was here. I hope this will not cause a problem, sir?"

"Well, it's not usual practice, I must say. We supply the horses for mounted combat. It must have been a quick meeting with Lord Fogarty after disembarking. You knew him previously of course, Mr Darcy?"

"No, sir."

"Well, how did you go about meeting his Lordship and loaning that fine horse from him in such a short time? Colour Sergeant Knight should have been there waiting?"

Patrick hesitated to answer. Hawk chose not to wait, as he'd already decided he need not know anything that might change his mind about this born-to-be officer.

"Well, I'm sure we'll work something out, Darcy. This way, please. I'll show you to your rooms. We've been having great renovations and extensions, you know. So, you Australians will be some of the first to have the privilege of using our newly appointed rooms. You will also have the pleasure of standing at attention before our King, as he is to grace us with his usual tour of inspection next week." Hawk smiled and, proud of this fact, he even stood straighter. "Once you've settled in, afternoon tea will be served at four pm. Don't be late. Any mail you have received prior to your arrival will be given to you later. You will have time to attend to this before you present yourself at the main office. Your formal introduction to the management and the officers who oversee your training will occur then. Are there any questions?"

"No, sir, I mean, not from me, sir," Patrick said.

He saluted, admiring Hawk in full uniform: tailored, black fine wool; trimmed lapels in red and gold; a red stripe down the middle and outside of each trouser leg; a stunning gold belt; highly polished black leather boots; and sword secured in a leather pouch on his left hip.

Later, Colour Sergeant Knight came to their rooms. He popped his head in and asked, "Is everything alright with you, chaps?"

"Yes, Colour Sergeant, just settling in," Thomas said. He and Patrick had been given a room for two and Peter had been shown a single room. William felt the need to comment, as he was quite stunned at their welcome from Major General Hawk.

"You know, you're dammed honoured to have Major General Hawk greet you personally. Normally he greets only lords or princes. I suppose Captain Forrester being out on fitness training and not being able to greet you may have had something to do with it."

"Hey, Willy, he's honoured to meet us, mate. We're very special blokes, us Aussies," Patrick said winking at Thomas.

"Yes, no doubt, no doubt at all! See you chaps at lunch then," William said, before disappearing for a moment, then returned. "Oh yes, nearly forgot. Captain Frederick Forrester and the rest of your platoon should be back at any moment. Until later then."

"Don't ya just love him?" Thomas said. "Hope they're all like him and Hawk. This place will be a breeze."

Chapter 10
The Truth

Two months later, and Patrick had performed the most gruelling training regime with ease. He was leading in the point score for the honours awarded to be the most outstanding cadet. However, Patrick had found his fair share of avengers and smiling assassins within the groups of officers and would-be officers. As only Patrick could, he handled them with intelligence, strength of character and physical ability, no matter which way they tried him. The word had soon spread that Patrick was not to be reckoned with nor his friend Thomas. A mild respect had also formed for Peter Mott, as Peter knew who to cling to for cover in a precarious situation. He was, therefore, reluctantly brought into the fold.

Colour Sergeant Knight remained a genuine admirer and a close confidant on behalf of the Aussie outsiders. They had copped plenty of jibing, including a near-miss of their famous ink bath. Once given the ink bath, the cadets were forced to run naked through the grounds while fellow cadets flicked them with wet towels. However, when they'd tried to initiate Patrick, not one cadet was left standing after he had avenged his attackers with karate. "There will be no ink bath for me, or my Australian friends. Do you hear me?" Patrick warned, as he stood above his groaning victims.

Finally, Patrick's first bundle of mail had just been delivered. One letter came from Jonathon, and one each from Angus, Nurse Helen, and his extended family, including Colleen and Bob. Patrick tentatively opened Jonathon's letter first, as he knew it would hold the truth of his family's secrets. Until now, Patrick had managed to put aside the haunting questions he'd asked Jonathon in his letter. His diminishing concern for news of the past had been mainly due to thinking of no one else other than Addy, who'd answered his letters only once since he'd been at Sandhurst. This was after Patrick had foolishly, it seemed, poured out his true feelings for her on paper. When writing back, Addy had been most diplomatic.

Dear Patrick,

My future as a doctor is paramount in my life and it has to be addressed first and most definitely before I become involved with a man as passionate as you seem to be. Although I must admit, I found you quite charming when we first met. One day soon, perhaps, we may meet in London and take afternoon tea at the Ritz Hotel. It is my favourite place for high tea.

He placed Addy's precious letter carefully in his wooden box along with his wooden soldiers.

Patrick opened Jonathon's letter.

Dearest Patrick,

I have received your letter dated the fourth of April 1910, asking for information about the Bakers' property. I do hope you understand that, yes, there are matters in your mother's diary that I'd wished to keep from you, until you were free from study and training to be an officer. I assumed you would be mature enough then to accept the past and move on without malice. In saying this, I now feel you will concern yourself further with questions still unanswered and it will worry you. Therefore, I will now tell you the facts of your birth and then you must put it aside and don't in any way take these things to heart, so as to make you any less a person than you truly are. And that is, my beloved son, a fine gentleman of strong character and a great Army officer-to-be.

Your genetic father, Cecil Birch, held your mother and her mother captive.

Jonathon went on to tell the entire story, beginning with his grandmother being sent to the Colonies, and finished by saying:

Your mother hid like a bushranger until she reached Mother Matilda's orphanage. The rest you know. I must ask once again for your forgiveness, Patrick, as by writing the truth, which I have never done, it's brought home to me just how I must have appeared to your beautiful mother. Please believe me when I tell you, if only Sally had told me the truth, I would have collected you in an instant and brought you home to be loved and cherished.

I beg you now, Patrick, do not dwell on the negatives. The love and respect everyone has shown you must tell you that you have shown no signs of Birch's genes. You are your mother's son, and no one would ever doubt it. Please, put this all behind you now and look forward to living the life your mother had wished for you. Margie and baby Millie send their love. I'm sure you will receive letters from all the extended family, and from Angus, as I have posted his letter along with mine today.

PS – Da's moved into our caretaker's cottage, and we are thrilled he took up our offer. He dines with us most nights, which is another blessing.

281

Your loving father,
Jonathon.

At first Patrick felt totally deflated with the truth about Sally, and hatred began to well up when thinking of Birch. He'd given Sally no hope for happiness, totally controlling her and everyone who'd entered his evil web. As Patrick became more emotional, tears trickled down his cheek. He was pleased Thomas was not there to see it although he may soon return. Patrick gathered his letters and left his room to find a secluded spot in the woods.

A giant elm tree gave Patrick refuge. He inhaled the clean fresh air, hoping it would clear his mind and heart from the hatred of a man he'd never known. After some time, he managed to rid Birch from his mind. Patrick's thoughts then turned to Addy and her being unmoved by his declaration of love. Never had he experienced this reaction from a woman. Every one of them had bowed before him. *I'm the invincible lover, the Casanova of the century. How can Addy resist what I've never ever told another woman?* Trying to wipe all worries from his mind, Patrick felt the autumn breeze playing with his hair, or what was left of it, after they'd insisted a good soldier must have his hair cut short. Patrick's argument to keep his curls made no difference. They floated softly to the floor, like pieces of his heart. Smiling at the memory he thought, *maybe even my hair's being trained to stand at attention, as my curls have disappeared. Strange how I felt so angry and hurt after finding out the truth of my birth father, momentarily wanting to kill him, and now sitting here, observing God's work and knowing in my heart Addy will be mine all in good time. I feel grateful.*

Straining his eyes towards heaven, Patrick blinked through shafts of sunlight. "Is it you, mother? Are you always with me, consoling me, making my life brighter?" With a tear in his eye, he could only imagine what she and her mother had to bear under the tyranny of the mad man, Cecil Birch. "I love you, Mother, and I'll make you proud. I promise."

It would be half an hour before training recommenced. Patrick looked down at his brother's handwriting. "Time for you now, Angus." Shuffling through his letters, he listed them: "You next, Mother M. Ah, my lovely Helen. Dear Colleen then you, my old mate, Da."

Patrick opened Angus's letter.

Dear brother Patrick,
That you will never be! Get it, 'Brother Patrick', ha ha. Now the joke is over, on with the news of the outside world! But before I do, I must give you my sympathy. You poor bugger, all tied up with early morning training, long nights on watch

duty, freezing your balls off in a cold-as-hell foreign land (even though they do call it the 'Mother Country'). I truly feel for you as I sit in the warm sunshine alongside my LOVING friend, Molly. I must now thank you, brother, for introducing us. She has not only pleased my senses as a man, but she has become one of my closest confidants, a very intelligent woman, our Molly.

Patrick laughed, "You little bastard."

I'm still spending my time (while not rolling around beneath the sheets with Eva)...

"Eva! One minute it was Molly, now he's into threesomes"? Patrick read on.

... debating the efficiency of Chinese medicine with the Superior Professors, they call themselves. I know better, of course. Just as well I have a black belt in karate, which I keep reminding everyone or I'd be bashed black and blue and my ego humiliated to the point of no return. Molly, plus father, have both pleaded with me to let the argument go and I should. But at this point in my life I'm going to stick to my principles until ignorance is eradicated. Yes, if I were a woman (and I know I'm not, now Molly and Eva have helped me to prove otherwise), I would most assuredly be a suffragette!

Life simply goes on and so do my studies. I've been accepted into the Adelaide University as one of the youngest and brightest students ever to attend. I tell no lies, Patrick, when I say it was indeed a ceremony. It seems I have made everyone proud. Apparently, my wisdom and IQ are above their comprehension of the everyday genius! I'm sorry, Patrick, I sound like a stuffed shirt.

I love you so much and miss you so badly that sometimes I cry on Eva's shoulder (lovely shoulder that it is.) Now I sound like a small child missing his teddy bear. Well, what the hell, you've always been my teddy bear. I hope you fall over and break both your bloody legs and your bloody arms, so then they'll send you home, you bastard—only joking. No need to ask how you're getting on, you're bloody brilliant at everything you do. Hope the libido potion is working! I'll have one for you. Well hello, Eva, ooh that's nice do it again, kiss, kiss, kiss.

Better go now brother, Eva's becoming excited!

Angus's letter was just what Patrick needed. However, one thing puzzled him: was he having a threesome with Molly and Eva, or had he acquired a taste for younger flesh? Thinking back, Patrick smiled at how one night had changed his brother. Angus had found his sense of humour and appreciated women for what they are good at, helping a man enjoy one of life's great pleasures. Patrick hurried to find Thomas then offered him Angus's letter to read. After having a good laugh, Thomas asked, "Have you heard from Addy, Pat? Will she meet with you in London?"

"I don't know. Hopefully, I'll hear from her just before we leave. Maybe."

Patrick was about to finish what he was saying when the all mighty trumpet blew. It put a stop to any further conversation as no man dared stand still after hearing it sound.

Chapter 11
The Mission

Young fit soldiers stood to attention in a sharp line, listening to the orders being given loud and clear for their next mission. Patrick shone like a beacon. He stood six feet two, looking magnificent in his uniform. Every muscle in his body had been tuned to its maximum after the solid physical training the platoon had done over the past months. Their new mission entailed searching out and capturing the enemy who had already left in time to be camouflaged among the forest green. Major General Hawk gave the run down on proceedings.

"Your enemy could be anywhere: in trees, under mounds of leaves, or pretending to be injured and crying out for your assistance before they let a hand grenade fly at your platoon. A pretend one, of course! However, they do make a darned awful noise." His lips curled up slightly before he returned to serious business. "Keep your wits about you at all times, men. You first-timers are up against our elite team. I don't think any of you will survive, let alone capture your enemy. However, if you do, you will be rewarded with an extra day of leave." This remark brought on a loud cheer. "ATTENTION! That will be enough, gentlemen. All pistols are filled with blank bullets. They will hit a man up to fifty yards, so remember to aim well. Last of all, take this mission seriously. It is not meant to be a game! This will be a fight for your life and to protect your fellow man!"

Silence prevailed while Hawk studied the faces of the young cadets, thinking he may find a show of humour. "Well then, I can see you're all taking this very seriously and you're ready for the battle. Good luck, but most of all, good soldiering!"

Patrick's Platoon Commander, Captain Frederick Forrester, was of English aristocracy. Unfortunately, he had a slight stutter and, despite years of speech therapy, he was still battling the problem. If you unnerved him and asked his name quickly, he'd answer, "Fed-wick For-for-aster, Caa-pp-tain, that is!"

Patrick had written to Angus about this problem. *Poor Frederick, his stutter can be funny, but if we're caught laughing, he gets very upset. If his condition is not completely cured—and soon—it will be the end of his battle career. In fact, he was accepted into Sandhurst only after his wealthy father who also graduated from*

Sandhurst made a large donation. You don't know a cure for stuttering, do you, Angus?

Patrick worried that this being their first serious campaign, important orders might come far too late from Frederick due to his stutter. And so, while packing their overnight rations, he spoke privately with Captain Forrester. "With all due respect, sir, perhaps you should use sign language to give your orders. It might confuse the enemy. If we're totally silent, then they won't know which way we're coming from.

"Bu-bu-t I won't know which w-way we- we-'re going!" Frederick spun around in anger when he heard laughter. "Who, who laug-hed?" he asked.

Thomas answered. "I'm sorry, sir, it was me, but it wasn't about you. It was because Patrick said we should use sign language." Thomas paused, trying not to laugh, before emphasising, "IN THE BLOODY DARK, SIR?" The whole platoon burst out laughing, including Fredrick.

With map in hand, Captain Forrester led the soldiers off. They had about half an hour before night fell, which would put them well into enemy territory. Forrester reminded them, "Any-th-ing is poss-ible through the lo-long c-c-cold night. We do-n't know if the en-emy w-w-will attack us w-with full force, k-kill-ing us all. Or they m-may g-g-give us until morning light, w-w-waiting, hidden, ready to p-p-pounce or kill us off one by one."

The fourteen young men crept in single file into the dark woods. In the eerie silence, they approached the boundaries of enemy territory just before nightfall and continued until Captain Forrester gave his orders in a whisper. "I-its b-best n-not to go any further i-into th-the woods. We-we have no m-moon to guide us. We'll sit here, with our b-backs t-together in a-a circle. Have y-your guns ready and b-bayonets b-by your side." Once they'd followed orders, Frederick whispered. "We'll h-have our b-bully b-beef now, then star-star-ting from me, every second man, try to sle-sle-eep for a while, then we'll cha-change over to the n-next man." The cadets passed this order around the platoon, without copying the stutter.

Patrick ate his rations but chose not to sleep. At his first real mission, he was too stoked, especially at the thought of the extra day he might get to spend with Addy if he was to capture the enemy. Before long, the entire platoon, except Thomas and Patrick, fell asleep and began snoring. Patrick sat alert, trying to listen above the snores for sounds coming from the enemy.

"I wish they'd fuckin' shut up, I thought I heard something. Shoosh. Listen, Tom." Patrick cocked his ear again. "No, it's nothing."

Thomas then noticed a red haze through the forest. "Look over there, Pat."

Patrick had to turn around to see what Thomas was talking about. "Through the trees, over there, Pat. It's a bloody fire!"

286

"Fuckin' arrogant bastards, they're probably playing cards and cookin' a chook. Ok, let's get 'em, Tom."

Carefully, they sneaked away from the ring of sleeping men. Patrick whispered his orders. "Take your boots off, Tom, and start walking to the right. When I give you a tap, I'll go to the left and throw my hand grenade in the fire then you throw yours. That'll frighten the shit out of them. When they jump up, I'll knock their blocks off with my kicks. We'll tie them up and march them back to camp just in time for supper."

Thomas, as usual, could hardly contain his laughter. To him it was not fair dinkum and, of course, he'd always see the funny side of things. Patrick put his hand over his mate's mouth, whispering, "Don't fuck this up, Tom. I need more time with Addy."

Everything went to plan. The group of six elite fighters never knew what hit them. First, the loud explosions in the fire and then what seemed like a giant centipede flying at them from all directions. Before they knew it, they'd been bound, gagged and smartly marched back to base. Patrick found it almost impossible to contain his pride when returning with his captured enemy. He saluted Major General Hawk and asked naively, "Sir, does this mean we receive an extra day of leave for each captured prisoner, sir?"

Ignoring Patrick's naive question, Hawk stood speechless before asking, "How on earth did you accomplish this, Cadet Darcy? Exactly how did this happen?"

"Sir, as you have said, sir, never let your guard down. I'm afraid our enemy did just that, sir. They underestimated *their* enemy, sir!"

Hawk saluted the two heroes. "Well done, Cadet Darcy, Cadet Norman." He then asked quizzically, "Do you think there may be something you have forgotten, Cadet Darcy, Cadet Norman?"

"NO SIR, Mission accomplished, sir!" They both answered.

Hawk smiled knowingly and then bid them goodnight.

Captain Forrester and his crew had continued to sleep soundly in the woods. However, in the morning they woke horrified to find Patrick and Thomas gone – they must have been captured by the enemy. After searching nearly all day for the cadets and their enemy, they decided to give up. Back at base, they were somewhat bewildered and then humiliated after hearing what had happened. It did nothing to endear the two heroes, Patrick and Thomas, to Captain Forrester or their fellow cadets, although Frederick could not help but feel a little envious. Frederick knew he was there only to appease his family. Previously, he'd told Patrick, "I've come from a l-long line of off-off-officers, Patrick, who n-need the family tradition to c-continue at all c-costs, it seems. If you can't b-b-beat them then join them, I s-s-say. Although I do realise if my s-s-stutter remains and I f-fail at being an apt leader by the end of the year, I will be relieved of my p-p-post."

He decided he would now confide in Patrick once again as, in his opinion, Patrick was a born leader and a brilliant, cunning fighter. Frederick knew he himself was not, although he had to admit part of him was also angry that Patrick had left his command and gone forth on his own to conquer the enemy. He'd also left the platoon without waking them after his victory, so they could all march back to headquarters together and share the glory. This, he thought, was almost unforgivable.

Frederick had been shamefully rapped over the knuckles for his lack of command in letting himself and almost the entire platoon fall asleep,

"UNTIL DAYLIGHT, YOU BLOODY IMBECILE," Hawk had yelled at him.

Patrick had thought long and hard about his own actions, realising what he'd done had placed a wedge between him and the other men. The night before leaving for London, he'd called for a truce with his platoon members, including Frederick. He stood to address the men.

"Sir and fellow cadets, I stand before you, ashamed at how I behaved on our last mission. It showed me to be selfish and immature. I do hope you can forgive me and take my word of honour that it will never ever happen again." Patrick turned to salute Frederick and said, "I will follow your orders, sir, and I will look after my fellow cadets at all costs. As was once said, 'All for one and one for all'." As he spoke, more for the implication than sincerity, Patrick was transported back to when he and Angus had lived with Da. The three musketeers Da had called them.

Patrick's speech brought three cheers, with every man lining up to shake his and Thomas's hand. Frederick waited until the men had finished, then after shaking Patrick's hand, said, "I say, Cadet Darcy, it takes a good man to know when he's been a bad sport and admit it. I know I will be standing behind you in battle one day, Patrick. You're a born leader! And if what you have just sworn to us stays true, then you may become a legend!" Frederick shook Patrick's hand firmly once again, followed by a salute.

Patrick was delighted that Frederick had not stuttered once during his address to him. "Sir, do you realise you addressed me without a stutter."

"Well, I'll be dammed! How ab-about th-th-at, hey."

"Yes, sir, thank you sir. You can trust my word. I have definitely learnt my lesson."

Patrick hadn't divulged to Frederick what Hawk had told him the morning after the training mission. Patrick had been let off lightly for his almost mortal sin of leaving his platoon. "The fact that you captured the entire enemy has lessened your discipline. Let it be a lesson to you, Cadet Darcy. We are a team; we protect and support each other. That is what an army of men is all about. United we stand, together we fall." Hawk had then softened his tone. "However, what you managed to accomplish was truly amazing, Cadet Darcy. But to leave your platoon completely out of it takes away your valour. Because of your actions, I won't be giving you any extra leave. I should be disciplining you further by revoking your leave." He looked severely at Patrick, then relaxed and continued. "But I'm sure you've learnt a lesson from this and will soon collect your fair share of extra entitlements." Patrick accepted his reprimand, knowing he'd deserved it.

The time had come for their first leave. Patrick was pleased that Lord Fogarty had decided that the bay thoroughbred should remain at Sandhurst in Patrick's care. Lord Fogarty had written to tell Patrick he had no need of the horse, as he had a carriage with suitable horses and a driver. The horse was to be used and cared for by Patrick on one condition: that Patrick and any friend of his could come and stay with him on their leave. He'd delight in Patrick's company and would enjoy talking with him of his old army days when at Sandhurst. Patrick, he said, would forever remind him of himself when he was young.

Patrick was quick to write his reply. He thanked Lord Fogarty and told him that he and Thomas would be honoured to accept his kind invitation. However, may he push the boundaries by asking, would he know of another horse that perhaps his friend, Thomas, could use while at Sandhurst? They'd prefer to ride to London rather than catch the train. One week later, a black ten-year-old ex-racehorse arrived, travelling behind a coach, with a note written by Lord Fogarty. *This old fella has won me quite a few races. He needs a good home now. Take care, until we meet on the first evening of your leave.*

L F

Chapter 12

Meeting Addy

Addy's letter arrived on the morning before they left for London, as Patrick hoped it would.

> *Dear Patrick,*
>
> *I will be able to join you for afternoon tea at the Ritz Hotel in London. I am free this Saturday afternoon, from four pm until five pm. I will then be collected from the hotel to attend Lord Harris's hunting weekend. However, I am sure an hour will give us enough time to talk over our mutual friends and family. I will be waiting in the foyer.*
>
> *Yours truly,*
> *Adelaide Watt-Stuart.*

Driven by nervous energy, Patrick packed his bag, saddled his thoroughbred, and yelled at Thomas. "Hurry up, Tom!"

The last two miles before they reached London had told on their horses, but not the riders. Both young men were fit and ready for anything. As they walked alongside their weary mounts, they began to talk about how Patrick would approach Addy. His outpouring of love on paper seemed to have done him no good. Addy had replied platonically only twice to his letters.

"How is it, Thomas, I can have any woman I want. But this, this? Well, I don't know who she is? She reminds me of Angus, so bloody high and mighty!"

Thomas waited for Patrick to continue about the only subject he wished to talk about. Thomas then witnessed a familiar cunning smile appear on Patrick's face. "What are you thinking, Pat? I know that look. Come on, tell me."

"All I'm going to say is look at what happened to Angus when he finally succumbed to love and lust when under the influence."

"Bloody hell, Pat, you can't do that. It's not always about you having your own way all the time, especially with a girl you say you love and want to be with for the rest of your life. Sooner or later you were going to meet a woman who didn't fall head over heels for you."

Patrick laughed, half-heartedly. "I know, Tom, I'm only joking."

To Thomas, yes he was, but in his opinion, Addy truly needed to throw away what seemed to him to be her shield of armour against intrusion into her body and soul.

Their first night with Lord Fogarty was enjoyable and entertaining. Good food, good wine and interesting company at the dinner party held in their honour. The grandfather clock in the hallway had struck twelve midnight before the guests began to bid each other goodnight.

Yawning, Patrick apologised for his refusal to take yet another port with Lord Fogarty.

"You are too kind, sir. It's been an unforgettable evening. And just think, one of the gentlemen Dad asked me to look up when I was in London is a friend of yours, and he was here tonight for dinner. It's truly remarkable. As they say, it's a small world, but on that note, I'll say goodnight and thank you once again for your generous hospitality."

Thomas followed Patrick with his thank-yous and went to bed. Both young men needed a good night's sleep.

That same evening Addy lay awake in her bed. Sometimes the cool of the night woke her, or a dream of returning to Hawaii or Bulkawa. Both places held her spirit. However, tonight she tossed and turned, thinking of Patrick. She didn't want her thoughts at this stage to be taken up with anything other than studying to become a doctor. Now, when remembering Patrick's handsome face, his charming smile, his lips, and him lingering with a kiss upon her hand, she found it impossible to prevent her heart from racing. Addy felt her heart had been lifted from her chest and given to Patrick the moment she'd laid eyes on him at the dock. Being scared of her feelings, Addy tried to calm her mind about their coming meeting. She forced herself to think of the fox hunt this coming Sunday. But with each jump she took, Patrick was there, smiling with those dreamy blue eyes.

At 3.45 pm on Saturday afternoon, Miss Adelaide Watt-Stuart sat in the foyer of the Ritz Hotel in London. Slightly embarrassed at being early, she decided it best to leave for a short walk. *I'll return later and make a late entrance, as a lady should.* About to leave through the enormous glass doors, Addy thanked the concierge who held the door open. Without noticing, she'd stepped straight into Patrick's path. "Oh, I am sorry, sir." Looking up into Patrick's smile, her heart soared and her knees almost gave way. Patrick held out his hand.

"You weren't about to leave, were you, Addy?"

"No, no, of course not. I lost my handkerchief. I thought perhaps I'd dropped it outside."

Her excuse was quite definite after she'd momentarily thought of one.

"Allow me. I'll have a look for you, Addy."

Stepping aside from the incoming guests, Addy stood admiring Patrick in uniform. *How can one man have so much charm and magnetism? His charm seems to have doubled from the first moment we met.* Taking a deep breath, Addy gathered her strength. She smiled and was about to apologise when Patrick apologised first.

"I am sorry, Addy, I wasn't able to find your handkerchief, but here, please have mine. Mrs Thomas, as you would have heard, makes these initialled handkerchiefs in her spare time. I have at least a hundred!" Patrick laughed and she along with him.

As they sat across from each other at one of the popular window tables, the afternoon sun highlighted Addy's flawless skin. Patrick sat mesmerised, lost in her presence, not really hearing a word she'd said until the waiter cleared his throat with a cough.

"Excuse me, sir. Will you be having tea or coffee?" The waiter stood with a pot in each hand.

"Tea, thank you," Patrick answered without taking his eyes off Addy. She'd been chatting constantly.

Addy thought that if she were to stop talking and gaze into Patrick's eyes, she would be lost to him forever. *Eventually I'd marry him, have his babies, and that would leave me with no time or energy to become a doctor.*

All Patrick could do was listen. He loved Addy's voice and hoped she'd never stop talking. That way he could admire her for as long as he wished. At one stage of the conversation, he did manage to come out of his trance in order to answer her question about Angus.

"Yes, that's right, Addy. He's at Adelaide University. He's one of the youngest students ever to be accepted. He's like you. He wants to be a doctor too."

Addy smiled sweetly, "I only hope to be a doctor one day. I need to study very hard. I'm not as bright as Angus. He must be quite a genius."

Patrick nodded, saying nothing, preferring to let her talk. He could then imagine kissing her lips, slowly undressing her, running his hands softly over her body, *I mustn't go any further with that vision or I'll lose control of my emotions.*

After she'd had a sip of tea and a tiny bite of her tea cake, Addy continued talking. "If I am unable to pass my exams to be a doctor, I will surely take up nursing." She hesitated. "I perhaps shouldn't say this, Patrick, but when I was a little girl, my mother and I went to visit your mother. It was the day we'd returned to Adelaide from Hawaii. Sadly, your mother had not long passed away. My mother had no idea until she was told by your step-mother, Marjorie. The sudden and sad news shocked my mother. I will never forget how she cried her heart out. It left a very deep impression on me." Addy paused for a moment, and noticing Patrick had looked away, she quickly finished what she was about to say. "I knew then I wanted to be a doctor. I needed to save as many lives as I could. Just like your beautiful mother."

Patrick turned his attention back to Addy. Her eyes dared to linger on his. "The passion has never left me, Patrick," she said softly.

The memory of his mother had brought a tear to Patrick's eyes. Addy handed him back his own handkerchief. "I'm so sorry, Patrick. I shouldn't have spoken of such things."

"No, no, please take no notice, Addy. I just thought how sad it is that my mother isn't here to see us finally together, her best friend's daughter with her son." He would have liked to have said falling in love with each other. He knew now Addy had feelings for him. It showed, with her not being able to look him in the eye for more than a second, and her continuous nervous chatter.

Laughing to himself at his own emotions, Patrick decided to change the subject. "Let's talk of more pleasant things, Addy. What about this fox hunt tomorrow? Any chance that Thomas and I could come along?"

The mere thought of him being so close to her for so long frightened Addy out of her wits. "I don't think so, Patrick. It's invitation only."

She'd replied far too quickly. Patrick raised an eyebrow. "Well, I'm sure if we were properly introduced, Addy, then things might go in our favour. Surely you could ask your friend to ask her father. If two young Australian gentlemen training to be officers at Sandhurst may join them, in a sport which they were familiar with in Australia, I think then the Lord of the Manor may just welcome us.

"I suppose so," Addy answered tentatively. "My friend, Clare, whose father is the owner of the manor and the master of the hunt, will be picking me up in her carriage." She then looked at her gold wristlet watch. "Oh my, it's nearly 5 o'clock. Clare will be here in five minutes. She's always punctual. You can ask her yourself if you like, Patrick, after I've introduced you to her, of course." *Now I've done it, now I've taken this further than I should. I know Clare will say yes. One look at him and she'll melt.*

Addy stood arm in arm with Patrick waiting outside the Ritz Hotel, when right on time Clare's carriage pulled up. A somewhat handsome, slightly horsey young woman stuck her bonneted head out of the window. "ADDY!" she called enthusiastically, and then in her upper-class brogue, asked, "And who do we have here?"

Amused at her friend's outgoing personality, Addy said, "Clare, I'd like you to meet Cadet Patrick Darcy. Patrick's a family friend from Australia. He's training to be an officer at Sandhurst."

Clare scrambled awkwardly from the carriage. "I'm extremely pleased to meet you, Mr Darcy!" Grabbing his hand, she shook it firmly.

Patrick laughed and responded, "And I you, Miss Clare…?"

"Harris, Clare Harris. So sorry, didn't give Addy time to introduce me properly. Always jumping the gun, Daddy says. Oh well, early bird and all that. Jolly good to meet you though, and are you able to join us for the hunt tomorrow, Mr Darcy?" Still holding Patrick's hand, Clare squeezed it.

"Actually, I was just about to invite myself," Patrick hesitated for a moment, "and also my friend, Thomas. We do love to hunt. Done an awful lot of it in Australia, you know."

Patrick was having a bit of fun sending up her well-bred English accent. Addy smiled at his attempt.

"Well, it's all settled then," Clare exclaimed happily. "Let us go and collect your friend, shall we? We'll all travel together. Daddy will be so delighted. He loves the military fellows. He attended Sandhurst himself, you know. Had to give it all up for the family business when grandfather died, keep the money flowing in. These damnable ancient manors and all their grounds; lots of hard work and money needed for the upkeep, you know." Clare noticed their concerned looks and giggled. "Oh don't worry, Daddy part-owns a shipping business that brings in millions every year. Money's no problem, not at all!"

Clare amused Patrick, to the point of him thinking she would make a good mate, in a blokey sort of way. *I bet she can ride a horse.*

Thomas had only just returned to Lord Fogarty's home after his prowl around London, where he'd tipped his military hat to any young woman who looked in his direction. He'd also checked out clean and respectable whorehouses, where he may just return that evening for his sexual pleasures. He looked out the window when he heard a carriage pull up. Patrick hurriedly explained the situation to Thomas and Lord Fogarty. Shortly after, Lord Fogarty was standing on the footpath and wishing them farewell.

"Tally ho, wish I were young and going with you, lads!" Lord Fogarty called as he waved them off. "See you Monday, gentlemen!" His heart soared at the mere thought of chasing the hounds again. He'd been a dashing young rider in his day, but sadly time and many falls had taken their toll on his body. "Just as well I have fond memories to cling to," he said quietly to himself as he painfully climbed the stairs leading into his home.

Their time together on the journey was hilarious. Patrick and Thomas had never met a girl quite like Clare Harris. Her confidence and down-to-earth humour left them astounded. They'd laughed their way through the tales she'd told, until night fell. Now their attention turned towards the flaming torches which lit up the walls of the grand manor. Driving the last quarter mile down the cobblestone driveway, Clare commented, "Just as well it's not winter and snowing. No good for the fox scent you know, although we'll miss seeing the bloodied patterns, squiggling across the snow." She'd said this with an animated blood-thirsty look in her eye.

Addy squirmed. The kill was not the part of hunting she enjoyed. She loved the freedom of the gallop, along with the elation of taking off and over an almost impossible jump, then landing safely. That was what the hunt was all about for Addy. To kill anything was not in her nature. However, Clare delighted in it, and Addy knew this.

Patrick was surprised that they'd even hunt in the winter. "How on earth do you manage to hunt in the winter, Clare? I thought it to be breeding season?"

"Oh well, not in the dead of winter. It sometimes snows in autumn and spring. Too many foxes, doesn't matter when we hunt them really. Young pups, old, in between. It's best to hunt on a clouded day, the sun kills the scent. Daddy just loves the chase. Don't use terriers any longer though, they'll wipe out the bloody lot. Kill the sport, they would!"

Footmen, housemaids and coachmen stood to one side of the entrance, waiting to welcome Clare and her guests. When noticing Patrick and Thomas gazing in awe of the impressive structure, Clare explained. "This manor was built almost four hundred years ago, on the cusp of the Tudor dynasty, to be exact."

Patrick lifted his head to see the highest tower, standing at well over one hundred feet, lit up by the flaming torches. "It's simply amazing."

Lord Harris stood at attention until Clare ran to him, nearly knocking him over.

"DADDY, DADDY, I have a wonderful surprise for you. LOOK!" Clare turned to beckon her three guests to hurry up, and she then introduced them.

"Of course, you know my beautiful friend, Addy, but you don't know these handsome young Australian men. They're Sandhurst cadets, Daddy." Clare took note of her father's approval, knowing that any young man in uniform would be welcome in his home. "Daddy, I'd like you to meet Patrick Darcy and Thomas Norman. They're Addy's family friends."

Lord Harris was most gracious in his welcome. He begged everyone to hurry inside, as the evening had turned quite cold. Clare moved along the row of servants, kissing each one on the cheek, addressing them by their Christian names. "How are you, Maude? How are you, Christopher? Has your mother recovered from…" and so on.

Lord Harris turned to Patrick. "I wish Clare wouldn't be so familiar and demonstrative with the servants." His face then donned a knowing smile. "Although I know who the servants would save first if there were to be a house fire," he chuckled.

Personal luggage was brought to the men's rooms by the footman, Oliver. Patrick and Thomas were to share a room where the fire had not been lit. Thomas couldn't help but comment. "Doesn't feel like autumn in here," he said with a shudder.

"I am sorry, sir," Oliver said. "We were not expecting you, however, the room should not take too long to warm up once I light the fire. I will also place a warming pan in your bed before you retire. Will there be anything else, gentlemen?"

"No, thank you, Oliver."

Oliver lit the fire and bowed graciously before leaving.

"Thank you, Oliver." Thomas then winked at Patrick, "You know, Pat, I could get used to this life," he said while falling into the folds of his feather bed.

"Well, just marry Clare, mate, and it's all yours. She's the only child, and I reckon she fancies you."

"Yeah, yeah, only because she knows Addy has her eyes set on you. Not a bad idea though, she'd be into anything, I think. Could be fun. Not the prettiest woman I've ever seen but she makes up for it with personality." Thomas's brow crinkled. "I'll think about it."

Patrick began prodding the fire, then stopped. "Do you really think so, Tom, about Addy, I mean? I didn't know if I were imagining it. She doesn't give much away."

Thomas sprang from his bed. "Mate, sooner or later she'll be all yours, trust me. Now I'm bloody hungry so let's go down for dinner."

The dinner table sat twenty, but not tonight. They were the only guests to accompany Lord Harris. "I always like to catch up with my dear daughter by sharing a quiet dinner alone before the hectic day ahead." He looked amused at their slight shock then laughed. "Although I must say, it's exhilarating to have your company this evening, gentleman, and you, of course, Addy. You are all most welcome, I must say." Lord Harris then raised his glass of fine red wine and made a toast. "To the younger generation and their quest for happiness through attitude and honesty."

Clare was the first to almost down her wine. "Here, here, Daddy. Well said. One cannot be truly happy unless one has the right attitude to life and, of course, being honest at all times. Jolly good toast, Daddy. Let's enjoy, shall we?"

Dinner began with a serving of smoked trout caught by his Lordship in his own stream, then venison and roasted vegetables, also grown and shot by his Lordship, and finally, spotted dick pudding was served with creamy custard. The conversation then moved to the den. It was informal and entertaining, mainly due to Clare and her remarkably quick wit. Their talk continued into the small hours of the morning. Lord Harris was shocked when glancing at the clock.

"Oh my, look at the time! We must be off to bed, an early start tomorrow or, should I say, in five hours' time."

Lord Harris rose from his leather chair, which was nearest the fire in the den. Once again it had amazed Patrick how small the world seemed, as in conversation he'd learned that Lord Harris knew of old Angus Darcy QC, the man who'd adopted Jonathon.

"I must tell you, Patrick, old Mr Darcy was a fine gentleman and a darned good lawyer. I knew all about your father, Jonathon, being adopted by Angus Darcy. Jonathon became an absolute credit to him when he graduated from Cambridge University. Topping the year in Law, I heard." Lord Harris seemed deep in thought before his next statement. "Always wondered what ever happened to young Jonathon. The Colonies, hey. Well, I'm so pleased to hear how well he's done."

Patrick thought about his own history and was reluctant to admit it, but chose to do so, after this gentleman had mentioned happiness through honesty.

"Lord Harris, I must tell you that I too was adopted, by Jonathon Darcy."

Without Patrick having to go into any more detail, Lord Harris placed his arm around Patrick's shoulder. "I'd like you to know, Patrick, I would have dearly liked to have adopted a son." He looked lovingly at Clare. "Clare would have loved it too. But my wife is from French nobility and while I adore her, she's a snob in the first degree. When you meet her, Patrick, down the track that is, as her Ladyship is in Paris at present." His round face squeezed up like an orange about to be squelched of its juice. "Well, I suppose, she's in Paris most of the time actually." He regained his humour. "Please don't mention to her Ladyship you were adopted, Patrick. She will have you divulge your underprivileged heritage in the finest detail. If she does not approve, then you may be sent to the gallows!"

Clare burst out laughing. "Daddy's only joking, of course, Patrick, but yes, poor Mummy's missed out on a lot due to her snobbery. I take no notice really. Apparently, I take after Granddad and I'm sometimes likened to his great friend, Lord Wilberforce. Now there's a wonderful man if ever there was one. He put those heartless fools in Parliament in their places. Always stood up for the downtrodden. Yes, he made darned sure humanity remained humanitarian and they all watched their manners!"

297

Addy had remained quiet throughout their dinner and now in the sitting room. However, Patrick thought her occasional quips were amusing and intelligent, adding another layer to her personality. Addy's heart went out even more to Patrick after his honest confession about being adopted. His knowledge on a wide variety of subjects, and his calm confidence, only endeared him to her further. However, what she didn't know, but suspected, was his many intimacies with women. Addy was determined not to be another notch in his belt. The looks Patrick gave her over dinner, she had to admit, set her heart pounding. Not only did Addy not trust him tonight, she didn't trust herself.

"Speaking of manners, I wish to thank you, your Lordship, for a wonderful dinner. I look forward to the hunt in..." Addy looked at the time on her gold watch, "nearly four hours. I must now bid you all goodnight, or good morning." Addy took Clare by the arm. "Come, Clare, you know I'm scared of ghosts. I'll share your room tonight if I may."

Not looking back to see Patrick's expression, she almost dragged Clare from the fire. Clare looked back, saying with humour, "Oh well, somebody has to protect her from such things. See you all soon."

"Red sky in the morning, shepherd's warning," Patrick recited, while resting his eyes on the magnificent sky throwing shades of pink across the green pastures.

Thomas rolled over, pulling the bed covers up over his head. "Please don't tell me it's morning already, Pat. I need more sleep."

Patrick felt euphoric, knowing he was sleeping in the same building as Addy. Savouring this thought and the sheer beauty of the pink morning, he felt as if he were somehow floating. Breathing in the country air, Patrick sighed deeply and then declared, "Oh, how I love thee, dear Addy."

Thomas shook his head. "Oh, for God's sake, Pat, what's wrong with you? You sound like you're in a Shakespearean play!" He then softened. "Did you go to Addy's room last night?"

Patrick returned from the balcony and sat on his bed. He chose not to answer Thomas's question, instead confiding, "You know, Tom, it's a strange thing. Part of me wants to make love to Addy forever. Part of me wants to rape her and part of me just wants to cherish her, look upon her as a china doll, too delicate to seduce. I'm confused as to how I should approach her. Now I'm here, I may have the opportunity tonight to seduce her. I really don't know what to do."

Placing his head in his hands, Patrick continued, "I've lost my nerve, Tom. She's got me scared and I've never feared anything in my life."

Thomas admitted to himself he'd never seen his mate like this. It unnerved him. "Patrick, you've got to get a grip of yourself. After all, she's only a woman."

"She's not just a woman, Tom. She's the woman I thought I'd never love. I bloody hate it. I wish I'd never met her; she's made my life so complicated. It was so easy fucking any woman I liked. They all fell at my feet. Now I'm her slave, I'd do anything she asked. I'd never tell her though. I don't know if Addy's scared of me, or she's just playing silly games."

"You haven't answered my question, Pat. Did you go to her room?"

"How could I? She slept in Clare's room, so I don't think she'd be in a threesome."

"Can't help ya, Pat. Never been in love before, mate, but it's bound to happen one day. Meanwhile I'm in for a bit of fun. What time does this hunt start?"

Patrick looked at his watch. "In an hour so we'd better get dressed."

"I'm so hungry, Pat, I hope they've killed the fatted calf."

"I can't eat, Tom."

"Oh shit, Pat, you've got it bad."

Tom jumped up, ruffling Patrick's straight blond hair. "Funny how your curls disappeared. You know what happened to Sampson when Delilah cut his hair?"

Thomas laughed until Patrick flicked him over the ear.

"Ooh shit, that bloody hurt!" Thomas complained while Patrick tried to kiss it better.

"Piss off, Pat, let me get dressed in this sissy English hunting gear. God bless Oliver. I'm bloody starving!"

Lord Harris left his room at the same time as Thomas and Patrick. The first floor, which was a horseshoe shape, held six bedrooms each with solid, carved doors. Normally, Lord Harris slept in his own apartment in another wing of the manor. However, last night he'd chosen the room adjoining the girls, with the boys' room further away. Patrick thought that if he were the girls' guardian he would've done the same.

"Good morning, your Lordship. Thank you for supplying our hunting attire."

"Good morning, gentlemen. I hear you do quite a bit of hunting in Australia, Patrick?"

"Yes sir, we must hunt the foxes and rabbits because they're vermin and in plague proportions. The English imported them, you know, and we could have done without them."

Lord Harris could not disagree but declined to discuss the matter further as they walked down to the grand dining room. Addy and Clare were already there. Patrick's heart skipped a beat at the sight of Addy wearing posterior-hugging culottes, only just acceptable in hunting attire for women then. Her long black hair was loosely tied in a black velvet bow. She wore a crisp white shirt with a gold brooch pinning down her frilly tog. Addy turned and smiled after placing scrambled eggs and a sausage on her plate.

"Good morning, gentlemen, I hope you don't mind but I like to eat early so I have time to warm my horse up before the chase."

"Good idea, Addy," Patrick said, as he walked briskly to pull her chair out. "Have you done much riding?" he asked once he'd sat next to her. He'd put barely any food on his plate and she noticed.

"Are you not hungry, Patrick?"

"Ah yes, but I keep it light before riding," he lied, his stomach a swarm of bees.

"You haven't answered my question, Addy," Patrick said.

She smiled before replying, "I've done enough riding to be able to stay on board, thank you, Patrick." Clare nearly choked on her bacon and was just about to sing Addy's praises when she felt a kick under the table.

"So you'll be riding with the second field then Addy, or what do you call them here in England, hill toppers?" Patrick asked.

Addy laughed. "Yes, that's what they call the second-rate riders." She finished her breakfast, stood up and declared.

"Well, I'm finished so please excuse me. I'll see you all outside in thirty minutes."

Patrick watched her bottom as it wiggled pertly through the doorway. Lord Harris witnessed the look on his face and silently agreed, however, he had to say the opposite. "Not sure if I approve of the new women's attire for the hunt, or their hurry to stride a horse instead of riding side-saddle!" He coughed twice to bring Patrick's attention back to the table.

Clare jumped up, kissing her father on the cheek, "I'll go and see if everything's in order, Daddy. Did you tell Oliver to make sure he served only the finest port for the toast?"

"Yes, of course, I did, Clare. That was your mother's idea, you know, before our last hunt. She didn't want to waste expensive port on second-rate citizens."

Lord Harris turned to Patrick, his voice a whisper. "Only one other lord coming, you know." He then thought a moment. "Oh yes, and a barred Member of Parliament, distantly related to a duke. Not the sort of company my wife would waste expensive port on." Laughing, he continued, "But a very good bunch of ordinary people, I must say!"

Twenty riders had gathered in front of the manor. Oliver had offered the finest port, serving it on a silver tray in silver goblets. The rush of alcohol sent a red glow to Patrick's cheeks and a heart surge; a good start for the hunt. He was excited, but with the alcohol taking effect, Patrick felt relaxed enough to introduce himself and speak at length to the other guests.

Addy stood enjoying her sherry before she mounted, sitting astride her horse. This act brought a murmur of disapproval from the older riders. Addy was not as disturbed by their looks or their comments as she was consumed by Patrick's charm and his outgoing manner. Admiring his physique, though slim, she could see his firm thighs and tight buttocks. With his broad shoulders, he sat square on his mount. He was magnificent. Patrick could feel Addy's stare, but decided not to look. He was sure if he did, his concentration and his strength would leave him.

"LET THE HUNT BEGIN!" called Lord Harris, a moment before the official horn blew. The first fielders gathered behind the Lord, while the second field stayed well behind.

With plenty of time to chat on their way to the fox's covert, Patrick was still trying to find out what field Addy would ride.

"I might just take my chances with first field today, Patrick," Addy said, bemused by his caring so much.

He was a little surprised by her confidence, especially when seeing her sitting astride her horse. He asked, "Are you sure? You don't want to be getting hurt, not with your final exams coming up."

Addy simply raised an eyebrow and cantered off to Clare who was riding alongside Thomas. They seemed to be getting on very well, with laughter punctuating their chatter. "Having fun are we, Clare?"

"Oh yes, thank you, Addy. Tom's such a good sport, he said he'd look out for me. You know, pick me up if I fall." Clare winked at Addy and then in a low sultry voice, she turned to Thomas, "I love strong men, especially officers. And one day, I'm sure, Thomas, you will rank the highest." Clare fluttered her most redeeming feature, her large brown eyes under long black eyelashes. Thomas fell into her honey pot. "Well, of course Clare, you wouldn't expect anything else from an Australian soldier."

Having to wait at the edge of the woods in silent anticipation had set the riders' hearts thumping. Then suddenly, the hounds barked so loud it shook the air. The first fielders took chase, helping the dogs force the foxes into the open. Branches snapped and some sprang back hitting the riders behind. Blindly, they allowed their horses to follow the pack until they focused once again. Fallen trees gave no clear passage with dense woods on either side of the rotting trunks. Every rider took the jumps, whether they were six feet or two feet high.

Lord Harris took the lead, with Patrick close behind. Momentarily he'd forgotten about Addy, until they were in the clear and she galloped up alongside. He turned and smiled.

"Look ahead, Patrick!" Addy warned, just in time for him to jump a fallen tree. Her horse sailed over it, landing in front of Patrick.

301

"Well done, Addy!" he said, his tone patronising.

Addy didn't need compliments or patronising. She was about to show him she could ride as well as any man, such was her competitive spirit. *I'm Jum Watt's daughter, and quite often I feel the need to show it.*

"They're quick foxes around here, Addy,' Patrick said, just before they took the next jump.

"Yes, I think Lord Harris breeds them fast for extra excitement."

Next thing they were galloping through a stream, laughing as they climbed the bank on the other side. The two became oblivious to the riders behind. They were alone, except for glimpses of Lord Harris about fifty yards in front. For a second, Patrick thought of heading Addy off into the forest to be alone with her. *Perhaps I'll find out if I'm wasting my time. If my heart breaks with Addy's refusal, it'll mend and I'll be able to get on with my life and be freed from this bloody stupid game she seems to be playing.* Suddenly, he thought about strategy. It always wins the war. *If I fell and pretended to be hurt, Addy would either stay with me and be upset, or she'd continue and promise to send for help.*

Superego was not a contender for Patrick. "Honesty unto one's self is all that's needed to make a man a man." Da's words would forever be instilled in Patrick's heart. Therefore, a simple fall from his horse would not endanger his soul and he would know the truth one way or the other. Patrick saw the ideal jump directly in front. He urged his horse to take off far too early. The horse's front hoofs cleared the obstacle, but his back hooves clipped it, bringing them both down. Unfortunately, what Patrick hadn't counted on was the horse rolling on top of him. He lay winded on the ground. Addy jumped off her mount and ran to him.

"Oh Patrick, what a silly thing to do. You should've known better!" she scolded, as she sat him up and rubbed his back, hoping it would help him breathe.

"Come on, Patrick, breathe deeply, you're just winded, I think."

Patrick did. "I think I've broken my ribs. It hurts like hell."

"Let me see," Addy said, softly probing his rib cage. "Yes, I think you have. What possessed you to take that jump far too soon?"

"Please don't force me to tell you, Addy. You won't like the answer." He tried hard to be brave and put up with the pain in his chest, but Addy was determined to find out.

"Try me, Patrick."

"Ok Addy, I love you. I needed to see if you'd stay with me when I fell, or if you'd leave me and continue with the hunt. Are you satisfied? I'm a bloody fool."

"Dear sweet Patrick, I appreciate your honesty and please believe me when I tell you." She hesitated when seeing the longing in his eyes. "I love you too…" He went to interrupt. "Please, listen to me, I can't let myself be taken. I've made a

302

solemn oath to my parents and myself that I'll become a doctor before anything else in my life…"

Patrick tried again to interrupt but she wouldn't let him. "You have to understand that if I let myself love you as much as I want to, my future will be changed. I know it will. I know exactly what I must do with my life. Call it fate or a sign from above, all I know is, I have to study hard to become a doctor."

Patrick grimaced with the pain.

"Poor Patrick, do your ribs hurt that much?"

He then managed a feeble chuckle at his own stupid act. He held onto his broken ribs and through pain he assured her. "Addy, I know I'll love you until the day I die. Please just do what you must, and I'll wait."

She kissed him on the forehead. "How could I ever love another man, Patrick? Your love and understanding are all I'll need to see me through my studies. You really do understand, don't you Patrick?"

"Yes," he nodded.

"I promise this will be for the best, Patrick. I wouldn't be able to live with myself, or be truly happy, unless I follow my calling."

If Patrick's breath had been cut short with his broken ribs, Addy's passionate kiss took it away completely. He then remembered hearing those same words from another girl he loved—his Betty, Sister Madeline.

Chapter 13

Recovering with Charlie

One month later, not only did the pain in Patrick's chest prevent him from training, but he had to sleep sitting up. This made his life at Sandhurst frustrating.

"I'm so bloody tired of myself, Tom. But when I get the doctor's pass I'm going to concentrate on being the best cadet to ever set foot in Sandhurst. I have to, especially now I've got Addy to impress." He smiled but then realised he'd handed Thomas a putdown. "Except for you of course, Tom, you'll be hard to beat with the point score." Thomas gave him a knowing smile.

"I'm happy for you, Pat. I told you that Addy had feelings for you. You'll end up married, I know. And you know what? I'm falling for Clare. She's so funny she actually said she'd 'allow me further exploration into her interior' next time we meet! Can you believe she actually said that? I really like her, Pat, and she makes me laugh. My heart doesn't race when I see her, but I find her attractive and I'm happy whenever she writes me a letter, or telephones me. And how magic are telephones, Pat? I still can't believe it. We're able to talk to each other from miles apart. Of course, with a name like Thomas, no wonder Edison was the one who invented the telephone!"

Patrick felt truly happy for his friend, even though his own romance had been put on hold. It seemed Addy was too busy studying to come to the phone or write as many letters as Patrick wished. There was one consolation though; she signed her letters now with "All my love, Addy."

Peter Mott continued to stick like glue to Patrick whenever he could, although he'd become close to Cadet Travis Bourke. Both creeps, as Thomas called them, took delight in playing stupid tricks on Patrick. They'd run away with Patrick's bath towel while he was showering, or they'd throw cold water over the shower door so Patrick would run out naked and clip their ears.

"Patrick, I'm telling you, they're both perverted, and they're after you. Watch out, mate, or they'll get you one dark night," Thomas warned.

"Fuck off, Tom, they're just kidding around. It doesn't worry me. Anyhow, I reckon he wouldn't do those things if he hadn't found a friend to play with. I don't think he had a childhood. Being bought up by that imbecile father wouldn't have been easy. He's just reliving his childhood. Let 'em go, don't worry about them."

Thomas continued to worry. He suspected Patrick had taken their antics far too lightly. It may give them the wrong impression. Thomas then chose to shut up about his fears, as he knew his constant reminders might insult his best mate.

In the first two months back at Sandhurst, disappointments were many and rewards few for Patrick. Firstly, his broken ribs had got in the way of his defence of the Sandhurst boxing championship. On Patrick's behalf, Thomas had put up a brave fight, only to be knocked out cold in the second round. When he woke up, the first person he saw was Patrick. Thomas mistook his look of concern for disappointment. "Sorry, Pat, I let you down."

Patrick had also missed another important battle between their enemies. Then there was heartbreak when Patrick's bay thoroughbred went down with a severe case of colic and died during the night. When informed, Lord Fogarty was sympathetic and understanding, promising to send him another horse he'd recently found. Patrick told Thomas after hanging up the phone.

"The horse sounds like a bit of a mongrel. Apparently, he's got a touch of draught horse and Welsh mountain pony in him. Oh yes, and his mother's an Arab. A very unusual mix, mate," Patrick smiled and shook his head. "Lord Fogarty never told me where he found him. He just said his name's Charlie and he was undernourished, so he took him in. But he says he's fattened him up now, and he's supposed to be pretty smart."

Some days later Patrick had some exciting news for Thomas, "I've been teaching Charlie tricks. I tell y', Tom, he's amazed me with how quickly he's learnt. I reckon I could teach him anything. And because I'm still out of action, I'm going to do just that. Maybe I'll put on a show, lift the moral. What do you reckon?"

"If anyone can do it, Pat, you can. Go for it."

The Saturday evening before Patrick was passed fit to return to duty, he'd called all who wished to see his wonder horse, Charlie, perform his amazing tricks. After he got permission to do it, Patrick chose Colour Sergeant Knight to usher the men to their seats in the quadrangle. The first-year cadets took the back row and the highest-ranking officers sat in front. Lighting was not needed as the days were still long, and so the show began.

The gramophone began to play a marching tune just before Patrick and Charlie appeared. They walked side by side to centre stage then turned to face the audience. Both lifted their legs in time to the music. This amused and enthralled everyone, including Major General Hawk. After the music and applause stopped, Patrick asked, "How old are you, Charlie?" With his hoof striking the ground, Charlie counted six, and Patrick gave him a cube of sugar as a reward.

"Have you ever won a race, Charlie?" Charlie shook his head from side to side.

"No? Why, Charlie, are you not fast enough?" Charlie nodded his head up and down; another cube of sugar.

"Charlie, can you go to Major General Hawk, take his hat off and then bring it to me?" Once again Charlie nodded his head, then walked to Hawk, took his hat off and brought it back to Patrick – another sugar cube. Patrick inspected the hat, looked apologetically at Hawk and said, "Oh, I am sorry, sir, it's a little wet around the edge. Charlie, can you wave your tail to dry the Major General's hat?"

Charlie spun around and waved his tail. At this, the audience doubled up with laughter.

"Now please take the hat back to the General, Charlie." Charlie straight away placed the hat on Patrick's head. The men went hysterical, including Hawk. "Charlie, I'm not the Major General—YET! Please take it back to Major General Hawk." And so he did, placing it squarely on the Major General's head then returned to Patrick for another cube of sugar.

"You've been a very good horse, Charlie, and I've given you sugar cubes. How many cubes have I given you?" Charlie stood for a moment, as if he was thinking about it. Then with his hoof he struck the ground four times.

"THAT'S RIGHT, CHARLIE, what a smart horse you are!" Patrick said loudly, while applauding Charlie. As he did, Charlie reached in to Patrick's pocket, pulling out the bag of sugar cubes. He trotted off to his stable with the bag in his mouth. Patrick simply smiled and bowed his head to the deafening applause and cheers.

After Lord Fogarty heard Patrick's story, he owned up. "I saved Charlie from a circus train, Patrick. He was skin and bone. Yes, he was a very sad sight indeed. But I knew there was something special about him. Well done, lad, you've certainly brought out the best in him."

Patrick was relieved now that he could breathe without pain, so he resumed training with urgency. He took on every mission and every order with such intensity that he was almost at breaking point. His horsemanship and riding skills had towered above his instructor's. This had been evident from the platoon's first riding class, when the Captain had given orders. "Those who think they can ride well, stand here. Those of you who think you can only ride, stand over there. And any smart-arse bastards who think you can outride me, come and stand next to me!"

Patrick, noticeably amused with the Captain's remarks, was told to stand with the smart-arses before he had time to choose. The Captain then proceeded to put on a show to amaze all the cadets. Unfortunately, the two smart-arses who rode before Patrick performed dismally compared to their Captain. In their defence,

Patrick said, "That was a little unfair, sir. It seems they were given tough-mouthed, uneducated horses, sir."

"Well then, Mr Darcy," the Captain ordered, "you choose your mount among this lot then!"

Patrick was shown a herd that appeared to be unbroken. Walking about the yard, he soon won their confidence, gently stroking their necks while whispering to them. He then chose one he thought would be the most likely to buck. The Captain's face lit up. "We're in for a show now, lads!" he said to the cadets.

Patrick took his time to saddle the sixteen-hand brute. Finally, he placed the bridle carefully over his head, attached a long lead to the bit, and lunged him around in a circle. The horse bucked beautifully for some time. When Patrick thought he was all bucked out, he gathered up the reins and put his left foot in the stirrup. He then stood upright, bouncing his weight in the iron before throwing his right leg over and easing himself in the saddle.

As Patrick's horsemanship became apparent, the Platoon were transfixed. He sat effortlessly to a few good bucks before the horse calmed to Patrick's feel. His sensitive hands soon mouthed the horse with finesse and then man and beast became one. The Captain remained quietly impressed but outwardly arrogant toward Patrick.

As everything concerning Patrick's ability was reported to Major General Hawk, he called Patrick in to his office. "Cadet Darcy, I've called you here today to ask you just how far you want to go with your Army career."

"To the top, sir," Patrick answered, saluting as he did.

"At ease, Darcy, this is an informal inquiry." Hawk smiled briefly. "However, due to trouble brewing with Germany and the talk that Britain may ally with France if a war breaks out, I feel the United Kingdom needs outstanding officers, as you will be, Darcy. We need strong officers to lead the way into battle. Therefore, I would appreciate your answer about where you will keep your allegiance. Will you be remaining in England once you've graduated, or do you intend to return to Australia?"

"May I sit, sir?

"Yes, please do, Darcy."

"I understand your concern, sir, but it will depend. You see, I've fallen in love with a young lady here in England." Patrick took on a dreamy faraway look for a moment before he continued. Hawk leant back in his leather chair, waiting to hear what may be a long story.

"I've known of Adelaide Watt-Stuart, sir, from when I was very young. Her mother is a close friend of my family. Addy, as we call her, lived mostly in Hawaii. I'd only ever seen pictures of her and it was purely by chance that I met her for the first time when I disembarked. I must admit it was love at first sight. For both of us it now seems."

Hawk took a moment to think about Patrick's arrival at Sandhurst and the story of the bay thoroughbred tracking behind the coach. "Did that bay gelding have anything to do with your meeting Miss Watt-Stuart?"

"Yes, sir, it's a long story…"

Hawk stopped Patrick from going any further. "Please, another time. You were about to give me your decision based on Miss Watt-Stuart?"

"Yes, sir, my decision will be made when Addy has chosen a university. She's going to be a doctor."

Hawk sat to attention. "A doctor! That's a pretty big claim for a woman."

Patrick smiled knowingly. "Yes, sir. But you don't know Addy, sir. She's like no other woman I've ever met. She's delicate and beautiful, but she can ride a horse as good as any man. She's confident and empowered. Yes, that's what she is, she's empowered. Addy is her own person. I love and admire her for that. I'll marry her one day, sir. But I need to be as close to her as possible, until she graduates and then we will definitely be married."

"I admire you, Patrick," Hawk nodded his agreement. "I must say, it is indeed a new age for women, finding their place in society. My sisters had only marriage to look forward to. Now it seems the doors are open to all professions for our gentler sex." He sat in reflection for a moment. "When, may I ask, will you know about Miss Watt-Stuart's decision, Darcy?"

"I won't know until the end of my cadetship, sir. Until then, I will be the best possible soldier I can be. And I'll certainly keep in mind the trouble that may lie ahead for England. After all, she's our mother country, the country most of us originated from, so my allegiance is very strong."

Hawk stood to shake Patrick's hand. "You're going to make a fine officer, Cadet Darcy." He then smiled, almost lovingly. "Oh, and another thing, my wife is intrigued with the story of your horse, Charlie. I told her, on my own presumption, of course, that you wouldn't mind performing a private show with Charlie, for her and some of her lady friends?"

"I would be delighted, sir."

Escorting Patrick to the door, Hawk said, "I don't know how you do it, Darcy. You seem to have a way with everything you tackle. But the way you've trained that horse—bloody brilliant. I hope you stay with us, Cadet Darcy."

Patrick stood to attention and saluted Hawk before skipping down the stairs. The news of a war brewing had excited him. *There's nothing I want more than to fight in a war. Well, make love to Addy excluded and without either, I know I'd rather die.*

The next day, Patrick received an urgent letter—from Jonathon.

Dear Patrick,

It is with great sadness I must inform you of Da's passing. What has touched us further is the following day, your old pony, Sergeant, lay down next to Da's cottage and never woke.

You would often see the two searching together for just the right piece of wood for Da to whittle. It seemed as if Sergeant could talk to Da in his own fashion. Sergeant would stand beside the veranda watching Da as he whittled away the wood he'd carve into wooden toys. Da would speak to Sergeant, and it seemed as if the pony understood every word he said.

I know the miles between us are many, Patrick, and the mail is slow. Therefore, I will write the words I think you may have expressed at his funeral. I will have said them for you by now.

I owed my initial guidance to Da. He taught me to address all things with good intentions and honesty. Without Da, I would not possess my knowledge and understanding of horses. I loved Da as my father and respected him as my mentor. He will be sadly missed but never forgotten. Each time I touch a horse, Da's spirit will be with me.

I can only hope I have covered your feelings, Patrick. I know how saddened you will be, and I wish I could be there to console you.

Your loving father,
Jonathon

Patrick sat with his letter in hand, weeping, his eyes red and swollen. As he folded the paper and placed it in his wooden soldier's box, memories flooded back—Da's sparkling blue eyes holding a hint of mischief and the practical jokes he loved so much. He'd nearly always ask Patrick to join him in tricking the girls and Mother Matilda. Their first practical joke was putting a large dead spider on the girl's toilet seat. Patrick had shown Da the frightening black creature, lying dead in his boyish hands. Da soon thought of what to do with it, and poor Lizzy was the first to run screaming from the toilet with her pants down around her ankles. "Just as well we all wear long skirts!" Mother Matilda had yelled, before she chastised them both.

Patrick thought of how each Sunday, without fail, Da would bring the legs of lamb to roast, plus Ma's apple pies, and how every now and then he'd trick the girls. Da would ask them to fetch the apple pies from the back of the cart, which he'd actually taken out before and hidden in the shrubs. He delighted in the girl's horror when they reported back to him. "The pies are gone, Da. They're not there, someone must have stolen them!"

"Oh, don't be silly, girls," he'd say, "I put dem dere meself, t' be sure."

Meanwhile Patrick would run around the back, place the pies back in the cart, and then hide.

"Now go have another look, girls. Ya must be blind!" Da would say. He and Patrick would laugh until their sides ached.

"You're devils. That's what y' are!" Mother Matilda would say, but with the hint of a smile.

Patrick could sit reminiscing all day about Da and their adventures together. However, he'd have to put it on hold. The trumpet had blown.

Another training regime was announced, this time strategically planned by Cadet Peter Mott and his partner, Travis Burke. They were to be in charge. Major General Hawk addressed the assembly. "These two first-year cadets have passed their first exam on strategic warfare with honours! At ease, and show your approval." Reluctant applause was heard.

Hawk was not surprised at the response, but at the same time he needed to give Peter and Travis some credit. He'd also hoped it might encourage their comrades to be at least more accepting of them, because most cadets obviously shunned them.

On this particular training session, Captain Forrester's platoon was the enemy. As they were to be hunted by the elite troop, only the very best plan would help them to survive. Peter and Travis had come up with a brilliant idea. Travis arrogantly declared, "We'll dig trenches and then cover ourselves with leaves and branches. This will produce an illusion and when the enemy approaches, we'll surprise them by firing from under our camouflage, killing everyone, of course!" He saluted Captain Frederick Forrester.

"Well done, chaps. Let's get going then, shall we? I hope you have enough shovels, Cadet Burke?" asked Captain Frederick.

"Yes sir, we have, sir." He nodded to Peter who then ran to the nearest tool shed. Upon reaching their destination, they began digging, but a little too slowly for Frederick's liking.

"Come on, chaps, put your backs into it!" Frederick ordered.

"Another sentence without stuttering, sir!" Patrick called from his trench, being the first to be dug and ready.

"W-w-ell, what d-do you kn-know," remarked Frederick.

"I think, sir, when you concentrate fully on something other than not stuttering, you in fact don't stutter, sir."

"Thank you, Darcy,"

Patrick smiled. "Not at all, sir."

Two and a half hours later, the elite team set off from the barracks expecting, as usual, to hunt down and capture FF troop. Since their first humiliating capture by Patrick and Thomas, the elite team had managed to recoup their moral within the time it took for Patrick's broken ribs to heal. They'd won every battle in that period.

As all FF troop's trenches were deep enough to cover the troops, the men waited silently, hidden below fallen tree branches and forest debris. Silence brought with it nervous anticipation for these yet-to-be warriors, who were still novices at confronting and beating a formidable enemy. Their muscles began twitching and stomachs churned with the thought they may be badly injured in this battle. They worried about whether the trenches looked natural, or whether they were sitting ducks for the well-trained eyes of the elite team. These questions filled their minds until they heard crackling leaves and sticks crunching under enemy boots. The sound became louder. Frederick, well hidden in the middle trench, was ready to signal when the enemy reached close range.

Suddenly, Frederick shouted, "FIRE!" All enemies were either shot dead, or bayoneted within minutes. It had been a resounding success. Later, the victorious platoon celebrated by downing two flagons of rum which Patrick had managed to smuggle in. The widow, Peggy Delaney, owned the nearby coach stop where she sold ale, and accommodated the cadets with the occasional sex romp. As Patrick was not being able to perform his usual duty due to the pain in his ribs (this was his excuse), Peggy spoiled Patrick by going down on him. As he lay back and luxuriated in the pleasure, Addy's beautiful face was the only image in his mind.

Weeks had passed since the evening of the platoon's united triumph. Now with a decent notch in their belt after boasting their well-planned victory, Peter and Travis gained the confidence needed to be part of the team. They had also assumed an air of smugness and took delight, it seemed, in whispering and smiling whenever Patrick passed by. Patrick would merely tip his hat, return the smile and keep walking. This made Thomas feel ill. The teasing in the shower block also continued. Patrick just shrugged it off as mucking around and sometimes he'd walk naked back to their room, demanding his towel back.

"I'm telling you, Patrick, you'd better watch yourself. Those two creeps are up to something and you'll be the brunt of it!"

"Jesus, Tom, I don't know why you worry about them. What do you reckon they can do to harm me? I'd kill them both with one blow!"

Under his breath Thomas said, "That's what they want to see you do. Blow. Bloody queens!"

As Patrick walked away, Thomas warned, "It'd be alright to kill them, Pat, but you'd be thrown out of Sandhurst and hung from the gallows. And they're not worth it, mate!"

After that warning, Thomas did notice a change in the two. Their childish games had stopped and Patrick smiled toward them no longer. There'd been an incident between the pair that Patrick had witnessed. It made him feel sick, but he kept it to himself.

Chapter 14

Graduation

Two years had passed and now Patrick stood at attention to accept the highest award given to a graduating cadet, the Sword of Honour. Standing alongside Patrick, Thomas accepted his Overseas Cane, presented to cadets from foreign lands who'd excelled in their training.

Luckily, the snow that had been forecast held off. This allowed Patrick to clearly see the broad smile on Addy's face. He knew Addy's exams for entry into medical college were to begin next week, so her taking time to come and see him graduate was touching. It was the only award Patrick needed. Hats flew in the air immediately after the new Second Lieutenants had been relieved from duty, free to celebrate with their friends and loved ones. The ones who were able to make it, of course, as Jonathon was most upset he was unable to be there. He'd written to Patrick.

We are truly disappointed we were unable to make the journey, Patrick. If it weren't for Margi having difficulty with her second pregnancy, we would have been so proud to have seen you presented with your sword. I'm sure I speak for Angus as well. Unfortunately, his final exam allowing him internship into Adelaide Hospital is on the same day as your graduation.

Please accept our sincere apologies, Patrick.

Patrick felt let down after reading the letter. However, Addy's company was the most important. She kissed him on both cheeks and congratulated him, her eyes watery with unshed tears. "I'm so proud of you, Patrick. Imagine the highest scoring cadet ever to attend Sandhurst, and achieved with two months out of action." Addy's soft lips lingered on his. Patrick's heart skipped a beat, wanting and needing to make love to her like nothing else mattered.

"That was a kiss from Mummy, Patrick. She said to give you a kiss of congratulations."

He laughed. "I think if your mother kisses like that, Addy, then I'm in love with the wrong woman!"

She slapped his arm. "PATRICK!"

Clare wasted no time jumping into Thomas's arms. She whispered, "Oh Tom, I love you. And if you take your uniform off later, I'll take a good look, just to make sure I do."

Lord Harris knew his daughter well. "What was that, Clare?"

"Never mind, Daddy. I have to keep some secrets from you."

Lord Harris put his hand forward to shake Thomas's. "Congratulations, Thomas, well done. I must say, I never reached anywhere near the heights you two gentlemen have when I was here." He thought for a moment, "How many years ago was it now?"

Clare shook her head impatiently. "Too many years ago, Daddy, now let's have some fun. Are they serving alcohol, Thomas?"

Lord Fogarty hobbled along with the aid of his walking stick to join the group.

"Well done, yes, well done indeed, gentlemen." After shaking hands with both young men, he suggested, "Where does an elderly gentleman get a decent whisky around here?"

"In the main reception hall, sir. Come, I'll show you the way," Patrick said, before taking Addy's arm in his. He gazed up to feel snowflakes landing gently on his face. *Confetti from heaven*, the euphoria of this moment set him in a time warp, and for a moment he felt weightless, as if being carried by angels on an out-of-body experience. His spirit stood alongside his mother looking down upon him and Addy. This moment was as real to Patrick as graduating to be an officer.

"Patrick, Patrick. Would you care for a sherry?" Lord Fogarty's voice had broken his trance as they stood in the main hall among hundreds of chatting people. Patrick chose not to disclose his experience to anyone. It had been a cherished memory, one to place in his soldier's box.

"Is sherry all they're serving, Lord Fogarty?" Patrick asked.

"Unfortunately yes, and I think we'll be limited so let's make a run for it. I know a tavern nearby where we can buy the finest Scotch whisky in England."

The tavern sat not far off the road heading toward London. Small and cosy, it gave shelter to a few local farmers who were finishing their last mouthfuls of warm ale before leaving. A bearded, ruddy-faced shepherd, the last to leave, tipped his hat and pulled his collar up before he opened the door, allowing snow to drift in around his feet.

"Time to be gettin' home and bringin' the sheep in. I tink it's gonna be settin' in for the night," he gestured towards the snow outside. They all nodded in agreement.

Then Lord Fogarty ordered the bar tender, "Your best Scotch whisky all round, thank you, sir!" then remembering in an instant, "Oh, I am sorry, ladies, would you prefer a sherry or ale?"

Clare answered immediately. "Scotch will be fine, thank you, your Lordship. What do you say, Adelaide?" Clare gave Addy a look, as if to say, 'Agree with me'.

"Yes, whisky will be fine, thank you." Addy smiled sweetly at Lord Fogarty, who for a fleeting moment felt young again, while he was lost in her beauty. Thinking to himself what a lucky young man Patrick was, his thoughts became words, "Yes, indeed very lucky." Coughing after realising what he'd just said, he explained, "What I mean is, we're very lucky to have reached here before the snow thickens."

They all agreed then their conversation turned to the army traditions in England, compared to the somewhat makeshift army in Australia. Something Patrick would dearly love to do, he said, was to return to Australia and become one of the founding officers at Duntroon. Excited by the idea he continued, "Duntroon is the newly appointed Military College in Canberra, Australia's national capital. My father's written me a letter after he enquired about the college." Patrick noted all eyes were upon him and so he asked. "Would you like to hear what my father has written?"

"Yes, yes of course, Patrick," Lord Harris answered.

"Well, then, I'll read a little."

Duntroon is the new Military College in Canberra. It's in desperate need of young officers such as you, Patrick and Thomas, of course. It would be a perfect situation for you to return home, considering how very much the family misses you. I feel, in time, that Duntroon will produce fine young officers. And I'm sure you will soon be one of the high-ranking officers in charge of training the men, especially now with your Sword of Honour to confirm your expertise!

Other news Patrick chose not to disclose then, because he had already read it and it was personal.

Mother Betty is expected home any moment to return to the orphanage. There she will teach English, taking over from Sister Lizzy who has now left the order to be married. Millie is looking forward to her new sister or brother. Marjorie says it's a boy, because he's already causing her grief with his kicking and moving around all the time. She said he must be playing cricket inside her tummy!

Colleen and Bob are slowing down to the point where Marjorie helps them every chance she gets. Your brother, Angus, has had his fair share of differences with the hierarchy of the medical profession. He's still hell-bent on proclaiming the wonders of Chinese medicine as being the saviour to all mankind. I must say it frustrates the university lecturers to the point of asking him to leave the lectures. I wish you could talk some sense into him, Patrick. He's threatened to go and live in China! Even Doctor Liu has pleaded with him to let it go and to concentrate on western medicine until he graduates. Sometimes I don't know how to handle Angus. He's rarely at home. He has close friends, he tells me, but that's all he tells me, I don't know who they are. He says they understand him. Do you think his strange behaviour comes with being a genius? I seem to have lost all communication with him.

The short of it, Patrick, is we all miss you terribly and need you. I know Canberra is a long way from Adelaide, but with the 'change-over express of the six-horse coaches every two hours', you hop from one to the next, making it seem not so far away at all. However, I'll leave you to make up your own mind, as I always do. I know you have Addy to consider now. Bernadette and Barney are delighted you two are getting along so well. (I think you may have told me a little more about Addy than she may have told them about you). And so the letter went on for some pages more.

Patrick thought it an ideal time to put Jonathon's questions to Addy. After he'd read only the Duntroon part of the letter, he read the final paragraph aloud.

Do you know at which university Addy will study? You may tell her from me that the Adelaide University would welcome her with open arms. Doctor Forster would be delighted to take Addy under his wings, he's such a fine, well-respected man. He's now taken to lecturing medicine at the university, and demonstrating operating procedures. I have taken the liberty to enquire into Addy's internship, that is, if Addy chooses Adelaide as her study base.

Patrick looked at Addy pleadingly and asked whether she had decided which university she'd attend to finish her medical degree. Would it be here in England or Australia? She explained to the group, avoiding eye contact with Patrick. "I have to pass my final exam before I choose a university. It depends really on which one will accept me, I suppose. I'm afraid I'll be unable to make a decision for at least two months."

Patrick had already made his and Thomas's decision. "We'll wait for you, Addy. We plan to share the next two months staying with you, Lord Harris, and you, of course, Lord Fogarty. That is, if Thomas and I are still welcome?" Both senior men nodded. Patrick continued, accepting that as their answer. "We'll wait and see if Addy joins us on our journey home, or Thomas may just have to travel home alone, as I'm determined to stand by Addy." Patrick then had to admit, "However, I'll remain in England only if Addy wishes." He took note of her joy in his remark.

"I would now like to propose a toast. I do wonder where we two young Australians would have ended up if it were not for the kindness and hospitality shown to us by you, gentlemen. Here's to Lord Harris and Lord Fogarty." Glasses clinked and the toast was drunk.

Nobody had noticed a plump, rather common-looking woman, who'd crept up behind them and asked, "Excuse me, sirs, madams, pork pies on the menu f' supper. Is anyone interested?" She was the tavern's busy cook, barmaid, and housekeeper. When no one answered, she stepped to the fore, asking the group politely once again if they would like to have supper. Then suggested, "We 'ave three rooms to let. I don't think you ladies and gentlemens will be goin' anywhere in this storm." She peered out of the tiny window to see only the whiteness of the snow falling.

"Hubby's put the 'orses in the barn for the night, so yer's may as well eat and stay. I'll be lightin' the fires in y' rooms now." Nobody said a word. They just watched in silence as their orchestrator left them. Then simultaneously, whether it was the alcohol, or the unusual situation, they laughed as a chorus.

Lord Harris was the first to speak. "Well then, it seems all settled; we are here for the night." He raised his glass. "Here's to our future as good friends and allies!"

The night continued in merriment, but every now and then, under the influence of alcohol, someone would tell of some personal drama, which would be accompanied with, "Oh dear, what a shame, that is a sad story." Each time after such a story was told, another would come in with a funny quip to cheer them up.

A small wooden piano sat in the corner of the room. Malt hops, turned upside down, hung from the beams surrounding the bar. Many treasured artefacts adorned the mantles above the two enormous fireplaces at either end of the room. Addy had found out that most of the figurines had been gifted to them by grateful travellers for the care given them in their stay. There were tiny porcelain moulds of Tudor manors, hunting dogs, miniature mugs and children holding rabbits.

To stretch her legs and take a closer look, Addy walked over to admire the figurines. Patrick joined her, seizing the opportunity to be alone for a moment. It gave him the time to ask Addy her thoughts on him returning to Australia, and perhaps leaving her here in England to pursue her career. "Addy, since reading my father's letter, I've had time to reflect on what I want to do and what I really should do."

Addy played the game of being preoccupied with the figurines, stroking the smooth porcelain. She didn't need a confrontation now. Her heart and her head were forever in a constant battle over her love for Patrick and her need to be a doctor.

"Of course, I want nothing more than to stay with you, Addy. I've thought of a way to make things easier for us." He hesitated, knowing she would probably not accept his offer, but he wasn't going to die wondering. "We could be married here in London, Addy. I'd never stand in your way of being a doctor. I'd have my own profession, but if we were to marry, it would make me the happiest man on Earth. I'd stay in England at Sandhurst to be close to you, and we could meet whenever possible."

Patrick's proposal strummed Addy's heart. The last thing she wanted was for him to leave and go home to Australia. But thinking this, she knew if he stayed and they married, it wouldn't be long before she'd give up her quest to become a doctor. She would surely give up her dream in exchange for the passion and love she now suffered silently for Patrick. Giving in to her need to please him, make love to him, care for him and have his children. It would take precedence over everything she'd planned in her life. Firmly, she decided she'd not relent, she would stay strong to her convictions until after graduation. *Yes, it is for the best Patrick leaves me and goes home to Australia. I need to be left alone to study, with no temptations swaying me, at least for a couple more years.*

Placing the tiny figurine back down on the mantle, Addy turned and looked Patrick in the eye. Her expression told him she loved him with every part of her being. "I will marry you, Patrick." She then realised it was cruel to see his immediate elation, so she continued quickly. "But not now. I'm not ready. I know what will happen. My love for you is so strong it would take over everything I've ever wanted and as you well know, it's to be a doctor. It has to come before anything else in my life."

Not believing she'd been so cogent with her words, especially with the alcohol weakening her defences, she studied his face. His disappointment seemed paramount, and her heart went out to him. She simply adored him, she wanted to undress him, savour his magnificence and beg him to take her virginity. She was all his and would be for the rest of her life. Addy's constraint on her feelings were paper thin now.

Patrick's heart fell, but defeat was not in his nature. "May I kiss you, Addy?"

Why she uttered her next words, she would never know. "Kiss me later, Patrick. I know Clare won't mind spending some time in Thomas's room." Shocked and thrilled at what she'd just insinuated, Patrick ushered her back to the table.

Supper was hard to swallow for Patrick. Not because it wasn't delicious. It was simply his anticipation of heaven to come. *Keep the old gentlemen inebriated. We don't need any unexpected interruptions.*

"Gentlemen, here we are, drink up. This is a very fine red." Patrick urged them on, pouring wine into the glasses of the already tipsy Lords. He then congratulated them. "A fine wine you've chosen well, my Lords."

Only sipping on his wine, Patrick chose to drink water to wake up his senses. Addy followed suit, although she thought perhaps if she didn't top up the nerve-calming liquor, she may just renege on her promise. She'd already been cruel, so how could she let Patrick down again? This one time would give Patrick a memory to hold onto when she sent him back to Australia, alone. And for herself, in her moments of needing his love so badly, it hurt. However, the question remained within Addy's logic and better judgment. *Why am I about to do this?*

With dinner complete and enough alcohol consumed to make an elephant drunk, the two elder gentlemen awkwardly climbed the stairs to their room, singing as they did. Once at the top of the landing and in slurred speech, Lord Harris ordered Patrick, while swaying his index finger pointing to one of the bedrooms. "You sleep in that room with Thomas, Patrick. You two ladies lock your watch. I mean your beds. I mean your doors!" Waving his finger around at the four young people, he said, "I'm watching!"

Before he almost passed out and just before Patrick steadied him and helped him into his bed, Lord Harris smiled up at Patrick, "Kiss me, my love, why do you leave me all the time?"

Lord Fogarty had already collapsed on his bed. Patrick covered them both and left the room as both men began snoring.

After knocking softly on Addy's door, Patrick heard, "Come in." Addy stood at the foot of the bed, her shallow breathing quickening as Patrick began kissing her neck.

He whispered, "The first time may hurt a little, Addy, but I promise the pleasure will be worth the pain. You were made for me to love. You are so amazingly beautiful. Just relax and let me take you to a place you've never been."

Addy believed him; she had no other choice. Her decision had been made. "What if I become pregnant?" she whispered innocently.

"You won't, my love, trust me. I have a method to prevent it."

Relaxing a little more with this knowledge, Addy enjoyed Patrick's sensuous touch. Undressing her slowly and then himself, he lay her naked upon the bed and stood admiring her perfect body. She smiled into his eyes, too embarrassed to look anywhere else. Patrick just looked, adoring her, savouring her beauty for what seemed an eternity.

"Please make love to me, Patrick," her voice almost a quiver with fear.

She's precious, too fragile to be played with just yet, Patrick thought. He lowered his body over hers, kissing her lips softly while parting her legs with his, he gently entered.

"Relax, Addy, it'll be alright, it'll only hurt for a second."

She cringed as he broke her hymen. Patrick then lost control, giving into the longing he'd held on to for so long and until he was gone to the glory of the moment, he then collapsed by her side.

"I'm sorry, Addy. I'm so sorry."

Addy felt as if she'd just been raped, her own needs not thought of in his attempt to satisfy only him. She felt cheated.

"You hurt me, Patrick, there was no other sensation and it was all too quick."

He held her tight, rocking her back and forth, and trying to soothe her.

"I'm truly sorry I hurt you, Addy. I was in another place, I needed you so badly and I couldn't help myself." He kissed her on the head as she lay limp in his arms. "I know you know nothing of sex or making love, Addy. You're so innocent. Please forgive me. I would never hurt you intentionally. It won't hurt next time, I promise, I'll go slower and bring you to orgasm. I have to admit, I'm far from being a virgin, but I've never ever truly loved a woman until I met you."

Addy pulled away from his embrace, shocked at his admission of being a philanderer.

"Please listen, Addy, I want to be honest with you. I've had sex with many women, but it meant nothing, nothing at all. I'll love you and only you, for the rest of my life."

Addy thought he was being sincere, and melted once again into his arms. "I believe you, Patrick, and I love you too. I feel such a fool. Can you teach me the art of making love and sexual pleasure? Will it always hurt?"

Patrick laughed, his chest vibrating against her breast.

"No, Addy, it won't hurt and there're many ways to please your lover," he said light-heartedly. "I will now give you some tantalising experiences that will send you straight to heaven, my dearest!"

She giggled.

Leaning forward he kissed her nipples, dancing his tongue around until they sat erect. This aroused her senses, until teasingly, he stopped and sat up. "But first I must ask you to cleanse yourself of my sperm, by infusing this fluid into your vagina."

Addy sat up, horrified.

Smiling, with his head to one side, Patrick asked, "You don't want to fall pregnant? Please do as I say, then you'll be rewarded with a trip to heaven." His sexy smile persuaded her.

For the next half an hour, Patrick slowly, almost clinically explored every inch of her body, while explaining all about eroticism and the feeling she was about to have when he did this, or that. Playing childlike, he made her giggle when he began to tickle and then blow his warm breath on her stimulated nerve endings. Finally and gently, his tongue offered her a new sensation. Addy writhed and moaned with the pleasure until she orgasmed for the very first time in her life. She gave out a soft scream before he slid up to whisper, "I need to enter you again, Addy, I'm about to explode."

Still in awe of her orgasm, she whispered, "Can I relieve you in another way, Patrick? I still hurt a bit."

Christ, she knows nothing, he thought. Reaching for her hand, he then guided her in the right way to bring him relief. She settled into the slow rhythm. Addy enjoyed her control, smiling seductively into his eyes, until his body became tense under her final stroke. Patrick's deep sigh of satisfaction sent her heart racing, and a feeling of total freedom overtook her. Addy's lips, her heart, her sexual being was now uninhibited, thanks to her love of Patrick. She kissed him passionately and then began to laugh.

"Do I have to wash my hand, Patrick, in case of pregnancy?"

They both laughed until a knock on the door startled them. "It's only me, Clare. Can I come in?"

Addy drew the quilt up and Patrick put his trousers on.

"Give me a minute," Addy said. "Yes, come in."

Clare seemed in another world, her face flushed pink, and she smiled up at the ceiling. "We're in love, Addy. Thomas and I are going to be married." Dancing around the room as if she were already doing the bridal waltz, Clare wanted to hold Addy and dance together.

"When and where will the wedding be, Clare? Is Tom going to live in England with you, or are you going to live in Australia? Tell me, Clare, please tell me everything."

Patrick put on his shirt and gathered the rest of his clothes. He kissed Addy, congratulated Clare and went straight to Thomas. "Is it true, Tom? Have you asked Clare to marry you?"

Thomas lay on his bed smiling. Without looking at Patrick he answered hypnotically, "Yes, I have."

"Well, I'll be dammed, so what are you going to do, stay here in England? Or take your lovely bride home to Aussie land?" Patrick paused while Thomas pondered the answer. No answer came, so Patrick continued. "I reckon Clare would fit in very well in Australia, She's such a great girl. She'll make you happy, Tom. What am I saying? She already makes you happy. So you've made the final decision tonight, did ya, mate?" Patrick gave Thomas a punch on the arm and a wink. He was still in a daze but answered.

"Yes, I did. I never thought Clare would be so, so, sexy. All that gung-ho charm and quick wit certainly turned very feminine, once we were alone and naked. I love her, Pat, I really love her. She's my mate, she makes me laugh and now we've made love, I don't ever want to stop making love to her."

Patrick shook his head in earnest, but laughed on the inside and teased. "You know, Tom, I'm almost tempted to wake up the old boys and tell 'em the news so we can have a celebration drink!"

"Don't you bloody dare, Pat! We have to keep this little episode very quiet, or we'll be kicked out of town."

"I'm only joking, mate, good on you though. Isn't it funny we had to travel half way round the bloody world to find the women we love?"

"Yes, I know, Pat, but there's still a long way to go. I'll have to pass Clare's snobby mother's interrogation first."

"I wouldn't worry if I was you, Tom. You have nothing to hide and anyway Lord Harris is the only person whose blessing you need. And I know for a fact that you have him all tied up. He thinks you're a splendid young man. I heard him say so to Fogarty."

The next morning brought with it a clear blue sky, headaches, love sickness and permission to marry. All of the above were discussed over a hearty breakfast of sausages, eggs and bacon. Lord Harris held his aching head in his hands and listened while Thomas asked for his daughter's hand in marriage.

"Oh, dear me, my head, I can hardly see straight. Did I hear you right, Thomas? Did you say you want to marry Clare? I can only say one thing young man; you don't know what you're letting yourself in for!"

"Oh Daddy, please be serious. Thomas and I are in love. Please give us your blessing."

Lord Harris rose slowly from his chair and shook Thomas's hand. "Please forgive me, Thomas, I'm not feeling very well this morning and this news has come as a bit of a shock. I won't ask when this decision was made between you two. All I will say is, you have my blessing, Thomas. I have never seen my daughter so deliriously happy. Happy yes, she's always happy, but I know in my heart you're the right man for her. I wish you every conceivable happiness and good fortune." Lord Harris then kissed Clare who'd jumped up, holding him tight, and crying tears of joy.

Lord Fogarty then suggested sagely, "Let us wait until next week to begin the celebrations shall we, I'm really not feeling well this morning."

Patrick chose not to announce his engagement to Addy, thinking the older gentleman might just smell a rat, seeing that the cats had been fast asleep while the mice played. One too many engagements this morning might set their tongues wagging and their minds befuddled.

Back at Sandhurst, Patrick tied Charlie and Thomas's horse, Freddy, to the back of Lord Fogarty's carriage. They looked forward to their future time together in London, especially when Lord Fogarty promised him, "I will lead you into an expanse of culture, my boys. We will attend operas, the theatre, and art galleries, not to mention the races at Royal Ascot. My filly, called Somehope, will be running there this coming Saturday. I'm delighted Addy has promised she will attend the race meeting with us. We'll have a wonderful day."

Chapter 15

Good and Bad News

Lord Fogarty's palatial apartment now felt like home to Patrick. His allotted bedroom reminded him of his own masculine room back home. Memorabilia and trophies sat on every available shelf. He smiled, remembering his own childhood. He'd had a wonderful night's sleep and now he lay in bed thinking he was the only person at home. He knew the cook had taken the day off due to family business, and James was given a free day for personal shopping. Lord Fogarty had gone to visit his sister, and Thomas had left early for Harris Manor. Patrick now had time to think and consolidate what Jonathon had written about him going home to Australia and being part of Duntroon. This morning Patrick also dwelled on his love for Addy. *I hope I pleased her and I've shown her a little of what she can look forward to for the rest of her life. I'd hate to think I hurt her though.* "She'll be fine next time," he said aloud, then made his way to the kitchen.

Patrick made toast and a pot of tea before sitting to read the *London Herald*. The headlines read, "War with Germany is imminent". In that moment, he had a vision of returning to Australia. Premonitions like this would come to him from time to time. He shook the vision away and returned to reading the paper. It was then he heard a loud knock on the front door. It made Patrick think he was not dressed to answer it.

"Oh well," he said before opening the door to greet a rather stout middle-aged man who introduced himself as a Mr Roberts. Mr Roberts said, "I'm calling to speak with a Mr Patrick Darcy. I'm a friend of his father."

"I am Patrick Darcy, sir. Pleased to meet you, Mr Roberts." Patrick shook his hand firmly.

Mr Roberts appeared to be around fifty to fifty-five, with a receding hair line, lamb chop sideburns, a ruddy complexion and a rather large pot belly. Patrick couldn't help but think of the difference between this man's condition when he was probably the same age as his father. While Jonathon's hair had turned grey at the temples, it was still mainly dark, and his physique was just the same as when he was a young man. This gentleman looked as if he'd eaten and drunk all things that were not good for his health. *Just as well Angus isn't here*, Patrick thought.

Patrick excused himself to go and dress before he settled back into the library with Mr Roberts, who spoke eloquently. He went on to tell Patrick that he'd attended the same university as his father, Jonathon. Humorous tales of their youthful adventures were relayed and laughed about. However, this gentleman seemed to Patrick to have something else on his mind, or perhaps he had a nervous disposition. Shifting constantly about in his chair, Roberts would suddenly look out of the window and rub his hands together, or give a shallow cough. His continuous signs of uneasiness gave Patrick reason to wonder if Mr Roberts may have some bad news to deliver and perhaps he was having trouble relaying it. Patrick chose only to observe and wonder. After more than half an hour, Mr Roberts asked Patrick questions.

"Are we alone? Do you think we may be interrupted sometime soon?"

"We're alone, Mr Roberts. The staff have been given the day off, and Lord Fogarty has gone to visit his sister. And my friend, Thomas, has ridden to Harris Manor? Why do you ask?"

"I need to tell you something, Patrick. It's about your family matters." Mr Roberts then lowered his voice to a whisper, Patrick lent forward to hear him clearly.

"Your father, Jonathon, has written to ask me if I could do some investigating work for him," he said, hanging his head a little and looking from under his eyes at Patrick.

"It was not my intention to give you anything other than good news. It's only that your father, Jonathon, needed to know two things. Firstly, where your birth father originated from and if there were any news of his own family. I have therefore done a thorough and successful job in tracking down your birth father, Cecil Birch. I now hold the truth to his past." Mr Roberts took a sip of water. "It seems that Cecil Birch, your birth father, whilst in England had kept only one step ahead of the law with his business dealings. Finally, he escaped the clutches of the law by fleeing to Australia, Adelaide to be exact, with enough money to live comfortably for the rest of his life. The good news is Cecil Birch was from a noble family. However, his father became a dreadful alcoholic and gambled away most of the family fortune. Cecil's mother became bitter and twisted. She'd left Cecil in the care of his unloving nanny, who in turn, left him with his drunken father, who thereafter abused Cecil physically and mentally." Mr Robert's sighed and relaxed a little.

"I suppose one should show a little mercy for Cecil Birch, the way he turned out, especially after all the abuse he suffered as a child. I know your father thought it best to tell you this, so you may find some compassion for your birth father." Mr Roberts paused for another drink of water and, noticing Patrick's quiet reflection, he continued.

"However, I do have some very good news, Patrick. It seems there's a decent estate to be claimed. It was left by Cecil's father, your grandfather, Lord Harold Birch. Apparently, he had a windfall with his gambling just before he passed away. The money was a substantial amount, enough to save his family property, consisting of one thousand acres in the Cotswolds along with a rather rundown manor. There's also a plentiful supply of stocks and bonds, which may help with the restoration of the manor. The estate, by law, is to be held in a trust for a fifty-year period. This is before it becomes possible for our King and Country to claim it, or until a substantiated male member of the Birch family comes forth. This has not happened as yet. I have therefore searched all avenues to find another heir. There appears to be none—other than you, Patrick. Yes, you are the only male heir of the Birch family." Mr Roberts sat back, smiling broadly.

"Yes, I'd say the inheritance is all yours now, Patrick! So, we can set the wheels in motion to claim it!" Patrick showed no emotion. Digesting this information would be a slow process. He'd never wished for anything more than what he already possessed, although he thought it would be fun to take Addy to show her their future home, maybe? With a little more enthusiasm, Patrick looked up and asked, "And what of my father's family? Jonathon, I mean. Have you any news, Mr Roberts?"

"Well, that's a different story, Patrick. The Duke and Duchess themselves are not willing to talk to me, or anyone else, about their disinherited daughter. That would be Jonathon's mother, of course. They said they wish no further investigation as to what happened to her, or any of her offspring. They disowned her the moment she'd left with, what they called a lowly bred stable boy who dared call himself a horse trainer. I strongly believe that Jonathon could fight their decision in court and become the receiver of his due inheritance. That is if he wished to do so!"

Patrick smiled a knowing smile. He also knew Jonathon's father had no remaining relatives left because he'd told Patrick this many years ago. "If you really do know my father, Mr Roberts, you would know he wouldn't even think of it."

"Yes, quite right, I do know him very well, Patrick, and I have missed him very much. You know, I had a rather bad stutter at university when your father befriended me. Most students bullied me. I'm forever grateful for his help in ridding me of the stutter and giving me his friendship. He truly is a wonderful man, your step-… sorry, your father."

Nodding in agreement, Patrick then offered him a whisky. "Time to celebrate, I think, Mr Roberts. It appears I may be wealthy in my own right after all!" Raising their glasses for a toast, Patrick said light-heartedly, "Not that it matters to me. But what I am intrigued about is how my dad cured your stutter. You see, our Captain Forrester at Sandhurst has a stutter. It will keep him out of leadership in war time. He may have to accept a desk job, so I'd like to help him."

The conversation then took a turn, and revealed to Patrick what was needed to help Frederick Forrester be rid of his stutter. At last, after two hours of discussion, Patrick shook Mr Roberts's hand and thanked him for his information and also his promise to continue the work needed in delivering Patrick's inheritance to him.

"Well, well, lord of the manor I am," Patrick proclaimed after he'd shut the door. Excitedly, he decided to ring Addy and share his good news. Picking up the brass telephone receiver, he dialled the operator and asked to be put through to Badminton Ladies College. It took only a few minutes before he was talking to Addy.

"Hello Addy, what a great invention this is!"

Aghast, she answered, "Patrick! You didn't pull me away from an exam to talk to me about the invention of telephones!"

"Oh please, don't be angry, Addy. You know how much I love you and want to please you."

"Don't you please me, Patrick! Our school Mistress told me it was urgent, I'm in the middle of an exam, so just tell me why you've telephoned!"

"I have just now been informed, Addy, that I have become a wealthy man. A friend of Dad's is a private investigator, a Mr Roberts. Dad asked him to find out any information he could on my English family. It seems I'm now the sole heir of a thousand acres in the Cotswolds, including a manor. And shares and bonds."

Addy replied with little more understanding. "That's wonderful news, Patrick, but I must return to my exam. Goodbye. I love you." She then hung up the receiver.

Patrick stood miffed. "Well, you'd think she'd be a little more excited." But not deterred by Addy's reaction, he asked himself happily, "What now? Time to spread the news. I'll write letters home and then I'll ring Tom to let him know. I don't think Lord Fogarty's sister has a telephone, so he'll have to wait."

His phoning Thomas came to a halt when thinking, *Thomas may still be under scrutiny from Clare's mother*. Patrick chose to write his letters first. After doing so, he thought it an appropriate time to phone Thomas.

"Hello operator, please connect me with Harris Manor."

Humming a tune, he waited until the female voice on the other end spoke in French. Patrick had learned enough French in his school years and recently at Sandhurst to get by. And so he asked if he could speak with Thomas Norman.

"*Oui*," was her reply, and then silence prevailed for a moment until Lord Harris came to the phone.

"Yes, who's speaking, please?"

"It's Patrick, Lord Harris. I've just telephoned to give Thomas some good news, sir. News I'm finding very difficult to contain, seeing I'm all alone and have nobody to speak with." Lord Harris lowered his voice. "Please come quickly, Patrick. You can tell Thomas all about your news then as we need help with my wife. She's not so thrilled with the idea of Thomas marrying Clare. Come and spread some of that delightful charm of yours. There's a good lad." He hung up, not giving Patrick the opportunity to accept or refuse the offer.

Never one to leave a friend in need, Patrick rose to the challenge. After writing a note to Lord Fogarty outlining his good news, and where he was heading, he locked the apartment, ran to the livery stable, saddled Charlie, and trotted out of town to Harris Manor. Charlie was just about done in from the long hard ride and seemed to deliberately rub his sweaty nose down Patrick's uniform. "I don't blame ya, mate, I'm a real bastard sometimes. Still, ya gotta keep fit, Charlie!"

After being escorted inside by Harold, the butler, Patrick was introduced to a well-kept, highly made-up and beautiful woman, Lady Harris.

The group settled down to high tea. These occasions would forever remind Patrick of meeting Addy for the first time at the Ritz Hotel. The Australian larrikin in him now found it amusing. All those dainty cakes, cucumber sandwiches and aristocratic little fingers pointed outwards, as they sipped on their half-filled undersized bone china cups of tea. *Give me a tin mug full of strong black Billy tea and a loaf of damper with treacle any day.* This afternoon, however, Patrick felt he should act as a gentleman should, mainly to help his best friend, Thomas.

After the courteous small talk, the family began to lead back into the obvious argument that had preceded Patrick's arrival. After they worked their way nervously through three pots of tea, many plates of sandwiches, and tiny cupcakes, Patrick began to see the reason for the uncertainty. He was sure it was to keep their mouths full to prevent them from saying what they truly felt. They seemed to have kept their hands to themselves so as to prevent a murder which, Patrick was sure, may happen at any moment, especially when Lord Harris declared for the tenth time, "Thomas is a fine young gentleman." That added more fuel to the argument.

"And just because Thomas is not a blue blood, my dear, does not mean he is below our daughter. After all, your own mother was a nude model for male artists!"

With that, the indignant Lady Harris rose from her chair and threw her serviette over the cake that Patrick was about to reach for. He sat back, watching her theatrics with amusement. Her head flung arrogantly upwards, she declared, "I will 'ave you know my mama was a model for the French aristocracy!"

"Yes, my dear, that's how she received her title, Baroness de Nude! And where was it she came from, before she married into nobility?"

Patrick spat his tea out, laughing and apologising at the same time. He then wiped up the mess with his serviette. Thomas and Clare looked at each other blankly. They were still no better informed as to whether they would be married or, perhaps, whether her parents would divorce over it. Lady Harris hitched up her organza skirt and stormed out of the room.

Lord Harris looked to Patrick. "Can you offer a suggestion, Patrick? Could you perhaps talk some sense into her Ladyship?"

"Me, sir? I don't really know her Ladyship. I've only just met her. What could I possibly say?" Patrick shrugged his shoulders.

"I don't know either, Patrick, but you seem to have a charm about you that women simply cannot resist."

"With all due respect, your Lordship, I don't want to make love to Lady Harris, so my charm may not affect her."

"Oh, I know that, Patrick!" Lord Harris was beginning to lose his patience with the whole situation. "Just put in a good word for Thomas and his family, that's all I ask. Will you do that much for us? You know all of Thomas's good points and his fine upstanding family in Adelaide. If anyone can charm her, it's you. Please see what you can do for us."

Reluctantly, Patrick left the room. He found the tempestuous Lady Harris in the ladies sitting room on her pink chaise lounge, weeping and blowing her tiny nose into a lace handkerchief. Patrick then wondered just how useful a piece of lace was to blow your nose into. Creeping towards her, he asked courteously, "May I sit with you, your Ladyship?"

Immediately, she stopped crying, moved to one side, and smiling her sweetest smile, she said, "Oui", and tapped the seat for him to sit as close as possible. Patrick followed her orders, and turned to face her. He was about to tell her that she was making a big mistake when her Ladyship grabbed his face and planted a long sensuous kiss on his lips. She then stood up and whispered in a sexy voice, "Do not leave, *mon chéri*. Meet me in my room at midnight and I will give my blessing for your friend to marry my daughter." Puckering her lips, and with her eyes half-closed, she insinuated an interlude which Patrick would most definitely refuse.

After she'd left, Patrick sat astonished at her provocative display. "Oh shit, what a bloody mess." With head in hands, he prayed silently, *Should I use strategy or honesty? Please, mother, show me the way.* Looking up, he saw a young maid smiling down at him. He hoped she'd been a witness to what had just happened.

"What is your name?"

"Mary, sir."

"Did you hear what her Ladyship just said to me, Mary?"

"Yes, I did, sir."

"Then you will vouch for me if things turn ugly, because I have no intention of going to her Ladyship's room."

"Yes, I will vouch for you, sir." Looking around to see if anyone else was listening, the girl added, "She's a very mean lady; I don't like her. Nobody does."

Patrick's blue eyes lifted to the ceiling. "Thank you, mother." He then handed Mary a pound note. "Here, please accept this money for your honesty, Mary, and now please go and tell Lady Harris that the young gentleman has just told you he'll be unable to meet her tonight. He has a prior engagement. And also tell her if there's any trouble, he'll spill the beans. Now please go and tell her exactly what I've told you. Thank you, Mary."

More than pleased with the money, Mary placed it down the front of her uniform and hurried off in the direction of her Ladyship's bedroom.

Feeling pleased with himself, Patrick then went to find his friends. "Her Ladyship has agreed. You should go ahead with the wedding plans."

The shocked expression on Lord Harris's face pre-empted his next question. "How on earth did you talk her into the marriage in such a short time, Patrick?"

"As you say, your Lordship, I have charm. Now I must beg your pardon as I have to return to London immediately."

"Please stay, Patrick. You can't be riding back to London in the dark. It looks like it could be snowing soon and you haven't told us of your good news."

Patrick shook hands with Lord Harris. "I am sorry, sir, but I must leave. My news will wait until later. I have pressing business in London."

"Well then, you must take my carriage. My footman will drive you home. Leave Charlie here, and Thomas will return with him tomorrow. Isn't that right, Thomas?"

"No, but thank you, sir," Patrick said. "Charlie and I have weathered storms before. If I leave now, we may miss the heavier fall." Then Patrick strode away and rode into the night.

Chapter 16

Angus in Trouble

The morning after that eventful day, a telegram addressed to Patrick arrived at Lord Fogarty's apartment. He opened it tentatively. *Telegrams rarely bring good news.* On this occasion, after reading the short note, his thought came true. Jonathon had written, *Patrick, return home immediately. Trouble with Angus.*

Patrick's heart fell with a heavy thud. His father's order to return home would put an end to his own plans in England. His mind began to spin. Addy's exam results and then her decision about which country she would prefer to live would affect him greatly. There was also Thomas and Clare's wedding to think of. As far as his own army career went, Patrick felt his loyalty was heading toward staying in England, especially since Thomas would definitely stay once he'd married Clare. Not to mention his newly acquired manor and grounds. He wanted at least to witness the property begin to thrive again. *This trouble with Angus must be totally out of Dad's control for him to beg or order me to return home, and straightaway.*

Lord Fogarty was eating breakfast in the dining room when Patrick walked in. The look on Patrick's face told him he had a real problem.

"Is there something wrong, Patrick?" he asked kindly.

"Yes sir, I've just received a telegram from Dad. He says Angus needs me. It appears he's got himself in some sort of trouble. I can't believe it really. And what's more unbelievable is why Dad can't cope with it, whatever it is."

"Is that all your father had to say, just some sort of trouble?"

Patrick handed him the telegram. "That's it, sir."

Lord Fogarty took his time reading it. "Will you telegram your father for more information? Or will you simply take his word for it that it must be of the utmost importance to ask you to travel all that way home?"

"Yes, I will, sir. I would never question my father's authority. I'll have to go to the travel agency and see when the next ship leaves. As I said, sir, it must be a very serious problem if Dad needs me home urgently."

"Yes, of course, Patrick. James will be at your service with the carriage if you are in need."

"No, thank you, your Lord, I'll take Charlie out for a ride. He loves the ride through the London parks."

Patrick would miss so much about this cultured city, especially the buildings, which were so ancient and so different compared to Adelaide. He'd admired the parklands surrounding London city with their manicured brilliance. Walking paths and riding tracks wound their way through what Patrick thought may be the finest and most interesting parklands in the world. London would be etched in his heart forever, after all, this was the place he'd first met Addy— in the flesh, so to speak. This was also the first country to help him realise his lifelong dream of becoming a soldier.

Charlie trotted along, snorting and whinnying to other horses, especially the odd pretty filly. It seemed Charlie thought himself to be handsome, when in fact he was not. However, he made up for it with character and intelligence. Patrick would be nearly as sad to leave Charlie as he would Addy, such was his love for this rare horse.

When Patrick enquired at the travel agent, he was surprised to find the first ship bound for Australia would depart in two days' time. He had no alternative, after the urgency in Jonathon's telegram, then to book his passage home. After sending his reply telegram to Jonathon, asking for more information about Angus, he took Charlie for another ride through the Royal parklands. Pulling him up after a two-mile hand gallop, Patrick dismounted and sat under an English elm. He fiddled with the reins while confiding in Charlie his heartbreak in having to leave him and Addy behind.

"I'll come back soon, Charlie, don't worry. But when duty calls, well, I'm afraid I have to go. I'll make sure Thomas or James takes you out every day for some exercise, and I know old Joe at the livery stable loves ya, mate. You'll be well looked after. You're a bloody genius, you know that, Charlie." Patrick gave him a scratch on his forehead. "You've got all the kids around London begging to see you do tricks. It's a bloody wonder your teeth haven't fallen out with all the sugar cubes they give you!"

Charlie showed his teeth by curling his top lip up to his nostrils. "Hey mate, feel like a ride to Badminton school?" Patrick asked, and Charlie nodded his head, yes. "No, too late today, Charlie. I'll ring Addy and tell her we'll be there tomorrow to say goodbye." With these words, Patrick choked back tears as anger stirred deep within him.

"Why in the bloody hell did Angus have to get himself in trouble? What's the bloody problem? Why couldn't Dad sort it out, eh Charlie?" After he had filtered all questions about this matter through his mind, he was feeling in need of a whisky. When he'd returned to Lord Fogarty's home by late afternoon, Patrick suggested a drink. Sitting comfortably together in the den with Lord Fogarty's finest Scotch whisky, and soothed by the dancing flames of the open fire, Patrick confided his dilemma to his friend.

"There are too many ends left untied here in England before I have to go home, your Lord."

Lord Fogarty, whether it be the alcohol, or the closeness he now felt with Patrick, became slightly maudlin at the thought of Patrick leaving him for so long. Patrick too felt that this older gentleman was a kindred spirit and he enjoyed his company immensely, especially his quick wit. Lord Fogarty, however, assured Patrick he would be delighted to deal with Mr Roberts to finalise Patrick's newfound fortune and property, and keep track of Patrick's stocks and bonds. A little cheekily, he volunteered to take care of Addy in Patrick's absence too.

"I shall endeavour to chaperone the beautiful Miss Adelaide Watt-Stuart to any official engagement that she may need an elderly gentleman to attend with." Lord Fogarty raised his glass for a refill, his face becoming redder by the minute. The alcohol and the heat of a well-stocked fire had brought on his sleepy disposition. After yawning, he assured Patrick once again he would keep all important issues close to his heart and mind.

Thomas had returned late from Harris Manor to a somewhat sombre welcome. He then asked cautiously, "Why such a sad mood?"

Patrick explained to Thomas his almost devastating news. Thomas was gobsmacked. "I don't believe this, Patrick. I was about to ask you to be my best man at my wedding."

Patrick embraced Thomas. "Mate, I couldn't be happier for you. So, her Ladyship did agree after all?"

Thomas stood rigid, a bit miffed. "Why are you so surprised? After all, you were the one who charmed her into it."

"Oh, no reason, Tom, just thought she may have changed her mind." Patrick's relieved smile hid his secret.

Thomas then recited the details of the wedding in what appeared to Patrick to be an officious manner. "Well, for your information, she did not change her mind. We have set the wedding date for next April, so I'm not going home to Australia. I cannot possibly go home now. I shall return to Sandhurst and then take leave for my honeymoon. Clare and I will be married at Harris Manor on the third of April. We will then take our honeymoon on the maiden voyage of the newly built liner, *RMS Titanic*. It will be leaving from Southampton on the tenth of April. Lord Harris, as you know, has shares in the shipping company which built her, and so he's booked the honeymoon suite for us."

After his ceremonious announcement, Thomas returned to being the Australian larrikin. "So, mate, only the best for yours truly now!"

Patrick was amused by the change in Thomas's demeanour, and voiced his wishes. "I'd love to be joining you with Addy. But when the family's in trouble, Tom, I must stand at attention. Nothing I can do, mate, so I just hope I'm not too late for whatever it is."

Patrick stood silent for a moment, once again feeling slightly apprehensive about his urgent call home but he declared his loyalty. "I know Dad wouldn't send for me unless it was really urgent."

Thomas understood Patrick's concern, and gave him a friendly punch in the bicep. "Whatever it is, Pat, you'll fix it and be back here in no time." Thomas's eyes glistened with emotion. He held back tears as he embraced Patrick and whispered, "I love ya, mate."

Lord Fogarty wobbled about, struggling to raise himself from the chair, when James the butler entered to say, "Supper is served, your Lordship."

"Very well, thank you, James. Come, gentlemen, let us partake of some French Burgundy with our roast beef. A splendid wine, yes splendid, I purchased two cases on my last visit to Paris."

The next day, as Addy sat alongside Patrick on one of the many bench seats within the school grounds, she wept after hearing the news. She wanted so badly to hold Patrick and beg him not to go, but was unable to do so, being under the watchful eye of her teacher, Miss Rose. Keeping up her pretence of decorum, Addy said through clenched teeth, "I cannot believe you're going home tomorrow, Patrick. It's only one more month until I'll have some idea as to which university will accept me. Can't you go home then and not tomorrow?"

"I'll see, Addy. If a telegram comes from Dad before I have to leave, it may throw some more light on the situation. But please try and understand. You don't realise all that my father has done for me and what an amazing man he is. He would never ask me to go home unless it was urgent. I love you more than anything on earth, Addy. But this may be life or death for my brother, and I love him too, he needs me, so I'm sorry, Addy. I must go."

Patrick could see in her eyes that she was longing to make love. However, being watched closely by the spinster teacher who had accompanied Addy from her classroom, it gave Patrick no opportunity to kiss her passionately as he wished.

"Is there any escape from our spy, Addy," he whispered.

"Perhaps. I'll stand now, Patrick, and you go as if you're leaving for good, but first, shake my hand platonically. Lunch break will be soon, it will give me the chance to slip away. About half a mile north into the woods, there's a small vacant stone house. It will give us shelter. I'll meet you there in about half an hour."

Smiling sweetly Addy then bowed her head while shaking Patrick's hand.

Patrick easily found the house. Dismounting Charlie, he began to tie the reins around a tree trunk. Charlie gave him an indignant look and Patrick laughed. "Ok, Charlie, just hang about, we don't want anyone to know we're here?"

Inspecting the stone walls of the shepherd's hut, Patrick ran his hands over the rough ancient stone, imagining the life of the past inhabitants. He wondered how many times they had made love under this roof, of which only half remained. This thought took him back to Addy and how lately, when he glanced towards a beautiful woman, it was only to substantiate the fact that, yes, she was beautiful, but they were never as beautiful as Addy. He knew something had changed in him since their first night together. He'd taken to relieving himself, rather than going to a whorehouse. He didn't mind, at least he felt faithful to Addy. Looking at his watch, Patrick said aloud, "Not long now."

He turned towards where he heard a rustling sound outside. Addy appeared, her face flushed after running all the way. Breathless, she fell against his chest. "I can't stay long, Patrick. My friend is diverting Miss Rose. I think she may suspect something." When she lifted her head, Patrick could see Addy's expression was of love mixed with disappointment.

"I adore you, Patrick. I don't want you to ever leave me."

As she kissed his lips, she felt a longing so strong it became electric. His erection pressed into her loins, arousing her. Lifting her dress, Patrick then pressed Addy's softness against the stone wall. His heart was pounding when he realised she'd removed her bloomers.

Smiling into her eyes, he softly stroked her, and Addy moaned with the pleasure. She undid the buttons on her bodice, and Patrick began kissing her breasts. Aching for him to enter, Addy begged, "Please, Patrick, I need you. I'm ready."

Don't hurt her, he thought, as he lifted her body up against the stone wall. He began thrusting carefully at first. Feeling Addy relax, he went deeper. Sighing with delight at this new tantalising experience, Addy kissed his lips, whispering as she did, "Oh, it's so good, Patrick."

"I'm not hurting you, am I?"

"NO, it's beautiful. Don't stop, please don't stop, Patrick."

With her body tingling and about to explode, Addy soon cried for joy, as he released his pleasure along with hers. She slid down the wall, and breathed out the words, "I'll marry you, Patrick, just stay with me. Please don't go. I need you."

"Shush, please Addy, you know how much I love you, but I don't want to be the one responsible for breaking your dream. Remember, you're going to be a doctor and save lives. I'll return just as soon as I can and then we'll be married, I promise. I love you with every drop of blood in my veins, you know that. There will never be another woman in my life except you, Addy."

They shared one last long embrace before leaving. "I'll write every day, I promise. You best go now. Here's the potion. You know what to do with it?"

Addy nodded yes, turned and rushed away.

Chapter 17

Adelaide, 1912

Life-draining heat hit Patrick as he stepped down from the steamship. It was the fourth of February 1912. Jonathon stood on the dock alone, wiping the perspiration off his furrowed brow. His solo appearance was mainly due to the temperature reaching one hundred and five degrees Fahrenheit. Patrick hurried across to Jonathon when he spotted him standing all alone. Before embracing him, he studied his father's face. Looking deep into his soulful brown eyes, he thought they showed great sadness. This he hadn't seen since his mother, Sally, had died. Despite the heat, they held each other close for some time. With his head lowered into his son's chest, Jonathon felt almost embarrassed by his inability to solve Angus's problem, but at the same time, he was desperate for Patrick's help.

"I'm so pleased you came home, Patrick. I fear we'll lose Angus if you can't do something to turn him around." Jonathon then raised his head to look at Patrick and began to tell him the truth.

"Angus has been experimenting with drugs. He's become addicted and I'm afraid there is no convincing him to give them up. It will ruin his life and eventually kill him. I'm sure. This is why I couldn't write the whole truth in a telegram. It's illegal, Patrick!"

When Jonathon's eyes welled with tears, Patrick embraced him again, trying to console him. "Try not to worry, Dad. I'll do my best. But I won't know how to handle Angus until I see him, but I promise I'll do my very best. I didn't come all this way for a half-hearted effort." For a moment, Patrick was shocked by his father's admission, and worried Angus's drug habit may have gone too far for him to be able to help. Not wanting Jonathon to notice his lack of confidence, he changed the subject.

"Now let me hear all the good news, Dad. There must be some since your last letter." Patrick then saw what he'd hoped for. A smile crossed Jonathon's face and he'd begun to relax a little.

"Of course there's good news, Patrick. Margi will have our second baby while you're here. In fact, she's due next week. Millie is growing up; she's a real character is our Millie. And dear Colleen and Bob are well and going strong! Well, that's with a little help from Margi. We are so proud of Mother Matilda. She has done a wonderful job in turning around the boys' orphanages here in Adelaide. They are now run with compassion and are believed to be a good place for homeless children to be brought up in. Thank heavens. Mother Betty, as I still call her, has taken over the orphanage school at Brinton. She's more than happy to be home after her time in India. Betty seems very content in her work with the Lord."

He then struck a serious note when returning to Angus's problem. "Doctor Liu has tried very hard to bring Angus into a state of self-honesty. I'm sure he blames himself for Angus's obsession with drugs. However, I do my best to convince Liu otherwise. He's been such a loyal family friend, and if it weren't for him, I would have surely died all those years ago. I don't need to remind you of that, Patrick. There's so much more to tell you, and I can show you a few new surprises when we reach home. But we'll have just a small family gathering to welcome you home first."

As they walked towards a black Ford motor car, Patrick slowed up his pace, as Jonathon quickened his to open the lid of the boot. Patrick stood a little shocked at what he thought to be a racing machine. Jonathon smiled widely, his brown eyes sparkling, "Come on, Patrick, this is my new motor car!"

"Well, well. My dad—the racing car driver, hey?"

"Yes, I suppose you could say that as I do like going fast. Not too many of them around, you know. I was one of the first in Adelaide to purchase a motor car. Put your bags in the boot, Pat."

Patrick did just that and then inspected the shiny paint. Running his fingers over the smoothness of the metal, he knocked his knuckles on the bumper bar a few times. He opened and shut the door twice using the silver handle, and then declared, "She's a beauty, Dad. You'll have to teach me how to drive it. I've driven one of the new trucks at Sandhurst but never a flash car like this."

Jonathon cranked the rotary starter in front of the motor, and it began with a hum. "Jump in, son. Let's go!"

With the suffocating heat beginning to engulf Patrick, he took his hat off quickly and let the wind blow some welcome relief.

Jonathon glanced across at him. "You've lost your curls, Patrick!"

Patrick raised his voice above the engine noise. "Yes, after they cut my hair short for the first time, the curls disappeared. I kept a couple of locks. I don't know why; maybe I'll place them in mother's diary. I also brought back some dried heather."

Jonathon simply nodded and smiled, looking back at the road. As they drove up their driveway, Patrick was astounded to see an enormous welcome home sign. He choked back tears.

"This is a nice thought, Dad. No doubt Margi organised it? How many people do you have coming to welcome me home?"

"Oh, only the extended family. I thought you may be too tired from the trip for a big crowd."

Then why did Patrick get a sneaking feeling that it might be more like an extravaganza? No, perhaps not. When he entered the foyer, there was only a heavily pregnant Margi, Colleen and Bob, and the new housekeeper, Jane. With nobody else at home, the silence was almost deafening. Patrick hoped his disappointment hadn't shown, though Margi seemed to have noticed. She embraced him and loudly exclaimed, "WELCOME HOME, PATRICK!" Suddenly, people appeared from the coat cupboard in the foyer, and many more from every direction. Patrick stood overwhelmed; his old school friends were there, also his mates from the polo club and the jumping club. Even a few young boys whom Patrick had helped teach karate, as well as a few old girlfriends who'd kept in touch when he was at Sandhurst. Only today they were accompanied by their boyfriends, whom Patrick also considered his friends.

Doctor Liu soon pushed his way through the throng of well-wishers, flinging himself into Patrick's arms, crying real tears. This touched Patrick. Feeling it was an apologetic embrace from Doctor Liu, Patrick whispered in his ear, "Don't worry, Doc, we'll help Angus get over this together."

Bowing backwards, Liu held his arm out to make way for Betty. Tall and slender, and in her full white nun's habit, she was more beautiful than Patrick could remember. Her flawless peach complexion illuminated her hazel eyes. Her grace flowed over him like the hand of God. The look she gave Patrick told him that not only did she now love him pure of heart, but she was a messenger from God. Yes, the love in Betty's eyes was not the same as the last time when she'd climbed the stairs in this home, looking down at him, like a woman does when she needs her man. He was now witness to her sublime peace. They embraced, it seemed forever, without a word needing to be said.

Once he'd left Betty's arms, an unfamiliar middle-aged man with a mass of greying blond curls smiled a familiar smile at Patrick. Immediately, he saw his mother in his Uncle Paul's face. Paul thrust his large calloused hand out to greet Patrick. "Hello, Patrick, I'm ya Uncle Paul."

Patrick embraced him as if it were his mother, they then laughed together.

"Well, it's about bloody time, Uncle Paul!" Patrick was amused at their likeness and eager to meet the younger identikit male standing beside his uncle. "And who's this young man?"

"This is my son, Jum," Paul said proudly.

Patrick shook Jum's hand. "Pleased to meet you, Jum. I'd say you have a lot to live up to with a name like Jum, mate."

"So they tell me, Patrick."

Patrick studied Jum's features, noticing the similarity with his own. "Must be a strong family gene somewhere; we all bloody well look alike!" The three men enjoyed a good laugh.

"Did you come all the way here just to welcome me home, Uncle Paul?" Patrick wondered why now, why not when Sally had needed him, why not when they were the only blood relations he had, except for Angus. The odd letters from Paul and his father, Ted, always included a promise to visit Patrick, but their meeting had never eventuated.

"I'm truly sorry, Patrick. It's been one thing after the other stopping us from coming down to Adelaide. You know how it is. Life just takes you on a journey, sometimes it gets out of control and most times, all you can do is go with the ride."

Patrick knew this very well, especially now, when even though it was great to be home and to see so many familiar faces, his heart and body really needed to be in England with Addy.

"But I promise, Patrick, this won't be the last you'll see of us. Young Jum wants to join the army. He holds you on a pedestal, especially after hearing about your cadetship and how you won the Sword of Honour. We're going to consider Duntroon on our way home. I just thought you may have a talk with Jum, you know, fill him in on the facts about army life and what to expect."

"I certainly will. It'll be my pleasure, Uncle Paul. You're staying a few days, I hope?"

"Yes, for a week. Your dad's such a gentleman. He said we could stay as long as we liked. Especially since I'm going to be a great-uncle, well, sort of, with Margi's baby due next week." Paul's eyes glistened, most probably due to the memories flooding back of Sally and her baby daughter. Patrick took hold of him once more. "Great to see you, Uncle. We'll talk some more later. I'd best spread myself around."

Taking Jum's hand in his, Patrick said, "We have a lot to talk about, Jum. I look forward to it."

Patrick became overwhelmed with so many people coming to welcome him home, especially nurse Helen. She was now sporting a huge diamond engagement ring, which she smartly waved at Patrick. "He finally bought you a ring, Helen. Lucky bugger, he is."

Helen had kept up her letter writing to Patrick, happy to share a unique friendship. Love and respect for each other, between ex-lovers, she thought, was seldom found. Helen had fallen in love with a young (virgin) doctor and she, being most near to the female version of Patrick, introduced the young doctor to exotic lovemaking. Helen had confided with Patrick in previous letters, "Maybe I've overstepped the boundaries with my uneducated lover. My darling doctor has decided to cool off the affair for a while." Her next letter revealed more. "My darling has now realised he cannot live without my slow sensuous seduction of his body. And so he's asked me to marry him. Thank you, Patrick, for your advice."

"Have you brought him here to meet me, Helen?"

"No, you'll meet him soon enough, a bit too crowded here today," Helen said, just before she was pushed aside by a large mass of bodies moving towards Patrick. Continuing to shake hands, Patrick eventually welcomed all of his friends and family, all except Angus and young Millie.

Above the noise and chatter, Jonathon announced loudly, "I have one more big surprise for you, Patrick!" Nobody, at this stage, had left the foyer so Jonathon motioned his arm towards the main staircase. "May I FINALLY introduce to you, Patrick, after all these years, Bernadette and Barnaby Stuart!" Applause echoed through the home and Patrick's heart skipped a beat, as for one fleeting moment, he thought it was Addy gliding down the stairs. Bernadette's stunning beauty gave Patrick the reason for Addy's amazing good looks. Although Bernadette, he had to admit, was slightly more exotic with her dark olive skin and jet-black hair.

The only person Bernadette had eyes for was Patrick. She walked directly to him, her hand out for him to shake. He instead held her hand to his mouth and placed a lingering a kiss. Bernadette smiled, knowing then exactly what her daughter saw in this charming young man.

"Patrick, it's so good to finally meet you. Welcome home. May I introduce my husband, Barnaby Stuart."

"Pleased to meet you, sir." Patrick's strong handshake impressed Barney as did his presence.

"The pleasure is all mine, Patrick. We've heard so much about you from Adelaide. Congratulations on your achievement at being awarded the Sword of Honour at Sandhurst and with two months out of action, Addy tells us. Well done."

"Thank you, sir." *I'm off to a good start here. Breaking the news of my engagement to Addy later in the day should come easy.* His attention was suddenly taken away by a small dark-haired girl climbing down the stairs who then stopped for a moment to view the crowd, her chin resting on the banister. Millie then stood up, filled her lungs with air, and called out, "What about me? Where's my bruda, Patwick!"

Patrick excused himself from Bernadette and Barney. Running up two steps at a time, Patrick gathered Millie in his arms, kissing her all over the face until she giggled at his attention.

"Hello, Patwick. Did you come home to see me?"

"Of course, I came all the way from England just to see you, Millie!"

"Well, dat's good, 'cause my mum's gunna have anudda baby and I'll need someone to play games with me!"

Patrick could not believe what he'd just heard from this precocious child, and the indignant pout that went with it. "Oh my, but haven't you got it all worked out, Miss Millie!" Patrick then carried her downstairs where he announced, "Millie and I are thirsty, hungry and need a swim in the pool—all at once!" He turned to face her. "Isn't that right, Millie?"

"YES, PATWICK!"

The rest of the day proceeded with good food, good wine and a little cooling off in the newly added swimming pool. Laughter continued to spill into the open spaces as friends recalled good times. Come twilight, Patrick relaxed with Bernadette and Barney around the pool where together they watched the sunset. A moment's silence prevailed before Patrick remarked, "It's hard to believe Addy will see the same sun rise as we see it set. I miss her so much." Bernadette noticed Patrick's look of love when he spoke and so took the opportunity to speak first.

"Addy tells us, Patrick, well, she sent a telegram to ask Barney and me to remind you to ask us for her hand in marriage while we're all together. I hope you haven't changed your mind?"

Patrick, a little shocked but relieved, nearly choked on his next words. "No... no, of course not. I was just about to tell you of my deep love for Addy. And I hoped for your blessing in our marriage. You beat me to it, Mrs Stuart."

Bernadette laughed, while looking into Patrick's eyes, she held his hand. "Barney and I would be overjoyed to accept you as our son-in-law. God bless you, and please call me Bernadette."

Leaning forward she kissed him on the cheek. Patrick then stood for Barney to shake his hand.

"Congratulations, Patrick, and welcome to the family." With one hand still shaking Patrick's, Barney placed his free arm around his shoulder, and pulling Patrick closer, he whispered in his ear, "If she's anything like her mother, you'll be happy for the rest of your life."

This statement slightly shocked Patrick, especially coming from a well-educated, cultured gentleman. However, Patrick knew exactly what Barney meant.

Bernadette asked for no repeat of Barney's comment; she could imagine it was meant for Patrick only. Smiling sweetly, she asked, "I think it may be time to make an announcement, before anyone leaves. Don't you, Patrick?"

Barney stepped in. "I'll go with you, and we'll both tell Jonathon. He won't be surprised, I'm sure, or have you told him already, Patrick?"

"No, I was going to ask your permission first, sir."

"Well then, I think we should let Jonathon have the honour of announcing it. We've been looking forward to it."

"Of course, Barnaby," Bernadette agreed.

With the announcement of Patrick and Addy's engagement, champagne was served to the delight of all.

Eventually, Jonathon and Patrick were left alone. They sat opposite each other in Jonathon's favourite sitting room, the room where he'd proposed to Margi. Their house guests had retired for the night, after Millie had her way. She'd refused to go to sleep until Patrick read her three of her favourite bedtime stories.

"Our Miss Millie will have you wrapped around her little finger, Patrick."

"Too late, Dad," Patrick admitted.

As Jonathon let out a sigh, an apologetic look creased his face. "I'm so sorry I had to call you home, Patrick, and Angus should have been here to welcome you. But in his defence, Angus did say he would be here when the crowd died down."

Patrick also let out a sigh, after thinking of his plan to turn Angus around. "If he's not home soon, I'll go fetch him."

"But you don't know where he is, Patrick."

"I've got a fair idea. You have to promise me though, especially after bringing me home at a most inopportune time…"

Jonathon opened his mouth, ready to explain.

"No. Please don't worry about that now. I do need you to let me use my own methods in ridding Angus of this drug habit though. Hopefully I'm right and what I'm about to do will bring him to his senses, enough to return to university and finish his medical degree. Or better still, go to Duntroon to finish his studies there."

Jonathon thought that to be a wonderful idea, then noticed how Patrick looked totally worn out. "Why don't you go to bed and find Angus in the morning. You look very tired, Patrick." Patrick smiled at the thought of his father's constant gentle care of others, which hadn't worked on Angus. *Stubborn little shit he could be at times.*

Today, Patrick had learnt something of what had been happening with Angus and how others had been treating him over this fiasco. It seemed it was with kid gloves. When Patrick spoke to the people who knew and cared about Angus, they all seemed to have excuses for him.

"Don't upset the genius; he may just get worse."

"Just try and talk some common sense into him, Patrick. After all, he's so intelligent."

"It will only be a matter of time before he realises what he's doing to himself."

"It's only an experiment. He needs to learn all there is to know about drugs and medicine, and he's so smart."

"Leave him alone, he'll wake up soon. It's just a phase."

"All geniuses go off the rail sometimes; it comes with the condition."

Patrick had heard it all today. However, he had his mind made up on how to wake Angus up to himself. Patrick had to stake his claim on his brother's recovery as soon as possible. He wanted to return to England and Addy, so he insisted. "If you don't mind, Dad, I'd rather go now. I'm ok and you need to stay with Margi. By the looks of her, she may go sooner than you think."

"Oh really?" Jonathon said, shocked. "Do you think so, Patrick?"

Jonathon began to panic a little. Patrick laughed as he rose to leave, giving his father a kiss on the cheek. "Don't believe everything I say, Dad, but you'd better stay here just in case. If Angus isn't where I think he is, then I'll come home and go look again in the morning. Don't worry if you hear me come home with him." Patrick stopped to think for a moment. "Is the tool shed still in the same place?"

"Yes, of course. Da actually mended it just before he passed away. Why?"

"Never mind, I'll look at it in the morning." Patrick kissed his father good night once again. "Now go to bed, Dad, and don't worry, I'll hitch up the buggy, if that's alright?"

"Of course, but why don't you take the car, Patrick. I'll show you what to do. It's not difficult. If you've driven a truck, you should be able to drive a car easily enough."

Jonathon jumped up from his chair all enthused about the motor car. He then proceeded to show Patrick how this new-fangled machine worked.

Patrick drove straight to Molly's establishment. It was ten o'clock when he arrived, still an early hour for the ladies of the night. After seeing Molly's home well lit, Patrick jumped from the car and strode the few steps to the door. His entrance was reminiscent of Jum Watt. Molly sat in the parlour talking to a well-dressed middle-aged man, who obviously didn't want to be recognised. He hung his head, gathered his coat and left in a hurry. Molly knew the reason for Patrick's explosive entrance but chose not to move. She smiled and tapped the empty space next to her. Seeing the anger in his eyes, Molly tried to calm him down first.

"Hello Patrick, welcome home." He pecked her on the cheek and she laughed, "Dear me, you've been well and truly hooked, young man. Normally I'd have my bloomers dragged off me by now, so she must be special!"

Patrick, not in the mood for sweet talk, tried to be polite. "Molly, it's good to see you. You're looking lovely as usual." The tenseness in his voice left no illusions about his reason for visiting. However, Molly possessed enough sense to get straight to the point.

"Patrick, you have to hear me out before you go dragging Angus home. He's had a lot to deal with. His mind doesn't work like yours and mine. He's a genius."

Patrick nearly exploded. "If I hear that fuckin' word one more time I'm going to kill someone!" He stood with his fist clenched, demanding, "Where is he, Molly?"

"Patrick, you can't deal with him while you're so angry." Molly stood holding his arm. "We're trying to wean Angus off the drugs. Please understand, he just didn't want to face you, not today, with all the people there. Leave it until morning. Please, Patrick, I'll make sure he comes home. Please don't lose your temper. You'll regret it if you do."

Patrick stood, glaring at her. Never had Molly seen such venom in his eyes. She knew there was no convincing him.

"I'll take you to him, but only if you promise, if he's sleeping, you'll let him be until morning and don't hurt him. Please, Patrick, don't hurt him."

He said nothing, but Molly noticed he'd softened with her pleading. "This way."

Patrick had walked this corridor a hundred times before. However, the sound of muffled groans of sexual pleasure did nothing to his senses this evening. The same exotic perfume lingered in the air, enticing him, but now he belonged to Addy and his mission was to save his brother.

A candle flickered and danced the reflection on Eva's bedroom wall, giving enough light of Angus sitting up in bed. He had his left arm wrapped around Eva's shoulder while his right hand held a long tube that led to a small tin. He inhaled the fumes surging from the apparatus, then blew them towards Patrick. The stench filled Patrick's lungs, and he coughed before managing a wry smile.

"Hello brother."

Angus, a little surprised at Patrick's entrance, peered through bloodshot eyes. "Patrick, it is you. My hero brother! You've returned to talk sense into me, eh? Well, what you may or may not remember is, I'm a genius. So how can you or anyone else make more sense than I do? Nobody can. I'm the smartest boy in town!" And he inhaled another puff.

Giggling like an idiot, Angus turned to Eva, kissing her passionately. Patrick waited patiently, "Aren't you going to get up and give your big brother a hug, Angus?"

Angus laughed, "I'm in the nude, Patrick. I always sleep in the nude these days."

Patrick threw him a pair of trousers. "Here, put these on, Angus. Come on, give me a hug, you know I love ya, mate."

"Ok, you're the boss, Pat. I love you too." Angus lurched from the bed and stood unsteadily. Somehow, he managed to put his trousers on. Walking to Patrick with his arms out for an embrace, Patrick simply and cleanly knocked him out. Angus fell backwards on the bed like a swatted fly. Patrick then threw him over his shoulder, and turned before leaving. "Good night, ladies. Say good night, Angus."

Smiling her approval at Patrick's method, Molly opened the door.

Chapter 18

Tough Love

"Patrick, do you think this is wise?" Jonathon asked. His concern for Angus being locked up in the tool shed, especially in such a heat wave, had become the focal point of their lives.

"Dad, look at me," Patrick said. "I'm sitting here in the heat too. Angus has food and water inside and a bucket with his shit in it, which I empty every day. And every now and then, he gets a bucket of water thrown over him to keep him cool." Patrick whispered, "He's lucky it's not the bucket of shit." He smiled up at Jonathon. "I won't leave him, I promise. Go look after Margi because she needs you more than Angus. Let me take care of him."

"Well, if you think so, Patrick, but I really think we should try talking to him again. It's been over a week now."

Patrick laughed, frustrated at his father's constant concern and softness. "I talk all bloody day long to him. Remember, I've been here too, sleeping out with the bloody mozzies eating me alive. No more advice please, or I'll be on the first ship back to Addy!"

Jonathon then realised once again what Patrick had given up to come home. And how Patrick was losing patience with his molly-codling concern. "Quite right, Patrick. Do what you think is best, son. I appreciate it."

The wood shed was positioned under an enormous white gum that shaded it from the soaring heat. The shed was far enough away to be out of sight from the watchful eyes of their house guests. The true story had only been told to Barney, as he'd discovered their secret unintentionally. Barney then became a trusted confidant, and in turn, told Bernadette a white lie. "Yes, my dear, Patrick is working on something very special with Angus. They don't want to be disturbed."

Whatever it was, she couldn't imagine, as Patrick was the only one who made an appearance at dinner time. When he'd finished, he'd take a plate of food to Angus in the shed, prompting Bernadette to ask, "What sort of experiment is it, Patrick? It must be important if it keeps you and Angus working all day and night?"

Patrick, always quick on the defence, explained, "You could say it's a matter of life or death, Mrs Stuart, I mean Bernadette. It's still an experiment, but it might just save a life." Patrick's eyes travelled around the table to see if he'd convinced their guests.

"Still, it's very unusual," Bernadette muttered under her breath. Paul and young Jum had a sneaking suspicion as to what was going on, but said nothing. As soon as Bernadette and Barney left for Bulkawa, Patrick informed Paul and Jum of his attempt to have Angus free from drugs. Paul, although seeing the seriousness of the situation, was nonetheless amused at Patrick's "prisoner of war" tactics and said so. "I haven't looked at it in that way before, Uncle Paul. I'm pleased we can at least have a laugh about it. The capture of my little brother, hey! Don't let Dad see us laughing about it, or he'll release him immediately. It's good of you to bring me down a cold beer and I do appreciate you sitting here for bloody hours. Although, I suppose, it's given us time to catch up on our family heritage."

Nothing had been hidden from young Jum. Sally's secrets were discussed in the open and, of course, the news of Patrick's fortune awaiting him back in England. "The fortune was some compensation, I suppose, for the dreadful life he gave my grandmother and Mum. I only wish they'd lived to benefit from it."

Young Jum had become even more respectful and admiring of Patrick after their heart-to-heart talks this past week. Angus had also stopped begging to be released. Perhaps the only option Patrick had given Angus was reason for him to think. "I'll gag you, Angus, if you don't shut up! Just listen to how normal, drug-free blokes talk! You can join in the conversation if you want to be sensible. We can hear you."

Sometimes Angus did speak, especially when they spoke of Sally. Finally after fourteen days, and after Paul and Jum had left for Duntroon, Angus begged Patrick to be released. "I stink, Patrick, my skin's crawling with fleas, please let me out. All my apparitions and nightmares have stopped, as have my tremors. I'm clean of drugs. I tell you the truth, Pat, and I will never use them again. Please, brother, let me out."

Angus's last sentence and the way he'd said it convinced Patrick he may have won the battle. Slowly the door creaked open, Angus immediately lifted his arm to protect his eyes from the blinding sunlight. His voice cracking, he said, "Thank you, Pat."

"Oh fuck! You stink, Angus!" They burst out laughing, tears falling down their cheeks. Patrick held his nose with one hand, and pulled Angus to his chest with the other. "You go back on drugs, Angus, and if they don't kill you, I will. You fucking little bastard!"

With the same intention, the brothers ran and jumped fully clothed into the pool, splashing and playing as they did when children. Their play was disturbed by a cry from Jonathon, who was running towards them. "Quick, come quickly, Patrick! Margi's water's broken. You'll have to drive the car to the hospital!"

Then Jonathon stopped and stood dumbfounded. He suddenly realised Angus was in the pool. Without speaking, Jonathon walked like a robot towards Angus, his arms stretched out and eyes welling with tears. Springing from the pool, Angus held his father so tight and long, Patrick had to remind them both that Margi was about to have a baby. "I'll hitch the buggy, Dad," Angus said soberly. "I'll meet you at the hospital." He then smiled, realising he was dressed only in the trousers he'd been abducted in. "I'll get dressed first."

Meanwhile, Patrick, still in his wet clothes, started the car. He was suitably dressed after the heat of the day had dried them. Jonathon carefully escorted Margi into the back seat and sat holding her hand, comforting her with little hand pats.

Jane, their new housemaid, cum-nanny, held Millie in her arms, saying, "Mummy's going to the hospital to have the baby now."

"I know, Jane, her water's broken. It's to give the baby a wash before it comes out."

Jane shook her head and rolled her eyes. "Another genius in the family."

After a perfect delivery, Margie's perfect baby arrived six hours later. The next morning Jonathon brought Millie into the hospital to see her baby sister. "Look, Millie, a baby girl," Jonathon said. "We'll name her after Colleen, because she's so strong and healthy."

To Margi's surprise, the baby girl was born without a cricket bat between her legs, as she'd put it so many times. "I could have sworn she was a boy!" Nonetheless, Margi was happy with another girl, and with Miss Millie singing sweetly to baby Colleen, Jonathon felt life was good.

Of course, the atmosphere surrounding the birth gave way for Patrick and Angus to bond once again as friends. The conversation arose several times of Duntroon, especially after Uncle Paul had telephoned Patrick with great news. "Jum's been accepted into Duntroon. He's so excited, especially since he's able to continue his studies as an engineer. It's an amazing place. They hold studies for nearly all professions. I asked them about internships for doctors and they said they're more than welcome. So, Patrick, have a think about talking Angus into army life."

After the two brothers discussed it, Angus eventually agreed to Duntroon, although he begged Patrick to go with him. "I need you, brother. You're my rock. Do you think you could talk Addy into coming home and taking up her internship in Adelaide Hospital? I could help her. Please give it a go, Patrick, please send her a telegram. Just ask her. Would you do that for me?"

Patrick didn't have to consider long. "Yes, it'd be perfect, Angus. Addy could live here with Dad and Margi while I'm in Canberra. It's not the usual type of marriage, but this marriage I don't want to live without. I know now my home will always be in Australia. My property in England can wait."

After Jonathon inspected the official documents about Patrick's property, he had a word with Patrick. "Mr Roberts's integrity is beyond reproach, and what is also in your favour is Lord Fogarty seems to have taken an interest in the manor, as a 'hobby', he says. Mr Roberts has also written to me. He says Lord Fogarty has promised to inspect the work's progress on fortnightly visits to the property." Jonathon laughed as he read on. "He's even taken the privilege of choosing his own apartment within the grand manor."

This news had also made Patrick laugh, especially when he explained to Jonathon what an old character Lord Fogarty truly was. "I miss him, Dad, I know I could have counted on your contacts in London, but I think fate took a hand with our chance meeting. He's a generous and funny man. We're like kindred spirits. It's just amazing how we met and immediately got along so well."

Jonathon enjoyed listening to Patrick's happy reflections, Patrick then asked Jonathon, "What is it about life, Dad? It seems to send us the people we really need just when we need them."

Jonathon sat gazing out the window. The cloudless blue sky and the shimmering heat rising off the parched rye grass held his heart. He felt a sense of belonging; he was meant to live in Australia. Patrick waited patiently for Jonathon's thoughtful answer. "And life takes them away again. Just like your mother and her wildflowers. You should to learn to appreciate every moment, Patrick, and every person you meet. You will know then it was all meant to be. It's all you'll have to take with you, son, the lessons and the memories." Jonathon smiled lovingly at his son, his friend.

The next morning, Patrick opened the door to a delivery boy who handed Patrick a telegram from Addy.

I have no other choice but to return to Adelaide, Patrick, I'm pregnant. However, I'm determined to go through my internship at Adelaide Hospital. The baby will be cared for by a live-in nanny so I can continue my chosen profession.

Patrick took no notice of her blunt, well-laid out plans. Instead, he was overcome with the joy of Addy's pregnancy and her coming home. He began embracing all who came near, including Colleen, who'd been visiting her namesake and was the first to be lifted off the ground.

"Oh, put me down now, Patrick, I'm too old t' be lifted up in the air. Put me down!"

Bob stood next to her, laughing. "It'll do ya good, doll face. Now tell us what's made ya so happy, Patrick?"

With sheer overwhelming joy, Patrick yelled, "Addy's coming home. We'd better make wedding plans immediately. She's pregnant!" His voice was so loud everyone in the mansion could hear. Walking and talking almost to himself, Patrick's thoughts became words, "I'll telephone Bernadette. Yes, I'll telephone her." Pausing for a moment, he asked Colleen, "Do they have a telephone at Bulkawa, Mrs T?"

"No, I don't think they do. You may have to send a telegram, Patrick."

"No, I won't do that. I'll drive there. Are you coming, Angus?" He turned to Angus, who'd just arrived after hearing Patrick yelling.

"Bloody oath, brother. Nobody goes to Bulkawa without me!"

Patrick had a sudden thought: this would actually be his first visit to Bulkawa. Also, perhaps Bernadette and Barney may not be too impressed with their unmarried daughter becoming pregnant. He stood still, sobered by the thought. "Oh Christ, they may be upset, maybe we shouldn't go, maybe we should send a telegram first, Angus?"

In that moment, Jonathon walked through the front door waving a telegram in hand. "Well, what's all the excitement about?" he asked, seeing the entire family had gathered in the foyer.

Miss Millie announced, "Anudda baby, Daddy. Do we have woom?" Jonathon didn't seem surprised at her comment.

"Who's your telegram from, Dad?" Patrick asked, still on a high.

"Well, who do you think? It's from Bernadette." Jonathon's expression gave Patrick the feeling Jonathon was not happy. Patrick's heart fell. *Of course they don't understand how much we love each other. How hard it would have been for me not to make love to her under the circumstances of me leaving for Australia. I never forced her to have sex. No, no, that's not right, I'll take the blame. I didn't have to seduce her, I could've held her respect and her love even if I had refused to make love to her that night, or at her school. Oh shit, she mustn't have used the potion.*

The room seemed to spin, and Patrick's heart pounded at the reprisal he feared was about to be delivered.

Jonathon cleared his throat and read aloud. "Dear Jonathon, although Barnaby and I wished for things between Addy and Patrick to be in a different order, it seems we are to be proud grandparents. Congratulations to us all." He folded the telegram slowly. Every eye was upon him and every heart, waiting in anticipation of his next words. He looked up and around at his loved ones. A Mona Lisa smile brushed his face.

"It seems love is all we need. This home and all who live in it will stay true to that principle above all things. I know that without love, we crumble and fall." There were deep sighs of relief all round, as everyone shared the joy and congratulated Patrick once again. Although in a state of happy delirium, Patrick would not allow today's news to overwhelm his duty to his brother. He chose to sleep in Angus's room that night, as he'd done since releasing him from his prison, and would continue until they went to Duntroon. He knew instinctively Angus's addiction may never leave him entirely.

Because of his excitement about Addy's return, Patrick found it difficult to sleep so he was half-awake when he heard Angus creeping out of their bedroom. He chose to wait a while. *Perhaps Angus is just getting a drink of water or a late-night snack in the kitchen.* But his instincts told him something else. *No, get up and follow him.*

A full moon gave light enough for Patrick to see Angus walking towards the horses, and gathering a saddle and bridle from the tack room. Leaning against the door frame, with arms folded, Patrick watched his brother saddle his horse. Angus had no idea he was being watched; he was too preoccupied with his thoughts of escape for his night of sex and drugs with Eva. *I'll tell them I've just been for an early morning ride. I'll be back in time for breakfast.*

Patrick waited until Angus had mounted his horse and riding past before he pounced. Angus hardly knew what happened, and why, out of nowhere, he was being attacked by a flying assassin. As the brothers hit the ground, the horse took fright and galloped off up the road. After realising who it was that had him pinned to the ground, Angus spat dirt from his mouth.

"Fuckin' hell, Patrick. Now look what you've done. The bloody horse's bolted with my new saddle on!"

Patrick had to laugh. He sprang up and brushed the dust off his pyjamas. "This reminds me of when we played soldiers, Angus. Remember, I jumped out of a tree, and you shat yourself then, brother. Have you shit yourself now?"

"Oh, fuck off with your bloody soldiers. I was just going for a ride!" Angus saw the look of disbelief in Patrick's eyes and tried to explain, "But you..."

"No, brother," Patrick shot back. "I do understand and I know exactly where you were going and what you were about to do. You can't fool me. There's no escape!"

After saying that, Patrick felt a flow of compassion for his brother. "I'd hate to be addicted to something, Angus. Well actually, now I look back, maybe I was addicted to sex for quite a few years." He smiled at the thought and offered Angus a truce.

"I'll compromise with you, Angus. We'll get a bottle or two of Dad's best port and finish it. Then you can wank away. I won't look, ok?"

Angus rolled on the ground laughing, but also feeling anguish at losing his drug-infused sex with Eva. He wondered if he would ever be truly free of this agonising need.

Patrick watched, slightly amused, and said, "Best I can do, Angus."

"Well, get the bloody port then!"

Another two weeks passed, and it was the day the brothers would leave for Duntroon. It was also the morning when Patrick received another telegram from Addy. She'd delayed her return home, deciding to stay in England to attend Clare's wedding.

"Bloody hell, I can't have her travelling alone when she's that pregnant."

Angus only just caught Patrick's last words as he entered the foyer. "What's that, brother, no problems, I hope?"

Patrick turned to tell Angus the news just as Jonathon appeared, wearing his leather cap, dust coat and goggles, all enthused about driving the brothers to the coach stop. He looked from one to the other. "Are you ready for your coach journey? They won't wait for you, you know. If we're not out in front of the post office in ten minutes they'll be off!" Jonathon thought for a moment and continued happily. "Well, if they don't wait then I'll just have to run the coach down in my racing car!"

The smile soon left Jonathon's face when Patrick told him of Addy's decision to stay longer in England so she could attend Clare and Thomas's wedding. Jonathon then worried that Patrick may make a dash to be there. He'd witnessed the strain on Patrick's face and knew how much he was missing Addy and, of course, he would be concerned for her safety. He responded without delay.

"Patrick, let me send a telegram to Bernadette. I'm sure she will go immediately to England and accompany Addy home. That is if you think there may be a problem with her travelling alone. Please go as planned with Angus. He needs you."

Jonathon squeezed Patrick's shoulder, assuring him of what he'd said was sincere, if not desperate. Patrick took to heart the pleading look on his father's face, and Margi's; he knew she too felt the strain they'd been under with Angus. It seemed to Patrick that he was their only hope for Angus.

"Let's go, Dad. Don't want to miss the coach."

Millie cried, "Don't leave me, Patwick. You stay too, silly Angus!"

"Amazing observations, that child," Patrick said, as they kissed her on either cheek.

Angus accepted Millie's comment graciously. "Goodbye, Miss Millie, I promise I won't be silly anymore. I love you."

They had just enough time to send the telegram to Bernadette at the post office before Jonathon watched his beloved sons spring onto the coach. "Good luck, and telegram me on your arrival." He stood until the coach faded out of sight. "Like one page closing and another opening."

Smiling, he cranked the rotary starter on his car. "Home now to my wife and daughters. Almost two different lives I've led." Jonathon suddenly realised how lucky he was. Singing Angus's silly goat song and thinking how Millie loved it too, Jonathon had been truly amazed how Millie had learnt the words so quickly. The only difference was that when Angus sang it so many years ago, he had a squeaky voice, whereas Millie has such a lovely voice for her age.

Chapter 19

Goodbye, Tom

Patrick wrote to Jonathon after they'd settled into Duntroon.

Dear Dad,

Having time to talk with Angus on our journey was a blessing. Although sometimes we had to whisper, with the coach being full of travellers, but that's only when we spoke of VERY personal matters, of course.

We found the coach trip amazing. So many properties springing up along the road, this country is growing at such a fast rate. And to think how organised and quick the trip was, stopping only for a ten-minute toilet and food break, then into the next coach. If I weren't so hellbent on being a soldier, I wouldn't mind owning and running a coach line. We were duly impressed.

We are also impressed with the running of Duntroon. They've taken all the best points of training cadets from the English and American military academies. The grounds are perfect for our warfare games and the higher-ranking officers are fair and just with their discipline. All in all, we're happy.

Angus, it seems, is content with being an army doctor. He says he'd always wished to travel and this was one way to do it. Our travelling could be much sooner than expected with talk of Australia joining Britain, with their war in the Middle East and Germany ready to invade France. He's keen to be part of the war effort. "To mend men" he calls it. I'm more than ready to go, I'd hate to spend my life as a pretend soldier and never see a battle.

I enjoy being in charge of a platoon, and for those cadets who want to, I teach them karate. I explain to them that it's another form of combat which may come in handy. As Doctor Liu says, it's more about control of the mind and the body rather than the fight. Angus has enjoyed sparing with me to show the young cadets just what can be achieved with this ancient art. And I've instilled in them the mind control it takes to achieve the ultimate victory.

It's sent a welcome reminder to Angus on how not to waste your life and your talent. Mother Matilda would be proud of us as we go to church twice each Sunday.

This also helps Angus stay focused. I'm so happy Bernadette and Barney have made the dash to England. I know how independent Addy can be, even stubborn sometimes. I'm sure I'll be saying "Yes dear, no dear" for the rest of my life once we are married. I have permission of leave to be home for Addy's arrival in May. Angus will join us for the wedding, two weeks later. After all, I said to the Commander, I cannot possibly be married without a best man so he relented and gave permission for Angus's leave. The gardens at home should be in full bloom after the recent rain. Let's hope it stays for the wedding.

Before I put my pen down, I sadden at the thought that Thomas and Clare will have spent the first night of their honeymoon aboard the Titanic *and Addy and I were not married alongside them as planned. We would have joined them on the cruise, for sure. I remember the story you told Angus and me, of you and Jum sharing your wedding. Maybe one day Addy and I may sail on board that amazing liner, with Thomas and Clare, maybe for our joint wedding anniversary. At least Addy was there at their wedding. Thomas wrote and said, "No expense had been spared for their wedding celebrations." I've given them my manor to live in when they return, Dad. It's not too far from Sandhurst, so Clare will be able to visit him when she can and Thomas will come home to "Darcy Manor" as I've renamed it.*

Maybe one day we'll all travel to England and spend a season there. Who knows what life has in store for us. You've surely had your fair share of changes and different roads to travel, Dad.

On that note I will bid you peace of mind. Please don't worry about Angus; he's doing very well. Actually, he's astounding everyone. They say, "How does such a young man have so much knowledge about everything?"

One more thing, Young Jum is a champion cadet, with more energy and power than a bloody steam train. He's flying through his physical training and he's excelled in war strategies. I'm proud to be his cousin. Uncle Paul and Aunty Mildred will be coming to Adelaide for our wedding. I'm really looking forward to it. I just can't wait to put my arms around my beautiful Addy.

Your loving son,
Patrick

Three days after Patrick had sent his letter to Jonathon, he sat in his quarters, totally heartbroken with the tragic news of the *Titanic*. "Unsinkable!" Patrick kept repeating to Angus. "Mainly only women and children survived, they say. Jesus, I hope Tom's safe, Angus. I can't believe it. How could this happen? What a catastrophe, how could this possibly happen?"

The life had left Patrick's eyes. They looked empty as he paced up and down his room. He couldn't help but visualise Thomas going down with the ship. Clare crying, begging him to come with her on the lifeboat and all the time, Thomas brave in doing his selfless duty, staying behind to help women and children.

"You know, Angus, there were only half the number of lifeboats on board that should have been there. Can you believe that?" It made Patrick feel sick. "Fucking arrogant idiots. How can anybody assume anything to be so indestructible? It's plain bloody murder!"

Putting his arm around Patrick's shoulder, Angus tried to console him. "I'm sure Tom's safe, Pat. Try not to worry as it'll be days, maybe even weeks before we know the names of the survivors. You may be married before you hear anything. Tom's parents will let you know as soon as possible. Try and think positively. You have so much to look forward to. Addy's on her way home with Bernadette and Barney, and there are definitely no icebergs on that journey." Angus's attempt to humour Patrick was not appreciated, so Angus removed the smile from his now healthy complexion and continued. "Just think of Addy and your wedding. There's nothing we can do but pray for Thomas and Clare."

Three weeks later, Patrick received a letter from Thomas's parents in England.

Dear Patrick,

It is with great sadness that we inform you of our son Thomas's death by drowning. Clare has survived the tragedy because Thomas gave her a knockout blow to the chin before placing her on the final lifeboat. Clare had refused to leave Thomas and between the two of them, they managed to save hundreds of lives. Clare is still in shock. All she seems able to say is, "Thomas knocked me out."

We have solace in knowing our son was a true hero, and will always be remembered as one. A special hero's medal is to be presented at Sandhurst. We will receive it proudly on his behalf. We're staying in England with Clare for the time being until she's recovered enough to resume her life.

We are pleased fate has sent you on a different journey, Patrick. Thomas wrote to us, saying he wished you and Adelaide could share your wedding with him and Clare and then honeymoon together on the Titanic. *We are consoled by the fact that you and Adelaide did not share their fate. God bless you and Addy on your upcoming wedding.*

Yours sincerely
Margaret & Thomas Norman, Senior

Another two days passed and more letters arrived from England. It was the day Patrick was given early leave to return home due to the circumstances of his friend's death. The first letter Patrick opened was from Lord Fogarty.

My dearest Patrick,

I can only imagine what sadness you must be feeling with the loss of Thomas, your best friend and closest confidant. I'm able to inform you, however, Thomas will receive the full military commemoration of a hero at Sandhurst. I will be there to represent you. I send my most heartfelt sympathy and love.

   Your friend always
   Lord Fogarty.

Patrick dried his eyes before opening Lord Harris's letter.

Dear Patrick,

Words cannot express how saddened we all are at Thomas's death. Even my dear wife Bridgette is heartbroken, as, like you, Thomas charmed her, in particular the night of the wedding, when he made her laugh with his flattery. He danced every second dance with her.

I will miss him terribly, as much as I would my own son. To think now, owing my daughter's life to Thomas makes it doubly hard to bear. I must say the only glimmer of humour, if there can possibly be one, is Thomas having to knock Clare out to save her life. I'd say he knew her well.

I must regretfully add, I had attended the final meeting to complete plans for the Titanic when all things were finalised with the safety measures. I, along with two other of my good friends and business partners, stood against the majority in their decision to not supply ample lifeboats on board. Sadly, we were outvoted, as the majority kept saying, "This ship is unsinkable! It would be a waste of money, time and effort to spoil the ship's exterior with ugly life boats that will never ever be necessary." It is of no consolation, I know, but surely it will make others think more clearly about safety first before rebuilding such a ship.

I leave wishing you every happiness in your future with our lovely Addy. If I'm able, I should love to accompany Clare to your wonderful country one day. I'm sure if Australia breeds fine young men like you and Thomas, it may just be the place not only to visit but also to live.

   Until we meet again.
   Yours sincerely
   Lord Harris.

Before entering the Adelaide-bound coach, Patrick embraced Angus, hiding tears on his shoulder. "This should have been a time of extreme happiness for us, Angus. With you well over your problem and me looking forward to seeing Addy and then marrying her."

"I know you're drowned in sadness now, Patrick, but time will heal you, brother." Angus held his brother close once again.

Patrick felt relieved to be stepping off the coach. Dusting down his kersey uniform, he took off his officer's cap, tapping it against his trouser leg to free the dust. Looking up, he spotted Jonathon—faithful, kind Jonathon, waiting patiently outside the Adelaide Post Office. Patrick dropped his army bag and threw his arms around his father, sobbing without shame. He then dried his eyes, asking for the car keys.

"I'd like to drive to Glenelg Beach, Dad. I need a long walk along the sand. Will you join me? I haven't done much talking lately. I don't know what to say, or how to express my sorrow, except for crying. I'm afraid I'll be classed as a weakling if I don't stop."

Jonathon smiled and wrapped his arm around Patrick's shoulder. "It's only natural, son. I was the same when your mother died although I needed to be alone to grieve. Some people need the company of others in their time of mourning. I was lucky all those years ago when old Mr Darcy needed someone. And that was me. I wouldn't be walking alongside you today if it weren't. God knows where I'd be."

Jonathon stood gazing into the shimmering horizon of the Southern Ocean, hoping this sad time for Patrick would soon pass. Somewhere out there lay his future happiness. The woman he loved was sailing home to be with him.

"Can you see Addy sailing towards you, Patrick?"

Patrick smiled, almost laughing, "No, Dad."

"Do you believe she's sailing home to you?"

Patrick's eyes flashed with surprise. "Yes, of course I do!"

"Well, that's what life is really—believing. Believing whatever comes our way is meant to be. Trust me, it's all a divine reason and all we have to do is accept it. Addy is your next blessing, Patrick. Who knows if death is not a blessing? Who knows where we go when our soul leaves this realm, or why we have to leave. So, all we have to do is believe it's all for some divine reason."

For the next hour they walked in silence. Finally, Patrick accepted what Jonathon had said.

Many soul-searching weeks passed for Patrick. Now on this glorious day, he stood smiling into every face disembarking the steam ship at Port Adelaide. Most people returned the smile, seemingly humoured at his contagious happiness. His heart almost stopped on seeing Addy, looking more radiant and beautiful than ever. Addy's hand rose, shading her eyes from the sun, then pointing toward Patrick, she turned her head slightly to tell Bernadette he was there. Addy removed her pretty straw hat and waved it at Patrick before running to him.

"Be careful, Addy, please don't run," Bernadette called out.

They held each other tight before looking into each other's eyes. Patrick kissed her with the passion built up from great love and loss. It seemed they needed each other more than life itself. Kissing her hair, her neck, her sensuous mouth, Patrick became excited with Addy's return of passion. Addy was oblivious to Bernadette tapping her on the shoulder.

"Addy, Addy, we best go now. Jonathon's here to take our bags."

Their obvious love and electricity for one another gave Bernadette a heady reminder of her passion for Jum. She knew very well what her daughter was thinking and feeling. However, Bernadette knew they could not stand there all day, becoming the centre of attention.

After Bernadette greeted Jonathon with a kiss on the cheek, her eyebrow raised, she commented, "I think we should bring the wedding forward, don't you, Jonathon?"

This remark brought about a knee-jerk reaction from Patrick, "Yes, why don't we get married on the way home, Dad? We can still have the wedding reception next week. We need to be together right now."

"Well, you don't have to be a psychologist to work that one out!" Jonathon said bluntly.

And so to the church they drove, praying all the way that Father Frank would agree to marry them on the spot. Well, let me tell you, Father Frank had never heard of such a thing.

"You want a wedding now, right now, at this very minute? I'm sure even God would be shocked. And what, may I ask, is the reason for the change in dates, Jonathon?"

Father Frank needed no verbal answer as he observed the two lovers kissing passionately in the background. However, Bernadette and Jonathon pleaded their case to Father Frank.

"Mmm, I see," Father Frank said with glasses hanging off the end of his ruddy nose. "Alright then, but I wouldn't be doing this if it weren't for you, Jonathon, and you, Bernadette, being loyal Catholics and fine upstanding citizens as you are. Do you have the ring?"

Jonathon looked down at the gold wedding band he'd given Sally on their wedding day. He'd never taken it off his little finger since the day Sally had died. "Here, Patrick, this ring was your mother's wedding band. She'd want you to have it." The father and son embrace gave Father Frank another reason to perform this ceremony on the spot.

A pink aura seemed to radiate from them as they finally said, "I do." And then out of nowhere, a lone choir boy sang "Ave Maria". His clear sweet voice sent shivers up the spines of the small group. Father Frank, noticeably surprised after this inspiring rendition, asked the young boy, "And what brought you here today, Teddy? Rehearsals aren't until this evening."

"I don't know, Father, but I just started walkin', and before I knew it I was here. I watched you marry these two nice people and just thought I should sing that song. Was it good, Father?"

Father Frank ruffled Edward's hair. "It was more than good, Teddy, it was heaven sent."

After their warm welcome home by Margi and Millie, Patrick immediately excused himself and Addy. "We wish to take an afternoon nap, if you don't mind. We are extremely tired. Isn't that so, Addy?"

"Yes, of course, Patrick, we're very tired." With an unmistakable glint in his eye, Patrick carried Addy effortlessly up the stairs. As he did, he smiled at Jonathon's remark.

"Why do I feel so dispensable at the moment?"

Miss Millie promptly commented, "They won't sleep tonight. I don't if I have a sleep in the day."

Addy was more than anxious to make love. She began to strip, while Patrick stood amused at her eagerness before holding her hands down. Tenderly he kissed her mouth, her neck then stroked her swollen belly, sliding the slip over her shoulders exposing her perfect breasts. With one tug the slip fell to the floor. She couldn't wait for Patrick's viewing today; Addy needed him badly. She almost ran to the bed, begging him. Patrick straddled her, placing his arms under her back, he then rolled Addy on top. She giggled.

Patrick's love of slow eroticism became Addy's delight in her need of sexual pleasure. They'd played games with each other's fantasies and for the week before their wedding reception, they hardly left the bedroom. When they did, it made even the bravest person uncomfortable when watching the heat rise between the two of them, before they'd run up the stairs to begin again.

Chapter 20

The Power of The Press

Mrs Adelaide Darcy was now keeping herself busy with her studies and her internship at the Adelaide Hospital. Her spare time was mostly taken up with writing to Patrick, about everything, especially how she was missing him terribly.

However, she wrote, I have found solace in working alongside Doctor Forster, who has taken me under his wing. Sometimes, I think he is amazed at how a young woman like me could be so strong and confident in this gory practice of operating on the bloody insides of people, or cutting human legs off with a saw, etc, etc. Yes, nothing seems to bother me. I've relished the challenge of everything set before me and to think I'm pregnant and the talk of the town, it seems. I am sending you the article written about us, Patrick, just in case you haven't received it.

The article began, "WOMEN DOCTORS ARE NOT SO RARE IN ADELAIDE HOSPITAL". The Adelaide Hospital over the years has given a home to the great Doctor Phoebe Chapple, who was born in Adelaide 1879 and was one of our tireless workers with the poor and underprivileged. Also the very first woman doctor in Adelaide, Violet Plummer, was certainly a woman to pilot all females in their pursuit to become doctors. Now Mrs Adelaide Darcy has joined the ranks of women doctors. She has said, and I quote: 'I have always felt it to be my destiny. I am at home because my heart is where it should be'." The article continued on for some paragraphs with their story:

"The recently appointed Judge and Magistrate, Mr Jonathon Darcy, the father of Patrick Darcy, first met Miss Adelaide Watt-Stuart in England. They later married at Mr Darcy's residence. The young newlyweds, we were told, knew about each other in their childhood. However, it seemed they were never destined to meet until Patrick disembarked from his ship in England, where he was to begin a cadetship at Sandhurst. Yes, it was only by mere chance that they had met. After Patrick Darcy completed his training to become an officer at Sandhurst, he returned to Australia and is now stationed at Duntroon in Canberra. Patrick Darcy was awarded the Sword of Honour at Sandhurst. Whilst he was in England, Jonathon Darcy, Patrick's adopted father, traced Patrick's deceased birth father's family heritage, and therefore, informed Patrick; he was the sole heir to a small fortune. I'm sure I speak for the entire Adelaide community when I wish Patrick and Adelaide Darcy every success and happiness in their future together."

The article did not mention Patrick living in an orphanage until he was nearly eight years old or how his mother came to leave him there. Or the fact that Addy was pregnant before they were married. Jonathon had assured the journalist, with not so much a threat as a commanding tone, "I will give you the story if I am the only narrator." He'd therefore dictated to a budding cadet journalist, who was happy to accept Jonathon's condition. So, while being informative, the article did cut some very important corners.

Cecil Mott, after reading the story, threw the paper down in his prison cell, seething with hatred for the Darcy clan. It was Judge Jonathon Darcy who'd finally sent Mott to jail for bribery and for abusing his wife physically and mentally to the point that she was incarcerated in a mental home. Faced with a prison term of ten years, Cecil Mott swore he would eventually bring the Darcy family down and so began his plan. Working through his son, Peter, who'd remained happily at Sandhurst, he wrote a letter.

Peter,

If you call yourself an accomplished spy, then get to work on Patrick Darcy. Find out about his birth father, a Mr Cedric Birch, who migrated from England to South Australia the mid-1800s. Patrick has recently been left a manor house and a small fortune in England. This legacy has come from his genetic grandfather's estate.

His son, also Cedric Birch, settled on a property forty miles south-east of Adelaide. It was eventually sold as a deceased estate after his mysterious and undisclosed death. Also track down Ruby Tompkins and her daughter, Emily. I'm sure there was some fishy business between Patrick and Emily before Ruby sold her hotel and left town in a hurry.

Leave no stone unturned.

Your father,

Cecil

Chapter 21

Good Tidings

Winters at Duntroon, it seemed, were nearly as cold as they were at Sandhurst in England. Patrick huddled over the small fireplace in his room. His favourite thing to do after Mass each Sunday morning was to warm himself by the fire while reading each letter he received. Addy's letters he would usually read first, but today, for some reason he was anxious to open Lord Fogarty's letter.

Dear Patrick,

Arriving soon by ship (most probably before your first child is born) will be your beloved horse, Charlie. He misses you terribly, and when I told him I didn't think you would return to England to live, I could see his heart begin to break. He immediately went off his feed and became quite forlorn. Charlie has now picked up considerably since I told him of his journey to Australia, so as to be with his 'mate', as you Colonials put it.

Thomas's parents, I know, will be on the same ship and I'm not supposed to give you another surprise, as you may not have received Lord Harris's letter yet.

Patrick looked through his mail; yes, of course, one from Lord Harris. He had a sneaky suspicion of what news it held, however he chose to return to Lord Fogarty's letter, smiling with happiness of Charlie's arrival. Patrick continued to read.

I must say, if I weren't so old and crotchety I would have also taken the journey with Clare. Oh dear, now I've let the secret out. This journey will do Clare a great deal of good, I think, to be with her best friends will lift her spirits. Also, her training to be a nurse alongside Addy will give her something to think about, other than Thomas knocking her out. Clare has such a bright happy personality. She now smiles about the fact that Thomas saved her life. I'm so sorry, Patrick, for what you and Thomas will miss together. I'm sure, however, you and Addy will be able to help Clare once again to find a purpose in life and to be useful. She was never one to be, as her mother is, a beautifully kept lady.

Patrick placed the letter on his lap, thinking as he watched the flames of the fire flicker and dance. This news was something Addy had definitely kept a secret. *Clare, a nurse? Well, I'm sure she'll cheer her patients up with her great sense of humour and her gung-ho approach to life.*

He returned to the letter.

Have you heard of Germany's impending invasion of France, Patrick? I wonder if you chaps will step in to help your mother country. Trouble brewing everywhere, it seems. Just yesterday I read in the papers that the Middle East is our main target, due to England having to protect its oil supplies. England's treaty with the Ottomans was based on having a free passage of oil to and from England. If this agreement falls apart, due to conflict about the Arabs siding with Germany, it will also no doubt affect all other colonies of the British Empire. I have no doubt Australia will be the first country to send troops; darned fine soldiers, the Australians. This is when you will shine, Patrick, and I'm not surprised with the news that you have been promoted already. You are such a fine soldier and a fine young man. You are bound for greatness.

So, now with the secrets off my chest at last, I rest my pen.

God bless you and your family,

Your sincere friend,

Lord Fogarty.

The letter Patrick chose to open next was from Lord Harris. It held much the same information about the likelihood of war, and his request for Patrick and Addy to take good care of his beloved daughter, Clare.

Clare feels so very close to Addy, and she has always felt the urge to be a nurse. Why not in Australia with Addy to support her, and to help her through her mourning for Thomas. Not to forget her studies, therefore, I am more than happy for her to go to Australia and perhaps find a new beginning. Clare's mother, of course, was horrified. But as you know, we do not take much heed of what she says.

Lord Harris finished by promising one day soon, he'd come to Australia and visit Clare, and he'd look forward to meeting Patrick's family.

Addy's letter, as usual, was loving but while she had her mind filled with medical challenges, she tended to become almost clinical, making Patrick feel secondary in her life. Perhaps he'd made her feel the same way, when explaining how proud he was of Angus and his turnaround with drugs. And how much Angus was now concentrating on being a great doctor. He also went into detail about young Jum's many achievements and how he was excelling in Patrick's mounted regiment. He filled her in on Lord Harris and Lord Fogarty's letters, especially the part where Charlie would be arriving on the same ship with Thomas's parents. He finished by saying, *you have my heart in your hand, Addy. I only wish my body was with it at the moment. I miss you beyond all comprehension,*

> *Your loving husband,*
> *Patrick*

Addy was now nine months pregnant and still working hard in the Adelaide Hospital. She was bent over a dead body to see what Doctor Forster was trying to explain. He'd become a little angry when giving his comment. "This man's ruptured appendix could have been prevented! He was incredibly brave but stupid. He obviously told no one of his pain until it was all too late." Just as Doctor Forster said this, Addy felt warm liquid flow between her legs. She asked him calmly, "Can this inspection of the appendix wait, Doctor? My waters have just broken."

A fellow intern laughed a little at Addy's calmness but, at the same time, quickly pushed the bed trolley forward. Addy was then smartly removed and taken to the delivery room.

Concentrating only on her breathing, she kept the excruciating pain to herself, giving only slight grunts with every push. The clock on the wall had now told Addy she'd been in labour for two hours when the baby's head appeared. One last push and the crying baby girl was handed to her. With sheer relief and overwhelming joy, Addy held her perfect baby girl, and remembered how she'd promised Patrick that if it was a girl, they would name her Sally. And so, Sally Clare had just been born.

Bernadette, upon entering Addy's hospital room, thought her daughter looked more radiant than ever. Happy tears trickled down her cheeks when Addy handed her the just-bathed and smelling-like-heaven baby Sally.

"Absolutely perfect," Bernadette whispered, kissing Sally on her forehead. Bernadette nestled the baby's head into the nap of her neck. "Oh Addy, she's beautiful and you were so brave, Doctor Forster tells me. I'm very proud of you, my darling. We've sent a telegram to Patrick. He's been given leave for a week. He should be here the day after tomorrow. But the week includes his travelling time to and from Canberra but I suppose it's better than nothing," Bernadette said, beaming smiles at her first granddaughter.

"I just can't wait to see him, Mum. I wish at times like this we'd chosen a normal life. Why is it we are both so strong and need to follow our own dreams? It hardly seems fair, when we love each other so much. I hope he understands me hiring a nanny so I can complete my internship."

Addy hadn't really thought twice about doing this, however Bernadette shuddered at the thought of a stranger caring and feeding her first grandchild.

"Patrick may not mind, Addy, but I do. Can't you take at least six months off?"

"No, I cannot, mother. I have to complete my internship, so please don't start with me. You know I've wanted this all my life. If I give up now, I'll never go back and I'll regret it forever."

Their conversation was disturbed by the door opening and Jonathon peering in. "May I come in, ladies?"

Early next morning, Patrick arrived back in Adelaide. After creeping into Addy's room, he stood beaming at baby Sally sleeping in her crib. Leaning over, he kissed her blond hair. And then he turned to gaze at his sleeping wife, his princess. He lingered a kiss on her lips until she woke. Addy's eyes danced, still in awe of their tiny miracle.

"Have you seen her, Patrick? Isn't she lovely?"

"Yes, she is, just like you, Addy, although I think she has blond hair."

"Well, you named her right then."

"Yes, I think so." Patrick hung his head, thinking about how to tell her he would soon be sent to the Middle East. Addy noticed his expression before he had time to speak.

"What is it, Patrick? Have you something to tell me?"

"You know I've been put in charge of mounted volunteers. Well, now I have to gather them and go to the Middle East. It seems this war is a definite. The Australian Government's promised the Brits we'll send mounted troops to Cairo whenever they're needed. It may take longer than they expect to produce the horses and the men to go over there. But it's my job and we have to go as soon as we're ready. I'm not saying I don't want to go, as I do. I just hope you understand, Addy."

Addy pulled his face to hers and looked him in the eye. "Patrick, you didn't marry me because I needed you every minute of the day, or because I'm a weak helpless female. You married me for the same reason I married you and that is, we love each other. We will accept our fate unconditionally and forever, until the day we die."

She sealed her statement with a kiss, which set both their hearts racing. Laughing, Addy said, "I know what you're thinking, Pat, but no, not in front of the baby."

"Oh come on, Addy, I'll lock the door. And the baby can't even see yet!"

"No, not until you've actually given birth, Patrick! Take my word, I'm not up to it but maybe in a few days' time." Noticing the disappointment on his face, Addy kissed him again. "Now go and wet the baby's head. Get drunk. I'm sure that'll dull your senses!"

"Actually, I have to go to the dock and meet the ship. What a week this will be, Addy. My horse, Charlie, and Clare, plus Tom's parents, all arriving here today, just after baby Sally's birth. At least it'll take my mind off not having you, Addy." Patrick gave her another passionate kiss and she pushed him away.

"Go, Pat, before I give in."

"You're giving in? Well, let's begin, shall we?"

Addy laughed so much she woke Sally. "Oh there, there, little one. Mummy's here and Daddy is just about to leave. Now say goodbye to Daddy."

Chapter 22
Bribery

The following weeks proceeded in just the right order for the Darcy family and their dear friend, Clare.

"I simply love your Australian way of living. And I'm extremely happy in my training to be a nurse. I've come to think it is definitely my station in life!" Clare said.

Addy was more than pleased to have her closest friend working with her. And she'd hired a young, but experienced nanny, who was more than suitable to care for baby Sally. The entire family and Clare all living under the same roof at 'Wild Flowers' offered a perfect environment for raising children. The three girls were surrounded by caring loving people, including Colleen and Bob, who were delighted to be part of the nursing team, bandaging scuffs and soothing bruises, as Millie was running now, Colleen was toddling, and Sally would roll about giggling at their antics.

Doctor Liu paid many visits to the home, bringing with him his papier mâché toys and magic tricks. However, his magic never quite tricked Miss Millie. She usually worked out how he produced things from thin air, it seemed. This would prompt Liu to say, "You vely crever, Mirry, just rike Uncle Angus."

Patrick was kept busy, gathering volunteers from around South Australia, who would become part of the Light Horse. He loved every minute of it, especially since his horse Charlie was accepted into the Light Horse Brigade. Patrick had been stationed near Adelaide for some time. There, he'd sorted out the horsemen who were tough enough to succeed in the extreme conditions of the desert. Being stationed so close to home suited Addy and Patrick. Their fever-pitch desire for each other was accommodated at every available opportunity. They'd search for anything that could give cover for their lust. This game amused them both, especially the time when the nurses in the hospital tried to unlock the door to the linen closet, but couldn't.

While life was good for all the Darcys in Australia, back in England the white ants had begun gnawing to bring them down. It began with a letter from Lord Fogarty.

Dear Patrick

I shall begin by saying it seems a waste for only a caretaker and a gardener to live at your amazing residence in the Cotswolds. However, I may have found a solution.

I have recently had the pleasure of meeting two lovely ladies who you know as being dear friends from Australia, a Mrs Ruby Tompkins and her daughter, Emily. I shouldn't say this, but her daughter is quite plump. Ruby Tompkins is indeed a very charming lady and said she had found my whereabouts through your good friend, Peter Mott, from Sandhurst. Ruby knew of your marriage to Addy and the birth of your daughter. Ruby also confided that she wished many years ago for you to marry her daughter. She said, Patrick, you would remember it at as being a time when you were possibly too young to be serious. However, the proposal of marriage you gave to Emily was just before she had an unfortunate illness in which she lost a considerable amount of blood. Just between you and me, I think you have chosen your life partner far more wisely.

This brings me to the point of asking, would you be interested in leasing your manor and grounds to Ruby Tompkins. She wishes, if the war does not interrupt her plans, to turn the manor into an exclusive hotel for only the rich and famous to frequent. Her plans of welcoming overseas guests to stay at this palatial manor, I must say, sounds wonderful. I must also add, the money spent on the structural damage, plus the overgrown garden, not to mention refurnishing the manor, leaves us with very little funds to keep maintaining the property. Perhaps, Patrick, you should consider Mrs Tompkins's offer. She seems genuine and very keen in her desire to live there.

Until we meet again.

Your friend always,

Lord Fogarty.

Patrick's stomach churned with mixed emotions after reading his letter. *I won't give this news to anyone. I have to think seriously of what Ruby and Peter Mott may have to gain from me and whether it's worth the battle in denying Ruby the manor. Do I really care about the manor now, now that Thomas is not there to live in it with Clare? Would Addy like to live in Darcy Manor and raise our family? Perhaps Ruby's request is innocent enough. God knows when I'll need it for my own use. As far as I'm concerned, it stands only as a monument of redemption.*

Patrick received more letters that day, but as always, he'd chosen to open Lord Fogarty's letter first. Fingering through the rest of his mail, he was slightly shocked and not entirely happy about opening a letter from Ruby Tompkins.

Dear Patrick

I have recently introduced myself and Emily to your dear friend, Lord Fogarty. I have kept our past problem discreet from the Lord at this time. However, I must now inform you of the truth.

Emily has never fully recovered from her dreadful experience with you and Angus. Would Jonathon know how many years it would be that you and Angus would spend rotting in jail for aborting Emily's baby? Emily's had nightmares ever since her heartbreaking experience, dreaming of you, Patrick, and her dead baby lying next to her. She's taken to eating everything in sight just to dull the pain a little. How could Emily possibly find a husband in her physical and mental condition?

I have decided that you will allow Emily and me to live in your manor for as long as we wish. I intend to turn it into a whorehouse. If you don't like it, Patrick, you should go and visit Cedric Mott in prison, where your father Jonathon has sent him. You could then see if you'd like a life locked up in prison, rather than your blessed life now. I think Lord Fogarty might just like to hear the real reason for Emily's overweight condition, her never-ending chatter, and her nightmares, which were brought on by you, Patrick, and, of course, Angus aborting her baby.

I have recently received news from a close friend who owns a cattle station in northern Australia. He said that they hired a station hand named Bob and his Aboriginal wife, named Dawn. Apparently, Bob knew your mother and grandmother very well. I, for one, cannot imagine why you weren't left your birth father's property in South Australia? It's funny how Cedric Birch's death was never reported. I wonder why?

Every ounce of Patrick's control was needed now. His blood boiled with anger at her threats. *How dare she threaten me? My father's a judge, she'll have no chance against us, and how can she prove anything? I won't succumb to her threats of exposing this to Lord Fogarty. Oh Jesus, I hope she hasn't done that already.* He took a deep breath, trying to clear his mind; imagining the worst would only lessen his control of the situation. He must remain calm. A small part of him then began to feel sorry for Emily.

Was I so cruel to Emily just for my own gain? It was so many years ago now. I remember feeling guilty for taking the life of an unborn child. Although my guilt soon disappeared, Emily's mental condition, it seems has worsened.

Patrick had only to think of his own daughter, alive and healthy. He may have had another daughter, only he'd killed her. He rested his head in his hands, feeling confused and sick. *I need to talk to someone, but who? It has to be somebody who knows me well and who'd understand that I was a different person then. Dad? No, not Dad, he's got enough to worry about. Angus is too fragile to be reminded of past mistakes. Not Doctor Liu, he'd feel guilty for agreeing we'd done the right thing in being rid of the baby. Mother Matilda would be most unforgiving, I'm sure. Addy doesn't need to know, especially after having our baby.*

Patrick then said out loud, "Betty! Yes, Betty! She'll know what I should do and she knows me better than anyone." He immediately placed all his appointments on hold for the day. He'd phone Betty (Mother Madeleine) at the orphanage to see if they could meet. She'd be sworn to secrecy and surely forgive him. He knew she would.

Mother Betty was still not used to the telephone, although she thought it a wonderful invention. She was unable to work out how any mortal being could possibly hear her from so far away. "HELLO PATRICK," she yelled.

"You don't have to yell, Betty, I can hear you," he replied.

"Oh, I am sorry, I'll never get used to this telephone AND I SUPPOSE YOU'LL NEVER GET USED TO CALLING ME MOTHER MADELEINE."

"Very funny, Betty. I need to talk you, and it's urgent." Patrick's statement and tone of voice set her back a little. Once over her surprise, Betty answered, "Well, Patrick, I was planning on travelling to Adelaide tomorrow. I was hoping to see baby Sally and, of course, Millie and Colleen after my meeting with Mother Superior, Matilda. I should arrive by eleven o'clock. Where shall we meet?"

"I'll meet you at the coach stop, Betty, and we can take a walk in the park."

"That will be fine, Patrick. I'll see you then."

For the first time since Thomas had died, Patrick was unable to sleep. He'd tossed and turned until Addy eventually kicked him out of bed. He'd also for the first time in his life refused her advances. His worry of what he should or should not do plagued him and would continue to do so, until he was able to speak with Betty, of that he was sure. Finally, Patrick fell asleep on the floor where Addy had thrown him a pillow and a blanket.

Waiting at the Adelaide coach stop, Patrick remembered his first journey back to the orphanage with Angus. How intelligent his younger brother was then and yet so naïve. Yes, Angus knew the facts about world politics and on many subjects including most machines that one could name, but not the facts of life. Patrick's guilt returned. He'd led Angus astray, as he'd done with Emily. She was not the brightest girl in town and Patrick had taken advantage of her. In fact, he'd taken advantage of many young women, but never Betty. Patrick could have gone a lot further than just kissing her neck and feeling her small breasts. *Why didn't I? Why didn't I fight the Lord for Betty's love?*

"I'll give you a penny for your thoughts, Patrick."

He looked up. "You really wouldn't want to know my thoughts, Betty."

"Yes, I think you're right, I probably wouldn't. Let's walk to the park, shall we?"

It was a fine day for a walk. Perfect spring weather presented an array of blossoms as they strolled and talked about the weather, Addy and the baby, then they finally sat on a park bench. Moments passed in silence before Betty smiled into Patrick's sad blue eyes.

"May I hold your hand, Patrick?"

He thought this a perfect moment to tell her of his mortal sin, the one he'd never disclosed to anyone, except his accomplices. Patrick placed his hand on Betty's. She brought it up to her mouth and kissed it. Closing her eyes, she prayed silently. Patrick watched her lips move while her eyes remained closed.

Once Betty finished her prayer, she smiled at Patrick and then placed his hand back on his lap. "God is with you, Patrick. He knows of your sin and He forgives you. This is because you have come to me to ask for His help and His forgiveness."

"But you don't understand, Betty, I've committed a shocking sin. It was when I was young and selfish."

Patrick faltered for a moment. "I… I have to tell you I was responsible for aborting a baby."

Betty placed her finger to her lips and closed her eyes once more. Patrick said nothing, just watched as her lips moved silently once again. After some moments, Betty turned to him with a look that reached into his soul.

"The Lord says the child is with Him. He forgives you, Patrick. You must now tell the truth to the one you love and respect most of all and then all will be well and good."

Betty smiled and held him tight, whispering, "I have loved you, Patrick, in the way a woman loves her husband, and the Lord knows, but He has forgiven me." She held him apart and finished her message sombrely. "The Lord will be with you when you tell your father of your sin."

Why was this prayer from Betty all that Patrick needed? He felt his guilt had been lifted. "I believe you, Betty. I'll tell Dad everything tonight. I'll face the consequences, whatever they may be. Dad will know what to do."

"I'm pleased, Patrick, but it's not my words. You have to believe that it's our Lord God. Remember, He's with you always, so whatever happens, it is His plan. Now, shall we go and see your beautiful wife and daughter?"

"Yes, but only a quick visit for me, Betty. I have to get back to work." Patrick looked into Betty's eyes once more. "Do you really still love me, Betty?"

She laughed out loud. "Yes, Patrick. It's my cross to bear, but our Dear Lord knows I love Him more, in a very different way."

It was the same evening, after the women had gone to bed, that Patrick could finally tell Jonathon the entire truth. Jonathon's expression after hearing Patrick's long heart-wrenching confession was unfathomable; Patrick was unable to judge his response. He'd have to wait patiently for the reply. He remembered what Sally had written in her diary about Jonathon having to weigh everything up carefully before he gave judgment. Sally had been correct in her prophecy of him becoming a judge, as Jonathon was now, and a well-respected one.

Patrick felt he may have softened the blow by first telling Jonathon his experience with Betty. He could see on Jonathon's face his story had touched him. Patrick also felt pleased that Angus was at Duntroon, as he alone would now pay the consequences. Not Angus, as Patrick had forced him to mix the potion. Doctor Liu had come home after the act and should be forgiven for his advice, due to his upbringing and culture.

Finally, when Jonathon delivered his judgment, his expression hadn't changed from blank.

"I had suspicions about this unfortunate event, Patrick. I did hear rumours, but chose to dismiss them. I feel now it is in the past and there is nothing we can do to change things. However, I do feel you owe this girl, Emily, and her mother, Ruby, something for all the heartbreak and trouble you've caused. I feel, or I know, you have repented and you have a fine career and a loving family to consider. They should not bear the brunt of any gossip or heartbreak. I shall therefore write personally and officially to Mrs Tompkins. I will explain to her your offer. I will not mention her threat of blackmail towards you. I will not mention her daughter's abortion, or her accusations against you and Angus. I will say that after speaking with you at length, Patrick has decided to help you, Mrs Tompkins and Emily, with your difficulties, by giving you the manor house and the grounds to live in for as long as you wish. Patrick truly feels for Emily in her unfortunate state of mind and wishes you to use Darcy Manor free of rent and in any fashion you so choose.

However, Patrick will not be obliged to pay for any upkeep. The fact that you, Mrs Tompkins, will no doubt run a successful business from the premises leaves Patrick to state that all personal ties and obligations for maintenance of the manor should be completely your own and the only correspondence to Patrick should be through his lawyer, who is yours truly, Jonathon Darcy, Magistrate.

In actual fact, madam, Patrick wishes you and Emily all the very best in life. He trusts you will find Darcy Manor more than comfortable to live in for the rest of your days if you so wish. Patrick will at no time disrupt your life with the sale of the property. He will at no stage come to officially inspect the manor, or to show his presence in so much as visiting the manor. He wishes you and Emily to not approach him personally, unless you are invited to do so. Furthermore, if you at any time wish to leave the manor and never return, then all items belonging to Patrick Darcy will be listed beforehand. As in ancient artefacts, furniture and paintings, they shall remain the property of Patrick Darcy. Patrick is also willing to negotiate. If the property is well maintained and you wish to take leave of the premises, Patrick will then reimburse you with twenty-five per cent of the value of Darcy Manor." Jonathon took a deep sigh and then continued. "This will have to be worded correctly, Patrick, and then, of course, it will be drawn up as a legal document."

Patrick threw himself at his father, holding him tight while sobbing. Jonathon smiled, patting him on the back. "Come now, Patrick, you're a grown man, a brave soldier, remember?" Jonathon thought for a moment. "You know, the only thing that bothers me is the mention of Peter Mott. I wonder if his lowlife father has something to do with this blackmail and with Ruby knowing about your mother's entanglement with that degenerate Birch." Not often did Jonathon make a mistake without thinking what he was saying. "Oh, I am sorry, Patrick, I never ever feel Birch had anything to do with you. You are my son, not his. I am sorry."

"No Dad, it's me who should be sorry. Maybe I do have an ounce of him in me. Or else how do you explain my behaviour with Emily?" Patrick chose not to disclose any further information to Jonathon about his well-planned seduction of Ruby. One day perhaps he would tell him, if need be. But the fact that subject had not raised its ugly head was a blessing.

"You were very young, Patrick, and I must say, you had more than your fair share of testosterone. I will tell you once again that I'd heard many rumours but chose to ignore them. Perhaps I was a little jealous of you. I'd never been that way, the way you are, so passionate about life and love. I know it may sound silly, but being so conservative, as I am, and weighing situations up all the time before reacting, can make one feel that they do not possess the passion one needs to enjoy life to its fullest."

Patrick laughed, saying, "Dad, you're not serious, are you? I look up to you as my god, my mentor. I'll never meet anyone like you. I wish I were more like you. You're full of love, and you're intelligent, calm, fair, loyal, caring and just the best bloody father in the world."

Jonathon smiled. "Thank you, son. Now let's hope this letter, which I will send tomorrow afternoon, shall be accepted by Ruby Tompkins in the good faith it was intended. I knew you wouldn't mind giving up the manor. You never seemed excited about the place anyway. And with Ruby looking after it, your stocks and bonds will accumulate again, without draining them for the upkeep of the manor. I will write to Lord Fogarty and tell him that the ladies are our friends and they need help which we are willing to give. I will then write and thank Mr Roberts, who will always remain my dear friend, and inform him that we will no longer need his services with the running of the property. However, I shall wait until after we hear from Ruby Tompkins before I inform him of that. Now let's go to bed, Patrick, and pray she accepts your offer and takes it no further. I need to have my wits about me when I write a legally-binding letter in the morning. Mrs Tompkins and Emily will have to sign an agreement on which we state the terms and conditions. Then that should be the end of the story, and we can only hope and pray so."

Chapter 23

The First World War, 1914

Britain teemed with wounded soldiers during the First World War to the point where civilian volunteers were called for, especially those who could well afford to give shelter and comfort in their homes. Under these circumstances, Ruby Tompkins became much more compassionate. After agreeing with the contract drawn up by Jonathon Darcy, she'd set to work at being an upstanding citizen, something she'd aimed for all her life. With Patrick's generous offer, Ruby kept to her original plan, the one she'd told Lord Fogarty. Therefore, Darcy Manor was opened as a refined hotel—not a brothel. "Only good comes from good," Ruby finally admitted to her daughter. This was after Emily had become engaged to Sergeant Brian Pierce, who'd returned from the war in France, blinded by shrapnel. Ruby had set up Darcy Manor as a hospice for injured soldiers and Emily took an immediate shine to Sergeant Pierce, spending many hours reading him stories and catering to his needs. It seemed he loved Emily's constant chatter, as it would guide him to where he wanted to go. He also felt at home, nestling into her ample bosom while experiencing shell shock episodes. This pleased Ruby, as with her burden now lifted, Emily's happiness had been returned.

Lieutenant Peter Mott ceased further investigation into the Darcy Clan, as his father called them. Peter was far too busy with strategic warfare in the Middle East—spying, in fact. Jonathon had since paid a visit to the prison where Peter's father, Cecil Mott, was incarcerated. Jonathon warned him to call off his bloodhounds, or his prison sentence would be lengthened.

The total round up of light horsemen from each state and territory of Australia had boarded their allotted ship. A massive Australian and New Zealand flotilla then gathered to create an awesome sight of power and urgency when docked in Albany, Western Australia. On the first of November 1914, the flotilla sailed away from the Australian coast. Patrick felt elated as his dream would soon become reality.

Weeks of mundane chores, feeding and caring for horses in cramped humid conditions continued to maintain a sober atmosphere on board the ships. But when the news spread that the war was advancing into nearly every corner of the world, the men began to think their cocky adventure to play war games might just become serious. This was especially so when they were told that the most destructive German warship, the *Emden,* was not far off their line. The most formidable warship in the Australian flotilla was the *Sydney*, a converted passenger cruiser. Its brave captain went full bore to find the *Emden* in an all-out attempt to send it to its death and, after a long ferocious battle, it did just that. Her victory had raised the morale of the soldiers and officers to fever pitch. Then on top of that there was more good news. It was announced that the Light Horsemen would not have to bear the brunt of the English winter for their training, as they'd been previously ordered. They would now set up in Egypt, in a place called Maadi, south of Cairo. They rejoiced by nearly emptying the ship's beer supplies. Young Jum was the first to comment after the welcome news. "I reckon if us Aussies can brave some of the hottest bloody weather on earth, riding for miles around the bush all day, this'll be a breeze, mate. I hate the bloody cold, so let's get to the desert!" A chorus of hearty agreement echoed through the steel walls of the ship.

Any solid ground felt like good ground to Patrick and his men, and they disembarked gratefully onto Egyptian soil in December 1914. Although another trip lay ahead for the men and their horses, this time it would be by train to reach their final destination—Maadi. As they travelled through the desert, the soldiers were amazed to see the Pyramids gradually appear. It all seemed surreal to the Aussies. They sat in reverence of such an incredible and ancient human feat.

"Jeez, they're bloody amazing. How the hell did they build 'em, sir?"

"How the hell do I know, Private? I'm just here to fight, not to learn how to build Pyramids." This made Patrick's men laugh, something he was able to do easily, as he was well liked and respected.

As he stepped down from the train, Patrick gave Charlie a big hug. "Gidday, mate. What do ya reckon we're in for here, hey?" Charlie snorted, seeming to know the reason. Charlie was one of the lucky ones as many horses had died on the sea journey, and the rest only looked in reasonable condition.

Patrick stood gazing around at the small town of Maadi, thinking it resembled an oasis in the desert. Desert roses and bougainvillea bloomed, plus any other variety of plant which could tolerate the extreme climate. The wives of the English officers who lived there permanently had succeeded in creating a homely, suburban atmosphere, which seemed a little out of place in such a strange land, but Patrick felt welcome. The English residents were friendly and hospitable towards the Aussies which made for a pleasant time before the battle.

Months of desert training and acclimatising brought the Light Horsemen to a point where they begged to fight, but were told to stand at attention. "Until orders come from the bloody Poms," they'd cuss. The Commander of the Australian Light

Horse, Harry Chauvel, was under his own orders from the British hierarchy. Chauvel had visited Patrick's regiment soon after their arrival and many times since. A small man but large in presence, Chauvel held a genuine interest in his men and their horses, which struck an immediate respect within the regiments.

Chauvel had said he was conscious of the Australians thinking they were only there to be owned and used by the British, but he assured them this was not the case; they were fighting for their own country and if this war was not won, it would duly affect Australia. All he wanted was his men to do their duty courageously, stay alive and return home. Of course, he had his own constant battle with the higher ranking British officers to prevent his men being used as pawns.

During this time of endless waiting, Patrick wrote home constantly.

Dear Dad and family,

Our long arduous desert training has been accompanied by a lull in battle proceedings. With my men now more than ready to fight, their eagerness is prolonged by the agony of waiting for the order to charge. The situation has caused a bad attitude in the men. They have begun to think they're here only for show and nothing else. This includes me. However, I'm here to keep the peace and to assure the men they will soon do battle with the enemy.

I've chosen the lighter approach to leading, so I've become a mate rather than a dictator. God knows it's a desolate and strange part of the world, and we need to bond as friends.

Lieutenant Jum Smith, my illustrious cousin, is beside me as my under-ranking officer. I know I've chosen well, the finest horsemen South Australia had to offer. And although most have come from properties, raising sheep and cattle, and have never seen war at first hand, I will be more than proud to go into battle with them whenever the order comes. They're tough and focused and I know what they're made of. I simply have to keep their energy contained for the battle ahead.

Love to all

Patrick

Back in Adelaide, Nurse Clare's heart was torn in two. The last thing she wanted to do at the moment was to leave Addy to join the war effort in the Middle East, however, she felt a real need to do so. The two women had cried and then argued with anyone in earshot about the fact nurses were the only women allowed to be sent to the war front. Women doctors from Australia were excluded.

Addy had gone to great lengths to find an opening for her to go to Cairo as a doctor. She protested on every front and now she'd gone to the top. Addy paced the floorboards and loudly asserted her case to the Army Replacement Officer in Canberra.

"How dare they say I cannot be useful in the Middle East? I'm a doctor, for God's sake. How could a nurse be any more useful than a doctor? We actually operate and save lives!" Addy yelled at the seemingly patient officer.

"Please sit down, Mrs Darcy," he said calmly.

A not-so-calm Addy replied, "First of all, you will address me as Doctor Darcy, not Mrs Darcy. I haven't studied all these years and passed with honours to be denied my title!"

"I am so sorry, but orders are orders and rules are rules, Mrs... I mean, Doctor Darcy."

Addy's eyes blazed with fury. "There must be a way around this!" she raged, more to herself than to him.

The officer paused for a moment before his expression became more hopeful. "If I may offer you a suggestion, Doctor Darcy, if you were to travel to England and enlist in the Royal Army Medical Corps, you may find they do send women doctors to the front. Or there is another option, Doctor Elise Inglis is leading a voluntary recruitment for women doctors to the front lines. They call themselves The Scottish Women's Hospitals for Foreign Service, the SWH in short. Oh and do not reveal that you're married, use your maiden name and I'm sure they would welcome you on board."

Flinging herself across the desk, she kissed him, then ran from the room, jumped in her car and drove nonstop to Bulkawa. She immediately told Bernadette who, in turn, felt like shaking some sense into her daughter. "How can you possibly think of such a thing, Addy? You have a daughter to think of! What if she loses both her mother and her father?"

Bernadette broke down crying. Barney held her close, looking pleadingly at Addy.

"I'm sorry, Mother, Barney, but I'm going to war."

Whenever she was at Bulkawa and called him Barney, not Dad, it felt strange. Was it because Jum, her birth father, was still here, simply lying low after what had happened to her in the swimming hole as a little girl? Addy was more than sure she'd felt his presence at times like this. She needed his strength now. *He would understand her.* Jum had always followed his gut feelings. Bernadette told her this many times. And this is exactly what Addy was doing.

As Bernadette's sobbing eased, she raised her head. Quite composed, she spoke in a manner that would amaze Addy. "Addy, you are your father's daughter and every bit as strong as him. I know you will do as you wish—you have my blessing." She'd felt and heard the words coming from her mouth, but seemed to have no control over what she'd just said. She had to smile and repeat, almost light-heartedly. "Yes, that's right, Addy. You're every bit as strong as Jum."

Barney had to agree, as he always did with Bernadette.

The decision for Addy to go to war had now been settled. After she returned home to "Wild Flowers" the same day, she sat content, knowing in her heart that baby Sally would be happy and well looked after by her nanny. As a bonus, she seemed delighted with the company of her two young aunties, Millie and Colleen, who kept her constantly entertained.

When Clare and Addy agreed to sail to England together, their travel plans were set immediately.

Chapter 24

Addy Joins the Fight

The very day they landed on the docks of London, Addy and Clare went to join the Royal Army Medical Corps. Addy then wrote to Patrick.

My dearest darling Patrick,

Clare and I have arrived in London. Lord Fogarty and Lord Harris were both here to greet us with a warm welcome. We went straight to the recruitment office to join the RAM, as they call it here. However, I being a doctor was refused the same as in Australia and so we took the next avenue and that was to join the SWH, The Scottish Women's Hospitals for Foreign Service. We have only two days to relax, and then it's off to training. I must tell you, Lord Fogarty is almost running these days after taking Angus's Chinese medicine. It's working so well on his arthritis he wants to enlist!

Have you met up with Angus yet? Is he still in Cairo? I thought perhaps they would have moved him closer to the front by now. Clare and I pray they will send us to Cairo, but France is on the cards. In that case, I shall feel this venture was not as I intended and that was to be near you, my love. However, I shall soldier on wherever, with the intention of saving as many lives as possible.

Our darling, Sally, is still only crawling. I think she would have perhaps walked sooner if it weren't for Miss Millie carrying her everywhere. The three girls are inseparable. Millie, of course, is the boss and makes Colleen and Sally sit and listen to her sing. You could say they are her captive audience. It is no wonder she has an amazing voice, after all, Margi definitely missed her calling as an opera singer. So my darling, all was well when I left Australia. Please take good care, Patrick.

Until we meet again, with all my love,
Addy

Patrick sat in the desert sand and kissed the letter from his wife. He then removed the photo he'd carried from his top pocket, the one nearest his heart.

Looking at her beautiful face, he wondered whether they would ever meet up in this hellhole. The heat and the flies were worse than anywhere in Australia, not to mention the ferocious and debilitating sandstorms which could blind a man. Cairo was certainly not the cleanest city in the world and the natives were a seedy lot. Prostitutes flaunted their half-naked bodies from the balconies of their cesspits day and night. Patrick shuddered at the thought. He then closed his eyes, imagining Addy's clean, sweet-smelling body and her tender touch, needing to make love to her. But at the same time, he wished her not to come to Cairo and take risks. He was thinking she should be safe at home, caring for baby Sally, just in case anything happened to him. However, he knew Addy well. She would follow the beat of her own drummer.

Patrick felt he was a confident leader, an elite fighter who'd had plenty of training. All his life he'd dreamt of becoming a soldier. But soon, as Da had said, it would all become a real-life battle. He hadn't even seen, let alone been a part of, a bloody battle as yet. He was definitely not scared, just anticipating the worst. Looking up into the heavens, Patrick prayed: "Mum, I hope you can hear me. I want to see my baby, Sally, grow up and I want to spend the rest of my life with Addy. Ask God to look after me, will you?"

Sitting alone with his letters and his thoughts, Patrick was conscious of his men around him. He knew they were restless and anxious to take the leave given. Jum ambled up to him and crouched on his knees. "Are you comin', cous? We're going to Cairo now."

Young Jum had become more like Patrick's younger brother and when not in hearing distance of the other men, he would always refer to him as "cous". Patrick smiled up at him. "Yes, of course, cous, can't let those larrikins get out of control. Somebody has to keep an eye on them!"

Patrick would now be forced to write his letter to Addy after his return from Cairo. Firstly, he'd write and welcome her to the battleground and then tell her; yes, Angus was still operating from the Cairo Hospital, although he would soon be transferred to Heliopolis. They were expecting an influx of wounded after heavy fighting near Cape Heles.

Charlie snorted his approval of them moving; he too needed to feel useful. Patrick smiled, thinking Charlie looked a little out of place within the regiment of bay Walers. His grey coat sometimes shimmered into the camouflage of the desert sand, whereas the other horses in the regiment stood out with their shiny bay coats. Patrick felt sure when he mounted that Charlie knew he was carrying important cargo, as he'd arch his neck and hold his tail up high. Cantering off through the hot desert sand, Patrick began thinking about where he was heading.

It is a proverbial den of sin, underhanded deals and, for the right price, as much sex as any man can handle. My men are wound up and anxious for action. I think they'll choose to take their pent-up emotions out in the brothels. They've become renowned for their drunken raids on the red-light district. The prostitutes don't want to be overpowered or outsmarted, so they've taken to stealing anything of value from my men while they sleep off their sex and alcohol binges.

When they arrived, Patrick warned his young cousin, Jum, "Just be careful, mate. Check your pockets before you leave."

Jum laughed, "How do you know I'm gunna spend my money there, cous?"

"Because you have my blood in you. Now go and have a good time but watch your back and don't get into any fights."

"What'll you do, cous?"

Patrick went on to tell him he was about to meet Angus at a popular bar in about an hour's time and then he finished by giving Jum another warning, "Just be careful, and give yourself a good wash after." Young Jum walked away shaking his head, and smiling to himself.

Patrick entered the dim, smoke-filled bar, thinking at least it was better than sitting in the bloody hot desert in the middle of nowhere. He ordered himself a beer and swilled it down. "Another beer thanks, mate."

The bartender studied Patrick's face. He then took a photo from his pocket, looked at it and looked back at Patrick with a smile on his half-shaven face.

"What's the problem, mate? Do you think you know me?"

"No sir, but a man, a short skinny man. English, Aussie maybe, wears Arab garb. He gives me this photo, says if you come in, I am to tell him you are here and then he meets you private."

The bartender leant over the bar so as to almost whisper, "If you don't want me to tell him, it cost money."

Patrick had no idea what he was talking about, but was inquisitive. "And do you know the name of this Englishman?"

"Yes, his name is Mott." The bartender had kept his voice at a whisper.

Patrick needed a moment to sort this one out. *What the hell was he doing in Arab garb? Why was he looking for me and why didn't he just write a letter if he had something to say?*

"Do as you like, mate. I know him but I don't give a damn." Patrick paid for another beer and took it to a secluded corner.

Angus arrived early, and when seeing Patrick, he beamed through watery eyes. They hugged for some time before Angus asked, "How goes the desert training, brother?"

"Bloody awful. I just wish they'd send us into battle; we're all ready and waiting. The morale of the men is the hardest thing I have to deal with at the moment because they're looking for a fight. And giving them leave to come to this place is asking for trouble. They get drunk and get into fights with the bloody Arabs. I wish to God they'd send us on a mission as I'd have more control over them then. What about you, Angus?"

"Oh you know, Pat, mending men. I had a letter from home. Dad says Clare and Addy are on their way here. No doubt about your wife. She's so determined! I think you met your match there, mate."

"I think you're right. There's no stopping her. Whatever Addy wants, Addy gets. Oh Christ, I miss her, Angus, I need a good battle to take my mind off her."

"Do you need some stuff for your libido, Pat?"

Patrick replied somewhat dourly. "No thanks, they give it to us in our tea, I think. Anyway, I can't even look at another woman. Addy's got me, for sure."

Angus changed the subject after seeing the depressed look on his brother's face. "How's Charlie handling the desert? I bet he's loving it here, being half-Arabian. Just like home, I suppose."

Patrick had to nod in agreement as his mouth was full of beer. He swallowed and then responded, "Charlie's happy as long as he's showing off his tricks or he's in training. Don't worry; he knows what he's here for!" He pondered for a moment. "But I'm sure the Arab in him definitely smells home."

From the corner of his eye, Patrick could see a small Arabian-clad man gliding to the bar, as if he was trying to be invisible. The bartender spoke to him and then nodded to where Patrick and Angus sat. As he approached, Patrick recognised those beady eyes, now darkened, and the thin lips which were almost covered by a full beard.

"Jesus, Peter! What the fuck are you dressed up like that for?"

"Keep it down, Patrick. I'm on a mission."

Peter glanced furtively around the room before he continued. "I thought I'd catch you here while I was in Cairo. I have important work to do and then I'll be off into the desert. That's all I can tell you about me. I just needed to meet with you, Patrick, and tell you face to face—I have changed my ways. I no longer write to my father as I have basically disowned him. I'm also sorry for any problems I may have caused between you and Ruby Tompkins." He hesitated for a moment. "And her daughter, Emily."

Patrick had almost forgotten about Ruby and Emily. He was tempted to tell Peter not to worry, it had been all sorted out, but Peter seemed anxious to finish and leave. "I'm truly sorry, Patrick, for whatever I have done to you in the past. I think my future in this war will prove I have changed for the better. I was very sorry to hear of Thomas's death. We gave him a hero's send-off at Sandhurst."

Peter hung his head, as Patrick held back his emotion. "There's one last thing I must say, Patrick. Thank you for not reporting the incident you witnessed."

Angus had been listening intently and so butted in. "What incident?"

Peter looked pleadingly at Patrick, his sadness still showing.

"Don't worry about it, brother. It was nothing."

However, Patrick did ask about Peter's mate, Travis. Peter said solemnly, "He was killed in France." Patrick simply nodded his head.

This short episode with Peter Mott took Patrick by surprise, especially the fact that before Peter left, he shook Patrick's hand quite firmly. Patrick then held his hand up, and looking at it, he said, "Well, what do you know, and to think Thomas once said a leopard never changed his spots." They watched Peter as he glided out of the bar.

After a few more beers, Patrick began to see the funny side. "You know what that reminded me of, Angus?"

Angus sculled his beer then coughed out the word, "No."

"You remember, in the films where the villain wore Arab garb and slinked around looking from under his blackened eyes. I swear he had bloody eye makeup on. What do you reckon?"

"Yes, I think you're right, brother. Now tell me about the incident, as Peter put it, the one you never reported?"

Patrick was reluctant to bring up the memory. However, he knew Angus would not relent until he was told the truth; it was the lawyer blood in him. And so the scene, when Patrick caught Travis and Peter together in a compromising position, was retold to an amused Angus.

"Well, well, we always knew it, didn't we, Pat?"

Patrick hung his head, somewhat ashamed he hadn't believed Thomas when he kept telling him about Peter's homosexuality and his love for him. "I'm afraid Thomas knew it before me. He kept telling me but I thought they were just mucking around. I didn't take much notice. Part of me felt sorry for Peter, especially the way he was brought up. Not like us, brother, love all the way."

Angus sat up, a little surprised at his brother's compassion for Peter. "You haven't got leanings, have you, Pat?"

"Oh fuck off, Angus. Why would I want to root that ugly bastard when I can still have the pick of any woman I want!"

"It's a wonder you haven't in this place. They're hanging out their windows, begging for it!"

"Not on ya bloody life, Angus! And get syphilis?"

"Well, you know, Patrick, the men who were sent home with it should have come to see me beforehand. I have a wash to help prevent the disease."

"Yeah, just like your anti-pregnancy potion that didn't work on Addy."

Angus raised an eyebrow at Patrick's remark. "I think perhaps Addy forgot to use it, Patrick. Doesn't matter anyway, look at what you both have, the most beautiful baby girl in the world!"

"Don't start me, Angus, I miss them so bad." Patrick stood to take their glasses for a refill.

Their night ended with them both drunk and singing the silly goat song, over and over, as they walked back to the Cairo Hospital, where Patrick soon found an empty bed to sleep for the night.

Chapter 25

Anzac Relief Mission

Orders came for Patrick's troop to move out. After nearly four months of training they rejoiced. They would have to cross the Nile River to reach their destination. The instructions were not exactly clear at first, on whether their mission would be a charge, or if they were needed to replace exhausted foot soldiers in their trenches at Anzac Cove. At least Patrick thought wherever, or whatever it was, it would be far better than sitting the war out in Cairo. As a place that begged his men to get into trouble, Patrick's farewell to Cairo pleased him no end.

After the long hot desert ride and then the almost perfect crossing of the Nile River, they boarded ship and were on their way to Anzac Cove. However, the final orders had been given about ten miles out from where they stopped for a prelim and a cup of billy tea.

The Commander of the Light Horse Brigades, Chauvel, had explained that this operation for the Light Horsemen was definitely not in the nature of their own mission. However, so many lives had been lost at Anzac Cove, and the foot soldiers who had been lucky enough to make it to the trenches were now exhausted. They needed desperately to be relieved so the Light Horsemen were to fight when and wherever they were needed.

This was the ultimate sacrificial order. This news did little to enthuse the Light Horsemen, mainly because the majority had not had any real training in trench fighting or foot soldiering. Their disappointment was obvious, not only within the mounted regiment but also their officers. This included Patrick, but he addressed them to lift their spirits.

"Well, men, let's kill 'em quick so we can fight another battle from horseback. Whether we fight on top of our horses or from the trenches, we'll win this bloody war—no matter how, no matter where!"

Patrick's words stirred his regiment, enough for them to focus on their real reason for being there. It was not only about riding horses, they were here to win this bloody war and get home safely, as soon as possible.

A group of horsemen were ordered to stay back and care for the horses while mostly the artillery group continued to ease their way into the allied trenches. Patrick gave Charlie a pat on the neck and warned his youngest platoon member, Timmy Walsh. "Guard him with your life, Tim. He's me best mate."

"Yes, sir. I will, sir."

Charlie gave Timmy a nudge and nearly knocked him over. Tim laughed. "I think he'll be the one lookin' after me, sir."

Aerial maps showed how and when to approach their mark. Leading the way, Patrick landed his men safely into the arms of the grateful Anzacs to be relieved. They changed over quickly and with no casualties apart from a few tired soldiers wounded by snipers. Luckily for them, they would be taken to the nearest stationary hospital and nursed back to health. Whether they had been wounded seriously, enough to return home or not, would be decided by doctors who were under strict orders: "Send them back to battle if at all possible."

Many Anzacs had been killed or wounded, due to the inhuman sacrifices ordered by British officers and to tactical blunders by war strategists. As the first night approached for Patrick's platoon, they got themselves ready in their trenches. He'd given orders for Jum to go into the nearest trench with four of his youngest platoon members, knowing they would be in safe hands. "No bloody rest for the wicked here," Jum said dryly.

Patrick joined his group of four as they laboured all through the night, digging deeper into the sandy soil trench. It seemed the more they dug the more earth filled it in. Nevertheless, they tried hard to keep the trenches at least six feet deep so as to cover their heads. Food was a welcome relief from the digging. Bully beef, and biscuits they'd break their teeth on were the main rations, but gratefully, cheese and jam were also supplied, which they'd make into a type of sandwich. It became Patrick's favourite snack to have with his tea.

Day after day, night after night, the deafening machine guns rattled on. Amidst the clamour of the guns, agonising moans from men injured by hand grenades or bullets periodically filtered through. This never-ending battle seemed to be going nowhere for Patrick. He knew the aim was to penetrate the enemy's barrier but each time a charge was called, an individual went stir crazy, made a run at the enemy and were inevitably shot dead. Patrick would take great risks in leaving his trench to attend meetings with his superiors. Each time he did, he amazed even the enemy snipers by using his Kung Fu agility to evade their bullets.

Weeks had passed with no gain in territory. The men endured extreme weather changes; on rainy nights being soaked wet, then chilled by freezing winds, then parched by a stifling sun. Their discomfort was made worse by being stuck in one place for so long; they were frustrated and bored. It was no surprise when the soldiers began a game of chance for a little extra excitement. They'd dare each other to lift their heads above the trenches. Sometimes they were killed or grazed with a bullet. Patrick called out to his men, "Any fuckin' idiot that does that again and survives will have me to take on in the boxing ring. Keep ya bloody heads down!"

They laughed dryly but some thought they'd take up Patrick's offer just to break the monotony. Then a familiar voice tested him, "Jesus, cous, I think it's about time ya did some Kung Fu flips and knocked a few of those Turks' heads off before they know what hit 'em."

Before Patrick had time to agree or disagree, his entire platoon, all in trenches nearby, called out to egg him on. "Yer, why don't you kill 'em with ya Kung Fu tricks. That'll get the dirty bastards movin'. They'll all leave real quick if ya kill a few of 'em with ya chop-chop-chop!"

Patrick smiled and called out, "Don't tempt me!"

"We're not tempting ya, we're tellin ya!"

A voice he didn't recognise yelled out just before the Turks began firing again, probably only to warn them that he'd better not try. Patrick slid down in his trench and sat deep in thought. The enemy trenches were only about fifty feet away. He'd already shown his ninja style agility to both the enemy and the allies. Would he risk his life for a show of supreme ego, or could it be done without too much risk?

The three nearest enemy trenches, he knew, held only a few Turks in each. On a moonless night, perhaps he could accomplish this act. Patrick's heart began to race with the thought. At last he'd be able to put to good use the martial art he'd studied and trained for all his life. However, word had just come to him; the Anzacs may have to run for their lives to the beaches anytime now. Chauvel had warned to expect a serious charge from hundreds of outlying Turks, possibly within the next twenty-four hours. Patrick's immediate instinct told him it would be sooner rather than later. And he was right; only hours after the warning, the Turks made their largest charge at the Anzacs.

After hours of intense fighting, Patrick was pleased to report he and his men had remained steady and had killed not only hundreds of enemy but the handful of Turks on their way to the Anzac HQ. This massive charge was part of a plan to kill top-ranking officers, including Chauvel at HQ.

More than three thousand Turks had been killed and many hundreds wounded, but Anzacs' dead and wounded was less than a third of that number. With so many bodies lying around, an armistice was called for to bury their dead. Neither side fired a shot until the job was complete. This gave Patrick time to read the many letters he received from home and from Addy now in Cairo. He opened Jonathon's letter first—all was well, particularly with the three little girls. "Life was a bowl of cherries", he wrote, "After Colleen discovered the three, well, Millie in particular, had eaten an enormous bowl of the succulent red beauties, only to vomit them all up over the new sandy-coloured carpet in the lounge room".

Simple everyday news from back home was enough to keep the soldiers grounded, and gave them reason for being there. Patrick laughed, as he could only imagine Colleen and Marjorie on their knees cussing, while trying to get the cherry stain off the carpet. He then spared a thought for not only his dead comrades, who would not return to their loving families, but for the faceless enemy. They too had families to go home to. He immediately shook the vision away. They were the enemy and had to be killed before they killed you. This was war, and he had been trained to win at all costs.

Patrick's heart raced as he opened Addy's most recent letter, the one which would tell him just how close she was to him. It read:

My darling husband Patrick,

I am finally here and based at the Cairo Hospital. Clare is at the moment greeting Angus after his return from Helios. Apparently, he saved many lives and cured the eldest physician here in the Cairo Hospital of his arthritis. Now he's in line for a medal, not for the arthritis cure, but for the men he's saved. Angus worked around the clock until he passed out with exhaustion before they gave him R&R. I can hear him in the background laughing with Clare. Just between you and me, I think there might be a glimmer of romance between them.

I can't wait to see you and hold you in my arms, Patrick, and to kiss you forever. Have you any idea if and when you may return to Cairo? Please don't take any unnecessary risks and keep your handsome head low in those trenches. I can't believe that is where they sent you; it's a waste of a great horseman.

There is a lovely little tavern at Point Said. A couple of Australian women have set up to make the men feel more at home. Clare and I go there and feel very safe to enjoy a wine or two. I must say you were right in saying Cairo is a den of vice, so many soldiers have been sent home after contracting syphilis. I'm so happy my darling husband only has eyes for me. I love you more than life itself, Patrick, and I pray we will be together soon; I shan't budge from this hospital until I see you, but please make sure it's not as a patient.

Your loving wife,
Addy XXXXX

Patrick hated becoming emotional when he read Addy's letters, but he soon laughed, saying aloud, "Christ, one minute I'm killing the enemy and the next I'm a sniffling wreck." Just for one second he wished himself injured so as to be taken to the Cairo Hospital to see Addy. However, remembering his mates who had been killed and whose families would never see them again brought him back to the reality of war, and to just how lucky he'd been.

Thousands of Anzacs had died in the various battles near Anzac Cove and now Patrick's troop had been called away to a more intense battle in the lower country, closer to the actual cove. Many different infantries had gone before them and failed. This gave the Light Horsemen a deep desire to kill with a charge, like in the Wild West days in the USA. The first wave of men, including Patrick and Jum, fixed bayonets. Close behind them ran soldiers with sacks full of hand grenades. At the tail, the pick-and-shovel brigade stood ready to dig deep and fast to secure their post. If this attack succeeded, the allies would have a clear way to take an important holding of enemy territory.

The bloody battle raged for days. A constant flow of Turks ran to replace fallen comrades. Continuous machinegun fire ripped up the dirt as soldiers ran to secure ground, their bullets and hand grenades scattering the air from all directions. When enemy grenades landed in the allied trenches, chosen Anzacs smothered them with layers of blankets or sacks, while praying to be able to defuse them in time. If they couldn't, they might lose a limb—or their life. A very brave and tricky business for these men. Sometimes they threw those grenades back at the enemy, even after one of their arms had been blown off.

In this attack, Patrick and Jum had killed more Turks than they had time to count. Mainly they used their bayonets though Patrick got even closer and dropped some with a few lethal karate chops to the neck. Eventually they were able to take shelter behind sand bags set up to protect the men while they dug trenches. After days of withstanding enemy attacks, the Anzacs finally held their ground.

Patrick and Jum sat outside their trench enjoying a break within an armistice period. In this time of relative peace, a tall lean New Zealand officer approached them. "Hey, you chups, are you the Darcy clan?"

Jum looked up to answer. "Well, sorta." He pointed to Patrick, "He's Patrick Darcy, and I'm Jum Smith, his cousin. What's it to ya, Kiwi?"

"We're runding up crack shots to go out at night and then come daylight to knook a fuw of the Turkish snipers from their perches. Unterested?"

Jum looked at Patrick who was obviously thinking about it. Jum answered, "Should be a breeze, mate. I can shoot the hole out of a needle, me old man says."

Patrick laughed. "He's not far wrong, Kiwi, and yeah, I'll join him."

The Kiwi coughed. "Will, I'm not sure about higher ranking officers?"

Patrick whispered to him, "Well, if you don't tell anyone, I won't."

The Kiwi Sergeant had refrained from saluting Patrick because of the danger of the officer being identified and targeted while in enemy territory, even if it were an armistice. He then gave them the good news. "I'm here to tell you sirs, if you cun clean up these snipers around here in a couple of days, it would be really good. Because I know for a fuct that you chups are being sint shortly to a holiday posting on the beach, time for a dup in the ocean and a game of cricket. What do you thunk of that?"

Patrick retorted, "I'd rather play a game of polo, mate. Miss my horse nearly as much as my wife."

The Kiwi laughed. "I know how you ful, I love the point to points myself. I nuver thought we'd be foot soldiers. I'm beginning to thunk it was a weste of tume bringing the poor blidy animals here. We'll only have to shoot them before we go home." He then hung his head.

After a moment's silence, Patrick said, "Nobody will ever shoot my horse. I'll pay for his passage home."

"Will, I hope it works out that way, sir, but I don't like your chances. If you could both find your way to HQ after dusk, you'll be given orders. See you both later thin." He left while the going was good.

When night fell, the ten chosen marksmen stood at attention awaiting their posting. A Lieutenant pointed his stick towards a rough map of the surrounding area. "Now, gentlemen, these are the best vantage points to kill as many snipers as possible. This operation, we feel, will be enhanced if bets are taken on you for your tally of kills."

It was said with such seriousness that Jum began to belly laugh. Pulling himself together he remarked, "Sir, can I lay a bet on myself?"

After this, Jum became odds-on to win, with Patrick to run a close second and so on. The bets were then made and written down between the officers and the chosen riflemen.

Jum had positioned himself before daybreak, not too far from Patrick. They'd camouflaged themselves with desert bush and grass whereas the infantry men had done nothing like that. It seemed they were making themselves an easy target for the enemy. And they were far too close to where the snipers' bullets were known to be coming from.

Although Patrick and Jum lay close to each other, they were still behind the known line of fire. Patrick should have been in charge but the other eight were infantrymen and took little notice of the Light Horsemen. Jum was the first to kill a sniper, who was about to fire at one of the infantrymen. He whispered to Patrick, "One down, cous. I just saved Stewie's life. He owes me a beer."

The dead Turkish sniper's mate quickly worked out where the bullet had come from. In no time, a single bullet whistled just over Jum's head. In retaliation, one of the Anzacs plucked the same sniper out of the tree with a single shot, straight through his head.

"Fuck! That was close. But a bloody great shot from one of our blokes; right in the head, cous," Jum had said just before he spotted another Turk running from one batch of scrub to the next. He took aim and waited. Finally, the Turk made another run with his gun aimed at the Anzac. This time Patrick beat Jum to the trigger. They laughed when Jum said, "You win the teddy bear, cous. Christ, this is just like shooting the ducks at the Adelaide Show!"

When Patrick heard a rustle in the bush behind him, he turned quickly, exposing most of his body, and in that split second a bullet just grazed his arm. Without Jum having time to blink, Patrick launched himself into the air with a ninja kick. Patrick's blows to the Turk's neck were quick, precise and lethal. As he scuttled back to be alongside Jum, Patrick asked, "Does karate count for a kill or do we have to shoot 'em?"

Jum smiled and shook his head, "Jesus, cous, I wish I was as confident as you are."

"You will be one day when you're as good as I am."

When the sun finally went down, they counted: one Anzac dead and twenty Turks down.

"A good day's rabbiting, I reckon, cous!" Jum said after they'd returned to their trenches for bully beef rations and to bandage Patrick's grazed arm. Having killed most of the snipers, Jum won the bet. But next morning, they were all back on the job for another week, until orders came for them to move out.

"Jesus, just when we were havin' fun," Jum remarked to his superiors. The two seemingly indestructible Light Horsemen had become unassuming heroes and were rewarded with a break at a beach post, as were hundreds of other tired soldiers. They were finally able to relax, enjoying something like a holiday at last. The Kiwi had been right.

Patrick found time to write home.

Dear loved ones,

After slogging it out in the trenches for months, we have been given a reprieve. We are now on a beach holiday, well, sort of. The men are playing plenty of beach cricket. They're laying bets on anything that moves, especially the mail rider's safety as he gallops along the beach to collect our mail and deliver our eagerly awaited letters and parcels filled with goodies. Thanks, Colleen and Margi, for all you send.

My right arm is in a sling after arm wrestling nearly every joker on the beach. So the tug of war and games are out for me at the moment. I can only manage a game of two-up! They reckon we've suffered the worst conditions of this war anywhere, and I reckon they could be right. Anyway I won't complain, seeing we're enjoying the sun and the sand. It reminds me so much of home. This break has lifted our spirits. We must remember we are the lucky ones, we're still alive.

Refreshed after two weeks off duty, Patrick received new orders.

"Lieutenant-Colonel Darcy, you are to be relieved of trench duties. This means you will return to battles of which you and your men have been trained for." When Patrick relayed the orders to his men, he was nearly deafened with their cheers!

Chapter 26

Addy On Duty

Two years had passed since Doctor Adelaide Darcy had taken up her position at Cairo Base Hospital. She wrote home.

Dear Mum and Dad,

I'm confident that I have become a valuable surgeon within the Middle East war effort. I work long hard hours, stopping only for a short break to get some sleep. I shower and then I return to save lives. I feel I've earned respect from nearly all the male doctors in the Cairo Hospital. However, I must tell you, after all the different injuries presented to me, there is one particular section which tugs at my heart. So many men have been burnt or partly blown up. I truly feel for them having to go through the rest of their life with a maimed face or with fingers melted together. It would be horrifying. And so I have made my decision. After the war, I will become a qualified plastic surgeon. I am aware this means I will have to remain in England to study further and I wonder if Patrick will be happy to live there once again. Baby Sally, of course, will have no choice.

When I'm not operating on soldiers, or writing letters to Patrick and others back home, I spend my time reading up on the advancements of plastic surgery and the new improved procedures in any form of operating.

Unfortunately, the senior chief surgeon at the Cairo Hospital, Doctor Bindley, is only interested in the old, tried, but not so true methods. He is the only doctor in the hospital who, I think, is not impressed with my skills or my up-to-date knowledge.

But all in all, I'm happy.

Love to all, Addy XXXXX

"It's like Bindley has brick-wall mentality!" Addy told Clare on one of their rare weekends away from the hospital. The two friends were enjoying a rest and a wine together in the Empire Club. Addy delighted in going there.

"Have you met Alice Chisholm and Rania MacPillany, Clare? I think they've done a wonderful service to the weary homesick soldiers. It feels like a home away from home. Don't you agree?"

"Yes, of course, I know them. And, speak of the devil, Alice has just blessed us with her presence." Clare smiled, nodding her welcome towards Alice.

"Now, where was I? Oh yes, I agree." Clare sipped on her wine and then commented again about Bindley. "It must be so frustrating for you, Addy, to see Bindley go the long way around things. You are so confident when operating, it's like you've done it all before in a past life."

"I know. I don't want to blow my own trumpet but sometimes I feel the same way, like I've done it all before. But what about you, Clare? You've taken to being a surgical Sister like a duck to water."

"Yes, I suppose I have," Clare smiled. Thinking about the operating theatre for a moment, she said, "I miss that silly Angus, you know, although sometimes I can't concentrate when I'm helping him operate. He makes me laugh so much. He's so bloody brilliant, not saying you're not a wonderful surgeon, Addy, but he just does the job like it's nothing to him. I suppose it's a type of arrogance. I wonder how long it will be before he overworks himself and passes out on the job again. Abbassia is not that far away. Maybe I should borrow a camel and go see him before it happens."

Addy was not surprised at Clare's suggestion. She knew Angus and Clare had taken time to slowly get to know each other, mainly because Thomas was still in her heart. Angus had told Addy about it so he said he'd approached Clare with compassion and an offer of friendship.

"You really do like him, don't you, Clare?" Addy had announced the obvious.

"Yes, I do, and my heart is beginning to mend and life's too bloody short, Addy. We get reminded of it every day here, and you know how I like to laugh. Angus makes me laugh, and I admire him."

Addy felt she too would like to hop on a camel and ride to see Patrick. It had been over two years since they had held each other. "Why don't we dress up as Arabs, buy two camels and ride out into the desert to see our men!"

Clare burst out laughing, "No more wine for you, Addy, but wouldn't that be fun. Daddy would love that story, if we survived!"

"How is your father, Clare?"

"Oh, sometimes I think when I read his letters he's fine. But if I read them again I can feel the sadness. It's a shame Mummy doesn't help him. She still trots off to Paris every chance she gets, even though it's dangerous for her. Daddy can't go with her, of course. I don't know why he married her. But then, of course, I wouldn't be here."

Clare chuckled. "How about you, Addy. How's the family in Australia?"

"Just the same. Sally is growing up fast. Miss Millie never stops singing and Colleen junior has apparently taken to nursing. She bandages her dolls all day long and whoever else that will sit still long enough to be wrapped. Jonathon and Margie are very well, as are all the extended family: Doctor Liu, Mother M, Colleen and Bob. It's a wonderful atmosphere for Sally to be raised in, but I do miss her terribly."

Addy paused, and then added, "Oh yes, you remember Felicity Baker from school. Well, she wrote to tell me she's back in England. She was studying opera at the conservatorium in London until the war broke out. Now she's helping with the war effort. Sadly, her father died recently. He was such a nice man. Mrs Baker wants Felicity to come home to Australia. But Felicity says no, she'll wait until the war ends and then she'll resume her studies in London. I can't imagine how Felicity won't be famous one day; she has such an amazing voice. Maybe Felicity will be a good contact for Millie when she grows up."

Addy laughed a little and then took another sip of wine, as Clare asked, "Didn't Mrs Baker have her eyes on Patrick for him to marry Felicity?"

"Yes, poor Mrs Baker, I think it was she who actually fell in love with Patrick when they sailed to England together all those years ago. Felicity had her mind set only on being an opera singer. She never did seem that interested in boys or men. Although she wrote to me recently to say she has found a suitor, who's also studying opera in London. Apparently, he has a magnificent tenor voice, so I'm really pleased for her."

Addy smiled at the thought and then Clare commented, "That's wonderful news, Addy, and I hope they stay together. I should like to see her sing opera one day. It reminds me of the story Thomas told me, of his journey with Patrick on board ship to England and the girl he met. Lucy Von-Heifer, if I remember correctly. Anyway, her father was a boxer on his way to England to fight for a world title. That was the one short romance Thomas regretted. He said he was bored, and what else does a man do on board ship but kiss a pretty girl? Just as well I came along and he could pass the news of our engagement to her father from a very long distance. I'm sure he feared the reprisal of her fighting father. Oh, I had to laugh."

Clare stopped, and as her eyes welled with tears, she sniffled, "I'm so sorry, Addy. I shouldn't go back there. I must get on with my life." Addy reached her hand across the table to comfort her friend. As she did, a young nurse approached.

"I'm sorry, Doctor, but we have wounded. We need you back at the hospital. And you too, Sister. I have the ambulance waiting outside."

Despite the fast driving, it took some time before they reached an overcrowded Cairo Hospital. Injured men were lying everywhere, in corridors and on stretchers outside the operating theatre. The Matron told Addy about it. "A supply train on its way to Cairo was derailed by a bomb that we think was planted by spies. The train carried urgent supplies of food and medicine, but also many English officers taking leave here. This seems to be another victory for the enemy, Doctor, as some of our very important officers will now be out of action with severe injuries."

In no time, Addy and Clare were in the operating theatre. The officer who now lay unconscious in front of Addy was Captain Frederick Forrester. The Matron explained his injury. "It seems he was catapulted into a door of the carriage. It doesn't look good, does it, Doctor?"

Addy concern for his condition was rising. "God knows how they moved this fellow here, Clare. They've probably done more damage to his spine. DRILL!"

Clare repeated, "DRILL," and handed it to Addy. Then she began to recall the soldier's name. "Captain Frederick Forrester! Yes, I remember him. I met him the day of the Sandhurst Graduation. He has a slight stutter. Poor man, he's a real sweetie."

"Yes, I remember him too, it's Freddy. Patrick tried to help him with his stutter. He must have overcome it if they sent him to battle. Let's save him, Clare, and find out if he still has that stutter."

The operation to relieve the blood accumulated around Frederick's brain was successful. Addy felt his C-2 vertebra had been severely damaged, but without doing an X-ray, she could not possibly know whether it had been dislodged or fractured. She needed Freddy to recover from this lifesaving operation before placing him under the X-ray. Addy was more than pleased she would now be able to make an accurate prognosis.

Addy worked through the night to save several lives and also patch up a few cheeky officers, one officer confessing, "It was I who derailed the train, Doctor, so I could see the famously beautiful Doctor Adelaide. I am not disappointed, you are absolutely stunning!" Addy ordered plaster for his broken leg, with extra plaster to be placed over his mouth.

Soon after her final patient had been mended, Addy chose to sit outside the hospital to watch the sunrise. Comforted by a cup of strong black tea, she daydreamed about Patrick, his touch, his tender kisses, his smell. She was sure she could see him riding towards her so she put the cup down. Was she hallucinating? Addy stood and shaded her eyes from the sun. *I'm so overtired that I'm seeing things.*

Patrick rode closer. Charlie snorted his hello and Addy felt faint, swaying with the realisation of the moment. As she staggered, Patrick leapt from the saddle and caught her before she fell.

"Don't say a word, Addy. I'm going to lay you down to sleep. When you wake, I'll make love to you all night." Addy was about to speak, but accepted Patrick's lips instead.

Patrick and his men had returned to Cairo for a week's leave, before their next mission. While Addy slept, Patrick returned to headquarters and kept himself busy by going over plans of attack with his commander. "Our orders are that several Light Horse brigades plus one hundred camels have been called up for the long journey. This will be our biggest charge so far."

When Addy awoke, their long-awaited evening had arrived. The overwhelming feeling of oneness between Addy and Patrick, and the beauty of the surrounding dessert, coaxed them to walk arm in arm under the allure of the full moon. Addy spread a blanket down and they sat close together. The evening chill gave Patrick further need to hold her closer while gazing up at the stars. A bottle of French wine sat embedded in the sand. Savouring this moment, they gave silent thanks to the Lord for simply being alive. Although a surreal euphoria melded their emotions for some time, Addy soon felt guilty about their happiness. A torrent of unnecessary deaths had taken a toll on her conscience. As she remembered the young soldiers she had been unable to save and how their families would grieve, she began to sob.

Addy couldn't help but think how different her life would be if she were to lose Patrick. This thought made her snuggle even closer to him and say, while sniffling back her tears, "I hate war, Patrick. Why are we like this? Why can't we be normal people? Live on a farm, raise our children and cattle. We would never be apart and we could make love every night."

Patrick laughed. "Christ, Addy, we'd end up with twenty kids!"

This broke her sniffling and she laughed; laughed so much she cried even harder. Patrick pulled up the spare blanket and began their slow sensuous lovemaking. After being sent to heaven, Addy gazed to the stars and warned God, "If You take away my darling Patrick, Lord, then I too will simply die."

When making love for the second time, Patrick let his juices flow. A little concerned, Addy asked, "Why didn't you use a condom, Patrick?"

"Please don't spoil my fun, Addy. You know I hate those bloody things. Just use the potion."

"I don't have any. Do you?"

"No, I thought Angus would have told you how to make it?"

"No, he didn't. Anyway, it didn't work when I used it at school."

"Well, Doctor Darcy, what can I say? The damage is done, or what I really mean to say is, I'm sure we'll be having another beautiful baby in nine months' time, so let us continue, my darling, and try for twins."

"That's not funny, Patrick. I don't want another baby. Not now."

Patrick spoke softly. "If you really don't want another baby, Addy, then Angus has an abortive drug and I know it works."

Sitting bolt upright, Addy was shocked at what he'd just insinuated.

"How do you know it works, Patrick? And do you think I would kill my own child, especially after seeing sixteen-year-old boys die on the operating table after being shot in this bloody stupid war?"

"I'm sorry, Addy, of course not. I wouldn't want you to do it. I just know it works, because Doctor Liu has told us they use it in China for unwanted pregnancies. Too many mouths to feed over there, and you can't blame them, poor little beggars. Anyway, they would only end up dying of starvation."

Addy wasn't so sure he was telling the entire truth. After all, she knew Patrick had sown his oats freely before he met her. She wondered: had he and Angus ever used the drug on some poor unsuspecting young woman? But did she really need to know, when this time alone with Patrick seemed heaven sent? However, two and two finally added up. Addy then knew very well that Patrick and Angus both knew about preventing pregnancies. Of course, they would know how to terminate them. Doctor Liu, she thought had a lot to answer for.

"Let's go, Patrick, I'm cold." She began dressing.

Patrick lay back and watched her with a wry smile. "You're not angry with me are you, Addy?"

She asked herself if she was angry, or had her eyes just been opened to another side of Patrick. Addy pondered for a moment, *I could never leave him; I'm totally besotted. If I look at him now I will melt into his arms once again. Whatever he did before he met me, I will forgive him.*

"No, I'm not angry. I'm simply aware of things I chose not to think about before."

Patrick knew women well, especially his wife. This was not the time to argue with her. *I'll let Addy continue arguing with herself about her suspicions. However, I know now to keep the secret about Emily's abortion forever to myself.*

Patrick tried to charm her. "As you say, my love, whatever you want. I'm here for you."

Giving him a venomous look, Addy almost yelled, "Don't patronise me, Patrick. I'm not your play thing, I'm your wife and a well-respected doctor. Don't ever forget it!"

He laughed on the outside but shuddered a little on the inside. "Christ, you're bossy, Addy. You frighten me when you talk like that." Jumping up to stop her from marching away, Patrick, still naked, grabbed her and held her close. "It's fucking freezing, Addy. Don't add to the temperature. Warm me up. I love you. I just thought if you were pregnant, you may not want to have the baby just yet. But personally, I want as much of *you* on this earth as I can possibly produce. Now kiss me, I promise you. You're my best friend; I respect and admire you, and I would never ever hurt you. Whatever I've done in the past is gone. My future is with you and our children. Please don't make me more scared of you than I am of the bloody enemy."

Patrick's last words hit home to Addy. She smiled and softened, while realising, yes, he was right; sometimes she could be aggressive. She kissed him before saying, "I believe you, Patrick, but I'm cold and you must be freezing!"

She stood back to look at the goose bumps on his amazing body. "Come on, it's warmer in my room."

He quickly dressed, gathered up the blankets and ran after Addy who was marching towards the hospital grounds. They slept in each other's arms until the morning light. Addy lingered her lips on Patrick's cheek, then slid her hand down to fondle him. "Patrick, are you awake?"

"On top, Addy," he said, half-opening his tired eyes.

Their recent memories of death and cruelty were soon forgotten in the bliss of their union. But only minutes later, a knock on the door prevented them from repeating the exercise.

"Doctor, the X-ray machine is ready for Captain Forrester. Do you want him to go now? His OBS are normal, he's awake and asking to see you."

Patrick sat up. "Is that Frederick? Does she mean Freddy?"

"Shoosh, Patrick. I'll be there soon, Nurse, I need to shower. Tell them to give me five minutes."

Patrick demanded, "Why didn't you tell me Freddy was here, Addy?"

Slightly angry, she responded, "I don't know, Patrick. I suppose not seeing you for two bloody years and then wanting to be alone with you and not having to think about saving lives—FOR ONE BLOODY DAY—might have had something to do with it!"

Patrick then realised how this war was really getting to her. "I'm sorry, Addy, I didn't mean to accuse you of anything. I'm just happy Freddy's still alive and he's here. So can I say gidday a bit later?"

Addy lent across the bed and kissed him on the forehead. "I'm sorry, Patrick, I didn't mean to yell at you. I adore you, my darling. You can say gidday to Freddy after the X-ray. I'll see you in about thirty minutes." Picking up her shower bag and clothes, Addy left Patrick lying in bed to remember the good old days and his time spent at Sandhurst with Captain Frederick Forrester.

Addy had read all about the X-ray machine, which she admitted was nothing short of a miracle. Previously, when Clare had assisted her with the first patient to undergo the machine, Addy said, "We have Coolidge to thank for engineering the finer details of Wilhelm Rontgen's original design and method of X-raying in 1895. This will be one of our greatest lifesavers in the war!"

And now with Freddy, Addy was able to confirm her opinion once again. "Doctor Bindley, I have X-rayed Captain Frederick Forrester. It shows he has a fractured C-2 vertebra. At this stage, he has no feeling past his waist and only slight movement in his arms, just enough to shake my hand."

"Yes, well, you'll have to give him the bad news, Doctor Darcy. He will never walk again."

Addy chose to take no notice of Bindley's doom and gloom, and went straightaway to tell Patrick he could now visit Frederick.

"Patrick, it's so good to see you again," Frederick said without the stutter.

Standing alongside Patrick, Addy smiled and said, "Tell me, Frederick, did I cure the stutter when I relieved the blood clot? Or had you freed yourself of it before coming here?"

Freddy laughed, as much as he could, with his head bandaged like a mummy. "No, Doctor, it was your husband, Major Darcy, who never gave up on me. He even sent me a speech exercise to follow after he left Sandhurst. Apparently, a fellow stutterer, a Mr Roberts, had told Patrick. Your father-in-law, Jonathon Darcy, had helped him with the same problem when they were at Cambridge together. I did what I was told and here I am without a stutter."

Freddy's expression then saddened. "And without any legs."

Addy spoke quickly, "Freddy, you must not give up on walking. You still have your legs. And I'm sure the fractured C-2 vertebra will mend. I'm not experienced enough to operate, but wait till the swelling goes down to see if you haven't regained the feeling in your legs by the time you're sent home to England. Then I'm sure an operation by a neurosurgeon in London will be able to relieve the pressure from the spinal cord. Time will tell if the cord has been damaged too severely for the operation to succeed. Unfortunately, the X-ray machine can only take pictures of solid objects like bones. It cannot pick up the spinal cord, only the vertebras."

Patrick then offered, "You're still here, mate, and that's the main thing."

"Yes, you're quite right, Patrick, and so are you, I'm pleased to say. Have you time to let me in on the amazing Australian Light Horse regiments? I must say it all sounds rather romantic. You fellows have become legends in your own lifetime!"

Addy excused herself, "I'll let you two gentlemen catch up on your battles. I'm so happy to see you awake and still with us, Frederick, not that I was overly concerned about your bleeding. Please don't worry about your legs. I'm sure you will mend and be walking around soon but don't tell our chief surgeon I said that. I'm not supposed to give any hope at all to our patients." Kissing Freddy on his bandaged head, Addy said, "And I'm not supposed to kiss the patients either."

"Thank you, Doctor, I'm sure you saved my life."

"Well, of course I did, Frederick, but only because you were worth saving."

Both men laughed. After Addy had gone, Freddy commented, "You are a lucky chap, Patrick. I hope you don't mind me saying so, but Doctor Adelaide is the most beautiful woman I've ever seen, plus she's a very fine doctor. Addy is to be marvelled."

"Yes, I agree, I marvel her alright, Freddy. Sometimes she's more frightening to me than the enemy. When she tells me to jump, I ask, how high, dear?"

"I'd jump very high if I was you, Patrick. You wouldn't want to lose her."

Patrick pulled up a chair and sat smiling at Freddy's ridiculous assumption. "I think the only way I'd lose her, Freddy, is if I was killed in battle."

The two men chatted about their time together at Sandhurst and the characters who they'd met. Peter Mott was mentioned, as Frederick knew of Peter's involvement in strategic war planning, or "spying", as it was also called. Frederick had bumped into Peter on odd occasions and told Patrick, "Peter seems to have made great headway in being accepted by the Arab tribes, talking them into supporting the allies."

Patrick felt quietly pleased. The glimmer of hope he'd once seen within Peter Mott had finally shone through. "Where did Colour Sergeant William go, Freddy? Is he here or in France?"

"I'm so sorry, Patrick. I thought you may have known. Willy was killed on his first day of action. He was trying to drag a young soldier to safety. He was shot. At least he didn't suffer. It was a clean hit straight through the heart."

Patrick hung his head, not wanting to show Frederick his emotion. But he had noticed. "Don't worry, Patrick. I've cried too for the mates I've lost. I pray to God this war will be worth the carnage."

Patrick sniffled and agreed. "They've fallen like flies around me, Freddy, some of them only boys, sixteen years old. You try and block it from your mind so it doesn't eat you up. I never thought I'd ever feel like this. I thought I was a gung-ho soldier, in for the fight no matter what the consequences. But reality soon hits home when ya mates are there right beside you one minute, talking about home and their families and then gone forever the next minute. Thousands of young lives lost and for what? A barrel of bloody oil and, you know, Freddy, there are so many fuckin' idiots in charge of this war. They don't give a damn about the loss of life. But I tell you one man I admire and that's Chauvel, our commander. I wish he ran the whole bloody show. He uses his head, not his men."

Freddy was listening with his eyes closed now. "Yes, I've heard about him, Patrick. He's a great man, but can we talk later? I'm a little weary."

"Of course, Freddy, I'll let you rest." Patrick needed to leave the hospital anyway. He had to meet his men and make sure they were not in too much trouble with the prostitutes and pimps. Also, Chauvel was preparing for them to move out of Cairo sooner rather than later. Patrick knew that Chauvel had always feared reprisals from the men's behaviour while in Cairo.

"A short visit to Cairo is all the Light Horsemen need," Chauvel had insisted for this particular rest in proceedings. He then added, "There will be reasonably safe places to set up camp on the way to Bir el Mazar. The men can rest a bit along the way."

Patrick reiterated the orders to Jum. "Bir el Mazar will be our next battle, Jum. They've rounded up over one hundred bloody camels to take our grub and water supplies. They reckon our Walers need about five gallons of water a day, but they seem to me to be able to manage on far less. Charlie's a prime example. I'm bloody lucky I've got him over here. I reckon he could carry three men for miles without a problem. The heavy horse in him, I think, gives him his strength and his Arab mother gives Charlie his desert savvy."

After Addy had left Patrick with Freddy, she went about her ward rounds until she'd got into an argument about a particular operation procedure with Doctor Bindley. Patrick overheard her as he approached the staffroom to say goodbye. Not sure whether to interrupt or not, he decided to walk away and leave a note on her pillow. *Dear Addy, please let someone else cover for you tonight, my darling. I'll be back at six. Love, Patrick.* As he walked past the room again, they were still arguing. By the sound of it, Bindley had no time for women doctors, or any new ideas on operating procedures. Patrick felt for Addy, as he knew the frustration of having to follow orders from an idiot ranked above him.

Walking through the streets of Cairo, Patrick noticed nothing had changed since he'd last been there. Drunken soldiers helped each other along the busy laneways. Lining the paths were street stalls managed by seedy characters selling anything and everything, begging for your money to buy their wares. Soldiers chased the odd prostitute down the road to retrieve what she had stolen from him. The smell of incense, strong tobacco, sour alcohol and donkey manure filled his lungs. Stopping at a street stall to inspect a gold chain holding a heart-shaped ruby,

Patrick bit the chain to see how soft the metal was and if it were solid gold. The ruby looked authentic but he would have to trust the stall owner whether it was.

After they had bargained, the Egyptian thanked Patrick and wrapped the necklace in a small piece of fine silk. Patrick was smiling at the thought of placing it around Addy's neck, when he felt a tap on his shoulder, he looked around to see Peter Mott. Although unrecognisable to most in his Arab garb and full beard, Patrick knew him straightaway. "Peter, it's good to see you again. It's been a while."

"Hello, Patrick, it's good to see you too. I've heard about your amazing efforts in the trenches and then in the Light Horse charges. Although I must say I'm not surprised. I only ever expected you to become a hero. I'll be accompanying you tomorrow when we leave on our next mission."

Peter noted Patrick's shock, then disappointment and tried quickly to console him. "I'm sure Adelaide will love the necklace. Have a pleasant evening, Patrick. I'll see you tomorrow."

Patrick stood motionless, deflated at the thought of leaving Addy so soon. He was hoping for another four days with her. But the warrior in him also looked forward to the battle. *I'd better go early to HQ and receive the orders.*

When first entering Cairo, Patrick had been told that "All resting officers are to return to the meeting place each afternoon by four o'clock, in case there are any changes in our proceedings." So, he knew that orders could come at any time to move out. Nothing in this war seemed fair to Patrick. But after nearly three years of being right in the middle of it, he thought how he was getting used to the ebb and flow of the battle charges and was unable to imagine himself doing anything else but fight in wars, even though, he admitted, the loss of his men would always be hard to bear.

Back at the hospital, Addy spoke with old Doctor Bindley after their argument. "I am taking the night off to be with my husband and you can sack me if you wish, Doctor Bindley, because neither heaven nor hell will take me from his arms!"

Bindley thought, *If the truth be known, I'm pleased to be rid of her, but only for a short time as I depend on her more than I'm willing to admit. Husband! Did she say "husband"?* He chose to let that question lie.

The day had been reasonably quiet for Addy. She'd checked in on Frederick several times to find him either asleep or in good spirits, especially after Clare had paid him a visit. But then Clare could make a cat laugh, Addy had told numerous people about her delightfully funny friend. She kept looking at her watch, wishing each time for it to show six o'clock. Come five o'clock, she bid farewell to her fellow doctors and nurses and left to take a shower. Pleased with the way she looked and smelt, Addy then sat at the desk in her room to write letters home.

Patrick too had dared go to a public bath and then trusted an Arab barber to give him a close shave. At precisely six o'clock he knocked on the door, which made Addy jump, as she'd been in another world while writing.

Opening the door, Addy took one long admiring look. "If you don't mind me saying so, sir, you are the most handsome sweetest smelling man I have ever seen."

Patrick handed her the small gift wrapped in silk. "The feeling is mutual, my love."

He watched Addy's expression after she'd unwrapped her gift. "Oh, I love it, Patrick, a symbol of your heart around my neck. I will wear it forever. I feel ashamed I haven't brought you anything." Her expression emulated her next words. "All I can give you is my love."

"I suppose that'll have to do, but can we eat first? I'm starving."

They chose to walk not too far away from the hospital. The bar in which Patrick and Angus had met quite often was close by, and renowned for its delicious lamb tagine. When Patrick walked up to the bar to order drinks, he was remembered distinctly by the bartender, who smiled, flashing his decaying teeth. "You big hero now. I hear all about you. You win the war on your own, they say."

Patrick laughed, "I wish, mate. Don't believe everything you hear."

"The curry and beer I give you free. On the house." He nodded toward Addy. "She your beautiful wife? She famous doctor too. She's the boss doctor, I think."

Patrick returned to their table and told Addy, "We best eat up quickly, or they'll come asking for our autograph. It seems we're famous."

Addy agreed, "Yes, it doesn't pay to be famous around here. We may just be kidnapped and held for ransom."

Patrick's face showed his worry. "Jesus, I didn't think of that. You're not in any danger, are you?"

"No, of course not. Anyway, I stay in the hospital most of the time. However, I'm not sure if some of the worst characters around Cairo may think about it. But if they were to kidnap me, they might have the entire allied forces upon them very smartly."

Patrick smiled, a little more at ease after Addy's assurance.

"You know, Patrick, I've been thinking about asking for a transfer, closer to the front. Maybe I could be with Angus. He's staying at Abbassia, or he may even go to Port Said. It's very safe there and I'm so fed up with Doctor Bindley, I need to get out of here."

Patrick didn't like the sound of her being any closer to the front. "I don't think they'll send you, Addy. This is as close as you'll get to the enemy. I know it's hard for you with old codgers like him. He'll never get out of the 18th century but don't put yourself in any more danger just to make him happy."

"It's not him I want to make happy. It's me."

"You just need a break, Addy, that's all. Why don't you go home for a while?"

Shocked with Patrick's suggestion, she responded, "You don't seem to understand, Patrick. I'm in the army too. I can't just up bags and leave whenever I wish. I'm in for the long haul, unless I become ill or pregnant. And pregnant I may well be!"

Patrick smiled coyly. "I'm sorry, Addy, you probably are. We'll have to talk about this. You know, whether we want our family to settle in Australia or England after the war. I know you have something on your mind. Whatever it is, you need to tell me now. Not that I have any intentions of being killed, but I would like to know if you've made plans for our future, or if we're gunna wing it, before I go into battle tomorrow?"

Addy was shocked again. "Tomorrow! I thought you were here for another four days?"

"I'm sorry, Addy, orders from the hierarchy. It's going to be the biggest mission so far so I can't talk about it. But don't worry. I'll be fine."

"That's easy for you to say, Patrick!" Her expression was a mix of surprise and anger. She continued, a little sarcastically. "However, I'm sure a hero like you will look after himself."

She then softened, held his hand and looked him in the eye. "Please come back to me, Patrick, and then we'll have plenty of time to talk about what we *both want* to do in the future."

Patrick immediately knew Addy had something brewing. "I'll do as you say, my love." He laughed at his own seemingly patronising comment. "But I'm not patronising you, Addy. Please don't scorn me. I know you have something on your mind; I'll let you think about it. I don't care where I live, as long as it's with you. Now finish your beer, then let's go and pretend it's our first time together."

"Not on your bloody life, Patrick, I remember it hurt the first time," Addy said with a cheeky smile. And then she wondered how Patrick would respond to her wanting to complete a plastic surgery qualification in England.

Their night of splendour, surpassed any love or lust they had ever experienced with each other. The mere thought that this may well be the last time they would ever see each other brought a raw and uninhibited passion to their lovemaking. They savoured every moment. Pleasantly exhausted afterwards, Patrick turned to kiss Addy, adding dramatic humour to his leaving, "Stay where you are, my love. I will remember you lying there, waiting for my return." He'd made her laugh.

"If only I could, Patrick. And if only you would return that quickly. I love and adore you, but if you don't come back, I'll kill you. Do you hear me?"

"Yes, dear, I'll come back, dear."

"That sounded patronising!"

"Yes, and I meant it. Please stop bossing me around, Addy, I'm a bloody war hero!"

She threw the pillow at him, and Patrick coped it, saying in a high voice, "OOH, please don't hurt me, Addy." Then he left.

Addy laughed and cried for some time before finding the strength to rise and face another day operating alongside Bindley. And to then tell him she would now pursue the opportunity to go serve at Saint Helios, or any other stationary hospital close to the front line.

Chapter 27

The Final Battle

Patrick and his men went forth as planned, only to take part in probably the biggest disappointment the Light Horsemen had ever witnessed. Before they reached Bir el Mazar, the Turks had already thrown down arms and retreated the very moment they had heard of the impending and almighty invasion by the Australian Light Horse madmen. So, when the Light Horse arrived and realised the enemy had flown the coop, Jum was moved to quip, "Well, that was bloody easy, cous! At this rate, we'll just have to show up and they'll all go running into the sea. It'll save a lot of ammo."

Over the following months, Patrick and his dwindling number of men fought more battles, not all of them as easy as Bir Al Mazar, of course. And not all were against the human enemy. Terrible sandstorms would suffocate any living creature unable to take cover quickly enough from the deadly mixture of tons of sand, driven by ferocious winds. The extreme heat sapped the energy and the resolve of the men and their horses. It seemed to fry the brains of those unable to cope with it, making men delusional until they could be cooled sufficiently to recover, or to eventually die. These unbelievable conditions severely affected more than a quarter of all soldiers and horses who fought in the Middle East.

Luckily, Patrick and Jum had avoided such a fate, and they were ready for the greatest battle of all, the Battle of Beersheba. Patrick explained to his men.

"This charge will be the most important charge so far. We must take control of the largest water supply in Arabia. These Beersheba wells date back to Biblical times. This includes the great King Solomon Well, the first and largest well, built over a thousand years before. The Germans are holding this hallowed ground, which will make or break our future in this war. Water, as you know, is liquid gold in the desert and we will surely die without it. So, it is our job to secure the water."

By the twenty-ninth of October 1917, the majority of the Australian Light Horse Brigades had gathered near Beersheba. Troops were scattered in the valleys around the perimeter of the city, making it difficult for the German air raiders to pick them off. As they waited for their order to mount and be ready for the charge, each troop felt the tension, like walking a tightrope, with each man longing to take part in this almighty battle. The mounted brigades that hadn't yet been part of a charge were itching to get going. But underlying their tension was the urgency to take control of water sources. It was no laughing matter; they were running out of the precious fluid. And the nearest water source for the horses and the troops was too far away from Beersheba for them to make it and survive the journey. Therefore, the men were unable to comprehend the seemingly complacent mood of the commanders, or really, one, the boss man—Chauvel.

Chauvel was known as a master tactician, and in this instance, it was to pay great dividends. He'd left nothing to chance; aerial photos had to be taken of the Beersheba's surrounds. These details were to be the most important factor in winning the battle, as the photos showed rolls of barbed wire placed around ninety-five per cent of the perimeter. Although the south-eastern approach was the only way in, it was plagued with holes dug especially to trip the horses. It would not be easy, but Chauvel knew very well they were almost out of water and so the decision to move immediately was forced upon him.

At dusk on the thirty-first of October 1917, the Light Horsemen were ordered to mount. Soon, hundreds of horsemen were feeling their adrenalin flow. As the dust settled, they gathered in a formidable line that stretched for over a mile from the top of the hill outside the city. Patrick sat tall in his saddle, his nerves tightening in his stomach at the prospect of being part of the most important battle so far. Charlie snorted, pawed his hoof several times at the ground while shaking his head. Patrick spoke calmly. "Yes, Charlie, this is it. The big one. You'll get some royal water soon, mate, so just hang in there."

Jum sat mounted close to Patrick on the right, and for the only time in their fighting life together, he saw the nervous anticipation in his cousin's demeanour. Jum put his usual light-hearted spiel on the situation. "Jesus, cous, I'm glad me mum made me eat carrots. I can see real well in the dark, so just stick with me."

Patrick had to agree. Night was falling fast. Things would be more difficult than they already were, maybe even impossible if they didn't get moving soon.

Chauvel had carefully chosen the officer to lead the advancement on Beersheba, Brigadier General Grant. Patrick knew he was many years his senior and had definitely earned the honour to show his courage and leadership.

Patrick then put his own ego to rest and remembered once again what Doctor Liu had told him. "Emotion and ego will end your life in battle. Only thinking with head belongs in battle." Patrick smiled at the memory. He wondered whether the troops would create a cloud of dust in their approach and with the fading light, Charlie might find it hard to line up the heads of the enemy, as he usually did when jumping a trench. Charlie would lower his hind quarters before landing. Most times this would give the Turks an upper cut to their chin with his hind hoof. An amusing thought, especially since he hadn't taught Charlie this trick. It seemed it was his idea. He stroked Charlie's neck again and for a moment became emotional with the bond he felt for his beloved horse.

A booming voice ordered the riders to move forward in preparation to charge. This was it—the wait was over. Hundreds of men and horses surged forward, making their way down the sand hills, across the hot desert sand, until Grant and his men built up to a fierce gallop to charge through the only available opening. Once inside the barbed walls, the Anzacs were met with machine guns, firing at random, culling the onslaught of scouts galloping in all directions. Turks were at the ready with bayonets, prepared to bring down horses that dared to jump their trenches. Some soon met with this agonising fate, leaving their riders to scramble for cover behind their fallen horses, as they fired their rifles or chased fleeing Turks to finish them with a bayonet.

Amid the dust and the darkness, Patrick found it nearly impossible to keep a close eye on all his men, although he could make out Jum who was always in front of him. After surveying the scene briefly, he was sure he'd lost at least five of his best, including young Timmy. Damn! Now he was determined to secure the wells. Using his pistol at close range, Patrick shot ten Turks. Some of them were about to kill fallen Aussie horsemen before they had time to go for their rifles. Jum was still in front of Patrick and jumping each trench like he was in the Grand National. Patrick managed a smile, knowing Jum had actually taken a bet with a fellow mate; he'd be the first to take out the krauts who guarded the wells. But what they didn't know was that the Germans were on the ready to blow up the wells if it looked like the Anzacs would take Beersheba.

The battle continued with hand-to-hand combat. Silver bayonets flashed down and came up blood red. As pistols blazed and rifles cracked, the Turks fell. About half of the remaining Turks dropped their guns and ran for the hills. The horsemen dodged sprays of machine gunfire while evading the bullets and small bombs from the German air fighters.

In the gloom ahead, Patrick could just make out a small building. He didn't know it was the water control room, nor that the Germans had lain dynamite fuses. And Jum was almost there—one last trench to jump. Patrick watched as Jum's horse took an almighty leap.

"Go, you beauty!" Patrick roared, just one second before Jum was shot and tumbled off his horse. No! Not Jum! He lay motionless where he fell. Still two trenches behind, Patrick was stunned. Jum still hadn't moved, focusing totally on Jum slowed Patrick's thinking. As Charlie jumped the next trench, Patrick could feel the force of a Turkish bayonet lift Charlie momentarily. The horse groaned as he landed, then staggered and fell with a thud, about twenty feet past the trench. Patrick rolled away only to see blood seeping from the gaping hole in Charlie's stomach. Losing control of his emotions, Patrick's fury became his demon. He ran towards the Turk with the bloodied bayonet, aimed and shot the culprit dead. Patrick took aim at two other Turks. One ran off but the other threw his bayonet to the ground, put his hands high above his head, and pleaded in stilted English, "Urrender, urrender."

This gave Patrick a moment to decide whether to shoot him, or let him go. His immediate thought was to turn back to Jum. But in that moment's hesitation, Patrick felt a knife being stabbed into his back and pulled out as he fell to his knees. Looking up at his faceless assassin, almost obliterated by the shimmering light of the blade about to pierce his heart, Patrick rolled over just in time to avoid the fatal blow and passed out.

Jum had only been winded when he fell from his horse, and his gunshot wound was not life threatening. He'd revived just in time to shoot the Turk who was about to end Patrick's life. Miraculously, Peter Mott appeared from behind a barricade and threw himself over Patrick to protect him. Jum then took control of Patrick's rescue after he'd summoned help from a stretcher bearer. Peter stumbled to Charlie, who was still alive. Peter knew many Bedouin tribesmen, one of whom was there with him. As they worked to help Charlie, Peter's memories of their days at Sandhurst came flooding back, especially of Patrick and Charlie's special show. It didn't matter whether you liked Patrick or not before that evening, you certainly had to admire his talent with horses, particularly this horse. Peter felt if Charlie died, a part of Patrick would also die.

The brown, leathered face of the tribesman furrowed into seriousness as he gave Peter the news. "I do not think I can save him."

Peter begged him to try, describing what a special horse he was: "He's like the God of all horses." This simple statement was enough to urge this wise man to do his utmost to save Charlie. Meanwhile, all around them, the Turks gave way and the battle was won. The horsemen had secured the wells by the time Patrick and Charlie were taken separately to their makeshift hospitals.

"It's a bloody miracle!" young Jum said when entering the stationary hospital to see Addy. Without Patrick knowing, she had wheedled her way into the front line. Her woman's intuition had told her that she must be there, and neither hell nor high water was going to stop her. In reality, the Army was desperately short of surgeons so her pleas were accepted.

Patrick lay unconscious, his complexion a pale grey, which led Addy to believe he was bleeding internally. Keeping a professional attitude towards her "patient", she inspected his wound, while deep inside, her heart cried with the thought that she might lose him. This was possible if the knife had cut through to his kidney, or perhaps severed an artery.

"I need to operate straight away, or he will die within a few hours, he's my husband." she said. With confidence in her own ability, and with a little of the Lord's help, Addy felt she could save him.

Doctor Larne, a little shocked with her confession, was not quite sure whether Addy would be able to handle the operation, and voiced his concerns. "I feel, Doctor, I should at least assist you, in case your emotions take hold of your focus needed to perform such an intricate procedure."

Defiantly, Addy stood her ground. "I am not, and I will not become emotional, Doctor Larne. I'm sure there are many more lives you need to be saving. I will not need your assistance."

Then she softened a little. "I know it may sound crazy, Doctor Larne, but I truly believe I'm here for this reason alone, to save my husband's life. I am quite capable of performing this operation without becoming emotional."

He yielded to Addy's reasoning and let her have her way, after noticing many more wounded were flooding into the tent.

For one fleeting moment before Patrick was to be taken into the operating tent, he awoke to see Addy's face. Smiling briefly, he asked hoarsely, "Have I died and gone to heaven?"

Addy put him at ease. "No, my darling, it's me and you know I'm no angel! I'm here on earth to save your life. Do you remember?"

Despite his pain and stress, he managed a little joke. "Please don't hurt me, Addy." Then he lapsed back into unconsciousness.

After she opened Patrick's wound, her worst fears were realised. "The dagger has severely lacerated the left kidney and cleaved the renal vein in two. Removing that kidney and clamping the vein is the only option to staunch the bleeding. The tip of the dagger has also scraped the corner of the spleen, causing major blood leakage into the abdominal cavity. The spleen's not damaged enough, in my opinion, to warrant removal, but I'll have to keep an eye on his bloods and pressure. If it deteriorates I'll have to open him up again and remove the spleen."

After three arduous hours of operating, Addy sighed deeply before relaxing a little, with the thought, *I've done my very best and with my prayers answered, Patrick will live.*

Over the next twenty-four hours, Addy completed many more operations and then was unable to sleep. She sat vigil beside Patrick's bed while praying every minute. She went over and over in her mind how she'd doubly cleansed the instruments and so on. Yes, she'd taken every precaution needed. Addy had checked and rechecked; she'd left no small bleeders. Now the hardest thing she had to do was to leave Patrick and operate on other injured soldiers.

As time passed, Patrick continued to slip in and out of consciousness. He now slept while Addy held his hand. She told stories of their happy days, as if he could hear every word she said, ending her sentences with, "I love you, Patrick."

Seven days had passed and Addy was still not sure if Patrick would survive. He'd been running a fever for the past few days and so she prayed. It was the only thing she could do. Knowing if his body was unable to fight the infection, there would be no saving him. Her concerns were gravest on the day Peter Mott had arrived at the hospital with bad news. Charlie had not survived.

He'd also brought Angus's Chinese tonic for cleansing the blood and fighting infection. Still dressed in Arab garb, Peter seemed to Addy to have a safe passport over the entire Middle East. She kissed him, and Peter blushed.

"Praise be to God," Addy said as she took the tonic from him, then placed her hand on Peter's bony shoulder. "And you too, Peter. God bless you."

His eyes welled with tears. Lowering his head to cover his emotion, he said, "I know you will understand, Doctor. I love Patrick too."

Addy did, although she was unable to understand his type of love, she accepted it. Peter then handed her a letter from Angus. She smiled and suggested Peter leave her for a while, "You should go and sit with Patrick, but please don't tell him about Charlie." Peter went to interrupt her, but Addy knew exactly what he was about to say. "I know you may think Patrick won't be able to hear you, Peter, but trust me, he will. When he hears anything about Charlie, conscious or unconscious, he'll know so please, don't say anything!"

Addy sighed with sadness, remembering Charlie, then turned her attention to Angus's letter.

Dear Patrick,

My beloved brother, I have good news for you. Clare and I have decided to be married on our first leave to Cairo. We have followed you and Addy by putting the cart before the horse! Yes, she's pregnant. We are so happy I can't tell you. Well, of course, you already know what a great girl she is, I love her to bits. Now that reminds me, I hope Addy has put all your bits back together successfully, as when this bloody war is over, we are going to do the proper garden wedding at "Wild Flowers". So, you had better bloody well live to be my best man, you bastard!

Love you, brother

Angus xx

Doctor Larne, while still a little wary about Chinese medicine, eventually agreed with Addy's suggestion to give it to Patrick. When seeing the results a few days later, he said, "I think we should order a truck load of this tonic to be shipped to all hospitals in the region! I have never witnessed such a transformation in a patient obviously suffering from a post-operation infection. Patrick's life has most definitely been saved by this amazing tonic. His temperature declined rapidly within the first twenty-four hours of his drinking the fluid. It is truly amazing." And now Doctor Larne was enjoying his conversations with a much healthier Patrick, one of the bravest young officers in the war.

Unfortunately for Patrick, his request to return to battle was refused. Both Doctor Larne and Addy insisted it would take him months to fully recuperate from his trauma. He had a three-week stay in the Cairo Hospital while in Addy's company; receiving her love and compassion in losing Charlie, as she too was allowed leave to be with him. Soon after, Patrick travelled back to London by hospital ship, and was given office duties until the end of the war.

That's where Addy returned to his arms.

Chapter 28

Home in Australia After the War, July 1927

After World War I, "Wild Flowers" became home to the entire Darcy family. Patrick and Addy's daughter, Sally, now a teenager, sat cross-legged at her father's feet, pen and paper in hand. She was asking Patrick about his involvement in the charge of Beersheba but he was not taking her questions seriously.

"Dad, please be serious. I have to finish this story for my school assignment."

Addy sat beside Patrick and, as usual, pulled him into line. "Yes, Patrick, the war was not that funny."

He responded, "You know it's the only way I cope, darling. Remembering the good times is the only way for me to keep returning to Duntroon."

Addy wished Patrick would dwell only on the bad times, so he would then leave the Army and they could settle down at Bulkawa and travel to Hawaii at least every second year. Addy had finally realised Australia was home. This had come about after the war, when she had returned to England alone, to study plastic surgery for twelve months. She became dreadfully homesick while there but she had put up with it until she'd completed her degree and then returned home. Addy vowed then, she would never again leave Patrick or Sally. Now, as she looked admiringly at Patrick, who was still very fit, however, she noticed he was beginning to show his age, greying at the temples and deep laughter lines around his eyes. She smiled, thinking it only added to his good looks, giving him character and distinction.

"I know, Patrick, and you're right, my love, but just this once, please tell Sally the truth and the way it really was when you were almost killed in Beersheba."

Patrick nodded, "I suppose I have the time, Sally. It could be a long story though."

She smiled. "Just give me the short of it, Dad."

"Alright, Sally, but are you sure you wouldn't like to write a book and be an author rather than a journalist?"

Addy interrupted them. "I'll leave you two at it. I have to meet Angus at the hospital. He has a patient he wants me to see and then I'm off to lunch with Aunty Clare."

Patrick kissed her goodbye and then began telling Sally his last war story. An hour later he had almost finished. "So the Light Horsemen finally succeeded in taking Beersheba. Most importantly, we prevented a young German man from pulling the lever that would have blown up the wells. We had some great men, brave fearless young men and the best soldiers in the world, I reckon. You know, Sally, I've learnt a lot from life, especially about following my instincts."

He dwelt for a moment, thinking about Peter Mott and how he'd done his utmost to save Charlie's life. "I must tell you, Sally. Peter Mott and I were enemies when we were young and at school together, although I couldn't help but feel a bit sorry for him. I think it was the way his degenerate father had brought him up. Your Uncle Angus and I were so lucky to have your Poppa Jon to love us and teach us the value of being strong in character and to have good principles. Peter wasn't so lucky."

Patrick fell silent for a moment to consider how Peter came home after the war to collect his mother and take her back to England. After explaining this, he said, "It made me happy to know he would care for his mother after the terrible treatment she'd received from Peter's father."

Sally could see her father was feeling a little proud of himself for always seeing the good in people before the bad. "What happened then, Dad? What did you do in England until the war ended?"

"Well, your mother certainly saved my life, as you know. She is the most amazing woman in the world, Sally. I am so lucky to have found her all those years ago on the London docks. It was fate." He sighed deeply before continuing. "Anyway, she did a wonderful job operating on me. Oh yes, and Uncle Angus gave Peter some Chinese medicine to deliver to me. It certainly got rid of the post-op infection, so I suppose he helped a little too." He laughed at his own kidding about the importance of Angus's input.

It was the way they were, Sally thought, always stirring each other.

"I must admit, Sally, I enjoyed the boat trip back to London and also the stay in hospital, where I recuperated for a couple more weeks. I then found myself an apartment in London and was put to work in the Army's bookkeeping division until the end of the war. The hardest thing I had to do was to wait to see your mother. It almost drove me crazy. I was so bored and so lonely. There were no battles to take my mind off her. Yes, it was the worst pain I think I had to endure for the entire war. That was until I held her in my arms once again."

Sally's blue eyes filled with tears. "I love you, Dad. You're my hero and you're the most amazing man in the world." She jumped up to hug Patrick.

"No, Sally, I'm no hero. I've just played the cards life has handed me. And I'm not proud of everything I've done. But I've tried to make amends for my mistakes. It's all we can do. We all make mistakes and I'm bound to make a few more before I'm done and dusted."

Sally sat beside him and held his hand. "Dad, one day, when you're ready, would you let me read my Nan's diary?"

Patrick thought about it. "Yes, I will. But it will be when you've passed your English literature degree at university."

"But I'll be around twenty years old then."

"Yes, and that's how old you'll need to be to read it. It holds some dark secrets, Sally. Your grandmother had a very sad beginning to her short life. One day you might write her story in a book. Now we best go and see what Jonathon and Margi have planned for the family reunion and your Uncle Angus's birthday on the weekend."

"How come we call them our family? We're not really related to Doctor Liu or Bob and Colleen. Even Mother Betty, I mean Madeleine, or Mother Matilda. And it's your birthday too, Dad!"

"Yes, I know, but the fourth of July is not really my birthday, or Uncle Angus's, but that's another story. Talking of extended family, you know they are as close to us as any blood relation could possibly be. You don't have to be of the same blood, you just need to have the same caring principles, and they were always there when we needed them."

Sally agreed, nodding her pretty head. "Do you think we could go to Hawaii this Christmas and stay with Granddad Barney and Grandma Bernadette? I just love it there. I'm getting better at surfing, you know, and Hawaii has the biggest waves in the world!"

"Yes, we are all going to Hawaii for Christmas, but please don't tell your mother."

His blue eyes creased and Sally saw a twinkle of mischief. "I have a surprise for your mother, Sally. I want to tell her in Hawaii. But I'll tell you now. That's if you promise to keep it to yourself?"

"Yes, of course I will, Dad. What is it?"

"I'm going to retire from the Army this year, just before Christmas. Your mother also wants to retire and take her turn at running Bulkawa before we get too old. I think I'm ready to help her. Well, work alongside her, I suppose." A frown showed his concern for this idea. "I hope she doesn't get too bossy."

Sally hugged him tight. "I'm so happy, Dad, and I'll finally have my parents together all the time. This is great news; I can't wait to tell Millie and Colleen."

"Oh no, please don't, Sally. They'll let the cat out of the bag, for sure."

"I'm only joking, Dad. Of course, I won't tell anybody. So is Lord Harris, I mean great-uncle Anthony, bringing Mrs Baker to the barbeque. I think he really likes her, don't you?"

Patrick smiled, remembering when Jonathon took a trip back to London to handle Lord Harris's divorce for him. And now, the fact Lord Harris calls himself a true-blue Aussie makes him laugh. Although he did retain his family manor in England, he now spends half of every year in Australia, so as to be close to Clare and his grandson, James.

Unfortunately, Patrick's dear friend, old Lord Fogarty, had passed away before he could make his promised trip to Australia. Addy was in London when he died and represented the Darcy family at his funeral. Addy also kept in touch with Felicity Baker, who had certainly become renowned for her sublime operatic voice. She wrote to Addy many times while she travelled the world singing in the most popular operas. She delighted in her mother, Edwina's, happiness, since meeting Lord Anthony Harris in London and didn't mind her choosing to keep his company rather than travelling with her. Felicity had suggested to Addy that she thought Edwina and Lord Harris seemed very well suited and wedding bells might be on the cards. Felicity had also promised Miss Millie she would be her mentor in her future opera career. Ever since then, Miss Millie had sung her scales all day long. Jonathon had thought it wise to turn one of the many bedrooms into a music room, along with soundproofing the walls.

Young Colleen clung very close to Aunty Clare these days, as she too wanted to be a nurse more than anything. Clare delighted in her company, especially seeing Colleen had become so close to young James. He was more like the little brother they never had, rather than a nephew. The same as Sally had been, in being more like a sister, rather than their niece.

Life was now simple and good for Patrick and Addy. They surprised everyone by having what some would call a mid-life baby, conceived while holidaying in Hawaii. They named him Patrick Jonathon Darcy Junior.